Siri Sahaj Kaur

About the Editor

PAUL ZAKRZEWSKI (pronounced *Zak-shef-ski*) is a writer, editor, and literary event curator. As director of literary programs for the Jewish Community Center in Manhattan, he runs a popular reading series featuring new and provocative Jewish writers at the KGB Bar in the East Village. He is also an editor at *Heeb* magazine, a Jewish pop culture collective, which was nominated for Best New Title in the 2002 *Utne Reader* Alternative Press Awards. He lives in Brooklyn, New York, and can be reached at www.lost-tribe-fiction.com.

LOST TRIBE

LOST TRIBE

Jewish Fiction

from the Edge

Edited by

Paul Zakrzewski

Perennial

An Imprint of HarperCollinsPublishers

"There's a Kind of Hush (All Over the World)" Words and Music by Les Reed and Geoff Stephens. Copyright © 1966, 1967 (Renewed 1994, 1995) by Donna Music, Ltd., and Tic Toc Music, Ltd. All rights for Donna Music, Ltd., in the United States and Canada controlled and administered by Glenwood Music Corp. All rights for Tic Toc Music, Ltd., in the United States and Canada controlled and administered by Songs of Peer, Ltd. All rights reserved. International copyright secured. Used by permission.

Individual copyrights and permissions listed on pages 545–548 constitute an extension of this copyright page.

HarperCollins books may be purchased for educational, business, or sales promotional use. For information please write: Special Markets Department, HarperCollins Publishers Inc., 10 East 53rd Street, New York, NY 10022.

FIRST EDITION

Designed by Nicola Ferguson

Library of Congress Cataloging-in-Publication Data is available.

ISBN 0-06-053346-3

03 04 05 06 07 WB/RRD 10 9 8 7 6 5 4 3 2 1

In memory of
Adam Low (1969–1999)

"So *[said the doctor]*. Now vee may perhaps to begin. Yes?"

—PHILIP ROTH, *Portnoy's Complaint*

Contents

Acknowledgments

I'd like to thank a number of people without whom *Lost Tribe* might never have happened:

The contributors, many of whom agreed to participate in this collection even before it had found a home. I believe these writers represent several important directions for Jewish writing in the new century, and I'm honored to have worked with each one.

My editor, Kate Travers, who has been a tireless promoter of the book from the beginning. The unity of *Lost Tribe* is due in large part to her, as she pushed me to see past the disparate voices and toward a coherent vision. And thanks to Susan Weinberg, Leslie Cohen, and the rest of the staff at HarperCollins, who not only eagerly embraced *Lost Tribe* but provided me with the chance to realize this vision.

My agent, Henry Dunow, a model of perseverance and courtliness, whose advice and encouragement gave me an enormous lift at a crucial time; also Jennifer Carlson and Rolph Blythe, of the Dunow & Carlson Literary Agency, for their help along the way.

An anthology is a group project in more ways than one. Thanks to all the agents, editors, and administrators whose efficiency helped to make the permissions-gathering process a relatively painless one; in particular Nicole Aragi and Robert Preskill for their many instances of advice; Virginia Barber, who approved an important permission and statement during a difficult time; and Frederick Courtright for his guidance. A special thanks to Kristin Lang at Darhansoff, Verrill, Feldman, who represents several of the writers in this book, and who cheerfully went beyond the call of duty at each new turn. Similarly, several professional contacts have lent their time and support to this project. Carolyn Hessel of the Jewish Book Council is a staunch advocate for new Jewish writers, and has made invaluable suggestions along the way; Simon Lipskar of Writers House provided an early road map; and Loolwa Khazzom and Cindy Greenberg reached into their vast Rolodexes to help put me in touch with a number of potential contributors.

I've had the good fortune to be surrounded by friends and institutions that have each helped, in their own way, to shape my life and this book. My colleagues at the Jewish Community Center of Manhattan, in particular Karen Sander, Joy Levitt, and Debby Hirshman, gave me the opportunity to pursue my interest in contemporary writing and Jewish issues. Pearl Gluck was a driving force behind the JCC's KGB Bar Series. Melvin Jules Bukiet, Denis Woychuk, and Dan Christian, whose gracious spirits animate the stellar KGB Bar, and can be counted on to provide pearls of wisdom (and the occasional free Bud). Jennifer Bleyer and the rest of the crew at *Heeb* magazine have inspired me to keep thinking about what really matters to young Jews these days. A special shout-out to Daniel Belasco, Joanna Smith Rakoff, and Jeff Sharlet for their generous acts of friendship.

I want to thank my family, including my parents, Gabriel Zakrzewski and Allison Burko, and my brother, Richard, and stepsister, Nadine, along with Janina Roth and Peng-Sang Cau, for years of love and support. Extra special thanks—and a kiss— to two babies who have grown alongside this book for the past year: Kasia Zakrzewski and Lucca Metzger-Goehlert.

Finally, for debts too numerous to catalog here, my thanks to Rebecca Metzger, the most amazing discovery I ever made at KGB Bar—or anywhere else. I love you.

Introduction

I trace the idea for this anthology to a reading series called "Bad Jews." One cold February night a few years ago, I found myself at the first of these readings wondering what to expect from anything with such a name. "Bad Jews" sounded playful, even funny, but would the writing be half as clever as the name? Would I hear some poorly imagined account of life in a nineteenth-century shtetl? Or a half-baked memoir about sexual escapades masquerading as fiction? That the series was held at the KGB Bar, I took to be a good sign. Tucked away on the second floor of a rambling, nearly anonymous tenement building in New York's East Village—its owners installed a small, street-level neon sign only a couple of years ago—KGB exudes the sort of well-worn authenticity you associate with left-bank Parisian cafés or nineteenth-century taverns. For a long time the meeting hall (and watering hole) of the Ukrainian Labor Home, a gathering place for Ukranian socialists, the bar retains a quirky communist décor with Soviet-era photographs and posters covering its red and black walls, busts of Lenin and Stalin brooding over the bar, and a large blood-red hammer-and-sickle flag pinned, like some strange, giant bird, to the old tin ceiling.

That night the place was packed. Twenty-somethings squeezed into booths or into spaces on the floor near the podium, their short, tidy hair and stylish, oval-framed glasses half-illuminated by tea lights. Regulars crowded at the old wooden bar. Off to one side, looking somewhat out of place in their sports jackets, wool skirts, and yarmulkes, sat a flock of middle-aged newcomers. A sense of anticipation animated the bar—all the more obvious when the curator, a young journalist named Jeff Sharlet, stepped up to the podium and the conversational buzz quickly died off.

The series was the brainchild of Sharlet and novelist Melvin Jules Bukiet. Not long before, Bukiet had approached the Jewish Community Center in Manhattan with the provocative idea of creating an altogether different breed of Jewish literary experience. "Bad Jews" would combine unconventional writing in an unexpected setting, aimed at a crowd that hungered for new Jewish events. In one sense, the series was part of a wave of edgier Jewish programs sprouting up in cities like New York and San Francisco, intended to reach unaffiliated or disaffected Jews in their twenties and thirties. One literary series which began around the same time featured spoken-word poetry slams, while another—held in the basement of a former kosher winery on the Lower East Side—opened its stage to emerging Jewish writers. However, "Bad Jews" soon set itself apart by creating a place for established literary talents to revel in more controversial, even subversive, material glossed over elsewhere. For example, the first reading featured a writer, Ellen Miller, who had never been introduced into a Jewish context before. Yet Miller's first book, *Like Being Killed*, which recounted the story of a young Jewish heroin addict living amid the faint traces of the old Lower East Side, was clearly a Jewish novel. The book also featured other topics not commonly associated with Jewish fiction, including sadomasochism and AIDS.

I had stumbled across the reading at a time when I was searching for my own Jewish roots. I had been raised, perhaps not atypically, in a wealthy but overwhelmingly Christian setting—this on the outskirts of Toronto, Canada. Being one of only a handful of Jewish kids in my high school, I had always associated being Jewish with a sense of life on the margins—despite bar mitzvah and years of Reform Temple Hebrew classes. By the time I had graduated college, I'd severed nearly every religious or cultural tie. But not for long, as it turned out. A sense of identification with Judaism had remained, however buried, and this began to reassert itself during my mid- and late twenties—a time in my life when I had experienced a dizzying sense of dislocation and loss engendered by my parents' divorce, among other events.

By then, I'd moved to New York, a city with the biggest concentration of Jews outside of Israel. I discovered a contemporary urban culture that excited me: progressive, ironic, queer-friendly, Yiddish-inflected. I was introduced to the music of the Klezmatics, a group of world-class musicians whose protests about the AIDS epidemic and paeans to marijuana are cloaked in a jagged, gorgeous fusion of klezmer and jazz. I saw the plays of Tony Kushner, who had recently adapted Ansky's classic *A Dybbuk* with such electrifying stage props and performances that it brought home the terrible loss of Eastern European Jewry in a way no TV special or Hollywood blockbuster had been able to do. And I discovered a number of literary events, such as "Bad Jews," at which young writers grappled on stage with questions of identity, history, and authenticity.

The name "Bad Jews" might put some *alter kacker*'s nose out of joint, but like most Jews my age, I grinned at its playful humor, its intimations of sexual, even religious, promiscuity. Beneath the flippant joke, however, I discovered a deeper meaning. Jews have risked the label of "bad" throughout our history, no more so than when we've elevated the quest for truth and justice above other considerations. A century ago, socialist Jews from Eastern Europe earned the label as they agitated for workers' rights, marching on Union Square to help end unjust child labor practices. A half-century later, college students risked this identification—and far worse—when they joined the Freedom Riders in the South to protest the inhumanity of segregation. More recently, the label has clung to women who've argued for a more egalitarian liturgy, or who've exposed the sexism that still plagues our institutions. At different times throughout our history, we've been "bad Jews" when we've helped to expand and redefine Jewish identity: when we've cheered for Abraham

Joshua Heschel in Selma, Lenny Bruce on the comedy stage, or an orange on the seder plate.

In the realm of contemporary Jewish-American writing, Philip Roth may be the most famous "bad Jew" of all. Throughout a forty-year career, Roth has enraged critics and earned fans with novels that offer brilliant, explicit, and outrageous dissections of Jewish identity. Long before the neurotic antics of *Seinfeld*, Roth had lampooned the values of the Jewish middle class in nervy, ambitious stories such as "Goodbye, Columbus," and "The Conversion of the Jews." But it was with *Portnoy's Complaint* that he captured the contradictions of Jewish identity with a ferocity and abandon heretofore unseen. Henry Roth, Delmore Schwartz, and Saul Bellow might present the lives of the immigrant generations as a tough but potentially redemptive struggle— but Roth and his narrator, Alexander Portnoy, don't find much in the experience to *kvell* about. When he's not busy recounting raw but funny encounters with teenage masturbation and shiksa goddesses, Portnoy ruthlessly catalogs the humiliation visited upon children of immigrants like himself, indignations inflicted by his suffocating mother, his feckless father, or his clueless rabbi. Roth once remarked that he was completely surprised by the public outrage that greeted the book, yet the reaction was a measure of how accurately he'd hit his mark. Critics might pounce on the book's untrammeled misogyny, or the tiresome nature of Portnoy's seemingly endless malaise, but one thing is certain: *Portnoy's Complaint* may still be the best yardstick by which "bad" Jewish writing can be measured—and Roth himself a good prism through which to view a new breed of Jewish-American writer.

From the podium at KGB, Jeff Sharlet introduced the first "Bad Jews" reading in a Rothian tradition of irreverence: "Tonight's readers are only the latest in a long series of troublemakers, like Sholom Aleichem, Molly Picon, Lenny Bruce, and—" here Sharlet paused—"Amy Fisher." For the next forty minutes, Ellen Miller transfixed the crowd with a story-in-progress, "In Memory of

Chanveasna Chan, Who Is Still Alive." Set on an Ivy League campus during the early 1980s, the story depicts a harrowing encounter between a working-class Jewish student, Beth Tedesky, and a socially awkward, but strangely compelling Cambodian refugee. The audience laughed as Miller recounted Beth's attempts to navigate among other campus outcasts, including a needy drama queen and a sexually aggressive Orthodox Jewish freshman (the son of Holocaust survivors) who plays upon the sympathies of his innocent dates. As Miller drew to the story's conclusion, however, some in the audience shifted uncomfortably in their seats.

Abandoning her Cambodian friend in a campus movie theater, Beth Tedesky flees to a ladies room to compose herself. Standing before a mirror, she contemplates her "pale Jew-girl" looks. She amuses herself by imagining a line of beauty products to enhance her features—and highlight the centuries of persecution to which her pale Eastern European complexion has been heir. *Shtetl Girl*, as the imaginary line is called, comes complete with a lipstick, *Pogrom*, a perfume, *Kristallnacht* ("the bottle's stopper might be a cute, sparkly, shattered Star of David."); there's even a moisturizer, *Creamatorium*, and a clear astringent for overnight use, *The Final Solution*.

After the reading, many in the audience weren't sure what to make of passages such as this one. Some were troubled by the story's morbid humor, others by the satire on Orthodox Jewish impropriety. The questions circled for a short time around KGB: Is her depiction of the slippery Orthodox freshman meant as a slight to Holocaust survivors? Is the story's humor anti-Semitic? Is she a self-hating Jew? Certainly Miller had lived up to her billing as a "bad Jew"—in every sense of the term. She'd risked outraging her audience by rejecting piety to describe Jewish persecution, breaking an unspoken taboo among Jews in the process. More significantly, she had depicted complicated emotional themes without retreating into the safety of self-righteousness.

A couple of years ago, long after the Klezmatics, Tony Kushner, and "Bad Jews" had helped to expose me to a new, vibrant, urban Jewish culture, I went to work for the Jewish Community Center in Manhattan. As literary director, it fell on me to run the KGB reading series each month—even though by this time the name, and to some extent the focus, had changed. Yet as I listened to the new and emerging writers who took to the podium at KGB each month, I was struck by a particular quality, something in evidence from the very first "Bad Jews" reading—and that is a sense of just how much new Jewish writing has changed over the past decade or two. More than thirty years after Philip Roth shocked readers with his frank, unflattering portrait of a 1950s urban Jewish upbringing, many new Jewish writers find no character too strange, no ritual too remote, no subject too taboo, to tackle in their fiction.

Call them the "post-Roth" generation. Just as Philip Roth once gave the Jewish community a double hernia—and a jolt of shock and recognition—with the publication of *Portnoy's Complaint*, so too, many new writers flirt with controversial topics such as sex, materialism, assimilation, and religious intolerance, not to mention the contentious legacy of the Holocaust, to create an authentic mirror of Jewish life today. Some, raised in Orthodox settings, are particularly attuned to the conflicts found in religious lives. Others, perhaps more committed to a cultural identity, explore the social contradictions of our time. Funny, raw, dark, even transgressive: these writers have reinvigorated Jewish fiction with their attention to contemporary dilemmas often ignored by others.

For nearly a century, Jewish writers focused on the story of immigration and its aftermath. But most Jews are no longer immigrants, no longer poor and marginalized. (Those that are have a very different story to tell from the earlier sagas of greenhorns.) Rather, Jews are among the most potent groups in American life, politically powerful and materially wealthy. At the same time, we are perhaps more splintered than at any other time in America. We are rent apart by religious affiliations, political differences, and social values. It is into this fractured landscape that a new generation of provocative Jewish writers has emerged. These are writers who take for granted the diversity of the present day in a way previous generations, tied up with the anxiety of being children of immigrants, never could. Many of the stories in *Lost Tribe* emerge from a growing sensibility among young Jews, one shaped by a broader acceptance of gay and lesbian Jews and Jews of color, of feminist liturgies and new spiritual practices, of a Jewish identity not based solely on an identification with Israel or the Holocaust. And it's a sensibility that suggests shifting literary allegiances, too. The writers in *Lost Tribe* are as likely to be influenced by the metafictional antics of Donald Bartheleme and Stanley Elkin as they are by the magic realism of Bernard Malamud and Cynthia Ozick.

The stories in *Lost Tribe* reflect many of the complicated themes to be found in Jewish life today: the tensions (and distance) between the religious and the secular; the search for an authentic identity, the complexity of modern ethnicity, the rise in alternative spiritual practices and mysticism; the rise of political as well as religious fundamentalism. For the sake of an interesting as well as coherent anthology, I've split the book into three sections, each devoted to a broad theme that reflects a crucial aspect of contemporary Jewish identity.

The stories in Part One, "Love and Sex After Portnoy," explore contemporary relationships. These are new variations on an old theme, the tension between individuals and their sexual partners, families, and communities. Some of the stories in this section portray characters whose neurotic sexuality has by now become a staple (some might say a cliché) of contemporary Jewish identity—but with a twist. Suzan Sherman's "Knitting One," can be read as an amusing inversion of Alexander Portnoy's WASP fetish. And there is more than a hint of perverse sexuality in Gabriel Brownstein's "Bachelor Party," which depicts the peculiar male ritual of one-upmanship, along with a disturbing game of Nazi role-playing. Equally biting is Gary Shteyngart's

"Several Anecdotes About My Wife," a look at two immigrants who can't seem to fit into New York, one from Russia, the other from the Midwest. Though the story's subject matter is similar to that of Shteyngart's popular first novel, *The Russian Debutante's Handbook*, the mood is much darker, the outcome for Shteyngart's young Russian slacker more uncertain.

In a gentler, but equally fearless way, Nelly Reifler's "Julian" explores the intoxicating intersection of puberty, sex, and death against the backdrop of a modern Jewish family. Ehud Havazelet's "Leah" is, similarly, a sensitive investigation of sex and love in a religious Jewish setting, this time among cousins in an Orthodox community in Queens, New York. Like a number of the writers in *Lost Tribe*, Havazelet is something of a storyteller in the realistic mode. Yet his uncanny ability to inhabit the psyche of his female narrator, and the lengths to which his story goes in depicting two very different paths (one secular and rebellious, the other religious and obedient), seem particularly modern.

If "Leah" depicts the constricted opportunities for Orthodox women in a quiet, nuanced way, then Nathan Englander's "The Last One Way" takes the opposite approach. The story of one woman's attempts to gain a divorce (which in ultra-Orthodox communities requires the approval of the husband) is a grim and harrowing tale, complete with surprising snippets of Hasidic violence. Indeed, while reviewers delighted in comparing the stories in Englander's bestselling debut, *For the Relief of Unbearable Urges*, with those by Malamud (and describing Englander himself as "Singer on crack"), his stripped-down style is reminiscent of the contemporary American masters, such as Raymond Carver and Thom Jones.

What is the link between Jews and memory? That's the question posed by Rachel Kadish's "The Argument," the magnificent story that closes Part Two, "Dreams, Prayers, and Nightmares." In a sense, every story in this section is concerned with the question of memory and loss—indeed, most are contemporary responses to the biggest loss of all, the destruction of European

Jewry. Yet these stories don't claim any direct relationship to the Holocaust; rather, they explore the complexities of remembering.

Sometimes, it's all too easy. The eponymous character in Peter Orner's "Walt Kaplan Reads *Hiroshima*, March 1947" is a young man who never made it to the front during World War II but who readily imagines the horrors of atomic (and by implication genocidal) destruction. In a contemporary setting, Binnie Kirshenbaum's "Who Knows Kaddish" provocatively links the destruction of European Jewry with another kind of loss, that of Jewish heritage through assimilation. Meanwhile, Michael Lowenthal's "Ordinary Pain," Ellen Umansky's "How to Make It to the Promised Land," and Aimee Bender's "Dreaming in Polish" touch on the difficulties encountered in imagining the Holocaust. The boy who hungers for the status conferred on victims of historic injustices in "Ordinary Pain" is engaged in a frightening revisionism that's all too real in recent times. The teen at summer camp who participates in a frightening re-creation of the Warsaw Ghetto in "How to Make It to the Promised Land," gets more than she bargained for—and leaves the reader to wonder how easily we dehumanize one another. And the narrator of "Dreaming in Polish" punctuates reports of her father's illness with accounts of a visit to the Holocaust Museum in Washington, D.C., attempting to reconcile herself to both kinds of loss.

Some of the stories in this section have only the most tangential relationship to the Holocaust. It seems nearly incidental that the old cemetery caretaker in Steve Almond's "A Dream of Sleep" may be Eastern European, and possibly a survivor, until we realize he's living a kind of life-in-death. Judy Budnitz's "Hershel" is nearly a shtetl folktale, although peculiar symbols (such as a baker's oven) threaten to pull the reader out of the realm of the imaginary and back into history. The naive narrator of Aryeh Lev Stollman's "Die Grosse Liebe" recounts his mother's sentimental attachment to the eponymous prewar love story—while other, seemingly trivial, details point to a much more disturbing chapter in her WWII–era history. And Dara Horn's "Barbarians at the

Gates" is an absorbing account of a young boy's visit to an Amsterdam museum in 1938, a visit colored not only by his father's cruelty but also by the reminders of public anti-Semitism.

The search for identity—personal, historical, and religious—dominates the stories in Part Three, "Mystics, Seekers, and Fanatics." In Jonathan Safran Foer's "The Very Rigid Search," a young Ukrainian translator and his grandfather chaperone a young American around the Ukrainian countryside. The American (self-reflexively called Jonathan Safran Foer) is engaged in a fruitless search for his family's ancestral shtetl. The story is a rich act of literary ventriloquism—the narrator's hilarious malapropisms, not to mention his grandfather's petty anti-Semitism, helping to fuel much of the comedy. At other times, the personal quest underscores a deeper search for cultural identity. This is also the case in Gloria DeVidas Kirchheimer's "Goodbye, Evil Eye," a story in which two young cousins search for the grave of a relative and discover the nuances of Sephardic Jewish culture in the process.

Some of the stories in this final section examine the contemporary allure of Jewish mysticism, while others examine the struggle between religious identity and the secular world. Simone Zelitch's "Ten Plagues" is a postmodern retelling of the Exodus story, exposing hidden emotional dimensions of an old familiar story. In Myla Goldberg's charming, eccentric "Bee Season," an otherwise unremarkable girl discovers a nearly mystical talent for spelling bees—a gift that helps to unravel the delicate balance of forces that bind her quirky suburban family. And in Ben Schrank's "Consent," a young man's search for his father's secret life is entwined with two intoxicating relationships, one with a mysterious woman, the other with Jewish mysticism. Soon, he comes to see how hidden forces—molded by the hands of others—are helping to shape his own golem-like existence. Meanwhile, Joan Leegant's "Seekers in the Holy Land" depicts the darker aspects of a young man's search for spiritual enlightenment in the ancient Israeli city of Safed. Tova Mirvis's "A Poland, a Lithuania, a Galicia" is an amusing look at how one family copes with a young man's religious transformation. And there's a mystical revelation embedded in Jon Papernick's "The King of the King of Falafel," as the humorous battle between two falafel stands escalates into potentially deadly violence.

A quarter of a century ago, literary critic Irving Howe concluded that the Jewish American novel was dying out, much like the immigrant generations whose stories had fueled the genre for so long. Though most critics—like most readers—have since dismissed the sentiment as hopelessly dated, similar attitudes creep into assessments of new Jewish writing with alarming frequency. One critic blames the lack of any genuinely "American" Jewish topics for the dearth of contemporary classics, while another faults our era's rampant materialism for softening up the rugged ethical core—the so-called "meshuga spirit"—that once marked Jewish literature.

It seems strange, then, to consider how many talented Jewish writers have recently emerged to share the literary spotlight. Nathan Englander, Myla Goldberg, Jonathan Safran Foer, Tova Mirvis, Gary Shteyngart, and Aryeh Lev Stollman are only a few of the writers in *Lost Tribe* to have debuted in the past five years. It's clear that while some critics carp about the very existence of American-Jewish writing, readers themselves have discovered those novels and stories that move beyond the focus of mid-century Jewish fiction. These tales struggle to make sense of Hasidic violence, Nazi fetishes, the Holocaust industry in America, Cambodian genocide, spelling bees, JuBus, *ba'al teshuvas*, mystical revelations, and warring falafel stands—in short, they are stories that mirror the complexities of contemporary life. I hope the stories of *Lost Tribe* will do for readers what "Bad Jews" once did for me: gather together the provocative fiction of a new breed of Jewish writer—and showcase tomorrow's great Jewish writers today.

—*Paul Zakrzewski*
December 2002

PART ONE

Love and Sex
After Portnoy

THE LAST ONE WAY

Nathan Englander

I

Electrolysis promises permanence, hair killed at the roots.
As far as Gitta could tell, in eighteen years of weekly visits not a single hair had been dissuaded from growing. Still she crossed to the Italian edge of Royal Hills each week and lay back on the cracked Naugahyde table in Lili's makeshift salon. They talked. Lili shocked and plucked. Then Gitta made her way home red faced and tender, the crisp sting of witch hazel humming in electrified pores.

Gitta never blamed Lili, not her stiffening fingers or boxy outdated machine. She never expected results. Her life was one of infinite patience and unfinished business, an existence of relations drawn out.

Quick she didn't look for either. The only quick she had known was her shiddach. One flit of a date in the lobby of a Manhattan hotel and the next month married. For that bit of economy she had paid with eighteen years of miserable marriage and eighteen years separated, waiting for Berel to give her a divorce. She was Royal Hills's agunah, their woman in waiting—trapped in Jewish marriage by loopholeless laws. Not to think that New York State did for her better. A state with no no-fault divorce. Even the blessing of the gentile court she couldn't get. Her reasons weren't prima facie. The judge was not impressed. What more should she have to say than she didn't want to be married? Idiot rules. No-fault in itself an idiot concept. Anyone who's experienced will tell you the same: when a marriage fails, always, always there is fault.

———

Up on the stool, switches flicked, the circular bulb of the magnifying light crackled while the gases fired up and raced round the tube. Lili pushed the light into place—Gitta's halo. She then witch-hazeled the glass center, witch-hazeled the needle, witch-hazeled Gitta, and leaned in.

"I went to the kabbalist," Gitta said, "went to the rabbi. Useless both."

"And who said useless from the start?"

"Still, I thought," Gitta said. "Better to try the others one more time. Mystical numbers, I brought. A kabbalist's feast. Married at eighteen for eighteen years. And now eighteen years waiting for a divorce. One second it took to explain. Clear as I'm telling you."

"Easy numbers," Lili agreed.

"I got the same as they've been giving all along," Gitta said. "The rabbi wanting to know if there was someone else, if I'd fallen in love, if, God forbid, I was pregnant. The kabbalist, no better. A blessing at the end, much mazal and a healed marriage and a house full of children. Fifty-four years old and wishing me children. And me with a hot flash in the middle."

"They're waiting for Berel to die of old age. They'll bring you a divorce when they can trail in the mud off his grave along with it. Enough is enough. If he needs to die for you to live, then see to it yourself." For emphasis, Lili sank in the needle and hit the pedal twice, shock-shocking Gitta and tweezing out the freed hair.

"I picture it done, sometimes. Berel face-down behind the supermarket drowned in a puddle, or in his apartment with a broken neck, by a broken ladder, an empty fixture hanging from the ceiling, and a lightbulb broken in his hand. Accidents. Who would guess? No trail from him to me, from me to you, from you to a husband with a cousin who knows people who do such things."

"It's a simple transaction, Gitta. Berel's life spent to buy back yours. At this point, a fair price to pay."

"Terrible. Terrible talk. There is still the matchmaker. A saner idea."

"Who's been saying matchmaker from the start? You want business done, do it in a business way. You don't go looking for some rabbi's sympathy, you go to the source. If this guy made the match, let him undo it, and let him know there are more permanent solutions. Trust me, it's not killing but the prospect of killing that gets things done."

"And if it doesn't?"

"Then there is killing. Win-win situation. For once. For Gitta. Win-win."

Looking at her now, Liebman remembered her then. He was a pious man and not one for staring. But the matchmaker, well, he is part of a highly specialized field, like the doctor. He is forced to look, to see, with honest eyes.

His memory confirmed what he saw before him: a woman not easy to match.

This was not just a cruel judgment, not because so maybe one of her eyes was a little higher than the other, and one of her breasts a whole lot lower so that it pointed out and down and looked like it was embarrassed on its own about the condition and trying to sneak behind Gitta's back to hide. It had nothing even to do with her trademark hirsuteness.

What Little Liebman could not afford to ignore was her nature. A generous person might pretend not to notice. But it's the matchmaker's job to know. Gitta Floog had always been different, and it threatened everyone. And for all the unfairness she'd seen in her life, Royal Hills somehow looked upon her thankfully. A sad case, but always someone has to suffer. Better it was Gitta. Somehow, underneath, they thought it. Gitta got what she deserved.

For this prevailing, unspoken feeling, Liebman felt worst of all. In thirty-six years of successful matchmaking she was his only agunah. And to his only agunah he owed his success.

Little Liebman had long trailed Heshel the Matchmaker begging a chance to make a match on his own. Drinking tea one afternoon with all the big machers, Heshel had called Liebman over, thought it would be funny to give his mascot a shot.

Slurping at his tea, biting through a sugar cube clamped between rotten teeth, Heshel pulled Liebman onto his knee. "Shmegegge," he said, "I've got a job for you. The Floog girl needs a man." And in the way matchmakers joke privately, he added, "The time has come to cut off her braids and trim down that beard."

Liebman skulked off. He did not kid himself about the task. At a more delicate age Liebman's own father used to slap him on the back of the head and tell him to drink some milk, to learn some more Torah. "Not a hair on you and already the girls in your grade have mustaches like they've learned the Gemara once through."

To everyone's surprise, Liebman had married her off—and in one date, yet. Parents began sleeping better, no longer worrying over the boy with the short leg, the girl with the port stain, and, worse, the children with selfishness and anger etched in their eyes. Liebman's business was airborne. For a short while, until the neighbors whispered about the noise from the newlyweds' apartment and the loveless look to the husband and his head-hung wife, it was true glory for the new matchmaker.

Gitta had long since become his shame. It was bad for business to have her standing there with arms crossed and tapping a foot, Gitta Floog on display in front of his dining room window. Liebman sighed. He waved her forward, rushed her down a hallway. Gitta expected no less. She followed him into a back office with a ratty couch and a file cabinet, a dingy room off the alley.

This is how Little Liebman the matchmaker found himself alone with Gitta Floog trying to convince him to undo what he'd done.

"Forty years ago, Gitta. My very first match."

"Why me for practice? Why my life sacrificed to get started

yours?" She dropped down onto the crumpled sheet spread over the sofa.

"A good rate, Gitta. Even for a first match. Even for then. A symbolic commission, I took, if ever there was." He did not say what he was thinking, did not mention the miracle he had performed. Nothing nice to say so he said what he could. "Forty years is late for a customer to come back."

"Thirty-six, first of all. Eighteen married, eighteen waiting for Berel to break."

"So thirty-six. Still a long time for the customer to return."

Gitta stood up, moved close to Liebman. She looked down into his eyes.

"A hammer," she said. "At Sears they will replace a hammer for life."

"This is because of volume, Gitta. Where there is volume people can afford."

"So I'll pay," she said. "Same as a match. I'll pay you to unmake a wedding, same as to do."

Her eye swims over the glass, swells and softens, runs suddenly long. Then precision focus and Lili's steady gaze. This is how Gitta knows her, through snippets of clarity and a collection of ever-warping parts, her view from the underside of the magnifying light. Gitta was thinking about this and ignoring Lili's diatribe, when Lili said, "Stubborn hair," and turned up the power on the machine.

"What do you mean, he doesn't want to get involved? We have involved him already. The day he introduced you to Berel he involved himself. Tell him that, Gitta. Tell him when Berel shows up dead, he'll have no trouble understanding he's in."

"I can't do any of this."

"Then plan B. Gennaro?" Lili screamed to her husband. "Gennaro, get over here." They heard his footsteps as he approached the curtain that split the rest of the room from the salon.

"What?" he said through the fabric.

Gitta propped herself up on her elbows. "Do not, Lili. Do not start this yet. Not as a joke, not as a threat. Because I really might want it. If we do it, we do it for real."

"What?" Gennaro said.

"Put on the rice. Go put on the rice for dinner." They were silent while he walked off. Then Lili whispered, "You go explain to that midget. You go tell the matchmaker that he better beat a divorce out of your husband before you make the problem disappear. Tell him whatever you need to tell him, Widow Floog. Because you've got three choices. The matchmaker, Gennaro's cousin, or shutting your mouth. If you're never going to do anything, then save us both some energy. At least keep your mouth shut so I can do my work."

Lili guided the needle. "Back to the matchmaker," she said, and she pressed the pedal and held it down until Gitta thought she saw smoke.

Knocking did not bring him so Gitta looked round the alley for something with heft. Next to a Dumpster she found a pipe with a joint on the end and tested its weight. This she swung against the metal door at the back of the matchmaker's apartment. Each blow left a dent and made a noise that carried. She raised the pipe for a third swing when Liebman peered through the grimy window and then opened the door to the back room. He had an arm raised. Gitta was a large woman, and even a small foe with such a weapon—well, he would not put anything past her. The old suspicion.

"Put that thing down." Liebman cowered. "I've got a front door, too, you already know."

"Not trying to complicate," Gitta said. "Not trying to make extra trouble for you. You hide me in the back room, I'll keep myself hidden. I'm interested only in finishing our business."

"Business we don't have. You want your money back you can have it. I admit your match was no success."

Gitta dropped the pipe, pushed past Liebman, and made her way to the crumpled sheet on the ratty couch.

Liebman wrung his hands. "I can't help you," he said. "What could you be back for but to hear it again?"

"Do you know what my life is?" she said. "Do you know how it is?"

Liebman thought about this. He sort of did, he thought. He kind of knew. She was trapped. She was a woman anchored to a foul husband, a married widow or maybe a divorced wife. He was also aware of the superstition that surrounded her, mothers stepping between Gitta's crooked gaze and their newlywed daughters. She was a woman who raised whispers. Yes, he thought he understood.

"I know they talk about you," he said, "that all this time and they still talk."

"You think I don't hear the nonsense." Gitta turned red. "They treat me like a witch. They say Berel snapped, chased me around the house with a razor, and kicked me out in a rage. They say I made a deal with the devil and was suddenly free of hair and husband—but like any devil deal it went horribly wrong." She covered her mouth. "I got rid of it to be pretty. The day I left. Got rid of it to maybe meet a new husband, have a child or two, and start a nice life."

"And?"

And what should she tell him, that Berel had won if winning meant ruining her life and losing meant seeing her happy and free?

Gitta told him what she needed to see the job done: "Maybe it *is* late, Liebman, maybe, you think, sad. But I'm here to tell you"—she smoothed her skirt, looked away—"Gitta Floog has fallen in love."

"Can't be," Liebman said, so surprised he didn't consider the insult involved.

"A shock, I'm sure. But such things happen on their own. Even to me. I'm in love, Liebman. And like our mother Sarah, even the greater wonder, I'm pregnant. When my period did not come, I thought it had gone, but fifty-four years old and I discover it's otherwise."

"Not Berel's?" was all Liebman could say. The scandal!

"A genius you are, Liebman. A detective. No, it's not Berel's. But the father is in our community, a hot-tempered man." She went on, though Liebman looked as though he might die. "We won't have our baby born a bastard."

"Then there really is a man?"

"Modern times, Liebman. Modern times. Still, in some form or another there's generally a man. Listen to me, he has found someone from outside, someone to make me a widow. Berel would be dead already if I hadn't begged a chance to talk with you. My companion is already decided. 'On Liebman's head' is what he told me. 'The whole mess, it's butter sitting on Liebman's head. Only Little Liebman can keep it from melting into his eyes.'"

"Who is he?" Liebman buttoned and unbuttoned his collar.

"When it's done, you'll know. You'll be the first invited to the wedding. Right now, though, it's time for violence. Only two facts that concern you. We'll kill him and I'm pregnant. So take your pick. Take your pick for what's more urgent. Take your pick for why it needs to get done. But the butter sits on your head, softening already."

Not long after Gitta stepped out of the alley, looked both ways, and crossed the street, a new rumor about Gitta Floog began to spread. Maybe it was someone who looked down from a narrow bathroom window with the banging of the pipe, or the sometimes homeless Akiva peering out from a Dumpster when the back door closed. Any number of people might have seen Gitta step out of Liebman's alley into the bright light of day. But the base of the rumor, the meat of it, well, only one person, only Little Liebman, could be guilty of letting it slip.

Proportion was the first thing to go. Even before the rumor had reached proper dispatch it ballooned past belief and had to be scaled back to an absorbable size. There were stylistic variations, of course, but one detail stuck, providing the rumor with unassailable authenticity. It was the addition of Liebman's name as father of the child and Gitta's secret man. It was a twist Liebman hadn't thought of, an advantage of which Gitta hadn't dreamed.

From that instant on, no one needed it over more than Liebman. What parent would trust a matchmaker caught up in a scandal? How to let him judge a prospective son-in-law's character if he can't seem to manage his own? No, the deal was done. Liebman was fully involved.

II

Three windows faced the street in Gitta's efficiency. The one over the dormant radiator was open a crack. On the other side of the long room was a kitchen area, the front door, and a panel with the buzzer in between.

It was after the first beating, and Gitta sat in a chair in the center of her apartment. This was the best she could do.

Berel was screaming outside. His voice carried up the three stories and made its way through the crack in the window. It was a terrible effect. Gitta's blinds were drawn, and the voice, localized and harsh, taunted her from that corner, as if Berel were somehow floating outside her window and yelling in. Then he'd pause—a second's silence—and the buzzer would start screeching on her other side. Again, this sense of his presence, Berel standing in the hallway leaning on a button right outside the door.

She had no television and no radio. She couldn't concentrate on her reading or the Psalms. So she had pulled a chair to the middle of the room as far as she could get from Berel on both sides.

And she sat there, head in her hands, trapped between him.

Lili flicked the switch on her machine and hit the side panel until the power light glowed.

Gitta was spread out on the table.

"Repetitive nightmares like my father used to have about Siberia. Sometimes Berel comes through the window and sometimes through the door. It's an elopement. Berel is in a suit. I'm gowned and veiled and clutching a bouquet. Every night he carries me away, either by the door or down a ladder, always with the flowers in my arms. And always, whether from their windows or lining the hallway, the neighbors are watching and wishing us luck. From the outside it looks like perfect romance. And I can see why they confuse the bride's weak moaning—all of them smiling and waving at my call for help. They stand there cooing while Berel rips my dress off, tears it all off right there in front of them, everything but the veil."

"Under the veil?" Lili wants to know. "What's under the veil?"

"Hairless," Gitta says. "No prettier or uglier and can't tell you my age. But hairless, hairless I am sure."

Lili smiles at that, goes after a stray follicle between Gitta's eyebrows, lands the needle, strikes a nerve so that Gitta's left lid flutters and she feels a strange comfort, as if her face has been split appropriately and magically in two.

"He showed up again after the second beating, showed up out my window, buzzing at my door. This time he stayed longer. It was supposed to improve, Lili, but it's made my life only worse. Every bit of punishment he gets, he takes out on me tenfold. Hard-hearted, my Berel. That's what the matchmaker says. He keeps calling to tell me Berel will never give in."

"And what do you say?"

"I say exactly as we practiced: 'There are two ways to free an agunah. One is for the husband to give a get. And the other, to bring proof of his death. One way or the other, Liebman. One way or the other.'"

"Oh, that's good, Gitta. That last 'one way' is very good."

———

Berel was returning from a night trip to the supermarket. One moment he was walking and the next in a car with four other men—his groceries left spilled on the sidewalk.

The men wore children's plastic masks with tight swirls of yellow hair and red, red lips, little Queen Esther masks on each one. But the disguises did not sufficiently cover their grown-up faces. Black beards burst out from behind bulbous rouged cheeks. Sidelocks stuck out like pigtails from under elastic bands.

They punched Berel and smacked him before anyone said a word.

Then the one in the front passenger seat, the smallest by far, turned to talk to Berel, restrained between two Esthers in the back.

"Hard to find people willing to beat you anymore, Berel. Not out of mercy, but because it's become such a chore."

"Such a tiny, tiny thug," Berel said, "I was wondering. And then the familiar voice. Since when are you so bold, Little Liebman, as to place yourself at the scene of the crime?"

"Maybe this time I don't leave anyone to talk."

Little Liebman motioned to the two Esthers and they wrestled Berel onto his stomach and taped his hands to his ankles so that they might carry him like a bundle. The one on the right unlocked his door. "This ride," Liebman said, "I'm making it clear. Tonight we make progress."

"You want progress, Liebman? I've got some of my own. As soon as you let me loose, I'm headed straight for the newspapers. I'm going to tip the goyim off to the injustice that goes on."

"The newspapers?" Liebman laughed. "Yes, have them report it. Just the kind of Jewish story the papers love."

"It will ruin you, Liebman."

"If only you heard the rumors. My name is already ruined. Let them run it on the front page. In New York you'll find no sympathy for a man who enslaves his wife. The feminists will bring me a medal for beating you. The mayor will put me on a float in the Thanksgiving Day parade."

The car headed out on the highway, a change in rhythm. Every few seconds a seam in the road so that the smoothness of speed was broken, the constancy interrupted by a rhythmic *thuck*.

The car door by his head opened and Berel was lowered toward the flowing script of road. He worried not over disfigurement but loss of senses, being rubbed clean of eyes or tongue, being rolled into the alley without his ears. Berel screamed into the wind and was pulled back in.

"Now give the get or we head out to drown you at Jones Beach. Two to hold you under the water and two kosher witnesses to watch."

"You won't do it," Berel said. "You're a matchmaker, not a murderer. You understand the sanctity of unions. Like in nature, Liebman. Like it says about pigeons. You kill one, you have to kill its mate. To make it kosher you've got to kill both, me and Gitta both."

Berel was once again lowered. Dangerously close. A pebble shot from a tire hit Berel in the cheek. He moved his tongue to try and find it in his mouth, sure the stone had cut through. They lifted him back in.

"With arranged marriages," Liebman said, "a good match is as difficult as separating the earth from the sky. Don't you think? A wonder they ever hold."

Berel buried his face in the warmth of the right-hand Esther's lap.

"Gitta is desperate, Berel. Desperate. At this point she feels it's your life or hers. And we can't have another generation ruined by this marriage. Royal Hills doesn't need another mamzer. No, we cannot have a bastard born because of you."

"A bastard?" This was too much. "If she's pregnant, I'll tear it from her womb." Berel went mad, fought like a tiger, put on quite a show for a man with arms and legs tied behind his back. There was a struggle to control him. They slammed Berel's head against the door until Liebman screamed for them to stop. He thought they might knock the life from the body, as if the soul were a filling to be loosed from a tooth.

"Are you still with us, Berel?" Leibman held on to the back of his seat.

Berel nodded, licking his lips.

"Any chance you're thinking clearly now? Might you reconsider before we kill you?"

"That's what you'll have to do," Berel said, perking up. "Like in the American ceremony. Till death do us part."

Liebman pulled off his mask and rubbed at his eyes. He nodded to the men.

This time when Berel was lowered out the door he felt the car speed up and the grip tighten on his hair. The one with his legs used maximum control. And like artisans attending to that final detail, Berel's head was forced to the grindstone, his face to the road. For an instant. For a touch. The Esthers took off a perfect circle, a sliver—not deep—of Berel's nose.

Berel screamed outside her window, taunts and threats, declarations of a love he'd never shown. And his refrain, "Why do they beat me?" This—as if he couldn't come up with a reason—he yelled again and again.

Gitta had things she would have liked to scream. She'd have liked to stand under the window of every Jew in Royal Hills and scream at the top of her lungs, demand to know why her divorce needs an excuse or a consent, anyone's help at all.

After Berel left, Gitta carried her chair back to the table, put on a sweater, and wandered over to the bridge. She followed the walkway, gazing out at the river, the traffic speeding by on her other side. This was the old decision Gitta had pondered. Not life or death for Berel, but traffic or river, traffic or water, to which side should she dive?

Little Liebman handed Gitta an apple and leaned against the file cabinet. "Showing already," he said, looking at her stomach.

She stared back at him, the corners of her mouth turned down. She didn't appreciate the familiarity and didn't trust Liebman's invitation. It was the first time he'd asked her over since the beatings began.

"Every nightmare has its end, Gitta. Berel has come to his senses."

"Nonsense. What, he promised a divorce while you twisted an arm? He came to my house after, same as always. Floated outside my window screaming in my ear." Gitta lowered herself onto the couch as if she were indeed carrying extra weight. She sniffed at the apple. "When he throws the get in my face, Little Liebman, then I'll know it's done."

"We put a fear into him and he wouldn't budge. We dumped him in the alley half dead and still swearing he'd never see you free. Then three days ago he shows up here, then yesterday, and again this morning. Each time more remorseful, each time clearer in what he had to say. It's the little mamzer that got him," Liebman pointed at his belly. "Not for you or himself does he have any mercy, but only for the unborn. The suffering of the father, he said, should not be borne out on the son."

"Suddenly there is sense?"

"He's never lied before. Stubborn and coconut brained, he runs around spouting nonsense. But never has he agreed falsely to a divorce. He too, like you, thinks there is some trick. He says meet him once and tell him to his face that you carry another man's child. He doesn't ask for the man's name. He doesn't want to hear a tiny heartbeat or see a note from a doctor. He says, after the degradation of how he learned, he will only bring you a divorce if you tell him about the baby yourself."

Lili bent a needle. She put down the wand and fished around for a replacement, talking all the while and working herself into a rage.

"Eighteen years it takes you to build up the courage and then you buy into nonsense like this. I'm coming with you, Gitta. I'm going to strangle that bum myself."

"The matchmaker is right. Berel's never lied."

Lili slid the magnifying light out of the way and moved her face right to Gitta's so that crooked eyes crossed.

"You're meeting in a hotel, fine, perfect. But let me tell you something, Berel's not offering you a divorce, Gitta, he's offering an alibi. Why not have it so, when he leaves, a gypsy cab jumps the curb and runs him down? You can be the first to scream, to yell in a lobby with one hundred witnesses, while Berel is hit-and-runned right outside."

"I lived with him for too long not to know what goes on in that miserable mind. Berel is finally tired. He is going to give me my divorce. Soon I'll have my life back and then who knows what I'll do? Get to work on those roots, Lili. I might yet find romance."

Yes, she is bitter. Her second date in fifty-four years and again with Berel. Again in the lobby of a Manhattan hotel. Her corpse will rot, she is sure, without ever having anyone hold open a door.

Gitta stepped down the three stairs into the deep, narrow lobby, chose a couch and a chair unoccupied by any of the long-legged, knife-chinned men and women—so smartly dressed and fortified.

Before she had sunk fully into the chair a waitress approached. Gitta ordered a crème de menthe which she would not touch. Her way of paying rent for sitting.

Over the years, Gitta had crossed the street more than once to avoid Berel, hurried into the women's section or out a side door to escape a confrontation at shul. This wasn't the first time she'd laid eyes on him since, but as he made his way down those three steps, her only lover in a lifetime, her husband and tormentor, she realized that she'd not uttered a word to him since she'd left.

He'd gotten old. His beard was full of white and his cheeks hung loose on his skull. And then there were the bruises. She could see the blood-black of one under his beard and the more shocking perfect scab on the end of his nose.

"I came to ask you," he said, in a voice detached, as if sending a message with this Gitta to take back to his wife, "if you'll give me the child."

Gitta chewed at her bottom lip, lowered her chin. Despicable from the start.

"Not this way," Gitta said. "I say what you want to hear and you give me what's left of my life."

"I'm allowed to ask, no? Denied so many things, you couldn't expect I wouldn't ask." He was sad, suddenly. She could see. Amazing. How many crimes produce only victims, Gitta wondered, everyone claiming innocence and everyone hurt.

The waitress put down a napkin and set a glass in front of Gitta.

"You've fallen so low that you eat in a trayf hotel? So adultery is not your only sin?"

"It's only a drink, Berel, and I've yet to touch it. And what I do is none of your business. I want from you only one thing."

"And I wanted from you only one thing. The duties of a wife fulfilled." He did not change his tone, but the old, loose skin began to tighten, his rage, as from an organ ruptured, began to seep into cheeks and purple tongue, spread through the broken veins of his nose. "All I wanted. To see my name live on."

"Wasted energy, Berel. You hear me say it and then you give me a divorce. Agreed? Just as you told Liebman."

Berel snorted at that.

"What is my word to Liebman who beats and degrades me and is said to be the father of your bastard child?"

"What is this, Berel? This is not what was planned."

"No, neither did I plan a life of misery because of you. I was about to give you a divorce, you should know. Thought it out, talked to my rebbe, I was literally on my way over to arrange it the first time they pulled me into that car. Later, even with those Nazis hounding me, I saw it was time to give in. Then Liebman told me you were pregnant."

How he knew her, understood how to tear her in half, not Lili's peaceful, electric-needle magic, but how to tear her whole being apart, rip her brutally in two.

"You weren't ever going to give anything," she said. "This is another of your tortures."

"Shaming me, making me a shame in my community, and you talk of torture. What does a whore need a divorce for when she sells herself either way?"

Gitta went hot with panic. Her recurring reality was as bad as her nightmares. It was supposed to improve. Somehow, sometime, her life was supposed to get better. She grabbed at Berel's sleeve and pulled him close.

"There is no baby," she said. "My own trick. I've been loyal all these years." Gitta tried for a smile but got tears. "Now you must," and she was crying, "must," and she was yelling, "must give me a divorce before I die."

"I only came for the truth," he said. And like that he was up, shaking her hand free, and taking the three stairs in a stride.

Gitta stood and watched Berel push his way round the revolving door, saw a handsome young man pop out in his place.

She tried to imagine the high-pitched screech of brakes, the car hitting and thumping, the gypsy cab racing off into the night. Gitta could call Lili from a phone booth and see it over with before morning. She could wake up knowing he was gone and say her prayers with fervor. Because she could take it, she could live with his murder.

Gitta unzipped her wallet and shook her head.

How close he comes, her Berel. His whole life a near-death experience, teetering on the blade of her courage.

She thought too of Liebman, who said he knew, he felt, suffered right there along with her. Even when she makes a denial, even when no baby comes, he will still be tied to the rumors. Royal Hills would make it fit, with an adoption, a miscarriage, a hairy dwarf child not well and locked away. Let him know from it, she felt. She did not feel generous. Did not at all care.

Then Gitta thought of herself, the years remaining, the end of this life. Let it be short, she thought. Though she knew she would see a hundred and twenty years. It would be like in the old wives' tales, corpses laid to rest still growing thick, yellow nails and wiry hair. And this Gitta knew, folktale or not, would be her doom—buried, waiting, the wrong man's ring going loose around her finger, and a scholar's beard growing and growing. Roots buried deeper than even Lili had dreamed. Hair growing from bone.

Nathan Englander

I had a right-wing, xenophobic, anti-intellectual, fire-and-brimstone, free thought–free, shtetl-mentality, substandard education. During some formative period or another, I had basic theological questions. None of the men in charge of my religious education were equipped to deal with them. And so I began to look elsewhere, I began to read literature. Simple as that. And the same with creativity. If it wasn't actively quashed it was surely helped toward atrophy. I started writing because it was the one thing that I had the tools for. The single available outlet. If we had a decent blowtorch at home, I might be a welder or an industrial sculptor or a pyromaniac. But the two decisions, to give up religion and to dedicate my life to the writing of fiction, are very different. I refuse to have writing equated with rebellion. I had a specific experience growing up that steered me away from one thing and toward another. They are mutually exclusive. Yet, I admit, they bleed into each other. Stories such as "The Last One Way" deal with a lot of these issues of religiosity and identity and morality. The religion leaks into the writing. And I guess the writing leaks into the religion as well. I am a pro when it comes to ritualistic behavior, everything prescribed and timed and struc-

tured, everything right or wrong. And once I got serious about writing, I discovered that I'd adopted a lot of these forms. You write hard every day, six days a week, and on the seventh you rest. My own Sabbath. For a long time Sabbath fell out on Tuesday. Nonetheless, a day of rest makes sense.

Several Anecdotes About My Wife

Gary Shteyngart

I am pleased to make her acquaintance

I met Pamela Tannehill at a conference in Midtown Manhattan. We were working for different non-profit agencies in New York. Her non-profit was known throughout the industry for its wavering commitment to social issues, mine for its slothful, dreamy staff. I was sitting in the front row discreetly doodling into my notebook how I would look if I were better-looking (a proud and aquiline nose pointing down to a well-formed, constructive chest; thick legs that could bear a rich man's weight) when I heard a tired, older voice—older, I say, but with some of the inflections of American youth ("Umm . . .")—asking about a difficult subject: the resettlement of Hmong tribesmen in Ulster County, New York.

I turned around and saw my wife-to-be, a pretty freckled face, parchment skin tautly drawn over two cheekbones, downcast gray eyes that for some reason flickered when she hit upon the hardest consonants (Z, K, R), and below that an angry little mouth that was steadily working itself into a frenzy over this Hmong business. Also, she had no chin.

Later, the conference broke up over lunch, and some of my colleagues, mostly social workers and public administration people, went outside to talk about their loneliness. I too felt suddenly bereft and ready for a solid good cry, when Pamela Tannehill touched my arm and told me she had heard of me from a co-worker, an American Jew named Joshie. Apparently, Joshie had said that I was one for witty remarks.

"Ooof," I sighed, confused and, for some reason, rather hurt by this compliment. I suppose I like to think of myself as a serious and private person, one who can be amusing at parties but is basically *of a sadness*. "Joshie likes to talk," I muttered. "But truthfully, I don't think I'm such a funny one."

"Come again?" said Pamela Tannehill. She reached over and lightly slapped my fleshy chin, making me flinch. I had just turned twenty-nine and was already starting to fill out here and there. "Did you just say *truthfully*?"

And she laughed at me.

We went to a pallid little Japanese restaurant where I further tried to play the comic type by waving my hands around a lot and smacking my lips after tasting the hot sake. I really wanted to please her. But the real comedy was my scarf, which kept falling on the floor to the growing hilarity of two Japanese businessmen at the next table.

"You're such an idiot," Pamela Tannehill said and smiled her kindest smile. She had thin Anglo lips and wispy eyebrows, a little nose and sad, old wrinkles around her eyes. There is some warmth here, I thought, as the sake clouded my chest and buffeted my groin. "Tell me about yourself, you freak," she said. "Like, what's up with the accent?"

I explained to Pamela Tannehill what kind of a creature I was. My melancholy pedigree. I talked openly about how my family, the Abramovs, had come to America in 1979, along with the 50,000 other Soviet Jews who had taken to the air that year. I scrunched together a fistful of empty soybean shells to better demonstrate how we were pressed into so many Western jetliners, herded through the glorious transit points of Vienna and Rome finally to alight on these American shores, to fill Brighton Beach and other parts of Brooklyn and Queens with our stale, humid bodies. The tale ended at its logical terminus: the interna-

tional arrivals building at JFK, where my family was greeted by
our co-religionists, two older women named Hadassah and Berl,
who gave us a booklet about the Ten Commandments, a ride to a
dirty motel room in Queens, and some cheese.

Pamela Tannehill dispatched her grilled eel and cheerfully
appraised my furry person. "And your name is really Leonid?"
she said. "Like Leonid Brezhnev?"

"They call me Lionya," I informed her, wiping my eyes with
the cuff of my shirt. It had been years since my last good talk
with a woman.

"Lit-tle, lit-tle Lio-nya," she sang. "Lit-tle, immigrant Lionya. Such a sad and lo-nely Lio-nya . . . Hey, little Lio-nya bear!
Why don't you come home and paw me a bit? You have no idea
just how neglected I've been . . ."

Pamela Tannehill makes love to me

She would seethe. Or perhaps hiss. I have never heard a woman
create such a sound, which to my mind was a combination of the
gentle American *ph* and the lusty Russian *sh*, both sounds sucked
backward through her teeth, her face twisting into an unlikely
grimace.

"*Phshhhhhh* . . ." Pamela Tannehill said as she mounted me a
week after we had met at the non-profit conference. I was the victim of a horrible flu, lying in a puddle of my own sweat, wondering about the quality of my breath, a sick man's breath, which
was gently blowing across her lock-jawed face. "I'm going to eat
you up," she seethed. "You little . . ."

"Oh, God," I said. She was screwing me. Our first time in
bed, after the conference, I had been too scared to take off my
shirt, lest she spy how flabby and unfit I was for that sort of
thing. But now I was completely naked and helpless beneath her,
her healthy rural girl's body making a mockery of my own. "I
need to—" I said. "Pamela, I need to—"

"Now *you* fuck *me*," she said. She turned around and put her
ass in my face.

"Please," I said. I was looking for a tissue to blow my nose in, my moustache was wet with flu.

"Go ahead, little Lionya," she said. "Pound me!"

"I can't."

"Pound me, you filthy immigrant bear!"

"Oh, honey." I grabbed hold of this ass, which was the real Middle-American article I had once known in college, with a kind of pre-ass pouch between the back of the thighs and the ass proper, and then the two side-flaps that one pulled to give the woman extra pleasure.

"*Phshhhhhh,*" Pamela Tannehill hissed as I found a way inside her, wayward drops of my sweat and effluvia forming a distinct Cyrillic И on her back, which is similar in sound to the English *I*. "Mmmumph!"

Later that night, after she had been kind enough to bring me a bowl of hot Udon noodles for my cold, she told me she had a boyfriend. "It's not what you think," she said. "He won't make love to me anymore. He's sick of me." The term "make love" was more surprising than the admission of a boyfriend. She smiled in apology and as she did I realized that she had not actually spent the last ten minutes crying silently, but rather that she had a constellation of beauty marks beneath her eyes which in the shallow half-light of her apartment—provided by a flickering plastic torchère in the kitchen and the green Brooklyn moon sinking into the Gowanus Canal—looked like mascara tears.

"Kevin will always be in my life," she explained to me that night as I spooned her with my wet body on the futon. "And there's nothing you can do about that, sweets." She was speaking of Kevin Weisman, an aspiring young poet from Mahwah, New Jersey.

They met twelve years before we did, after Pamela, at the age of eighteen, had fled her family home with a black man. Ach, what can I say? An unfortunate life. As soon as my Pamela Tannehill was born in the easternmost part of Oregon state, her father left the family and she was poorly raised by an assortment of hicks, one of whom was her mother. Young Pamela had sex with black men when she was as young as twelve and her relatives would beat her for it, until the day she had had enough and bused herself across the country with her beau. In 1986, when I was taking my board exams and dreaming of a small Midwestern college thousands of miles away from my befuddled parents, Pamela arrived at the New York Port Authority with her lover, who, upon seeing with his own eyes just what kind of place New York really was, promptly left her as well. "Men just lose interest in me after a while," Pamela confessed to me that night, cradling her empty chest, "so I'm very realistic about my prospects."

She found Kevin Weisman after getting a job as an au pair in New Jersey. The patriarch of the family she worked for took time out of the Passover Seder to molest her in the solarium, and on the second night of the Jewish holiday she ran outside to find college-bound Kevin pruning an azalea in the backyard next door. They talked through a chain link fence separating the property of Pamela's master and Kevin's parents. I suppose when you're young in this country, and you're pretty—which Kevin and Pamela both were, ruggedly so in their youth—and you've been basting in the same cultural references and the same sense of entitlement and ennui, the differences of regionalism and class can be cut to pieces with, say, an inside joke about a television star who happens to be a midget, a sip from a common can of soda pop, a lonesome, furtive caress across the buttocks or genital area followed by a teenager's endless kiss.

Truthfully, this is just guesswork on my part, because when I was eighteen and growing up in a Long Island suburb under my parents' roof, it was not often that I had the chance to be alone and flirtatious with a beautiful American woman like Pamela Tannehill. But I have a feeling that my wife kissed Kevin Weisman that very night, that she even managed to swing herself over the chain link fence and let him go inside of her. And after they had satiated themselves amid the Weisman's garden, I imagine Kevin must have talked and talked in the loud, funny way of

American Jews about the salient points of his life: his love of horticulture and poetry, his overarching need for the warmth of his mother, the films of Laurence Olivier (whose manners he adored), and his plans for building a truly inspiring birdhouse out of birch.

And she must have told him, in so many words, about her life, because the next day the Weismans bought her out from the neighbors next door, and she spent the next ten years under that family's downy wing. They showed her how to build a middle-class life—Olay protective cream for the face, summer drives to Jacob's Pillow in the family's AMC Eagle, the art of a raucous family fight in which everyone goes to bed with their sense of moral imperative intact. They even paid for her to attend the popular New York University, where she studied social work administration, the caring profession practiced by the Weismans both.

"They are my family," Pamela Tannehill told me. "You never had to be reborn into another family, Lionya Bear, so you don't know anything. But if the Weismans ever found out about us . . . No, it's just impossible. You should know that right away."

And that night, shaking from the chilly after-effects of flu and sex and my simple, rather uncultured hatred toward Pamela Tannehill and her New Jersey boyfriend Kevin, I agreed with her.

Lionya loves Pamela

Fully clothed, we looked like your average young Brooklyn couple, second-rate hipsters in retro garb hunting and pecking through a pancake brunch at Harvest or perusing the two dollar rack at the Community Book Store. Naked, on the other hand, we were a sight to behold—Pamela a giant blond squirrel with her great bushy tail puffed up behind her and I a tiny, dark Semitic savage, genital in hand, standing glumly by her side in the mirror. To imagine that I could take her from behind or scale her pale supine bulk required unusual anthropological perspective, akin to imagining a love affair between a kangaroo and aardvark caged side-by-side at the municipal zoo.

But scale her I did. To mutual delight. Pamela, as she herself admitted, had been sexually neglected by Kevin for six months now (he needed his space, the bastard) and I had essentially been neglected for the past six years since breaking up with my college girlfriend. Thus, to borrow Pamela's words, our constant fucking "filled a need."

Not to say that Kevin Weisman was missing from our relationship.

Before Kevin I had been, loosely speaking, an animist. I worshipped a few memorable rocks and trees in Central Park, I worshipped the living spirits of my ancestors—my angry immigrant father, my nervous immigrant mother, crazy Grandma with one foot always in the grave—and I worshipped the spirit of the age, the sloppy fashions, the high-pitched political to-and-fro, the dubious drugs that had all but rewired my central nervous system. Kevin was my first brush with monotheism. He was my God. He was invisible to me, but His word was law.

His was the deep-timbred, phoney-English voice that I heard on Pamela's answering machine ("You have reached the residence of Kevin Weisman and Pamela; presently, neither of us is *in situ* . . .") His was the stern, all-knowing visage that surveyed our lovemaking from Pamela's bed stand, even while a slightly more bemused Kevin-god smiled at me from the bathroom wall, giving my mortal bladder an acute sense of shyness.

When Kevin called, and he called every few hours, I was exiled to the kitchen, my ear pressed to the negligible door as Pamela addressed Him in the quiet, obedient tone of a henpecked first-grader. "Yes, of course, that's okay . . . What time is good for you? Do you think I look too fat in the green dress? How about I just wear black?" When Kevin wished to "drop by" I had to scramble to get my clothes on, often dismounting Pamela in the process, getting in a few last humps before being zipped up and rushed out the door. I swear, in the moments before His arrival,

Pamela exuded the smell of lilacs. She spontaneously smelled of spring.

On weekends, if the weather was clear and Kevin wasn't staying over, Pamela and I would saunter out of bed and go for long walks. As we left the confines of her minuscule studio apartment with its Kevin icons and constant collect phone calls from Mahwah, New Jersey, I felt my mind go empty and free, my lungs replenished by the unlikely perfume of industry and trees, that strange, sour Brooklyn air. Out amid the Greek revival houses, the fluted porch columns of her borough, I goosed her in the middle of the street with my wide-open greasy palm; I licked her freckled nose at the corner of Atlantic Avenue and Court Street; I begged her over and over to say "I love you." She refused, of course, but I liked hearing myself repeat those three ridiculous words to her. When you ask for something often enough, I learned, even a refusal can seem like an acceptance.

At times I would weep about Kevin, our jealous and vengeful God, and beg Pamela to choose me in his stead. Here were some of the things she said.

"Relax, cowboy."

"No matter what I do, I'll end up hurting you. That's just a given."

"Don't give me that I'm-too-delicate-for-your-worldly-ways bullshit . . . Coy little mother."

"When it comes down to it, I'm all alone in the world."

"I've cried a lot before and it doesn't interest me."

"I don't want some stranger sifting through all the evidence and then condemning me" [on the subject of seeing a psychiatrist].

"You're too hard on yourself. Why don't you just chill out, Lionya Bear."

Pamela comes out into society

I decided to take her advice. Perhaps it was time to *stop being so hard on myself*, to, vernacularly speaking, *take it easy*. Now in my youth, I had attended a gentle, easy-going Midwestern college (its name would be familiar to many a reader) and as a consequence I had some friends who fitted a progressive portrait of America—two blacks, one Asian, an American Jew and an Anglo. Interestingly enough, all but the Anglo were women, as this gentle college was very woman-friendly (not to mention Lionya-friendly; oh, how well I had fared there!).

And so I decided to throw a little cocktail hour for my friends in the depressing Delancey Street hovel where I lived. It gave me something to do: I put on a pair of gloves and cleaned the toilet; I chased the dust bunnies out the door with a broken broom handle; I bought the latest compact disc featuring the Senegalese rapper MC Solaar plus five bottles of Vinho Verde and some sheep's milk cheese. And I almost managed to convince Pamela that she was going to have a good time. "As long as I don't have to play the loving girlfriend all night," she said, pulling on the moth-eaten sweater that had accompanied her on the Greyhound bus from eastern Oregon. "God knows, I'm through with that."

"You just be yourself," I said.

My apartment was, all told, no more than a queen-sized futon ringed by a couple of folding plastic chairs. A framed poster of the boyish-looking Soviet cosmonaut Yuri Gagarin took pride of place among my meager possessions.

Pamela and I sat in the center of the futon, my friend Kai-Ling, a freelance shopper for badly dressed technology executives, directly to my left, and Nancy and Christa, two slick, voluble Memphis natives just returned from a year in Paris, to my right. The Jewish woman and the Anglo were laughing it up in the kitchen, and we left them alone (alumni rumor had it they were going to marry each other, bring little pale babies into the world).

From the beginning, I had intimations of disaster. Pamela glared at the innocent Kai-Ling with a compressed fury that seemed to cast an orange glow across her corner of the futon, as if someone had introduced a lava lamp into the proceedings. She spent the first twenty minutes of our little party trying to burn a hole in Kai-Ling's combustible leather pants with her strange gray eyes. Finally, when I asked K.L. (who, on the occasion of my cocktail party, had sewn me a cute amoeba-shaped throw pillow), to pass the sheep's milk cheese, Pamela struck her lap with both fists and blurted out: *"Let him get it himself!"*

Near-silence. Nancy and Christa stopped their amiable French chatter in mid *bon*. Even MC Solaar grew quiet and pensive on the compact disc player. "I mean . . ." Pamela said, shaking her head at me, "He just always . . . *wants* . . . He *wants* things . . . He *wants* . . ."

Now I had had many discussions with Kai-Ling, a fellow immigrant like myself (Guangdong Province to my Leningrad), about how we should face up to the authority of the native-born, but the brisk tone in Pamela's voice had stilled Kai-Ling's hand even as it skirted the edge of the cheese plate. My friend looked at me with simple social terror, while I desperately tried to fudge an expression of encouragement. "Kai . . ." I said hopefully and lifted up one leg. In the hush of the room, we could hear Pamela's breathing.

And then, wordlessly, with a shudder of childhood fear still pulsing about her lower lip, Kai-Ling picked up the cheese plate and handed it to me.

"No trouble," she whispered. "Here you go, Lionya."

We all exhaled.

In retaliation for the Passing of the Cheese Plate, Pamela drank six glasses of Vinho Verde in rapid succession and started to pal around with Nancy and Christa. She called them her "sisters" and threatened they would have something called a "throwdown." The two black women, vaguely familiar with urban expressions, but more in tune with the Afro-French stylings of MC Solaar, smiled amiably and brushed back loose tendrils of their Paris-coiffed hair and tried to talk about Foucault's *Discipline and Punish*, a dog-eared copy of which was keeping my coffee table level.

"You *sistas* are all right by me!" Pamela said, scowling at Kai-Ling, who was quietly trying to explain to me the theory behind her amoeba pillow, a miracle of single-cell organic design. "I dated lots of black guys in high school and, let me tell you, those boys *knew* how to treat a woman . . . They were like *for real.*"

"Excuse me," Christa said. She put her drink down. "What did you just say?"

"Nuthin', sweet pea," Pamela giggled. And then she started kissing Nancy.

"Um," Nancy said.

"You have such beautiful skin," Pamela cooed as she sank her lips into Nancy's cheeks. "It's like cocoa butter," she said.

Nancy had always been something of the class clown—I still remember the weekly riots she instigated in our Zora Neale Hurston seminar—and so I expected from her some kind of delicate but appropriate joke, a mild rebuff, a playful slap across the backside.

But that night she just sat there, her lips pursed together defensively against Pamela's warm, inquisitive nose; one arm flailing in the air as if she was trying to hail a taxi. She was entirely at a loss. We were all stuck, in fact. Our gentle Midwestern college had always encouraged lesbianism in all its manifestations. What could Nancy do?

The kissing of Nancy probably took up no more than three minutes, but it was the centerpiece of the evening, the way films about the *Titanic* are memorable not for the obligatory love affair between the ill-fated cook and the thoughtful debutante but for the final scenes of the great ship rearing up its doomed prow over the Atlantic.

"*Bozhe moi,*" I whispered in Russian.

"*Mon Dieu!*" Christa seconded, clutching at her purse strings and jumping up from the futon, lest she be loved by my Pamela in turn.

"Honey," Nancy finally said, pressing a restraining palm into

Pamela's forehead, lifting her up a bit so that we could all share in the sight of an older woman's unhappy, lipstick-splotched face, the face that I loved. "Please . . ."

"You don't know what it's been like for me," Pamela was saying matter-of-factly. "I have nothing. Nobody. My father gave me away. I'm all alone in the world, sister. I never even went to a fancy college like Lionya . . ."

I considered pointing out that Pamela had in fact been sent to the popular and expensive New York University by the caring Weismans, but as I was unhinging my dry mouth in preparation to speak, Pamela suddenly withdrew from the tender pleasures of Nancy's face and threw her wine glass against the refrigerator where it exploded in spectacular fashion. *"Why don't you just fuck her?"* she screamed at me, her hands shaking, her left eye shot through with the red tracery of a burst corpuscle. "You think I don't see? Sitting there all cozy with your legs rubbing up . . . Why don't you fuck your little Kai-Ping in front of us? C'mon, sisters, let's all watch Lionya fuck his little whore. You want me to get a video camera?"

The smallness of my apartment ensured that Pamela was on her feet and out the door before Kai-Ling could say a word. I hastily pursued Pamela, just as the two lovers in the kitchen (the Anglo and Jew) were peeking out, turtle-like, at the unfolding drama, buttoning up each other's shirts, mouthing their happy dismay.

I ran down the stairs and into the rainy March night, following the slap-slap sound of Pamela's slippers against the wet pavement. Despite her fairly thick legs, she was an unusually fast runner (and a healthy woman all around, I'm pleased to say). Soon there was so much distance between us that I worried I would never catch her up, never comfort her in my hairy arms, never tell her there was nothing between Kai-Ling and myself, that we were essentially just good friends who had had an American college experience together. Later that night Pamela returned to my apartment and begged for me to hit her. "Smack me 'cross the face," she hollered in some strange accent I could not place. "Be a man, Lionya, and teach me something."

I could not do as she asked.

We talked throughout the night about what had happened, as the remains of the sheep's milk cheese gurgled away on the coffee table (by the morning's light we threw it out altogether). This is what I learned from our long night together: apparently, seven years before, Kevin had had a brief affair with an Asian woman, an affair that had caused some serious damage in his relationship with Pamela. Thus, in Pamela's world view, women of Asian descent were not to be trusted. "They come to this country with one thing in mind," she said: "Men. They come here to take our men, Lionya. That's all they're good for . . . Believe me, she'd throw you over as soon as someone more attractive came along. Or someone richer. Or more American. That's what happened with Kevin's little slut. He came right back to me with his tail between his legs. I'm just trying to save you some heartbreak, buckaroo."

We both laughed at this, although it was hard to say why. I felt vaguely complicit in something I didn't like, but by this point I just wanted to get Pamela snug in bed and to get some sleep myself. Of course, I called Kai-Ling to apologize the next day, but, for various reasons, we managed to drift apart in the years to come.

Pamela Tannehill, my only friend

And yet, for the next seventy-two hours or so, I was a happy man. Pamela treated me to her best side. She was truly contrite. "I'm sorry if I embarrassed you in front of your black friends," she wrote to me in an electronic mail message. "I really liked them. Especially that cute Nancy. Christa was kind of quiet, though. Shy, I guess."

"Sorry to be such a shit to you," she said, after saying some things to me at brunch. "Self-pity is one of my favorite hobbies, in case you haven't noticed. What a bore I am, huh?"

"I hate that you feel so bad, sweetie," she whispered to me over the phone, after I had been ejected by the second coming of Kevin. "Wish I could come over and pet your black curls and kiss your sweet furry face."

So, you see, she was coming around; trying to understand my feelings; not such a difficult woman, after all; every relationship is troubled at first.

And then, of course, there was the time she comforted me. The time I had my episodic little breakdown on the subway.

We were taking the train to see a comic film about the difficulty of falling in love in a modern London neighborhood. We were holding hands for some reason, when I heard, seated next to us, a Russian family speaking heatedly about cellular phones.

They were Soviet Jews of the least cultured kind, from Odessa perhaps, or one of the outlying Soviet Absurdistans where some of our people had settled for hard-to-understand reasons. They wore cheap leather jackets. The mother was a peroxide blonde in her fifties, whose heavy mouth articulated the careful, soothing sounds I know all Russian women are capable of (I'm thinking, in particular, of my mother during her best days). The son was a balding, oily Russian nerd of about twenty-two while his father, the patriarch, presented a more secure version of his son—fully rounded, his enormous nose bent at several junctures, the look of understood wealth in his eyes.

I winked to Pamela, trying to imply how evolved I was by comparison to my co-nationals, how I wore only the most fashionable Manhattan-style clothes, but she failed to notice.

Meanwhile, the post-Soviet cellular phone conversation was heating up. "Six hundred minutes," the son kept saying, anxiously waving his hands in the subway air. "And the weekends are free! And that's long-distance too . . . You can call Izya in Los Angeles. We can each have a phone for thirty dollars a month!"

The family was caught up in these figures. Thirty dollars. Six hundred minutes. These figures cut and hurt, they tempted and teased, they somehow managed to bring out a hundred collective years of Soviet pain and ten collective years of American uncertainty. Finally, the patriarch put an end to the discussion. "Sasha," he said to his boy, "The problem is, little son, you don't want to learn. *You have to learn*. You have to work part-time and go to Hunter College three days a week. Otherwise, how will you get a profession?"

The son started whining some more about his cellular plan, but then the mother switched out of her kind woman's voice and spoke conclusively: "Don't compare what Americans get and what we get!" she said. "We are not like them! We are not like other people! How can you think we are like Americans? When will you grow up already, idiot?"

The forcefulness of this woman's voice made me tremble. I am not sure how memory works, but I do believe there are wispy force fields of desire and history that enfold Manhattan, a simple result of the number of foreigners that inhabit the island and cannot express themselves in their true language at any given moment.

Yes, unexpected memory. For just then, in the subway car, at the sound of the woman's voice, I stumbled upon the quiet image of my father consistently punching my face—first punch, lean back, watch my hand scramble to cover my face, find an unprotected space for the fist to lodge, left hand tight around my shirt collar, second punch. We lived then in our first American apartment—a garage sale assortment of bric-a-brac plus a coveted Romanian coffee table and a pair of lacquered footstools. I was a small, pale boy who stuttered in English and ate baloney sandwiches in the school bathroom to avoid my lunchroom colleagues, the throaty native-born boys who whispered things about me in their urban patois and tried to steal my beautiful sheepskin coat.

Father was punching my face for algebra problems I had failed to solve in school, while my mother's voice colored the background with its insistent tone, the tone of the subway mother now before me. "Don't hit the head!" my mother had pleaded to my father. "Ai. Ai. Are you crazy? He has to earn money with his head . . . He'll have bruises! I beg you! Hit the stomach." Also, the methodic, reasonable look of the subway patriarch reminded me of how my own father had approached his punching—soberly. With no outward malice in his eyes. For therein lies a major difference, I believe, between the kind of discipline I received and the kind doled out to my post-Soviet peers. *My father was never a drinker and so he did not punch my face when drunk.* His punching had a very specific purpose, grounded in cultural relativism, which was to make me a better student and a more conscientious person. In this way, I believe he had succeeded.

Pamela Tannehill didn't ask me why I was crying violently, hunched over on the subway floor, my beautiful polyester golf pants (a gift from Kai-Ling) smudged beyond repair. People were laughing. This must have been an unprecedented outburst for the genteel No. 6 train, and the Russians in particular were making some cutting remarks about my girlishness.

Pamela took me to her house and cancelled her evening date with Kevin, the first time she had done so and perhaps the last. I slept for three hours inside her embrace—she must have ignored the constant ringing of the phone, the thunderclap of her New Jersey God—and when I woke she gave me a slice of banana pie to eat. "Tell me," she said.

"What?" I said.

"Anything," she said.

So I told her. She smiled and kissed my cheek. "This is what our parents do," she said. "This is why neither of us will ever, ever, *ever* have children."

"Mm-hm," I lowed.

"But I thought your parents were educated," she said. "I thought educated folks didn't get physical. I thought everything they did was subtle and interior."

Drowsy, bereft, dribbling banana pie on her bedspread (usually a punishable no-no), I explained to Pamela that my father, along with his dozen cousins, had been made fatherless by the Great Patriotic War, that they were raised by the men who had managed to avoid battle, the violent, dour, second-tier men their mothers had brought home with them out of loneliness. I brought up the familiar cycle of violence we hear so much about.

But Pamela wanted me to explain myself further, which was, in itself, a pleasant surprise (it wasn't often that we were talking about me).

And she was so lovely just then. So ready to listen to me and feed me.

She was, I thought, my girlfriend.

This is what I told her. The story of my father in America. The story of my papa and the girl we both loved.

Post-Soviet mutants on parade

To begin with, my father and his relatives were—as my mother would always remind me—of simple village stock and were quite keen on survival; that is to say, lessons could be learned from the way they prospered.

Only my father had gone to university, but the rest of his family did even better than he did. They ran gasoline excise tax schemes out in New Jersey, built fantastical European-grocery-and-bootleg-Russian-video empires in Forest Hills, cornered markets in improbable goods—man-sized containers of Riga sprats, coupon books promising the bearer free drinks in Belgian hotels, vials of horse tranquillizer bound for the Israeli market.

They set my father up with a tiny factory—light manufacturing, you could call it. Within this blighted space on an asphalted stretch of Nassau County three Caribbean women bound together the pages of wedding albums.

I worked at our family's wedding-album factory all through high school, answering phones in my struggling American accent, while my father ran around yelling at the poor Caribbeans and doing a passable impression of the harried immigrant male suffering a heart attack twenty-four hours a day.

"Getting married is a special time," I found myself telling all sorts of amorous Long Islanders over the phone. "There are many tender moments you'll want to preserve. I would definitely recommend the silk moire linings and genuine leather cameos."

"Tell them about good screw!" my father would holler, sweating all over his desk.

"Oh, yes," I said, "I would be remiss if I didn't mention our special reinforced stainless steel screw, which, post binding, allows pages to lie flat."

I don't think I ever sold an album to anyone.

The Caribbean women, all in their fifties, did their binding in complete silence, each bent over a portable fan (no talking or air conditioning was allowed). When not binding, they risked their lives running across the highway to fetch my father a never-ending supply of cigarettes and coffee. For twenty minutes a day, they clustered around a folding card table eating pigeon peas and rice. I could hear them muttering in low voices during their allotted break time and occasionally throwing a conspiratorial glance my way as if to prove to me they weren't entirely beaten.

One summer, a daughter, Lissette, replaced her mother for the season. She was a smart, handsome teenager, with a sweet lisp and a shy way of smiling that she was learning to use to her advantage. After a month spent bearing the brunt of my father's seasonal anger (during July, the temperature in the factory approached 105 degrees Farenheit), I was shocked to hear Lissette ask him for a college reference. Equally shocked, Father demanded to know what she had read that summer. She softly lisped a couple of names.

"I have never heard of such person," my father sneered. "I am supposing this Achebe fellow is no Tolstoy. If you want to go to university, young girl, you should read Russian literature, *real* literature, not book by Chinese mandarin or Indian chief." But eventually he relented and had me type up some of Lissette's better qualities—her punctuality and hygiene—on a Fordham University recommendation form.

"I bet that *obezyana* will get a full scholarship," he told me later. "This is simple socialism. How can she afford to wear such a fancy blouse when I pay her almost nothing? If only she would give me a foot massage with those long monkey fingers . . ."

August approached. My father and I started preparing ourselves for the IWPC, the International Wedding Photographers Convention in Cleveland, Ohio, an important annual event in our field. We put together our best album samples, hand-polished a dozen of our *specially reinforced stainless steel screws*, and worked on the logo for our booth.

"Big Memory Never Die," my father suggested, "If You Preserve Such Memory in Abramov Album."

I was a fan of the word "tender" and suggested "Tender Memories Never Die."

"Maybe *die* is too negative," Lissette said, wiping sweat off her chest with a towel. Because of the equatorial heat in the factory, she had lost a lot of weight in two months and her body now had an erotically angular quality. I must confess that lying in my bed I would sometimes press my penis against the sheets imagining her sweet smile and sweaty chest next to me. "How about 'Tender Memories Live Forever,'" she said.

"Yes!" my father said. "I like the word 'Live.'" It has positive connotation for marriage." He smiled at Lissette, smiled with the crinkled-nose happiness he reserved for the rare occasion when something good happened to him in America. "Yes!" he said. "And you deliver slogan in clear, forceful manner! Maybe sometime you can talk to customer on the phone, because Lionya still has big Russia accent . . ."

I was a bit hurt by his comment about my accent and by having to share my phone duties with Lissette, but she did manage to sell thirty albums in one day (thirty more than I had ever sold), and when the time came for the IWPC in Cleveland my father surprised the entire factory by announcing that Lissette was coming along. "A black girl is still an American girl," he told me. "She understands things that we cannot. Do not be afraid of her. If you want, I will put her in a separate hotel room so that there will be no strange problems."

The convention was held in Cleveland's I-X Center, a kind of space-age barn near the airport which boasted the world's biggest indoor Ferris wheel. As in summers past, we had a lot of trouble setting up our booth and my father punched me several times on the neck and shoulders because I kept failing to do it right.

I wanted to do it right. My mother had told me that the convention was a time for me to support my father. He was scared of the other attendees, their perfect English, their easy, knowledgeable shop talk, the way their sports jackets settled around their shoulders just so. He got very drunk and sad during the complimentary IWPC stir-fry, a prime time to network with other suppliers, and I don't think we made any meaningful professional connections that year.

Lissette, on the other hand, was doing very well. While my father and I sat to one side of our booth, two dismal immigrants unhappily eyeing our own wares, our protégée drew in several of the younger specimens from the trade who flirted with her and came away with bundles of our rosy brochures. "You've got to see our stainless steel screw," Lissette crooned. "It's specially reinforced! Check *this* out! The pages lie flat!"

My father and I stared at her silently. I think we were both attuned to the same aspect of Lissette, the way her deep dark eyes (a mythical attribute in Russian cosmology) would gaze into the middle distance and then lift up toward some imaginary horizon, as if measuring the distance between the warm, brutal islands on which she was born and the shores of Lake Erie where she now hawked wedding albums for a depressive Russian. I knew my father kept calculating similar distances himself. I knew he did not believe in his present life for a moment. His family, his home, his business—how could he account for any of it?

The IWPC was ending. My father stole two bottles of vodka from the farewell dinner and drank them down in our hotel room. "We have had a very good convention," he said, sprawling nakedly under the covers. "This is a good industry to work in. You can meet nice people from all over the nation—California, Salt Lake City, Raleigh-Durham-Chapel Hill . . . Hey, you know what we should do now? We should go out and get some whores! We'll line them up and take our turns thrashing with them, father and son! We'll take them from the back."

"Yes," I said, non-committally. I could see my father's erection rising to form a significant tent under the covers. I remembered how we had once climbed a small cliff near Yalta, in the Crimea, a cliff that resembled an old man's face in profile. My father gave me a cardboard medal, the Order of Lenin for Socialist Mountain Climbing. He had drawn a crude picture of Lenin riding atop a mountain goat on it. I was maybe nine then.

"Let me ask you," he said, "Are you still a boy?" He threw down the covers and stuck out his hairy chest as if to show me what it meant to be a man.

"No, I have twice had an Italian girl from school," I lied to him.

"A little Sophia Loren," he sighed. He was not usually a drinker and I don't think he knew what to do with his drunkenness. "Your mother and I thought you were only a boy," he said. "I'll tell you, the first thing I did when I became a man was hit my stepfather Valentin right across the face . . ." He laughed at this memory, picked up an empty vodka bottle and gave it a proper shake. It was still empty.

"I would never hit you . . ." I started to say.

"You know what?" my father said. "I've been training Lissette. I've been giving her Chekhov stories to fill her mind. Sometimes I can't believe how kind I am to this poor black girl. Have you ever read the novel *Heart of Darkness*? It's by Joseph Conrad, a good writer of Polish descent . . . Ah, but what do you care about our stupid Lissette, when you've got your Gina Lollobrigida at school."

But there was no such Italian girl, unfortunately. All I could think of was Lissette at the factory, her sweaty chest hovering over my hungry nostrils, her soft New World palms pressing into my shoulders when she passed by my desk. How I wanted her! Yes, her chest and her palms, and also her general non-Russian benevolence, her deep dark eyes gazing into the middle distance.

I was sixteen years old and growing tired of being a boy.

I turned off the lights and imagined our Lissette lowering herself on top of me. For about an hour I pressed my penis into the hotel mattress with Lissette's smooth, young body in my mind, and then I must have drifted off into sleep. I remember my dreams distinctly: we had scaled that small cliff in Yalta and my father was congratulating me for my manliness and bravery, my commitment to keeping the Soviet cliffs of Crimea safe from the Enemy. He was kissing my cheeks and calling me by the diminutives of my name that I have always loved: *Lionchik, Lionen'ka, Lionechka.* All those silly, tender Russian permutations.

When I opened my eyes it was early morning, and the casual Ohio sun was ascending to light up the forlorn cube of the Cleveland Hopkins Airport Marriott. I could hear my father's voice urgently whispering the diminutives of my name. I turned to him, my heart filled with a forgotten filial warmth. But his bed was empty.

After a brief period of dislocation, I realized that his voice was coming from the next room. My father was crying out my name. Only it wasn't my name . . .

Lissa! my father was whimpering. *Lissen'ka! Lissetochka!*

Half asleep, a somnambulist in a pair of stained white briefs, I stumbled out to the hallway. The door to Lissette's room was slightly ajar. Hesitantly, I gave it a slight push, and was straight away confronted with the unlikely sight of my own ass, an ass I knew well from the locker-room mirror at school, vigorously pressing down into a woman. There it was: the same caved-in posterior with a jaunty trail of thick, curly hair running up the middle, culminating in a spooky hollow at the base of the spine.

And there she was beneath him, Lissette, making a series of sounds, a pathetic *ukh, ukh,* almost Russian in timbre, that made me worry my father was hurting her, but also an emphatic *ah! ah!* that was unlike any sound I had ever heard.

I stood there. Not because of the sight of my father, but because I was entranced by the white bottoms of her feet hanging in the air, much whiter than I had suspected, bouncing up and down in tandem with my father's angry rhythm. Suddenly, I wanted to kiss those tiny white soles. I wanted Lissette to know who I was. I wanted her to shout my name and to cry out for me: *ah!*

If only my father had known the truth of the matter. The way I had watched her eat pigeon peas with a hand cupped beneath her spoon. How I had borrowed Toni Morrison's *The Bluest Eye* from the library. How I had requested an application form from Fordham University where she was applying. Lissette Townsend, kind and beautiful, the white bottoms of her feet making half-circles in the air, the room filled with her soft moans . . . All my life I had been waiting for her.

Pamela Tannehill, my wife

Now that Pamela Tannehill understood me, now that she knew we were fellow sufferers, I began to pressure her to cement our relationship at Kevin's expense. Two years after we first lay together, Pamela and I moved into a little walk-up tenement apartment in the Boerum Hill section of Brooklyn. I was so in love with her that often I could not look at the world around me without experiencing a joyous convulsion, a happy blurring of vision (later this was diagnosed as an anxiety disorder, and I was given pills to take). Each morning, I left the apartment for work a little earlier than she did, and walking down the stoop, passing the Jamaican cafe where we ate curried goat on the weekend, I felt a great proprietary peace, knowing that the woman I loved was still ensconced in the musty tangle of our bed sheets, her sleepy gray eyes ringed with my morning kisses.

We had it all worked out. Weekdays were spent in our apartment. After work, we'd cook up lamb and couscous, listen to the amiable droning of National Public Radio, read the more interesting parts of *Harper's* magazine, and make loud love on all fours before going to bed. It was a pleasant time and I could feel our affection for each other growing.

The weekends she would spend with the Weismans. I imagine there was a lot of embracing between her and Kevin, maybe a few smooches on the lips, some footsie under the dinner table, but no sex. Kevin slept on the floor of his room, and would scramble into bed with her when his parents knocked on the door to wake them up in the morning. I'm not sure what they did as a family (once she brought me seashells from the Jersey shore), but after I had called the Weisman house one weekend to tell Pamela how alone I felt, Kevin apparently said to her: "I don't want that man calling this house ever again."

This instigated a terrible row with Pamela. She was very honest about the situation. "What can you give me?" she said, spitting into her palm, a vestigial gesture from her childhood years. "Huh? Can you give me a family like the Weismans? They saved my life, you know. Are your freaky, fucked-up immigrant parents going to take care of me? Look what they did to you, Lionya Bear."

I was surprised. We had once had brunch with my parents and I thought it went rather well. My mother held Pamela's hand and said: "Pamela, it is very nice for you that you have such white skin." (After my sojourn at the gentle Midwestern college, my mother for some reason believed that I was going to marry a black woman.)

And my father added: "Yes, we could never imagine our Lionya with such a beautiful girl," a remark so heartfelt that it made Pamela blush.

But at the end of the meal my father had performed his customary fumbling with the bill, whispering the amounts in his strange greenhorn dialect, while my mother, in her callous, Russian way, had implied that as a woman of thirty she had been prettier than Pamela and dating more successfully. "One time, I went with head of Leningrad musical conservatory, another time with Sergei Sukharchik, famous alpinist!"

Come to think of it, Pamela had cried after the meal and, in one of her horrible attacks of low self-esteem, once again begged me to hit her. That was one of the last meals we ever shared with my parents. But this was also a time when our relationship continued to deepen. In fact, we were so into each other that even spending the weekends apart (her with the Weismans, me alone at home) often proved painful for us.

One day, after Pamela Tannehill had cried in my arms all night because she said that nobody cared for her—not me, not Kevin, not anyone else in the world—I had sent an electronic message to her workplace. *You should know, Pamela,* I wrote, *that I love you very much.*

My Little Lionya, she replied, *You are quite dear to me, but I am wary of the binding effect such tender statements can have on the parties involved. I'm not the slightest bit interested in hiding the truth from you or getting into some sort of ugly mess once again (story of my life, huh?). I hope these many qualifications do not diminish in any way your open-hearted declaration of love for me. Okay?*

I printed out that message on my office's best bond paper and carried it around with me for many months. Actually, I carry it with me still. I know that her many caveats are a little off-putting, but they simply reflect the careful way in which Pamela Tannehill considers matters of the heart. Someone with a history like hers cannot afford to be hurt again, the way Kevin Weisman hurt her when he refused to have sex with her after twelve years of intimacy. Still the message speaks for itself, I believe: *You are quite dear to me.*

Three months after I received this message, three years after we had met each other at the non-profit conference, I asked Pamela Tannehill to marry me. She took two weeks to consider my proposal and finally said she felt she had no choice but to accept (under the condition, of course, that her arrangement with the Weismans would continue in perpetuity). "I don't want to lose you," she sobbed. "No one treats me like you do."

We settled for a simple municipal ceremony. By this point I had lost all the friends I had made at the gentle Midwestern college and Pamela also could not come up with any friends of her own, so, somewhat idealistically, we decided to ask Kevin to be our witness.

After two years of loving Pamela, I finally met Kevin Weisman. I finally met my Maker. He was one of those five-and-a-half-foot Jewish-American men about whom everything is big—a bulbous nose twisted by schoolyard violence, a single hairy brow dripping with early-morning virility, enormous hands that hammered together birdhouses and could have easily ripped me apart as well. He spoke with the aplomb of Sir Laurence Olivier in one of his celebrated Shakespearean roles.

"There's no need for histrionics," Prince Hamlet of Mahwah told me at our first meeting, after I had started raging about this triangular mess we had gotten ourselves into, about how my wife would never really be my wife. "Pamela and I will be special friends forever," he said, "because from the moment I declared her mine—and rarely do I make such declarations—the gods decided it was so. You should feel lucky that you'll never have to carry her weight alone the way I did for twelve years. Aren't you a lucky fellow, now?"

"You fucking bastard," I said. I wanted to speak brilliantly but was terribly drunk and could not help sounding like a simple fool. "You fucking—"

"Now, now," Kevin said, clearly delighted by the quality of his *tut, tut* voice. "No need to get nasty now, sport. I'm your best man, after all."

I had never hit a fellow before, so after I had lunged at Kevin across the room, I found myself quite unsure of what to do with my clenched fists. Kevin showed me. He beat my face for a good five minutes—he seemed to excel at dispassionate beatings, like my father—until, in a simple defensive measure, I bit one of his hairy knuckles. "Aw, shit," Kevin said in a distinctly un-Shakespearean turn.

After the City Hall ceremony, he bought us rotis and a pitcher of wine at the Jamaican cafe and gave me as a wedding present Michel Leiris's *Manhood: A Journey from Childhood into the Fierce Order of Virility*. It was a warm June day and I thought Pamela looked beautiful in her snappy velvet dress and a charming straw boater threaded with one daisy. Kevin wore a polyester suit and rep tie. Only I had opted for a traditional tuxedo.

We cried and fought all through our honeymoon at a Vermont inn and after our return to the city Pamela opted to spend an entire week with the Weismans. She came back happy and disdainful. Apparently she and Kevin had done funny impressions of me during the course of the week; in particular, they liked to dredge up the remains of my Russian accent, the way the word "attic" left my mouth as "addict," for example.

But for the next year or so, Pamela softened. She must have sensed my singular sorrow at her teasing and cruelty and I was once again reminded of the two things she had said in response to my wedding proposal: "I don't want to lose you" and "No one treats me like you do."

Even Kevin, it turned out, felt bad about what had happened between us and wanted to start a correspondence with me. He had abandoned birdhouse-building as an occupation for the time being and wanted to concentrate on his poetry. To wit, he was highly influenced by the Polish Nobelist Czeslaw Milosz and wanted to see if I, as an Eastern European, had anything to offer him in terms of my own sadness and despair. I tried to oblige him, but our correspondence was tenuous at best. It was difficult to immerse myself in Kevin's poetry, which was a kind of suburban updating of Greek myth, centering around Zeus's wife, the goddess Hera.

"Rising from the alfalfa-strewn lot/forty yards behind the Super-K-mart/Hylonome—female centaur lover/'browser of the woods'/bow before the queen of heaven/protectress of children in childbirth/spread my mother's legs/But know this, Hera/I will not come inside you/I will not clip the wings of moths."

Finally, Pamela told me that Kevin had a new plan. As a poet, he needed to be around other poets, which was difficult to do at his parents' house in New Jersey. There was a little bar near Atlantic Avenue where some of Brooklyn's finest young poets gathered to exchange their verses and "shoot the shit." Wouldn't it be wonderful if instead of her going over to the Weismans, Kevin could come by on weekends and indulge himself in the life of the New York poet? Yes, it would be wonderful, I said, but how could he pursue this delicate kind of life with me puttering around the apartment all day, blasting Rachmaninov with my morning coffee, noisily lamenting the Week in Review section of the Sunday *Times*, and constantly coughing to clear my chest of phlegm (I was often sick)?

True, it would be difficult for him, she agreed. But what if I were to spend my weekends at my parents' house? It was clear to Pamela that our marriage was driving a wedge between me and my parents, and she didn't want to be responsible for a thing like that. And so I left for my parents' Long Island estate. The Abramov manse was a nice, goofy, immigrant's house—mock-Tudor wedded to Dutch colonial with some Moorish influences thrown in as if to announce that the owners were real Americans, unencumbered by modesty or shame, who could damn well do as they pleased with their private property.

The first few weekends my parents were honestly shocked to see me, but soon enough they warmed to my presence and the opportunities it afforded for them to unbosom themselves to me. I learned in the course of four weekends that my parents were deeply unhappy people, that the cause of their unhappiness consisted of approximately thirty per cent Social and Cultural Dislocation Brought About By Immigration and seventy per cent Their Son's Failure to Be a Successful and Loving Son. They were at least relieved that I had managed to find an attractive wife on my yearly income of US $52,900, and they prayed each night to Yahweh that she would never leave me and that we would soon have babies.

One Sunday, after an afternoon spent on the patio watching my father glower at me from behind a stack of wedding-album samples, I decided to try to relieve some of my loneliness by going home three hours before I was due. All through the long ride on the Long Island Rail Road, I worried that coming home before I was expected was a kind of acting out, of invading the space of others. And my uneasiness was justified, for when I walked into our apartment, I immediately spied Kevin Weisman and my wife, the goddess Hera, lying together on the sweaty corner futon where she and I usually lay. At first, there was the usual range of unhelpful emotions: I was pained and debilitated, cut to the quick by their loud self-involvement, the unruly sight of two familiar bodies stuck together in the late summer heat, the stillness of the room punctuated by his whimpering and her pleading . . . But surprisingly, with the endurance of a Soviet citizen queuing in line for sausages, with the trembling resignation of my parents' son, I found myself oddly inspired by how hard they were working, both of them red-cheeked and winded, as they faced up to the difficulty of the task before them.

Before I could say a word of reproach (and what, really, can one say?), I had turned around and walked out the door, leaving them to themselves.

Pamela Tannehill's fierce order of virility

Shortly after Pamela Tannehill and the newly erect Kevin Weisman sued me for divorce, I found that I had no place to live, and so I decided to set up house with my parents for a few months (I was starting to see a therapist at this time, who, incidentally, found this idea perturbing). It wasn't so bad. Both my parents were working long hours, and I, having recently lost my job, was left to my own devices for most of the day.

The Abramov estate had a comforting effect on me. I had

some pleasant memories of coming home to this house from the gentle Midwestern college and impressing my parents with my grades (my father actually kissed me on the mouth when I got a perfect average), and also of breaking a condom with my college girlfriend up in my bedroom, which had made me feel quite virile and long.

I remember the last time I introduced a woman to Casa Abramov, my honeymoon with Pamela Tannehill. We had borrowed my father's station wagon—the words ABRAMOV'S SUPERIOR WEDDING SYSTEMS stencilled on both sides, an unintended irony—and were going to return the car to Long Island and take the railroad back to Brooklyn. As mentioned, we'd been fighting all through our stay at the Vermont inn, Pamela accusing me of not being Kevin, of not knowing the things he knew, the names of North American trees and shrubs and marmots, or, more practically, how to drive a car or haggle over the room service bill with the proprietor of a humble country inn. She drank three stolen mini-bottles of Stoli on the drive down, and I think both of us were secretly hoping we would crash into one of the highway's formidable cement dividers, maybe take a little hospitalized breather from each other.

Speaking of breathers, as we pulled up to my parents' house, I found myself suddenly short of breath. "I can't get through this," I wheezed. "I can't see my family right now." Also, my eyes were red from crying and this would be unacceptable to my father. Gasping, I tried to explain the situation to Pamela.

"We'll be okay, bucko," she said, stuffing her mouth with an entire container of breath mints. "Just let me do the talking." She winked at me, a clever, angry smile building in both corners of her mouth. "*And* the breathing," she said. (Her joking often inspired me.)

My mother had set up a table of fishy Russian appetizers "for the newlyweds," and was decked out in her flashiest cosmetics and shoulder pads, looking exactly like the owner of a quasi-Moroccan-mock-Tudor-Dutch-colonial house. Sometimes it was hard for me to remember that she was essentially a small tired woman whose parents ate their share of horsemeat during the siege of Leningrad and whose hands still trembled when she handled a fifty-dollar bill.

My father was relegated to a lonely corner of the vast dining room table and allowed to speak only when spoken to. This was a few months after my mother found the letters from Lissette. Mother told me she was considering the financial ramifications of a divorce (too costly, said their accountant), and presented me with a bale of letters as evidence. The letters were actually quite beautiful. That strange young Lissette was taking a course on Tolstoy at the university and was comparing my father, quite improbably, to both the sweet-tempered nobleman Levin and the dashing Count Vronsky. "Does that monkey think she's Anna Karenina now?" my mother spat at the delicate blue-lettered script. It turned out Lissette had been seeing my father for over three years.

On the day of our return from the honeymoon my father was glancing at me sullenly, motioning for me to pass the sardines and the vodka. My breathing problem was hardly easing and I was trying to reinvigorate my battered lungs with a bottle of chilled white wine. Pamela, meanwhile, was getting properly soused with whiskey. "So, Mr. Abramov," she said. "What's up?"

My father grabbed at this rare opportunity to speak. "My pretty new daughter," he mumbled, a monumental green vein bulging across his forehead. "I was just now thinking, Pamelachka . . . Do you know what it is, the meaning of your name?"

"My name?" said my wife, laughing. "You mean *Pamela Tannehill?* Oh, it doesn't mean anything, Mr. Abramov. I'm just white trash, that's all . . ."

"Ah," my father said, although he had clearly not understood my wife's meaning. "No, I was thinking, that, mm-hm, deh . . ."

"Speak English already!" my mother shouted at him, stabbing a sturgeon with her fork.

"I was only thinking," my father said, "that Pamela means in Greek 'sweet like honey.' See, Pamela, as a young man I was aspirant to the faculty of philology at Leningrad State University . . . Hmm . . . So, Lionya, when you are addressing your wife, you are saying to her that she is 'sweet like honey.'" He managed something like a laugh.

"Well, that's very nice of you to say," Pamela told him. They briefly smiled at each other across the table. "Sweet like honey," Pamela whispered to herself, pleased. She finished her drink and poured another.

My mother decided to steer the conversation to her favorite topic, the lightness of Pamela's skin and hair. "Now I was thinking," she said to Pamela, "that perhaps when you bear us children you will dilute some of Lionya's dark blood. Look at his black hair! Just look! He is like an Armenian. *Or worse.*" She stared balefully at my father, the acknowledged Master of Miscegenation, the betrayer of our sad, marmot-faced tribe.

"Oh, I like my Lionya just fine!" the generous Pamela declared, rocking from side to side.

"Really?" My mother was shocked. "But our son is nothing! He makes nothing! I am embarrassed to discuss him with friends. I am only proud of his beautiful wife."

"Don't say he's nothing!" Pamela suddenly shouted. "He's my husband! How can you say he's nothing . . ." She lowered the neckline of her blouse and stuck out her neck, whereupon a giant black hickey glimmered for all to see. "Look!" she shouted. "Look how he ravished me last night! Is that nothing? Answer me!"

My parents did not have a ready answer to this question. We sat around the table, silently eating, Pamela giggling to herself and sipping more whiskey. "No, it is something," my father finally said. "It is really something."

I let out a concerted wheeze.

Meanwhile, an important event was taking place. Pamela had abandoned her fork and was scrounging under the table with her right hand, a glass of whiskey in the other. After she found what she was looking for, after my pants had been soundlessly unzipped, after I was partly naked under the table and fully cupped in her hand, I let go of my fork as well.

Recently, I have asked my therapist to reappraise the meaning of humiliation, to try to find something a little more favorable, a better fit, a more inclusive definition, at least as far as the post-Soviet immigrant male is concerned. For sitting at my parents' table back then, growing larger, my wife's hand massaging the organ that cinched us together, my cheated mother snorting into her fish, my disgraced father dreamily considering something in the folds of his cotton napkin—his forbidden Lissette?—I felt, oddly enough, in full possession of my lungs.

I take in a long breath, enjoying for a change the American smells of the house—the odor of burnt rubber and spent electricity that lingers over the enormous television console; the heady scent of lemon spray that keeps the kitchen sparkling with possibility; the aromatic, cloying discharge of newly cut grass that hangs over the back acre.

Believe me, I am home.

Gary Shteyngart

Being an ex-Soviet, Russo-Judeo-American immigrant writer is not all borscht and laughter for me. In some ways, I'm trapped in the past. Nothing would make me feel better than sloughing off all that excess baggage and joining the new post-Bellow, post-Roth (Henry and Philip) direction of Jewish-American literature. But, as a circumcised immigrant, I have no choice other than to write about the strange hairy creature inside me, this Lionya Abramov who scrambles my days and shatters my nights. To rehash the old immigrant narrative—what a job, eh? Who would want it? And yet there's something comforting about it. Post-Lenin, post-Stalin, post-Hitler, post-Brezhnev, we Russian Jews are a ruined and shattered people, and yet we have a beauty all our own. We may very well be the last immigrant Jews in this country who have a foot in both worlds, the megashtetls of Moscow and St. Petersburg, the overstuffed bars of Orchard Street in New York.

JULIAN

Nelly Reifler

Julian balanced between the rungs of the cast-iron gate. He held the stationary fence and swung in a slow, small arc back and forth. The iron hinges squeaked. Rebecca was rummaging in her purse for the keys. When she found them, she pushed open the front door, then turned and waited for Julian to get down from the gate.

When Julian hopped down, he took a couple of uneven steps away from his mother and the front door, dragging his right foot behind him.

"Come on, time to go inside," said Rebecca.

"Today, in Yard," Julian said, "I learned to limp."

"Please, Sweetie, you can play later," said Rebecca.

Julian's father, Herzl, had said he would try to make dinner. When Rebecca and Julian entered the house, there was no smell of food being cooked, no heat coming from the kitchen. Julian ran past his mother through the living room and back door, into the garden.

Herzl was in the hammock, curled up sideways, with his knees pulled up to his chest. One arm was hooked over his head, and the other covered his eyes. The ground around him was stained black from the summer's mulberries. The hammock was big and stretchy, woven from bright green cotton string. Herzl's body weighed it down in the middle, so it supported him just above the ground and folded over him. Julian thought of a picture book they had at school about monarch butterflies, and the fields of jade-colored cocoons hanging off thousands of milkweed plants.

Julian dropped his knapsack and jacket on the ground and ran to his father. He pushed the hammock, but could not move it. His throat closed and his heart pounded. He pulled the taut ropes and looked at Herzl, then reached out a finger and poked him.

"Gentle . . ." whispered Rebecca behind him.

Herzl opened his eyes. Julian let out his breath and almost laughed. He waited for Herzl to smile or wink. He wanted his father to pull him onto the hammock, he wanted to get tangled in the stretchy webbing and fall onto his father's belly. But Herzl just looked at him; his eyes were the only part of his face that moved, and he looked Julian in the eye.

"Hi, Dad," Julian said. He made himself sound sullen and removed, like a teenager on TV.

"You didn't make dinner," said Rebecca. Then she added, "It's okay."

"I'll make dinner," said Julian. "I'm going to make dinner. I'm a good cook, Dad, right? I'll make omelets!"

"I'll make dinner," Rebecca said. Julian heard her close the door partway as she went inside the house.

Julian backed away from the hammock. His father pushed himself against the fabric and turned himself around. The hammock tipped and he sat just inside its edge, crouching, feet on the ground. Julian could see how his father had changed: his skin did not fit his big bones, it hung slack on his chest and belly. The treatments had given him rashes and had made his hair patchy. Julian stared at his freckled scalp.

He reminded himself again of that time long ago, when he was just a little kid. Herzl had taken him upstate to the sculpture park. He had been strong, and he had lifted Julian onto a couple of the giant metal monsters and taken pictures of him. Julian knew this had happened because one of these snapshots was framed on his grandmother's wall. On the way back into Brooklyn, they were stopped at a red light. Julian saw two figures in the doorway of a building. He pulled on Herzl's sleeve and pointed. A tall, thin man was bent over a tiny old lady, who was holding her pocketbook to her chest. "Wait here," Herzl had said to Julian, and he pulled over and got out of the car. Julian pressed his face to the window and watched Herzl go and talk to the man; they seemed to argue. The woman backed away and opened the door with several keys. Julian was watching her when he heard shouting and saw someone run past the car. Then he didn't see his father, and then he realized Herzl was lying on the ground. Julian started screaming inside the car. He tried to open the doors, but Herzl had locked them all. Some people came over and were brushing Herzl off as he pushed himself up to sit on the sidewalk. Julian kept screaming. Herzl gave the keys to someone to let Julian out. He ran over to his father, who was talking with the people around him. Julian leapt at his father from behind and clutched onto his head. He buried his fingers in Herzl's pale woolly hair. Julian hardly remembered the rest of the night. The important parts of that day, Julian reminded himself now, were that his dad had lifted him up and taken pictures of him; that his dad had saved a lady from being mugged; that his dad had been hurt, but was okay, and had sat up all on his own.

Herzl was rubbing his hands together and Julian could see the crisscross pattern of the strings on Herzl's arms. There was a sketch pad under the hammock. Next to it was Herzl's pen, which Julian loved to use. It was a special pen, a Rapidograph filled with India ink. Julian looked at the pad, but from where he stood, he could not make out the drawing on the page. It was small and dark and seemed to be quite detailed. He squatted to get a closer look, but Herzl reached down and closed the pad. Julian felt himself blush. He thought he had seen wings in the picture. Was he not supposed to look? Was there another new rule?

On Friday evenings during the school year, Julian's Uncle Maurice—Herzl's brother—came over with his son Peter. This visit would be their first since May. The doorbell rang at eight o'clock. Herzl was resting upstairs in the bedroom. Julian ran down the front hall in his socks, sliding the last few feet. He opened the door and let in his uncle and cousin. Uncle Maurice was divorced, and he was religious. He and Peter wore crocheted yarmulkes which were held in place with bobby pins. Maurice bent down to hug Julian, while Peter leaned back into the shadows near the door. He was twelve and he had recently experienced a growth spurt. He was covered in a new padding of flesh, and his black hair hung down to his chin. He wore his shirt untucked, had fancy suede sneakers, and carried a leather backpack. He said "What's up?" to Julian. His voice was husky.

Julian took Uncle Maurice's hand and pulled him into the hot, humid kitchen. The window to the garden was steamed over. Rebecca wiped her forehead on her sleeve, then turned to receive Uncle Maurice's hug. Rebecca's hands were coated in lentil loaf batter and Julian watched them dangle in the air behind his uncle. They were caked in a drying brown crust.

There was a big rectangle cut out of the wall between the kitchen and the living room. Julian could see Peter kneeling on the rug, flipping through Herzl's record collection.

"How is he?" Maurice was asking Rebecca.

"I don't know, something happened this afternoon. He was in the backyard with Julian—" Rebecca began.

Julian walked out of the kitchen and went to kneel next to Peter, who was inspecting a Frank Zappa record he'd taken out of a faded cardboard jacket. Julian remembered Peter prying open a clamshell once on a trip to the beach, forcing it open to see the live clam. Julian had been content to look at the pretty outsides of shells. Peter liked to open things up and touch them.

Peter handed the record to Julian and said, "Remember when we went with your dad to the radio station?" Julian nodded. Herzl's friend Al was a DJ at WROC. They went the night Al did a phone interview with Frank Zappa, and Peter had gotten to ask a question on the air. As he took the black vinyl disk from Peter,

Julian saw his own slender, bony hand, with its thin skin and just a few silky blond hairs—and he saw his cousin's hand, his thick fingers, tough, chewed nails, and two skinned knuckles.

"Do you want to play?" Julian asked his cousin. His voice came out high and fluty, like a faraway child's.

"Where's your dad tonight?" asked Peter.

"Taking a nap," Julian said. "He'll wake up for dinner."

"Let's go up to your room."

The walls of Julian's room were covered in posters from *National Geographic World,* mostly fish and frogs. There was also a souvenir picture from the *Nutcracker Suite* that Julian had meant to take down before his cousin came over. He knew that Peter's walls were painted red and had pictures of Bob Dylan, Albert Einstein, and the kibbutz in Israel that he'd visited. Julian opened the door to his closet, so that it almost completely hid the Sugar Plum Fairy. He leaned against the closet door. Peter locked the door to the room.

"I'm not allowed to lock the door," said Julian.

"Don't you have any privacy around here?" asked Peter.

"Yeah . . ." Julian's voice disappeared. He sighed.

"At my mom's place," said Peter, "there are no walls, just big canvas curtains hanging from the ceiling. It doesn't have rooms, just 'spaces.' I'm having problems with my mom right now." Julian remembered Peter's mom from a long time ago, at a party, holding a cat.

"Do you still have turtles?" Julian asked.

"Yeah. But they're old. They don't move around a lot." Peter suddenly sounded weary and he flopped down on the floor. Julian flopped down, too. Peter then half opened his eyes and said, "I brought you something. I don't know. Maybe you wouldn't like it."

Julian tried not to sound eager. "What is it?"

"I found it in the neighbor's recycling," said Peter. "Actually, I found a lot of them."

Julian felt himself clasping his hands together like a beggar. Peter reached into his bag and pulled out a manila envelope, which he tossed to Julian. Julian caught it. He opened the envelope and pulled out a magazine. *Penthouse,* it said. Julian froze. He looked at Peter.

"It's so funny," said Peter. "Look inside. It's really, really funny."

Julian opened the magazine to the first page. On one side was an ad for menthol cigarettes, on the other a table of contents. Julian squinted so everything blurred.

Peter pulled himself across the rug to Julian's side. He giggled and opened the magazine to the middle. It rested on Julian's lap as Peter flipped through the pages.

Julian heard the door to his parents' room open. He heard his father pad into the bathroom, using the cane. Julian's stomach contracted.

"This is the one," Peter was saying.

"My dad is up," said Julian.

"It's okay. The door's locked, remember?" Peter nudged Julian.

Julian was overcome by it suddenly: the thing he'd been trying not to think about all night. It had happened earlier in the day, when he was out in the garden with his father. Right after he closed the little sketch pad, Herzl had pushed against the hammock to stand up. He was up for a second, and he reached his hand out to Julian. Then he toppled over and lay there on the grass breathing hard. "Get your mother," he'd said, and as Julian dashed into the kitchen, he wondered if Herzl's hand had been about to squeeze his shoulder apologetically or hit him. Rebecca had helped Herzl up. "You have to go upstairs and lie down," she had said.

"I can't lie down forever," he had said.

Peter nudged Julian again. "Look at this."

Julian looked down at the page. His armpits tingled. He heard the toilet flush, and the door to his parents' room closed with a click. Peter nudged him again. Julian let his eyes focus. It was a picture of two women on the back of a horse, which was standing in a meadow, chewing some grass. It was a beautiful horse, sleek and brown, with a black mane. One of the women was blond and slight and she wore a white shirt which was unbuttoned to her waist. A globelike breast pointed toward the sky. She wore nothing on the bottom and she leaned back against the horse's neck. She had no hair between her legs, like a little girl. The other woman straddled the horse facing her, leaning forward on the horse's back. She held a black riding crop and her tongue pointed between the first woman's legs.

Julian looked over at his cousin. Peter now had a very serious expression on his face. Julian looked back at the picture. He heard a spatula on a pan downstairs.

Peter said quietly, "I think that one looks a little bit like you."

"Her?" Julian put his finger on the blond one's face. Peter nodded, and pushed Julian's finger away. Julian felt an ache in his thighs. He felt his testicles shift. He heard his mother's footsteps on the hardwood stairs. Rebecca called to them, "Dinner'll be ready in five minutes, kids." There was a pause, and then the footsteps descended. Julian could smell the lentil loaf. He looked at Peter, and Peter was looking at him with a strange, agonized grin. Then Peter stuck out his tongue, making it pointy like the woman in the picture. Julian stuck out his tongue, too, and leaned toward his cousin until their tongues were touching. Julian's penis pushed against his underwear. Peter put his arm around Julian's shoulder and pulled him close. Julian felt Peter's tongue, large inside his mouth. Julian thought of the Sugar Plum Fairy and moved his own tongue around. Soon they were hugging each other and lying down on the floor. They touched each other's shoulders and arms.

Then it was over. Neither pushed away, they just parted and went back to leaning against the wall. Julian inspected Peter's face. It was red and shiny. Julian still ached between his legs. He glanced down at the crotch of his cousin's pants, but they were very baggy, and Julian couldn't see anything.

"Think about something sad, and it'll go away," said Peter.

Herzl did not come down to dinner.

Rebecca asked Peter about the skateboard he was making. Peter talked about planing down the wood, picking out a finish, and why small wheels were better than the old fat kind. Then Uncle Maurice told them about two-headed tulips that had been found growing next to Three Mile Island. "How can we pray to a God who creates these things," he said. No one answered.

"Everything in the world is somehow meant to be—" Uncle Maurice continued, gesturing around the room with both his hands. "I accept that, or I try to, anyway. But think about it— normally, those bright flowers are the most prized and beautiful part of the plant. Then when you multiply them, they become bizarre—just *wrong*. Who is it that decides these things for us? Is there something we're supposed to learn? If anyone knows, please tell me."

Under the table, Julian's feet moved rhythmically. He was practicing his limp.

After dinner, Uncle Maurice and Cousin Peter went upstairs to visit Herzl. It had been months since Peter had seen his uncle. Maurice had visited after the surgery, but Peter had been in soccer camp. Julian helped his mother fold the tablecloth and make tea. When Maurice came downstairs, Peter was not with him. He explained that Peter was in Julian's room, spending some "alone time."

Julian dashed upstairs. He wanted to tell Peter to take the magazine, that it was too dangerous having it in this house. The door to his room was closed. Julian knocked.

"Who is it?" Peter's voice was muffled.

"Julian."

"Come in," said Peter. Julian pushed the door open. Peter was lying on the bed, on Julian's old *Star Trek* quilt. When he sat up, there were glossy tear stripes under his eyes. Julian closed the door behind himself and sat down on the edge of the bed. He was very near to Peter. Peter sniffed and wiped his nose with the back of his hand.

Peter said, "Your dad is sick."

"I know," said Julian. He looked at the Starship *Enterprise,* zooming across his bed.

"I mean, I knew he was sick, but," Peter whispered, "is he going to die?"

Julian looked back up at his cousin and he wanted to beat him. Peter was weeping, and the flesh on his body looked raw and tender. Julian's arms jerked, and for a moment, he felt he would punch Peter in the face, kick him in the belly, push him out the window to fall like a stuffed dummy into the garden.

But then Julian slid off the bed and onto the floor. He pulled his knees to his chest and wrapped his arms around them. He imagined a crisp, sunny autumn day. He imagined walking through a field of milkweed plants. As he walked, the plants started to grow. They grew taller and taller, until they were like trees around him. In his mind, he crawled up a thick stem to a fleshy leaf right below a brown pod. A thousand silk threads encircled him until he was sitting in a bright green capsule. He would hibernate in there, wait until spring. He would not come out until the time was right.

Nelly Reifler

I wrote the original version of this story when I was in graduate school. At the time, I was in love with a man who had lost his father to cancer at a very tender age, and I could sense somehow what the combination of that terribly slow and gruesome rending and the con-

current onset of puberty had felt like for him—and how it lived on in his body.

I remember a complaint that a couple of the non-Jewish members of the class had: they said that the mother, Rebecca, didn't seem warm and loving enough, not like a real Jewish mother. Thank God for my classmate Rachel, who jumped in and said that the Jewish mothers she knew weren't always warm and loving—they could be remote, neurotic, distracted, irritable . . . just like all mothers. While I was writing "Julian," I felt very close to this family—they were very real for me. And the record collection, the lentil loaf, the way that the characters speak to each other—for me, these add up to a specific kind of contemporary Jewish family life.

The character of Uncle Maurice is someone who has rediscovered his Jewishness. He talks about the flowers at Three Mile Island and wonders aloud (rather dramatically) what kind of God would do these things to people and the world in general. But he has been through a divorce, his brother is dying, his son is on the verge of becoming a man, and at an intimate, personal level, he has found some kind of reassurance in returning to a tradition that will never give him comfortable answers, but which will allow him to keep struggling to ask big questions. There's something naive-sounding about those questions when a grown-up asks them aloud at dinner, and yet we all ask them silently every day of our lives.

KNITTING ONE

Suzan Sherman

K nitting is a series of loops." This was written on the chalk-board when Dotsy first entered the classroom. I must be in the right place, Dotsy thought to herself, though there was no teacher in sight who would have jotted a sentence like that one down, and there were no other eager, first-day-of-school students.

Bulletin boards lined the walls and a few stray pens littered the floor—it was a classroom like any other, which for Dotsy contained a certain charm, hearkening back to elementary school, when multiplication tables and cursive penmanship were still thrilling subjects to be learned. The desks had been moved into a makeshift square formation, and Dotsy sat down at one that was much too small for her. She promptly poked her knee on the sharp metal edge, sending a shock of pain up her leg.

Two weeks before, when Dotsy registered for Knitting One, she'd been given a list of supplies to bring the first day—two #10 knitting needles, one skein of light-colored, medium-weight yarn, and thirty feet of measuring tape—all of which she took from her overstuffed handbag and placed in a jumble on the desk in front of her. None of these things had been easy for Dotsy to find; in searching for them she came to the conclusion that knitting had practically petered out—to the people of New York City it was not unlike cave painting and other prehistoric arts.

A couple of women walked into the classroom just then; they were about Dotsy's age, in their early thirties, and were talking and laughing together. Dotsy concluded that they must be friends. Never could she have convinced any of her girlfriends to take a course like this, as their greatest domestic achievements were heating cans of soup and sifting clumps from their cats' litter boxes. Dotsy watched the women sit down across from her do exactly what she had done; take their supplies from their bags and place them on their desks, staring in stunned amazement at their ability to find knitting needles—like fossilized bones dug up from the earth. They shed their coats, bulky layers of down and wool, and waved away the winter static from their long, blonde hair. Then they pulled off their mittens in quick, identical gestures to reveal their engagement rings. Enormous diamonds glinted fiercely at Dotsy, like an accusation—*you are not one of us*, the white rocks seemed to scoff in the cool, hard fluorescent lighting—and Dotsy did feel more than a mild twinge of jealousy.

Dotsy had never been married, nor had she ever been engaged, though she'd had a boyfriend, Dale, for two years who had recently broken up with her. Absolutely devastated, Dotsy needed something to do with her hands, which moved so frantically lately, like a bat's wings, until they finally landed on something. She would make little braids from the hair on her head, a strange Pippi Longstocking style, which, when she untwisted it, became an awful, wavy frizz. The fringes on her scarf had since turned into a glob of tight knots—Dotsy needed to order this behavior into something practical, hence Knitting One.

Dotsy found herself constantly replaying the final moments of her relationship with Dale; he sitting her down—for a talk, as he put it—and she naively interpreted the formality of this gesture as Dale preparing to propose. With a silly little grin she pushed her left hand, bare of any jewelry, up to Dale's face and stroked his hair as he began—"I know we both wanted to make this relationship work, but . . ."—and with this dangling conjunction Dotsy felt her stomach begin to fall. "I'm sorry to have to tell you this Dotsy, but we're just too different from each other."

Dale and Dotsy were different, that was true, but Dotsy had always found their contrary opinions amusing, something to tease the other lightly about, though Dale never had much of a sense of humor. Blond, tall, and handsome, his chest as wide and hairless as the Ken doll Dotsy had played with as a child—he was the type she always went for. And WASP men tended to like Dotsy back; they were like opposing forces which, after some initial tensions, had clung desperately to each another, like magnets. Over the years Dotsy had held numerous WASP hands in her own, warming their tepid palms, and at first this heat of hers had been a turn-on. Little did these WASPs know that just beneath the surface Dotsy's Jewish blood boiled furiously, ever ready as it was to bubble over, burn and blister their skin—perhaps even leaving a scar.

Dating WASP after WASP continued to backfire on Dotsy—her mother warned her about being stung one more time, as if she were covered with bites that she scratched until bloody, as if one more WASP welt would be deadly for Dotsy. In each relationship the same dynamic recurred—Dotsy paced around in circles, always in an angst-ridden fret about something, while her boyfriends sat on her couch, their blond hair in perfectly sculpted coifs, staring at her coolly, a gin and tonic in hand, with their pinkie fingers outstretched like pestilent stingers.

Everyone tried to get Dotsy to date Jewish men. Her mother, her friends, even her WASP ex-boyfriends. She relented a couple of times and went on blind dates they'd set her up with. But they were all the same; even more neurotic than Dotsy. They rattled on, obsessed as they were with their smothering mothers, while becoming tipsy on one Cosmopolitan—an effeminate pink drink that they ordered with extra Triple Sec, to make it sweeter than the syrupy Manischewitz they drank once a year at the Passover seder. After the second round Dotsy would help her dates off their bar stools and hail them a cab—she was already mothering them!—and then would flatly refuse to see any of them again. The only appealing aspect of Jewish men were their brains, but those were hidden beneath wiry brown mops of hair, unless they were balding, which many of them were. They were thin and pale, like brothers Dotsy never had. They were too high-strung, a term Dotsy's mother used for her father when he was still alive— he'd had a fatal heart attack when Dotsy was nine. The worst part of all this was that Dotsy could imagine these Jewish dates of hers forty years later, as old, shriveled men in yarmulkes, davening in the synagogue she'd gone to as a child. She winced at the thought of leaping onto this homogenous, Jewish merry-go-round, dizzily circling around and around.

"Perhaps you have some sort of self-loathing," Dale had said to Dotsy, this suggestion a hint of disturbance between them, which, at the time, Dotsy had not picked up on. WASPs were quite subtle, much more subtle than Dotsy was.

Another stereotype: Jews don't boat. Dotsy wasn't sure why this was, but it was true. She had never set foot in a boat until Dale took her out on his parents' sailboat. She had gazed in admiration at Dale's arm muscles swelling and buckling as he pulled on the ropes to tighten the sails, the boat skirting flawlessly over the water. It was a clean and wholesome experience, completely new to Dotsy, who lay on the stern basking in the rays, her cheeks turning pink and warm, while Dale's blond hair glistened like plated gold. What would her mother be doing at that moment? Dotsy wondered—either playing canasta for pennies with her Queens neighbors, or watching a *Jeopardy!* rerun.

A speedboat whizzed by them just then, making waves that headed straight for Dotsy and Dale, causing the sailboat to lurch up and down. Dotsy's stomach turned over on itself, like a flipped pancake, and a ripple of nausea crept from her stomach to her throat. With the taste of sour bile on her tongue she leaned over the stern, gagging until her half-digested lunch spilled from her mouth. Dotsy hoped Dale hadn't noticed this ungainly sight, but how could he not?—the sailboat was not exactly a yacht. Dale had purposely ignored Dotsy's retching and the dreadful smell that came afterward—another wonderful WASP trait when compared to Dotsy's family, who pointed out any personal flaw with relish. Dotsy's vomit had rested like flotsam on top of the waves, and Dale had stoically maneuvered the sailboat against the wind, until the vomit became smaller and smaller, a nearly invisible spot against the water's shimmering surface.

Another stereotype that was true: WASPs feel guilty about sex, while Jews feel guilty about everything else. To "do it," as Dale described sex, he had to be completely inebriated, and would then insist Dotsy dress in outrageous latex outfits. With a pleading look Dale would then ask Dotsy to spank him, just this once, though it had turned into a daily ritual, as routinized as brushing and flossing. He would bend over in his usual way, and Dotsy would pat his behind halfheartedly, all the while considering herself the perfect example of healthy sexuality. Dale, of course, did not agree, as they never agreed on anything. He had just presented her with another outfit—a nurse getup this time, and a long, ridiculous needle to prick him with—which Dotsy had teased him about. To get back at her Dale had said flatly, "You know, you're not so normal either. You have a Nazi fetish," and Dotsy had been utterly shocked by this accusation.

But in retrospect perhaps Dale was right, as he tended to be about everything, considering each of his words so carefully, while much of what came out of Dotsy's mouth was drivel, fat on a steak to be cut away. Secretly, Dotsy was slightly titillated by images of the German SS—their cool arrogant air, their demonic blue eyes, their shiny black boots, demented and dangerous, which would stomp on anything in their path. Dotsy had never admitted this to anyone, not even Dale—she had never boldly presented him with props—a swastika armband, for instance. Yet how had Dale known about this fantasy of hers? She remembered showing him a selection of photographs of her exes once, and they did not look much different from him—a troop of blue-eyed blonds whom Hitler would have held up as perfect Aryan specimens.

When Dotsy spoke to Dale on the phone recently he revealed he was already dating someone new. "She's Protestant," he said, "and we're very happy together."

Dotsy now stared at the women sitting across from her in class, mesmerized by their composure, their perfectly erect postures, their barrettes that secured their blonde hair behind their ears, and wondered, is this the type that Dale is dating? Whatever they ended up knitting—scarves or sweaters or socks—Dotsy knew these women, who were surely WASPs, would proudly present their woolen bits to their fiancés as neatly wrapped Christmas gifts. How typical, how Martha Stewart, how *whatever*—Dotsy dismissed them, these WASP women; as perfect as they were, they were perfectly readable. Dotsy had figured them out fast and discarded them like an easy crossword. Each week she would have to watch these two—the Twin Marthas, as Dotsy had come to nickname them—merrily whispering back and forth the most minute details of their upcoming weddings. This was not exactly the knitting spinsters club Dotsy had assumed this class would be. She had envisioned a group of single women like herself, whiling away the hours knotting bits of yarn into coherent clumps. The other students—ten in all had milled in—sat silently, staring down at their supplies, which they as yet had no idea how to use, except to poke at their skeins with their needles, like puncturing an oversized hors d'oeuvre, a puff pastry with two tremendous toothpicks.

And then a woman entered the classroom who marched purposefully toward the chalkboard and stood there, facing everyone. She took off her coat and wrote beneath "knitting is a series of loops," the words *Deborah Schwartz*. "This is Knitting One," she said in a low, raspy voice while scanning the room, a small cluster of women; her students. Deborah Schwartz had the

carefree, thrown-together style of an aging hippie. Her acces-
sories in particular revealed this—the long, beaded earrings that
danced around her neck, and the chunky amber necklace she
wore, which Dotsy found herself staring at, attempting to understand the appeal of amber. What was it?—dried-up tree sap with
petrified insects suspended inside of it.

Deborah then gave a short speech, as teachers sometimes do
the first day, about her life, and how she had come to be their
Knitting One teacher. For years she had taught knitting at this
very school, and before that she had worked for *Stockinette*, one
of the leading knitting magazines, making complicated patterns
for photo shoots. As she spoke she persistently pushed a stray
strand of her salt-and-pepper hair back behind her ear—the rest
of it had been pulled up in a round, puffy bun with two
mahogany chopsticks sticking out. Dotsy imagined Deborah
unpinning her hair and going to work on every last strand, until
she'd knitted an impromptu hair stole to wear around her shoulders. But then Deborah's speech hit the wrong key when she
said, "*Stockinette* was a long time ago, before dear Jeff passed
away."

Dear Jeff? Who was Jeff? What did he have to do with any of
this? Here was an odd bit of information, but Dotsy and everyone
else in the class would shrug it off, they would all just try to forget about it.

"Okay, everyone, take out your needles and yarn. That's
good, it looks like you all bought light colors. It's hard to knit
dark when you're a beginner."

Hard to knit dark. Dotsy wrote this down in her journal. She
kept track of everything by jotting it down, fixing it in time, lest
she forget something that might be meaningful. Dotsy was a
writer of sorts, a journalist by trade, and made her living writing
celebrity profiles, though some of the people she wrote about
were more esoteric than others. For instance, she was scheduled
to interview a matchmaker rabbi the following week for an

anthology called *Brooklyn Jews*. This rabbi was not exactly a celebrity, but at least Dotsy was getting paid well.

Deborah held up her needles for everyone to see. In her hands they looked like conductors' batons, and with one flick everyone would break out in song. "Now, go like this," Deborah said, demonstrating the first step, how to attach the yarn to the needle. "Like this," she said again, taking the yarn off and repeating the same fluid motion, absolutely indiscernible and so far away from Dotsy. It had all happened so quickly, and as she studied the abstract movement of Deborah's hands, Dotsy found that she could not imitate them. Watching and doing were two very different things—her own needle and yarn quickly became a tangle, and when she pulled to tighten what she'd done, the stitch that she'd concocted promptly disappeared. Everyone else had already gotten the hang of it—their yarn hung loosely off the side of their stick, mirroring exactly what Deborah had demonstrated.

* * *

"You're taking a knitting class? Dotsy, I can't believe this. Jews don't knit."

Dotsy's mother was always one to make generalizations like this. Generalizations were fine when Dotsy made them, but coming from her mother's mouth they were baseless accusations. What her mother said made absolutely no sense—of course Jews knit. Before sweaters could be bought at Bloomingdales and Bergdorf's, Jews did not just stand around shivering in tight circles until the conclusion of long, frigid winters.

What was wrong with knitting, anyway? Her mother just didn't understand—Dotsy needed a tinge of WASPiness, a stinger of sorts to sink into her skin. It really was a benign drug, knitting was—now that Dale was gone.

"Mom, my teacher is Jewish for God's sake—Deborah *Schwartz*."

Dotsy immediately regretted telling her mother about the

knitting, as she should never, ever tell her mother anything that mattered to her. That was the primary rule of being a daughter. Why was she always forgetting this? When Dotsy slipped into a mood where she confided in her mother, opening up and expos-ing her feelings, fragile and tentative as they were, it always ended up backfiring. Her mother would huff through the phone in disapproving tones regarding her daughter's "lifestyle." Already thirty, not yet married, and the biological clock ticking loudly, incessantly—and not one grandchild for Dotsy's mother, not one token of appreciation for all she had done for her only daughter. Dotsy's mother poured guilt over her like a warm, brown gravy while waiting impatiently for the next cycle to begin— this single career-girl stint had gone on for too long: Dotsy's mother was bored.

"Couldn't you have taken a course where you'd meet men?"

"Like what mom? Mechanics 101? Carpentry?"

"Men don't need to take courses like that. They already know what to do with their hands. From their fathers, it's passed down to them."

"The same might be said for knitting," Dotsy retorted, "but you never once bothered to teach me."

"Jews don't knit, dear, in case you forgot what I just said. We're Jewish—try to remember that."

How could Dotsy forget? Her mother wore that huge Jewish star around her neck, the points of which stabbed Dotsy in the chest every time she hugged her mother, the occasional times she went to Flushing to visit her in the same apartment in which Dotsy had grown up. Over the years she had received a hefty share of toilet jokes when people asked where she was from—*Flushing! Get it?*—they'd say, as if she'd never heard that one before.

At one time Flushing had been a predominantly Jewish neighborhood, but within the past five years it had transformed into a miniature Korea. Out of nowhere signs appeared in Korean, as all the people walking down the street were Korean, speaking to one another in Korean, pushing and shoving Dotsy's mother as she tried to find a piece of ripe fruit in the supermarket, if she could even find the supermarket anymore, everything had changed so quickly, overnight it felt like. Dotsy's mother had stubbornly refused to move away, and now she was the last Jew in Flushing, it seemed. Sometimes her mother would wail into the phone, "Dotsy, Flushing is like a foreign country now!"

Dotsy was certain this was why her mother had dug out her Jewish star from the bottom of her jewelry box—she had never worn such an ostentatious chunk of jewelry when Dotsy had been a child. She wore it as if to remind her neighbors who she was—as if she were a *Mayflower* Pilgrim, entitled for having landed in Flushing first, before the Koreans had. Dotsy's mother's Jewish star was so heavy it was like a rock hanging from her neck; people could use it to jump off a bridge and never resurface again. Who needed a gun or a bottle of pills when there was Dotsy's mother's Jewish star; it was also a stabbing knife to draw blood. Dotsy noted it had begun to affect her mother's posture, stooped over as she was whenever Dotsy saw her; a little hunchback had begun to form—and almost before her eyes her mother had grown old.

Dotsy told her mother that she had to get off the phone, she had to cut the conversation short before she might divulge anything else and dig a deeper hole for herself. But Dotsy knew that at one time mothers had taught their daughters to knit; daughters would sidle up to their mothers to learn the moves, as pie- and bread-baking and other lost arts had also been taught. Daughters did not have to pay someone—as they do now—to stand in front of a classroom and play the part of a surrogate mother. Once a week, for an hour and a half, Deborah Schwartz was now Dotsy's mother of sorts. And the Twin Marthas, mere strangers who Dotsy might have bumped into with annoyance on the street, had miraculously metamorphosed into Dotsy's sisters. Mismatched as this family was, the Marthas were the sisters Dotsy never had.

* * *

The second week of Knitting One mirrored the first in many ways. Everyone sat in the same seats as the week before, marking their territory in what had once been an unfamiliar classroom. The Marthas chirped together discussing flowers, most likely their wedding bouquets.

To pass the time until Deborah arrived Dotsy brought along a book written by the matchmaker rabbi she was to interview the next day. *Jewish Women* was a resource for her to garner ideas, questions she might ask about the Orthodox lifestyle. But reading it was a terrible struggle—it was like medicine going down, a sweet red cough syrup tasting vaguely of chemicals. The book explained the purpose of a Jewish woman's life simply and succinctly—to marry, and then give birth to as many babies as she could; this is what God had said. Dotsy swallowed hard to take in each word, knowing full well that this rabbi would immediately deem her life purposeless; after all, Dotsy was not taking Knitting One to make booties for her babies—this was not the purpose of moving two sticks around—it was more of a hobby. Actually, it was like therapy for her.

And then Deborah Schwartz waltzed into the room, dressed in a formless purple smock, reminiscent of what people wear when they get their hair cut. "Okay, everyone," she said, "take out your swatches."

What initially appeared to be a simple and straightforward homework assignment—knit a three-inch square in medium-weight wool—had been more difficult than anything Dotsy could have ever imagined. There was a beat of hesitation before everyone dug through their bags for their humble assignments, their knitting badges, their little woolly squares. Dotsy looked down at what she'd made; it was a useless thing—not big enough to be an oven mitt, but perhaps it could be used as a coaster for drinks. Deborah then began circling the room. She nodded her head at the Twin Marthas' work, perfect beige things, perfect to rest gin and tonics on, until the glasses beaded with perspiration and the wool would again smell like sheep.

Deborah lifted the swatch of a student sitting next to Dotsy and examined it. "It's a bit tight," she said. "Loosen up." And with that remark Deborah smacked her on the back encouragingly, like a couch to a football player. Deborah's comment seemed to go to the heart of this woman, so tense did she appear, her arms and legs crossed so tightly that they were contorted into knots. Her blouse was buttoned up her neck, and her veins throbbed visibly through the thin, white fabric.

Dotsy's swatch, she knew, had problems. A spider's web was what it looked like, with a knotty glob in its center, as though a fly had mistakenly flown in and gotten tangled, before finally dying there. It had become clear to Dotsy, in observing her own and other people's homework assignments, that how one knits is a clear reflection of one's personality—and like the loops and slants of a signature, can so be analyzed.

Deborah pointed to Dotsy's swatch. "This is a bit all over the place," she said. "You need to develop an even stitch. Do you know how one does that?"

Dotsy had no idea. Develop a completely different personality perhaps?

"Practice, practice, practice," Deborah rasped. And then Deborah noticed the book Dotsy had been reading, sitting on her desk. "What have we here?" Deborah said. "May I?" And before Dotsy could say a word, Deborah began flipping through the pages of *Jewish Women*, with the same awful expression Dotsy had had.

"You know Jeff grew up in a strictly Orthodox family, too," Deborah said, pointing to a page. "They never approved of me— not ever—even though I nursed him to the end. His family was so righteous, and yet they abandoned him."

Here we go. Jeff had emerged again.

What could anyone say? Who was Jeff, anyway? Dotsy studied everyone's pained expressions, which unanimously appeared to say, *We are sorry for your loss, but this is Knitting One, not a bereavement workshop.*

Dotsy wanted Deborah to put her book down, move away from her desk, and go on to the next person. But instead Deborah's eyes focused in on Dotsy, and she frowned at her, as though Dotsy too was Orthodox and somehow in cahoots with Jeff's family—as if she was their long-lost relative. Dotsy wanted to shake her head and explain, no I am just a freelance journalist, this is for an article I'm doing. I am just like you, a secular Jew, grieving the loss of a man—Dale!—even though he isn't exactly dead. But Deborah, it seemed, would never like Dotsy; she had already decided that her student was, as she put it, uneven. And Dotsy would never like Deborah, this mother she had paid a registration fee toward. Meanwhile, the Marthas sat smugly in their seats, running their fingers over their perfectly knit stitches. Dotsy felt resentment bubbling within her; clearly she was not one of the favorites in here. So this was what sibling rivalry felt like. Dotsy was relieved to have been an only child, at least up until this point.

*　*　*

"Tell me about yourself, Dotsy. Tell me why you are here." The rabbi's eyes were wide, and he stared at her curiously while stroking his gray beard. Some yellow crust was stuck in the whiskers by his mouth and Dotsy found her eyes lingering there. Children screamed in the background, and through a crack in the partition where she and the rabbi sat Dotsy could see them, seated at a table and eating from Styrofoam bowls. Next to the children was a makeshift ark that probably housed the yeshiva's Torah scrolls. This was not a fancy place—the children ate in the same room in which they prayed. The building itself was a depressing and dilapidated structure, made from yellowish bricks that had begun to erode; at any moment it felt like the whole place could collapse into dust.

Dotsy had already explained the reason for her visit twice to the rabbi on the phone, when she'd initially made her appointment to come out to Canarsie to interview him. "I am writing an article for a book," she said, even more slowly this time. "It's called *Brooklyn Jews*, and the editor thought you would be a good subject—she met you once, at the Holocaust Museum."

"Ah-hah, I see," said the rabbi, leaning back in his chair, though clearly he was still confused, as he did not appear to remember this editor from the Holocaust Museum at all. Presumably he did not receive many visitors to his yeshiva, particularly from Manhattan. It had been a grueling trip for Dotsy; an hour-and-a-half ride on the express bus through the most desolate sections of Brooklyn. She had waited almost half an hour in the freezing cold until the bus finally arrived—a hollow, drafty, rickety piece of machinery—though the driver had been friendly enough, relieved probably, to finally have a passenger for the journey. Dotsy was the only one.

"And why, may I ask, did the editor pick you to come here?"

Dotsy had no idea. The editor was a friend of a friend, and though Dotsy had never written about Jews per se, she was Jewish, so why not her? What was this rabbi trying to get at, assaulting her with these questions? That was Dotsy's job, not his. She placed her tape recorder as close to the rabbi's mouth as possible, and authoritatively pressed the record button.

"How old are you?" the rabbi asked.

Dotsy frowned and looked at the tape recorder, which appeared to be working. The little round light on it glowed red, and the tape inside turned around. "I'm thirty," she said flatly, not knowing why she had divulged this bit of information to the rabbi.

"Thirty!" the rabbi exclaimed. "You don't look thirty. You look like you're still a child. You look twenty, I'd say. Twenty-two. You're very preserved. And very pretty, too."

He looked Dotsy over. She was wearing an outfit she'd found in back of her closet, something she hadn't worn in years, a pleated flower-print dress that went down to her ankles. She had chosen this dress specifically for meeting the rabbi; she would dress as the Orthodox women did, covering every last bit of skin, as Dotsy did not want to offend. That morning, as she studied her outfit in the mirror, she thought, *I look just like a yeshiva girl.*

"Are you married?"

"No, I am not married. But Rabbi, I should be asking you the questions here. I really want—"

"Don't you see?" the rabbi said, interrupting her. "Don't you see why you are here? Fate has brought us together, my dear. I am a matchmaker and you are a single, Jewish girl. Fate has brought us together. I will have you under the *chuppah* within a year!" The rabbi was clearly excited with the prospect of setting Dotsy up with someone. This is what he loved to do. Beads of sweat had sprung up on his forehead.

Dotsy pressed stop on the tape recorder. She was trying to stay calm, maintain some semblance of professionalism in the face of this absurd back and forth. "Just a second here, Rabbi. I want to make sure that this machine is working." Dotsy rewound the tape a bit, and listened to her high-pitched voice say defensively, "No, I am not married," the background sound a hiss of screaming children.

"And I know someone, Dotsy, I know someone just perfect for you," the rabbi continued. "An accountant. How does that sound?"

This was unbelievable, this rabbi was uncontrollable, he could not stop setting Dotsy up. She could never explain the truth to him—that Jewish men did nothing for her. Without waiting for her reply the rabbi said, "I am being rude. How could I not offer you something to eat? You must be hungry. Wait one second, I'll get you something." He got up from his chair and opened the partition, the sound of screaming children magnified now; there must have been a hundred of them crowded into the other room. Dotsy shifted her legs. She looked down at her dress. She couldn't wait to tear it off when she got back to Manhattan. How much, exactly, was she getting paid for this?

The rabbi rushed back into the room and placed Styrofoam

bowls heaped with egg salad in front of her. "Here, eat," he urged, handing her a white plastic fork. "It's very good."

But Dotsy was not hungry, she had eaten before she'd come. She wanted to ask the rabbi questions. She had heard from the *Brooklyn Jews* editor that the rabbi was a Holocaust survivor, and though it was probably not an easy subject for him to discuss, Dotsy wanted to know, had he been in a concentration camp? Did he have a number on his arm? What were his experiences with the Nazis? And if she dared, she might have pondered, were they as devilishly handsome as their photographs? With the rabbi's answers in hand Dotsy would dash back to Manhattan and write her article, but at the rate this was going she wouldn't be home until after dark. Dotsy shoveled a bit of egg salad into her mouth—it was sticky yellow stuff, cold as ice and ruined with too much mayonnaise—and swallowed without chewing. This egg salad, she observed, was what was caked in the rabbi's beard.

"So, what do you say about the accountant?"

"Really, Rabbi, I don't want to be set up with anyone. Anyway," she decided to add, "I prefer men who are creative."

"Creative? You can 'go out' with men who are creative, but they are not the marrying kind. Let me tell you, I know from experience."

Just then Dotsy felt a stabbing cramp in her stomach and held her hand there, covering it up.

"What's wrong, Dotsy? Are you all right?"

"Just a little cramp, Rabbi, I'll be fine."

"Eat a little more egg salad, to line your stomach." He nudged the Styrofoam bowl closer to her.

"No, Rabbi," she said, pushing the bowl away, a bit annoyed now. "The egg salad is probably what's causing this in the first place."

"I doubt that," the rabbi said shortly, clearly insulted by the insinuation that the food he served—kosher food!—was making Dotsy ill. She immediately regretted her words. She imagined the rabbi punishing her by refusing to divulge anything of interest about himself, and the Nazis, now.

Another sharp pain stabbed at Dotsy, and she felt a rush between her legs. It was then that she knew her cramps were not from the egg salad at all. As usual she was not prepared for this—she hadn't been keeping track, she was uneven, just like her knitting teacher had said. Dotsy's period seemed to arrive at the most inopportune moments, as though her body was purposely trying to humiliate her. She felt it, sticky and warm, the blood soaking into her dress. From reading *Jewish Women* Dotsy had learned that the Orthodox consider women's menstrual cycles "unclean," and husbands did not have sex with their wives on those days. Most wives were consistently pregnant anyway, popping them out like toast, and if they weren't, they were bathing in a ritual pool to cleanse themselves—a *mikvah*, wasn't that the word for it?

"I am sorry to have to tell you this, Rabbi, but I think I've stained the upholstery of your chair."

"A little egg salad? That's not a problem. We'll get it out with some soap and water." Without another word the rabbi hurried out of the room—he seemed to relish these distractions, as a means to avoid divulging anything about himself. With the rabbi gone Dotsy stood up, and sure enough a purplish black splotch of blood had soaked into the chair. She touched the back of her dress and it was now all over her hands. Dotsy's flow was exceptionally heavy; it burst out and oozed down the sides of her legs like lava from an active volcano.

The rabbi rushed back into the room, his forehead wet with sweat, and a sponge in his outstretched hand. Dotsy wanted to take the sponge and wipe it across the rabbi's head. "Where is it, Dotsy? I'll give it a little rub and it'll be all clean again."

"I think I should do it, Rabbi." And when he looked down at the chair his eyes widened, as though he'd just witnessed the bloody gore of a horror film. He muttered *oy goytenu* and leaned against the wall.

Dotsy tried to explain, in case the rabbi might not understand. "It's my period, Rabbi. Please, I am so sorry, but with some cold water it should be fine. Just wait outside, I'll have it like new in no time." And without another word the rabbi handed the sponge to Dotsy and exited the room as she went to work rubbing at the blotch, which appeared to only make it worse, spreading the color all around until the upholstery had a pinkish brown hue. She bent down on her knees, and scrubbed at it harder, and when she looked up she noticed that the tape recorder's red light was on. This moment had been saved; she could play it back if she really wanted to.

The door cracked open an inch and Dotsy could see one rabbi eye peering in. "Dotsy," he whispered, "as you know, rabbis have very busy schedules. All the time I am running here and there. I have to leave for the airport in ten minutes, to pick up my sister-in-law. She's coming in on a flight from Israel."

"But, Rabbi, I came all this way, and I haven't even asked you one question yet." Dotsy stood up, the soiled sponge in her hand. She immediately leapt to the assumption that there was no sister-in-law, no flight from Israel, as he had not mentioned this before—the only flight was the rabbi's, from Dotsy's menstrual blood.

"I will be in Manhattan on Thursday night, for a singles mixer on the Upper West Side. Perhaps you'd like to come, or we can meet afterward, for dinner. In the meantime you can give some thought to the accountant I mentioned."

"Let's just forget about the accountant, Rabbi. I'm here to see you."

"But Dotsy"—the rabbi winked—"I'm already married." He opened the door a crack wider. "I will call you and we'll set up a time for Thursday."

"Rabbi, I can't do that. I have a class on Thursday night."

"A class. How nice." The rabbi brightened. "What are you learning?"

"Knitting."

"Knitting? Who needs to knit if you don't have a baby?" The rabbi wrinkled his brow. "Don't you know what they say about Jews, Dotsy?" He was talking to her now like a teacher, his voice a bit too loud, as if she were one of the yeshiva children.

Dotsy parroted back her mother's generalization, "Jews don't knit."

"Right, Dotsy, that's right." He smiled at her, for the first time since she'd arrived.

"So we'll meet after your class. I'll come to you, wherever you will be. I'll go out of my way, the way you did for me."

Dotsy had been taking a nap when the phone rang. Still groggy from sleep, her first thought was that the deep, male voice on the other end of the line was Dale. "Oh hello there," she said saucily. "Nice of you to finally call. How are you doing, anyway?" And before he could answer she decided to tease him. "I'll bet you and your Protestant girlfriend eat ham and cheese sandwiches every day together."

There was silence at the other end of the line. Had this statement been funny? Dotsy hoped so. She did not want to appear to Dale as bitter and raw as she felt—like she'd eaten a lime, her mouth puckered and sour with juice.

"Ham and cheese sandwiches? I think I have the wrong number."

Oy goytenyu. Just then Dotsy knew who was calling her.

"Oh hello, Rabbi," she said, shifting her tone to that of a professional freelance writer. "I don't know what I was just saying. I must have been dreaming or something. I just woke up from a nap."

"A nap in the middle of the day?" The rabbi clearly thought that was strange. "Are you feeling all right, Dotsy? Dreaming about *treif*—this is a nightmare, not a dream."

"Rabbi, please. I just woke up."

"So, you and me, Dotsy, Thursday night?"

"You and me, Rabbi."

It sounded just like a date—another date with a Jewish man, and this time with a rabbi no less. Begrudgingly, Dotsy had made a plan to meet him after Knitting One. She'd given him the address and room number of her class, and from there they would venture to the Second Avenue Deli, one of the few kosher restaurants still left downtown.

*　*　*

Dotsy had been practicing her knitting. She had gotten so good that she could knit while talking to her mother on the phone. And when she dropped a stitch she'd patiently rip out the entire row and start again, until her fingers were sore from the needles' pointed tips. At least what she was unraveling was yarn, and it was not herself who was coming undone.

From her apartment window where she had perched herself, the balls of wool at her feet like large, multicolored stones, Dotsy could hear car alarms blaring and horns honking and people in drunken stupors on the street corner, screaming curses and other insults. These people were so modern, and so deeply disturbed compared to Dotsy, who was perfectly content to be sitting at home knitting and humming to herself.

Once or twice Dotsy had brought her knitting with her on the subway, where her fellow passengers had stared at her moving hands in nostalgic fascination. Some had switched their seats to be closer, and to reminisce about their grandmothers' moth-eaten sweaters that, to this day, they still could not throw away.

"Who are you making that sweater for?" they would query. "Your husband? Your child?"

"Myself," Dotsy would say shortly as she looked down at her hands, the needles clicking along.

———

By the time the third class rolled around Dotsy had already completed the front of her sweater. Every minute of her spare time had been taken up with it. Made from a pinkish purple wool, she had even experimented with a simple pattern. She looked forward to presenting it to the class, and to receiving praises, as the Twin Marthas surely would for theirs. Dotsy was prepared, even, and composed—Dale, if he could see her, would be proud of her. In a sense, this knitting class was like a WASP finishing school.

When Dotsy walked into the classroom everyone was already there, and Dotsy saw that someone was sitting in her chair, looking down at a rather ratty lump of wool with yellowish flecks in it. Suddenly a head shot up and looked at her.

"Dotsy! Hello!"

It was the rabbi, sitting there, and the wad of wool on Dotsy's desk was actually his long, graying beard, as though by spreading it across the table he too might participate in class. What was he doing here? Everyone was staring at the two of them, the shock on Dotsy's face apparent. "My Jewish singles mixer was canceled," he explained. "Not one person showed up, so I thought, why not? I'd come here and sit in on your knitting class."

Deborah, standing in the front of the room, rasped, "Guests are not usually allowed in class, but I suppose I could make an exception this once." She frowned disapprovingly, and pointed to an empty seat for Dotsy across the room. "Let's begin everyone. Show me your assignments."

The Twin Marthas, using a beige wool, had made an elaborate pattern called "the seed," which Deborah admired. The woman sitting next to Dotsy had used a hot magenta wool, a heavy-weight skein, which she held in front of her like a breastplate. "A very interesting fiber," Deborah said encouragingly. Dotsy lifted up her own assignment, spreading it out for Deborah in her hands. "My, Dotty, you're really coming along," Deborah said, as though surprised by her progress. It wasn't quite the response Dotsy hoped for—she had called her Dotty—but at least it was positive.

"That's wonderful, Dotsy!" The rabbi exclaimed enthusiastically, out of nowhere on the other side of the room. "Maybe you could make me a scarf. It gets a bit chilly at the yeshiva this time of year."

Everyone's eyes turned to the rabbi. He was an off-putting presence in a room otherwise filled with women. It was as if he'd burst unannounced into a women's bathroom or dressing room as the women stood there, motionless and in shock, their clothes in a pile at their ankles. Dotsy held up her forefinger and made a slight *shhh* sound, which the rabbi, it seemed, had not picked up on. He raised his hand. "Teacher," he called. Deborah was looking at the beginnings of another woman's sweater. "Teacher," the rabbi said again.

"Yes? What?"

"I see your name on the blackboard. Schwartz, does it say? You're Jewish?"

"I am, but I don't see what that has to do with anything," Deborah said shortly, looking down again at the student and her wool.

"Ah-hah," the rabbi said, leaning back in his chair, taking all of this in. He studied Deborah with a mixture of what appeared to be fascination and repulsion, as if she were an exotic insect—she was wearing another purple smock, and moved her hands in front of her chest, hunched over like a purple praying mantis.

"What I'd like everyone to do is continue knitting their patterns while I go around the room to correct your postures and see that your movements are fluid. You all need to relax a bit, loosen up. It will make the knitting go faster. Here, let me demonstrate again for you." Deborah was showing off now—she was knitting without even looking at what she was doing. A peculiar little smile descended over her face just then, and she added, "Jeff would always tell me how beautiful I looked when I was knitting."

Oh my God. Jeff. He could not stay out of this. Everyone looked down at their needles, embarrassed for this display, except for the rabbi who said, "Jeff? Who is Jeff?"

Deborah's eyes settled on the rabbi, her smile widening. She apparently welcomed the rabbi's question, as she wanted to talk about Jeff constantly. The class had become a Freudian therapy session for Deborah: her students were blank screens who listened politely to her free associations.

"Jeff was my husband who died. Five years ago already. He was the sweetest, kindest man. I miss him so much." It looked as if Deborah was about to cry.

"That must be very hard for you. I meet plenty of widows and it is a difficult situation to get used to. But—" the rabbi paused for a moment as he considered his words—"there is always hope. Fate has brought me into this room."

Dotsy knew what was coming now.

"Fate has brought us together, Deborah, and it is time now, for you to start seeing someone new. Jeff would want you to be happy, don't you think so?"

Deborah sniffed, and appeared to soften a bit as she looked the rabbi over, considering him, as if he were asking her out.

The rabbi explained, "I am setting Dotsy up with a nice Jewish accountant. I am sure that I can find someone for you, too. A widower, perhaps. I just need to consult my files." He listed his credentials: "You see, I am a matchmaker by trade, besides being a rabbi."

"To be honest, I really don't know if I'm ready, Rabbi. I appreciate your concern, I really do, but I would not be good for anyone right now. I'll have to think about it."

"Nonsense! A good Jewish man, he can solve any problems you may have!" The rabbi dug through his pockets and handed Deborah his business card.

Dotsy was about to gag. She had repeatedly told the rabbi that she would not go out with the accountant, and here he was, flaunting that he had planned out the rest of her life for her. Everyone else in the room appeared fascinated by this exchange, as they watched the two most unlikely people earnestly conversing.

Just then one of the Marthas chirped, "My fiancé is a CPA as well."

"Oh really?" the rabbi said. "But he's not a Jewish accountant, is he?"

She flipped her blonde hair away from her face. "He is, actually. Look at the beautiful diamond he gave to me." The Martha stretched out her hand for the rabbi to see—flaunting the rock, which reflected in a thousand different directions at once. It seemed to shoot Dotsy right in the eye, blinding her like the high beam of a car. "Jewish men are the best," she continued. "Harry treats me so well."

What was happening here? The entire structure of the class had broken down, despite Dotsy preparing so carefully for it.

"Are you Jewish?" the rabbi said skeptically, studying her blonde hair and pixie nose. Like Dotsy, he seemed to not like this Martha girl.

"No, I am not Jewish. But maybe I'll convert someday."

"Not Jewish," the rabbi said, meditating on this fact for a moment. He shook his head in disapproval, discrediting the perfect composure of this WASP girl. Dotsy was beginning to relish the absurdity of this. "There are not very many single Jewish men in the world. We don't need people like you coming in, making ham and cheese sandwiches, and taking them away from us." The rabbi raised his voice a bit then. "Do you know what you are?"

The room bristled with tension. Dotsy found herself chuckling beneath her breath.

"I am getting married," the Martha said proudly. "That is what I am."

"You are a shiksa, a stealer of Jewish men."

It looked like Martha was about to cry. She wiped her beige, woolly gin and tonic coaster across her eye—and Dotsy did feel a satisfying tickle of pleasure at the sight.

After class everyone from Knitting One rushed to the rabbi's desk and urgently demanded his business card, except the Twin

Marthas, who skulked silently out of the room. He handed them out, one after another, and to Dotsy it looked like the beginning deal of a high-stakes poker game. She heard Deborah Schwartz insist, "The man I date must like knitting. Some men are terrified of needles." A couple of women ventured to ask if the rabbi had any photos of the accountant on hand. Dotsy could not believe this. Granted, she had no interest in the accountant two hours before, but with the sudden appeal the rabbi had garnered, her date with him seemed like a gift. The rabbi, the Messiah of Jewish single men and women of Manhattan, had finally arrived.

It was ten o'clock by the time Dotsy and the rabbi got out of the classroom—they were both too bleary to do any sort of interview, though she'd finally relented to one date with the accountant, who the rabbi mentioned offhandedly was named Moses.

Of course, the date was a disaster. Moses looked exactly like the rabbi, minus the beard and thirty years. His chest was as hairy as any mammal—so much for the hard, tanned, plastic ideal of Ken. Wiry black strands escaped from Moses' shirt collar as he sat across from her at the dinner table. He had taken her to a very nice restaurant, one Dotsy had never been to, with green leather booths and dim lighting—so dim Dotsy could barely see what she was eating. An exotic formation was piled precariously high on both of their plates, and when the accountant dug into his portion the whole thing came toppling down in a mess. The waiter came over then, asking if they wanted drinks, and the accountant sheepishly replied that he'd try a Cosmopolitan.

"I'll have a double vodka straight up," Dotsy said, bracing herself for another dizzying ride on the Jewish merry-go-round, composed of stilted, boring snippets of conversation until Dotsy settled on a topic that she knew would be of interest.

"Tell me about your mother, Moses," she said, leaning forward in her chair. The vodka had already begun doing its work, lowering her voice and giving it a slight slur. Asking a Jewish man about his mother reminded Dotsy of the climactic scene in the film *Frankenstein*, after the lever had been pulled and sparks flew perversely through the air. When the smoke cleared the monster's eyes had opened—miraculously, life had emerged from a lump of dead tissue. And so it was with Moses, who immediately perked up, and recited a long, sinewy monologue, which began in his mother's womb. From there he babbled on in the most minute detail, concluding in the present day, when Moses' mother had cleaved her son to her bosom in a crushing good-bye hug before his date. Dotsy was properly entertained, her hands folded in front of her as she listened to him. It was at least half an hour later when Moses finally paused to take a sip of his Cosmopolitan, and Dotsy immediately flagged down the waiter with a white napkin in hand, as though she were surrendering. When the check finally came, it rested face down next to Moses' plate.

Afterward Dotsy felt a certain smugness—she had controlled this date like a drive down an easy road, street signs and stoplights exactly where you'd expect them. She had opened the door of this metaphorical car of hers and emerged unscathed, or so she thought at first. But after she said good-bye to Moses with a half-hearted peck on the cheek, and hopped into a cab, it was then that the tears began to fall. Why was it that she couldn't settle down with a Jewish man? What was wrong with her? Dotsy touched her head, and then began massaging her scalp until her hair became a big frizzy thatch—so much for the composure Knitting One had briefly offered.

Dotsy could easily conjure next week's class, with Deborah Schwartz and all the other women flushed and beaming from what they considered a good toss in the sheets with a nice Jewish man, while the Twin Marthas, the shiksa stealers of Jewish men, would be so ashamed of themselves that they'd become Knitting One dropouts. Their sweaters would surely remain sleeveless, hidden in back of a drawer, before they eventually threw them out.

————

Dotsy sat down on her mother's couch, which was covered in a plastic slipcover. The couch appeared to be brand-new, as there was not one stain or wrinkle, though it was at least as old as Dotsy, but much more preserved. Photographs cluttered every surface of the living room, all of them of Dotsy in various stages of growth. There was Dotsy at age twelve, holding up her first bra—a pink, stringy thing with cups so small they could have only held up a couple of walnuts. Dotsy's face, which had turned a bit green over the years, looked absolutely humiliated; her mother had captured this mortifying moment with a hard snap of a button and a cruel white flash.

And then there was a photograph that Dotsy had completely forgotten about, as she had never remembered seeing it displayed in her mother's living room before. It was Dotsy at the age of ten, in a Halloween costume, when she'd insisted on dressing up as a nun. This had so shamed her mother that she'd dragged Dotsy to Corona, a completely different neighborhood, for her to trick-or-treat. She still remembered her mother's attempt to curb her in a more appropriate costume direction, by showing her a photograph of a Hasidic rabbi, and urging her with the words, "Look here, Dotsy. You can put on a big beard instead of a habit. What do you think about that?"

Dotsy wiped a tear from her face, she was crying again, when in the midst of this memory her mother came into the room and sat down on the couch next to her.

"You look so pretty today, Dotsy. What did you do? Streak your hair? Is that a new sweater you're wearing?" Dotsy's mother's touched the sleeve and said, "I think you've got a stain on it."

"Mom, this is the sweater I've been telling you about for months. It's the one I made. In Knitting One. What do you think?" Dotsy stood up and twirled around so her mother could see it from every angle.

This was the first time Dotsy was wearing her sweater. When she'd initially sewn the pieces together she realized it was a bit too small, and had frantically soaked the sweater in warm water and then pulled at it, widening the stitches as Deborah had suggested. When it dried she barely managed to push her head and arms through the holes, and when she did, she could hardly move her arms up and down. The sweater began cutting off her circulation, like a strangling tourniquet, and the wool was rough and scratchy, irritating her. Despite these problems it was such a relief to stand in front of her mother with it on. Unlike the Twin Marthas, Dotsy had made a commitment to finishing her sweater; she had followed through, even though it wasn't exactly a long-term relationship.

"It's pink. Right?" Dotsy's mother said, again touching the sleeve.

"Yes, it's pink, Mother." The mushy, weepy feeling that had befallen Dotsy while her mother had been in the kitchen was quickly replaced with the usual defensive and agitated posture she took with her, as she knew full well that any vulnerability she expressed would be twisted and dissected by her. Dotsy could feel her body heating up—sweat broke out and collected beneath her arms, ruining the sweater's perfect woolly animal smell. Her mother's apartment was always too warm.

"Mom, I want to ask you something. Why is it that you have this photograph of me dressed as a nun out here? You hated it so much when I insisted on that as my Halloween costume."

Dotsy's mother took the photograph from her daughter and held it in her hands, staring at the image with a blank expression. "Be careful," her mother said, "you're getting your fingerprints all over the glass." She rubbed it on her sweater until it was clean and clear again.

Dotsy waited for her mother to answer her question, wanting so much to receive an explanation. Why was Dotsy who she was today, and not someone else, a wife and mother in the suburbs, say? She couldn't exactly blame her mother for the present state of affairs, now could she? That would be as simplistic as Moses' monologue from the night before. She was still a bit fuzzy and slow from all the vodka she'd consumed, though Dotsy's mother hadn't appeared to notice that her daughter had a hangover.

Dotsy watched her mother study the photograph of her as a ten-year-old covered in a black sea of cloth. A plastic rosary hung from her neck, the beads and cross a greenish color that glowed ominously in the dark. Her eyes were closed—Dotsy must have blinked as her mother took the photo—though it looked like she was deep in prayer, and Jesus, her spiritual husband, was touching Dotsy's head from above. As her mother held this image so close to her chest, her eyes were also closed, and the Jewish star she wore banged against the glass, sending an odd, high-pitched ring up into the room. It was like an alarm clock about to exert its full force, which would stun both of them into a wakefulness neither had experienced before.

Suzan Sherman

"Knitting One" is based on a mix of autobiographical experiences all tangentially related to Judaism—a subject I rarely grapple with in my fiction. A number of years ago I took a knitting class, like Dotsy, the protagonist of "Knitting One," but dropped it before the semester-long project, a wool sweater, was completed. In my story, knitting—a seemingly archaic, grandmotherly hobby that's had a recent resurgence among young people—becomes a "religious" metaphor for Dotsy, a single, assimilated Jewish woman who only dates WASP men. Also like Dotsy, I once attempted to interview a matchmaker rabbi for an anthology of Jewish writing, but the rabbi was so intent on setting me up with a Jewish man that I never wrote

the article. Orthodox Judaism and knitting—two seemingly dis-parate threads—are literally tied together in "Knitting One," result-ing in a twist on the present-day dilemma of whether or not to date a tribe member. (I've since finished knitting the sweater—miraculously, it fits.)

LEAH

Ehud Havazelet

1

As far back as I can remember, Leah was preparing herself for marriage. Not for love, exactly, not for romance—unlike the rest of us, with our dewy notions of cars and cigarettes and boys' broad shoulders—but for marriage, for sacrifice and a lifelong abiding. She was my cousin, a week older to the hour, a thin girl with rich, pleated hair, searching eyes, and olive skin taut over bony points, flat inconcealable planes. She was polite and diffident, so you could never tell what she was thinking. She was starved for attention and consequently did everything to avoid it. She lacked what I later understood to be intensity, and in my family that was the greatest lack you could have, but she saw everything. That is my memory of those years, of life as it happened, vivid and unexplained, and Leah off to one side, not missing a beat, silently watching us all.

Before bed—we were young girls, eight or nine—Leah recited a prayer her mother had taught her, asking God to protect the unknown boy who would grow to be her husband. She prayed for his safety, his moral development. She prayed God would give him brains but not a swelled head, good looks but not vanity, money but a sense of charity, decorum. She prayed he was off in his own room these nights, praying for her.

When we played Barbie dolls, she didn't take hers to the beach, or a dance concert, or a picnic, where they could lie under some shady trees. Her dolls were endlessly married, set up in modest houses with patios and backyard grills. They were in shul together, at holiday meals, their plastic heads bowed in gratitude over the bread. My Barbies, even then, were restless, insurgent. They borrowed the family car without asking. They smoked cigarettes behind the Dream House. Partly to annoy Leah, they kissed constantly. Hers brought babies home from the hospital in little bonnets, did good works for the Jewish Sisterhood. They wed and grew old serenely, they emigrated to Eretz Ha'Kodesh—the Holy Land—they even died (usually Ken, after a long, uncomplaining decline), Bridal and Malibu Barbies, Midge, and Barbie's sidekick, Skipper—minus the arm our neighbor's dog had chewed off—all gathered solemnly around a shoebox grave to weep.

At the time, of course, I didn't find Leah mysterious, even interesting, just odd in that painful, embarrassing way cousins, whom you didn't get to choose any more than you did brothers, could be. Even at that age, she had a capacity for misery, she seemed marked for it, and too young for knowledge of luck or instinct or plain irrefutable fate, I sensed she would be in for a hard time. The one thing we knew about Leah was she wanted to be married; and the one thing we knew about the world was it would never happen, not to her. About this, about some other things, we were wrong.

My grandfather was a rabbi, his shul, with its high-set sea-green windows, and the brass eternal flame flickering before the velour-draped Ark, three blocks from home. My mother and I sat to the side, a few rows back, in the women's section, while David weekly climbed the steps to be with our grandfather at the front. Here I was allowed only on special occasions, when, if no serious prayer were being conducted, girls might join the boys in the main sanctuary.

Rabbi, scholar, community statesman, my grandfather was acknowledged family leader, but his status was tested constantly by Simon, my mother's uncle. If not himself a spiritual adept,

Simon was Brooklyn's fourth-largest Chevrolet dealer, with a lot on New Utrecht Avenue and another in Bensonhurst. At the shul, Simon was alternately president of the congregation, chairman of the building fund, secretary of the men's club. He was devout, in his way, thinking he could outdo anyone in adherence and good religious sense. He loved biblical commentary and nothing would make my father go silent and grim around the mouth quicker than one of Simon's obscure finds, offered usually at mealtime, in mock humility—"I'm not a rabbi myself," Simon might say to a Shabbos guest, "but anybody can read."

Leah's mother was Simon's younger sister. She had married late and had one child, about whom she worried with a fanatic devotion. She was a flighty, kind woman, my Aunt Esther, given to overexcitement and meticulous superstition. She had prayers—and she taught them to Leah—for rain and drought, thunder and lightning, for the moon in its four quarters, for dressing in the morning and undressing at night, prayers for a new pair of shoes, for an old one, for perspiring, for headache, for your time of the month, for someone else's, for killing the chicken, plucking its feathers, and putting it in the pot. Aunt Esther sewed a red thread into Leah's underwear because this would bring a good husband, and when a one-eyed neighborhood cat named Duke picked among our trash cans, she would spit three times and make us turn to the north. For six months she was possessed by the spirit—and the heartburn—of an acquaintance of hers from Detroit, a recently deceased stenographer, a vindictive person, she told us, impossible to get along with. She walked around holding a blue bottle of Bromo-Seltzer, belching mournfully into a handkerchief. From my grandfather she begged an exorcism, until he threatened to banish her from the congregation.

Friday afternoons, school let out early. In the alley between the houses we played baseball with my brother—whom Leah voicelessly loved—and Barry Diamond, me in jeans and a sweatshirt (I was allowed to change after school) and Leah (who wasn't)

in the long-skirted cotton dresses her mother sewed, with the
woolen knee socks and black shoes. They wouldn't always let us
play, not when they were about the manly business of making
believe they were Yankees or Mets, and when they did allow us,
it was mostly to laugh, to make comments between them as if we
were deaf or too stupid to understand. That was boys. But I liked
baseball. I liked the running and being outside. I liked the sting
of the bat in my hands when I hit the ball, and I liked watching
the boys hit it, occasionally, over the hedge into Mrs. Cohen's
backyard. I liked knowing that soon it would be sundown, all of
us indoors, a veil of silence and muted light drawn over the day
as Shabbos approached, but now we were running, filling the air
with our shouts, free.

One day we were girls against boys. It was autumn, you
could feel the weather changing. Above the garages, wind shifted
the oaks and sycamores and we stopped to watch as the leaves
turned, filling the big trees with red and yellow light. Soon it
would be time for my brother to dress for shul, for us to go in and
set the table. The boys spent a lot of energy mimicking us, splay-
ing arms and legs spastically, meaning to imitate our girlish inep-
titude, while we said nothing about the mighty swings they
took, hitting air, or the balls that bounded under their gloves,
between their legs. Baseball was their game, and if we wanted in,
we had to put up with them. But that didn't mean we had to lose.

The boys made smug concessions—they'd pitch easy to us,
they'd play short in the field. They'd pitch left-handed, Barry
offered, and blindfolded, David said. "C'mon," I said to Leah.
"Let's show these fools."

We did. We scored a run in the first when Leah, closing one
eye and swinging from her heels, hit Barry's garage on a fly, a
ground-rule double, and then came home when the puffing red-
faced boy chased a grounder of mine all the way to the swing set.
My brother didn't like to lose. He didn't like to play fair unless he
was winning and could make a show of it. David was a boy constantly on the edge, of laughter, of panic, of some unaccountable

act of friendship or some meanness that would leave you stunned. I never forgot I was around him, and Leah watched him as if the sun rose over his shoulders every morning.

He could be nice. Before the game started he had shown Leah how to hold the bat, bringing his arms around her to demonstrate the correct angle, flaming her cheeks a pretty red. She stood there, holding the bat, his hands on hers. "You see?" David said, and she nodded, but I knew she wasn't seeing the bat, or the green garage door she faced. She was off in some landscape of her own, with his voice as company. "Good," David said, not unkindly, when he let her go. "At least you look better than my sister."

Now, down by a run, he was angry. He flipped the ball in the air to himself after Leah scored, and when she laughed suddenly at his grim expression, he managed Brooklyn's most grudging smile.

Why was any moment in any day suddenly the last straw to boys, the ultimate line in the sand, pride staring down disgrace? I thought he was ridiculous. I thought of saying something funny, something to ease the tension. We all felt it. Barry was trying, jumping foot to foot behind David, saying, "He-ey, batta-batta-batta, no-o batta-batta," pounding his silly mitt. But with David you always thought of saying something; you never did. Some invisible signal he gave off warned you to keep away.

I think Leah was enjoying herself. We hugged at home plate, and when she fell in the field next inning, dirtying the side of her blue dress, I thought she might go inside to admit the damage to her mother, but she just shrugged and pounded Barry's mitt as she had seen him do. We held them to a double and came up to bat in the second and—daylight quickly draining from the trees—final inning.

David seemed all right. They were still down a run, but they had the bottom of the inning, plenty of time. As I came up they made jokes.

"Show her your scroogie," Barry said.

"You think? It might make her cry."

"Show it to her once, man. Give her something to remember."

Adrenaline. Annoyance at my brother and his motor-mouthed friend. Some melancholy in the fading light that signaled the coming end of the year. I don't know. The ball met the bat with a feeling I had never had before. I swung right through it. I connected with it, as the boys would say, as if everything—the ball's flight, the tracking of my eyes, the slow acceleration of the bat in my hands—were the progression of an inevitable mathematical theorem. I creamed it.

A low liner, the ball pierced Mrs. Cohen's hedge more than cleared it. But there it lay in her azalea patch, at the end of a little furrow it had dug, a home run for all to see.

Leah and I hugged and ran around the bases together. I told her it was easy, to go up there and do the same thing. Then I looked at David. He waited for the ball, glove raised, and when Barry flipped it to him, he held it in his hand, looking to the side, his fringe of brown hair concealing his eyes.

Leah could sense his anger. She walked up to the plate and asked him if she was holding her bat correctly. "That's fine," David said, not looking.

"C'mon, Leah," I said. I could hear the nervousness in my voice. "You can do it."

The pitch came hard, high over Leah's head. It bounced once on the cement and then off our house at the other side of the alley. I ran to get it.

"What was that?" I called, angry now myself.

"A pitch," David said. "A slider, if you really want to know."

"Good one," Barry said behind him. "Now show her your scroogie."

I picked up the ball and thought of just going inside. This was how it was with my brother—at any moment the showdown, the crisis unavoidably arrived. Instead, I threw it back, over his head intentionally, and sat on the steps of our back porch to watch.

There was no way Leah could have gotten out of the way.

David turned, lifted his leg in the manner I'd seen them practice with Barry's older brother. He brought the ball close to his chest, gathered himself, and threw as hard as he could. The ball hit her squarely in the face, with a sound like a piece of fruit dropped on a wooden floor. It made me sick even as I heard it. She fell straight down, the ball rolling feebly behind her, down the alley toward the street.

We reached her at the same moment. David helped her sit and Barry took the bat from her. I stood with my hand over my mouth.

"Are you all right?" David said.

"No blood," Barry said, leaning in to see. "That's gotta be good."

"Shut up, Barry," David said. "Leah, are you okay? Where did it hit you?"

A purple bruise was already spreading under her eye. I wanted to take the bat to him.

"Can you stand?"

"I'm all right," Leah said, and she let him put his arms under hers to help her.

"I'm sorry," David told her.

"I'm all right," she said again.

He helped her up. When he let her go to brush off her sweater, I saw the expression on her face. She was looking at David. In her eyes not the pain or shock I expected to see, but something else, something I didn't understand. It was as if she'd been waiting years for her turn to be hit in the face with a base-ball. She looked at him with forgiveness, with wonder, even joy. I pushed him aside and put my arm around her.

"Good job, superstar," I said.

He shoved me from the back. "You think I meant to hit her?"

"You hit her, David," I said, turning around with Leah a moment. "You hit her and you knew you would, or could. You knew."

I took Leah inside and our mothers, draping the thick white

cloth over the table for the meal, came running. Aunt Esther took one look at Leah and began opening and closing her eyes rapidly.

"Mom," I said, "she's going to faint."

"No she isn't," my mother said. "Esther, go into the kitchen and get a cold compress. With ice."

We were all late that night, the men to shul, the food to the table. As Leah and I stood in front of the candles while our mothers said the blessing, I could hear my father calling David in the yard. I heard him go up and down the alley, calling, his voice rising each time, then finally David answered and the shouting began. Then there was quiet, which could only mean my father had hit him. I knew the neighbors were listening, quietly pulling back their curtains to watch. I felt sorry for David, I always did, but now this night and what had happened would be about him. I looked over at Leah. They had held ice over her eye for half an hour. It was swollen blue and below it were the distinct imprints of three stitches from the baseball. She was praying, swaying slightly from side to side. Her eyes were closed and her lips moving slowly, something like a smile playing over them.

2

We moved to Queens later that year. By fourteen we were smoking joints in the space between the garages and by fifteen I was involved with a boy from around the corner, Albert Fogel, who wrote love poems and planned to be an optometrist and wanted me to go all the way. He was a tall boy, with a diffuse smile and thick curly hair like a cushion for my head, my hands. I would lie with my head on his chest, listening to the breathing sounds, the unerring thump of his heart, while he smoked Winstons, read Marvel comic books. He copied out an e e cummings poem for me, complete with the famous inverted characters, and seemed so certain I would catch him in his poetic larceny that I didn't have the heart, and told him it was his best poem yet.

He wagged his head at me, side to side, I swear he did, that loopy smile, perhaps starting to think if I believed he wrote it, maybe, somehow, he had. He kissed me and told me he loved me. Did I *know* he loved me, he asked. I know, Albert, I said, of course I know, and kissed him back. I wouldn't go all the way with Albert Fogel because he would leave me then, that's what I knew, and the night I finally loved him, that's just what happened.

It was a Saturday, the night of his senior dance. The family had gathered, as they often did since my grandfather's death, at our house for the weekend. Albert had left early to meet me, made off with one of the table arrangements—a black-eyed Susan and two daisies minus petals, like missing teeth—and a six-ounce bottle of kiddush wine. As Albert had gone into the storage room to lift the wine the band was playing "There's a Kind of Hush," a popular song from a few years back, and he was humming it now. Inside, they were doing the after-Shabbos rituals, my mother and Esther finishing the dishes, putting them in the cupboards, Uncle Simon's boys, maybe Leah, on pillows in front of the TV. We did that every Saturday night, the same shows, movies in rotation, redress to the prohibition on TV the day before. David talked constantly about the shows we couldn't see—*Twelve O'Clock High, Wild, Wild West*—as if an entire culture was out there and we, hostages to religious zealotry, were being kept from it. From the windows on the shifting breeze I could hear the women talking in the kitchen, the rasp of the TV as the credits for *Chiller Theater* rolled—a hand lifting from a steamy swamp, six fingers waving—and behind it, classical music from the living room, where the men sat with newspapers and listened to Rubenstein or Heifetz. Albert began singing, "All over the world, you can hear the sounds of lovers in love." We sat on a front seat Barry and David had pulled from a derelict Buick the summer before, the flower arrangement beside us in the dirt, our feet on the tin milk box where we kept our stash. We held hands and looked at the sky between the trees. To the east, a faint glow was gathering, moonrise over Flushing Meadow.

We settled in comfortably and watched the view. Albert sang

the song for me, but he couldn't remember the words. "So listen very carefully, da-da-da and dee-dee-dee what I mean . . ." We kissed and when Albert put his hand down my shirt I let him, we'd done this many times, and he left it there contented, under my bra, as you might leave a hand in a pocket. Albert drank the wine and I rolled a joint. When he passed it back to me there was a purple ring around the lip end, residue of the sticky wine. That was Albert.

"Penny for your thoughts," he said.

He killed me. "I don't have any change, Albert."

"Really. What are you thinking about?"

"Nothing. I'm not thinking about a thing."

"You must be," Albert said. "It's Saturday night, we're together. I'm graduating high school next week. I mean, we're in love, aren't we? You must be thinking about something."

"I was just thinking," I told him, "how nice it is to be here with you, smoking this joint and hearing my mother in the kitchen, while Mothra attacks Tokyo, just being here with you and not thinking a thing. That's what I was thinking."

But Albert was pensive. We shifted on the car seat, I leaned into him, smelling the warm woolliness of his shirt. He put the wine down on the ground and looked at me before he spoke. This wasn't easy, what with his hand, my wire-supported bra, the shallow car seat, but Albert managed. He took my hand with his free one.

"Rachel," he said. "What do you hope for?"

"Hope?"

"Yeah, you know, what are your dreams? Where do you see yourself in ten years?"

"Ten years? From tonight? I don't see myself anywhere in ten years."

"Okay. What do you hope for now, then?"

"Well, right now I'm hoping your hand doesn't fall asleep."

No, Albert said, he was serious, and he was, looking at me with slow, blinking eyes. "All right," I told him. "Okay."

So as the moon rose through the trees, as my mother's voice

in Yiddish mixed with the screams of Japanese teenagers running from a forty-foot moth, I told him lies I hoped he wanted to hear. I hoped for these things: a nice home, a tree-lined street, a backyard with shade trees, maybe room for a garden. A career, I told him, some service kind of thing, nurse or teacher, you know, people work. He seemed happy, so I went on. A good marriage, with a man I could admire. Friends, women I could talk to. Midmorning, after the chores (did I really say chores?), they would come over to my patio, or I would go over to their well-lit kitchens, the breakfast dishes still glistening in the drying racks, and over coffee we would discuss tuition, how fast kids went through clothes, recipes. Albert had his smile back on. He gave my breast a soft companionable squeeze. Travel, I continued, Italy and France, Hong Kong. Copenhagen, I threw in for the sound of it, Budapest, for no reason at all. Sri Lanka. And children, of course, several, boys and girls, matching sets. Larry and Lulu, I'd call them, Minnie and Mo, but this was going too far for Albert and I kept it to myself.

He reached for the bottle and nodded, his eyes above me somewhere, where he saw me in a trim apron in some sunny kitchen alcove, cutting meat for stew, pausing to look out the window and count my blessings.

"Yeah," Albert said.

He was a sweet boy, the only boy I had known who would listen to me, no matter what I said. I liked the way his man's body seemed to have caught him by surprise, the way he clunked around in his brown work boots, as if his feet were things he had to carry, the way his flannel shirts hung out of his pants, part man's indifference, part boy's unaware sloppiness. He liked to hold me, I could tell from the way he shifted, settled his arms around me, moved so there was room for me on his chest. In polite ardor, he would recite his poetry: "High upon a windblown crag, I climbed to think of you, And there, amid the roiling clouds, my melancholy grew . . ."

I told Albert I hoped we could see each other after he went

off to college. When he looked at me, I turned away, concentrated on relighting the joint. I passed it to him after taking a long toke.

"Sure," he said. "You bet."

Then he spoke of his dreams, I'd heard them before, to be an optometrist like his Uncle Danny, go to conferences in Miami Beach, live in a home with a circular drive. I knew the rest—he would move out to the Island, learn to play golf, date blond girls who'd never heard of Queens. At restaurants, they would pour his drink the minute he came through the door, and they would call him by first name. He would marry somebody whose dream it was to marry an optometrist on Long Island and who would buy them coordinated outfits. They would actually have kids named Minnie and Mo. They would be happy.

He was sweet and earnest and the night was fresh and full of breezes. He loved me, he said. Did I *know* he loved me? From inside I heard the teapot whistling for tea, and Mothra, having devoured the populace of several towns, had retired ominously to the hills. The moon, white as a dinner plate, shimmered upward in the sycamore behind the house. Albert swung the bottle like a small pendulum between his knees. It was one of those spring nights they tell you invoke newness, rebirth, possibility, but which to me are always edged with sadness, full of time's passing and the many things that will never be. I know, I told Albert. I love you, too. I took the sugary wine from him and finished it off. I took his hand out of my shirt and then unbuttoned it. I kissed him on the mouth and undid my bra. The look of surprised delight as I pulled him onto me I will always remember.

When he got up from the car seat to stretch in the blue moonlight, he told me he had just that day been accepted to a college upstate. They had a major in optometry and eleven fraternities that allowed in Jews. It would be so great, he said, buttoning his clothes. Soon, I would be old enough to drive, I could save up for a car—heck, my rich uncle would probably *give* me one—and I could drive up every other weekend to see him. It would be so great. He lit a cigarette, lay back near me, his bil-

lowy Afro nudging my neck like a small pet. When he fell asleep
with the cigarette in his mouth, I took it and smoked it down,
looking at the moon laced with thin gray clouds.

I heard laughing behind us, then voices, Barry and David,
back from wherever they had wandered, talking to someone else.
"There's no rats in here," Barry said. "There hasn't been a rat in
here for weeks." As if he were already in his home and heard the
gravel crunching up front, my first love Albert jumped up from
the Buick seat to welcome guests.

"Hey," he said, before they had made the turn to see us.
"We're over here."

David came first, holding a pint bottle. "Oh," he said. He
looked back at Barry. "They're over here."

Barry pushed past him and said, "So that's where you are.
Terrific. Now in case anybody is ever looking for you we'll
know." He moved past Albert and dragged the milk box from
under my feet. "You guys roll any doobies?"

Behind David, half in the shadow of the garage wall, was Leah.

From the way she stood, one arm extended before her, I realized Barry had been holding her hand.

"C'mon in," Barry said to her, "cop a squat. Hey." He slapped
my foot. "Shove over."

The tearing pain I felt when Albert first pushed into me had
mostly subsided, but when I had pulled my pants back on I saw
there was blood. I could feel it now, warm between my legs. I
didn't move.

David stood at the other end of the clearing, tipping the bottle to his lips. When the amber liquid hit the light, I saw the bottle was nearly empty. Albert kept his eyes on David as Barry took
Leah by the hand and brought her over to the Buick seat. "Here,"
he said, guiding her, and to me, "You wasted or something? Make
some room." She sat next to me and we exchanged quick glances.

"We were just hanging out," Albert said, moving a foot in
front of him as if there was a rock there to kick. "You know,
talking."

"Yeah?" David said. "About what?"

"You know, stuff. School stuff, summer plans, stuff like that."

"Yeah? You have summer plans, Albert?" David said.

"I usually wait tables at the Concord, you know, where my parents spend a few weeks. Sometimes I teach swimming."

"Swimming. Like, to kids."

"Kids, yeah. And adults. Anybody who wants to learn to swim, I guess."

I knew Albert would flip desperately for minutes around David, until, like a fish on a line, he'd give up and silently wait to die. I reached out and pulled him by the pants pocket onto the seat beside me. There was barely room. He was scared by David, which I found endearing, and a sign of good sense. David was deep into his glowering, sarcastic phase. He had grown his hair as long as he could without inciting outright war with my father and I saw him every day combing it delicately, then messing it up, over and over, until he achieved just the right look of accidental fashion. He was seventeen, smoked whatever dope Barry left for him, had some connection for Southern Comfort, maybe Barry's older brother back in Brooklyn. The liquor was nasty, sweet and sour and biting, like medicine, and I couldn't swallow a mouthful. But for weeks now David had been coming to the garages with pint bottles, the label with the Southern mansion and the riverboat on the front, drinking the stuff until he got sick in Mrs. Segal's irises or fell stuporously silent, hunching his neck deep into his collar, not saying a word.

"Want a hit?" He gave Albert an unfriendly smile and passed the bottle.

"Sure," Albert said. "Thanks, bro." I felt the shudder pass through him as he drank.

Barry was rummaging in the milk box, collecting papers, the Baggie of marijuana, the *Playboy* he used to separate the seeds from the buds. I saw Miss April, in a bow tie and fishnet stockings, spilling her breasts halfway across the page.

"Albert," Barry said, opening the magazine to the centerfold, "have you read the article in here on our flawed Vietnam policy? I tell you, it makes you think."

"No," Albert said, staring as the glandular marvel of Miss April unfolded in sections to the light. "I haven't read it."

"Albert," I said, taking his hand. "Don't speak."

Like a teacher at the front of the room showing a picture in a text, Barry displayed Miss April to each of us in turn, his grinning face stuck to the side like a salacious gargoyle. She was a blonde, not much older than me, I guessed, in a lacy shift that covered nothing, lordosing to beat the band, a pose only boys could find intriguing. I felt the oozing wetness in my pants, squeezed my legs together for the almost reassuring stab of pain it sent through me, and wondered what this cotton-candy phantasm had to do with the brief, breath-filled encounter (And there amidst the roiling clouds . . .), half pain, half pleasure, I had just had with Albert.

Once Albert had a sufficient study, Barry turned her to me, but I smirked at him. David, by the wall, ignored her, as if just one more naked woman today could hardly be of interest. But Leah, beside me, was rigid with attention. I was sorry I had not tended to her more. Normally, I would have, would have screamed at Barry and David to leave her alone, led her back to the house. But tonight I had other things on my mind.

Barry moved the pinup closer to her, holding it top and bottom. "This," he told Leah, "is what today's gentleman refers to as beauty."

I looked at her. Her face bore no expression beyond the stiff-jawed determination to reveal none. Her hands were in the pockets of the coat she wore, or was made to wear, even on this warm night. Leah, fifteen now, still rail-thin, still watching through soft, wary eyes, still dressed as she was when we were children—the heavy dress, black braids, the laced shoes and white stockings. I wondered what she was doing here. She never came out back. Another night, an earlier year, I would have protected her from this. She stared at Barry and Miss April without flinching.

"Put it away," I told Barry.

"Why? Aren't you an admirer of the female form?"

"Shove it, Barry," I said, and he leered at me, then Leah, even Albert, then shrugged and busied himself with the pot and the papers.

Leah looked at me, but with gratitude or fear or confusion, I couldn't tell. She sat on the seat beside me, her hands thrust into her coat pockets. It was a spring coat, had been fashionable when it was new, brown wool with big buttons in two rows down the front. I tried to catch her eye and smile but she had looked away. David passed the Southern Comfort back to Albert, who took a showy, manful slug. This time he nearly retched. Barry had rolled two fat joints and handed one to me.

Leah and I had grown apart, if you could say so—from what earlier intimacy had we deviated? We still shared the same room, weekends, when her family stayed over. We were still lumped together, the female support staff, assigned chores in tandem— set the table, girls, make the salad, iron the spread and napkins. And we still talked. Leah, not allowed to be around boys herself, was insatiable for knowledge of them. She never quite said as much but I could tell. When I started dating Albert, I told her. She wanted to see a picture. Who needs a picture, I said, he's around all the time. Wouldn't a picture be nice? she said. We could look at it in our room, together. So I got her one and she kept it by her bed, at night when her mother didn't know, propped up against the lamp. I didn't care. She asked me if he went to shul and I said I don't know, I guess so. She asked me if he was polite to me and I said sure, Albert was as polite as they came, and she asked me if we talked about the future and I said, yes, Albert talked about the future day and night.

When I told her Albert wrote me poems she demanded to see one. I found one and read it, declaiming, waving my hands around, and we laughed so loud David banged on the wall next door. Then I made the mistake of telling her I had let Albert put his hand down my shirt. She seemed genuinely shocked, and I was sorry to have upset her, but later, praying by the side of the bed, she kept glancing at me, and I realized she was praying for my redemption, which shocked me and kept me angry for two days.

She still prayed, sometimes so long and fervently I'd stay awake just to watch. She prayed for the boys facing off with the Arabs in the Sinai desert. She prayed for her father's gout to disappear. She prayed for Mort Sheinberg, a man from my grandfather's shul running for city council, and when Uncle Simon went into Maimonides for a hernia repair she kept a vigil into the night, all night, for all I knew, finally falling asleep myself in stupefied awe. She no longer prayed, at least out loud, for the welfare of her future husband, and aside from our talks about Albert's studies, his plans for the two of us, I never heard her speak directly about boys. When they dragged David off to a psychiatrist, for general recalcitrance, for mouthing off and skipping shul, she was nearly hysterical.

The grownups sat on the front porch and talked about him as if he had become a stranger, were gone already, committed to a life of crime or insanity, disappeared into the one-way hole of the goyim's world. In our room Leah pulled me down on my knees next to her, held me there. If we prayed together, she said, maybe we could help him. Fine, I said, and closed my eyes and listened to her fervid whispering. Then she asked if she could burn herbs in my room, and I ignored her and got into bed.

One night the spring before, she lay in bed under the covers, did not get out to kneel on the floor. After the final prayer, speech was forbidden. "Hear, O Israel, the Lord is God, the Lord is One." After that, silence. Those were the last words God wanted to hear from you that night. Aunt Esther told us this. She also told us that in the moment before birth God took each new child in his hands. He looked at it and kissed its forehead, which meant it would be born, alive and healthy, into our world. But his kiss also left a number, invisible, under your skin. This represented the words you were allotted to speak in your lifetime. Your whole life. When they were done, you were done, finished, no more, don't bother asking. Aunt Esther had an aunt, back in the Old Country, who had lived to be ninety-eight and couldn't utter a single word the last four years of her life. Could we imagine anything more terrible? This old woman—a happy enough individual in her youth—walking around scowling all day, holding a cup of cold tea. She knew what had happened. Well, Aunt Esther asked us, sitting on my bed and whispering, was that the future we wanted?

This night, instead of climbing out of bed after we'd finished reading, Leah lay under the blankets. I knew she wanted to talk. From somewhere in the street, music played on a radio. I couldn't hear the words or melody, but the rhythm came through, barely pulsing in my ears. I ran my eyes up the trellis of roses on the wallpaper, a pattern repeating until I lost sight of it in the dark near the ceiling. Then she spoke.

"I had my time," she said.

I didn't answer. I wasn't sure what she meant.

"My time," she repeated. "Last week, at school."

"You mean your period?" I said. "You got your period?"

"In history. I thought I had had an accident. I thought I had wet myself. I ran to the bathroom. I had to wait there two hours for the final bell."

"Oh, Leah, I'm sorry." I sat up in bed and looked over at her in the gray half-light. She lay still. I could see her hands motionless on her chest. I pulled the pillow from behind me and held it in my lap.

"I had my first one in gym last year. We were jumping over that stupid horse, you know? It was my turn, I got up from where we were sitting by the wall and I felt this trickle. But I was concentrating on the stupid horse, you know? On not making a fool of myself. So Sheila Schivelowitz announces to me and everyone else in the room there's blood running down my leg. 'Gross,' she says. 'Oh, my God,' she says, 'that is just so gross.' It was in my sneaker and everything." I fluffed the pillow and leaned over it toward Leah. "I flicked some right in her face." Leah looked at me and I laughed. "I didn't. But I wanted to. It didn't hurt. You know, cramps, a little, but nothing else." I tossed the pillow at her. "Anyway, cousin, welcome to the wonderful world of womanhood."

The pillow lay where it had landed, across her legs. She didn't answer and I thought—as I did often—I had said something to offend her. I looked out the window, across the driveway, where I could see the lit kitchen in the Segals' house. The brown Motorola radio on their table was playing music, it might have been a waltz. Every night I would watch them in there, Mrs. Segal ironing clothes, making coffee, which they drank from green cups while they listened to music from the radio. No one was in the kitchen now, just the radio playing soft music and a breeze shifting the corner of a curtain.

"Do you use something?" Leah said.

"For my period? Sure."

"Did you see a doctor?"

"For tampons? Why? I got some from my mother, then bought my own at Rexall's."

"Your mother knows?"

"Of course she knows. Doesn't yours? Didn't you tell your mother, Leah?"

"I found something in her drawer. I took it."

She got up from bed, went to her small blue suitcase, came over, and handed something to me. I was about to turn on the light when I remembered it was Friday night. The light from the windows was enough to see by. It was a puffy contraption, a long thin diaper snapped to a belt by metal clips. The belt was worn and beige, the white diaper downy with cotton, thick in the middle and tapering at both ends, where it attached to the belt. The napkin was long enough to wear as a headband.

"What *is* this?" I said.

"You wear it. In your time every month."

"You do? How? I mean why? Don't you know about Tampax?"

But this was the wrong thing to say, or not what she'd hoped to hear. She got back in her own bed and I, full of exasperation and self-reproach, went to my drawer and got out a tampon. We weren't supposed to tear anything, not even paper, on Shabbos, but I ripped the paper wrapping off and let it drop to the floor. I sat on Leah's bed and showed her how it worked, the string, the cardboard applicator. She looked at me as if she had no idea what I was talking about and I was so mad I would have pulled my nightshirt over my head and *showed* her, but she said, "Thank you. I see," and rolled over on her side to sleep.

"Oh, Leah," I said. "It's nothing, you know? I mean, it's not nothing. It happens to everybody, that's all." She didn't turn or make any response. From my bottom dresser drawer I got a handful of Slender Regulars and tucked them into her suitcase. I said "Good night," but couldn't hear her murmured reply. Later, as I was just beginning to dream of Mrs. Segal putting down the iron to dance around the kitchen with her husband, I heard the sheets rustle and the bed shift as Leah climbed out of bed to pray. I didn't open my eyes.

Barry was smoking one joint, holding the other. "This is killer weed," he said to Albert. "*Yo soy blotodo*, bro, *et vous?*"

"Killer," Albert agreed.

"I'm wasted. Like, okay, like, I wouldn't know my own head if I sat on it, you know? I mean, where'd you *get* this stuff, man?" He put a hand on Albert's knee. "Righteous bud, man."

Barry was on the ground, in the rubble and gray dirt. He lounged on one side, his head cupped in a hand as if he lay on a rug in somebody's living room. He offered the joint again to Leah, who had declined a dozen times, then passed it to me.

"I thought it was yours," Albert said.

"Mine?" Barry said through held breath. He had the other joint now and was contorting his face dramatically to trap the smoke in his lungs. "I live in Brooklyn. Where would I get weed like this, for Christ's sake!" He looked at Leah. "I mean, by gosh," he said.

"It's his," I told Albert. "He's just making fun."

"Seriously, bro," Barry continued. "This is A-1 marijahooch. You gotta cop some more, I'm begging you."

He half walked, half stumbled over to the car seat. He tried to squeeze in between Leah and me, but there was no room. He sat on the ground and dropped his head in her lap.

David had finished off the bottle, with some help from Albert, who now sat with his hands between his knees. From the way he looked fixedly at the ground before him I knew he was angry.

"Hey, Albert," David said.

When Albert did not respond David said it louder, then a third time, stressing the second syllable. "Hey, *Albu-u-urt*!"

"That's Alvin," Albert said, still looking at the ground.

"What's Alvin? Your name is Alvin?"

"No," Albert said slowly, "when you said Hey Albert just then, that's not what they say. They say Hey Alvin."

"Who says?"

"Those chipmunks. That's what they say," and he looked at David, nodding his head as if his patience were being sorely tried. "In the cartoon. They say Hey Alvin, not Hey Albert."

"Wait a minute." David turned to me. "Did you know his name was Alvin? I thought it was Albert. Didn't you tell me it was Albert?"

"It *is* Albert," Albert said, and I could feel him start to rise.

"Oh, sure, now it's Albert, a minute ago it was Alvin. You see my problem? How am I supposed to keep up?"

"David, you asshole," I said.

"That's Hey Asshole, isn't it, Alvin?"

"No," Barry said, half asleep, or pretending to be, in Leah's lap. "I think it's just plain asshole."

"Yeah?" David shoved himself off the wall and came over to the seat. "Well, what I mean is, Alvin, why it's so important and all, is just that my sister should know who's fucking her. That's just courtesy, don't you think? I mean, does she say 'Oh, fuck me, Albert!' or 'Oh, Alvin, that feels so good!' You don't want to get these things wrong."

Albert stood. "David," I said.

"I just want to know. Is she hot? When you fuck my little sister, Alvin, does she bring you pleasure?"

I was woozy from the pot, but not enough so I couldn't stand between them. I felt the blood move in my pants. "David, shut up. I'm warning you to shut the hell up."

"Why? It isn't true?"

"It's none of your fucking business is what it is, even if it was true, so just shut the fuck up."

"Oh, I see. Pardon me."

"Asshole," Albert said and moved toward him. David nodded broadly, encouraging Albert forward. I sat back on the seat.

Then Leah gave a quick moan, a swallowed shout. Barry had his head nestled in her lap. A joint smoldered half smoked in his lips. His hand, moving, had disappeared under the folds of Leah's skirt.

"There," Barry said, contented. He smiled dreamily at her and lay his head back down.

Albert threw a punch at David but missed, grazing his hand on the stone garage wall. David stepped over the milk box and shoved Albert hard against the opposite wall, where his breath left him in a rush. When it returned to him he started to shout.

"You fuck! I'll get you, you fuck!"

Immediately my mother's voice reached us from the kitchen. "David, what are you doing out there? David?"

David stood in front of Albert with his hands at his sides. He held the empty liquor bottle before him, then let it fall to the ground. He smiled at Albert, taunting him until Albert stood and swung again. He missed, but the third time connected, hitting David hard in the mouth. Blood was on David's face, from his mouth or Albert's hand, I couldn't tell.

"Hey, look, Alvin," David said, touching his face. "You got me."

He walked over to Barry and yanked him up by the shoulders. "Party's over," he said. "Say good-bye to your friends." Albert, giving David and me one look together, tramped off through the garages one way while Barry and David headed off the other. "You bring the doobies?" Barry said.

"Yeah, I got 'em."

"Hey, man, watch it," we heard Barry say. "You're bleeding on me."

Leah was sitting beside me, still rigid, her hands inside her pockets. I leaned over and pulled the skirt of her coat around her. She made no sound, no movement. I wanted to cry. I wanted to hold her and be held and cry with her. When my hand touched her, on the way to her pocket, she flinched, and I looked at her, saw her lips moving. I lay on the car seat, my head brushing her coat, my feet hanging over the edge.

"Well, cousin," I said. "It's me and you again."

She didn't answer me, and by the small rocking motions she began making I measured the duration of her prayer. After a while she sat still. I didn't know if I should say something to her. I hoped she would say something to me. She didn't. She got up and went indoors.

The moon, framed directly above me between the garage roofs, was a bright disk, an opening and closing eye. I watched it, clouds rippling before it high in the wind. What had Leah prayed for? Vengeance? Absolution? Understanding? I never understood what you were meant to pray for. In shul we thanked God for healing the sick, bringing in the crops, crushing our enemies. We bore witness: Hear, O Israel, the Lord is God, the Lord is One. Was that what she had prayed? Nighttime's prayer, the last thing God wanted to hear from you.

I lay on the car seat, hoped for a while Albert would come back. I listened for him. He would be smiling, embarrassed, putting the whole thing behind him with a joke. That crazy brother of yours. He would hold me, he would hum songs in my ear. I would listen to his poems, I would let him make love to me again if he wanted to. Upstate was a dumb idea, he'd tell me, he wouldn't be going after all. He would stay.

But Albert didn't come back. It was getting colder. Soon my mother would be calling, or worse, out looking for me herself. From the yelps and hurrahs of Uncle Simon's boys I could tell Mothra had succumbed in flames, the countryside was safe, the villagers could return to their homes. I lay there watching the moon in the clouds until I heard my mother say my name, a quiet question from the kitchen window, as if she knew I was close by and could hear.

3

Leah's first marriage was a neat disaster.

Rabbi Solomon Memmel was a short man, with small glittering eyes that fastened on what he saw. When the food went around the table he watched it, as if unbelieving that any would remain by the time it reached him. When he lifted his hat to wipe sweat from his forehead, his yarmulke peeked through, stained pink to purple, and his mouth, through his thick ungainly beard, was a wet red hole glistening with teeth. Rabbi Memmel had a small, ultra-Orthodox congregation in Williamsburg, where they called him Reb Shlomo. He encouraged everyone to call him this, even my father, ten years older than he. "Call me Reb Shlomo," he said to me, with a damp hand leading me to the couch in my mother's living room. Passing me the cake, the lemon slices for the tea, he sat so close I had to keep moving my legs.

Reb Shlomo lectured us about the responsibilities of the Jewish wife, about the rites and sanctities of marriage, including the marriage bed. He leaned into me, smiling confidentially, and gestured at the bowl of fruit. As he talked he peeled an orange by sinking a thumb past the knuckle in the soft meat, then tearing outward. He announced with satisfaction that Leah was a good girl, modest, dutiful, a hard worker. She understood—and he looked around the room here, as if to suggest not everyone did nowadays—what it meant to be a Jewish wife. Wiping his hands on a napkin, he told me I would be welcome in their home any Shabbos of the year, weekdays, too, and when I showed him to the door, he took my hand again in both of his, fixed me with his moist gaze, and whispered, "Now we will be family."

The marriage was annulled within two years. I never learned the whole story, though the fact that Leah remained obstinately without little Memmels surely played a part. I heard from my mother, who sadly shook her head, of Leah showing up in tears at Aunt Esther's house in the middle of the night, without a coat or change of clothes or money to pay the cab; of prayer sessions, with incense; of entreaties to rabbis for an exorcism of the child-killing spirit Aunt Esther believed had encamped in Leah's womb.

I was off in college then, a small school in Ohio. I didn't get back East often, and when I did, too much urgency was focused on me—my hair, my clothes, my friends, my life—to talk about my cousin. She wasn't going to have an argument with me, my mother said once, before I'd shrugged my pack to the floor, but if I came into the house again without a brassiere on, she would send me back to Ohio for good. And those boys—Paco and H., long-haired boys in sunglasses who had dropped me at the house, given me a kiss, each of them, waved to my mother happily, and driven off without a word—they weren't Jewish, were they? Weren't there any Jewish boys in Ohio? And what was I telling her, his name was H.? His whole name? What kind of name was H.? I could have asked for money for a bus, I didn't have to ride halfway across America with boys with names like secret agents.

Later, in the kitchen, after watching me unpack my things in bated sadness—where were the nice dresses I left home with?— she would tell me of Leah and Aunt Esther, but not with much spirit, her worried eyes coming to rest on me, the kitchen falling silent around us.

Leah's second marriage was more placid. An old man named

Miller—older, my mother insisted; yes, I said, older than any-body else still living—a retired fur cutter on a good pension in Rockaway Park. Even my mother had to admit it was odd that such a young woman—Leah was twenty-three at the time—would agree to the match, but everyone saw how the old man loved her. He redecorated their entire flat in the latest colors—burnt-orange shag for the living room, pale lime for the cabinets and trim in the kitchen—installed a new range and refrigerator, an auto-drying, pot-scrubbing dishwasher. While Leah sat in the living room he would insist on serving guests himself, shuffling in slippered feet to the kitchen to prepare the tea and cut the cake, whistling quiet old-man ditties to himself. When he talked about his long solitude—he had lost his first wife nearly forty years earlier—and about how happy Leah made him, his eyes would swell red at the edges. "My *neshomale*," he called her, "my little soul." For two winters he took Leah to Miami Beach, deluxe accommodations, strictly first-class—I wondered if they ever ran into Albert Fogel there—and they sent picture postcards of the Millers, Mr. and Mrs., in chaise longues on immense white beaches, in sunglasses, matching robes, funny hats.

To no one's surprise, except Aunt Esther, who took to her bed for a week, Mr. Miller died. After returning from Florida their second winter, he sneezed once or twice, ran a slight fever, was told to stay off his feet. Leah pushed fluids, boiled soup, blasted steamy showers in the bathroom for his runny nose. In a week he was dead. On a Sunday morning she found him, slumped in his chair by the window, wrapped in the blue robe with the hotel monogram on the pocket, the Yiddish paper fallen in his lap. He looked so peaceful there in the sunlight she didn't think to disturb him at first—what really was the rush, now?—until the strangest thing happened, no one had ever heard any-thing like it.

As she watched from across the room, a black bird with yel-low eyes and strange red feet, like a sparrow but bigger, flew in the open window and landed on Mr. Miller's head. It stood there, pecking at his few gray hairs, until Leah, horrified, ran to the kitchen for a broom.

And this is what sent Aunt Esther to her bed. Couldn't we see? It was a dybbuk, as plain as the nose on a dog, a dybbuk, the old man's foul spirit—yes, he *seemed* a quiet old gentleman when he was alive. Who knew?—roosting on the corpse, leering at the young wife, pecking like a balabos there on the warm dead head. A disaster. Had Leah touched it, Aunt Esther kept asking. Had it looked her in the eye; worse, spoken any words? No, Leah reported, it stood on Mr. Miller's head until she shooed it with a broom. She gave it a bad scare, she thought, and it knocked Mr. Miller's glasses off in its escape, but after a short breather on the curtain valance it had flown back out the way it came in.

After a brief examination Esther's rabbi proclaimed the new widow free of all visitation, demonic or otherwise, except the grievous luck we had all predicted for her, and Aunt Esther, with great trepidation, dragged herself to the cemetery. She would go nowhere near the grave, however, and stood ten feet off with the men who would fill in the hole, one holding a shovel and reading a magazine, the other in a slouch cap, chewing an unlit cigar.

So my first year out of art school, apprentice and lover to a Manhattan stained-glass artist who monthly retired, told me sadly we were finished over a bottle of Chianti, called his broker to put the studio up for sale, then got back on his meds, hired more help, fired his broker, took me off in the middle of the afternoon to a downtown hotel to make love with the TV on, then order room-service pizza and urge me into the shower so he could call his wife in White Plains, I was not entirely surprised to receive an invitation to my cousin's third marriage. The sober stationery had a bare black garland around the border, some puny leaves, and was covered with a lengthy Bible quotation about the joy of wedlock. "The hour of the songbird is upon us," it proclaimed in block letters. "The call of the dove is heard in our land." I immediately got on the phone with my mother.

"It's terrible," she said. "This one will be worse than the

other." "Which other?" I was about to ask but she went on. "He's a scholar, God help her, a serious man." And all the way across the river I could see her shaking her head. "That poor girl."

Bernard Finkel was indeed a serious man. At twenty-six he had already received his rabbinical degree, authored nine scholarly articles of his own, four in Hebrew, and, with his professors at Yeshiva and the New School, co-edited a lively volume of essays on the decline of moral standards in the Jewish family. He was of the new breed of learned men, adept at contemporary discourse, a modern at home in several languages and literatures, one who out of clear-eyed zeal, not some weak-kneed atavism, cleaved unto God's Law in all its terrible majesty. He was thin and ascetic-looking, and had the preoccupied gaze of a man with too much on his mind. He was discussed, consulted, admired. He was invited to shuls to deliver Shabbos sermons. He was on panels, talk shows, was photographed with a gloomy assemblage of religious leaders convened to discuss ethnic relations with an assistant to a deputy mayor. He suffered shattering headaches, epic insomnias. No wonder. Who could sleep after so much thinking? Only tea and warm toast could anyone, even Leah, coax into him, though she was often asked—Aunt Esther, who was terrified of the man, told my mother this—to stand behind his desk chair and rub his closed eyes with her fingers, lightly, making no sound. He was a great catch, this was obvious: where in the whole city would you find another like him? And that he would marry an older woman—Leah and I were barely twenty-eight— showed him to be a man of sound character as well as searing intellect.

But something troubled Aunt Esther. At the engagement lunch Esther never emerged from my mother's bedroom, and a constant shuttle of family ranged from the kitchen to the back of the house until only Uncle Simon, my father, and I remained at the table with the guests of honor. We were eating honey cake and fruit. Uncle Simon had had two slices, was eyeing a third. Bernard Finkel sat in his suit and hat in front of his untouched cake—he had sliced an apple and carefully placed a section in his mouth—looking like a man at an interview for a job he knows is beneath him. Uncle Simon was very interested in Bernard Finkel's rabbinic views on finance, and was becoming his closest ally. He was just asking Bernard what kind of car he drove when my mother called me from the room.

On her bed lay Aunt Esther, a dampened handkerchief on her forehead, another forgotten in the top of her blouse. "She's fainted twice," my mother told me.

"Three times," Aunt Esther said feebly from the bed.

"I only saw two."

"You were in the kitchen," Aunt Esther said. "I couldn't wait."

My mother leaned out the doorway to look down the hall, shaking her head.

"I can't do it, sweetheart," Aunt Esther said to me, taking my hand. "Darling, I beg you, I haven't got the strength." She pulled me onto the bed near her. "One more minute, bubele, a little mercy, please." She closed her eyes and breathed. "Don't worry, I'm coming. Just help me up. Is he gone yet?" And she tried to sit up, if lifting one wrist can be counted as such, then succumbed, eyes fluttering.

"Number three," my mother said from the door.

From behind closed eyes, Aunt Esther whispered, "Four."

After Mr. Finkel had gone away, Uncle Simon came and sat on my mother's bed, where Aunt Esther lay recovering with a small tray of chocolates and candied fruit, and pronounced Bernard Finkel a rare animal, a biblical scholar of the first rank with—and this was truly unusual—a good business sense. He thought he might put him in an Impala. What was all the commotion, Uncle Simon wanted to know, glaring at us balefully. Rabbi Finkel had some fascinating ideas on what the Law had to say about running a modern automobile franchise, but we had missed it and it was too subtle to re-create.

The bride was purchased a gown, snow-white, by her husband, who also determined the menu, the guest list, the flowers, and the music. For a honeymoon they would travel to Boston, where Bernard had an appointment and had purchased a house, which he described to Leah with vivid detail, so she could see it in her mind's eye. He had, Leah told my mother, thought of everything.

At the wedding, the women sat in the bride's dressing room while in another room the men gathered with a bottle of Scotch to review the marriage contract, discuss the ancient rites of property transfer—of bride from father to husband—dowry, payment. Leah's father, my Uncle Lew, had been dead for years. My father stood in as surrogate proprietor, but he was nervous around Bernard Finkel and his intellectual friends, and I had glanced in the room, seen the black-coated backs of Bernard's friends leaning over a table, and my father, an empty whiskey glass in his hand, hovering nearby.

In the bridal chamber, a room walled completely in mirrors, maroon velvet, like a walk-in jewelry box, I watched as Leah had her hair combed by Miriam Finkel, Bernard's younger sister, whose own hair, henna bright, was festooned impressively from all sides of her head. On the vanity before them were atomizers, hair sprays, tubes of gel, cans of mousse, a pink travel case stuffed with makeup. Bernard wanted a floral bouffant, Miriam explained around bobby pins in her teeth, and it was not going well. She tugged Leah's hair like she was hauling in an anchor, constructed something first to the left, then the right, then the left again, pausing only to stare in the mirror one outraged second, then tear the whole thing down to begin again. At her feet, small piles of daisy and lily-of-the-valley were ground slowly into the carpet.

On a couch to the side, my mother held Aunt Esther's hand and Aunt Esther held a bottle of smelling salts. She looked grimly arrayed in a white suit—courtesy of the groom. She had agreed to some sedation and stared stonily ahead of her, as if she had been invited to view her own destruction, not see her daughter wed a third time.

My mother, too, seemed agitated. There had been some commotion, raised voices in the attached powder room when I had first arrived, and when my mother and Aunt Esther emerged together, Esther was red-eyed, tottering in her new silk shoes, and my mother was erect with anger. When Esther saw me, she put some spirit in her wobble.

"Esther, don't you dare!" my mother said, and Aunt Esther found the seat where she was sitting now. I had gone over to offer a kiss and congratulations. She grabbed both my hands and started to pull me down, crying. My mother, her mouth a straight line, nabbed a girl who had come in to lay out more towels and ordered a pitcher of whiskey sours to be brought in.

"Ma'am," the girl said, "the bar's not open."

"I'll give you five minutes," my mother said.

She had replaced me by Aunt Esther, taken her hand, and when the whiskey sours arrived, she ignored them. I didn't. Though the sweet fizzy mixture was nauseating, I sensed this might turn into a day that required some fortification. I drank one, offered one to Miriam, who had no time for it, so I drank hers, too. Leonard, my boss/lover, who needed the narration of talk shows to drown out his guilty bleatings in bed, had taken up with a new glass cutter in the studio, Stephanie—"She's got a fine steady hand," he told me. I'll bet she does, Lensky—younger than me, who watched him with that secret, limpid, adoring look I was absolutely disgusted to recognize from my own face in the mirror barely a week earlier. Not even a bottle of Chianti this time. After pouring several glasses and offering them around, I drank one at a time from the five cocktail glasses on the tray, and watched Leah's torment.

She was beautiful. It shocked me to see this. She was as pale as ever, but the harrowing thinness had left her. She seemed, after all this time, to have grown into her body, and it was softly contoured, lovely. She had breasts, nearly obliterated by Miriam in powder, but there they were—I had from time to time admitted to passing fits of nostalgia for the pre-braless days, junior high, when you could change shape weekly, courtesy of Maiden-form and Kleenex, and there would be boys who would have stepped over you bleeding in the street the day before regarding you all of a sudden, stopped in their tracks, prayerful hunger on their silly faces—and here was my cousin grown to womanhood, somebody's dream date, somebody's wife. Her eyes, looking occasionally at me in the mirror, were—I was unprepared for this—happy.

I wished then we were back in my room, years ago, saw us perched on the edge of our beds in the dark, holding pillows and whispering, the doorframe outlined in light, the sounds of grownups on the other side. "What's happened to you, Leah?" I wanted to ask. I realized I wanted to talk with her, to tell her about Leonard. I hadn't spoken about Leonard with anyone, but I wanted to tell Leah now, how I was sure I'd lose my job, a job I needed, how he had told me just today it was so painful to see me now, how he kept looking over my head, couldn't look me in the eye, and other things, the little "hunh"s he gave out when we were making love, the way he screwed up his eyes and made me hold completely still so he could come undistracted, the way he patted his semi-flat stomach and liked to sit around in striped bikini briefs. All this I wanted to tell Leah, waiting to marry her thin-lipped rabbi, but here, today, I could say nothing. The pitcher was empty and Miriam Finkel was cursing under her breath when, after a particularly savage tug to Leah's head, she had snapped her second comb. I went over and put out my hand. Miriam looked at me a wild moment, as if she would plunge into my hair next, then exhaled, surrendered the half comb and brush and left the room with two bobby pins still vised between her teeth.

"I can do a French braid," I told Leah, "sometimes."

She smiled quietly in the mirror.

"They're going to live in Massachusetts," Aunt Esther said from the rear of the room, as if someone had asked a question. "Cambridge. In Massachusetts. You know it?"

"Yes," my mother said absently.

"That's where they'll be. In Cambridge, Massachusetts. He has an appointment."

"I know," my mother said.

"He bought a house," Aunt Esther said. "A yellow house. Three floors. I saw pictures. In the garage you could put at least two cars."

"How's that?" I asked Leah, pulling the hair back to show her what I intended. With hair like hers, I'd have worn it down, wedding or not. She nodded, and for a few moments I made believe I knew what to do with the pins, the spray.

"She looks beautiful," my mother said. "Esther, wake up, tell her she looks good."

Esther nodded sadly.

"Bernard found us a house," Leah said to me. "I haven't seen it yet. It's near the campus, so he can walk to the library."

I shook my head enthusiastically, a barrette between my teeth.

"If only Elazar was alive," Esther said, meaning my grandfather.

Leah and I paused, looked at them in the mirror. My mother straightened her hat, sat stiffly. "Yes," she said. "Well, he isn't."

Esther took two deep breaths, opened and closed her eyes, and slumped against my mother, who pushed her ungently away. *"Genug shain!"* she said. "Esther, enough!"

"He wants children right away," Leah was saying. "He says it's already late, most of my child-bearing years are behind me."

From the couch, a soft groan.

"He's a distinguished man, Leah. You must be very proud."

She smiled again.

I was braiding her hair now, moving down her back. Before I had thought about it I heard myself say, "David called. To say congratulations."

"He did?" She turned around in the chair to look at me. "I'm glad. Where is he now?"

"Out West," I said casually, as though I knew more but was deciding to be vague. Actually, that was all I knew. He had quit architecture a year earlier, about the same time his marriage had collapsed. When he had come back to tell my father he had left the firm the argument had carried them out of the house, the shouting bringing out the neighbors, until a man from across the street had approached with his hands in the air and David had run toward the subway. That was the last we'd seen of him.

He called from time to time to say hi, relate some funny anecdote about the town he was in, the job he temporarily held, twice to ask—though he never really asked, somehow managed to let me know an offer would be accepted—to wire him money. He was heading out to Oregon now, or Washington, anyway, the Coast. What would he do? He would know when he got there, and he would call. "He's still traveling," I told Leah.

"You know," she said. "It's silly, on a day like this . . . I used to hope . . . I mean, when we were young . . ."

Her hair was done. Before me in the mirror, swimming above her head in the five whiskey sours I had poured into me and in the tears that unaccountably pushed their way into my eyes, was an image of the three of us as we had never been—I knew that—children together, unworried, sharing spacious and sunlit days. I shook my head. The whiskey would make me sick. "I know, Leah," I said. "I know."

I wove a spray of white belled flowers into her hair and turned her from side to side so she could see. A knock and then outside the door a soft voice said, "Time."

I walked to the front of the chair to look at her and bent down to kiss her lips. "You do," I said. "You look beautiful."

She looked at herself in the mirror.

"He sent flowers," I said, gathering up the pieces of comb. "From Seattle. They should be here by now." He hadn't, of course; had reacted to the news about the marriage with no more than a snort, but I'd sent an arrangement in his name. With a funny note, "Don't forget your favorite cousin."

"Ready?" I said.

The sanctuary was full, and when we entered, Aunt Esther and my mother first, then me, then Leah and my father, they all turned to look. The violinist from the band took up a Yiddish air. The old ladies from my family were in tears, gazing at us, bright with hope and sadness. On Bernard's side, strangers, though behind his aged mother and the bonfire of Miriam's hair were several empty seats. Ahead stood the rabbi in his white ceremonial robe, under the flowing canopy, prayer book in his hand.

Everything was ready. But the groom, who should have been waiting under the canopy, was missing. I looked at my father, but beyond a certain stiffness around the mouth could see nothing in his face. We stood to one side to make room for Bernard and his attendants, and waited. The violinist had come to the tune's end, but after a moment of silence that seemed to swell into the room, he began again. Leah took my hand.

In the front row, as if moved by the lugubrious melody, Aunt Esther began to sob, and my mother worked the bottle of smelling salts into her hand. I gave my father a questioning look but he had his teacher's face on, calm, unreadable. He gazed steadily up the aisle at the rear doors. The rabbi held the prayer book open, busied himself turning the pages. On a small table beside him, the wine, brimming in the glass for the wedded couple to drink, vibrated almost imperceptibly.

Two chairs were knocked to the ground as the doors to the rear burst open, and Uncle Simon strode in, holding a piece of paper above his head. He took two steps and stopped, breathing loudly, glaring at us all with pop-eyed wrath.

"Woman!" he shouted, and waited for the room to fill with his voice. "What have you done!"

He stood there, both arms upraised now, seeing himself, I'm sure, as an Old Testament prophet summoning God's destruction. But he had used the same pose for an ad in the local paper—Fifty Cars Under Twelve-Ninety-Nine!!!—holding in each fist the dollars his lucky customers would save. I saw now he had the Hebrew marriage contract in his hand.

"A lie," he proclaimed, "an insult," and he began walking slowly toward the front of the hall, as people rose from their seats. "An outrage before God."

People were standing by their seats now. The rabbi, a professional smiler, looked up mildly, though he couldn't keep wrinkles from gathering near his eyes. Bernard's deaf mother looked about happily and Miriam leaned into her ear. "I told you," she shouted. My mother had her arm around Aunt Esther now, who sobbed openly. My father walked quickly to Uncle Simon, pulled him aside, and talked with him in strained whispers. The rabbi joined them. I saw him look back at Leah. We were the only two left under the canopy. Leah held my hand, did not move, and looked down at the floor, where the wineglass lay wrapped in a linen napkin, waiting to be shattered by her husband at the ceremony's end.

Uncle Simon made a dramatic turn and walked from the room, nearly tripping on an upended chair by the door. My father came up to my mother and Aunt Esther.

"Is it true?" he asked.

"Yes," my mother said.

"The contract says she's a virgin? A woman who has had two husbands?"

"Yes," my mother said quietly. "How did he find out?"

"You knew?"

"Just a few minutes ago. How did he find out?"

My father stared at her, uncomprehending.

"About Memmel," she said. "About Miller."

"Simon. They asked Simon to look at the contract."

"They who?" my mother asked.

"They who? They, who do you think, they? The friends, the professors. Someone got suspicious, someone started asking questions."

Esther let out a small whimper, and for the first time since

Bernard Finkel had entered the picture I heard my father raise his voice at her. "A woman's married two times already and her husband's not going to know? Who thinks like this?" And he looked up the aisle now, where not a person was still sitting.

My mother shrugged, raising both her palms as if to say nothing could be done now, or to tell my father enough had been said. Aunt Esther was in full collapse beside her, shaking with near-silent moans.

Then, as if this was his cue, the doors to the rear exploded again and Uncle Simon made his second entrance, arms full of coats. "Come," he declaimed, in the general direction of his wife but loud enough to include us all. "We're leaving this place." Behind him were Bernard Finkel and several serious-looking men in black suits. They moved up the aisle like Jewish Secret Service men, they didn't look left or right. Bernard gathered up his mother, an old woman in a huge brocade gown who came docilely, still smiling, used to being moved from place to place, like a potted plant. To Leah, all Bernard said was, "I'm disappointed."

Then they were gone, all of them, Bernard and his mother, Uncle Simon and his wife, his boys, grinning delightedly over their shoulders, Miriam, who, after glaring at Leah a moment—as if nothing would surprise her from a woman whose hair wouldn't take a back comb—stomped noisily from the room. The news spread quickly, a buzz filled the air. The violinist, looking unhappy, picked up his instrument to start again. Then a woman I did not know ran up and whispered in his ear. He dropped the violin from his shoulder and looked at us. People, as if they had to choose sides, either left the room—this was the majority—or huddled near my family, what was left of it, looking shamed.

I didn't know where to look. The rabbi, beside us, was gathering up his papers and book, hurrying, as if he meant to catch up to the departed crowd. My father was gray with rage, looking at him and away, and my mother stared out patiently before her as if she were on a steamship, land days and days from view. I thought I might laugh or I might sit down and cry. I watched the swinging doors at the rear of the room, heard loud voices beyond them, Uncle Simon's the loudest, apologizing, assigning blame. Leah had not raised her eyes from the floor, but the expression on her face was composed, unsurprised. "I asked her not to," she said, looking only once at her mother. She still had not let go of my hand.

Then, as if on a cue of her own, once the crowd scene was ended, a groan, a guttural plaint, and, for the first time since I had known her, my Aunt Esther really did faint. She collapsed to the floor and lay there, mouth open, head back, her thick wig lifting slightly from her mottled white scalp.

One of her arms nudged the linen napkin slightly, releasing the water glass—not a wineglass, after all—inside. No one moved. The glass rolled across the room in a wavering line until it reached the far wall and the baseboard heater, where it came to rest with a tiny click.

4

My guy was a cabdriver, a chess player in Washington Square Park, a Rumanian on an expired visa who read philosophy paperbacks in three languages, phoned his mother in Bucharest every Sunday, wearing a clean shirt and tie for the occasion, and sold nickel and dime bags in the park so we could shop at Balducci's once in a while, eat at Panetta's Steak House on Fourth Street, and dance—we did this twice—to the Harmony Makers Jazz Band at Roseland uptown. His name was Alex. I loved him.

We had plans. Summers hiking in the West, a flat on the Left Bank where he would pursue his philosophy degree while I waitressed evenings, did my stained glass all day. We would traverse the world by sea, following Magellan's route. We would open a bagel shop in Rio. We would spend some time among the Hopi or the Navajo or whatever tribe would have us—Alex wrote away for information. We would live wherever we decided to, Alex said, wherever the life was, and when we had money we would send for his mother and sister to join us in New Orleans, Dubrovnik, Montevideo—if not in time for the wedding, then for the christening of the grandchildren.

The police said he was lucky to survive such a beating, that anyone who would fight three men so hard for fourteen ounces of marijuana was either lying or had a serious wish to die. They were guys we knew from the park, just young guys who hung out, sometimes bought dope from Alex, sometimes shared beer with the rest of us. They danced to the conga circles, they checked out the girls. They had names, but I didn't know them. It was a Tuesday, early spring, the grass starting to push through the pounded dirt, everybody's juices running. They were all in the park. Alex would go there after getting off shift, to mellow out, play some chess, talk with the local philosophers. He was besting the old Belgian with the beret and the Chihuahua for the third consecutive game when these guys came over and lingered, that look on their faces. "Sure," he probably said to them. "I got you." After the game, he invited them up to get high, to sample the wares. There was an empty Budweiser 40-ouncer in the stairwell, Alex had probably shared this with them on the way upstairs. What happened next he wouldn't tell me or the police. He had been stupid enough to leave the pot with the money he was saving under the bed—all of it, just rolled up in rubber bands and shoved in a box under the bed like some farmer from the Old Country—and maybe it was seeing the bills that set these guys off. Maybe it was something he said—if he was angry Alex was capable of saying anything. Maybe they had it planned all along. All I know is they called me at the studio, told me to get down to St. Vincent's right away. "What is it?" I asked, not able to breathe. I was standing near the round window overlooking the street. I watched people talking, entering stores, waiting for the light, trying to get myself to breathe. "What's happened?"

"There's been an assault," the nurse told me, and gave me his name. Behind her I could hear a siren and loud voices.

He was on a bed in the emergency room, hooked up to a whole wall of machines, smiling at me like it was an elaborate joke. "They have good drugs, your American doctors," he said, grinning around a broken tooth. He had a fractured wrist, a contused kidney, four broken ribs, a blood bruise behind one eye the doctors said could leave him brain-damaged if the swelling was not controlled. His arm was broken in six places, he would need to wear a pneumatic cast for two months and then have surgery. He smiled and waved me over with his chin. He looked comfortable, stoned, amused. His face was so blue and battered I couldn't even touch him. I just stood in the doorway and cried.

The studio I worked in, maybe to help me get out of town for a while, sent me on assignment to Baltimore, where they had contracted to clean the windows of an old Presbyterian church. It was absorbing work, the crew was friendly and liked the job, they even got me to go for margaritas one night in a dive across the street. After three weeks I took up my mother's constant suggestion and gave Leah a call. She had lived in Baltimore almost four years now, was married to a man I'd never met, had two little boys I'd never seen. "I knew you were here," she said. "I was hoping you'd call." She invited me for the weekend, for Shabbos—the new husband wasn't a rabbi, thank God, but a lawyer—but I said no, I didn't do that anymore, and Leah changed the invitation to the following day. So on a Sunday afternoon I borrowed a car, put on a dress for the first time in months, and followed Leah's careful, elaborate directions out to the suburbs.

They lived in a two-story house on a gently curving street lined with young trees. There were hydrangeas out front, a bank of irises to either side of the door, and around the side of the house a rope hammock slung between two maples. There was the smell of barbecue in the air, and a radio played the Orioles game next door, where two men were carefully re-oiling a driveway with big push brooms. The older man stopped to wipe his forehead and waved his cap at me.

The door was opened by a boy in a plaid shirt and a large yarmulke, his hair crew-cut on top, wrapped in small peis around his ears, where it had been allowed to grow on the sides. He looked at me seriously a moment, then left the door open and ran into the house, calling for his mother. Leah said, "I'm coming," and the little boy stopped in a doorway up the hall to stick his head out and peer at me sideways.

In the moment it took her to walk to the door, I fought the urge to run, get in the car before anyone else saw me, drive, not back to my hotel, not back to New York, just somewhere away from here, fast. There was a nameless rebuke in her happy face coming toward me, in this quiet street with the ball game drifting from the radio next door. Then Leah threw her arms around me, and with the older boy leading the way and the younger laboriously pushing a plastic truck into the hall before us, she brought me inside.

I sat in the living room with the older boy, Joseph, while Leah called her husband in from the yard. Through the sliding rear door I saw him put down pruning shears, and he waved to me from the kitchen, a large man sweating freely behind a thick brown beard. He smiled and tugged at his shirt collar to indicate he was going upstairs to change. Leah and the younger boy, Sam, were in the kitchen, preparing food. Joseph sat on the sofa opposite me, his sneaker soles straight out before him. He held a brown bear with a battered white nose in his lap.

"I know who you are," he said.

"I know who you are, too."

"This is Bo, my most famous stuffed animal."

"Hello, Bo," I said.

Joseph shook his head. "He doesn't talk to people."

Alex had been gone two months. He was gone five days after the beating, still dizzy, still pissing blood, only out of the hospital thirty-six hours. Someone had asked some questions and Alex was convinced the police had turned his name over to Immigration, and it was clear, at least to Alex, he'd be jailed for the drug charge—though they'd found less than an ounce in what was left of our room—then deported anyway. He was leaving for Bucharest, if he could find the money. There was no choice.

We had just come from the hospital. We were standing in our kitchen drinking iced tea. It hurt Alex to sit down, jarred the dressing around his chest, and he tended to knock his pneumatic cast against the table, which the doctors told him wouldn't hurt but did. I had taken the week off from work, made us a lunch of soup and cold salads from Balducci's. I had bought a checked cloth for the table and some flowers from the cart on Sixth Avenue. I had made a sign in block letters and funny designs, "Welcome Home!" but the place, the "crime scene"—for two days yellow police tape had barred me from the door—didn't feel exactly like home anymore, and I had left the sign in a drawer. I had done what I could with the bedroom, though the blood in the carpet would never come out, and the glazier had not come to replace the window as he'd promised. In the cab Alex had told me he was leaving. Now he poured his tea into the sink and with one clumsy hand found the Scotch in the cupboard. I could have helped but I didn't. He opened the bottle by holding the cap in his teeth, poured a glass full, and smiled at me. "I have no choice," he said, and took a long swallow. "This way I beat them to punching me." He laughed, wincing through the pain. "Is joke, no?"

There was no one I could talk to. My father didn't know about Alex; I was sure my mother had kept the information from him. She had disavowed all knowledge, too, telling me one Sunday last summer in Central Park. Alex was going to join us at Bethesda Fountain for a picnic, his first chance to meet my parents. I was at the subway stop with the basket, and when my mother came up the steps alone, without my father, I grew concerned, but she looked festive in a blue summer dress and I hugged her gratefully and took her arm. But she wasn't staying. There on the avenue, with tourists unloading from a bus behind us and the summer breeze buffeting our dresses, my new straw hat, she told me as long as I was with this man she would rather not know about it. She looked me in the face, then turned away and said if I didn't care what I did to my own life I could at least care about the pain I caused others who loved me. She kissed me solemnly on the cheek and was gone, down the stairs, lost in the crowd of people blinking their way into the sunlight.

When Alex met me by the fountain, I had thrown away the hat, the picnic, basket and all. I couldn't talk to him at first. We walked around the park until it grew dark and lights came on in the high buildings on the avenues. We walked down to the duck pond, then up to the reservoir and back, not talking, until at Sheeps Meadow Alex stopped me and took me by the shoulders and held me hard until I could begin to cry.

So I had no one to call. David knew about Alex, was ambiguously sympathetic—"My God, you made a *picnic*?"—but he would just magnify it into an age-old pattern, a constellation of familial pain in which David's star burned most bright.

Alex called Bucharest several times, spoke loudly to his mother, had a shouting match with someone he later told me was an uncle. He had been drinking since early morning, had smoked some hash the police hadn't found in the freezer, was washing down pain pills with Scotch every half hour. When he finally screamed something into the phone and hung up, he turned to me with a tight smile.

"They have no help," he said. "You must get money for my plane."

I did. I emptied my bank accounts, including one he didn't know about, where I had been depositing forty dollars a month for our future travels. I reserved the ticket over the phone, packed his heavy leather suitcase, his box of books, while he supervised from the couch.

At Kennedy Airport the following day he boarded the plane, his head in a big colorful Rastafarian cap I'd bought to cover the swelling, his shattered arm in its cast sheltered up near his chest like a sleeping child. In the coffee shop he had talked about sending for me in a few months, about meeting in France in a year, but I wasn't really listening and soon he stopped. As he went through security he tried to wave, but a stewardess came up behind him, jostling him down the ramp. I saw him try to turn, but he couldn't, and then I began waving. He couldn't see me but I waved anyway. All I could see was the festive woolen hat, concentric rings of yellow and red and green bobbing down the walkway. I waved until it was out of sight.

The younger boy enjoyed planting his feet in his father's lap and tugging with both fists on his father's thick beard. Avram, Leah's husband, didn't seem to mind. We ate sandwiches with coffee in the kitchen, except for Joseph, who explained that Bo wasn't hungry and he would eat when Bo did.

"Will Bo be hungry soon?" Avram asked.

"I *told* you, he doesn't talk to people!"

"All right," Leah said and put a sandwich in front of the boy, who soon took a few bites and asked for milk.

We talked about the neighborhood, the religious school the boys would have to be bused to across town. Avram seemed to know all about me, which I found touching, and the delight he took in his two boys, the quiet way he watched Leah, made some age-old verity in me dissolve away, made me glad for my cousin and at the same time made me know I couldn't stay here very long. After the meal, Avram took the boys upstairs for a bath, and Leah, as we had done all our lives, cut lemon, boiled water, and brought tea in glasses to the table.

"You have a beautiful family," I told her.

"Yes," she said, and I was grateful she didn't say any more.

"How's your job?" she said. "Still making windows?"

"Well, cleaning them most of the time. I like it. I'm good at it and I like the work."

We sat in Leah's white kitchen, with its sink and stove under

gleaming copper-bottomed pots in the center of the room, with
the soft garland of flowers circling the wall near the ceiling, with
the long shadows of late afternoon reaching across her flower
beds and the children's toys left in the yard, with the tea steaming between us, and suddenly I wanted to tell her everything
about Alex, about my life with him, about the idiotic dreams we
half believed in. I wanted to tell her how his thick red hair had so
many cowlicks he wore a hat most of the time rather than wrestle
it with a comb, how his beard tended to grow inward, piercing
the skin and causing painful blisters, and how I would tease the
hairs out gently with a pin. I wanted to tell her we liked taking
baths together, using a huge pink sponge, the kind they use at
car washes, on each other's backs, that we liked to go see Chinese
movies in Chinatown, no subtitles, how the Chinese women
would knit and talk back at the screen, how the kids would play
in the aisles, sometimes come right up and climb in your lap, how
vendors walked up and down during the movie and sold sweet
candied noodles out of little trays. He was a large man, I wanted
to tell her, but somewhere he had learned how to dance, and he
had taught me, and he would talk with anyone—if someone
stopped us on the street for money he'd ask what they needed,
where they would spend the money, until I dragged him off,
handing out dollar bills as tolls to reach home. I wanted to tell
her he snored like a diesel engine, was the only man I ever knew
who liked to hold me after we made love, how he thought he was
a talented cook when he was a terrible one, how he liked to sing
Jimi Hendrix tunes when he had no idea of the lyrics. I wanted to
tell Leah I loved Alex and he was gone and memory was a tricky
thing to live on; it shifted on you like cards in a deck, until you
didn't know any longer what it was you were remembering.

Our last night we propped up the bed with a milk crate we
found near the elevator—one of the legs had been knocked off in
the fight. Alex was in great pain, and had been through a bottle
of Scotch. Now he was drinking red wine and talking to me in

Rumanian part of the time. He had gotten very angry when I couldn't find his Husserl essays and when I asked him if he wanted any of our travel books he said I should keep them. I said I didn't think I wanted to and he said fine and opened the front door and threw them into the hall. He had followed them out and taken a long walk while I finished packing. When he came back he was silent and I took him to bed, undressed him, changed the bandages over his eye and on his chest, bathed him with a damp cloth and warm water. He was asleep when I finished. I found some music on the radio, took off my clothes, and got in next to him, listening to the music and his thick breathing.

Sometime in the night he woke me. He was unable to move without wincing, so we kissed for a long time. I tasted Scotch on his breath, wine, and his skin smelled of smoke. I moved, kissed him on the hair, the cheeks, the shoulders and neck. I whispered nonsense in his ears. After a while he stopped kissing me back. I had drunk most of the wine, Alex had taken more pills. He said something to me, too quiet for me to catch, as I slid down his belly to take him in my mouth.

I was making love to him when he said it again. "Jew."

"What?" I picked up my head.

"Jew. Jewess. Daughter of Abraham."

"Alex, what the hell are you saying?"

"Daughter of martyrs. Miserable bone-faced Auschwitz to teach us all how to suffer."

I was sitting in bed now. I tried to get out, but Alex caught me by the arm and dragged me back. He pushed my head back toward his penis.

"There. You see?"

"Let go of me, you fucker," I said.

"What do you see?" he said angrily, this time pulling on my hair.

"You," I said. "I see you."

"This is uncircumcised cock. Look." And he reached down

with his other hand, I heard him groan and he lifted the half-erect organ closer to my face. "Uncircumcised cock of infidel dog. Cock of dog. Is what your mother saw."

"No, Alex," I tried to say, but with a call of pain he sat halfway up in bed and forced my mouth down over him.

Leah asked about David. He was married again, I told her, had a little boy just about Sam's age.

"Cousins," Leah said.

I drank some of the tea and Leah went to get more hot water. She had started to gain weight after the second child. She thought it was funny, after a life of praying she could put on some weight, her prayers had been answered all at once. Her hair was short, and I was relieved obscurely that she had not covered it with a wig. She wore a white blouse with a blue skirt and battered Adidas on her feet. She moved lightly around the room, called up the stairs when Joseph yelled a question from the bath, and watched me patiently during my silences.

"It's nice to see you this way," I told her.

"Yes?"

"Like this. Happy, I mean."

"I am," she said. "And I hope you will be."

"Oh, you know, I have my moments." I stood to help her with the kettle.

At the table she spooned sugar into her tea. Then she said, "It was always easier for me," looking down at her teaspoon, turning it in her hand.

"What?"

"Easier. I always had an easier time, or I always thought I did."

I had no idea what she meant. I remembered the trussed and constrained child, the timid girl who could not choose her own clothes, where she went, whom she talked to. I remembered her inability to hold even a simple conversation, and her eyes, always wanting. I had been the free one, I had been outdoors, unsupervised, able to speak my mind, my convictions.

"I don't think that's true," I said. "I always . . . I'm sorry, but I always pitied you, Leah, you had so many rules, so many fears."

"Yes, that's true. I was afraid of everything. But somewhere in all those rules and superstitions and fears, I understood what I wanted, I learned what would . . ." Here she paused, looking for the word. "What would be enough."

"I'm glad," I said. Something was in my throat, a pressure building behind my tongue. I tried a sip of the tea and looked at her, then away.

"I'm sorry," she said.

"And me?" I said. "What did I learn, Leah?"

She pushed the saucer of lemon slices aside and reached across for my hand. I pulled back, lifted the warm glass near my face.

"You never learned," she said quietly. "I've watched you my whole life and you've never known what would be enough for you."

"That's not fair," I said. I heard Joseph running upstairs and Avram's voice calling in Yiddish. I thought of Alex walking away from me toward the plane, of my father, who had not spoken with me since I had come home the night after Alex left, in tears, and he had learned of him for the first time. He had prayed for me that night, prayed to God and to his ancestors for guidance, for forgiveness. I thought of my parents, steeped in sorrow like good Jews, of Leah, emerging from it and looking back at me from her remote and inscrutable calm. Where in all this had I asked for too much? I thought of what Alex had called me. "That's not a fair thing to say to me," I said, standing at the table.

"I'm sorry," Leah said, rising, too, "I didn't mean . . . All I meant was . . ." And again she paused, and I raised my voice.

"What? All you meant was what?"

"All right," she said, and sat down, looking at me. "It's not about wanting, I don't think. Everyone wants. It's about looking around and finding the world, I don't know, sufficient. You saw everything, nothing slipped by. Maybe you saw too much. You saw right through people's words, what they meant to do, to the ways they failed. You always had to forgive them. I saw less. I had less to forgive."

Sometime later Avram came down and said the boys were ready to say good night. We followed him upstairs, where the boys, one in train pajamas, the other in a red suit with a smiling dinosaur across the shirt, were saying their prayers. They said good night first, Joseph throwing his arms around me, and putting his lips on my face. They got into bed and said the Shema, the prayer Leah and I used to say before bed. Then they added the prayer David had been taught, the prayer for boys. "May the angel who keeps me from all evil bless these young boys and speak of them in my name and the names of my forefathers. And may they grow to prosper in the heart of their land." I stood in the lit doorway near Avram, while Leah sat on Sam's bed, and wondered if in other dark rooms somewhere there were little girls praying for these boys, praying for their future husbands. And I wondered who prayed for those girls.

Downstairs, they invited me to spend the night, to stay and listen to some music or sit on the patio out back. I shook my head, said I had a crew who would sit and drink coffee until I showed up and got them started. They walked me to the door, came out to see me to my car. The night was fresh and still, the oil from the drive next door shone dully in the moonlight, and from somewhere behind the house I could hear wind moving in the trees. Leah and I kissed. She made me promise I would call soon and kissed me again. Avram shook my hand warmly and put his arm around Leah there on the walk. I got into my car, turned on the ignition and lights. They waved as I pulled away from the curb and I waved back. But at the corner I stopped, looked in the rearview mirror, where I could see them still standing on their walk. They looked around the street a moment, Avram picked something off the lawn, and they moved back toward the house. I watched until I was certain they were safe indoors, then slowly slipped out the clutch and turned the corner.

Ehud Havazelet

We moved from Jerusalem to New York in 1958, when I was two, and I grew up in the tight-knit, occasionally airless Orthodox community in New York, where the privilege and burden of a well-known family name were constant markers. My own determination was simply to fit in, to be an American boy. I remember staring at the kitchen clock when I was four, delighted in the knowledge that I had successfully forgotten all my Hebrew except for one word—the word for bicycle—and once this was expunged I would be as American as Barry Perlman and Marshall Berkowitz, kids on the street. I was wrong, of course.

In 1967 my father and I were still debating whether to fly "home" to help out in the war with the Arabs, but it ended before we could make our plans. In 1973, at the outbreak of the next war, I was a freshman at Columbia, and arrived late to shul on the day they were raising money to send to Israel. The usher took a look at me through the glass doors, locked against children and noise, saw my long hair and disheveled clothes, my sleepy, arrogant teenage demeanor, and must have decided I was one of the reasons everything seemed to be going so suddenly wrong. He wouldn't let me in, though all I had come to do was pledge some money. I gave him the finger and before I knew it he had me by the neck against the wall, I'm cursing him loudly, the congregation spilling out to the foyer to break us up.

My cousins became doctors, lawyers, rabbis, made aliyah, *and stayed in New York to teach. My rabbis were Jerry Garcia and Wes Montgomery, later Bernard Malamud and Flannery O'Connor. I moved all around the country, settled as far from the world I grew up in as I could without leaving the continent entirely, and like Malamud, who also lived in my small town and taught at the same school, I've returned to New York in my stories, to the family contradictions and battered loyalties that still abide.*

BACHELOR PARTY

Gabriel Brownstein

Jake's divorce has got me remembering events of a few years ago: that night before his wedding. It's not so uncommon, I guess, for brothers to fight at a time like that. And my brother—well, I've never known him.

Jake is twelve years older than me. In his early thirties—just before he got married—he became Jewish, by which I mean yarmulkes and Shabbos. This seemed odd at the time because when he was in high school, who knew? Take a look at his yearbook picture: the feathered hair, the cocky grin, football helmet under his arm. Then Dartmouth, then UCLA.

When he got hitched at our parents' place in Cold Spring Harbor, the affair was full of ritual. The night before, however, Jake let in some American secularity: boys, booze, cigars. Two A.M., the party had dwindled down and it was my brother and his old college buddy Larry Abrams, who for some reason had put on a skullcap to match Jake's—I think for Larry it was some kind of gag, a freshman beanie—and me and our cousin Tibor. Tibor has always been a strange guy: skin the color of buttermilk, big glasses, thin hair that flies in too many directions. He laughs at inappropriate moments, picks scabs off his face. I feel for Tibor, I'm repulsed by him, and in those days I worried I was too much like him. Just home from my first year of college and the semesters had not gone comfortably.

The porch light was out and Tibor was rocking in his seat. I was a little drunk and a little buzzed on account of some pot

Larry had slipped me. A little out of place, too, a little anthropological, peering at the strange macho bonding of the Dartmouth alums. Jake assimilates into any crowd—businessmen, intellectuals, athletes—and that night he shifted out of enthusiastic Judaism and into American guy-hood as easily as if his ego were one of those cars that at a push of a button pops from two- to four-wheel drive.

Larry cracked jokes for him. They weren't even jokes, but something more primitive and private. Larry said, "Milking the cow," and Jake snickered. Larry said, "Butter biscuits, man." My brother shook his head. "Sand in my bed," that was another good one. I must have been staring too intently, because Larry adjusted his skullcap and glanced my way. "You getting all this, Kenny? Taking notes?" Checking out my brother, looking for a reaction. "You working on your novel, Ken?" Larry's jokes, elbows to the ribs. He'd heard I'd taken a class in creative writing.

Larry broke out some more cigars and opened a bottle of brandy and it was clear we would be on the porch for a while. He leaned over and lit the cigar that was in Jake's mouth.

"You must be scared shit," Larry said.

In my family, Jake has always had a reputation for cool. "No. I can't say scared. Maybe you mean anxious? But I'm not anxious."

Somehow this made Tibor laugh.

Larry said, "Tell me something, Tibby. You ever gotten laid?"

White Tibor went whiter.

I said, "Hey, Larry."

"Kenny the college man. Ken." I guess Larry took my point, that it wasn't the time to ride Tibor. "Ken," Larry said, and he leaned back, elbows on the porch. "I hope *you* are getting laid. Every night. Because that, my friend, is the true value of undergraduate education."

He had no idea how much I had to learn.

"My advice to you, Ken, is don't go looking for a girlfriend. Don't fall in love and don't be particular. But you're a Garbus. I don't need to give you advice. Probably prowling the sororities right now. Or do they have sororities where you go to school, what, Green Tofu U.? Shagging the hairy-legged hippy chicks. Let me tell you," he said confidingly, "your brother here, my boy Jake, he might act like quite the religious scholar, but when I knew him, this guy—well."

"Larry," said Jake. "You don't have to—"

"Must I make a list? Reese Crawford? Sabine Bourgeois? The heiress, Winona Van Den Leider? Kappa Sigma Phi? Jake Garbus, man—Long Island Lothario, Kosher Casanova, circumcised scoring machine—"

"I—I have had sex," Tibor interrupted.

"Sure," Larry said. "Sure."

Jake puffed on his cigar. I pictured him trotting up sorority stairs, my brother's athlete's legs and BVDs and some girl in a bra giggling up in front of him. When he was in high school, I once caught Jake posing in front of the bathroom mirror, flexing his pectoral muscles. With me, it wasn't exactly trying on my mother's lipstick or putting a ruler to my schlong, but I have never been a confident guy.

"You and Monica do it, right?" Larry tossed down one brandy and started work on another. "I mean, being with this whole Jew thing. I don't want to be offensive. But how far do you carry it, Garbus? You? With the little missus?"

"He doesn't want to be offensive," Jake told the lawn.

"Okay." Drunken Larry. "Now he's Mister I'm-not-going-to-dignify-that. But in my day? May I ask something?" He coughed. "Garbus. Okay? Best sex, man, tell me right now. Best sex you ever had."

"Monica." Jake, ever easy.

"Go to hell."

"We don't have that," Jake said, "in our religion."

"Okay." Larry turned to me. *Okay.* Larry, big and shambling with his tie loose and his suspenders emphasizing the sandbag of his gut. Professionally, he trades Third World debt.

"Okay," he said. "Groom's not talking. So you then, Kenny." Brandy sloshed from his glass. "College shenanigans out in that liberal New England outpost. Tell us about freshman year."

"Actually." I looked down. It wasn't my habit to talk. I was the only man in the world with my problem.

A pretty face on a sophomore in sandals brought tears to my eyes, and that Saturday before I had left Vermont for my brother's wedding, Padgett Hastie (who was on the field hockey team and in my Marxist Theory class) had spread her legs for me under a poster of Tracy Chapman, and then all that was solid melted into air. For a second there, in conversation, I felt as I had in her bed: my poor brain flying the white flag of surrender.

"No way?" Larry understood. "You never did it?"

"Um—"

"A virgin? You must be, you *must*—"

"Hey," said Jake. "It's okay. He's eighteen years old. Lots of people haven't done it at his age. Besides, it takes guts—"

"Guts," Larry acknowledged.

I resented my brother for coming to my defense. And Padgett Hastie. A redhead with a raccoon's mask of freckles. "Everything okay?" she asked as I stuttered up above her. "Kenny?" And then did I peel off the condom? Yank up my underwear? Padgett kissed me and her attentions made for an extra heaping helping of shame.

"Guts," Larry said. But he had had too many and was looking for a fight. "Mr. Groom," he said. "Contestant number one," he said. "We need to know the best sex you ever had. I don't think the judges can accept your answer to the question as it was previously posed. *Bachelor Party*." As if it were the name of a game show. "We are here to talk about—"

"Larry," Jake said, "why don't you answer the question?"

"And compromise my role? That would be like Pat Sajak, like, 'Pat, do you want to buy a vowel?' You don't see guests ask dick of Alex Trebek. No." Larry stretched out his arm, reading from an imaginary question card. "You are the leading tang-taker we know," he said. "Our own sultan of salami-stuffing, the great vandalizer of virginity, and so, now, as you go now to retire your roaming steed, we ask you to enlighten us." Larry, steadying himself. "We who have admired and watched your career. Garbus, tell us about your greatest, most satisfying bouts. Your intended—Ms. Monica Schneibaum—we'll call that off limits. But we need information, and tonight. Judges, am I right?"

I stayed quiet, so far out of my depth. Tibor, big glasses on his little face, said, "I could t-tell stories, man."

"At least I didn't bring a stripper."

My brother sucked on his cigar. "You want me to embarrass myself?"

"I've never seen you embarrassed, Garbus."

"You want me to tell you something for old times' sake?" I could see the outline of Jake's face, his curls, the glint of the bobby pin on his white knit skullcap. "Something to freak out the kids?"

"Hey," said Tibor.

"I'll tell you," said Jake. "I'll tell."

My brother left the house when I was six. His room went untouched until I was thirteen. It was like a special exhibition he curated, a diorama, object lesson to my junior high misery: Successful Teenage Life. Shelves heavy with trophies, A+ book reports in the desk, lipsticky letters from old flames. The holy box of Trojans in the drawer of the night table. I'd sneak in there when my parents weren't around and I'd look at the letterman jackets hanging in the closet, the yearbook with hearts drawn on his face, and I'd wonder.

Seventh grade, I got the shit kicked out of me, and then I would haul my ass out of a garbage can and look at my brother in the school trophy case. He held the record for the two-hundred-yard dash and was pictured with a championship football team. Math teachers reminded me all the way up to senior year. Old Mr. Albertson. "You're really Jake Garbus's brother?" He remembered Jake on account of some statewide prize. "You don't look like him. But obviously, you're bright. I think you could take a lesson from Jake. Apply yourself as your brother did—and really, it doesn't have to be in athletics. There's no telling how far you will go. . . ."

Report cards came home, my mother retreated into herself. She saw me as some misted-over genius. My father got mad, threw books, threw telephones. Mysteries of genetics. Jake's got dad's big shoulders and curly hair. He's got a profile, and sitting out on the porch the night before his wedding, I saw it embossed on the night sky.

"It's nobody you know," Jake began. "No one any one of you might remember—"

"You're going to tell me better than Callie Cannel?"

"It was during my postdoc." Jake ignored Larry. "When I had moved from California to New York. I was going to work with the preeminent man in the field, Victor—let's call him—Himmler. But names have been changed to—"

"To Himmler." Larry, deadpan.

"Yeah." My brother, the world's smoothest liar, or embellisher, or (who knows?) maybe it was true. "The work was to be in his labs. I was his chief assistant, a great move for me, careerwise, but socially it was strange. I had been in Los Angeles, UCLA, for years, and even though I was a biologist and a graduate student and by definition a nerd, well, I knew a couple of people in the film business and my social life was easy. You'd be surprised how many aspiring actresses want to sleep with someone just because he's *not* in movies." I pictured Jake in a Venice Beach bar, more confident, predatory, and handsome than any of the young actors or producers' assistants. Jake all the while pretending to be some sweetheart of a guy. "I was working on a cure for cancer. I got a lot of mileage out of that."

"I tell you." Larry. "All the angles. We should be taking notes."

"I don't b-believe . . ." Tibor, petulant.

"What?" I said.

My brother ignored us. "I came to New York and even though I grew up here on the Island and am an East Coast man by nature, well, the city felt cold. I didn't know too many people. I had never really lived in New York. Also, working for Dr. Himmler, I had the feeling that it was time to get serious in my life. I rented an apartment in Queens. I had to change subways to get to Columbia, so I woke up early. I worked out at the university gym before heading to the lab. Then I came home late and reviewed my notes. I would lie alone in bed reading journals and sipping seltzer. I didn't drink, I didn't smoke. Celibacy did me wonders. Dr. Himmler was scrupulously neat, perfectly devoted, absolutely careful. Before him, science had been academic to me, something I knew I could do well. It was a little like football—I didn't choose it, it chose me. But with Dr. Himmler that changed. He presented an elegant world, a world defined by the aesthetics of the laboratory, and I wanted to be a part of it. People think a man like that, with his achievements and Old World dignity, would be unapproachable, but with me he was kind. He accepted me—a twenty-four-year-old Jewish schmuck from Long Island— as a colleague."

"You screwed the Teutonic oncologist?" Larry.

Jake sighed.

I pictured this grandfatherly, severe mentor. Undoubtedly, there had been someone like that. Thin head, rectangular jaw. Deep lines in his face and his gray hair carefully combed. A tie beneath his lab coat, the lab coat replaced at the end of the day with a sports jacket. Really, in my life, I have never had anything against Germans.

"He was kinder to me than I had any right to expect," Jake said. "He invited me to his house for dinner. He introduced me to his wife, Greta, a handsome, neat woman in her sixties—"

"You did the hausfrau?" Larry, mock aghast.

"Please." Jake's hand shot out and I thought he was going to smack Larry, but he just tapped him on the ridiculous yarmulke.

"Dr. Himmler introduced me as Jacob Garbus, a young fellow who takes his work too seriously, and since I have never in my life been introduced that way, I was flattered and didn't object." My brother, he'd be diffident in the doctor's home. "Dinner came in courses. There was soup with dumplings, then rabbit served with potatoes and greens. After each course, Greta cleared dishes. She took her apron off each time she came back from the kitchen. I offered to help but was shooed away. How do I explain? I'm no clod. I know which is the salad fork, which spoon is for coffee, but I don't live my life by those rules, and I got self-conscious about the way I handled the cutlery. My knife clanked the plate. I made too much noise."

"Do I remind you at this point"—Larry, the peanut gallery—"we were talking about getting laid?"

"They lived in a three-story town house in the West Eighties. They owned beautiful rugs and gorgeous antiques; there were books everywhere. I have to admit I was surprised. Dr. Himmler was a prominent scientist and Columbia probably paid him well, but this was a house that would have suited a financier. I must have let my surprise show—I wasn't half as smooth as I wanted to be—because as we sat down in the living room for coffee and cigarettes which I refused—he smoked, yes, the great oncologist smoked vicious unfiltered European brands—he told me the story of the house. His wife was washing dishes and that sound made a pleasant background. Apparently the mansion had fallen into their laps. Thirty years earlier, Dr. Himmler and his wife had rented the basement apartment. Their landlords in those days were an elderly couple named Miller and when the old folks became infirm, Greta Himmler tended to them, very decently and out of sheer neighborliness. She cooked their dinners. She tended to old Mr. Miller after his stroke, to Mrs. Miller when her arthritis was so bad she could barely walk. The landlords died childless, but before Mrs. Miller passed on, she gave the Himmlers—and Greta was pregnant then—a deal. They bought the town house for a song. I could hardly believe this. In New York, you know, real estate is the stuff of high drama, of miracle. Dr. Himmler laughed when he told the story and then said he had no right, no right to be so lucky."

"And you two passionately embraced?"

Jake continued. " 'Who is living in the downstairs apartment now?' I asked. And Dr. Himmler answered with a twinkle. 'My daughter,' he said, and he showed me the picture."

My brother shut his eyes. A light went out upstairs. In the glow of suburban street lamps, passing cars, and burning cigars, my brother was a silhouette. Tibor picked up a stick and began swinging it.

All that week, I had wanted to call Padgett Hastie out in her parents' Jersey home but was too frightened of what she might think of me. I guessed my brother would have screwed Padgett happily; or maybe, worse, wouldn't have screwed her at all—not cute enough, too stocky. Or maybe in his new orthodoxy he would have disapproved. A shiksa.

"Kristina was dazzling," Jake said. "She was absolutely dazzling. I don't mean like sorority girls or aspiring starlets, I mean the real thing. Here was a simple snapshot of a girl and her parents, a countryside somewhere in Europe; they were all dressed in shorts. Dr. Himmler, of course, had his oxford shirt tucked in, and Greta wore epaulets on her shoulders. The girl had her sunglasses pulled up on top of her blond head and she had raised her arm in the air like she was celebrating something. It was a very ordinary photograph and yet she seemed in a different frame than her parents; she seemed not just more alive than they did, but more vivid, more . . . I'm not expressing it well." Jake leaned back, and though we could hardly see him, we heard his voice, that throaty, confident voice of his. "Have you ever seen one of those Shakespeare films with English actors and American movie stars? Have you ever noticed how the players from the two countries can be in the same shot—Keanu Reeves and Kenneth Branagh are in the same room, standing there, but it feels like a special effect that has been pulled off unsuccessfully? The actors speak the words and mean them, while the movie stars yank themselves out of the picture with each word spoken. It's like there is a hard line drawn between, and it's not just because of the movie stars' failings but because they are juxtaposed with something more real, more artful, more expressive, than they can ever hope to be. This photograph worked something like that. Beside the liveliness of their daughter, the Himmlers barely seemed real—or maybe they seemed too real, too ordinary, too prosaic. I must have gasped."

"The plot thickens," Larry Abrams said.

My brother nodded, sucking on his cigar. Ash glowed red.

"Dr. Himmler called to his wife. He said, 'Greta, darling, invite Kristina upstairs.' And then she came. And then the parents disappeared. They served their daughter to me after dinner, like she was a wedge of lemon meringue pie."

Jake woke me up the morning of his wedding, putting on his phylacteries by the piano and singing. That rich cantor's voice of his. I had given up my bed to Aunt Mimi and was lying on the living room couch. My left eye hurt like hell.

My parents' living room has big glass doors that look out on the porch and the lawn beyond, so morning sunlight shines right in and Jake was praying and bobbing in his blue flannel pajamas, unshaven. So fucking handsome, he could have been a movie star. Prayer shawl over his shoulders, leather wrapping his arm and forehead, looking out at the porch where the night before he had told his crazy sex stories.

Why did he wake me up with those prayers? My face hurt like a bitch and later I took two aspirin and used an ice pack. Why couldn't he just pray in his bedroom? With his yarmulke and tefillin he was draped in the full authority of his religion and I couldn't say to Jake, as any American brother would have, "Hey, will you knock that off?" Also, it was his wedding day. His wife-to-be, Monica, was taking a ritual bath. I pretended to sleep. Sonorous Hebrew ranting all around me. When he was done, Jake snapped his book shut and he looked down at me and smiled.

"Coffee?"

My face with the imprint of his knuckles. What do you do with a brother like that?

On the porch, his voice had been burned and bruised by the cigars and brandy. It got so dark I could only imagine his curly head. Also, I imagined Kristina, the oncologist's daughter. I felt pity for her even before Jake's story began.

"She cannot have been so hot," Tibor snorted. He was a shadow out on the lawn, swinging his stick. "I mean, what—she was like, like Claudia Schiffer?"

"Shut up," Larry said.

But Jake put a restraining hand to Larry's chest. "Claudia Schiffer," he lectured Tibor, "has her hair recut by Hollywood stylists for a single posed shot. She wears hundreds of dollars in makeup and is photographed only under the most flattering light, and then by highly paid cameramen. She wears the best clothing and terribly uncomfortable undergarments that pull and push her body so it's thin in the gut and her tits puff up. She's photographed a hundred times, the best of those shots are selected, the best poses, and then they are airbrushed and recolored and made more perfect. There are committee meetings about whether Claudia's panties look better in pink or blue. Kristina Himmler—the girl I am calling that name—was flesh.

"Larry." My brother gripped his friend's shoulder. "I don't know how to explain. Ken, you have to trust me. Tibor. Kristina was the easiest conquest of my life. And let's be honest: Girls have never been hard." My brother. "But her attraction was the kind of thing that explodes vanity. I cannot tell you what she saw in me. She was fun, delightful, the kindest, sweetest girl I have ever met. She was not particularly interesting or ironic or artistically gifted. She had beauty and kindness and that was it. But if I may, I'd like to get crude here for a minute."

"Please," said Larry.

"I could have said, 'Blow me,' the moment we met, and she would have gotten down on her knees and sucked."

"Some guys." Larry Abrams shook his head.

"Are you kidding? This girl was crazy. But I couldn't get enough. She wanted me. I was powerless—"

Larry nodded solemnly. "That Nazi bitch."

They fucked right there, on the Oriental, twenty-five minutes after her father left the room. Jake said something like: You live downstairs? The girl said something like: So you're my father's student? Then she was getting rug burns. So the story goes. They went to the kitchen, to tidy the dishes, and did it again on the ceramic floor, mismatched pubic hair all creamy and meshed. Jake on his back, hairy legs up against the dishwasher, trousers in the sink, and pale pink Kristina with the hem of her dress clenched in her teeth—

I couldn't believe what my brother was telling me. It shocked me, by which I don't mean I was offended, but like a jolt of static fuzzed my brain. Those days, I tell you, so uptight: I didn't talk about such things, couldn't.

"We tried to behave like human beings," Jake said. "You know, we'd go out for dinner. We would discuss the weather and the classes she was taking. Kristina studied social work at Hunter College. We would converse, but then in the middle of dinner and as if by some secret pact she would get up from the table and then I would follow her and before you knew it, I was banging her against the men's room door. Thump, thump, thump—then we'd walk out past someone who really had to take a piss, the two of us blushing and tired. We'd bring home moo shu pork and do depraved things with plum sauce, right there, downstairs, in her parents' house. She would giggle, she would shout like a demon, and then the next morning her father would invite me up for coffee and he and I would sit together and read the newspaper like civilized men, except I couldn't stand up when Kristina entered the room on account of my raging hard-on."

"Plum sauce?" asked Larry.

"She had a perfect face, a face at once childlike and womanly. She had wide eyes and a wide mouth and a smile that rose against her cheeks. She had a perfect pan and she liked it if I pulled her hands behind her back and pressed that face into anything: a pillow on a bed, sand on a beach, mud in a parking lot. The girl wanted to be demeaned, and by me. Had she done these things before? I have no idea. She would show up on a date in a white dress with little blue flowers. Her hair would be washed and combed and shining. You know that fine net of stray hairs that sometimes settles above a beautiful head? She never had that fine stray net. A girl so clean and white and fine, and all she wanted me to do was sully her."

"Sully," said Larry. "The words he chooses."

"This is total bullshit," said Tibor. "This is something I read—I read it in *Penthouse*—*Penthouse Forum*. Did did you read that, Ken? I mean, I think—"

"Tibor," said my brother. "Give me that stick." And Tibor did and my brother chucked it end over end into the lawn. "Now, please," he said. "Please listen."

Religion and ethnicity, in my family when I was growing up these were facts like the carpeting. Passover, we once celebrated release from Egyptian bondage with take-out falafel, baba gannouj. My parents went to services sometimes on the New Year and sometimes on the Day of Atonement, and when they used to drag the kids along we would all feel uncomfortable together. Both sons had bar mitzvahs, Jake's with pretty girls. But you know how it is in the suburbs. We tiptoe around holiness the way our ancestors did around sex. We have special places for it, we avoid them.

I'm no anti-Semite. And I have the usual apportion of feelings toward my older brother: admiration, envy, worship, hate. I remember seeing Jake play football at Dartmouth, seeing him fly in from the secondary and clock a quarterback cold. I remember the way the underclass girls reacted to his name at college graduation. When I was eleven, he'd come home from L.A. and he enjoyed making fun. I was hitting adolescence. My big nose, my weak chin, my glasses.

"Starting to look like Grampa Abe."

My brother, the Greek god.

"We were competent, scientific men. We injected rats with carcinogens. We monitored progress, examined data and DNA and renegade cells, we counted death rates and measured tumors and kept it all clean and crisp and beautiful. We faced disease in civilized abstraction; we could quantify death. Then at night I would take his daughter to my apartment in Queens and stick jalapeño peppers in her mouth and whip her behind so my belt left streaks on the ivory globes of her ass. She wasn't inventive but she was always game. Kristina flounced around my apartment without pants. She would hand me something hard or cold—a squash racket, a Popsicle—and as if coincidentally bend over or spread her legs."

Who remembers dialogue as it happened? I'm doing reconstruction here. At the time, like half these words must have bounced off my forehead. No way they were getting to my brain. A freshman home from college—I played with my snifter, I fidgeted on the porch.

"The family invited me on picnics as if I were an ordinary boyfriend, as if Kristina and I were to be engaged." My brother in happy tennis whites. "We drove up to the Bronx Botanical Gardens in their BMW. Greta brought an enormous wicker basket full of wine and crystal and china and sausages and breads and home-baked pastries. The next day, then, Kristina came to my apartment with the same basket, this time filled with toys she had bought in Greenwich Village, little metal clamps and leather. She took off her clothes and began to fasten these restraints together, to take them apart, a little demonstration—my naked stewardess showing off the not-so-safety gear."

Larry laughed. I tried—nervous distraction—to count the thumps Tibor's chair's legs made on the wooden porch.

"When her parents left town for two weeks in October, Kristina wanted me to screw her in every room of their house. So we did. With her father away, I was on my own and sex had crushed all my hopes of diligent study. I spent as little time as possible in the lab, left most of the work to graduate students, and went on a methodical sexual rampage. We did it in the foyer, knocking over the coat rack. In the living room, I sat in her father's chair, while she undid my fly, raised up her skirt, and, sitting on my lap, fucked me, all the while feigning conversation with make-believe guests. In the dining room she bent over the table, took a banana from the fruit bowl, and shoved it in her mouth. She wore her mama's apron in the pantry."

"The judges are scoring this high," said Larry.

"Just wait. I'll give you more than you can take."

"That what you gave her?"

Did my hands cover my face?

"Listen: I did her on the stairs and in her father's study and her mother's studio, playing with the paints and brushes. And we did it in the hot tub and in her old single bed surrounded by stuffed animals and pictures of Baryshnikov. In the den, we screwed to MTV. Finally we got to the third floor, her parents' bedroom, actually a suite with French doors and the walls all painted brown. The furniture gave the room the feel of an importer's showroom, everything massive and wood. Curtains on the windows made as if it were a country estate. And Kristina stood girlishly tracing her naked foot across the tassels of the purple rug, waiting for me to undress her.

"This was something of a consummation for her. I understood that implicitly. I undid the little buttons on her back, helped her arms out of their sleeves, and when her little blue dress dropped to the floor around her, I offered gentlemanly assistance as she stepped out of the charmed circle her clothing had made.

"The bed had no canopy but four carved posts. On the walls were black and white photographs, ancestors and weddings. God, was I exhausted from fucking all day. And I suppose with all lovers—even the most beautiful—there are moments when one views their bodies almost clinically. You know you are being objective, seeing them as they are. So I saw Kristina then, the scales of attraction falling from my eyes, and I thought with cool detachment that nothing could be more lovely than her legs. I ran my hands up the arches of her feet, and then her ankles, the calves, the knees—the muscles' curves, a child's soft skin on a grown-up body. I got to the thighs. I began kissing, half wondering where the hell the imperfection might lie." Jake paused. "Bang, bang." He pumped a fist. "Bang, bang, bang, bang. The old bed is creaking. We are damp, our bellies suck and kiss. We rock with the bed. And she is coming and I am totally in the driver's seat, like I believe I could fuck again all night until tomorrow, but her teeth grab my nipple and I am lost, but maybe even then, in the midst of my orgasm, maybe even then—because I was spent, really, I can only do it so many times in a day, my balls were burning—maybe even then bells were ringing. I rolled off onto her parents' mushy mattress and not into blessed postcoital satisfaction but something much more—"

"You were freakin'," said Larry. "Warning siren: Woo woo. Get me the hell out of here. 911."

I wanted to leave the porch.

Tibor coughed. "This is such a load of crap."

"Shut up, Tibby," said Larry.

"I sank exhausted into their old mattress, thinking: Okay, the attic and the roof deck and then what comes after that? And Kristina snuggled under my arm, all that blond hair. Then she said it: 'I love you, Jacob.'"

Larry knew everything. "You fuck 'em, they fall in love."

"And I had no response. I looked up the long, pointing finials of the bedposts, with their intricate squares and carvings, and the peaks like angry flower buds. I looked at the old oak dressers whose mirrors reflected squares of shadows and the frames of photographs. She was waiting for me to speak. I flicked on the lamp on the bed table. Japanese white porcelain, a seascape: I saw a pack of Gitanes next to a copy of *The Periodic Table*—there were some old brown hardcovers but the Primo Levi was in paperback, all dog-eared, with a playing card for a bookmark. 'I love you,' Kristina said again, as if I hadn't heard her the first time. So I reached for the cigarettes, to give my mouth something to do. I lit up, and pretended to examine a Learn to Drive matchbook. My bare ass against the sheets, I was scared shit, irrationally, and trying to keep my cool, and smoking and studying the room. I patted her head. I didn't want to lie.

"I looked at their wedding pictures, Greta with a streaming white train and Victor young and very thin. I studied her jewelry case and the stacks of correspondence on his dresser. I would stare at anything then so as not to look at Kristina. There was an African mask hanging above a picture, of a street scene in a long-ago European town. And then I finally noticed it: the gray face with the high cheekbones, the knobby forehead, the hollow eyes, the heavy lids whose lashes seemed to have been burned off, the lipless, damnable, clever mouth—"

I was so out of it, I thought maybe he was giving us a new way to see the girl.

"Please," said Jake, "don't look in the Columbia University directory for a Professor Dr. Victor Himmler. The names have been changed, as I told you. But Dr. Himmler had been Nazi Youth. There were UJA letters on his dresser—payments for family sins, I guess. I saw those letters when I got up from the bed, buck-naked and smoking, to get a good look at their famous ancestor: a man in a khaki uniform with familiar insignias, and I wouldn't have been able to match the name with the face if the name hadn't been all around me.

"'What the hell?' I said. And this was my response to her 'I love you.' Kristina, flustered in that great four-poster bed, was halfway to tears.

"What came out finally, after fragmented sentences from both sides, me pointing like an ape at the photograph of the Nazi, was her saying, explaining for her parents' sake: 'You would not want us to forget?'"

"Goebbels," said Larry Abrams. "Was the name really Goebbels?"

"We fought there, for the first time, really fought, me naked in the elegant bedroom and Kristina sobbing about how it's all right that I don't really love her, it is enough that she loves me. Then she ran down the stairs, leaving me alone with those glowering photographed Nazi eyes, while I poked around for my socks and underwear.

"I went home that night to my place, rode out to Astoria on the R train, and I felt as if Eichmann and Hess were sitting on either side of me, quiet, gentlemanly commuters, perusing the *Post*, the *Daily News*. And then I got in my little single bed, anxious and exhausted, and I had the most awful dream."

Me? I have never lived in *The Sorrow and the Pity*, much less *Schindler's List*. Padgett Hastie wrote a term paper about the Congo, Belgian mercenaries filling up barrels with the severed hands of black kids—I don't say this to put events of World War II in context. I grew up in Long Island, *that's* my context. And to this day I pray at night in a way that's embarrassingly New Age Protestant American—one on one, extemporizing to The Big Guy as if He were my imaginary best friend. I don't know why Jake's story made me so angry. Was it because I was so damned uptight? About sex, about Jews, about mystery? Did I expect more from him? Less? I didn't quite believe his story and I still don't, or if I do it's as some kind of hyperbole that blends Jake's ambition with his fears and something angry that he wanted to shove in all of our faces: Larry's, mine, Tibor's. Back then I was intimidated by Jake in a different way than I suppose I still am: that he could so easily and publicly talk about fucking, so confidently display his religion, his yarmulke, confident like he was playing football, flying forward in full body armor. I didn't know what to do with his talk.

And then this purported dream about which he told us next—that night in his bed in Queens Jake saw himself in Kristina's place, dressed in a German officer's World War II uniform. Kristina's head was shaved and she was wearing a concentration camp suit and he was barking orders and she was obedient.

"I told her about it," Jake said. "My nightmare. This was a week after the incident in her parents' room. I had been avoiding her, but that day I had come back to the Himmlers' town house to pick up some papers. It was the afternoon—I was hoping not to see her. But Kristina surprised me by being there, fixing lunch in her parents' kitchen. I remember being shocked by the way her jeans and her T-shirt showed off her body—those innocent, those alluring curves. Were things okay, she wanted to know, between us? She was licking mayonnaise off her fingers. Was I avoiding her?

" 'I didn't mean to pressure you,' she said.

"We were in the sitting room, standing on the rug on which she and I had first fucked. And I was nervous and a little afraid and couldn't quite face her. So, by way of describing my discomfort, I told her my dream. She stepped closer. She tossed her blond hair. She wasn't tentative—though my guess is she was a little scared of me at that point, waiting for me to dump her—and she, Kristina, said—God—she said, 'Okay. We can do that if you like.' "

Larry said, "Do you still have her number?"

"Oh, please," said Tibor.

Do girls like that even exist?

"I left that day," he said, "like right then, after her offer. It was too much for me. The whole thing seemed so—but she called me, she called me. Friendly, sexy Kristina left messages on my answering machine. I wanted to dump her, I wanted to go back to the way things had once been. Things had gotten out of hand.

I knew I should stay away, but you know how it is, you always go back one more time. She phoned and said, 'I'm not making demands.' She said, 'I have a surprise for you, Jacob.'

"So one day—maybe a full year after I had met her—I left the lab a little early and walked downtown through Riverside Park. It was late fall and I had on a pea coat over my lab clothes. My sneakers and jeans were in a bag. I remember the blue sky, the bare trees, my breath making clouds. I walked over on West 89th Street to their brownstone, and Kristina greeted me at the door. She wore lipstick and a pale yellow dress and smiled.

"I was full of misgivings, but I showered as I always had after I got to her place from the lab. That was routine and a psychological necessity after all those tumors, all those rats. In the past, she had sometimes come into the shower with me, but not this day. She was outside, in her bedroom, preparing my surprise. So I scrubbed and the place got steamy and the glass doors of the shower fogged and I remembered the German officer's face, and I thought, Big deal, big fucking deal, so what? Her parents wake with their guilt every morning, and she loves you. Is this a burden you can't bear? I catalogued my worst, most far-fetched fears—that she was her dad's instrument, that she was signing her cunt over to me like it was a UJA check, some form of psychosexual reparations—and I thought, What a load of crap. I let the water run over my head. You can't hold family history against someone. We are modern, liberated New Yorkers. That's what I thought. I turned off the tap. I wrapped a blue towel around my waist. I walked through the little kitchen and into her bedroom, and there was Kristina at the foot of her bed.

"Her hair was all over the floor. She had shaved it. And on the down comforter was the actual object, I tell you, khaki with insignias—"

"Ab-," Tibor said, "absurd."

Larry said, "This is clearly some fucked-up kinky bitch."

I said, "A woman would do that for you?"

"For me?" Jake said, indignant. "Of course I couldn't put

that on. And she was on the floor, sobbing, bawling, a beautiful bald nude surrounded by her own marmalade hair, naked and soft, her breasts like a teenager's, her ass full. You have never in your life seen anything like that, or if you have, God bless you. I stood there with a towel around my waist. I think I wanted to say something like 'What the hell are you doing?' but what came out, if I remember, was a cross between a stutter and a gasp. I tell you, I ran. I was tying my shoes on West End Avenue. I tucked in my shirt on the subway platform. I left the lab clothes at her house."

Was that it? What my brother wanted, what he feared, what he knew? I leave it to you to dig through the layers of possibility, the desire, the paranoia, the lurid grotesque. But at the time I heard his story, I was frustrated, I was angry, I was a mess.

"I don't know what Dr. Himmler thought afterward: That his daughter was suddenly bald? That I was gone from her social life? I don't know. He said nothing about Kristina to me, and he never invited me to his house again. Still, we worked side by side. These things, I suppose, do happen, affairs between the protégé and the mentor's child. Things do sour. He was very—is the word *understanding*? I'm not sure. I know neither what drove his actions toward me, nor to what degree he was conscious of his motivations. I was good at my job. And at the end of my postdoc, Dr. Himmler wrote me a letter of recommendation, a letter that I am sure secured my subsequent appointment at Hopkins, a letter which in no small part made my career. And he never stopped being good to me. He even gave me coauthorship of our study. He didn't have to do that—nobody does that. Was it all penance? I don't know. Was I his Jew? I never asked. I did good work for him. I'm not saying I didn't deserve the credit I got. Then, before the study came out, Dr. Himmler was diagnosed with lung cancer. I never visited him in the hospital. I didn't go to the funeral. I stayed away. I couldn't face it, you know?"

"And the girl?" Larry asked. "Still looking for Jewboys to fuck?"

"She lives in Israel." My brother sighed. "No shit. She works with deformed Arab kids."

Tibor laughed.

I looked to my brother in the darkness. I wanted him to say something to me, to tell me one more thing, maybe some explanation—was there a point to this story, a lesson? Did he feel guilty? Did he feel wronged? But more than that, I wanted to be one of the guys, or even the special guy, the one who understood. When I spoke I did it mostly to break the silence, or maybe to find a place by Jake's side.

"And this," I offered, "was why you have become so orthodox? Such a Jew?"

"Oh, for Christ's sake." Jake turning nasty. "Take it easy, Ken."

I looked at his yarmulke, its knitted pattern, blue and white, letters in Hebrew I couldn't read. I don't know what overcame me; I had an impulse. I just grabbed it right off his head, chucked the skullcap out onto the lawn, and the thing lofted like a Frisbee.

Jake looked up at me, gape-mouthed. He stood. And that's when he did it, no change of expression. Boom, punched me right in the eye.

At the wedding, I made excuses. Told my mom I had slipped the night before, banged my face against a doorknob. And after the ceremony, I offered a toast full of shit. Like, Jake was the one man I admired most. My dad bit his trembling lip, so proud. "His courage," I said. "And boy is he being courageous now." The kind of thing people say at weddings, ha ha. The bride was charming all dressed in white, and Jake wore his skullcap as if it were a crown. He gave me a hug when I was done rhapsodizing and then I saw his life spreading out before him, justified at all margins: Dr. Jacob Garbus, pillar of the community, father, oncologist, mensch. I could never imagine his divorce just a few years later: that he would leave Monica for this Raina Zweig, a colleague's wife, a few years older than he, a member of his congregation.

The band began to play, a stage in a backyard. Under the tent the family danced in a wide circle, legs stomping to the beat. My mother laughed, my father sweated. I looked at Jake, whom I hated right then irrationally and more than I can express. Still, I smiled and clapped. Just like everyone else, though underneath it all my dark soul imagined him doing different steps in a different costume, a riding crop in hand and a bald girl on the floor in front of him.

Gabriel Brownstein

I wrote this story after reading something disturbing in the Village Voice. *It might have been in journalist Dan Savage's column, and was about black and white interracial couples playing slave and master sex games—a short leap then to Jews and Germans playing at being Nazis and camp victims. I think the story is about role-playing, assimilation, and being haunted by history.*

PART TWO

Dreams, Prayers,
and Nightmares

WHO KNOWS KADDISH

Binnie Kirshenbaum

i) First there is this business with the yarmulkes

The rabbi wants my father, my brother, and my Uncle Alex to wear yarmulkes even though we are in a non-denominational funeral home, which is nothing like a synagogue. This funeral home is indeed a house, a white colonial set behind a circular driveway and maple trees. It's a house which speaks in well-modulated tones of the affluent and the understated. It is the only funeral home in town not affiliated with an Episcopal or Presbyterian church.

My father is too dazed to do much of anything. Say what you want about them as parents, my mother and father loved each other, and her death, which came fast and out of the blue in the shape of an aneurysm to the brain, has rendered my father a mess. He accepts the satin skullcap as if it were delicate and unexpected, a daisy or a baby bird, and he holds it cupped in his hands as if it were something he must be careful to not crush. Ren, my brother, slips his yarmulke into his jacket pocket. Ren is a Buddhist. Buddhists do not wear yarmulkes, and my Uncle Alex, who is functional but insane, a professional pip, says, "No. It will muss my hair." His hair is a rug. A toupee, although one of quality so that you can't necessarily spot it from a mile off.

The rabbi is clearly out of his depth here, and fearing he might cry, I take the yarmulke from my father's hands and place it on his head. It's off center, but it's there. Then I turn to my brother and my uncle and I say, "Put the fucking hats on."

Certainly none of us had called this rabbi to lead my mother's funeral service. "No rabbi," my mother had said. Whenever my mother attended the funeral of a Jew, she would come home and say, "Promise me. When I die, no rabbi." The reason she gave for not wanting a rabbi to officiate at her funeral was this: Who wants some person who never so much as laid eyes on you to go on and on, in that singsong way, about what a devoted mother you were. "And they always bespeak of the deceased as a committed member of Hadassah and how her matzoth balls were so light they could float on air. Ugh," my mother made a face. "Hadassah. Matzoth balls. No rabbi." Such was the reason she gave.

The real reason my mother did not want a rabbi officiating at her funeral was that she feared an elegy delivered with an intonation, that singsong way. My mother cringed at the thought of her friends and neighbors subjected to an accent unmistakably Yiddish. My mother was resolute in her conviction that the Jews of Europe were peasants, and not just any old peasants, but ignorant peasants. Which was why my mother had no use for my father's side of the family. My mother's family emigrated to New York at the time of the Civil War. "We're real Yankees," my mother was very fond of interjecting into any conversation.

From the moment I was old enough to listen, my mother told me repeatedly and with emphasis, "Your father's sisters are so stupid." My mother would get off the phone with one or another of them and shake her head. "So stupid." As we rarely saw my aunts, I had no reason to think otherwise until only a few years ago when at a gallery opening in Chelsea who should I run into but my father's eldest sister Tessie. The daughter of her friend was one of the artists in the show, and together Tessie and I looked at the paintings. To be honest, if I had been alone, I would have done a once-around-the-room and out-the-door. The paintings didn't interest me much, but Tessie interested me enormously, the way she stopped at each canvas and looked, tilted her head left, then right. The way she remarked on color and mood and texture and the way she wondered what the paintings meant, what the artists were trying to say without words.

The minute I got home, without even taking the time to take off my coat I called my mother and said, "You won't believe who I met at a gallery opening. Tessie," to which, no surprise here, my mother said, "That stupid woman."

"But she's not," I said. "She's not stupid at all. She's sharp and bright and curious. Why do you say she is stupid?"

My mother let go with an exhalation of exasperation at having to explain the obvious. "For crying out loud," my mother said. "She drinks tea from a glass."

Through discreet inquiry I'd learned that this rabbi came with the funeral home; he was part of the arrangements made, along with the coffin and the rows of folding chairs, and although I do think we ought to, generally speaking, honor the wishes of the dead, I suppose it's okay to let him go on with it because if he has an accent at all, I'd place it from New England. He is asking us questions about my mother, to give him material to go on. "She taught high school English," I say.

"She loved animals. Especially Maine Coon cats," Ren says, and Alex tells the rabbi, "My sister was a perfect size eight. Her entire life. A perfect eight," and then the rabbi asks us, "What was her Hebrew name?"

My father starts up weeping, "I don't know. I don't know," as if realizing again what is gone cannot be retrieved. My brother shrugs, and I'm wondering, a Hebrew name, do I have a Hebrew name. Not that I know of, but could I get one? And could I pick my own the way Catholic kids get to pick one at Confirmation?

I was enormously envious of that, of choosing for yourself a name from the list of saints' names, and that wasn't all. I coveted the medal, the small silver medal, with Mary embossed in powder blue enamel, that all the Catholic girls wore around their necks. But most of all I ached to sport the smudge of ash on my forehead as if it were the accessory worn with sackcloth. Oh, to be a martyr, and Ash Wednesday left me longing. Jews, as far as I knew, did not have martyrs unless you count the whole lot of them.

Ritual and ornament tempted me, but my family, we had none of that. My parents said we were Jews but we lived like Unitarians, and celebrated the secular trappings of Christmas—tree, stockings, Santa, elves, lots and lots of presents. Easter we reduced to the bunny, egg, and candy-in-a-basket bit. We celebrated no Jewish holidays because as far as we knew, they weren't any fun.

It is not known to me exactly how far back the Jew-eschewing went on my mother's side of the family, but her father was an artist who supported his family by painting portraits in oils. He did these paintings under an assumed name, James Sander, because New York rich people didn't want Joseph Saperstein's signature on their portraits. They did not want an original Saperstein.

But even all of this does not prepare me for the story my Uncle Alex tells in response to the rabbi's inquiry as to my mother's Hebrew name.

First a word about Alex: Until he retired four years ago, Alex designed costumes for the Metropolitan opera. A career tailor-made. Alex has flair, an eye for color, a touch for fabric, and an intuition for the overblown. There is much of the diva in Alex, and the man loves a tragedy. The more dead, the better, but they must be well-dressed dead to qualify.

It was this adoration of tragedy and style which led Alex to his hobby turned passion turned obsession. Alex collects items, things—souvenirs, ashtrays, menus, postcards, correspondence to and from, silverware, plates, towels, fixtures, anything, you-name-it—from ocean liners that sunk. His Gramercy Park apartment is a shrine to the *Lusitania,* the *Mauritania,* and that great tragedienne-of-the-deep, the *Titanic.*

According to Alex, the airplane is responsible for all that is wrong with the world. By *wrong,* Alex means that no one dresses anymore for the opera, that women no longer wear smart hats to lunch, that B. Altman's went out of business, that there is such a

thing as fast-food, that elegance has been replaced by casual
wear. Alex refers to the sneaker-shod hordes as "steerage."

Like I said, he's functional, my Uncle Alex, but insane, but if
my mother had a Hebrew name, it is only Alex who might know
it. However, Alex is telling the story of his own name, how he
came up with the name Alexander Sebastian which is not the
name on his birth certificate. Obviously this is not news to me.
Long ago, I'd figured out that Alex had changed his name, that
my mother was a Saperstein but he was not.

He was Alexander Saperstein until his eighteenth birthday
when he would get himself a new name, but which name he
hadn't yet decided. He'd come up with a number of possibilities
which he'd sounded out loud—Hello, I'm Ander Stone—and also
he worked on the signatures, Algernon Sage and Albert Sapier,
which would be pronounced as if he were French, *Al-bear
Sa-pee-ay*. He was determined to keep his original initials because
his shirts and pillowcases were monogrammed.

This is the part of the story that is news to me: August 1946
and two weeks shy of Alex's eighteenth birthday, he went, as he
did most days, to the movies. "That's when Hollywood was Hollywood," he tells the rabbi. "Those were the real stars, Bette
Davis, Joan Crawford, Greta Garbo, Ingrid Bergman."

It was Ingrid Bergman, along with Cary Grant and Claude
Rains, who was starring in the movie Alex went to see on that
day. "*Notorious.* Marvelous picture. Superb. Have you seen it?
International intrigue. It was just after the war. The character
played by Claude Rains, who by the way I think was never better." Here, Alex stops to deliver Claude Rains's infamous line—"I
married an American agent"—and then picks up where he left
off. "Claude Rains played none other than Alexander Sebastian.
It was perfect. I could keep not only my initials but my given
name. Alexander. Alexander Sebastian. It's refined and memorable, don't you agree?"

In the movie *Notorious* Claude Rains played Alexander

Sebastian who was a Nazi. My uncle took the name of a Nazi—
fictive, but a Nazi all the same—as his own name.

The rabbi is dumbfounded, as if stricken with something like
that which afflicted Lot's wife.

ii) It's not a real unveiling anyway

It's my father's wish to hold the unveiling on the date of my
mother's birth rather than what is customary. We're calling it the
unveiling, but it's not really. For one thing, there's no veil to
unveil, and there's no rabbi to officiate nor friends and neighbors
to witness. Just us. My father, Ren, Alex, and me. And Alex
refuses to get out of the car because he's wearing suede shoes,
suede like butter, and earlier in the day, it rained.

"I can see from here." Alex is in the back seat of my father's
BMW, and he keeps the car door open for a wide-angle view.

We, the remaining three, walk from the car to the grave. For my
father, these few steps constitute a hike. My father never walks. A
true suburbanite, he drives to go across the street, even. My mother
was the same way. That both of them were born and raised in the
city is yet another fact erased or grown vague, remembered as if it
were the remnants of a dream or déjà vu from another lifetime.

Not long before my mother died, she expressed interest in
visiting the Tenement Museum on Orchard Street. "For nostalgic
reasons," she said, and I laughed and asked, "Whose nostalgia?
You lived on Riverside Drive."

When I moved to the city, to a walk-up not all that far from
where my father was from, my parents considered this a serious
come-down, yet another indication that I was something of a failure. "Do you get hot water?" my mother asked.

"Is the toilet in the hall?" my father wanted to know. Period-
ically, my parents would come to visit me, although they did not
come often because, for one thing, the city involved walking.
And as if they didn't know better, in the city they behaved like
rubes. My mother wandered around with her purse wide open,

and my father would park his car on the street and neglect to lock up, as if Eighth Avenue were the same as Sycamore Lane. Also, my parents were not keen on visiting me because they had hopes for me which were not at all realized. To see me, to witness it on my turf, was to re-experience the disappointment. They wanted me to have their life, only more so. They'd hoped I'd have a husband taller than my father, a house slightly larger than their own, and children with light eyes.

"Didn't it ever occur to you," my mother once asked me, "that I might like to be a grandmother?"

"No," I said. "I can't say I ever gave any thought to that, and I can't imagine a worse reason to have a child. Why don't you bother Ren about this?"

If I was something of a disappointment to my parents, Ren barbed the dart. It wasn't so much that he became a Buddhist, but that he was a devout Buddhist and a house painter. A Cooper Union dropout, Ren exchanged oils on canvas for latex matte on walls. He says he likes painting houses, the expanse of the walls, pure. Plain white walls. That is his specialty. Despite explanations to the contrary, my parents insisted Ren was a Moonie. A fanatic, and what in the world possesses him to vacation at the Zen monastary, to holiday in silent retreat? "He's never going to meet anyone that way," my father said. "Even if he sees a pretty girl there, it's not like he can strike up a conversation."

Although I always stuck up for Ren in this area—let him believe what he wants—the truth is that Ren's Buddhism gets on my nerves. Frankly, I think it's a crock, fake, the way he goes on with those conundrums, the koans, as if there is real meaning for him in a riddle with no answer.

In his bedroom, Ren has an altar where he keeps jasmine incense, a candle, a seashell, and daily he puts a fresh flower there. Ren has flowers with him now, to place on my mother's grave, which is all wrong. Jews don't leave flowers at the cemetery. It's not how we do it, but Ren's brought flowers, wildflowers, as if he doesn't know any better.

Then again, he probably doesn't know any better. Why should he know any better? Ren was not even bar mitzvahed, the significant event in a Jewish boy's life, because my parents associated it not with a boy becoming a man (that's what puberty was about) but rather an ostentatious party where inevitably the roast beef is stringy and the string beans almandine are cold.

And true, my mother would've preferred the flowers. She wouldn't have much appreciated the small stones, rocks, pebbles, we're supposed to collect from the soil and place to rest on the headstone. So Ren leaves his flowers on our mother's grave and my father wipes the tears from his eyes and that is end of the unveiling which is supposed to signal the end of the mourning period, a period which, for me, has yet to begin.

iii) The Kaddish is recited at the grave

Today, waking me God-awful early, Peter said, "Where would you like go?" He had opened his map of southern Germany and a guidebook.

"Nowhere." I pulled the blanket over my head. Tourism is not why I am here. I'm here for the sex, and while maybe across the Atlantic Ocean is a long way to go for that, trust me on this, it's worth the effort.

"How about Swabia?" Peter says. "You've never been to Swabia."

Peter is the specimen Heinrich Himmler had in mind with that breeding program plan. The perfect Aryan, and he—Peter, not Himmler—is one of those men who gets even better looking with age.

Also, for a whole host of reasons, Peter considers me something of a deity, a goddess, my body an altar upon which he bestows offerings and atonements. It's all quite delightful for me, and he revels at what he considers his great fortune, that I am twenty years younger than he, that I am what he calls an intellectual (the German equivalent to movie star), that I am from

New York, and—most significantly—however marginally, I am a Jewess.

All too often, the sight-seeing Peter suggests revolves around exhibits of Jewish artists, monuments commemorating the Holocaust, and sites of former synagogues which are now parking lots decorated with memorial plaques affixed to concrete pylons. He is dying to take me to a concentration camp, but I catagorically refuse to go the same way I also refuse to go hiking in the Alps and kayaking along the Isor. Thanks but no thanks. So we compromise and look in on castles and cloisters and cathedrals and the houses where this one lived and that one died and so-and-so ate a schnitzel.

So Swabia, the region west of Bavaria, it is. We are not seeing all of Swabia. It just seems as if we are. Peter is highly energetic and robust, which is good in bed, but out of bed, it can get on my nerves.

Nonetheless, my only regret about having a German lover is that I hadn't thought of it sooner.

This has been no kind of day for all this sight-seeing. It's been raining on and off, and there is an icy chill in the air. Truly miserable weather, and I feel as if I'm coming down with something for sure. My throat is growing sore, and I ache. I want very much to go back to Munich, to shed my clothes, which are damp and cold. I want to be in Peter's bed, cozy under the duvet. "Can we please go now?" I plead with him, and finally we walk back the way we came through the narrow and cobblestoned streets of Schwabish Hall, which really is a cute place the way the buildings tilt and lean with age like very old people and how some of them are hunched over too. Also, I liked the museum here, how its depiction of life in the Middles Ages went so far as to place taxidermied rats around the straw and burlap bed. That made for a nice touch.

Peter's car is parked outside the medieval city walls, and by the time we reach it, I am shivering in earnest. Peter puts up the heat, and while he drives, I stare out the window. It is dusk, the light is shrouded in purple, which makes the air look even colder than it is.

No more than two kilometers down the road which will eventually lead us onto the autobahn, we pass a cemetery, and I speak before I think. "Look," I say. "There's a Jewish star on that headstone." Given Peter's proclivities, it should come as no surprise that he slams on the brake and then backs up, but I didn't mean for this to happen, for him to stop the car to gawk at a Jewish star on a headstone. Only he won't be talked out of it. He parks the car parallel to the row of headstones on the other side of an iron fence. There are a dozen or so of them in this first row, all marked with the Star of David or Hebrew lettering. I can recognize that these are Hebrew letters, but I can't read them.

We walk, on our side of the fence, the length of the row pausing to read the dates of birth and death; death which came in 1917, 1918, 1921, but Peter is not content with this much. He is determined that we enter this cemetery, that we inspect all of it, and so in the cold and the rain, we trudge up a hill to find the gate. I'm muttering about the weather and about how my feet are getting soaked, and Peter fiddles with the latch to the gate, which is not locked but stuck. When he gets it open, he steps aside to let me go first.

On this far side of the cemetery another row of headstones mirrors the row below. Only this group of Jews—Isadore Rothstein and his wife Ruth, Emanual Apfelbaum, Leah Oppenheimer who died six months after the death of her daughter Charlotte—checked out in the late 1920s and into the mid-thirties. With Charlotte and Leah Oppenheimer as the exceptions, they were a hearty lot and lived long lives.

Between these two rows of gravesites rests pretty much no one. An expanse of land dotted with two trees and a half-dozen headstones set seemingly at random. Naturally, Peter wants an up-close look at these too. The slope is sopping wet, and it is difficult to get our footing, although I'm having an easier time of it than Peter because I'm wearing high heels. High heels dig into the soil the way cleats on golf shoes do. Still, I say, "I wonder why there are no steps here," and Peter says, "There are. Look." He points to our immediate left, and sure enough, I can make out the barest outline of steps secreted under deep green moss inches thick.

We stop to read beneath the disappearing light that Leo Moser died in 1937, as did Albert Levy to his left, and Miriam Meyer. 1938 claimed Miriam's husband Otto and, behind him, Samuel Friedlander. Halfway down the hill, Anna Koppelmann's grave is alone. She was born in 1878, and she died in 1939 and that is the end. Then, there in 1939, the Jews stopped.

Clearly, they hadn't planned to stop. This cemetery, far more empty than not, is evidence that they planned to be born, to love, to marry, bear children, and they planned for their children's children; they planned to live and to grow old and die here because they got themselves plenty of cemetery plots for generations to come. Only there weren't any generations to come. Anna Koppelmann was the last Jew. As if, in 1939, the Jews of Schwabish Hall went the way of the Shakers and the pterodactyl. Which is, as we know, what did happen. Poof. Gone and never to return.

But I am here, and night has fallen now, and the rain comes with a bit more force. I ought to say Kaddish for them, for these Jews extinct. I want to say Kaddish for them, and I want to say Kaddish for my mother too. No one did that for her, for my mother. No one said Kaddish for my mother. I want to, but I cannot. Here in the state of Swabia, I stand before the grave of the last Jew, and I mourn because I do not know how to say the Jewish prayer for the dead.

Binnie Kirshenbaum

Although the circumstances and the characters in the story are fictional, I really did stumble upon such a cemetery outside the town of Schwabish Hall in Germany, and it did evoke in me a response sim-

ilar to that of my narrator—a profound sense of loss for what will never be. It was the first time that I really considered not those who died in the Holocaust, but the loss of a future for the Jews of Europe, which made me then think of American assimilation as another kind of loss, but loss nonetheless.

I see myself as a writer who is Jewish, which is not the same thing as being a Jewish writer. Maybe I'm not sure what being a Jewish writer is. Maybe a Jewish writer is an oxymoron. Is telling secrets antithetical to being a good Jew? Being Jewish is decidedly part of my identity, but not the whole of it. Jewish writer, woman writer, New York writer, this categorizing of writers seems parochial; literature, I hope, is universal. And the truth is, in matters of the faith, I am somewhat devout but barely observant.

HERSHEL

Judy Budnitz

When I was your age, back in the old country, they didn't make babies the way they do now. Back then people didn't dirty their hands in the business; they went to the baby-maker instead.

These days, these young people, they all want to do it themselves; they'd buy the do-it-yourself kit if there were such a thing. They don't trust anybody else to do it for them. And most of them aren't any good at it—baby making requires skill and training. These modern babies they turn out today, some of them are all wrong, and the parents keep them anyway. That's why the world's all mixed up these days. I haven't seen a baby in the last twenty years that could hold a candle to Hershel's.

Who was Hershel? He was the baby-maker in our village. He did wonderful work. People came for miles around to buy his babies. He was a good man, never cheated customers. They bought babies by the pound back then, and Hershel always gave them exactly what they wanted, not an ounce more or less.

Most people got one at about six and a half to seven pounds. A baby was a large purchase; people saved for years to buy one. Sometimes a very poor couple would buy a small one. Hershel didn't recommend this; the small ones were scrawny and underdone and often died. He made no guarantees. Once the baby left his hands, that was it. You couldn't bring it back.

Hershel seldom left his workshop. He rose with the cocks and worked all day. When the stars came out, you could see in his window the orange glow of a candle as he tinkered away far into the night. People had to come to the workshop to place their orders. It was a large stone building in the middle of the village and it looked like a bakery, with large ovens and chimneys like fingers pointing at the sky, puffing out white smoke and a sweet yeasty smell.

Sometimes a woman came alone to order her baby. More often she made it a big occasion, with most of the family tagging along. As Hershel emerged from the steam to greet her, the woman would say, Hershel, make me a baby. And Hershel would nod and say, God willing.

And then he would take the grease pencil from behind his ear and begin to make notes. A boy or a girl this time? he would say. How large? What color? And the woman might say, Brown curls, please, and a nose like my sister Sarah's, and a special mole in a special place so that I will always know she is mine. Hershel would write it all down and say, No guarantees, remember, no returns.

The parents would give him the money, and nine months later to the day, the baby would be finished. Sometimes it was what they had ordered. More often it wasn't. But it didn't matter, because Hershel's babies were such wondrous things that people fell in love with them instantly and forgot the specifications they had made. The woman cradling her new baby in her arms would say, Oh, I *did* want a boy after all, and I *did* want black hair, not brown, and *look* at his little nose like a sideways potato! Thank you, thank you, Hershel.

And Hershel would blush and stare at the floor and say, It is the hand of God. Whether he was being modest or whether it was an excuse for his mistakes, I do not know. I only know how wonderful the babies were, how fresh and new and perfect as he wrapped them up and handed them over the counter to the parents.

Once the babies passed over the counter, Hershel washed his hands of them. He said he was not responsible for how they turned out. He said once, I only make the outsides. The parents make the insides. I make only the seed. If they cultivate it, then it will flourish.

Did he ever miss the babies once they were gone? We often wondered. Hershel had no wife, no children of his own. His work occupied all of his time. He lived in a little room in the back of his workshop, empty save a bed and a table and a prayer book. He was not an old man, though he stooped and shuffled like one. His eyes were unreadable behind the thick glasses.

He was not secretive or mysterious about his work. He was fair to customers, never cheating them by filling their babies with water to seem heavier, as I have heard crooked baby-makers do. Hershel allowed anyone to come into his workshop to watch him work. During my childhood I spent many hours there, watching. The other boys came, too, and the girl named Alina. We felt more at home there than any other place.

The place was lush and steamy. The babies were sensitive and needed warmth to grow. Hershel began by making dough. He stirred together powders and liquids in a big wooden bowl, carefully testing its consistency. We did not know what went into the dough and could not ask, for as he mixed and poured, Hershel chanted prayers, one after another in a torrent, sometimes with his eyes closed.

When the dough was golden pink and about the consistency of an earlobe (Hershel once let us touch the dough, making us wash our hands first), Hershel then began to knead it. This was wonderful to watch. Though a slight man, Hershel had thick muscular arms built up over years of kneading. We watched the dough somersault and dance, and the ropes of muscles stood out on his arms and the sweat ran down his cheek, and we boys looked at one another and said, *That's* what I want to be when I grow up.

Then Hershel placed the dough in a bowl and covered it and left it to rise. When it grew to twice its size, he punched it down again. Twice he did this. Then he rolled up his sleeves, wiped his glasses, and began the most wonderful part. With his strong, sensitive hands, he began to shape the dough into a baby, chanting prayers all the while. As he shaped the head and neck and belly, he prayed for the things he could not shape: the heart and the mind and the soul. He caressed arms and legs into shape, he twisted fingers and toes and patted cheeks into place. Soon the complete body lay before him, dusted with flour. Except for the ears, which he had left as buds. They would uncurl and bloom during the baking.

Then he would slide the baby on its back into the oven. The ovens were clean and white and were kept at exactly 98.6 degrees all year round. The babies shifted and bubbled as they baked, rocking about on their backs. Some stretched; others curled up. Hershel checked them conscientiously but did not disturb them. After nine months (he kept careful records) he would draw them out either by the head or the feet. Nothing could compare to the sight of a new baby fresh from the oven, crisp at the fingernails, crying from the cold as Hershel held him aloft, checking for any mistakes in his handiwork.

I am Hershel's work. That probably explains why I've turned out so well.

Hershel claimed to have no bond to us. He said he had merely prepared us for our rightful parents, just a step along the way. Nevertheless, we were all attached to him. As children we brought him gifts: a flower, a drawing. Once I brought him a bird, frozen, cupped in my mittens. A pet for you, Hershel. Put him in the oven, bring him back! I said. He shook his head sadly.

When we were older, my friends and I supplied him with firewood for the great ovens. We invited him to our homes for holiday meals. He seldom accepted. He was a solitary man. Sometimes, though, we would glimpse him in the window, looking up from his prayer book to watch us tumbling in the snow.

Hershel never picked favorites. But secretly I hoped that he had liked me (even a little bit) more than the others, that he had blessed me with an extra stroke, a pinch, a little more attention than the others, in the making. I'm sure the others hoped the same thing, too: that Hershel had given them something special, an extra ingredient.

I thought, sometimes, that he watched me more than the others.

As I grew older, I began to look forward to the time when Hershel would make a child for me. But then the trouble came. We did not know then that it was a mere hint of what was to come.

The girl named Alina, she was beautiful. She was about my age, with hair to her waist and shining eyes. Hershel had made her, and I sometimes thought jealously that perhaps *she* was a favorite, for how could she be so beautiful if he had not worked longer on her and given her some extra spice?

As children we had played together. She had been daring, quick on her feet, skipping along the top rails of fences or turning cartwheels. Now that she was older she had to wear long skirts and cover her hair, but she was the same laughing red-lipped Alina dancing about on her long new legs, gypsyish and wild.

I dreamed of her. We all did. I remember waking in the night to hear my younger brother whisper *Alina!* in his sleep. He was only fifteen and still a boy. I lay awake, burning with jealousy over the fact that she could be dancing in another's head.

And then—I don't remember how it happened, how the man first saw her. Perhaps he was out hunting for sport and came through our village. Perhaps Alina was in the city visiting her relatives and he saw her there. Where doesn't matter. The man took one look at her and wanted her for his own.

It all happened so quickly. How could she refuse? He was a wealthy landowner with connections in the government. Her family was poor. He had ice-blue eyes and a set of iron teeth. He was very powerful. He owned everything. She had no choice really.

Then again, he was rich. He was powerful. He may have been handsome. So . . . she married. I do not know if she wished it or not. But she was gone and we all missed her. The clouds came down, the snow fell, and the sky did not clear. We suffered terrible nightmares.

And then we heard stories. We heard that he was cruel. That he left her alone for days. That he beat her. That he did not love her as a man loves a woman, but as a man loves a horse that is beautiful and good to ride. As the stories trickled out to us, we suffered for her.

Then suddenly she came back, wearing a long coat and a veil over her face. She did not go home to her parents. She went instead to Hershel's workshop. She burst in from the cold, dropped a heavy, clinking bundle on the counter, and said, Hershel, make me a man.

She looked at him and she knew he would not refuse. She saw that, like the rest of us, he loved her. But he could not act on his love because he was almost a father to her, and he could not love a daughter as a husband. And yet still he loved, and he dreamed, and his dreams spread to all the men and boys he had ever made, so that they all woke in the night with a chorus of *Alina!*

How did she know it? Perhaps suffering had sharpened her eyes. Perhaps Hershel had given her something extra that let her know his thoughts. She said, Make me a man. And he silently nodded.

She pushed the bundle toward him and said, Two hundred pounds' worth; I will be back in nine months.

She looked hard at him, her face chiseled sharp by desperation, and he longed to press again the cheek he had once pressed into shape. But she was gone.

Hershel rolled up his sleeves and began. He refused other orders and worked only on Alina's man. He worked for days in a frenzy, without eating or sleeping or praying. All his love for Alina and all his years of experience he poured into the colossal mound of dough. He kneaded it, wrestled with it, massaged it, the sweat rolling unchecked down his face and dripping in the dough. The massive body took shape beneath his hands. He labored over the face, carving out nostrils with his fingernails. When he was finished, the man was over six and a half feet tall. I don't know how he got it into the oven.

When Alina returned, she looked more ravaged than before. Again she wore the veil. Again she went directly to Hershel's workshop. Wordlessly, Hershel led forth the man. Alina stared.

He was a giant, and smooth and beautiful as a piece of Roman statuary. Hershel had no clothes to fit him, so the man stood wrapped in a sheet. The eyes were iridescent, like fish scales. Each muscle bulged firm and strong, and they lay together snugly like bricks forming a wall. Hershel had even drawn the lines in his palms promising long life and happiness.

Alina did not thank Hershel. She merely took the giant by the hand and led him into the night. Hershel dusted his floured hands against his apron and closed his eyes. He saw again her face as it had been a moment before, eyes lit up with joy. That moment, he thought, that look, it was worth any price. If he couldn't love her, Hershel thought, then at least she could be loved by something made by his hands.

I wish I could have told him that he had made *me*, and I could have loved her, too.

The news of what happened next, in the great house in the city, traveled back to us quickly. Such news always does.

Alina quietly led the man to her bedroom in the house of her husband. Her husband, she thought, was away. But the husband came upon them, the two of them, in the bed together, late in the night.

Alina was not frightened at first. Her husband was a slight man, and no match for her giant.

But her man lay unmoving, breathing deep and slow. The husband thundered closer and rolled his colorless eyes and shouted threats and obscenities. Alina then clutched at the man, called to him, tried to rouse him—but still he lay sleeping like a slab. And as she screamed and pounded on him and forcibly turned his face to her, she sobbed and cursed Hershel, for she saw in her hands the wide-eyed, uncomprehending smile of a newborn. And then her husband cut them both down with his sword.

That was the end of Hershel. As soon as he heard the news he closed his doors. The ovens went cold. And he disappeared without saying good-bye to all his children. We followed his footprints in the snow, but they stopped abruptly, like a sentence interrupted. We could not find him.

We grieved. The whole village did. For Hershel. For Alina. For the hundreds of beautiful unborn children that had been taken from us.

And we became frightened, for we learned that the other baby-makers in the surrounding villages were also disappearing, closing up their shops and leaving, or suffering strange accidents, or just *gone* suddenly, with food going cold on the table and the chair tipped over backward and the window broken. What about our *children*? we cried, but it was only the beginning, only a hint of the larger tide turning and building and washing over us, the days and years of blackness, of madness that you would not believe if I told you.

Afterward your grandmother and I had to make your father by ourselves. It was an awkward, newfangled thing for us. But I think he turned out all right. And then your father and mother, they managed pretty well with you. Your ears did not turn out quite as well as mine, I think. But they are good ears. They listen well.

Judy Budnitz

I was reading a lot of I. B. Singer at the time and wanted to write something in that style, a new sort of shtetl story. This story arose out of a number of other ideas as well. I'd read a story, I think from the Talmud, about how unborn babies have perfect and total wisdom of the earth and the heavens. But the minute a baby's born, an

angel strikes him on the mouth, causing him to forget everything.
This is why babies cry when they're born, for the loss of all that
knowledge. And that is also why everyone has a little indentation
between nose and upper lip, the mark of the angel's blow. That got
me started. Another image I had in my head was from a time when
I was being taught how to bake challah. I was told that the dough
was ready for baking when it had the consistency of an earlobe. And
I was fascinated by the golem legend, this superhero-Frankenstein's
monster creature, and wanted to write a version of that. I wanted to
write an answer to the child's query, "Where do babies come
from?"—a creation myth, but one that goes awry. And finally I
wanted to write a story about the Holocaust. But I felt I didn't have
the right to write about it in a specific, firsthand way. That seemed
presumptuous. I wanted to find a way to write about it indirectly,
obliquely, to cloak it in a fairy tale. So in "Hershel" the Holocaust is
a dark, looming presence, this monumental thing that destroys the
characters' world forever, something too terrible to be named. There
are many elements of this story that I didn't consciously plan and
only noticed later, like the irony, in the Holocaust context, of bring-
ing forth life from ovens.

A Dream of Sleep

Steve Almond

The caretaker's name was Wolf Pinkas. He lived with two cats in a stone cottage at the rear of the cemetery. The cottage, a squarish structure six feet high, had been constructed as a family crypt. But the wealthy Prussian immigrant who commissioned it disappeared without a trace before the First World War. Unable to sell the vault, the owners of the cemetery, a family named Gardner, converted it to a caretaker's shed.

In the years following World War II, when Wolf assumed the position of caretaker, the yard was a thriving concern. Its high walls, trimmed in ivy, showed the intensity of new brick, dainty blue benches lined the paths, and the ornate pattern of the wrought-iron gate shimmered like delicate, interlacing claws. The graves were styled in the Eastern European fashion, above ground, great slabs of marble or slate etched with names and dates and inlaid, as often as not, with small, circular photos of the deceased. On weekends and holidays, relatives came in clusters to set out flowers, votive candles, wreaths of hazelnut. They carried picnic lunches and sat on the benches and ate and laughed with the dead.

But the yard had since fallen from prosperity. The elder Gardner died, leaving management to the whim of his son, a young man with slicked-back hair. He informed Wolf he no longer had the funds to pay for caretaking services and security. "No one's buying plots," he murmured. "I'm sorry, Mr. Pinkas."

Wolf was a shy man, unaccustomed to speech. But he grew

visibly upset at the prospect of losing his job. His face flushed and his hands, unusually large for a man who stood barely five feet, began to tremble. "Them visitors," he said, speaking slowly, hoping to undo the effects of his heavy accent. "What are they gonna do?" A bargain was struck. Wolf agreed to accept a pay reduction in exchange for permission to move into the shed.

"You'll have to double as security," Gardner said.

Wolf, who was frightened of weapons and their use, quietly assented.

The young man removed a small whisk brush from his coat pocket and began dusting his wingtips. "Don't worry, sport. There's nothing but ghosts in this place."

Wolf said, "I suppose."

The shed had never been intended as a domicile and Wolf spent an entire autumn making it suitable for the living. He purchased a pot-belly stove from a nearby estate sale, placed a tin basin beside it for bathing, drilled holes in the roof for ventilation, built a privy out back, and conveyed the few furnishings from his apartment. The architect had been thoughtful enough to include several arched window slots, no doubt intended for stained glass, and Wolf constructed wooden shutters for these. On especially cold nights, he bolted the shutters and unplugged his tiny refrigerator from the portable generator and attached a space heater. In the warm months, he left the shutters open, so that a breeze might stir the room's air and sunlight lance its shadows.

Wolf spent his days clearing vines from footpaths, scrubbing the first coppery hint of rust from the gate, hacking at the eager weeds that threatened remote plots. There was also the problem of refuse, which on windy days drifted in from the street out front, where there was a trolley stop. As if by some act of willful mischief, bright papers found their way into corners of the yard, and so Wolf made a round before each sundown, jabbing them with a spear fashioned for this purpose. He worked methodically, without pause. Had he considered the larger aims of his work, had he been given to such considerations, he would have described it as a siege against the reckless mess of the living, which hoped to infiltrate and despoil the peace accorded the dead.

At night, he listened to classical music. He had a few dozen records, Chopin mostly, but also some Mozart and Bach, and an ancient crank phonograph in its own carrying case. He ate lightly, tea and toast in the mornings, a sandwich at lunch, rice or potatoes for supper, with vegetables. The most that can be said of his diet is that the bread was hearty, for he baked it himself, following a recipe printed on the side of the flour bag. He did, however, indulge his cats. Each received a can of tuna every other day.

He had not intended to keep pets. The cats had come to him. The first arrived soon after he moved into his cottage, simply appeared one day, puddled in a sunbeam near the stove. Wolf attempted to shoo it away. But the cat merely batted forward the carcass of a freshly killed field mouse, as if tendering the first card in an expected negotiation. Wolf hissed and stamped his feet. The intruder, a large orange tom, stretched languidly. Both ears were frayed and his left eye had been battered into a perma-nent wink, which lent him a rakish air. He departed, showing no great concern, only after Wolf advanced with a broom. This scene repeated itself the next evening, as it did each evening until Wolf relented. In a moment of whimsy, he named the cat Dempsey.

The second cat appeared two years later, a black smudge on the sill. Wolf noted its delicate ribs and nubby spine, and moved to the window with a bowl of powdered milk. The kitten limped off. Only when the frosts began did a scratch come at the door. The cat cowered against Dempsey and began attempting to suckle. Wolf named him Coal.

Each month, a small check signed by the younger Gardner appeared in the mailbox outside the gate. The next morning, Wolf walked the half mile or so to his bank, where he cashed his check, then continued on to the barber and the grocery store.

When the bank and barber closed, he climbed onto a trolley. And when the city's trolley service ceased, its tracks ripped out of the ground and piled like burnished femurs, Wolf found a bus to serve the same purpose. Asphalt and pavement seemed to wash outwards from the roads, inviting a greater flow of cars. The air swirled with acrid tar. Wires snarled overhead. In the near distance, cranes pieced together the skeletons of skyscrapers.

The law of entropy, which Wolf was used to opposing on his familiar terrain of plots and paths, went unchecked outside the gate. No matter how neatly men striped the center of the streets, no matter how bright the billboard promises, disorder grew. Wolf ventured out less and less, and the world returned this favor.

Doddering figures still appeared from time to time, and invariably praised the upkeep of the yard, sometimes even seeking Wolf out to comment on the garden he had coaxed from the sandy soil around his cottage. Wolf nodded at these comments and smiled and disappeared from view as quickly and courteously as possible.

But this older generation, which understood the importance of spending a few hours each week in the company of the dead, died off themselves and, though there were still unfilled plots for sale, younger relatives buried them in yards closer to their own neighborhoods. These suburban cemeteries looked to Wolf more like a species of park, acres of grass smoothed, as if to erase any unsightly wrinkles; small stone tablets marked the graves, or discreet plaques of the sort used elsewhere to announce historical sites. A road wound through the identical rows, presumably for those who sought a whiff of the dead while driving past.

Ironically, the decline in visitors increased Wolf's workload. For the care of individual plots, which had once been the assumed duty of relatives, now passed to him. It was he who ensured headstones were kept free of rubbish, the photos polished, and dead flowers cleared away. He enjoyed these tasks, which seemed to him the logical completion of a cycle to which he gave his life over contentedly.

Wolf was not a man prone to fancy. But sometimes, as he hunched to clean a sheet of marble, or set a bouquet of wildflowers at the foot of a favored pyre, he believed he could hear a faint voice on the breeze. Once in a great while, these happy apparitions appeared outside his cottage and hovered in the moonlight. When he played Chopin or Mozart, even Bach, they moved with cautious grace, wisps of cotton waltzing. The cats perched on the sill and watched.

After a lengthy period of construction, the road fronting the cemetery became a four-lane highway, and thereafter the surrounding neighborhood began a precipitous decline. Private homes were demolished and large, drab public housing projects built. During the cold months, after supper, Wolf lay on his bed and read in peace, the cats flung atop him like pelts. But when the nights turned warm, Wolf could hear young people in the park next door, inebriated laughs and shouts, bottles shattering against his brick walls, the snapping of firecrackers, or gunfire, which frightened the cats.

Increasingly, graffiti appeared near the front gate. Wolf scrubbed at these sinister symbols and, if they were impossible to remove, painted over them. He considered writing the younger Gardner a letter to apprise him of the problem, but decided instead to purchase additional paint himself, the same course he followed upon discovering that the blue paint with which he brightened the benches each spring had run out.

Gardner was a busy man, or seemed so, and his annual visits lasted barely long enough for Wolf to count the buttons shining on the front of his coat. "Sales have been a bit off," he observed, which both men understood to be an understatement. "Some orders around the holidays, maybe." With an expression of sour dread, he would then inquire if anything was needed, to which Wolf would respond, with a slight bow, in the negative.

One evening, after closing, a tall figure in a sagging suit appeared at the gate. He let himself in with a key and tromped about the place with a small device in one hand and a notepad in the other, so engrossed that he failed to notice Wolf's approach and nearly walked over him. The man leapt backwards, his suit seeming to follow a second later.

Wolf apologized.

"Quite all right," the man said, squinting. "Yes, Gardner mentioned you. Mr. Pinks, correct?"

"Pinkas, yes."

"You live on the premises, correct?"

Wolf pointed to his cottage.

"Yes. Well. I didn't mean to startle you. Ham Tallaway." He extended a soft hand. "Development commission. Just here on a routine inspection."

"Yes," Wolf said. "How did you get a key?"

"Why, Gardner gave it to me. For my inspection. I'd have rung the bell, but you don't seem to have one." Tallaway, laughed, at what Wolf did not know. "Anyhow, I'll just look around and be out of your way."

"Of course."

While the two men stood talking, Dempsey hobbled out of the cottage and nudged his body against Wolf's shin. He then moved toward Tallaway and pressed his muzzle against the cuff of his trousers, scenting. "What a nice kitty." Tallaway said, bending to pat him. "This retaining wall—you know if it's furrow-grounded, or overlaid?"

"I'm not certain," Wolf said. "I wasn't here when it was built."

"I see. Well. Don't let me interrupt you. I'll be done in a few minutes."

"Of course."

When Wolf returned to the cottage, Dempsey was gone. Only a week later did Wolf locate his body, a stain the color of pumpkin lying beneath a bush just inside the gate. The cat had hoped to spare him this discovery, but lacked the strength. Coal took one look at the body and scampered back to the cottage.

With his garden and the new varieties of dehydrated foods,

Wolf ventured outside less and less frequently. It was not necessary for him to leave the cemetery to observe the course of
progress. At rush hour, cars puffed past, exhaling smog, blaring
horns, skidding, crashing. Ambulances keened, police cars threw
colored light, planes shouted overhead, black boys loped by on
foot, carrying plastic boxes that boomed with cruel imitations of
music. Even the quieter moments resounded with electronic
beeps and metallic sighs, the chuff and heave of machines whose
sleep is never quite entire.

Against these, Wolf placed his wooden shutters and the
chirping of tinder in his stove and the music from his phonograph and his own persistent fears. He allowed ivy to overrun the
walls and the front gate, found comfort in the gradual obscuring
of highway and streetlight and wire. He removed the mailbox
and fed the envelopes dropped near the yard's entrance to his
stove. He surrendered his battle against graffiti. Then, without so
much as a letter to young Gardner, he bolted the yard shut with a
large padlock.

He had hoped to make the ruin outside his kingdom, that
against which he measured the order of his life, disappear. But
rather than reassurance, he felt oddly besieged. The murmurings
of the dead were no longer gay, but petulant, and their appearance outside his window meant the smirk of skulls and a clatter
of bones. His sleep grew restless with dreams.

Wolf had never before remembered his dreams. True, he
might awaken with a strange sense of elation, or dread, even
expectation. But as he swung his legs over the edge of his cot and
gathered kindling for the stove, as he drank his morning tea and
surveyed the yard, these feelings, the chaotic rhythm of them,
dissipated. He gathered Coal onto his lap, sipped his tea, then
began his daily regimen. And, as if by a gentleman's agreement,
all was forgotten.

Now he woke with distinct memories: a vulture gliding overhead on dusty wings, swooping down on Coal, its awful black
claws outstretched while Wolf watched from the doorway of his

cottage, unable to wrestle himself into motion. Other nights, Wolf found himself cast out, wandering a dark, featureless landscape: the stink of diesel and dead horses, eyes staring at him from dank basements, a journey with no apparent point of origin or destination, just one step after another into blue-black air.

Most disturbing of all was his dream of sleep. He could see himself in this dream; he slept peacefully. Yet he could also see images from his early childhood: families marched down muddy roads, his father falling, a heap on wet road, his sisters crying out for potatoes. Bombs dropped from the sky, turning earth to violent dirt, the dry pop of machine guns shoved bodies into pits, the smell of his nanny rose up around him and turned to ashes and settled onto his skin. Wolf did not understand: he saw and heard and smelled all of it. Yet he slept. Even as he rose to fire the stove, sixty years on, he could see himself asleep, in the garden his family kept, hidden away. He looked dead. But he was not dead. He slept. This terrible fact was all that seemed to matter.

One day, in the midst of mending a fissured tombstone, Wolf heard the strokes of a hacksaw. He found Ham Tallaway on the other side of the gate. Next to him stood a black man in a workshirt beginning to sweat through. The black man said, "What'n the hell?"

Tallaway stared at Wolf. "If you wouldn't mind opening the gate, Mr. Pinkas."

"Of course."

"You mean this crazy muthafucker had the key all along?" The black man scowled. "I been comin' out here for how many months, Mister Tallaway? And this old boy been ignorin' me?"

Wolf shied away. With a strained smile, Tallaway instructed his companion to return to the truck. It had been a year since his last visit, but Tallaway looked older. His jowls hung in gray wattles and his suit bowed around a new gut.

Wolf swung the gate open and Tallaway proceeded to the nearest shaded bench and sat. "We need to speak, Mr. Pinkas. I am sorry about my colleague, but you can understand his frustration. I myself have grown . . . frustrated by the situation. Mr. Gardner has sent a number of letters informing you of the situation, as has the city. But these, I imagine, you have chosen to disregard." He gestured with his chin toward the beheaded mailbox post and paused. "I understand that you have grown quite attached to your home and that your job is important to you. I can see by your care of . . . the premises, that you have been diligent in the exercise of your duties here. The cemetery looks quite well tended. But the city is now the owner of this land. Do you understand?"

"Yes."

"What I am saying, Mr. Pinkas, is that Mr. Gardner has sold us this cemetery. Sold it to the city."

"Yes," Wolf said. "I understand." He felt eager to return to his repair, fearful the grout would dry improperly.

Tallaway pulled a handkerchief from his pocket and dabbed his forehead. "And the situation calls for me, you see, to inform you that the city, as it should arise, will no longer be requiring your services. I'm sorry, Mr. Pinkas. It's nothing personal."

Wolf felt a kind of recoil, as if shoved backwards.

"We appreciate your dedication," Tallaway said. "I assure you this has nothing to do with job performance."

"What you mean? You will hire another man?" His tongue flustered at the words.

"No. You see, this property . . . the city needs this property. We have plans to build on this property, to build an arena. For sports, music concerts, *cultural* events."

Wolf said nothing, but his expression must have changed, because Tallaway quickly added, "The plans are already quite far along. If you had read any of the letters—"

"But this is a graveyard."

"I am aware of that, Mr. Pinkas."

"You can't move graves."

"We have already secured permission from those relatives we

could locate. You needn't worry, Mr. Pinkas. The interred and all existing markers will be relocated."

"But the graves," Wolf said quietly. "You can't move them."

Tallaway folded his handkerchief and tucked it back into his pocket. "It was my hope that you would include yourself in the process, Mr. Pinkas. But you chose not to. Construction won't start until after Christmas, so you have several months to wind up your affairs here. I have discussed the possibility of your obtaining employment with one of the municipal cemeteries. That is a decision, of course, for you to make on your own." Tallaway stood and walked to the gate. "I'm sorry," he said without slowing.

When, some nights later, Wolf heard the voices behind his cottage, he felt certain these were the dead, roused by Tallaway's visit. But the voices sounded young, mirthful, red tongues licking the night with laughter. Coal, who inevitably woke at spirits, lay beside the stove, a curled purr. Wolf rose from the cot and fetched his trash stick and his lantern and stepped into the night. Summer, with its languid breath, was gone, but autumn had yet to arrive. A fragment of moon hung in the starless sky.

Wolf heard more giggling, from the north corner of the yard. His footsteps carried him past the privy and the brass monument erected to honor the yard's wealthiest family, past the small clearing where Dempsey had hunted mice and toward a low wooden gate. Inside this gate, weeds rose around two rows of waist-high headstones. Wolf felt gooseflesh on his arms. When he first took the job, he made occasional forays to the children's graveyard. But these became more than he could bear: to be stared at by the mounted photos, eyes unblackened by fear, or forced to consider the bodies that lay inside each stunted mound.

But now he heard a sharp cry, which he took to be distress. He stepped inside the gate and made his way toward the back where, under a stand of cedars, he saw two figures intertwined. The bodies appeared to be wrestling, one atop the other. He stepped closer and lifted his lantern. They were not fighting at all. For a long moment he watched the boy's muscled back, watched him struggle with the pleasures of congress, arching and thrusting, grunting at satisfied effort, while the second figure breathed extravagantly, thighs fallen apart, ankles rising up, digging at the ropy muscles of her lover's calves. Against the crisp white of the cedar trunks, they composed a tableaux of brutal desire.

Wolf stepped backward, but in so doing stumbled on a root. The girl lifted her head and looked at him and shrieked. The boy ignored her distress and continued his exertions. But she shrieked again and he tumbled from her and they both lay, aroused now by fear, on the blanket they had set down. Bits of dried leaves clung to the girl's braided hair and her breasts jittered. She ducked behind the boy, who raised his arms as a boxer might and peered into the dull nimbus of Wolf's lantern. "Who the fuck out there?"

Wolf could smell what they had been doing, the slightly putrid scent of bodies happily opened. The girl reached to cover herself where she glistened. Wolf felt something punch at the inside of his ribs. "I am the caretaker here," he said.

"He crazy," the girl said. "Look at him, Boo. He crazy. He crazy like them murderers who kill they family. Keep him away from me."

The boy reached past her, for his clothes. "Come any closer and I kill your ass." He showed his teeth, a band of white interrupted by a single gold tooth. "I got a gun."

Because they spoke fast, Wolf had trouble understanding. But he saw they were afraid. The girl pooched her lips in and out, and the boy, for all his bluster, quivered around the mouth.

"I do not want to hurt you," Wolf said.

"Ain't nobody scared of your ass," the boy said. "You the one should be scared. I got a gun."

"This is private property," Wolf said. "A graveyard is here. This is not a place for what you do."

"Look at his face," the girl cried. "Boo, *do* something." She crawled behind a cedar trunk and struggled with a T-shirt.

"You have no rights to be here," Wolf said.

The boy seemed to consider this. He took note of the steel-tipped stick in Wolf's hand.

"This ain't no private property," the girl said suddenly. "They building an arena here. The city gonna build it. We got the same right be here as you."

But as she spoke, the boy was gathering the blanket and snatching up a pint bottle and dashing away. The girl scrambled after him, marking her departure with an emphatic spit. Wolf watched them retreat, sleek and graceful, as if they belonged to the night. He hurried back to his cottage and lay on his cot. But each sound now seemed suspect. He no longer trusted the rustle of branches, the wind's whistling route through the graves, the settling of his own cottage. He felt unprotected, angry, as if someone had stirred his gut to simply to test his reaction.

Toward dawn there was a faint knock at the door. Coal lifted his head. Wolf stoked the fire and pulled on his trousers and set the kettle for tea. He rubbed his eyes. He had slept barely an hour. The kettle started in. The knock became more distinct.

Wolf opened the door. The girl fell to the floor like a swimmer frozen in mid-stroke. Scratches raked the length of her forearms and blood from a gash at the knee ribboned her calves. Her T-shirt rode up around squarish hips, revealing the muddied seat of her panties and, where the fabric ended in a dainty frill, a tear in the skin. She looked at Wolf and began at once to sob. At the sound of her crying, she cried harder. Gradually the noise subsided. Coal strode over and dabbed his tongue at her cheek.

"What's happened to you?"

"I couldn't get out."

Not quite understanding, Wolf said, "Are you hurt? Was it the boy who did this?"

"It was your goddamn wall. It too high."

Wolf flew into brief, private panic. He wanted the girl gone, out of his home. "Now listen," he said, "You must get cleaned up. Your mother will worry. There is a place here for washing. Then you leave. I will leave the gate open."

The girl nodded drowsily.

When Wolf returned at lunch, he found her on his cot, wearing one of his undershirts, her dirty T-shirt thrown in a corner, Coal draped on the swell of her belly. With no great interest, she was inspecting one of his records. "Young lady," he said.

"You ain't got to tell me," she said. "Only reason I'm here is 'cause I slipped on that wall. I was just waiting 'round to say thanks."

"Yes. I appreciate that."

"I'm going," she said. And yet she did not move.

Wolf looked at her face, not obscured by darkness, nor contrived by hysterics. Her small features lacked sharpness. She was young. Twelve? Thirteen? "I could sue you," she said. "For reckless abuse and some other shit."

Wolf thought about his cache of twenty-dollar bills. Would she have had the ingenuity to check the tin hidden behind his bookcase? "Young lady," he said.

She stood, Coal tumbling and hitting the floor with a squeak. Wolf held the door open. But rather than moving to the door, she ambled around the cottage, as if distracted, as if he were the interloper and his presence an inconvenience she had chosen, for the moment, to tolerate. "Where you from?" she said.

"What do you mean?"

"You got a accent," she said. "Where from?"

Wolf shook his head. "What does this matter?"

"It don't. I'm just asking."

"I am asking you to leave."

"I *am* leaving." She smiled at him. "You from Mexico?"

"No."

"No?"

"I am from Russia," Wolf said, clenching his jaw around the word. "Then, for a time, I was in Poland."

"You don't look like no Russian. Them Russians are *big*. Where's your wife, anyway? You old enough to have a wife."

"You need to leave," Wolf said.

"If you had a wife she'd make you cut that hair, I tell you that right now. Hoo boy, you like one of them flower children. Like Rainbow Man or Sunshine or some shit. How old are you?" She wandered over to the stove and begun plucking the laundry line as if it were a guitar string. "Why you live here? It's *spooky* 'round here."

Wolf watched her uncertainly. He cleared a strand of hair from his face, as he had done a thousand times, but now, for the first time, felt a twinge of self-consciousness. "I left the front gate open." She shrugged. Wolf noted, with some distress, that she was the same height as him. "Go home. Your mother will worry."

"You got any Coke?"

"Young lady—"

"Any kind of *soda?*"

"Young lady," Wolf said, as firmly as his manner allowed. "This is private property. My home. I am a busy man."

"Yeah. Taking care of a bunch of dead folks. Real busy."

Wolf's cheeks reddened.

"All right, all right. I'm going. Don't get all crazy on me." She regarded him curiously, a girl staring from the body of a woman. Then she began at once undoing the buttons on her shirt front.

For a moment Wolf said nothing, only watched in flushed astonishment. Then he recovered his voice. "That is not necessary. No, please. Stop that, young lady. You may keep that. As, as payment. For your fall."

The girl looked down at the shirt, then over to her T-shirt in the corner. "Fine. You can keep mine, then. We trade."

"Yes. Fine."

She made her way slowly to the door, looking about distractedly. "Your cat pregnant," she said, before stepping outside.

"What?"

"Your kitty. She pregnant."

"No," Wolf said. "That is a boy cat."

"Look at her. She fat. She pregnant."

"No," Wolf said. "I feed him too much."

"That cat ain't no boy. It got nipples."

"The front gate is open. If you need bus fare—"

"Nah." She breezed out. "I don't want nothing from you. Anyway, this ain't no private property. The city own it. There's a sign out front."

"Do not come back," Wolf called to her. "I am warning."

That night Wolf smelled her, smelled her everywhere, on his clothes and on Coal and especially his cot, a smell like the oil applied to babies. He settled down and cranked his phonograph and attempted to clear his mind for sleep. But the smell interfered. He felt a longing that was not lust, but something less easily dispelled. He wanted to cry out. Coal, lying on the foot of the bed, meowed in alarm. Wolf rushed outside in his bedshirt. He stumbled this way and that, peering at nothing, at the heavy ink of night, at his garden, at the remnant of footsteps too small to be his own.

A week later she was back, her voice circling the treetops, then a deeper tone, that of a boy. Coal looked at him. But Wolf merely selected a record from his collection, an obscure chorale by Philip Emanuel Bach, and cranked his phonograph and listened to Moses sing in German, filling the cottage with somber promises, an end to the desert, the new milk of Canaan. For a moment he saw her eyes, and then her body, bent to its awful, animal purposes.

The next morning, he marched to the children's graveyard and stood between the two rows of headstones, like graying teeth. Their figures were sketched on a thin quilt. This he brought back to the cottage and cut in strips and fed to the stove. He drank his tea and struggled not to think any further about these interruptions. But she made this impossible, for she returned to the yard just often enough to keep him in a state of nervous expectation. It was as if she had gained access to his mind and, making it her mission never to be forgotten, appeared on the very night he managed to convince himself he was free of her.

Only in October, with the rains now steady, did her visits cease. As if to compensate, surveyors sent by Tallaway arrived and spent the afternoons tromping around the yard's perimeter, taking measurements. A helicopter hovered overhead one morning, dispatched to snap aerial photographs. Wolf lost the pleasures of peaceful sleep. The snows began. Drifts dusted the yard. The spirits that had once danced, now coiled outside his windows, sibilant as snakes, refusing to be consoled. The darkness distended, blurred. Wolf lost track of the days, or, more precisely, they seemed to lose track of themselves. He began harboring the conscious wish that he were no longer alive.

A notice arrived informing him of the yard's closure. He had thirty days to relocate. Wolf had nearly forgotten about the girl when, on a frigid night deep into December, her voice roused him. He took her screams, at first, to be those of ecstasy. But as they lengthened and rose in timbre, Wolf recognized other forms of abandon: pain and sorrow and terror.

The spirits assured him this was all a dream. He held fast to the rails of his cot and burrowed under his blankets and lay trembling, unable to determine if he was awake or asleep, if he lay in the garden of his boyhood or the graveyard that had been his home for forty years. Then Wolf heard the sounds of his life: Coal's thick purr, the hum of the space heater, the soft crackle of the phonograph needle dipping into the empty grooves at the end of a record. It had been a dream. A dream.

The girl's next cry drowned out everything, like an air-raid siren, but jagged, discordant, flawed in the way of things human. Wolf put on his coat and boots. The spirits called him a fool and a coward, turned themselves into black veils and twirled indignantly.

He found her on the ground, her legs thrown open, her monstrous belly heaving under a glaze of sweat. Steam puffed from between her legs. Her arms lay to each side, like sticks propped in the pegs of her shoulders. Every few minutes, her fists pounded the frozen earth. "Oh God," Wolf said. "Young lady. No. No. God, we got to get you to a hospital." He wondered if he might be able to lift her into his wheelbarrow. But she grew panicky when he tried to move her, tore at his arms. She wasn't going anywhere.

Wolf had never seen a baby born, had been a youngest child, and felt an instant revulsion at the prospect of having to play a part in birth. He told the girl he was going to find help, and started toward the gate. Surely someone had a phone and that would lead to an ambulance, a doctor. Wolf tried to move away, but the sound of her stopped him dead: she howled in the only manner humans can howl if they are to make themselves complete—not with motive, only as an expression of anguish so profound that silence is impossible. Wolf made it as far as his cottage, then turned back to her, with an armful of blankets.

He lay these under her, and over her torso. He shucked his coat and made of it a pillow for her head. He lowered himself between her legs. The smell of blood and waste punched into his nostrils. Her genitals were red and grotesquely swollen. He reared back and pressed tentatively at her stomach and told her to push. The girl buckled and thrashed. She clamped his wrist until the bone ached.

"Push," Wolf said. "You must push." The girl cursed him. "Push," Wolf said. "Young lady, please." The girl did push. Wolf could feel her clenching. And he felt the baby ease down, into the birth canal, could see how the girl's stomach sunk and her hips buckled and her vagina, engorged with blood, prepared to rend. Snow started in, flakes swirling and landing and melting on the girl's shuddering legs and Wolf's own reddened hands. "Please," he said. "Young lady, *please*." The girl seized up, let out a wheeze, then ceased moving. Her muscles went slack.

Wolf began to weep. He took off his nightshirt and held it out, as if its presence might coax the child. The idea suddenly struck him that the child was asleep. This was the problem. Wolf himself had slept through the trauma of his own birth; this is what his father had told him. "Your own mama dying and you slept, Wolfie. Peaceful. Asleep."

But if the baby was asleep, and his mother as well, how was the birth to occur? He jostled the girl, to no effect. He kneaded her stomach. Finally, his hand came forward and began unsteadily probing. It was not like touching earth, the wet rubber of her, the shit-slick hairs, the muck. His fingers slipped inside and immediately felt the baby's head. Her flesh held to it like the seal on a jar of preserves. He pushed in further and felt something hard against the baby. One of its shoulders was lodged behind the pelvic bone. With a sharp jab, Wolf wedged two fingers between the mother and child and tried to pry the child free. Blood and fluid spurted onto his hands, made the flesh slippery. The girl convulsed. He lost purchase.

For a moment, the situation seemed almost comical: he, a naked old man crouched in the cold, reaching into a stranger, trying to pry life into a world he wished mostly to leave. Again, he worked his fingers in and searched for the point of contact. He dug at the child's shoulder, felt his fingers cramping. The girl convulsed again and Wolf felt something give, collapse downward.

The baby's head appeared, a dark crescent, then a bit more, a forehead and nose smashed nearly flat. A second dark blotch appeared, a shoulder, and in a moment, a single moment, the baby slid out, as if sprung from a trap. Wolf held the body in his huge hands, watched it drip and paw the air, the umbilical cord dangling. He smacked its bottom once, twice, a third time, until he heard a sputter, its gums suddenly gaping around a wail. He swaddled the baby in his nightshirt, and set it on the mother's belly, beneath the blankets. He took her hands and placed them on the baby. "Hold," he said, then shoved one arm under the girl's back and the other under her knees. But she was dead weight now, unconscious. His attempts to lift her failed. He laid one hand on the baby and with the other dragged its mother, yard by yard, away from the cedars. The snow fell harder. His knees ached.

Blood rushed to the surface of his skin. The baby wailed and by this the spirits seemed cowed. He was alone with the girl and the baby and, at each step, an oddly invigorating pain.

Back at the cottage, Wolf placed mother and child on the mattress pulled from his cot and fed the stove the last of the kindling. With a jackknife, he cut through the umbilical and moved the baby, a boy, onto its mother's breast. His delicate lips rooted for a nipple, found it, suckled. Wolf boiled water and yanked a pair of britches from the laundry line and cleaned the girl as best he could, and the child. He placed tea leaves between the girl's legs, to ease the swelling. Coal wandered over and licked at the blood staining the stone floor.

Wolf pulled on his trousers and a shirt and ran outside to fetch wood. He was gone less than a minute. When he returned, he found the baby sprawled beside his mother. He had somehow been heaved off her, or fallen. Coal was cowering in the corner, his tail puffed. Wolf reached for the child, pressed him again to his mother's breast. The child was limp, unbreathing. His eyes were open but blank as stone. Wolf cradled him and ran to the door. Perhaps if he brought the baby to a neighbor, they could call the police or a hospital. But then, any fool could see baby's neck was broken. Wolf stood in the doorway.

The girl smiled a glassy smile of delirium. "You kilt my baby," she said slowly.

Wolf shook his head: "What happened? Something happened to this child."

"You kilt him."

"No," he said. Then again, louder, he said, "No."

"You a killer."

"No," he whispered. He stepped closer to the girl and set the baby onto the mattress, out of her view. "I didn't kill nothing. I tried to save. Do you understand? I did what I could."

She stared at the space where he stood. Her eyes flickered, then closed.

"I did what I could do, young lady. What else could I do?

You should have gone to a hospital, not come here. Why did you come here? *Why?* I did not ask for you. I explained, this is private property, my home. Why did you bring this into my home?" He looked at the baby and began to tremble. "I will not take the blame for this, young lady. I tried. I tried to save your child, and it was you who did this. You. Not me. You." His legs had delivered him to the other side of her, away from the baby and its broken stem. He put his lips to her ear: "How could you do this? You will never be forgiven for this. Never. Do you hear me? Never until you are dead."

But the girl couldn't hear him. It occurred to Wolf that he might be in the midst of a dream, that none of this was real, only an elaborate charade devised to torment him. He went so far as to turn away and strike his head against the stone wall. But when he turned back, the girl was still there, her feverish body tossing, and the baby beside her, still.

He sank to his knees and wept, remembering the sting of death, how a body might in fact bury itself in grief, for years or whole decades. And realizing this, he experienced for a single sweet instant what life might feel like unaccompanied by guilt or fear or dread. He had been a child, a child too young to do anything but sleep. Sleep.

Blue light seeped in the shutters. Wolf rose from the floor and walked to the door of his cottage and, in one curiously exuberant motion, leapt outside. He moved through the cemetery on an old man's legs, creaky but stubbornly alive, not seeing the grave mounds he had tended, the headstones touched with dew, only moving himself toward the gate, the city beyond, a hospital, a doctor, the pink thread of dawn.

Steve Almond

I wrote "A Dream of Sleep" after visiting an abandoned graveyard outside Wroclaw, Poland. I was struck by the dilapidated beauty of the place, and the strange sense of tranquility. Surely, I thought, a man seeking to escape the modern world would choose to live here. As to Wolf Pinkas himself, he is a Jew, though I decided not to tag him as such in the story. It's enough to know that he's a survivor. He might just as well have been from a family of gypsies or Communists. It is the job of art, after all, to recognize human suffering— and perseverance—not as products of history, but of the individual spirit. As for me, I'm proud as hell to be a Jew. But the stories I write (the best ones, anyhow) are about how people withstand their deepest fears and desires. And it doesn't really matter to me who they call God, only that I love them all, as they deserve.

BARBARIANS AT THE GATES

Dara Horn

In the opening credits of this imaginary film, Wilhelm Landsmann—or Bill Landsmann, in the subtitles—has just landed
in Amsterdam. Shipwrecked, if you will, or, more accurately,
landwrecked. Of course, "just" doesn't really mean much at this
point. How long has it been since the wreckage? A few months?
A few years? It scarcely matters. He will always feel as if he has
just arrived. Wilhelm has "just" become Willem, the second of
three names—the third being Bill—that he will use in a period of
less than five years.

His Dutch is abysmal. "His" Dutch. A European way of
speaking, he decides years later, claiming languages as one's own,
as if each person owned a little piece of German or French or
Dutch, or a great big piece, and some languages have more to go
around than others. In school he slowly picks up Dutch, but
Dutch doesn't pick him up in return—he can understand all the
insults the other children whisper at him, but be doesn't speak
back. German is his, or at least was his. But now he has stopped
speaking German, and as a result of "his" Dutch not really being
his, he speaks nothing at all. Instead he wanders around the city
of Amsterdam, silently creeping around its streets and wishing
he could somehow run away and go home.

All of Amsterdam reminds Willem of a rat trap. Crooked little
streets, crooked little buildings with hidden dead ends at every
turn. You walk home from school, a terrible place—although it is
Montessori, and therefore a Very Good School—where each

classroom is stacked on top of another and where they put the new kid, right after he arrives and despite the supposed "open classroom" philosophy, in a seat at the back of the room. (Willem didn't remain in that school. Kicked out by Montessori, he had to go to the Jewish school, and at the new school, speaking German was not only discouraged but expressly forbidden. By some quirk of fate, however, he found himself assigned to a seat at the back of the room even there. Someone always has to sit at the back of the room.)

The school is cramped, like everywhere in Amsterdam, so much so that Willem sometimes wonders if putting children in it is actually a waste of space—the floor level is always jammed, but since children are small, Willem thinks, they might have split each of the building's stories in two instead of having six feet of empty air above the children's heads, thus doubling the building's floor space without altering its height. Perhaps that would inconvenience a few teachers, but what of it? These are the things that Willem thinks about all day at school as he stares up at the ceiling, trying his best not to learn any more Dutch even by accident. Anyway, the extra air in the classroom doesn't help the fact that Willem sits in class each day jammed between his desk and the back wall and tormented on both sides by boys—Peter and Jan, they are called—who take advantage of the open education model to spit at him whenever the teacher turns around.

But then the whole city is like some ridiculous maze designed by a cruel psychologist who waits, watching you, testing you to see if you might take a wrong turn and receive an electric shock. You leave the school each day and walk home along the canals, where the big flatboats—reveling in their flatness in this upright, vertical city—seem to be grinning idiotic grins at you just like the boys in school. The boats, after all, are in the right place, while Amsterdam itself, a city built on seventeenth-century pilings of stone, is ever sinking into the sea where it belongs, and the boats themselves seem to know it as they chug their joyous way out to the North Sea. Meanwhile you are stuck on dry land, confined to the narrow streets, some of them walled in by crooked buildings, others open on one side to the freezing canals with cruel grinning boats, and all of them jammed with black bicycles ridden by old ladies in long frumpy skirts madly ringing their bicycle bells. Amsterdam belongs to these frumpy women, and you are forever jumping out of their way.

After you dodge the bicycles, though, you still have to negotiate your way through the tiny little streets, their corners, lampposts, and buildings occasionally marked with the city's seal—a badge shape with three simple letters in a vertical column: "XXX." At the Montessori School, before he was expelled, Willem learned that these three X's stood for the three trials of Amsterdam: flood, fire, and plague. Those X's glare at him at every interval as he wanders in circles around the city looking for a way out, as if to say, Not here, not now, not ever—and if you try to stand still, I'll knee you in the groin.

And if the streets aren't enough to make you feel like a suffocating rat, there is always home. Willem's building in Amsterdam is a canal house, one of the strangled town houses gasping for air along the city's river-streets. The canal houses each stand about four stories high, but are rarely more than thirty feet wide, with their side walls rubbing each other as they sink deeper and deeper into the city's soft false ground, leaning forward and backward like poorly trained soldiers falling out of line. Inside, the apartments are so cramped that each building has a giant hook protruding from its elaborate gables. These hooks are for pulleys, used for roping up furniture that won't fit through the narrow staircases and hauling it in through the windows.

The hooks stab at the thick blue air during the most oppressive moment of the day. It isn't exactly sunset, especially not in the winter months, but the moment right after sunset—the moment when the day has just disappeared forever, leaving behind a few ragged leaves and scattered regrets. The sky seeps like watery blue ink behind the buildings, but it's not the sky that smothers Willem. It's the lights. Along the brick walls at that moment, windows begin to light up like little slide panels, glowing white-framed pictures with tiny people in them, or yellow squares blurred by casually drawn shades. Each windows is its own separate could-have-been, a place he might have lived, a person he might have known, a scene he somehow missed. Instead he walks home through the blue ink, a lost merchant sailing across an uncharted open sea.

And then, at the door of the apartment itself, the test becomes a true challenge, just like a test on a rat who chooses one path for cheese and another for an electric shock. A choice of going in or not going in, of listening at the door to hear whether some anonymous moaning woman might be behind it, and if there is, of waiting in the suffocating hallway behind a corner, sometimes for hours, until you hear the clicking of shoes and laughter—and smell the perfume that smells nothing like how your mother used to smell, your mother who, you remember, used to smell only of coffee, or sometimes of fresh bread, but never of perfume—passing through the building's front door. One time, when Willem first arrived in Amsterdam, he walked into the apartment to find his father and a young woman sitting on the mattress on the floor, still clothed, and he passed through the room to get to his tiny bedroom on the other side. For this his father refused to serve him meals for a week. From then on Willem made a habit of sitting on the grimy tilted floor in the corridor, listening and waiting, torn between an aching curiosity to overhear as much as possible and the wave of nausea when he actually did. Only once in the countless hours of sitting in the corridor did he ever hear mention of himself. The door to his bedroom must have been left open, Willem realized, and the woman asked his father, in Dutch, if his son was living with him. Willem's father laughed and answered that Willem had been sent to boarding school in Switzerland. Willem wished he had. But by then the doors were almost all closed. The world was becoming a dark and grimy apartment vestibule, and Willem could do nothing but sit and wait in it.

Willem's father Nadav Landsmann had shell shock, from the war. He had even received a copy of an army-issued letter from a doctor stating that he had undergone psychological damage on the front, a letter he kept hidden in a drawer out of some sick refusal to throw it away, even though he went to great lengths to make sure no one ever heard about it, including his wife.

Nonetheless, there was something of his illness in the very fact that he kept the letter at all. One day when Wilhelm—back when he was Wilhelm, an old-fashioned name even then—was about eight or nine years old, he discovered the key to the locked drawer in his father's desk. First checking on tiptoe to be sure that no adult was nearby, Wilhelm scampered into his father's study in their old apartment in Vienna. He climbed up on a chair to better reach the drawer, an old wooden desk drawer crisscrossed with scrape marks, as if someone had been scratching to get into it. Wilhelm inserted the key into the lock with a fervor he could taste and turned it in slow restrained ecstasy, and was astounded and thrilled when the drawer burst forth, gaping and beautiful. Papers mostly, but ah, secret papers! No school compositions, these! Letters on official printed stationery, some of them, from places with unreadably long names. Long lists of numbers, more complicated than a web of tangled shoelaces, with return addresses in Switzerland. Telegrams, written in incoherent stunted sentences. And long brown-inked letters in Hebrew script—Yiddish, Wilhelm knew—written in a shaky hand. Wilhelm plunged his hands into the pile of treasures and pulled one out at random. A gem: a crisp yellowing sheet, typed and printed on letterhead with a giant seal of the Austro-Hungarian Empire, a horrifyingly dark, feathery eagle clutching clawfuls of spears. Wilhelm savored that picture as if it were a portrait of his mother, committing its every detail to memory. But quickly, so that he could move on to the text. And on he read:

Our diagnosis of Private Nadav Landsmann's psychological state reflects that Private Landsmann is experiencing sustained mental trauma of the type broadly
termed "shell shock." The condition varies in its effect
on patients. Some may require lifelong hospitalization;
others experience little disturbance in their civilian
lives. In Private Landsmann's case, the illness may
express itself, among other symptoms, in continuous
nervous behavior verging on paranoia, in sudden or
violent fits of temper, in obsessive or compulsive neurotic tendencies, or in the repression of normal emotional response. Further analysis will be necessary to
determine the extent and nature of Private Landsmann's
disorder.

Wilhelm Landsmann was blessed with a photographic memory,
and he quickly filed all the hard words away in his mind like a
spy memorizing a secret code, to hunt them down later in the
dictionary. Thrilled to the very bone, he continued reading:
"Recommended treatment may worsen the—"

Suddenly a giant hand dropped down from the heavens,
smashing the letter down into the drawer and slamming the
drawer shut. But the magic drawer wouldn't quite close, since
Wilhelm's fingers, unaware, were blocking it. And when the
hand noticed the reason why the drawer wasn't closing, slamming it once more wasn't enough—the hand slammed it again,
and again, and again, and again like cannon fire, faster and faster,
harder and harder, deliberately catching Wilhelm's tiny fingers
over and over, crushing them again and again until they jumped
out of the drawer like animals narrowly escaping a trap.

The shell shock was thus the easy way to explain why Nadav
shattered Wilhelm's mother's entire set of Royal Copenhagen
china one evening when he returned from work and didn't like
what she served him for dinner, or why he tore up one of Wilhelm's compositions for school—the one about explorers in the

New World—because Wilhelm had left his shoes on the floor, or why he still managed to convince nearly every woman he met, with little more than a smile and a flattering remark, that he was the one thing they needed to make their lives complete—and why, from time to time, he completed them. But only selfless people keep their illnesses to themselves. Others pass them along. Which is why it was Wilhelm's mother who wound up in a mental institution and first on the list of the doomed.

Like many undeserving people, however, Nadav had done extremely well in life, at least on paper. He was a handsome man with a Clark Gable mustache and truly captivating eyes—bright blue, though they had a certain hard edge to them that could almost cut you. Powerful eyes. After the war and a few long years of academic catch-up, he had managed to enter the university in Vienna, where he studied modern history, and after university he opened a successful business in upmarket cashmere sweaters. Much later in the game, to add insult to injury, he won the Viennese lottery. The papers, not yet propaganda machines but getting there, heralded his victory in headlines on their inside pages: RICH JEW TAKES VIENNA'S MONEY. Nadav was not interviewed for these articles, but someone who had known him from the university was on the masthead of one of the papers and had suggested this interesting angle on the usual lottery-winner story. It was still early. No one had stopped Nadav from winning the lottery. But he realized when he saw the headlines that the best thing to do with Vienna's money was to ship it out of Vienna, so on the advice of a friend in the business, he opened a branch shop in Amsterdam. He had studied some Dutch in university, inspired by a beautiful woman from Amsterdam with whom he had promptly fallen in love. (She went back to Holland and married a minister and he never saw her again. But she left him with Dutch.) Still, when he came to work one morning in Vienna to find the windows of his main store smashed, he stuck it out.

"Barbarians at the gates," Nadav muttered at the dinner table that evening. "We'll see how long we can stave them off." He had

recently finished reading yet another book about his latest obsession, the fall of the Roman Empire.

"What are barbarians?" Wilhelm asked, in a moment of
extraordinary bravery. He had heard his father use the word
before, distinctly remembered it, but when? Where? He regretted his question as soon as he asked it. Why hadn't he just waited
until later, and looked it up in the dictionary?

Nadav snarled. "People like you, you idiot, who know so little that their vocabulary doesn't even include descriptions of
themselves."

Out of hopeful habit Wilhelm looked to his mother for rescue, but she just sat there staring at her food, stirring it absently
as if she were eating alone. In less than a year she would be gone,
but she might as well have been gone already. Wilhelm copied
her movements, hiding from his father's face. His father pushed
his plate away and left the room, and his mother wordlessly got
up and began clearing the table, as if nothing had happened. This
was always how things went.

Later Wilhelm took out the dictionary. The dictionary—an
immense volume, not a children's book, with thousands upon
thousands of words—was without question his favorite book. He
liked reading just about anything, though most of the books he
wanted to read were still too hard for him. But the dictionary! He
could sit for hours flipping through its pages, reading the definitions, the etymologies, the sample sentences that made each word
seem like the cornerstone of a giant house of speech. Everything
in it was necessary, yet nothing was excluded. A perfect economy. By an early age, Wilhelm was convinced that every known
fact about the world was included in the dictionary. Why ask
people questions when the answers were all right here?

Wilhelm opened the dictionary with care, taking his time as
he turned the pages. After all, half the fun lay in the words discovered en route to the destination, the stones kicked up on the
path to reveal the diamond mines beneath. Since the word *Bar-
bar* was in the *B*'s, he turned right to the beginning, glancing at

the opening lines of the preface before he plunged into the words themselves. "Language," it read,

> is a people's most essential common bond, the one true voice of a nation. Yet the core of language lies not in a dictionary such as this, but rather in the living voice. Through the shared words they speak and hear every day, the people of a nation constantly acknowledge the lives and goals they share, their common destiny.

Idiots, Wilhelm thought once he had deciphered the text, stopping on some of the dictionary's back pages along the way to do so. They don't even like their own book. To the words, then. He passed by a picture of a man playing an accordion, squeezing his eyes closed as if to better hear his own music. In the same section he found another picture, this time of a rat-like animal with long strange thumbs, its arms and legs spread out in all directions as if flattened by a truck. The caption read, "Opossum mouse, *Acrobates pygmaeus*." The definition of *Acrobates pygmaeus*, listed under its Latin name, read, "A genus of marsupial animals found in Australasia, including the opossum mouse, which flies with the aid of its phalanges." This, naturally, meant that Wilhelm had to look up *Phalangen*, on the way to which he detoured to *Penis*, which was disappointing—"The male sexual organ; in mammals it is also the organ through which urine is expelled." *Phalangen*, meanwhile, had something to do with fingers. Staring at his own fingers, he found himself wondering whether there might be some people in the world who could use their fingers to fly, like the *Acrobates pygmaeus*. Wouldn't that be neat? Enough flying around now, though. He rushed back to the front of the book, this time directly to

Bar.bar

No picture. Immediately Wilhelm felt somewhat disappointed, since he had been half hoping that he might find a picture of

someone resembling himself. In the wake of this letdown, the
long series of derivations and grammatical details following the
word bored him. Onward he read:

> 1. Etymologically, a foreigner; a person whose language
> and customs differ from the speaker's.

Interesting, but not helpful, Wilhelm thought within the confines of his extremely meticulous schoolboy's brain. The people
who had smashed the windows were Austrians, after all, and
Wilhelm was Austrian too. And they and he and his father all
spoke German. So far, Wilhelm was not a barbarian.

> 2. Historically, a: a person who is not a Greek; b: a per-
> son living outside of the Roman Empire and its civiliza-
> tion; c: a person outside of Christian civilization.

Here things got muddier. Wilhelm ran down the list. Indeed he
wasn't a Greek, so that made him a barbarian according to 2a. But
his father wasn't Greek either, so who was he to go around calling
other people barbarians when he was one himself? That couldn't
be right. As for 2b, well, in school they had learned about the
Romans, who had lived a long time ago, in Italy. So Wilhelm certainly lived outside of the Roman Empire, and so did the people
who had smashed the windows. But again, so did his father.
Maybe his father was a barbarian after all. Definition 2c made
Wilhelm's throat hollow with nausea for a moment. It made him a
barbarian, that was certain. But if it made him a barbarian, then
it also made his father a barbarian. And it made the people who
had smashed the windows not barbarians at all. So—and here
Wilhelm's brain worked out the mathematics of it—if he was a
barbarian, and the window-smashers were barbarians, but his
father was *not* a barbarian, then definition 2c couldn't be what
his father meant. Hence Wilhelm was still not a barbarian. Wil-

helm suspected that something wasn't quite right about his calculation here, but he forged on nonetheless.

3. A rude, wild, uncivilized person.

Wilhelm sighed. The dictionary really did include everything. But luckily, something lingered below the definitions:

Note: The Greek word originally referred to speech, and it is possible that the word itself represents an attempt to imitate inscrutable foreign speech.

So the word was actually meant to sound as silly as it did? "Bar, bar, bar, bar," Wilhelm repeated to himself as he closed the dictionary, barbling his words as he went to bed.

The barbarians couldn't be staved off for long. Soon Nadav fled to Amsterdam, leaving Wilhelm's mother checked into her institution and thereby finding himself forced to take Wilhelm with him. Secretly, Nadav was dreaming of meeting that young Dutch woman again, of finding her abandoned by her husband, splashing in the water of the canals pleading for rescue, so that he could dive in and pull her up to dry land. He never would find her, but he kept looking for her, in the face of every woman he met strolling through the streets of Amsterdam, while his son barbled away at school, unable or unwilling to speak Dutch. Which brings us to the day in question. Roll film.

It is a Saturday afternoon, and Willem's father isn't home. He is sure to return shortly, though, as he usually does, to spend the afternoon in the company of yet another woman, which is always Willem's cue to leave before he guesses they might arrive. But for now the place is his. As usual, Willem sits at the small table in his father's bedroom, deciphering a textbook with his German-Dutch dictionary by his side. Biology is getting boring, though, and Willem has already skipped ahead in the book to the parts about human reproduction. He is secretly hoping for a school lesson on the subject, and he begins fantasizing about live demonstrations in class. Engrossed in his fantasies but restrained by the possibility of hearing his father's key turning in the lock at any moment, Willem sits at the table and stares across the room, dreaming. But then he notices that something on the other side of the room looks slightly amiss. Scanning the nearly empty room, he immediately determines what is wrong. The secret drawer of his father's desk—a different desk from the one left behind in Vienna, a smaller, dirtier one, but with a secret drawer nonetheless—has been left open.

Willem waits a moment, listening carefully in the silence. No one is out in the hallway, of that he is certain. Taking care not to make a sound, Willem pushes away from the little table and stands up, scampering across the room and deftly pulling open the drawer. It is almost too good to be true. There, lying right on top of the pile, is the letter with Private Landsmann's diagnosis. Willem hasn't seen it since they were in Vienna, but he barely needs to read it again. He practically knows it by heart.

The temptation is too great. Willem pulls out the letter, places it right in the middle of the empty desk, and closes the drawer. Then, knowing precisely what he is doing, he returns to the table, picks up his biology book, and retreats to his tiny bedroom, closing the door behind him.

In less than half an hour, he hears his father come in the door, talking with gusto to a laughing woman who steps into the apartment with a click of heels that makes Willem's heart flutter. Willem hears the door close and the echoes of playful kisses as he draws her further into the room. And then they both stop short.

"What's this?" he hears her say in Dutch with a giggle. "Is someone writing you love letters? You remember I can read German, don't you?" Willem stands up, leaning against his tiny window and still holding his biology book. He would cross the room to the door to hear better, but he is afraid of making a sound. He hears his father jump, lunge across the desk, and grab the letter from her hands with a laugh and a stuttered joke, but the words sound as if they are falling apart in his mouth. Willem smiles. It is almost as if, Willem thinks with stunted pleasure, his father has forgotten how to speak Dutch.

"I've just remembered," the woman says, far too loudly, "I have an appointment this afternoon. I'm sorry, but I really need to go now."

Willem's father stutters his protests, but he seems unable to find the right words. Soon his protests degenerate into begging, then into shouts, but there is nothing, nothing, he can do. The door to the apartment squeaks open, then slams shut.

There is a moment of silence, heavier than the thud of a club against a wall, and Willem's heart pounds so loudly that he wonders if it might be overheard. Then the door to Willem's room clicks open.

Willem remains in the same position he was in before, standing with his back to his tiny window, staring at his book. The apartment is silent. Willem feels his father's glare on him, but he doesn't look up to meet it. His father waits. Willem still doesn't look up. Then, without any warning, something crashes into Willem's chest and knocks him to the ground, smashing the window on the way. Willem sprawls on the floor, his limbs spread like the fingers of a flying phalanger, hearing himself squeal as he sucks at the air. As he opens his eyes amid the rain of broken glass, his pimpled cheek pressed against the floorboards, he sees his dictionary lying on the floor beside him, drowning in shattered glass. His father has thrown the dictionary at him.

Before Willem even regains his breath, his father grabs him by the shirt, lifts him off the ground, hauls him out the door and down the hall, and literally throws him out of the house, kicking him down the steps before slamming the door and locking it.

And so we find our hero, Wilhelm alias Willem, jacketless and freezing and flung out of his house, swung to the sidewalk against a lamppost that has just missed his groin. After a few minutes, he crawls back up the steps and bangs weakly on the door. No response.

Willem hates Amsterdam on principle, but there is something sort of gentle about it. The city is a maze, but at least it is a maze lined with small and interesting things. Bakeries, mostly. And chocolate stores. And candy shops. At the moment, though, the thought of food makes him feel sick and disgusting. He needs to throw things, to smash windows—not that he has the guts to actually do it, of course. Instead he gets up, slowly, and begins walking. He passes one block, then another. And another. And twelve or thirteen more. He turns a corner, then another one, then a few more, wanders even further, for what feels like days, then hurries along a canal. And suddenly, as if rising from the depths of the sea, a giant edifice appears before him. Like all good citizens of Amsterdam, Willem recognizes it immediately. The Rijksmuseum.

The Rijksmuseum, his teacher at Montessori once told their class, is the oldest museum in Europe. The Louvre and other museums may occupy older buildings, but those buildings were originally built as palaces, or train stations. The Rijksmuseum was the first building actually built for the sole purpose of housing a public museum. "In other countries, art was something reserved for the wealthy, for nobles and royalty, and it remained that way for a very long time," his teacher had said, facing the class and thereby giving Willem a short respite from the spitballs. "Here in Holland, though, we realized earlier than anywhere else that the fine and decorative arts should not be partitioned off for the upper classes. They are our national treasures. And that means that everyone in the nation shares these treasures of our kingdom, including all of you."

Willem raises his head until the back of his skull touches his neck as he stands before the giant edifice. The walls are brick, carved and sculpted, ornamented at every turn with arched glass windows and circular rosettes. It looks like a Gothic cathedral, or a towering palace, or a great train station. Funny how train stations look like cathedrals or palaces sometimes, Willem muses, when people don't even live in them—like shrines to the art of passing through. Willem is dazzled by the building's beauty. His feet take him closer to the great entry gate, drawing him step by absentminded step toward its magnificence. And then he bangs his shins against a makeshift sign on a sandwich board just outside the museum's gate. Stunned into alertness, he steps back and reads it, a hand-painted sign that probably wasn't official at all, that might well have been put up by hooligans just that day:

WELCOME TO THE RIJKSMUSEUM
No dogs or Jews allowed

Our hero stands motionless, staring at the sign, a barbarian at the gates. But he doesn't stand there long. Self-conscious twelve-year-olds—particularly underdeveloped twelve-year-old boys, the sort of twelve-year-olds that older people too often mistake for ten-year-olds, and justifiably so—always know not to stand around looking at something, because then someone nearby will notice you looking at it and use it to make fun of you. That's what happens with girls, anyhow. Not that Willem has any ability to talk to girls. It would have been hard in German. When he tries to speak Dutch, even the Jewish girls at his new school avoid looking twice at him. They flounce their little skirts, crossing and uncrossing their knees in front of his very eyes, deliberately almost. Like a slow torture. One girl, Jopie, has tortured him especially of late. Shining blond hair, glowing green eyes, perfect hands, and a hint of a slope beneath her blouse. She isn't Jewish, but her father is, and so she ended up at Willem's school. Late at night, he dreams about her popping out from around a corner in the city, dragging him into an alleyway, and stripping off her clothes in front of him. Meanwhile the boys at the Jewish school still throw spitballs at him whenever he dares step near her. In the daytime, he opens his mouth in her presence and finds it filled with heavy parchment, the words he wants to say written on scrolls under his tongue, in a forgotten language.

Willem walks back to the canal, turning away from the museum casually, glancing at the people on the streets and trying to act as if he were just a curious visitor, a tourist perhaps, just looking to see what this magnificent building is called. The part about dogs was also of interest to him. But the part about Jews? Of course not. As he turns in his attempt at casualness, he is almost hit by a bicycle. The old woman on it, dressed in a long paisley skirt like a school librarian, spins her head around like a witch to shriek evil spells at him in Dutch. His eyes focus on the street in front of him, and he ventures over to the water's edge to peer into the canal. It's a clear day, the sort of day so bright that it's practically insulting to complain of the cold, but he can't help burning with cold. A cruel day. His reflection looks back at him, his left cheek shimmering red from being scraped against the floorboards and his ears sticking out wildly from underneath his messy brown hair. Ears, he had read in his biology textbook, are one of only two parts of the body that continue growing throughout one's life. Unfortunately the other part was the nose. Being Jewish was a double curse. He examines his face, more with his bare fingertips than in the reflection—which, he notes with pleasure, is not quite detailed enough to pick up the little island chain of pimples alongside his mouth. No facial hair yet, although as he glances at the canal, he imagines that he can see a bit of a shadow on his upper lip, until a duck splashes into the water and makes his image disappear.

He pictures his father's dark mustache and rubs his own upper lip, suddenly tasting something bitter. But then he remembers something he noticed in his reflection before the duck landed. He waits until the ripples in the water dissipate and peers down at himself again. In the canal's waters, he looks like a dark young man, unhatted and unjacketed. But this young man seems much more ordinary than Willem has felt in the past few months, much more like every other young man on the streets around him. It takes a moment for him to realize why. Without his jacket, he no longer has his yellow star.

The image of this starless self enchants him. It is as if his reflection, plunged into the canal in the duck's wake, has emerged renewed from cleansing waters. Purified and anointed, he rises up and examines himself in the canal again. Suddenly he looks older, taller, more handsome. The people on bicycles riding behind him seem to turn their heads toward him in admiration, smiling and singing Dutch greetings, at least in the world reflected on the skin of the canal. He has become a grown man of Amsterdam, a lord of the city. He spins around and faces the street, smiling with confidence verging on arrogance. The city is his!

Across the street towers the monolith itself, the Rijksmuseum. Willem knows what to do. He marches right across the street without even bothering to look both ways for screeching bicycles. Let them cower before him! In an instant his lordship stands at the sign beside the golden door.

WELCOME TO THE RIJKSMUSEUM. Willem reads the words again and hears them as if they were spoken by his old teacher at the Montessori School, whom he imagines standing at the museum's gate, grinning and shaking his hand. "Welcome to the Rijksmuseum, my dear Willem! Your national treasures await you!" Willem pulls open the museum's heavy door like a bishop entering his own cathedral. A gust of heated air blows in his face, inflating his thin sweater and shirt on his skinny shoulders into flowing regal robes as he closes the door behind him.

Willem stands in line to enter the museum, posture perfect, head erect. He has urgent business to attend to; his national treasures await. The only problem, he suddenly realizes with embarrassment, is that his wallet and his yellow star travel together—one on the breast of his jacket, the other in its left-hand pocket. He has no money for admission. With shaking hands he searches the pockets of his pants. Not a single coin.

Bit by bit the line moves forward, and now the people directly in front of him have reached the ticket counter. In front of Willem is a large group, a family—a couple in their thirties, a father already balding and a mother with hair so blond it is almost white, both quite tall. They lean against the ticket counter, frowning and exhausted, while their—how many? Willem counts them—six children whine, play, and harass one another behind them. The youngest looks about three, a little blond girl with chubby legs bulging like rolls of dough between her red pinafore and her sagging white socks, and the oldest, a boy with dark hair and glasses swinging one of the younger boys around by the arm, about eleven. A girl of about five hides between her mother's legs, peeking out from under her skirt. Suddenly Willem has an idea.

"Two adults and six children," the exhausted father recites. Willem edges closer to the children in question, who are far too busy hitting each other to notice him. The little girl has concealed herself completely underneath her mother's skirt.

Willem waits, his breath held, as the ticket cashier leans forward over the counter, lowering his glasses and pointing with his finger as if tapping buttons on an invisible typewriter as he identifies each child. "One, two, three, four, five, six," he announces, handing the tickets to the father. The parents sigh with relief as the man behind the counter leans over to move the velvet rope, allowing them in. And Willem, whom the ticket cashier has counted as their mute fourth son, slinks in behind them.

Willem does not know what to expect of the Rijksmuseum. At first he is vastly disappointed. From the outset, as he wanders through the maze of endless galleries, it doesn't seem that different from the museums he once toured with his school back in Vienna. Lots of paintings of Jesus, mostly. Jesus as a baby, looking like a wrinkled, hairless old man shrunk to baby size. Jesus as a young man, with shining rays coming out of his head as people gather around him. But of course, mostly Jesus dying on the cross, moaning and bloody, jeered at by an ugly crowd and crowned with the letters "INRI"—a Latin abbreviation, Willem remembers having read somewhere, for "Jesus of Nazareth, King of the Jews." Willem walks by these paintings quickly. Then he turns a corner and enters what seems like a labyrinth of thousands of rooms filled with paintings just of fruit. It is amazing, he muses, how many ways one can arrange fruit in a bowl.

As the rooms full of fruit continue, however, Willem notices the galleries slowly being infiltrated by non-fruit, non-Jesus paintings. Portraits, mostly. Not much nudity, to Willem's disappointment. Instead the portraits show people sitting in dark rooms, their faces looking almost incandescent, as if light were not shining on them but coming from within them. Willem stares for a moment in fascination at a small painting of an old man, seated in an empty shadowed landscape, pressing his delicate white-bearded head against his palm. The title of the painting is given in Dutch: "blah blah Jeremiah blah blah blah," a wordy title that Willem doesn't feel like deciphering. The old man looks as if something tragic has happened to him, but what? Maybe his parents died, Willem thinks to himself, but then dismisses the idea. The man is old, after all, too old to mourn his own parents. But clearly he is upset about something. What?

The painting unsettles Willem. He tears himself away from it and moves on to another gallery, one filled again with those self-illuminating portraits of people in darkened rooms, most of them holding books or quill pens. There is almost always writing of some kind involved. In one painting a young woman who appears pregnant is holding a letter, looking anxious. Or more than anxious. Devastated, more like. Willem finds himself feeling sorry for her. But it's a comforting kind of sadness, like hugging someone who has fallen down or visiting a stranger in the hospital. Her problem, not his.

Countless fruit-lined rooms later, Willem comes upon a gallery with a sign beside its entrance. Suspicious of all signs now, he only glances at it, but the glance is enough to make him pause in his tracks.

POPPENHUIZEN

"Poppenhuizen"? A delicious word. Willem tastes it on his tongue, lets it dissolve in his throat like cotton candy. *Poppenhuizen*. Dollhouses?

At first Willem hesitates. Dollhouses are for girls, he thinks. Why would they be in a museum? Toys of old nobles, probably. There is a long explanatory plaque in Dutch, but Willem doesn't have the energy to try to read it—he catches only a vague date in numerals, "17th to 18th century." At any rate, he considers, the *Poppenhuizen* have clearly been classified as national treasures. Willem does a quick mental calculation. If one of his classmates should by chance walk by and spot him in the dollhouse gallery, he will never hear the end of it. But then he realizes something else. In this vault of national treasures, he has found a perfect sanctuary from the children at his new school, if that sign is really true. *No dogs or Jews allowed*. It probably wasn't official anyway, that sign, though. Nonetheless, Willem steps inside.

The dollhouses aren't really dollhouses, to Willem's vague disappointment. He was expecting miniature homes, shrunken bricks, tiny windows he could peek into. Instead, inside the gallery's glass cases stand elegant cabinets, each about three or four feet high, with polished speckled wooden doors flung open behind the display windows. The cabinets are divided into square compartments, a perfect grid.

But inside these cube-shaped spaces are outrageously beautiful miniature rooms. Parlors, bedrooms, kitchens, storage rooms, music rooms, nursery rooms, making each cabinet into a perfect replica of the interior of an elegant old-fashioned canal house. Here, for instance, is a sitting room. The windows against the cabinet's back wall are draped with perfect tiny velvet curtains, tied back with tiny golden braided ropes. Between the windows stand the fireplace, a marble mantelpiece, and then bookshelves, lined with row upon row of tiny, leather-bound volumes. Do they have real words inside them? There is no way to tell from Willem's side of the glass. In the dining room the tiny banquet table is set for a grand dinner. Each place is set with delicate blue and white china, complete with dinner plates, soup bowls, wine goblets, and tiny coffee cups. The cutlery is silver, and the ends of each tiny utensil are engraved with someone's monogram. Silver bowls of fruit, just like the ones in the museum portraits, sit in the middle of the table, their rims engraved with initials and dates. On the mantelpiece are silver candelabra. Ivory inlaid end tables stand like sentinels in the corners, holding tiny jewelry boxes. Upstairs, canopy beds with perfectly arranged pillows lie waiting for someone's miniature dreams.

Willem presses his nose against the glass until he almost feels as if he lives in one of the rooms. Suddenly he wishes that he could shrink, shrink, shrink down until he was the right size to fit in one of those velvet-covered chairs. Then he could step into one of the houses and run through all of it—sitting on all of the plush sofas, eating off the blue and white china with the silver forks, sitting by the fireplace and reading all of the tiny books on the tiny shelves, undisturbed. Or searching for keys in secret places, and then opening the house's countless secret drawers. Suddenly Willem notices something moving inside the room and shudders in fright. In a moment, though, he realizes that what has moved are his own eyes—his face is reflected in the gilt-framed mirror above the fireplace.

The real problem with Willem's plan to shrink himself down into the tiny rooms, of course, is that they are already occupied. Each of the houses is populated by little dolls, dressed in strange costumes, as if they are going out to a masquerade. But then Willem understands that the dolls are a few centuries behind the times. The men wear black trapezoidal hats and shoes with big

metal buckles on them, dark enough to blend into the upholstery
except for their starched white collars. The women wear little
white covers over their hair, and big dresses with lace bodices.

Yet there aren't quite enough dolls around. Each house seems
occupied only by a few dolls each, perhaps four or five at most.
But the bedrooms can accommodate more than that, and the banquet tables are set for many more. There must be more people
living in these houses, Willem thinks, who are simply off on a
journey somewhere. After all, these are the seventeenth and
eighteenth centuries, which means that Dutch people have places
to go. Willem thinks of the merchants of the house going off on
their ships to—where?

To India, of course, cruising off on voyages for the Dutch
East India Company, or to Indonesia or the South Pacific—the
"Dutch East Indies," they had learned at school—or to Dutch
Guiana in South America, or to Curaçao or St. Maarten in the Caribbean, all within the world of the great Dutch mercantile
empire. (In the past, everyone conquered the world for fifteen
minutes.) Willem imagines a giant ship with white billowing sails
pulling alongside the shore of some distant tropical island,
greeted by naked natives in hollowed-out log canoes. He pictures
the topless women for a moment, garlanded with flowers above
their completely revealed breasts, reveling in the thought. It is as
if he is there, touching them. And India—here Willem even con-
jures up the smell, and his eyelids droop as he takes a deep drag
of incense, blown out of some sort of exotic pipe as dark
women—also topless, he muses—make offerings to their gods.
Willem pictures a shipwreck on an Indian coast, the poor Western merchants lost in a land they never intended to explore,
thousands of miles from home. It is easy to picture the scene during daylight hours, Willem thinks. But what if such a shipwreck
had happened at night? What if they had washed up on this mysterious shore under a black velvet window shade drawn over the
sky, feeling for each other's hands and faces in the thick wet
night, crawling onto dry sand without knowing who might be

waiting for them on land at daybreak? Was that humid blind man's beach the farthest anyone could possibly be from a warm little glowing Dutch house?

Perhaps more likely, Willem thinks to himself, the dollhouse people would have gone to New Amsterdam, the Netherlands' greatest loss. And here Willem's fantasies run wild. He knows English from school in Vienna, reads his English-German diction- ary with passion, lust almost—he knows English better than Dutch, even though he doesn't often hear it spoken. But some- how when he'd stare at the map on the wall back at the Montes- sori School, he always found his eye wandering across the Atlantic, right to left as if reading a sentence out of the Hebrew Bible. Vienna was indiscernible on the world map from his exile at the back of the room; Amsterdam sank into a muddy delta of borderlines and riverlines, practically lost beneath the sea. But New York! Somehow Willem feels drawn to New York, his mind's eye climbing up the metal skyscrapers he has seen in photo- graphs, crawling through the cavernous canyons of streets. The slightest thought of it enchants him—the buildings so tall, the sidewalks so wide, the streets laid out in perfect rectangles so that no one could ever get lost or disappear into them, the blocks of buildings divided into neat columns and rows like a case of eggs. What fools the Dutch were to lose that little island, that case of gleaming eggs, brimming with people's eager lives always just about to hatch! The dot on the map with its loud black letters in Dutch, NIEUW-YORK, stood out like a stout peg on a coatrack, waiting for something—someone?—to hang on it. Would the dollhouse people go there, building themselves new glowing box houses for a new world?

No, Willem decides. He knows where they have gone. To the Barbary Coast, attacked by barbarian pirates, never to return. Some of them don't even make it that far. They leave Amsterdam and are apprehended by bandits, their throats slit before they reach Hamburg or even the Amsterdam city limits, their bleeding bodies left to freeze, staining the ice red on the side of the snowy road. Outside of this perfect little house, this glowing fed and heated sanctuary, barbarians were scratching at the gates, held off by nothing more than thin, wavy windowpanes of imported glass!

"Young man, you mustn't touch the glass. You could get shocked, you know."

The voice makes Willem jump. He has plunged so deep into his barbarian dreams that he didn't even notice the museum guard creeping up on him, uniformed in black, nightstick in hand. The guard is a fat man, with thick hands and a stomach lurching over his wide leather belt. His bald head peeks out from under his cap, crowning a pink face with bright blue eyes. He is breathing through his mouth, panting almost. As he lowers his face to Willem's height, Willem can detect a vague smell of fish on his breath. Instinctively Willem steps away from him, moving his nose just slightly away from the glass. The guard is joking about the glass being electrified, but Willem doesn't know that. Still, he feels a need to disobey this smelly man's orders at all costs. These are his national treasures!

Deliberately not looking at the guard and staying as close to the glass as possible, Willem focuses his stare on the dollhouse lavatory. In the split second after inhaling the sardine breath, Willem has decided that he will force himself to look at the dollhouse, even though he knows he can't stand looking at something while being watched. It reminds him of his father's constant lurking around the empty apartment, where Willem can't even open his bedroom door without eliciting insults. But to his surprise, Willem finds that the lavatory, which he had barely noticed before, is actually one of the most intriguing rooms in the house. On second glance, he sees that it is more of a storeroom than a lavatory. There isn't any plumbing, of course—this is, after all, the seventeenth or eighteenth century—but there are basins, basins upon basins, wide basins for washing, dented basins for shaving, round basins serving as noble urinals, all made of that blue and white china. Even the chamber pots are beautiful. All that water partitioned off, controlled, brought within the house's hallowed halls on condition that it stay within those basins. The house could flood, of course, if the water seeped in from the man-made ground. It probably did flood, in fact, since flooding was one of those three X's on the city seal. But within this room, one is safe from water's ravages. Thinking about all that water gives Willem a sudden urge to urinate. He pushes the idea out of his mind.

"You like those dollhouses, do you? I've never seen a boy who liked the dollhouses," the guard says, his voice curling up around the word "liked" in a way that reminds Willem of a tiny worm creeping unexpectedly out of a piece of fruit. Willem understands every word of the guard's Dutch. He feels his face going red, and a brief tremor between his legs. He opens his mouth for a second to answer and notices that his lips have dried together, fused by not talking. In an instant, though, he closes his mouth again. A horrible thought crosses his mind: Even if he wants to speak, he can't. Not just because his Dutch is awful but because his Dutch is awful in a particular way. If the guard hears his accent, Willem calculates, the game is up. WELCOME TO THE RIJKSMUSEUM: *No dogs or Jews allowed*. Was the sign outside the museum official, or was it not? Willem swallows, cornered by the guard's smiling stare. He looks at him and nods, then turns back to face the dollhouse. Better to seem like a girl than a Jew.

"Well, a boy who likes dollhouses. You know, I actually like them myself. It's amazing how much detailed work goes into them. The craftsmanship is equal to a lot of the better paintings in the museum, I think. Certainly better than all those still lifes of fruit bowls. If you ask me, they're undervalued as works of art."

Poor man, Willem thinks to himself. He glances at the man's left hand and sees no wedding band, only a set of sweaty fingers. Does he have a wife, Willem wonders? Children? Friends? Or had he been condemned to walk the earth in solitude, speaking only to old women on bicycles and stringy boys who sneak into museums? Willem shudders without meaning to, shifting his weight back and forth from one foot to the other. A little dance almost.

"Cold? We've been having horrible weather lately, haven't we? All this rain. I don't understand why people would spend the one nice day this week in a museum." The guard sniggers, a repulsive little noise. Willem shakes his head and leans his nose toward the glass once more, suddenly thinking again of how noses are one of only two parts of the human body that continue growing throughout one's life. Of all the things to keep growing. He glances at the miniature chamber pots again, wishing that the guard would go away. No such luck. Meanwhile the man has inspired him. He begins thinking about rain, about pouring watery rain, water flowing in and out of the chamber pots, water seeping through the dollhouse foundation, rain drowning out his reflection in the canal. Willem begins tapping his feet on the ground, more and more loudly. Something makes him impatient, makes him want to end this encounter as soon as possible. But what?

"Do you have to go to the toilet?"

Willem shakes his head no. But even the head-shaking goes on too long, becoming part of his little bladder-dance. He tries to stop tapping his feet and comes within instants of wetting his pants. Instead he pounds the floor again. The guard laughs at him and stoops down, an embarrassing stoop, to Willem's eye level.

"Well, you might not like talking, but you still manage to get your thoughts across, don't you! Look, I have to go to the john myself. Let's go together, all right? The route is too confusing for you to find it by yourself from here anyway."

And the two of them walk on together, until, halfway there, alarm bells go off inside Willem's brain.

The urinal. Suddenly, as they hurry through room upon fruit-filled room, Willem's entire future seems to be pending between his legs. In some ways, of course, it is a familiar feeling. After all, Willem is twelve years old, and at this point more and more of his thoughts seem to have their origins there. But this time there is real danger in it. In America, Bill will think to himself years later, people all look different, until you take off their clothes and discover that they are really all the same. In Europe, people all look the same until you take off their clothes and discover that they are different, irreparably different, differences scarred into their flesh. He can't very well run away now, though. Besides, he has to go.

Just before they reach the men's room, a woman in her early twenties struts through the corridor, her skirt hugging her hips and swishing around her calves as she swings each leg in front of the other. Willem notices. The guard nudges Willem, muttering down at him. "A knock-out, isn't she."

Willem nods and quickly looks to the floor. The last thing he needs at this point is to start fantasizing about some girl. The guard leads him into the men's room and the door swings shut behind them. No one else is there.

"You got a girlfriend yet?" the guard asks with a smile, his voice bubbling like a city fountain.

Willem feels his face turning red. He pictures Jopie and shakes his head. No.

The guard steps up to one of the urinals, unbuttons his pants, and starts babbling.

"It's rough at your age. It gets better, you'll see. I remember when I was about your age—well, a few years older really, when I was more of a man, if you know what I mean—and I fell so horribly in love with this girl. Her name was Lies, and wow, was she a knockout. Big on top, big on the bottom, slim in the middle, unbelievable. My sole purpose in life was to see her naked. I had a friend who lived across the street from her, and he had a little spyglass. I used to go over to his house with a bunch of other guys and we'd try to see whether she was home, just waiting for her to show up in the window. And she'd show up all right. The thing is, she knew we were there. She'd lean over by the window and start slowly opening her shirt, like she was really going to take her clothes off right in front of us, but then, right when she got to about the third button, she'd pull the shades. Right then!

Just to drive us nuts! Peter got her in the end, but boy, I would have killed for her."

Willem swallows, picturing the Peter who used to spit at him at Montessori. Peters always spit at people, Willem thinks to himself. It figures that the ones who treat you like dirt end up with the girl.

He steps toward a urinal, two down from the guard's, and opens his pants, terrified. A shameful lump of tortured flesh emerges, used for lewd thoughts at Jopie's expense, late at night after his father's women have gone home. In Willem's new school, they teach the Bible—sort of like in his old school at Montessori, actually, except this Bible is only about half the size. Most of the time Willem passes school time staring at the ceiling, or flipping through textbooks to find interesting pictures in chapters the class hasn't reached yet. The Bible the class uses doesn't have any illustrations—Willem has checked. But once as he was flipping through looking for one, a line in the Dutch translation caught his eye, in something called the Book of Job. The line was so strange that he copied it into his notebook, and he was sure he had mistranslated it as he converted it into German in his head. But that evening he checked in the dictionaries and found that the verse really did mean what he thought it meant: "After my skin has been thus destroyed, then from my flesh I shall see God."

The line was strange enough to make him turn to the beginning of the Book of Job to see if something there might explain it. He found no explanation, but what he did find—even though he had to translate it word by word, until he was spending almost all of his waiting time in the hallway working on it—swallowed him whole. Job, it seemed, was the name of a man who was "simple and upright, and feared God and shunned evil," a happy man, apparently, with happy children and prosperous flocks, who always thanked God for what he had. Then one day someone called "the adversary" (Willem wasn't quite sure about that part, suspecting something funny in the Bible's footnotes, yet he continued nonetheless) asked God, teasing him almost, whether all Job's good faith wasn't something of a sham, since, after all, Job didn't have much to complain about. God decided to let the adversary play with Job a bit, and this was where things started to get interesting. First, all of Job's flocks were stolen, and his children killed, through various disasters. Job, however, took this rather well, continuing his praise of God despite their deaths. Then Job was stricken with some sort of skin disease. The details here eluded Willem's dictionary skills, but it seemed that Job ended up sitting in a pit and scraping himself with a broken plate (and here Willem winced, remembering his mother's china smashed on the floor in Vienna). Three friends came to visit Job at that point, but as Willem read their names— So-and-so the Something-ite, Somebody-else the Somewhere- else-ite, Somebody-else the Nowhere-ite—he suspected that they weren't really Job's friends at all, but rather just some sort of emissaries, reporting their own boring points of view on why Job deserved all this hard luck. It was only then that Job rose up and cursed his God.

Willem found himself feeling proud of Job for this, and the so-called friends and their preachy arguments against the poor guy were making Willem angry. But then came the best part, when God answered Job "out of the whirlwind," roaring at him: "Where were you when I laid the foundations of the earth?" Where indeed, Willem wondered as he crouched in the hallway, where the house's sinking foundation made the floor slant down to the canal. But Willem never got to read the rest of God's answer to Job, because that night his father, furious with the woman who had just left the apartment before Willem came in, took Willem's book and threw it in the building's furnace.

At the urinal, Willem looks down at himself, at the purplish scar where his skin had been destroyed at his circumcision when he was eight days old. He thinks of Jopie and his face burns. He wraps his fingers around it further down than usual, trying to seem casual as he does his best to conceal himself, just in case the guard should glance to the side and notice something missing. *No dogs or Jews allowed*. Probably the sign wasn't even official at all, he thinks to himself, trying to steady his trembling fingers. The guard, however, is standing at his urinal whistling something, and doesn't take much interest in Willem. When Willem has arranged his fingers as best he can, he relaxes and begins to urinate. But then, as he glances down at his strangely intertwined fingers, one thumb on top of the other, he suddenly remembers something that happened at his grandmother's house long ago. And as he empties his bladder he feels himself about to cry.

Willem doesn't know where his grandmother's house was, but he knows it was far away, very far away—so far away that he and his father and his mother had to take a train at night to get there, in a special sleeping car in which he and his mother shared a bed. (Where was his father during the night train ride? Willem thinks hard but cannot remember.) It was scary riding a train at night, but also thrilling, like being in a boat on an open ocean. The porters would knock on their cabin door to ask if they needed anything, and his mother would smile and say no, nothing, thank you, in her public voice that sounded clear and whole, like a single tap of a spoon on a wineglass. And then the door would close and they would be alone together in their clean and glowing room, a box of light whizzing through an endless sea of darkness. His mother would hold him and play games with him, drawing pictures with him in a notebook until it was time to go to sleep. Then they would climb into bed, a funny bed with stiff white sheets and too many blankets, and his mother would turn out the lights, falling asleep almost instantly, as if she existed only for him during the day and then, secretly at night, returned to another world. But Wilhelm had no past, no other world to return to. His only world was the one inside the glowing sleeping car. And so he would press his nose to the windowpane and stare out into the darkness, where he immediately saw that the train wasn't actually going anywhere—he could feel it moving, sure, but outside the window was nothing but a blanket of blackness, a deep and heavy curtain drawn over the entire world. He would stare at that dark curtain until it terrified him, and then he would wake up his mother and tell her that he had had a bad dream. Each time she believed him.

His grandmother's house was also scary at night, but only on the outside. Outside the house—he had sneaked outside once while his mother was busy with something else, enjoying the brief moment before she noticed he was missing and raced outside to find him—he could hear the clopping of the neighbor's milk goat circling the tree where it had been tied when the fence was broken, and some other animals rustling about in their sleep, and he glanced back at the house, where he could see his grandmother standing at the stove by the lit-up window with a look of distraction on her face as she cooked. It was his grandmother's house, not his grandfather's. Wilhelm had never met his grandfather, and neither had Wilhelm's father—he had died before Wilhelm's father was born. His grandmother stood alone, framed in the window. Through the adjacent window, Wilhelm could see his father talking to her, frowning, pacing back and forth. It was strange, this view. Wilhelm knew it was one room, but if he hadn't been inside before, he wouldn't have realized it. It could have been just two little panels, a diptych, photographs framed side by side, not even related at all.

But inside the house it was cozy and warm and small and safe. Wilhelm's mother sat on the crooked wooden floor with him after dinner as he drew on blank pieces of paper with charcoal pencils his grandmother had given him. He had found some leaves during the day, and his mother taught him how to make leaf rubbings, laying the leaves on the floor (Wilhelm had wondered whether this offended the floor's dead wooden planks, but the leaves were from plants, not trees) and pressing against them with paper, scratching his pencils—gently now—back and forth and back and forth and back and forth across the paper until a leaf would emerge, magically, as if he had conjured it into being. Later, when he had made too many leaf pictures, he tried to trace his hand on the page. But it kept slipping off the paper, and soon his mother took his hand and gently pressed it down on the page for him, laying each of her fingers on top of each of his as he moved his pencil around their stack of hands, her thumb on his thumb. Her hand was warm and soft, and he felt, in each of his fingers where his touched hers, as if some gentle and beautiful current were flowing from her fingers to his. His pencil skipped, tracing her fingers instead of his own and catching their silhouettes on the paper. "See, now you're making an image of your own hand, but you're also making an image of mine," she said.

"Her image is yours and yours is hers anyway, you should know, because all men are made in the image of God," his grandmother suddenly said from her chair. Wilhelm's grandmother spoke in a funny way that you could only understand after you got used to listening to her, and sometimes not even then, with all the wrong vowels and weird words and phrases, as if she were reading from some strange old book. (Yiddish, that was.)

Wilhelm's father growled in German. "Mother, can't you stop filling the child's head with this barbarian trash?"

His grandmother snapped her head up and looked at Wilhelm's father. "Listen, young man, when you go back to your precious city, you can fill his head with whatever nonsense you want. But when I'm in this house I say what I mean." Wilhelm's grandmother was the only person who could talk back to his father and win his silence. And silent he remained until they returned to Vienna.

But now Willem stands at the urinal, holding himself with one thumb on top of the other, wondering whether or not he is made in the image of God. Is he even a man yet? No, that much is clear. And what God would stand at a urinal, an intruder in a house of treasures not his own, hiding his sex in his hands because he was afraid a stupid guard would see that he had the Covenant sealed into his flesh? Will any girl ever want him, with his skin destroyed? From his flesh, will he ever see God? Right now all he sees is his mother's face, and as the guard finishes and turns away, Willem squints to keep his tears from sliding down into the urinal's drain. If I ever get up the courage to talk to Jopie, he realizes, or to kiss her, or to kiss any girl at all, or to ask a girl to marry me, my mother will never know it. In that moment, he suddenly understands that he will never see his mother again.

The walk home from the museum is much too short. The city has grown dark. All around him, lights begin to flicker on in the houses lining the canals, illuminating the rooms inside them like little slide panels of distant lands. When Willem arrives at his own house, he sees that the light inside his apartment is also glowing. Inside, his father sits at his desk, writing on a piece of paper. His father raises his head for a moment, as if hearing something outside, but then returns to his writing. From his side of the window, he cannot see out. Willem rings the bell and pounds on the door, but there is no answer. His father knows he is there, Willem is sure, but that hardly matters. Willem is forced to watch and wait.

And so Willem watches. It is almost like a silent film. His father writes intently, squinting his eyes and furrowing his brows, pausing frequently, as if after every word. Willem is puzzled. On most days when he notices his father working at his desk—before ducking into his room again, before his father notices him noticing—he is amazed at how quickly his father writes. But now his father is sitting like a schoolboy, struggling to move his pen, his teeth clenching his lower lip, frightened. Like Willem.

The silent film continues as Willem's father puts down the pen to read through the page he has just written, slowly, moving his lips. After what feels like years, he lifts the page off the table, folds it carefully, and slides it into an envelope. And then the silent movie ends: Willem's father stands up and walks away. A moment later, he lets Willem in.

They do not speak to each other. Once they are both inside

the apartment, Willem's father turns his back to Willem and returns to his desk. But Willem has noticed something new in the house. Sitting on the table are five envelopes, each addressed, in his father's handwriting, to America.

Willem has noticed stacks of letters like these in the house two or three times before, but his father has always snatched them away before Willem could get a good look at them. But this time, glancing again at his father's back, Willem reaches for them as silently as possible and flips through the little pile. Five letters, yes, all going to America. Three to New York, and two to somewhere he has never heard of: New Jersey. But the names on the letters intrigue him even more. They are strange names, weird names, names like the ones he remembers hearing at his grandmother's house, long ago. Moyshe. Shmuel. Freydl. And all five of them seem to have the same last name, even though the addresses are all different. But they are also all American. Willem's father has written it in giant letters on each of them: "U.S.A." Who are these people? How does his father know them? Willem knows better than to ask questions. Instead he places the letters back on the table exactly as they were and slinks into his bedroom, shutting the door behind him.

He had been hungry before, and tired, and cold. But now, lying on his mattress on the floor, he can think of nothing but those letters. In Willem's dreams, the names on the envelopes come to life, five people dancing in a circle in some giant American house, and Willem dances in the center. Between their shouts of laughter, Willem hears the sounds of someone pounding on the door. It is his father, but they refuse to let him in.

As an old man, Bill Landsmann doesn't like movies. He prefers slides, leaving context to the imagination, writing his own script. Instead of a movie, Bill Landsmann might have presented, to anyone who wanted to see it, a single image: his father sitting in the window writing a letter, framed only by possibility, unaware that this moment was already buried under so many other moments that came after it—unaware, sitting behind the thin pane of glass, that he was drowning in all the choices that would ultimately destroy him.

Dara Horn

In my academic work, I became intrigued by how early modern Hebrew and Yiddish literature almost constantly makes reference to the Hebrew Bible, even while challenging the religious tradition. I wondered whether it was possible to create this sort of literature— using biblically anchored language within a secular text—in English. I wanted to create a different style for American Jewish literature, one more connected to the Jewish literary tradition of constant reference to ancient text.

In the Image is mainly a contemporary American story full of biblical allusions, although "Barbarians at the Gates" is not a good illustration of that. However, "Barbarians at the Gates" does illustrate something else I wanted to do: to separate the Jewish experience from the experience of anti-Semitism, to defy "Holocaust literature," which ultimately teaches that what is worth knowing about Jewish life is only that it ended. I also wanted to explore the deeper tragedy that everyone who doesn't read Yiddish has forgotten, which is that Jewish communities in Eastern Europe were already really, genuinely devastated twenty-five years before the Holocaust, during the First World War. And I wanted to show how, even in the most dire of circumstances, as Jews and as people, we alone are responsible for the choices we make and for kind of people we choose to be.

ORDINARY PAIN

Michael Lowenthal

Larry Blank feared he was as nondescript as his name. His nose was normal, not hawkish or wide, his hair the shade of soggy cardboard. He had dirt-brown eyes, freckleless skin. Each year he measured just what the growth charts would predict, so that in all of his class photographs—arranged by height—he was lost in the middle of the middle row.

If Larry wasn't particularly unpopular, it was because disfavor required being noticed. He had an official "best friend," Vance—who, as son of Larry's parents' bridge partners, couldn't shirk the obligation—but other than that, no one much talked to him. Like the Muzak piped into department stores, or the pastel wallpaper of doctors' waiting rooms, Larry seemed fashioned to elude people's awareness.

Above everything, it was the name: Larry Blank. The joke was so boring, his fellow seventh-graders didn't bother teasing him. They had names with history, badges of pride. Vance was short for Vanzetti, the wrongly executed anarchist, Vance's first cousin three times removed. Tanisha Jefferson's ancestors had been slaves at Monticello, and people shushed deferentially when she spoke of them.

At Mooretown Friends, where no one lacked for Volvos or summer homes, true status came from underprivilege. More valuable than country club credentials was the ability to claim membership in the disadvantaged—the groups lauded by their social studies text. Larry, resigned to his own blandness, wished at least for a heritage of oppression. But his name meant nothing—literally.

He complained to his parents. "Blank? What kind of a name is that?"

"Ours," his father said. "That's what kind."

"Okay, so maybe you were stuck with that. But Larry? It doesn't stand for anything."

"You're named after your grandfather," his mother explained, "but we didn't want kids to make fun. If we called you Ludwig, you'd have griped we didn't name you something normal."

"I wouldn't have," Larry insisted.

"Yes you would."

Larry knew little about his grandparents, who had died before his birth. They were German, he dimly sensed; they'd sold insurance. He asked if there were photos, and his mother produced a single snapshot, from Marienbad in 1929: his grandfather strolling on the promenade. The man was huge—three hundred pounds at least—but the bulk only added to his elegance. His pants flared up like a funnel, the trashcan-width waist hoisted by dainty suspenders.

Larry pictured himself as fat as Ludwig, so fat that strangers would stare. He climbed into his father's too-big pants and shirt, padded them with pillows until his mirror image bulged. It gave him an idea.

He went to the kitchen and wolfed half a package of Chips Ahoy! At the point when he thought he would be sick, he dunked two tablespoons of strawberry Quik into a glass, then filled it with half-and-half. He guzzled until his lips glowed pink.

Larry decided to forge a career as the fat kid. Obesity would make him the butt of bathroom graffiti, the target of playground taunts. He'd be the underdog; everyone would know his name.

And so he ate. He ate and ate, sneaking downstairs each night after his parents had gone to bed and gobbling cinnamon grahams smeared with peanut butter. He stuffed himself with

Snickers bars. Beer Nuts became a secret breakfast. He studied the fat content on nutritional labels, calculating how to ingest four and five hundred percent of his daily requirement.

But no matter how much he gorged, Larry didn't gain. Every day he weighed in on his mother's digital scale. One hundred four pounds, one hundred three—how could he lose in the midst of his pigging?! His metabolism defied all logic, a perpetual motion machine. It burned up everything he offered it.

After three weeks Larry quit, cursing his body as he'd cursed his name. He was a prisoner of his normalcy.

In a year he would be due for a bar mitzvah. His parents enrolled him in Hebrew school.

Larry had never thought of himself as Jewish. He didn't have curly hair like Jonah Greenberg. He didn't have the honking schnozz. And the Blanks were hardly observant. Once or twice they'd erected a Chanukah bush; most years they didn't go that far.

But a bar mitzvah, his father said, was nonnegotiable. He had done it, as had his father and his father, too, and now it was Larry's turn. Larry was perplexed by the sudden bow to tradition, annoyed that it would claim his time. With the fat project a resounding failure, he needed to find other avenues to distinction, and Hebrew school didn't seem a winning bet. Jews were plentiful at Mooretown Friends, probably more so than birthright Quakers.

But what choice did a twelve-year-old have? Hebrew school met Wednesday nights and Saturdays at the synagogue bordering the golf course. His parents gave him money for the cab.

Mrs. Hershman, the teacher, taught the "aleph-bet" and made them sing it to the tune of the "A-B-Cs." The language was difficult. Larry's voice cracked. He lip-synched and tried to look convincing.

The second hour of each class was modern Jewish history.

They started with the Inquisition, then fast-forwarded to pogroms. "Can anyone tell me what a pogrom was?" asked Mrs. Hershman. She rolled the *r* with an Old World accent, as if relishing an ethnic delicacy.

Miriam Goodman, a froggy little girl whose eyes floated on the verge of being crossed, raised her hand. "A pogrom is when they massacre a whole town of Jews just because they're Jews. It's a kind of unfair prosecution."

"Persecution," corrected Mrs. Hershman.

"Yeah, persecution. My great-uncle Boris was in a pogrom in Latvia. He and his sister were the only ones who survived. They hid in an outhouse for three days with no food or water and rats biting at their toes. But they escaped, and they saved the family candlesticks. My mom's going to give me them when I get married."

Mrs. Hershman walked over to Miriam and placed a reverent hand on her shoulder. "You should be proud of such tradition in your family. That kind of courage has allowed the Jewish people to survive through the centuries."

Other kids piped up with questions. "Were they down inside the outhouse holes?" "Didn't the rat bites get infected?" Miriam responded with the patient largesse of a movie star doling autographs. She told and retold the tale of Uncle Boris until it was time for class to end.

Slinking out, Larry seethed with jealousy. Even here, the spotlight shone away from him.

The next week was Zionism, and the week after that, the Holocaust. Mrs. Hershman passed out time lines of Hitler's rise. A glossary defined *Judenrein, Reichstag, yellow star*. The students had secured parental signatures to see "a film of disturbingly explicit nature." In grainy black and white, they viewed corpses stacked like cordwood, heaps of shoes and eyeglasses and shorn hair. Women stood shivering before the camera, their naked breasts shrunken bags of skin.

When the movie ended, Larry heard sounds that might be crying. "Six million murdered," Mrs. Hershman said. "Think how lucky we are to be alive."

"Did you know anyone who was killed?" asked Ethan Taub. He was the only one in the class worse than Larry at the aleph-bet. In elementary school he'd been held back two grades.

"I'm too young," said the teacher, turning on the lights. "But my parents lost many loved ones. I'm sure your parents and grandparents did, too. Later, we'll be doing oral histories. But does anyone know right now what happened to their families in the Holocaust?"

No one raised a hand, not even Miriam Goodman. The fluorescent tubes ticked expectantly.

"Well, thank HaShem if no one here has tragedy in their family. But this is still our collective tragedy, as Jews." Mrs. Hershman tugged the movie screen's cord so that it snapped up with a ghostly vinyl shriek.

Larry thought of the living ghosts in the wartime footage, stick-thin men with grotesque blowfish stomachs. He thought of the paunch he had tried to cultivate. "My grandfather was from Germany," he blurted.

Mrs. Hershman's eyebrows perked. "Your grandfather? When did he come over?"

"He didn't," Larry said. "He died there."

The lack of sound that greeted this announcement was louder than any gasp. Larry felt tendrils of attention stretching for him. The room's walls seemed to tilt in his direction.

"I'm so sorry," said Mrs. Hershman. "It must be hard to talk about. Do you know which camp?"

Larry's pulse clogged the veins in his neck. His brain felt wobbly and wonderful. He picked a name from the movie: "Buchenwald."

"Yes," said the teacher, as if she'd known.

There were stirrings of amazement from his classmates. Ethan Taub asked tactlessly, "Was he gassed?"

"Now class, remember," warned Mrs. Hershman, "this isn't Twenty Questions. We're talking about a real person's life."

"It's okay," Larry said. "It's just, you know . . . I'm not used to saying stuff."

He was stalling. The truth was, Ludwig had died of diabetes in 1935, well tended in a Berlin hospital. Larry's father had been a year old at the time; his uncle Gene, two-and-a-half. Within six months, their mother had the family settled in Connecticut.

"He wasn't gassed," Larry said. "He was shot. In an escape attempt." He recalled Miriam's pogrom account, how each new particular burnished her gleaming aura. "My grandfather made it outside the fence," he went on, "but then he turned back to help his brother through, and the guards shot both of them. His name was Ludwig. That's how come my parents called me Larry—the same first letter and all. I guess I'm his namesake, or whatever."

"That's quite a legacy to live up to," said Mrs. Hershman.

"I know," Larry said, "I know it is."

After class, not wanting to squander his success all at once, he rushed past his thronging classmates to the street. He imagined the cab that drove him home a limousine.

Riding to regular school the next morning, already in need of another fix, Larry schemed ways to export his celebrity. In homeroom, he doodled Stars of David on his spiral notebook. *Jude*, he wrote in block letters, remembering the previous night's film. *Achtung, Shoah, Buchenwald.* He added approximations of Hebrew characters.

Nobody was biting, so finally Larry knocked his notebook on the floor. Tanisha Jefferson handed it back to him.

"What's all that mumbo-jumbo?" she asked.

"What?" Larry said, playing dumb.

"This. These stars. These words in Jewish."

"Oh, that. Just stuff about the Holocaust. Today's the anniversary of when my grandfather was killed."

Tanisha's jaw dropped so wide she almost lost her Bubble Yum. "Your grandfather got killed in the Holocaust?"

"Yeah," Larry said. "He was shot."

Two other kids screeched their chairs around to listen.

Larry followed the same script he'd invented at Hebrew school, only this time with added details. Ludwig had been the ringleader of an underground rebellion. Because of his cunning, seventeen men escaped, but then the guard they'd bribed ratted on them. That's when they made a run for it. Alone, Ludwig could have managed, but he had to carry his sick brother, who was so weak he couldn't support himself. They caught him at the fence and gunned him down.

By lunchtime, everyone knew. People fought for space at the cafeteria table. Trays of American chop suey almost overturned.

Larry maintained a pose of superiority. He would tell them— yes, he would—but first they had to settle down, because this was no circus sideshow attraction. This was history. This was remembrance.

Larry added backstory to his fantasy. To the gathered crowd he explained that Ludwig hadn't gone easily. When the Nazis came for him, he refused; he wouldn't open the door for a band of thugs. The Nazis broke in and found him in the kitchen, holding on to the massive stove. "I'm not leaving," he told them. "This is my home." An SS officer tried to pull him free, but Ludwig in his anger was too strong. A second Nazi grabbed him, then a third, but still Ludwig wouldn't budge. "I am not leaving," he repeated. "I won't let go." Finally, the officer grabbed a meat cleaver from the wall. With one clean chop he severed Ludwig's thumb. "What happened?" he mocked. "Why'd you let go?"

Larry paused to let the horror sink in. He took a bite of his American chop suey, now congealed to a gloppy mass. Its slimi- ness in his throat inspired him further.

"This might not be appropriate for mealtime," he warned. He was a genius. He couldn't stop himself. "There was this time in Buchenwald—that's the concentration camp they took him to.

My grandfather felt sick, probably from the soup they were fed, made with nasty sewage water. After dinner, when they got back to the bunkhouse he threw up. His hunk of bread wasn't digested yet, so the other prisoners dove and tried to steal it. That's how starving they were. My grandfather had to get down on the floor, too, and fight them for a piece of his own puke."

"Eew," Tanisha groaned, and dropped her fork. "I don't think I can take any more of this."

Someone assented, but everyone stayed put. Larry was now the sun around which they all revolved; they leaned phototropically for more.

"It's not pretty," Larry said, "but it's the truth."

Vance sat across from him, glumly gnawing a carrot from his brown-bag lunch. Larry figured he was peeved, because as his best friend, Vance expected first dibs on information. Later, Larry would apologize, explaining that he'd never mentioned Ludwig because the subject was too touchy in his family. He hadn't planned to blab, but then Tanisha asked.

Vance crumpled his empty lunch bag and hook-shot it into a trashcan. He stared at Larry. "I don't believe you," he said.

"What?" Larry said, even though he'd heard.

"I don't believe you. You're making it up."

"Oh shit," said Tanisha. "He's telling you about his people getting murdered, and you're calling him a liar? Oh shit."

Larry gripped the table's edge, so invested in the story that his rage at being doubted was genuine. "What don't you believe?" he said. "You think the Holocaust didn't happen?"

"Of course it happened. That doesn't mean your grandfather ate his own puke."

"What, you want a doctor's report?"

Larry chortled, hoping to persuade the others that Vance was ridiculous. But no one joined in. Vance's skepticism had tainted their credulity.

"Tell me this," Vance said. "Your grandfather died, right?"

"Yeah."

"And so did his brother. So how do you know exactly what happened in the camp?"

It was a good question. Larry wanted to shoot back with "How do you know about your dead cousin what's-his-name?" But Sacco and Vanzetti were pictured in their history book. Vance's claim could be fully documented.

Like spark plugs in a cold engine, Larry's synapses strained to fire. "There was a guy . . ." he said, out of nowhere, "a school-teacher. He kept a diary of everything. He wrote it down on the backs of envelopes."

"Uh-huh," Vance said. "I bet. And what happened to the envelopes?"

"They're . . . in the museum. The Holocaust Museum in the Smithsonian."

The name cast a hush over the crowd. The Smithsonian was the destination of the annual eighth-grade trip, the sparkling Oz that teachers dangled before them—mere seventh-graders—as inducement to two years of good behavior.

"I told you so," said Tanisha, plucking a walnut from her brownie. "The Smithsonian? No way could he be faking."

Larry shrugged as if to say, "Go ahead, check it out"—his triumph poisoned already with the terror that someone might.

But after that, no one challenged him. Even Vance deferred to his authority. What Larry discovered in the following weeks and months was that people didn't want to doubt their celebrities. They wanted, more than anything, to believe.

His renown was unprecedented. Calamity had visited their circle previously—one girl's father had nearly died two winters earlier until doctors gave him someone else's liver; Tanisha's Brooklyn cousin had lost two fingers in a drive-by shooting—but these were nothing compared to Larry's story. He found that Ludwig's misfortune, despite its distance of decades, was an end-lessly potent narrative, and that merely setting a given episode in the concentration camp exponentially increased its profoundness. Pain inflicted by the Nazis hurt more than ordinary pain. The Holocaust was the ultimate trump card.

Word of Larry's heritage spread. Kids he didn't even know found him at his locker and asked to hear the story of the cleavered thumb. Mr. Tisch, his social studies teacher, kept him after class to say, "Your grandfather would be proud of you."

Larry tattooed his wrist with a blue felt-tip pen: 6-14-42. This was Ludwig's number, he confided to Tanisha, knowing she'd have the whole school talking by fourth period. He made sure to roll up his sleeves.

The ploy worked so well that he forgot to wash the ink. At home that night, his mother grabbed his arm. "What on earth?" she demanded. "What is this?"

Larry had told her nothing of his concoction, so he simply confessed the truth: the number was his locker combination. She insisted he scrub clean before dinner. But the next morning he reapplied the numerals. He fended off teenage paparazzi all day.

People called him now. He got invited. Rob Swann, the soccer team captain, asked him to his birthday slumber party. The redhead from Life Science made a bid to be his lab partner.

Walking down the corridors, Larry felt fluorescent with importance. He was a tycoon of tragedy.

As the bar mitzvah neared, Larry grew studious. He possessed no knack for the material, but Mrs. Hershman suggested he dedicate the occasion to Ludwig's memory, and this incentive kept his focus sharp. His grandfather had been killed for his faith, the teacher said; learning the liturgy was the least Larry could do.

He labored over his Torah portion and his haftorah. He warbled the ancient melodies seemingly composed to taunt a boy at his change of voice. He practiced donning the tallis and tefillin—a silly-looking costume, but one, he realized, well suited as a conversation piece.

Each bar and bat mitzvah candidate was expected to prepare a speech. Mrs. Hershman advised that the students stick to a gloss on their allotted scripture, but she pulled Larry aside separately. For his recitation, she said, comments on the Holocaust might be movingly appropriate. She loaned him books to read: Anne Frank's *Diary of a Young Girl; Night*, by Elie Wiesel.

After boning up on the Final Solution, Larry decided that his choice of Buchenwald had been astute. When Mrs. Hershman first put him on the spot, he'd almost claimed Theresienstadt as the site of Ludwig's death; the lilting name felt good on his tongue. But now he learned that Theresienstadt, with its art classes and orchestras, was hardly even a concentration camp. Buchenwald wielded far greater prestige.

He was thrilled to find, in an oral history of Holocaust survivors, the line that he knew would make his presentation's high point. "If you could lick my heart," one survivor said, "it would poison you." Who could compete with such agony?

Larry's parents would be attending, of course, as would his uncle Gene, and he worried about their reaction to his zeal. Knowing the banality of the actual family past, might they question Larry's sincerity? But if he kept his comments general, without mentioning specific relatives, they should welcome his ethnic empathy. That was the whole point of a bar mitzvah! He rehearsed his cadence, his swell to the finale. Before the mirror, he nearly brought himself to tears.

When the day came, Larry was ready. His mother had bought him a suit at Brooks Brothers, a charcoal gray miniature of what his father wore to work. He had new black lace-up shoes, and his first-ever pair of non-tube socks.

In the car on the way to the synagogue, he sang to himself his memorized Torah portion. He understood now that the trick was to let your voice crack. He didn't flub a single word.

He felt the crisply folded pages of his speech, tucked into his jacket's inside pocket. The corners jabbed with his slightest bend or shift, but the twinge was good—it allowed him to practice wincing.

And then they were there, and Rabbi Kahn ushered them in,

and all of a sudden it was time. Larry sat on the bimah, tiny in the plush high-backed chair. The sanctuary fanned before him, the same sloping shape as his school auditorium and with a similar choky carpet-cleanser smell.

Larry gazed across the banks of seats: his parents and their friends and Uncle Gene in the front row; then behind them, the regulars from the congregation; and in back, dozens and dozens of kids from school. Weeks earlier, addressing invitations, Larry's mother had questioned his guest list's length. She didn't know of the new voguish Larry, only the quietly unremarkable boy she'd raised. "Honey," she said, "having so many friends is wonderful. But do you really think all of them will come?" Larry had been stricken with uncertainty.

But scanning the crowd, he saw that his fears had been unfounded. Vance was here, and Tanisha, and Rob Swann. His whole homeroom had come, and most of social studies. Everyone was here to see him.

The service dawdled like a tape recorder on low batteries. Stand up, sit down; stay silent, please repeat. Larry watched his schoolmates, some respectful in their monkey suits, others joking and trying not to laugh. If the wait was too long, Larry might lose them. Performance was such a delicate balance, he had learned, a dance of delivery and delay. Every audience had its breaking point.

Yes, he knew he was performing. And if at times his act had been so heartfelt that he himself almost believed it, he was aware, too, that there must come an end. Even if he managed somehow never to be debunked, the fact was that people got bored. Even the Holocaust, if overused, grew mundane. But what Larry hoped was that this day would be the cresting of the wave. He would surf the glorious edge, riding for all it was worth, and then, just before the crash, turn out to chase another swell.

At last it was time for the Torah reading. There were seven segments, of which Larry would chant only the last. The first six would be sung by the cantor.

There was a special cantor today, Rabbi Kahn explained, visiting from a congregation in New York. It was an honor to have such a distinguished guest. The man who'd been sitting on the far left of the bimah, whom Larry had barely noticed, rose and approached the podium.

He was short in the way of old people, as if a lifetime of exposure had shrunk him down. Everything was too big on him, his tweed jacket swallowing his arms, his *tallis* like a child's costume cape. In order to see the Torah, he mounted the wooden stool usually reserved for bar mitzvah boys.

And yet when he opened his mouth, the cantor was anything but small. He sang with the rough-hewn authority of a shepherd beckoning his flock, the kind of voice that makes microphones redundant. Larry wondered where, in that tiny chest, it came from.

The countdown began. Before each Torah segment, a different man was called to recite the blessing. The first two required special lineage and went to synagogue regulars, but the rest had been apportioned by the family: Larry's father's boss; Dave Foster, their next-door neighbor; Uncle Gene; Larry's father; and finally Larry.

Up the men came, offering handshakes like cigars, then down again when each portion ended. As his turn neared, Larry woozed with adrenaline. He slowed his breath, trying to locate a meditative calm. *"Om,"* he hummed silently, a mantra copied from the movies. *"Om, om."* He repeated the sound, again and again, until he sang, "I'm, I'm."

Then the wait that had seemed infinite abruptly found its end, when the cantor summoned him with an operatic flourish. Larry stood and straightened his jacket. He squared his jaw, as he had trained himself. He puffed his chest like Ludwig in the photograph.

Staring out into the congregation, Larry saw only a vague scrim of light and dark. The rabbi flashed a hidden thumbs-up below the podium. His father managed a nervous nod. Larry pretended not to know any of them. They were mere fans; he was the superstar.

He began the preliminary prayer, the rote formula locked on its perfect pitch. If he concentrated, he knew he could nail this. He would chant the blessing and the Torah portion, displaying his impressive competence. And then the real test: the pages tucked next to his hurried heart. He would speak of cruelty and devastation, but also of enduring hope and faith. He would explain the responsibility he felt—to history, to memory, to truth. He'd be fervent and unforgettable.

At the blessing's conclusion, the congregation called "Amen," their voices like a spotlight trained on him. Now the tiny cantor leaned in close. The man was even older than Larry had first imagined, his skin scored with lines that evoked the underside of an autumn leaf. "You'll be fine," the cantor whispered. "Follow along with me."

Until now, Larry had heard only the cantor's Hebrew. His English was edged with a foreign accent, so that "with me" became "viss me," a whip.

"Ready?" he asked.

Larry nodded firmly, he'd never felt more ready in his life.

Like a conductor preparing to cue the orchestra, the cantor lifted his *yod,* the miniature silver hand with which he'd guide Larry through the text. The antique was delicate, precise in its semblance of flesh. Larry fixed his sights on the metal finger. Focus, he thought. Full voice. Confidence.

The cantor scanned the Torah scroll for the portion's first word. Because Larry had now claimed the wooden stool, the old man had to stretch on tiptoe. He reached to his arm's limit, his wrist extending turtlelike from his jacket sleeve, and that's when Larry saw the numerals.

They looked fake at first. Mine were more real than that, he thought. But then he could see the depth of the tattoo, its dye etched into the wrinkled skin. After half a century the numbers were still clear, the dull purple of the stamp on a slab of beef.

"Go ahead," the cantor urged. "You can begin." He smiled, but in his face Larry saw the hollow-eyed victims from the Hebrew school documentary. The *yod's* disembodied hand was a ghastly skeleton.

Larry tried to retrieve his voice, but it disobeyed. He slumped against the podium. A folded corner of his speech poked his ribs.

"You can do it," his father coached. "Mrs. Hershman says you know it cold."

Larry glanced up and saw his teacher. He saw his mother, too, Uncle Gene, the kids from school. He wished he could erase himself.

"Please," said the cantor. "We must begin."

And then, somehow, because the show must go on, Larry did begin—shakily at first, his voice reedy and small. The cantor's pointing hand accused him and Larry closed his eyes to banish it, chanting the rest from memory. He missed a phrase, backpedaled, got it right on the second try. He eked the tune word by word from his tightened throat.

In a blink he was finished; he'd only made the one mistake. The rabbi pumped his hand with a hearty "mazel tov."

Now the speech was all that remained. Larry cleared his throat and began to read from his laser printout. He was aware of the words, but not of speaking them, as if he were a ventriloquist's dummy. He came to the section about the concentration camps. Buchenwald, Treblinka, Westerbork—the names must have sounded ludicrous in his trumped-up accent. He thought he heard a snicker, but it was only someone's sneeze. The audience sat rapt, credulous.

He pressed on, trying to ignore the cantor behind him, trying not to imagine what he'd endured. "To remember," Larry said, "is a never-ending duty. If we forget, then survival is meaningless." The congregation, spellbound, restored his confidence. He surged to the heart-swelling conclusion. "They say we're the Chosen People, but I think we should be a choosing people. Today I choose to remember what happened to our ancestors, and I choose to risk the same fate by standing up to say: I'm a Jew."

In the kiddush room downstairs, after the challah and wine were blessed, Larry was swarmed by awestruck well-wishers. There were hundreds, it seemed; they all wanted to shake his hand.

Mrs. Hershman requested a Xerox of the speech, saying it would be a model for years to come. "Totally cool," gushed Tanisha. "You made me feel it. It was almost worse than slavery." Vance offered a hug, and said, "Way to go, man. That speech should be in the Smithsonian."

And then, after Rabbi Kahn and some cousins from Florida, Larry looked up to the cantor's wizened face. On his chin shone a lurid dab of wine. Tears muddled his weary, knowing eyes.

"Son," he said, "I've seen more than I care to in my life. Humans doing inhuman things."

Larry braced himself. He feared his luck was spent.

"Sometimes," the cantor went on, "many times, I wished to die. But this, today. To hear a sensitive young man like you—it just makes me want to live and live!"

He drew Larry down, his hand gripping Larry's jaw, and pushed a wet kiss onto his mouth. The lips were rancid with kiddush wine and nicotine. If you could lick my heart, Larry thought, it would poison you.

His vision sizzled and shrank like a TV screen in a storm. He withered. He was going to be sick.

Excusing himself, he bolted to the bathroom, and wasn't quite to the sink when he threw up. He choked off his throat and swallowed back the bile, but specks of challah spattered the linoleum. A second retch, then only grueling air.

When the heaving subsided and Larry found his breath, he bent to the sink to rinse his mouth. Grains of vomit clung inside his cheeks. Larry washed and washed, even gargled liquid soap, but every swallow tasted just as bitter.

Michael Lowenthal

*Having written a story in which the name of the Holocaust is, as it
were, taken in vain, I feel the defensive urge to say: My relatives
suffered, too; my great-grandfather and my half uncle were killed in
the camps. But isn't there something sickeningly boastful in that
statement? A smug establishing of credentials? We live in an
identity-politics-crazed age of my-persecution-is-worse-than-yours
one-upmanship. Is it possible that this frenzy of boastful suffering
exacts a psychological cost on those who have no claim to victimiza-
tion? This question intersects with concerns raised by the changing
status of American Jews. Now that Jews (come on, admit it) are
disproportionately powerful insiders in almost every aspect of
American life, is a new generation deprived of the old frisson of out-
siderness? Do we miss standing in the spotlight of suffering? As
someone whose family was, yes, scarred by the Holocaust, but who
was born a quarter-century after the camps were liberated, and who
has never personally experienced even the slightest suggestion of
anti-Semitism, I ask myself these questions as I write.*

DIE GROSSE LIEBE

Aryeh Lev Stollman

T*he Great Love* was her best movie. I felt so happy watching her, no matter how many times I saw it."

As always in our house, when my mother described the movie in which her favorite actress starred, she spoke the language of her Berlin youth. Not the jumbled clacking of the crowded Scheunenviertel, noisy with the unsteady tongues of immigrants, but the soft, cultivated tones of the beautiful Grunewald, its grand villas overflowing with art and books and music, its gardens, its lawns sweeping down to quiet lakes.

When she pronounced the film's title—*Die grosse Liebe*—it sounded to me, a boy born and growing up in the vast present tense of Ontario, so unlike the marvelous emotion it was meant to convey. Despite the gentle refinement of my mother's voice, that sublime sentiment—that grand passion—seemed almost grating and unpleasant. The dense language of my home, the elaborate syntax of my parents' distant, and to me, unknown lives, suddenly became vaguely unsettling.

The revelation that my mother even had a *Lieblingsschauspielerin*—a favorite actress—was a complete surprise and came on the evening after my father's funeral. My mother had never spoken of actors or movies before. As far as I knew, neither of my parents ever went to the movies, although I was allowed to do so. And except for one other occasion, the days leading up to my father's funeral were the only times I could remember my mother leaving the vicinity of our house. She had never gone shopping or out for a walk. I cannot recall her ever taking me to school. I never thought to question this behavior. I had simply accepted it as an aspect of her personality. It was never discussed or explained, and I was rather comforted by her generally quiet and steady presence in my childhood world.

I was only twelve at the time of my father's unexpected death and bewildered by my mother's strange disclosure. She had never been very talkative. But she had, on that exceptional night in my life, suddenly opened a hidden door and—I could not know it then—would permanently and just as abruptly close it again.

"I saw *The Great Love* maybe fifty times the year it premiered. That was the year I stayed with the Retters. Herr Retter took me to his theater, the Gloria Palace, whenever I was sad and needed to get away. I learned every song by heart." My mother smiled and caressed one slender hand with the other. "Sometimes I helped with the projector. I was very mechanical." Here my mother paused and frowned. "The Retters had a daughter my age. Ingrid had dark brown eyes and long black hair. She was a big chatterbox and caused a lot of trouble. *I* was the one with blue eyes and blond hair." My mother gently smoothed a lock of this same hair from her forehead, shook her head, and smiled again. "Of course, like most girls we dreamed of being actresses."

When my mother described the movie in which her favorite actress starred, and whose songs she had memorized, we were sitting together on the living room sofa. The last visitor, an old woman neighbor, had just left. My parents had kept mainly to themselves, and there had been few guests at the house after the funeral. Those who did make the visit included several neighbors, the old woman among them, and some business acquaintances who knew my father from his jewelry store. The old woman had silently helped my mother put away the food that had been set up on the dining room sideboard and then clean up the kitchen. Before she left she took my mother's hand: "I'm very sorry, dear. It's a terrible tragedy. But God is the true judge and we must learn to accept His will." My mother looked at her blankly and said, "Thank you."

Years later, when my mother herself was gravely ill, I took a leave from college to take care of her. She would not allow herself to be admitted to a hospital or permit strangers into the house. I asked her about the old woman. I wondered whatever became of her. My mother lifted her head off her pillow and gave me a surprised look. "Oh, no. There was never such a person that day."

"But there was, Mother. She was our neighbor. I even remember what she said—"

"No, you must be mistaken. And now, Joseph, I'm quite tired."

But I know I was not mistaken and the old woman really did exist. Recently, however, now that I am well into my forties, approaching the ages when my parents died, and I think back to this late exchange with my mother, I find myself increasingly alarmed. I can no longer conjure up a single one of the old woman's features. Did she have a long or short nose? What was the color of her eyes? How did she wear her hair? I recall only a sense of her frail, ghostly movements, the vague disruption of the still atmosphere of our house, and her parting words. The details of our house on that day I remember vividly—the carved oak sideboard in the dining room where the food had been set out on silver platters, the speckled green tiles on the kitchen floor over which the old woman passed, and the claret moiré fabric with which the living room sofa was upholstered.

"In *The Great Love* she played a beautiful singer named Hanna. Oma—whom you never met—was named Hanna, too." My mother had rarely referred to my grandparents except to say proudly that they had been *angesehene Leute*—highly educated and cultured. Her father, she once told me, had composed art songs in the style of Hugo Wolf, and no doubt would have been famous had he not died, as she put it, *so vorzeitig*—so prematurely. "If you had been a girl, I would have certainly named you Hanna."

The night she told me about her favorite actress in her favorite movie, my mother never looked directly at me. Her eyes skimmed the top of my head and watched the pale blue walls of our living room as if she might be seeing the very same movie, projected there by memory's light. My initial unease at her elaborate reminiscence gave way to an odd comfort and excitement in hearing her talk to me at length as she might have with my father, even if she was in her own world. I had never before considered the mystery of my mother's youth and was now fascinated. I listened carefully and quietly.

While I was growing up, my parents' extreme personal reserve never seemed odd: rather, their conversations seemed dignified and appropriate. In their leisure they read books, or listened to records, mostly lieder and opera. We never went away on vacations. Often they spoke about my father's jewelry store. In the background I would hear references to "a wedding ring with six quadrillions" or "the young woman who bought the emerald pheasant brooch." Several nights a week my mother would go over the store receipts. She sat quietly at a small mahogany secretary in the den. A stack of papers would be piled neatly in front of her while she tapped her forehead with the eraser end of a pencil.

Somehow I grew up understanding that one did not ask questions of a personal nature, even to one's parents. I knew that surrounding every human being was a sacred wall of dignity and privacy. My parents never asked questions such as "What are you thinking, Joseph?" or, "What did you do today?" They never entered my room without knocking. *"Joseph, darf ich eintreten?"* my mother would say if she needed to do any cleaning. As far as I could tell she never entered my room when I was out of the house. And I am still taken aback, unsettled, observing people who talk too much, chatter, ask question after question.

My mother told the story of *The Great Love* in extensive

detail. After her death, I would increasingly find myself review-
ing in my mind's eye the scene of my mother's greatest confidence. When I tried to review this night in my mind, I would
realize to my great dismay that I had forgotten some small detail,
some tangential plot line my mother described, and with it, I felt,
some irretrievable clue to her life. Sometimes I would experience
physical symptoms when my memory failed me. I would break
out in a sweat, breathe rapidly, or feel dizzy. And now, years later,
the memory of my mother's description is further clouded by my
persistent and pathetic attempts to patch up those gaps, to move
through the doorway she had so briefly opened that evening.

The plot of *The Great Love* was—with its predictable twists
and turns, period clichés and movieland formulas—fairly simple.
And it was of little interest to me at the time.

Paul, a handsome air force pilot on twenty-four hours' leave,
attends one of Hanna's sold-out concerts in Berlin. That night,
after the concert, during an air raid, fate brings them together in
an underground shelter. They fall in love. But love is not easy in
wartime. The next day, Paul had to go on a dangerous mission.
Three weeks later, when he safely returns on furlough, they plan
to marry right away, but an unexpected order comes in from the
High Command. Paul must once again leave abruptly. Meanwhile
Hanna, disappointed but still hopeful and understanding, goes
on with her life and travels to Paris for her next concert.

"In Paris, Hanna stood on stage in the ballroom of a splendid palace, in front of hundreds of soldiers, many of whom
were wounded." My mother sighed. "I kept thinking to myself,
Did such places like that ballroom still exist in this crazy world?
Yes. Yes. Of course they did! They must. It was an absolutely en-
chanting scene.

"Hanna wore a black velvet gown with a silver leaf embroidered near the top. Like so." My mother traced an arc across her
own bust with her hand. "Hanna was so elegant, so charming, so
warm. She stood onstage before a small orchestra. Her accompanist, a sweet older man, played the piano. She sang a wonderful

song about how life had its ups and downs but in the end everything would turn out wonderful. And how she knew that one
day her beloved, her soul mate, would return."

There were tears in my mother's eyes. I had never before seen
my mother cry. She had not cried earlier that day at my father's
small funeral, nor had she cried when she came into my room the
week before, her face very pale and drawn: "I have very bad
news, Joseph. Papi was found dead in his store. We now must
survive together."

I asked her only one question that night we sat together on
the living room sofa.

"Did Father see the movie?"

My mother seemed startled by my interruption. "Oh, no.
Papi was in a different hiding place. We weren't married yet." My
mother dabbed her wet eyes with a handkerchief. The tears had
stopped. "Papi was afraid to go outdoors to come to the theater.
Someone might see him and catch him. But once when I was able
to go to him, I told him about it. At first he was annoyed. He
thought it all foolish, vulgar. Not something I should have been
interested in. 'They are wicked people!' he said. 'It's only a love
story,' I said. Then Papi said he was sorry and listened, just to
amuse me."

After my mother's death, on my first visit to Berlin, I watched
The Great Love over and over, perhaps five times, all afternoon
and evening, at a revival theater on the Kurfürstendamm. Each
time I had the strange feeling that my mother was telling me the
story as I watched it. Finally the manager came over to me and
asked if something was the matter. I said I had come all the way
from Canada to see this movie. He shook his head and walked
away muttering, "*Noch ein verrückter Fan*—Another crazy fan!"

After that a new memory emerged of my mother and her
favorite actress in *The Great Love*. It was, I knew from the start, a
false memory, but so insistent in nature that even now hardly a

week goes by without its coming to mind as if it had actually happened.

In this false memory, which has occurred to me ever since I first went to Berlin and saw *The Great Love* myself, my mother gets up from the sofa where she sat with me that night after my father's funeral. She stands up and begins to sing in the voice of her favorite actress. It is that woman's voice but darker and deeper, a voice that hovers between the Earth and the heavenly firmament, singing of miracles to be:

Ich weiss, es wird einmal ein Wunder geschehn,
und ich weiss, dass wir uns wiedersehen!

But in reality, my mother had been sitting the whole time. She never sang any lyrics. And I never in my life heard my mother sing.

Our house stood on a quiet street at the outskirts of town, and though modest in size, it was densely furnished with sofas and chairs, various mahogany and oak side tables, étagères, and lamps. Except for the kitchen, heavy draperies hung on the windows of every room, including the bedrooms. My mother kept the house meticulously clean. Though she never left the vicinity of the house, and had very little interaction with other people, she always dressed very elegantly, even lavishly. She subscribed to several fashion magazines to keep up with the latest styles. She ordered expensive fabrics from a store in Toronto and made her clothes herself. Often when she was working in her sewing room she would call me over. "See, Joseph, this is a very fine silk, touch it. Feel its weight. Chinese silk is better than Indian. Please hold it out for me so I can see it better," or "This cotton comes from Egypt, the land of Nefertiti, the best cotton in the world."

My mother was also particular about her thick blond hair,

which she brushed back from her high forehead and kept gently waved at the temples so it framed her oval face.

My father was always appreciative of my mother's efforts. "Ute, you are very beautiful tonight," or "How elegant you are, Ute," he would say when he came home from work.

"*Danke*, Albert."

My father did the household shopping on his way home from work. From time to time he brought my mother cosmetics, stockings, and even shoes.

Only once, before my father died, can I remember my mother leaving our house. One holiday, I believe it was Yom Kippur or Rosh Hashanah, when I was eight or nine, my father insisted we all go to the synagogue in town. I did not understand why, because we had never attended synagogue before and no one ever expressed an interest in doing so. I can still see my mother adjusting a small feathered hat atop her blond hair. The hat had a delicate veil that hung in front of her eyes. Before we left the house she glanced in the hallway mirror. She seemed pleased with her appearance. We drove into town for services. While we walked up the synagogue steps, my mother moved with an uncharacteristic awkwardness, constantly looking down at her shoes. I thought she was afraid of stumbling. At home my mother walked very erectly, her tall slender figure moving gracefully.

In the synagogue I stood between my parents and listened to the unfamiliar melancholy singing. I felt sad and bored. My mother leaned sideways and tugged discreetly on my father's sleeve. We moved out in single file from the crowded pew while the singing continued. Later, when we returned home, she looked at my father. She was pale and trembling.

"*Bitte, Albert, nie mehr.*"

"*Ja, Ute, nie mehr. Nie.*"

And we never did attend synagogue again.

When I asked her about that episode before she died, she said, "No. I never went into a synagogue, even as a child. We were never observant. Maybe you went with your father. Perhaps your father took you once. He was very nostalgic."

In my boyhood I began a beautiful and, I did not fully realize then, extremely valuable gemstone collection. I stored my treasures in a velvet-lined leather case that I hid under my bed. This collection was gently but persistently encouraged by my father. Over time he presented me with many precious and semiprecious stones: an oval-cut ruby, a sapphire cabochon, a violet garnet. "For your birthday," he would say, or, "For your report card." My mother would nod and add, "You must always keep the pretty things Papi gives you. You can take them wherever you go."

"They are like having *Lösegeld*," my father once said.

"What?" I had never heard that word.

My mother looked sternly at my father.

"Oh, nothing," he said. Later I looked the word up. It meant ransom.

Often I would study my collection under the jeweler's loupe he had given me, which I kept on the desk in my bedroom. He had shown me how to scan a stone's surface and, in the case of a transparent stone, its depths. "A small flaw is a big tragedy if you're a jewel," he was fond of saying.

Once in elementary school, I came home and told my parents that my French teacher, Madame Dejarlais, thought I had an extraordinary gift for languages and that this might be useful in choosing a career for myself. She was right—after college I took a position in Toronto as a translator for a Canadian corporation that was expanding its business in Europe. My mother smiled pleasantly. She was sewing a hem on a dress.

My father said, "That is very good news, Joseph. We are happy to hear it."

My mother looked up from her work. "Yes, of course. We are very happy to hear it."

The next day my father gave me a two-carat marquise-cut

emerald, the last gift I received from him. My mother said, "You must always keep the things Papi gives you."

After Paul safely fulfilled his mission, the one he was called to by the High Command, the one that postponed his marriage, he was given three weeks' leave. He traveled to Rome to surprise Hanna, who was rehearsing for her latest engagement. They were joyously reunited and decided to marry that very night. Suddenly, as they were making their plans, the phone rang. An officer friend asked him to help by joining a new and dangerous mission. This time it was not an order but a request. Paul instantly agreed to volunteer.

My mother's voice rose angrily as she described Hanna's reaction. "'Must you go *volunteer* and leave me just like that when we are about to marry! Without so much as an order! What about us? What about our marriage? Is that so unimportant? I cannot, I will not endure this any longer!'"

Then my mother's voice softened. She understood Paul's side as well. "Paul tried to reason with her. It was wartime and he had his responsibilities. 'And what is it you cannot endure,' he asked her, 'when so many awful things are happening in the world?'

"But Hanna remained stubborn and so they broke off their engagement. Paul, dutifully, left on his mission. After he was gone, Hanna sat down and cried."

The morning after my father's funeral my mother knocked early on my bedroom door. *"Joseph, darf ich eintreten?"*

My mother was wearing a sky-blue satin dress with long sleeves. There were white cuffs at her wrists and white buttons up the front of the dress. I remembered seeing the shimmering fabric when she was working on it in her sewing room, but I had never imagined the finished product. She appeared especially glamorous to me that day, like one of the models in the glossy magazines to which she subscribed.

"I will be back in the evening." She looked at me to see if I understood, and then added, "I cannot sell Papi's store. He loved it too much."

I was puzzled, not because of the sudden and astonishing discarding of what clearly was some form of phobia. I never thought in such psychological terms when I was a child. I was puzzled mainly because it was three miles downtown to my father's store and my mother did not drive. I could not picture her, dressed in white-trimmed, sky blue satin walking that distance, or for that matter, traveling on a bus, though it would have been simple to do so.

"I must go now, Joseph. The taxi is waiting."

For the next two years she went back and forth by taxi from our house to the store. She did not, as far as I knew, go anywhere else. I believe the store must have been for her an extension of our home. I took over from my father and did all the food shopping. My mother would give me a list with the brand names she preferred. Sometimes she asked me to buy certain cosmetics or stockings as my father had done for her. In her spare time she continued to order material from Toronto and make her own clothes.

My mother turned out to be a skilled businesswoman and was good with customers. She still sold jewelry as my father had, but she expanded her merchandise to include fine gifts, such as crystal and silver. Though at home she continued speaking to me in German, her English was much better than I had realized, and her accent diminished over the time she worked in the store. Occasionally I would catch her at home with her sewing, repeating some English word out loud until she was satisfied with her pronunciation. Once she caught me watching her. She smiled. "A good actress must adjust her accent for a new role."

My mother continued my father's custom of building up my gemstone collection. On the first anniversary of his death, she gave me a one-and-three-quarter-carat round-cut diamond. I examined it that night under my loupe. I scrutinized its brilliant surface table, the glittering facets of its crown and pavilion. Its depths were flawless and fine white. My mother asked if she could enter my room. She took the loupe and examined the diamond herself.

"Yes, it is really an excellent stone. You must keep it with all the things Papi gave you."

Sometimes after school or on Saturdays I helped my mother at the store. One day, near the second anniversary of my father's death, a short, dark-haired woman came into the store. No other customers were present. The woman wore expensive clothing, large sunglasses, and many rings on her fingers. She walked around the store, browsing. She looked at me, then my mother. My mother smiled. "May I help you, please?"

The woman answered in German. "Yes. Would you show me those bracelets?"

"*Natürlich*." My mother leaned over to open the display counter.

The woman took off her sunglasses and glared at the blond hair on my mother's bent-over head. "Feuchtman," she whispered. "Feuchtman." It took me a moment to realize the woman was saying my mother's maiden name. My mother had rarely mentioned it. My mother looked up. She smiled. *"Wie, bitte?"* To this day I don't think my mother actually heard or understood that the woman had just called her name. Suddenly the woman whirled around, her scrawny arm outstretched, her fist slamming into my mother's jaw with surprising force. One of my mother's teeth flew out, clattered across the glass top of the display cabinet and then fell to the floor.

My mother stood up. Blood gleamed at the corner of her mouth. She was so startled that she did not even bring up a hand to feel the damage on her face.

"Petzmaul! Verräterin!" The woman spat at my mother. "Bitch! Traitor! You are worse than they were! The evil informer-girl is finally caught!"

The woman ran out of the store and disappeared. I heard a

car speeding off, but I was too shocked to run out and look for the license plate. I did not even move from where I was standing.

Finally my mother spoke. Her voice was altered because her lower jaw was now swollen. I could barely make out what she said. When she spoke she did not look directly at me. Her eyes skimmed the top of my head as they did the evening after my father's funeral, when she watched the pale blue walls of our living room and told me about her favorite actress in her favorite movie. She whispered.

"Oh, no. No, no. She is completely mistaken. I would never have worked for them even if they tortured me. I would never turn anyone in. How could I? . . . I had to do something to save your father. . . . No. No. I myself was hiding the whole time, first with the Retters. . . ." She became silent. She wiped her mouth, then felt her jaw, opening and closing it slowly. She smoothed her blond hair back with both hands. She took in a deep breath and looked directly at me. "Well, no bones are broken. There is no need to see a doctor. You know I do not go to doctors. Why are you shaking?"

A week later she put the store up for sale.

According to city records, the Grunewald house, where my mother grew up, was destroyed during the war. Now, in its place, are pretty garden apartments with cobblestone trails meandering down to a small lake. The house of my mother's favorite movie actress in nearby Dahlem, across the street from a forest park, is now a retirement home.

A few years after my first visit, my company established a permanent office in Berlin. I requested a transfer. I thought of renting one of the garden apartments where my mother's house once stood, but none was available. Instead I found an apartment south of the Tiergarten and have lived here almost as long as my parents lived in Canada. At night, from my small balcony, I can see far across the lights of the Kurfürstendamm into the vast city. In *The Great Love* Hanna had a balcony, too. In one scene she stands there with Paul looking out at the sparkling night sea of Berlin. "It is like a fairy tale," she says, sighing.

"No," Paul answers her. "It is lovelier than a fairy tale."

I don't think it would be an exaggeration to say I have seen *The Great Love* more than fifty times. When I first moved to Berlin, I would see it any time it was playing at the revival houses, which was surprisingly often. Later, when it became available on video, I began watching it at home. I have also seen my mother's favorite actress in her other movies: *To New Shores, In the Open Air, Homeland*. But I have found these other movies boring and never went to see any of them a second time.

My wife never asks me questions about this peculiar obsession of mine. She thinks only that I am a crazy fan. There are so many other people here who are fascinated with my mother's favorite actress. She is a great cult figure. If you go to the clubs you are bound to find someone dressed up like her, singing her songs, "Could Love Be a Sin?" or "My Life for Love." My wife is glad I have not come to that. *"Ich bin sehr dankbur dafür!"* she says. I am thankful for other things. Though we have now lived together for many years, she does not ask me about my family, nor do I ask about hers. I like to think of our life together as in the present, so long as the present maintains its own sense of privacy. Even in *The Great Love*, Paul and Hanna do not ask each other questions of a personal nature.

Lately, now that I am approaching the ages of my parents' premature deaths, when I recall my mother on the night of my father's funeral, I see us sitting on the claret moiré sofa as *The Great Love* is projected on the pale blue walls of our living room. We are watching it together. My mother takes my hand and smiles. She is enjoying herself so much and she hopes I am, too.

After Hanna and Paul break up, Paul leaves on his new mission, the dangerous mission for which he has nobly volunteered. Hanna remains in Rome rehearsing for her big concert.

Her concert is, of course, an amazing success. As she walks triumphantly offstage, she is handed a telegram. "Captain Paul Wendland has been wounded but only slightly. He is in an infirmary in the mountains." As Hanna returns to the stage and takes her bow, she whispers to her accompanist that she must leave that very night.

"Hanna, when will you return?" he asks sadly, for he is obviously in love with her, too.

"*Nie.*"

My mother recited this "Never" with the same restrained tone of conviction, the precise note of love and hope that I later witnessed each time I watched her favorite actress in her favorite movie.

Finally Hanna arrives at an infirmary somewhere in the Alps. Snow-covered mountain peaks are all around. She rushes over to Paul, who is sitting on the terrace, one arm in a sling. "Perhaps, Hanna, we can try again to get married." He laughingly points to his bandaged arm. "This time I really have three weeks' sick leave!"

Hanna smiles. She takes his hand. "And after the three weeks are over?"

Paul looks up and she looks up, too. Overhead, the sky is so wide and breathtaking. Here and there, glorious shafts of sunlight break through the billowing clouds. And suddenly, in the distance, a squadron of planes appears. And there, of course, to those wondrous heavens, Paul must return. That is where his duty lies.

"Paul turned and looked into Hanna's eyes," my mother told me. "Their faces were so beautiful, so full of happiness, it gave me goose bumps. And then Hanna nodded. Yes. Yes. She would marry him."

And then my mother turned and looked directly at me for the first time on that extraordinary night in my life. I trembled ever so slightly at the unbearable tenderness of her look. "If I had been them," my mother said, rising from the sofa, "I would gladly have sacrificed all of heaven for love."

Aryeh Lev Stollman

Two different interests of mine came together in the writing of this story. Years ago I had learned that there was a highly sophisticated movie industry during the Third Reich, a parallel universe to the American industry, that produced emotional dramas and lavish musicals. I went to Berlin, my first trip to Germany, to research the topic in a haphazard way, looking for video recordings of old films. I became fascinated by the Swedish actress and singer Zarah Leander, the leading female star of Nazi German film, groomed to take the place of Marlene Dietrich, who had left for the United States. In a Berlin department store, I easily found a videotape of her 1942 hit, Die grosse Liebe—The Great Love—*which became the title of my story. At that time I had also been interested in a certain type of Jewish collaborator, the* Greifer—catcher—*who helped turn in fellow Jews in hiding. Some Jews in hiding did so "in the open," pretending to be Aryans with false identities and papers. The Nazis used other Jews to point them out. In the end most of the catchers themselves were killed, but a few survived.*

DREAMING IN POLISH

Aimee Bender

There was an old man and an old woman and they dreamed the same dreams. They'd been married for sixty years, and their arm skin now wrinkled down to their wrists like kicked-down bedsheets. They were maybe the oldest people in the world. They sat outside their house together, elbows touching, in the wicker chairs you'd expect them to sit in, and watched the people walk by. Occasionally they called out images from the night before to the gardener or to whoever happened to be passing. Most people smiled quickly at them and then looked back down at the sidewalk. And when night fell, the old man and the old woman walked into their bedroom, drew back the white sheets, covered themselves up, and shared what was beneath.

This summer was the one where I worked in the hardware store, and my mother talked only about going to Washington, D.C., to ride on the cattle cars at the newly inaugurated Holocaust Museum there. Apparently this museum had the best simulation of Auschwitz in the world. I didn't want to go; I was happy giving refunds to wives who'd bought the wrong pliers for their enterprising husbands. Besides, my mother and I had pretty much done the concentration-camp museum circuit by this point—looking at piles of hair in the Paris one the summer before, walking past black-and-white photographs in Amsterdam. I didn't like going, but she, somehow, craved it. I watched her hands tremble as she looked at the biographies pasted on the walls, and wondered what she was thinking.

My mother didn't have much to do with her day besides plan these trips; she taught, and kept her summers free, but I was very busy at the store, stacking bags of potting soil until they were all in perfect rows. I spent my afternoons scraping bird shit off a statue of a random Greek god that stood in the town's central square. The statue had ended up there inexplicably—no one, not even the oldest people, remembered when it arrived. It seemed to have simply grown up from the earth. My boss at the hardware store thought it was his duty to keep it shining, so every afternoon when business was quiet, he sent me outside, and I rubbed the dried white off muscled iron thighs, running my cloth down sinewy gray biceps. This was the only man I had ever touched so closely. I sang songs in my head from the Sunday morning countdown while I cleaned him. I kept songs going in my head because they were the easiest thing to think about.

At home, during the evenings, I took care of my father, who was sick and stayed in bed all day. My mother thought I made the better nurse. I told him all about my day, half-listening to my mother watching television in the next room, her wrist cracking and popping when she saw something she thought was funny. She did that instead of laughing.

My father liked to hear details about the store. He liked talking about hardware.

"Any wrenches back today?" he asked, arms flat by his sides, sticks.

"Yes," I replied. "Mrs. Johnson said hers was the wrong size, so we just traded that one in, and there was a man passing through who needed one for his car, he was having car trouble."

"Transmission," my father said knowingly, relaxing further into his pillow.

The old man and the old woman once dreamed that a pig drowned. As usual, they announced this to the neighborhood, listening closely to the sounds of their own voices. They rarely spoke in sentences, but instead called out the images in fragments, like young earnest poets.

"Pig," the old woman said.

"No breath," he finished.

"Pushing pig," she said.

"And brown and dead."

That day a farmer from across town heard them as he walked by, and when he arrived home his wife hurried out to tell him that the tractor had accidentally scooped up a pig instead of earth and thrown it headfirst into a pile of manure. The pig couldn't get its footing, fell forward, and suffocated. The farmer was disgusted and annoyed by the story but didn't think of the significance until he was on the toilet before he went to bed and then he remembered the old man and the old woman. And brown and dead. Disturbed, he told his wife about the prophets in the town, and she promptly told all the neighbors. When the news got back to them, the old man and the old woman just smiled and touched elbow bones closely, loose skin nearly obscuring the tattooed numbers on their inner arms.

I brought my father potting soil and put a pot of growing radishes by his bed so he would have something to tend to. He watered it maybe twenty times a day with an eyedropper, placing strategic drops near the roots—this would increase growth capacity, he said. And I told him plants grow more if you talk to them, so I'd find him, at odd hours in the day, whispering secrets into the damp dirt—about his dreams, about what it was like to be sick, I thought. About his first kiss and other stories.

But when I sat with him it was only me who would talk: Celia and her Anecdotes. He wanted to know, with a powerful urgency, what I did in fourth grade, because he'd been well then and hadn't paid attention to what I was doing. He was busy flying into enormous airports and doing deals. He dreamed, then, of having a son and playing catch on the lawn. Now I knew he thanked God he'd had a daughter. A son would be long gone. A son would be windswept in New York City, the warmth of red wine in his mouth, hands firm on voluptuous women while his father grew thinner and thinner in a queen-sized bed in the country.

I told my father about Reggie, the fat boy with a bowl cut that I liked in third grade and how I cried the day he moved to Kentucky, and I told my father about my former best friend Lonnie and how she had sex at fourteen, and how dumb that was of her. Fast-lane Lonnie. He settled himself back in the bed, and smiled as I talked. I could hear myself prattling, sounding so young and eager. I thought that if I were my father I would want to pat my head. Sure enough, when I kissed him good night, he rubbed my hair with his bony fingers, still steady and confident.

"You're a good girl, Celia," he said. "You're a little prize just waiting to be discovered."

"Oh," I said quickly, somewhat annoyed, "I'm not waiting for anything." Closing the door gently, I went into the kitchen and stared at things. Then I wiped the stove down until it waxed white and pearly under my cloth.

In the concentration-camp museum in Los Angeles you had to pretend you were a deportee, and choose between two doors: one for the young and healthy and another for feebler people that used to go straight to a gas chamber. I chose the "able-bodied" door and found myself in a stone room with twenty other Jews, all of us picking at our clothing. I didn't really understand why I was there, suffering through yet another museum, until I caught myself sending a hello to the ceiling. And then I knew I was visiting the dead people. I wanted to let them know I'd come back. That for some reason, no matter how much I wanted to, I couldn't leave them behind, loosened on the ceiling, like invisible sad smoke.

One day the old man and the old woman woke in a panic. They looked at each other and babbled something in Polish, the language they only used when they were scared. They rushed onto the porch and alerted a young gardener who was planting azaleas across the street.

"You," the old man cried. "Stop!"

The townspeople passing by, who revered the old man and the old woman as minor prophets due to the pig phenomenon, stopped and listened. The gardener wiped his dirty hands on the grass. The old woman was spluttering, her body stooped and visible through a soft yellow nightgown.

"No other gods before me. Or we're all dead. Town will die, die, die!" she cried shrilly, then fell back into her wicker chair.

The townspeople were instantly alarmed by the prophecy. They ran to the mayor who listened with studied concentration, stared at the floor, and then spoke.

"Town meeting," he announced in a firm, authoritative voice previously used only for the dog when it peed on the carpet. "We must hold a town meeting."

In a flurry, the townspeople were assembled. The gardener paraphrased what he'd heard. " 'No other gods before me or we're all dead, dead, dead,' she said." Due to all the anxiety, no one could really make any sense of the obvious until Sylvie Johnson, a Catholic who owned the potato store (all kinds—red, white, brown), spoke up.

"It's Commandment Two," she said calmly, pleased to demonstrate her Bible knowledge.

The crowd murmured in both recognition and feigned recognition.

"What do they mean by dead?" asked an older banker.

Everyone looked up at the mayor for some guidance.

"Hmmm," he said. "Hmmm." He looked out over the people. "Just follow it." He was humbled by the possible presence of God in his congregation. "Town dismissed."

Everyone streamed out of the gymnasium. By nightfall,

garbage bins all over the city were overflowing with sculptures from Africa and colorful masks from Mexico, anything that even slightly resembled Another God Before Him. There was much concern over the Greek god statue in the park; its base was wedged several feet into the ground, and therefore extremely difficult to move. Finally the mayor draped a white sheet over it, which seemed to satisfy the worried public. It looked like a piece of long-awaited artwork, waiting to be revealed.

My mother began taking long walks to nowhere. She would leave the house in the afternoon and call me two or three hours later from a phone booth. I would drive and get her. When we returned home, she would go straight into my father's room and for ten minutes she would love him beautifully, holding his cheeks, playing melodies on his hair.

I often wanted to be like my mother because she had long hair with red in it and to me that proved she was crackling inside. Somewhere in her there was a gene of impulsiveness, a gene I was sure I lacked. My hair was brown; at times I would dye it temporarily red for a week but it felt like putting a princess's gown on a handmaid. The breeding was not there.

Once when the sunset light came into the living room, my hair did turn red, really red, like my mother's. I watched it set my head on fire for several minutes, holding up strands and letting them fall. I felt I was in another country, where the air was so hot you could see it, and my back was dripping with sweat. I felt, for an instant, the absurd sturdiness of my legs and my back. Then I heard my dad in the other room, counting the drops under his breath as he watered the radishes, and I went to take a shower, to erase the red from my hair. I scrubbed my body fiercely with the soap, as if it were not mine, as if it weren't young, or soft, or wondering. I tried to imagine what it would be like not to want things. I tried to empty all the things I wanted into the drain and let them swirl away from me, silenced.

I came home from the store one afternoon and found my father had fallen out of bed onto the floor. He'd had some sort of seizure because his sheets were twisted into ropes near his feet and the radishes were broken on the carpet, a pile of dirt and terra-cotta. My mother was on a walk. I rushed to the phone and looked at it, then rushed back to him. He was breathing, I could see that, but his head was strangely tilted and he didn't respond when I said his name. I said his name a few times anyway, but I didn't want to touch him. I could see the strange black hairs on his thighs that were usually hidden by the yellow blanket. I stepped into the back-yard and ran and ran little tight circles around the lemon tree, lean-ing my head in to increase the centripetal force, trusting this would prevent me from running away. I wondered if there was a train waiting at the train station, going to someplace beautiful; I won-dered if the conductor had a mistress that he kept in the caboose. I imagined him stepping through the cars to reach her, train shaking, going to see her, going to make love to her in the shaking long train, and I kept making the train longer, pushing him back, ten cars, twenty cars, an impossible length before he can see her, and I pushed him and pushed him until I heard my mother open the front door. She went straight into my father's room. Running inside, I found her kneeling at his body, a hand on his leg, taking a pulse.

"Celia," she said. She was clutching a brown bag from the bookstore. I wondered what she'd bought.

"Here," I said.

She looked up at me. "Help me lift him up," she said. "He's okay."

Once he was in bed, he looked normal, like a regular sleeping person. My mother made me a hamburger and we watched TV for five hours. It was Tuesday night, a reasonably good TV night, which was lucky. Before I went to bed, I wandered briefly into my father's room; his breathing was calm. I stopped and fingered a baby radish buried in the mess on the floor. It was hard and red as a reptile's heart.

The old man and the old woman still dreamed the same dreams but she could no longer speak anything but Polish. Regardless, there were usually at least eight or nine devout followers sitting in front of their house, listening. As a whole, the town was now alert, on edge. Nervous about the commandment, people went about their day with great caution, trying hard not to make the irreparable goof. There was a moment of terror in the hardware store when Mrs. Johnson accidentally blurted, "Oh my stars," after dropping a wrench on her foot. Everyone held their breath and wondered if it was the end. Nothing did actually happen, but Mrs. Johnson hurried home in a daze, and parents hugged their children a little closer than usual that evening at bedtime.

  The old woman loved her audience, and didn't seem to realize that no one understood her anymore. She asked the gardener long complicated questions in Polish. But since his parents were immigrants too, he always nodded appropriately, and often picked a flower from the garden and gave it to her before he left. The old woman placed the flower in the hand she always shared with her husband, and they sat, quiet and patient, fingertips linked by the bloom.

One afternoon my mother went on a walk and didn't come back. By nine o'clock my father seemed confused because he kept asking me if the TV was on. An on TV was a sure sign that my mother was home. After a while I just turned it on anyway even though he could tell from his room that it was alone, blaring to an empty couch, a lamp turned off.

  By eleven, I was worried and drove by the bookstore looking for her familiar turned-out walk. There was no one but people my age, weaving through the sidewalk, heads on shoulders, the taste of beer in their mouths. I imagined fast-lane Lonnie, out with her boyfriend, her hand calm on the small of his back; I imagined my mother in Niagara Falls, screaming and laughing into crashes of bluish water.

When I got home my father was nearly asleep. He heard the front door and called out from the darkness.

"Ellen," he said.

"Celia."

"Don't worry, sweetie," he said. "She just does these things sometimes. Tomorrow."

"I should call the police," I said.

"No," he said firmly, "really. If by tomorrow this time we've no news, then okay. But she'll call."

I smiled. I knew he was wrong. But as a comfort, I stayed in the living room with the TV on all night, as she often did. I didn't really watch much, but stared at the reflected silhouette of my body in the TV screen, twirling my ankle sometimes just to remind myself that I was there.

The next night after dinner we still hadn't heard a word. I brought him milk and sat by his bed.

"She'll call," I said feebly.

"I know," he said. "She just does this sometimes."

"Yeah," I said.

"Really." He looked at me for a moment, touched my hair with his forefinger. "You're a pretty girl, my Celia," he said. "You ought to go out sometimes. You must be so sick of taking care of me."

"No," I said, trying to think of something to say. "No."

"Boys, any boys you like now?" he asked.

"No," I said again. "No boys." He looked at me and patted my head again. I could feel myself smile.

She called at ten. She was at a bar in Connecticut, on her way to D.C., to the museum, walking. She had a day or so more to go, and she wanted me to send my father on a train, bundled in blankets to keep him warm. She wanted him to meet her; they could go on the cattle cars together. She said her feet were already very blistered, and I imagined her relaxing into the cattle car, arm around my blanketed father as they prepared to experience simulated genocide.

"Put your father on the phone," my mother told me.

"He's asleep," I said. "We were both really worried. You didn't call. I was sure—we didn't know where you were."

"Is that Ellen?" I heard my father's voice, oddly strong, from his room.

"Put him on," my mom said.

"He's tired," I said.

"Celia," she ordered. "Now."

I brought him to the phone. He was delighted to hear her voice. I waited for him to be angry, to tell her how mad we were, but he didn't sound angry at all. Instead, he curled up in his bed like a teenage girl, and cooed into the receiver. I walked, disgusted, into the living room, and watched my ankle in the TV again until I heard the click.

"She wants me to take a train and meet her in D.C.," he said.

"Oh well," I said.

"But if I'm bundled up and in a wheelchair I should be okay," he said. "You know, we'll explain it to the conductor. It'd be fun to go on a trip."

"Are you kidding?" I asked.

"No," he said, "no, it could work. It's a little crazy, I know, but it could work. Your mother is walking to Washington—now *that* is crazy."

I stared at him. "It'll give you a break," he said. "You can have a little vacation from us."

I wasn't sure if he'd suddenly lost his mind. He'd been in bed for several months. He hadn't been outside for an entire season.

"Daddy?" I asked.

"I'll take a lot of vitamin C," he said. "It'll be fine. I'll go tomorrow. You'll take me to the train station?"

I walked to the door frame of his room and looked at him,

so thin under the many blankets that I couldn't see his body anymore.

"Really, Celia," he said, "I wouldn't try if I didn't think I could do it."

"Let's see in the morning," I said quietly. He smiled at me and clicked off his light. I stayed in the door frame for a few minutes, trying only to remember the words of radio songs, trying hard to fill my whole brain with hundreds and hundreds of lyrics. I cleaned the refrigerator but it was clean. Finally I left the house.

The night was warm and clear, all the lights off in the neighborhood, front lawns wide and empty. I walked through the streets counting the sidewalk squares over and over under my feet until I reached one thousand, which brought me right to the middle of the center square. And there was the Greek statue looming under its sheet. I stood quietly at its base, and looked around. The park was empty, only trees and circles of splintering wooden benches surrounding me. Even under the sheet, the statue commanded the space. I began to run in front of it, back and forth in tight rows.

"I'm going to do something," I warned, back and forth in front of the pedestal. Windows in the distance were dark, people sleeping, holding their wishes in tightly. I could hear my breath mounting as I ran faster. "I'm going to show him," I yelled, louder this time. The silence was great and empty. I ran for a moment more, faster, faster, then stopped abruptly in front of the base of the statue, and stilled my body. Breathing quickly, I grabbed a corner of the white sheet. I rubbed the corner over and over between my fingers, chafing my skin, until it climbed into my fist and I had a good hold. And then, with one fierce yank, I pulled the sheet off. It blew up high, like a gasp, then floated to the ground, collapsing and bowing behind the statue.

Uncovered, the god looked huger than ever—young, unbreakable. I put my foot on the top of the pedestal and pulled myself up. I climbed on his foot, then his knee, until I was high enough to face him. Holding on to his shoulders to steady myself, I moved in close, arms wrapping around his shoulders, pressing into his chest.

"Father," I whispered. I listened as my breathing slowed, and waited for something to change.

Aimee Bender

I visited Berlin for a few days in the fall of 1998. The couple driving me to a reading were discussing Germany's plans to build a Holocaust memorial. It was the source of lots of debate at the moment. "If you put it in one place," the German husband said, "then people come by, they give flowers, they go home. The truth is, all of Germany should be the memorial."

It seemed a very intense thing to say, to ask that the whole country hold it, in all places, at all times. But it also seemed right to me. Writing "Dreaming in Polish" was, in part, about trying to manage my own ambivalence about the Holocaust museums I've visited. On the one hand, I feel they need to be there, they serve a clear purpose. They can be visited by schools; they facilitate discussion. On the other hand, I feel (of course) we are at a loss to figure out how exactly to help people remember this chapter of history. How do you facilitate discussion of the undiscussable? I suppose one interpretation of "Dreaming in Polish" might include the idea that the mom, by going repeatedly to Holocaust museums, is also worshipping an idol, or having some kind of mediated experience, versus holding on to outrageous loss and horror in any real way possible. But, at the same time, maybe a museum is the first way to get a handle on what is almost impossible to hold. I don't know. I'm still wrestling with it.

WALT KAPLAN READS
HIROSHIMA, MARCH 1947

Peter Orner

He sits in a creased maroon leather recliner with his feet flat on the rug. The book is slender, nearly weightless in his hands. The door of his tiny study is closed. He reads by the light of a lamp that sits on a dark oak desk, now cluttered with a few opened books, face down. Otherwise the desk is tidy, with a lone paperweight in the shape of a terrier (the same one he once tried to glue to the hood of his Ford in a dig at Cy Friedman and his Cadillac DeVille), a heavy-duty stapler, a leather-bordered blotter, and a small framed photograph of his daughter as a baby. His wife, Sarah, gabs in the back yard with Erma Friedman—he can see them from the room's single window—the ladies stand, wavy dresses in the gust, by the huge boulder that looms oddly between the two houses. It is late afternoon, Saturday. He reads. By page 13 the flat nonchalant terrorless prose begins its scream. *Everything flashed whiter than any white.* He reads.

No one could say that Walt's not a patriot. In the war he was 4-F. Wife and daughter plus extreme asthma. So he joined the Civil Defense. His job was to make sure people retreated to their houses, to their basements, when the air-raid sirens shrilled. Walt Kaplan, rooted in the middle of Weetamoe Street with his steel helmet loose on his head, ordering and pointing. A starter's gun loaded with blanks jammed into the waistband of his pants, the idea being that if people didn't move fast enough he could fire into the air. Once he'd threatened to do it when that loony Roland Shutan refused to stop mowing his lawn. Walt had raised the little gun above his head but hadn't fired, and though the gun made him almost a soldier, he never liked the weight of it in his palm.

And though the 4-F made him a coward and he despised it with every ounce of his soul, he couldn't picture himself firing on anybody, even Rollie Shutan, even with a gun that shot only blanks. A man with a wife and daughter killing anybody. But didn't Melvin Zais have a wife and son, and didn't he die in Italy, a married hero with a son to worship his photograph? Didn't scrawny Mel Zais die with a gun in his hands? Mel Zais, who worked alongside him at J. J. Newbury's and later at his father's store, who lived at 618½ Tuttle Avenue his whole life, even after he married Irene and they had Toby, dying at Anzio with a gun in his hands, sweet Italian soil in his mouth and a single Fascist bullet in his temple. Now, in this thickened quiet of 1947, when he no longer is called to the street (he keeps the little gun in his drawer), he reads of Truman's bomb, more than twenty thousand tons of TNT, atomic, and Father Wilhelm Kleinsorge in his underwear. He reaches the bottom of page 48.

> To Father Kleinsorge, an Occidental, the silence in the grove by the river, where hundreds of gruesomely wounded suffered together, was one of the most dreadful and awesome phenomena of his whole experience. The hurt ones were quiet; no one wept, much less screamed in pain. No one complained; none of the many who died did so noisily; not even the children cried; very few people even

Walt stops near the top of 49, remembering the number, not folding in an ear. He balances the little book on the arm of his chair. Father Kleinsorge, no hero, a German Jesuit priest in Japan, a thin, lethargic, bent-over cornstalk of a man. The man was sickly even before what Hersey calls the noiseless flash. Walt leans his head back over the top of the chair and stares at the ceiling and knows it's lunacy, probably worse, sacrilege, an insult to the suffered, but he envies Father Kleinsorge. Envies him in his underwear in a country not his own amid the mute death, bodies under every bridge, on the banks of all seven rivers of Hiroshima. Frighteningly silent children coughing and dying in the smoke of Asanto Park. Sarah would say, Walter B. Kaplan, time to get your overheated noggin examined by Dr. Gittleman, some parts are grinding down already. And Father Kleinsorge clawing through the splintered wood of a ruined house for a voice faintly calling, and Walt Kaplan in the middle of Weetamoe Street with a whistle and a pretend gun. A child's toy. A track-meet popper.

He stands and walks the tiny room, pausing at the Kaplan Brothers' Furniture Store calendar that hangs on a thin nail by the window. His father, Max, and his two uncles, Irv and Yap, in fancied-up oval pictures, his father frowning, his little uncles grinning: Have we got a deal on a sofa and loveseat combination for you, Mr. and Mrs. Oblinski, yes, we do . . . A two-year-old calendar, still on February 1945.

Walt Kaplan, thirty-one years old and already his back hurts, his hair barely clings; he feels as if he's peeking through a crack in the door on fifty. A soft-spoken man who after a couple of drinks will laugh and tell Old Fall River Line stories for as long as his friends and brothers-in-law will listen. Built a bar down in his own basement for that very reason. So he'd never have to worry about the bar closing on a story. That, and with a bar in his own basement, Sarah gets to keep one ear on him, and so long as he can drink a little and mostly talk, he doesn't care that he never gets to go to Orley's. *Walty K.'s Home Front*, Alf and his brother Leon still call it down there. Three chrome stools with red vinyl coverings. Heavily varnished bar top and Walt's famous mermaid swizzle sticks hidden in a coffee can behind the old cash register. A big man, roly-poly since he was a kid. For the most part he carries it well—though stairs have always been a huffer and he fights to keep his shirt stay tucked. Loves and fears his wife, adores his daughter to death.

He doesn't ache for the bravery. The reaching into flames, so unfathomable—seared flesh sliding off grabbed hands and Father Kleinsorge, not repulsed, holding on to what was left and pulling. No, something far more simple. Walt's astonishment that Father Kleinsorge had vigor left to save. That his energy even half-matched his instincts. Walt stares at his dead father's now berating eyes. Then at his father's crumpled-faced brothers, the little bachelors who worked like dogs to please Max, who haunt the store even now, bitty wizened ghosts hovering among the lamps in the storeroom.

He thinks, I would have collapsed in a fat heap had they beat us to it and dropped it on Fall River. The Japs or the Germans.

The Civil Defense patrol captain for Ward 9 (Weetamoe Street to the 300th block of Robeson), me with my 4-F and cursed asthma and my Sarah and my Rhoda, and I would have wheezed and gasped. Would not have run from the chasing fire with babies in my arms. I am six years younger than Father Kleinsorge. I would not have saved my wife and daughter and the Minows, and the Friedmans, the Ranletts, the Bickles, the Pfotenhauers, the Eisensteins, the Corkys, and goddamn Rollie Shutans. A hundred thousand people writhing and shrieking, dying American style, the two onion domes of St. Anne's exploding, both the Quechechan and the Taunton blazing, and I would have been under the Ford, whistle in my mouth, gun in my useless hand—

Sarah knocks gently on the door. But as is her way—to remind him that her deference to his private study only goes so far—she says loudly, accusing, "What are you doing?"

"Reading, Sarah."

"Reading Sarah? What'd I write?"

He laughs. "Don't come in here."

"We're meeting the Gerards at the Red Coach at seven-thirty."

"The place that's shaped like a caboose?"

"Seven-thirty."

"Rhoda?"

"She's going to stay at Ida's. Gabby's over there. We'll swing by on our way home."

"Fine."

Sarah stays at the door for a couple of moments, stoops, and looks at him through the keyhole. His back is to the door, but he knows what she's doing because he heard her knees snap and her breathing sound closer. One time he taped over the hole with black masking tape, but she poked through it with a pencil.

"I said it's all fine, Sarah."

Her feet clump heavily down the stairs—his wife is no breezy chicken feather either. Without looking back at the little book, Walt opens his closet. He keeps his shoes and suits in his study. He picks up a shoe, takes it out of its felt sleeve, and inhales a big whiff of the polish. No smell like it in the world. All his shoes smell this good. Like taffy apples soaked in dye.

Sarah tromps back up the stairs. She didn't like something in his voice. As though their conversation through the door never ended, she says, "What are you reading?"

"Nothing, Sarah."

"Walt."

"About Hiroshima. The Hersey book."

"The one where we're supposed to feel sorry for the Japanese?"

He opens the door. "Sarah, you don't know."

His wife is crimson and anxious, standing in the narrow hall. She is thirty and raised a child during war (she used to send Walt out to trade vegetables for extra candy rations), got news of her sailor brother Albert's death at New Guinea in a letter from the War Department, her being his older sister, his closest living relative. Not to mention Pearl Harbor. Not to mention what the Nazis did to Jews. Who needs more sorry? We've got enough sorry as it is. This man. So swayed by newspapers and books as if they were God and everything those men wrote in them was always true. As if what they said were more true than her framed letter from the War Department: *With love of country and utmost valor*. Has to crack him on the head sometimes to pull him out from under that reading. And she used to watch him from behind the blackened curtains of the kitchen window, standing bow-legged in the middle of the street with that whistle and helmet playing General George Patton, warning neighbors in a tone of voice they never heard from Walt Kaplan before: *Citizens, if this was a genuine air raid, you'd have approximately six minutes and forty-five seconds*. Those days, when the papers shouted U-boat in the Cape Cod Canal and scared all the old fishermen out of their bananas. Everybody watching out for periscopes in their toilets.

Walt looks at Sarah, his face drained of color, bleached, like a drowned child. *Rhodas. How many thousand daughters reaching and that priest wasn't even in the Civil Defense.*

Sarah watches his stricken face, so close to hers, so familiar, so changing, withdrawing. His shoulders tremble. He's holding a shoe. Afraid of what, Walt? What? You beautiful cowering man, already old in the eyes. You'll die before I do and leave me in this house and the silence from the basement will kill me. Shhhhhhh-hhhhhhhh! You drunken whozits are waking the baby!

"Walt," she says. "Hold still. Hunk of sleep in your eyes the size of China. Telling me I don't know. Hold still." Sarah fingers the yellow schmutz out of the edge of his eye with a nail. Then she pulls her finger down his cheek and lets go.

Peter Orner

I imagine Walt Kaplan as the sort of person—too rare, maybe— who is as genuinely sorry for other people as he is for himself. I'm not certain it's all so straightforward as this, but my aim was sim- ple: to write Walt as a man who can hardly endure what he's read- ing. And this is the sort of reader you always want to reach out to, the sort you hope still exists, the sort who in the quiet of his own chair will bleed with your characters. I think in this story, I was try-ing to give a book a reader.

I wonder a lot about what sorrow does to us. Aren't we, daily, remaking ourselves? And doesn't sorrow destroy, but also build something new? I think of Kafka, alone in his office at the insurance company. I like to read his letters. All that constant anguish and yet he continued to reinvent himself over and over in letter after letter. He understood how differently people do their best to endure. Toward the end of his life, in a letter to Milena Jesenska, he wrote, "It's just that one man fights at Marathon, the other in the dining room."

In Memory of Chanveasna Chan, Who Is Still Alive

Ellen Miller

Across the hall, Charlotte was wailing again. As sure as Christmas, Friday night had descended upon the College campus—weekends had their way of doing that, coming back around with remarkable regularity—so the Weekend Weepfest officially had begun. The sound of her crying was unnerving. Crazy-making. For me, by now, its auditory assault was familiar. Familial. Powerful evolutionary forces worked behind that sound and its awful audibility. I understood that; I'd studied it. By eliciting instant, anxious vexation in the listener, by immediately elevating the listener's heart rate and blood pressure, an infant's cry—which possesses spectrographic qualities remarkably similar to those of ambulance sirens—is brilliantly adaptive for garnering attention. Maternal attention.

But still. My own mother, perhaps without knowing it, was a staunch Creationist who enjoyed saying that God made babies cute so mothers wouldn't strangle them when they cried. When I remember my mother, who is still alive, I remember irritability. I remember that at least once a day something that I did, several things that several people on television did, and every little thing that Dad did—which indubitably included his spawning, as if her body had nothing to do with it, and his befriending of me—made her grind her teeth, gnashing bone against creaking bone, clenching her whole temporomandibular apparatus, and declare with a horror that sounded newly minted every time: "Now *that* really sticks in my craw!" She'd say it about children who cried in

Kings Plaza, the local shopping mall, about babies who cried as they graffittied the walls of The Arch, the local Greek diner, with gummed-up, spat-out mashed potatoes, carrots, peas. "If that was my kid? I'd smack her so hard she wouldn't know what hit her. That little-kid shit really sticks in my craw."

For sixty-odd years, at a minimum of 365 times per year, at least once a day some real or imagined indignity bothered my mother sufficiently to get stuck in her craw. How can I not pity the woman, hobbling along, fat and bitter, trying to get around with more than 22,000 *things* stuck in the only craw she'd ever have? Twenty-two thousand things. A bit sad to picture her craw with 22,000 *things* sticking in it, sticking out from it, each craw-stick a shocking, brand-new insult. One solitary craw—alone in the universe, but attached to my mother—up against 22,000 *things*.

But nothing—"and you can believe you me, not one thing!"—stuck so deeply in my mother's craw as a baby's cry, so her craw hadn't a snowball's chance in hell of survival intact here, now, with Charlotte across the hall. My secular, Darwinist cosmology afforded me a more charitable interpretation of Charlotte's infantile tears than would my mother's Creationism. If crying was the helpless body's first desperate shriek—*Please! Notice me!*—then notice I did, because against my better judgment, against the higher reasoning presumed uniquely human among the animals, instead of strangling Charlotte I opened my closed door and headed toward her open one. Like her pair of long legs, Charlotte's door was generally open, and always flung gigantically open, while she cried.

I hovered outside her doorway, observed cautiously as she blubbered and shoveled tablespoon upon tablespoon of Coffee-mate into her lipsticked trap. Charlotte ate one meal every day: a jar of powdered, non-dairy cream substitute and a teaspoon of sugar-free jam for dessert. Only someone from big money, I thought, would spend 4,000 of Daddy's dollars—which, like his DNA, he had neither acquired nor earned, but inherited passively—on a College meal plan every semester, then eat nothing but condiments from a moldy mini-fridge. Only the spawn of countless generations of gentry, lacking even one individual who'd moved heavy objects for his livelihood, could afford the resulting fatigue and manufactured malnutrition.

A housing shortage had dumped us together. The College had accepted too many freshmen—*frosh,* as we were hideously but non-gender-specifically, required to refer to ourselves. In turn, too many freshmen had accepted their acceptances. The campus housing administration responded to the crisis by purchasing six New England mansions located way out on the campus's northern edge, across Route 66, far from the other students and buildings, to house us, the surplus. Our mansion was known as *Candyland*—a two-story affair with an architectural design seemingly lifted straight from a Christmas-kitsch catalogue. Candyland was a constant reminder of a good reason to love Jews: Jews just ain't quaint.

I'd once discussed—privately, of course—the blessed lack of Jewish quaint with a black girl, or African-American froshwomyn, who'd come to Candyland from East New York, a neighborhood overpopulated by dashed hopes and busted promises dealt by New York City to a generation of Puerto Rican and Southern black immigrants, the neighborhood from which the largest and earliest streams of Jewish and Italian migrants had committed white flight into Canarsie. Jocelyn Anderson had been surprised that I'd even heard of her subway stop: Sutter Avenue, on the LL line, four stations away from the LL's last stop—mine: Canarsie. Canarsie was the end of the line. The terminal Canarsie station's dubious contribution to U.S. cultural history was its serving as the location for Pat Benatar's "Love Is a Battlefield" video. Jocelyn had left crowded East New York to come to College and share, down the hall, with the only other black student in Candyland, a double room smaller than either Charlotte's or my own blessed single. Jocelyn's room was located opposite the highly aromatic bathroom serving all ten of Candyland's woperchildren. *Woperchildren*, because *woman* contained the offending syllable *man; woperson*, the offending syllable *son*. The door of the Woperchildren's Room bore two signs: one featuring the stylized Toilet Woman icon, with her universally recognizable yet featureless face, her ill-fitting A-line skirt, her raised, stiff shoulders, which suggested that it was no easy life being the Toilet Woman. The other sign, generously provided by a guy from downstairs, a born-again, teenage Right-to-Lifer, featured a pseudo-sonographic image of a fetus screaming in utero. The supposititiously crying fetus, Toilet Woman, and female bathroom smells greeted Jocelyn and her roommate whenever they opened their door.

Jocelyn had been a Fresh Air kid, then an A Better Chance kid; now, like me, she was a Scholarship kid. On a campus so open-minded and diverse that referring to a female five-year-old as a *little girl* instead of a *developing woperchild* had once earned me a public scolding from the College's radical feminist cult figure, any and all conversation about financial aid was tacitly forbidden. But in that one out-loud conversation Jocelyn and I vocalized a common distaste, an upward contempt for cutification while lamenting our situation in Candyland, whose corners cried out for dolls dressed in gingham and nestled in white wicker baskets, whose eating area begged for tea towels with country-duck prints, whose walls demanded samplers bearing *God Bless Our Home*—whose home? whose God?—stitched in needlepoint. I'd said to Jocelyn, "Thank God, I'm just so glad, that my people aren't quaint. You never see a Jew, for instance, wearing fucking *gingham*."

We cringed and laughed. She said, "True. I've never seen that. And the only time you see a black person wearing gingham is when she's a slave." For a while we worked not to piss ourselves laughing, then Jocelyn's eyes darkened to deadly serious. "Don't tell any white people here that I said that."

"Of course not."

"Or any black people."

"Of course not."

We could have been friends, but the silence around financial-aid status made Jocelyn and me impossibly shy around each other. By default I was hijacked into a poor excuse for a friendship with Charlotte Honeywell, for whom my preferred but unsaid name was *Across The Hall*. That's what she was—across the hall. That was her place, her purpose, her location on my mental map, so that was her name: *Ms. Across T. Hall*. With looks as WASPy as hers, her surname easily could have been *Hall*, the honorific, *Ms. Hall*, but it had so happened that no one had bothered to inform her that her Christian name was *Across*, her middle name, *The*. Across The Hall and I had an instantaneous freshman non-friendship arising from inevitability and convenience more than affection, from being exiled in Candyland, far from the rest of the campus, and from her desperate reaches toward commonality where little, if any, existed. In the first days of College, Across The Hall waxed overenthusiastic, declaring—as if friendship, unlike war, could be declared—our being joined forever with commentary that carried about as much real-world weight as, "You like oxygen? I loooooove oxygen! We're soul mates!"

Across The Hall glanced up now, furtively making certain she had an audience. I tracked one globular tear from her eye, down cheek to chin, where it hung unattractively before plopping and dissolving into her blouse's dry-clean-only fabric. It seemed clear then that the evolutionary adaptation of crying as the manifestation of distress in the young, as insurance for maternal care if the individual had lucked out in that particular department, surely must have included the selection of tears as the only bodily secretion that isn't too disgusting. If babies are *Homo Sapiens sapiens'* weakest members, and if crying is their universal distress signal, then in mammalian selection terms it behooved the species to adapt a distress signal that didn't involve revolting secretions. Tears are a clear, unclouded liquid. Tears do not adhere, congeal, or stink. Tears leave no stains and taste reasonably clean. If so much child abuse, including infanticides resulting from Shaken Baby Syndrome, stemmed from parental attempts to stop a baby's crying, what would happen to the hapless hypothetical infant who wept earwax? What mother would comfort the child weeping feces?

Would I have stood there, patient and stupid as a Labrador retriever, watching Across The Hall if she wept menstrual blood? Semen? Vaginal fluid?

Across The Hall probably did weep vaginal fluid or wish that she did, so as to facilitate the deposit of her densely pheromoned juices at every possible occasion. This week's weeping involved last weekend's dearth of sexual success stories. Today, Friday, she apparently had no beddable weekend prospects—which meant that at least in one way, I might get a day of rest. Every time Across The Hall got laid I lost sleep; her operatic moaning and my own disgusted agitation kept me awake. The afternoon after, she'd swing her door open to air out her room and boast. Each time, upon her door's grand opening, the air in the hallway between us would fill, inexplicably, with her unmistakable but baffling post-coital personal odor signature: grilled cheese sandwiches.

She clicked on high heels to her full-length mirror, banged the Coffee-mate onto the desk where she spent hours each day before her mirror studiously applying makeup to her makeup. She tossed her curls, which were so heavily viscid with residual layers of aerosols, gels, and emulsions that after the emphatic, adolescent tossing gesture, the curls reverted instantly to their original shellacked position. Only a great, uninteresting mystery of chemistry allowed her hair to move at all.

Still staring into her colorfully reflected rendition of her own features, she inhaled dramatically, as if summoning courage, faced me. "You know what you can do for me? *Si'l vous plaît*. A favor. I was talking with Chan, and—"

"—Stop there. I heard you crying, so I came over. Not to find out what I can do for you. And here's what you can do for me: Don't ever mention Chan."

"Let me explain my predicament. I've been spurned. Spurned by God."

"For crying out loud. That's what the histrionics are about?"

"I've spoken with God. God has spurned me." I busted up laughing. Across The Hall whimpered, "You laugh in the face of my torment. I'm talking about God."

God was Charlotte's name for a spiky-haired blond boy from L.A. with whom she'd been in unrequited love since her first day of French class. Her weeping spasms had worsened markedly two weeks earlier, when God had stopped showing up for French or for meals in the dining hall. Across The Hall had scrawled—in black, inch-high, magic-markered letters on my mandatory but mortifying freshman accoutrement, the message board on the door, with its infantilizing, ubiquitously embarrassing cartoon depictions of Garfield, Ziggy, or at best, Snoopy—"I've looked everywhere. I cannot find God."

On her door's message board, using its detachable, Velcro-bound pink pen, I'd replied: "Perhaps Nietzsche was right, and God is dead."

She batted a stiff tendril of hair from her eyes, then looked despondently down to hasten its descent back to its permanently lacquered home position, the tendril's inevitable return apparently illustrating her life's futile, immovable tragedy. "I went to the dining hall in case he showed up. And he did! I wasn't psyched; I was ecstatic! I was having a religious experience. My first chance to approach God, you know? So first I go to the bathroom to check my makeup and hair."

Charlotte shampooed, styled her hair, and applied fresh cosmetic products to her face only on Sundays. The other six days were a matter of accumulation onto that first foundational layer. She slept wearing makeup, in case God—or one of His earnest College-boy acolytes—popped by for a midnight poke.

"Then I go up to him and smile, you know, all crooked and

sexy, how guys like it. I go, all casual, really really *cazh*, the way guys like, not too eager—"

"—Not much. Wouldn't wanna look desperate."

"Bethie!" No one had ever called me that. "Be nice to me, okay? So I'm all *cazh*. I'm like, 'Hey, listen, if you were sick or something and you want to look over'—and he goes like this." Like an elementary school crossing guard, a transit cop rerouting traffic, or a Supreme, she shot her arm straight out in front of her torso, rigidly horizontal, parallel to the floor. Her fingers, with their thickly bejeweled rings, strained to hold a sharp perpendicularity relative to her arm. "Like, God said, 'Halt!' Then you know what he said?" Her chin assumed the texture of grapefruit skin, and her forehead wrinkled until her cosmetics cracked like an old plaster cast. "God looked me over," she sniffled wetly, "did that signal, and said: '*Please*.'"

"Bethie, I've never suffered such humiliation. Just, just explain it to me. Why would God treat me that way? I mean, I know you're a virgin so you're probably not the right person to ask." She looked at me sympathetically, as if I were extracting the pity, then sat backwards on the chair, her front pressed against the chair's back, skirt hiked—the way guys apparently liked it—legs parted at a forty-five-degree angle, knees and thighs flanking either side of the backrest. In the open space between the chair-back and seat, I saw an old menstrual stain—a Rorschach print on panty hose, shaped like the Indian subcontinent—on her stockings' cotton gusset. "But who knows? You're street-smart. Maybe you understand men even better, since, unlike me, you're not blinded by passion. Tell me honestly. What do men think when they meet me? What would be, like, say, the first two things a man thinks when he meets me?"

"That's simple."

She smiled too excitedly, leaned farther forward. "Ooh, you are a smart cookie!" No one had ever called me that. "I knew you'd have something wise to say. Tell me tell me tell me."

"Well, the first he thinks is: 'Do I want to fuck her?' And the second thing he thinks is: 'Can I fuck her? If fucking her is something I decide I want to do, what are my chances of getting it done?' That's about it."

"Maybe that's what men think about women in general, but I'm talking about me. Specifically me. What do men think when they meet me?"

"No one's exempt. Anyway I didn't make the rules. I just work here."

"You really think all men think that way?"

"No." I paused for thought. "Definitely not." I cleared my throat. "I just think that men who don't think that way pay for it with their lives."

She shut up then. I turned to leave.

"Wait. How do you know how men think if you've never been with one?"

"You've reversed it. It's because they think that way that I've never been with one."

"You should get to know some men, Bethie."

"Sounds great—especially if I then get to ball up in the fetal position and spoon-feed myself Coffee-mate while sobbing hysterically."

She grabbed her spoon and Coffee-mate jar, prepared to chow down. "Date women then. I've been thinking about women lately. I mean, like, sexually."

"That's very fashionable of you."

"Before I die I'd like a woman to make love to me."

"That phrase—make love *to* me. That's as sickening as that petroleum by-product you eat." I rubbed my eyes to wipe away the sorry sight of her. "Wouldn't 'make love *on* me' be more accurate? 'Make love *at* me.' 'Make love *despite* me.'"

She licked her lipstick, crunched Coffee-mate, smiled. That my prospects for sexual viability appeared more abysmal than hers seemed to cheer her. She wrinkled her nose and grinned slyly, twinkling several thousand dollars' worth of cosmetic dentistry. "Well, enough theories. Back to the original plan. It's a perfect idea. We can help each other. Be mutually supportive. I need to take care of myself tonight. Put my own needs first for a change. Stay in and lick my wounds."

The picture of Across The Hall naked from the waist down, doubled over, performing auto-cunnilingus, was aggressively unpleasant; naturally, its very undesirability made it stick in my visual field. I knuckled my eyes, those trouble-making, offending orifices. Fuck the poetry-schmoetry about eyes as mirrors of the spirit, windows to the soul, portals into the truth. Eyes were gelatinous holes, admitting any and all invading images: *eyesore, easy on the eyes,* were common locutions that glanced toward the eye's uncommonly infinite potential for penetration. That its emissions, tears, weren't disgusting was cold comfort relative to the great danger the eye confronts: the unrelenting risk of polluting sights, like that of Across The Hall licking her own open, red gash.

"It's beautiful!" she said, "so reciprocal. I'll stay here to look after myself, which, after what happened with God, is what I need to do. What's in it for you?"

"Glad I asked."

She smiled colossally. She had smears of lipstick on and clumps of Coffee-mate between her expensive teeth. "Getting out! That's what you need to do."

"Save your breath. The answer's 'no.'"

"You work too hard. You need a break. We've established that."

"We? Listen, how about I leave for twenty minutes? While I'm gone you and me can have a real private conversation. A nice little *tête-à-tête,* as you would say. Then when I come back you can tell me what I said."

"Just please let me finish. You need a break from work, and I need a break from my life's hardships. So, like, a few days ago I told Chan—"

"Charlotte!" I exclaimed. I actually exclaimed. Usually people claim to exclaim only in print. In my sixteen years I hadn't heard much authentic, out-loud exclaiming, but this time I heard myself, and it was empirically accurate to say that I exclaimed. Then, without any sadistic or conscious command from my brain, my arm and hand formed the Supreme- and God-like *Stop!* sign. "If I was willing to do you a favor before, which I wasn't, all I need to know is that Chan's involved and I'll tell you, without any fear of changing my mind—no. The guy's a nightmare."

"He's nice."

"Okay then. He's a nice nightmare. I'd rather eat bark than be in the same room he's in."

Chanveasna Chan lived, without a social skill in sight, downstairs with the guys. I avoided him. He was embarrassing—and not just because he was on scholarship. He didn't know how to speak; he only knew how to blurt. To spurt. Nothing he said was a clear, declarative statement, but instead a rapid-fire, spat-out sound. "Spudtz," he'd sputter. "Fliddyipp. Brertzatatll. Duffugugg. Spupp." His English itself was fine, taken word by word, but his loud, burpy, blippy, start-and-stop delivery made talking to him a seriously vigilant occasion, as there was no predicting when his next eruption of rapid, consecutive splutters would froth forth. Chan was a saucepan, full of bubbling speech-soup, word-bursts randomly popping, the pan's contents perpetually on boil.

Back in late August, on the first day of orientation, everyone in Candyland gathered in a groovy little circle for cursory introductions. Typical freshman crap. "I'm going to study bio and then cure cancer." "My favorite band is Squeeze." "You dick, Squeeze sucks. The Stray Cats rule."

My turn came. "I'm Beth Tedesky. That's about it."

There was a long silence. Across The Hall broke it: "Wooooow. That's soooooo intense."

A fey, poet-turd of a guy, wearing more kohl eyeliner than Across The Hall did, said, "Really interesting. Quite a powerful, stripped-down statement. One can't help but think of Beckett." My thinking-inside-voice offered advice from home: "You Beck

it. You brought it." Candyland's resident advisor, Hugh, a senior
with an amusing little major in ethnomusicology, who was there
to help and relate relate relate to us as an older peer, looked
thoughtfully up and to the left. "Okay." He bobbed his big Hugh-
head like a tom turkey. "I can see what Beth's getting at here."

Hugh's name tag read: "Hi! My name's Hugh!" I would've bet
good green money that not a single time in my hometown's
history—not once, since the late sixteenth century, when Grand
Sachem Penhawitz, the chief of the Canarsie Indians, whose name
looked and sounded strangely and presciently Ashkenazic, sold
Manhattan to Peter Minuit for twenty-four dollars paid mostly in
wampum; not once, since 1939, when the Works Progress
Administration declared Canarsie, which took its name from the
Algonquian word for *fenced land*, to be "a sparsely settled community laid out in dispiriting flatlands, smoked over by the perpetual reek of fires in the vast refuse dump at its western end";
not once, since the 1940s, when Simone de Beauvoir rushed to
Canarsie from her transatlantic ship's dock, because she'd heard it
was a "worker's district"; not once, since the 1950s, when the last
of Canarsie's vacant swampland, Brooklyn's last, most- and best-
avoided frontier, was finally drained and dredged to build not
homes, not *houses*, but *housing* for working families, people like
my parents, who were then still pent up in pestilent tenement
quarters; not once, since the 1970s, when Frank Zappa sent lis-
teners into stoned laughing fits with a monologue, narrated
above his song about the fur trapper in Alaska, with the words,
"I picked up a handful of yellow snow, and I rubbed it into the
fur trapper's eyes in a circular motion with such force and verac-
ity hitherto unknown to the citizens of Canarsie"; not once, since
1974, just before Dad died, when he reported overhearing a conversation between two carpenters on his job site, in which one
said, "If you can nail that piece of wood in there, I'll give you
Canarsie," and the other, who was holding a big hammer and a
big handful of masonry nails, said, "No freakin' way. Canarsie? I
wouldn't nail Farrah fucking Fawcett for that shit-heap," and

threw his hammer and nails to the ground while the whole construction crew cracked up—not once, not one single time, was
Canarsie ever called home by a person named Hugh.

Across The Hall had winked at Hugh. *Hugh*. Hugh wasn't a
name. It was a noise. But then, Canarsie wasn't a place. It was a
punch line.

After my turn came Across The Hall's. "I'm here to study
the-ay-ter. Acting is my trade," she said—as if she would recognize *a trade* if it raised and dangled her dangerously off a fork-
lift's power-operated, pronged platform, dumped her onto a
loading dock, and left her there to perish.

Next Chan erupted: "I call myself Chanveasna Chan since I
came to here, United States, San Francisco, on boat. I am from
Cambodia. My parents were killed in front of me. They were doctors. They read books. Before they were shot in the face in front
of me they had to pay for the bullets. I was a small boy. Don't
know how old. I hided for a very long time. They closed all universities. They killed everyone with eyeglasses. With wristwatch. Clock. Calendar. It was always Year Zero. Every day was
Monday. I only guess how old I am. Never know. Never sure.
Maybe twenty-seven. I give myself my name. It means 'lucky
moon.'"

Everyone seemed grateful when Hugh cut Chan off, with the
toothy WASP politeness only a Hugh has, by effusively thanking
him. For sharing and for shutting the fuck up fast. But even after
we returned to the typical autobiographies—"I'm waaaaaaay into
Dungeons and Dragons," and "But does no one here share an
admiration for the profundity to be found in Joy Division?"—
the mood had clouded. Chanveasna Chan's presence lingered. The
weather in the lounge seemed to have changed, as if bad precipi-
tation was oncoming. Just as contaminants in coughs and sneezes
dispelled only after the passing of fifteen long minutes, permitting anyone nearby to inhale them, incorporate them into his
own bloodstream, I sensed that the spat-out sounds Chan had
sloppily ejected, and their message—you bring your biography,

and the particular *you* that your particular biography authored, here, with you—were infectious agents, molecular structures of disease that dispersed, like a real stinker of a fart, too slowly.

Whatever the infection, I didn't want to catch it, but after the circle broke up for milk and cookies, which I'd never before eaten—WASPs, I soon discovered, were the only people who drank milk, whole glasses of it, in adulthood, with meals—I surveyed the excited new students. From afar I examined every youthful face and understood that Chan and I—a freshman at sixteen, as I'd skipped one year of elementary school and one of junior high thanks to the generosity or apathy of Brooklyn's public school system, and I'd saved money for College from off-the-books, below-minimum-wage, after-school jobs I'd held by violating child labor laws since I was twelve—had never been, and would never be, their age.

Now, back inside Charlotte's sex-pit, I insisted, "I'm not interested in charity projects."

"It's just a movie. I promised I'd go."

"Precisely. You promised *you'd* go. It's your gig. Deal with it."

"It makes sense for you to go. You've both been through so much. With your dad and everything? It'll be inspirational. You'd learn from each other. And it's not like he'll expect anything afterward. It's not, like, a date."

At her mention of Dad I started absently rapping my knuckles against my forehead. I spoke over the sound. "There is absolutely nothing to learn from Chanveasna Chan. The only lesson you learn from being traumatized by the Khmer Rouge is this: how to be traumatized by the Khmer Rouge. And just because he's been traumatized by the Khmer Rouge doesn't mean he doesn't like to get a little pussy."

Human eyes hold ten mere microliters of lachrymal fluid before they spill, as Charlotte's did now. "I can't go. I'm too depressed. He'll be all by himself."

I scratched at my scalp. Pulled hairs out from the base of my neck. Twirled a strand by my ear. Checked my wristwatch.

Wished it was too late. Ten after seven. Twenty minutes until the movies started.

"What's the fucking movie and where is it?"

A. T. Hall, *A.T.*, as her Best-Friend-in-a-Box—a product, me, similar in its utilitarian spirit and function to the old-fashioned, all-purpose household cleaning fluid called Janitor in a Can— named her for short, although her nickname around campus, which she pretended not to know about, was *Fashion Disaster*—hoorayed, jumped up and lunged in for a hug, shouted, "You saved the day!" My impulse, which I contained, was to mutter, "Please," halt her in her tracks with the much-maligned, God-like hand signal, and repeat something my dead Dad often said: *Don't trust people who try to save the day. The day is always too late to be saved.* "No huggie-wuggies. No theatrics. Just information, please."

"It's *Splash*. A nice, light movie. You two'll be so cute together. You're both so small. It's at the Science Center. You like that." Friday and Saturday nights two movies played on campus: one in the Science Center's big lecture hall, the other at The Cinema Society. Not *movies*, not *films*: *cinema*. I disliked seeing movies there. Too much pressure to have a transcendent, high- minded, artistic experience. Science Center movies were typi- cally more mainstream and seldom subtitled. The Cinema Society favored anything French.

I grabbed my jacket.

Heading downstairs, where Chan waited, I passed Andrew Plotkin, who was on his way up. As always he wore his yarmulke, knitted, he said, by his beloved Yiddishe mama. We stopped on a step and appraised each other. "Just back from services?" I asked. "Feeling low?"

He shook his drooping, heavily burdened head heavily, like a latter-day Job. "I thought I'd see what Charlotte was doing. I need to talk to someone."

Two Fridays earlier Plotkin had knocked on my door. Could he come in? Talk awhile? He'd just returned from Shabbat ser- vices at the campus chapel, which was actually a Methodist church. A traveling-road-show rabbi drove in from three towns over, blatantly violating dictums against operating machinery on the day of rest, to lead Shabbat and High Holiday services—as long as the Jewish ceremonies didn't interfere with Catholic Mass, general goyish holidays, or the charming New England weddings for which the College profitably rented out the chapel. Plotkin had plunked onto my bed, invited himself to lie down. He was upset and needed to rest his head. He loved and hated Shabbat. Services reminded him of growing up with his parents, both Holocaust survivors. His bottom lip quivered. He asked me to hold him. From my chair I'd replied that I was willing to listen. He talked at great length about his parents, about Dachau, about Survivor's Guilt, about Second-Generation Survivor Syndrome. Shabbat services were very, very hard for him. Why didn't I accompany him some Friday? Why couldn't we be Jews together? Would I give him a back rub? Could he give me one? When he got to the part about the medical experiments, he blubbered, reached for my hand, stroked the bluish inside of my forearm, moving upward to my shoulder, neck, chest. So much for the prohibition against sex on Shabbat. As I'd jolted to standing, sufficiently enraged and ready to remove him violently if it proved necessary, I recalled having read the label on a tiny bottle of one of Charlotte's contact lens products: *Artificial Tears. For Lubrication Purposes Only.*

I did some mental arithmetic. College was in session eight months a year. Shabbat came every Friday. For the observant, of which I was not one, a week seemed to have about three obscure Jewish holidays. Since most of the holidays were depressing, after four years Plotkin would have had 128 Shabbats and 384 holidays to play his Holocaust card, to run his trauma number. On a campus with 1,200 women—mostly well-intentioned, gullible WASPs who'd never before spoken to real-live Jews, let alone someone as Exotic and Intense as the first-born son of Dachau survivors—Plotkin's traffic in shtick and sympathy offered excellent odds for the sexual success of a pockmarked

yeshiva boy with subadequate personal hygiene, to whom I now
offered my well wishes: "*Shabbat shalom,* you sick shit."

Downstairs, I told Chan that Charlotte wasn't feeling well. He
didn't seem to mind silence as we walked. Then, halfway across
campus, he blurted, "Charlotte says your father died when you
were young." Stunned, my eyebrows hit my widow's peak. Had
Across The Hall coached him in advance, recommended my dead
Daddy as an icebreaker? "My parents died, too. Shot in the face.
Right in front of—"

"—I know. You told us."

"People forget." The lenses of his oversized eyeglasses
flashed crazily, catching beams from lamps on the Green. I considered his pleasure in wearing glasses publicly, in loving his
studies, in living for his brain after his parents were shot for having theirs. Chan awoke at 4:30 every morning. I'd leave Candyland an hour later to shelve periodicals in the science library—a
premium campus job at $4 an hour—and I'd see him sitting in the
lounge, where he studied while eating breakfast: one bowl of
rice, one bowl of tea. He'd finish by eating the last grains of rice,
plunking his spoon and pouring whatever was left of his tea into
the rice bowl, swishing it around, and drinking it all up, wasting
nothing, leaving no mess, cleaning his two bowls and one spoon
in a slurp.

The whole time he'd smile a bit, as if telling himself a cease-
lessly amusing private joke. While his morning meal was so
lovely in its self-sufficiency that I couldn't help but watch him,
the sight of him eating alone in the lounge nearly reduced me to
a puddle on the floor every single day. My memory's eye would
involuntarily see Dad on a job site, before he died when I was
eight, from blood poisoning, from thirty years' exposure to
industrial chemicals, mostly paints containing an oily, poisonous
benzene derivative absorbed through skin called aniline blue.
Aniline blue sounded like the title of a song or a poem, the name
of a daughter or a lover. Aniline blue killed him. But before that,
at 11:30 every weekday morning Dad would open his lunch

bucket and prepare to eat his meal—two-turkey-on-dry-toast sandwiches, an apple, a cookie, a thermos of black coffee—along a temporary fence, high up on a scaffold, atop a wall half-demolished by a wrecking ball, alone. The man who drinks alone in public can be tragic, heroic, pathetic, but he's always granted his adjectives. There are no words for the man who eats alone in public. The man who eats alone in public has no adjective. He exists outside language, outside the entire kingdom *Animalia*, because all the other living creatures do each other the honor, the grace, the social favor of sharing, disrupting, or wrangling each other's meals. The poor bastard who eats alone in public? He's done for.

Chan yawned. I asked, hopefully, "Too tired for a movie?"

"I worked hard today. I am tired, but I am glad that soon I will see Darryl Hannah."

"You like her?"

"I like Darryl Hannah very much." His private smile and eyeglasses flashed again, the lenses like Zany Zappers. I composed a mental note for Ms. Hall's message board, which became a letter: Dear Charlotte. Chan is an ox. I am an ox. We work all day. We eat the minimum of cud required to keep us working, driven by blind duty, blind terror, and also by the knowledge that hard work—making a *living*, a *livelihood*, a *life*—is a strange and surprising privilege. Oxen work hard for food, for survival. Oxen ultimately pay for their labors with their lumbering, lummoxy lives, but never, ever underestimate the ox's cosmology. Behind the slow, stupid, brown eyes of any ox, eyes that apparently comprehend exactly two things—toil and more toil—exists an inner galaxy, a universe, of perception. An ox experiences the subtlest nuances of hunger, exertion, desire, strain, gravity. An ox knows the accurate heft of things, the hued particularities of muscle fatigue, the sweetness of well-earned rest, relief, and respite. And Darryl Hannah.

In the lecture hall we settled into our seats, watched the other students laugh, flirt, sneak six-packs. I couldn't get it up to make chitty-chat with Chan. Having exhausted the subjects of Darryl Hannah and dead parents, anything I said might have sunk to the bottom of a bottomless historical hole. Eventually I'd fall and get trapped down there with it. With him.

The room darkened. Chan sat up erect and I slumped, each of us anticipating Darryl Hannah flopping around in her mermaid suit and arranging our seated bodies correspondingly.

No mermaid. A skinny brown boy—definitely not Tom Hanks—wore a black helmet and sat on a big, floppy-eared buffalo as a plane flew low overhead. A vast field, green with the phosphorescence of young grasses. Blue hills. Words: An Enigma Production. Enigmatic that these cool colors—blue water, hills, skies, green jungles, meadows—looked so violently hot. Sounds: propellers, explosions, sizzles of fire, an earth that appeared to have crashed into the sun.

"This is *Splash*?" I demanded. "I think we should be at the other place."

Black storm clouds. Chan's face didn't shift an inch from its direct confrontation with the screen. "Charlotte said Science Center."

I said, "We're in the wrong place." We were. We were in deep shit. We were in the warm, dark womb of a movie theater, and very bad things were happening there. We bathed in, then absorbed, the light and sound waves whose job it was to transport us—by penetrating our optical, auditory, neuronal passageways, whether or not we'd consented—to this very bad place. Words appeared first in white letters, then each letter turned a terrifying orange-red, a color I recognized as the color of heat itself, of heat visible inside the lit inner chambers of car lighters. The letters, larger now, title-sized, burned themselves into the screen.

The Killing Fields.

"We're outta here, Chan. Let's go. We're leaving. Now. We're leaving."

"No!" he shouted. A frosh-squad turned and shushed him. "I stay," he hissed.

His eyes fixed themselves to the screen as movie-time elapsed, and images passed through us, their ingress, the eyes. An infant's corpse, burned to a black crisp, abdomen open and blackly red. Bombs detonated. Machine guns fired. Cars exploded. Chan didn't look away. When a group of prisoners were blindfolded, knocked to kneeling with the rifle butts of soldiers, and shot in the back, Chan exclaimed, truly—"Oh!"—and slapped his eyes with his palms, kept them there, pressing in hard. Then he doubled over, his chest flattened against his thighs. He sat unmoving in that position during some minutes I spent deciding what to do.

An affectless American actor said, "Anything I eat has to be absolutely dead." A prisoner was shot in the face. A Cambodian actor explained to an American, "I do love my family."

I leaned over so that Chan's head and mine were level and whispered at him. "What are you, high? Are you nuts? Don't do this to yourself."

Chan whispered, "I must."

I whispered, "Fine. Then don't do this to me. Don't wipe it on me."

He whisper-shouted, "You go. I will not mind. I stay here."

"You're not even watching."

"I cannot watch. I am not watch, but I stay. You please go. I stay here." Chan's English was breaking down, but Chan wasn't. He removed his hands from his face—a wet, authoritative man's face—and in a single, slow, controlled rise he sat up. When his torso and thighs formed a right angle, his eyes looked directly at and into mine. "You see, this is first time since I was small boy, don't know how long, twenty years maybe, never sure, only guess, never know, that I have heard the sound of anyone speaking in Khmer." In the dark Chan's eyes were steady, calm, wet, almost happy in their absolutism. Behind his berserk eyeglass lenses was something new and hot and raw and dangerous and not to be fucked with. "For very long time I not hear any sounds of this language. Khmer."

The frosh-squad turned, glared, noticed that Chan's face was shining with long, slow tears and not a little mucus. Then they apologized humidly and too much. One kid actually wrung his hands. Chan whispered, "We stop talking now, so that my parents can listen to our language. Khmer." He placed his face back into its private shelter of palms and woven fingers.

I needed—and fast—another of Charlotte's contact lens products, her *Multipurpose Solution*. I sat for a while, then bolted up the aisle and out the lecture hall's door. The doors swung shut but failed to seal in the cataclysm. The Science Center was blessedly silent, except when it wasn't: except when there was shelling, screaming, rat-a-tat-tat spraying of automatic fire, and voices using a language of loud, clipped, staccatoed reports. Was the chopped and fractured Khmer issuing from inside the lecture hall what Khmer always sounded like? Or did all voices, universally, regardless of language or land, bang themselves out this way in emergency, a vocalized Morse code for naked fear? The answer didn't matter to Chan, who'd been flown by this language to the place where he was most mutilated and most solid: Home.

I was very glad not to be there.

In the bathroom, after a nod toward the ever-tense Toilet Woman on the door, I splashed cold water on my face and noticed my hands shaking when I tried unsuccessfully to zip up my jacket for the long trek back to Candyland. My face in the mirror looked even paler and bluer than usual. The mirror's surface was flecked with smears of lipstick—smudges in rose-pink, coral, plum, brick, burgundy, and one perfectly puckered kiss-shape in a nearly black blue, the shade of a day-old bruise—from so many College girls, like Across The Hall, making themselves beautiful, putting on their faces, for movie dates. I'd have to murder the harlot Charlotte later, especially if I found out that she'd dumped me with Chan to pass the evening fucking Plotkin instead. A pity. Since I'd also have to kill Plotkin I'd serve time for double homicide, but for the greater good of the community they needed to disappear, and I was the one to make that happen.

I imagined Across The Hall here in this bathroom, gazing into the marred mirror, blithely applying yet another layer of lipstick to the layers that were preexisting, like a condition, an inch of it caked onto those red, puffy, red lips, always shiny, overglossed, slightly parted. Those lips were her face's central red hole, a void at the core, surrounded by dark, damp-looking curls, voicelessly shouting, "Look, world! Check it out! My face is a cunt!"

I looked as if I'd just walked barefoot all the way across Russia from Bialystok, as if I'd washed up like ocean detritus near the Bering Sea, which separates Asia and the United States at their closest points, and trudged *borves,* my feet shoeless bloody stumps, over the Bering Strait, which during the Ice Age—when the Bering's sea level fell by several hundred feet, turning the frozen strait into a land bridge connecting Asia to North America—provided the most slender of passages over which innumerable plant and animal species had migrated in search of their next temporary homes.

Back in this public bathroom, in the more recent Holocene epoch, I looked like the dog's dinner. Charlotte was always chasing after me with powders, creams, brushes, and pencils, but none of her stuff matched my coloring. If she ever would live to let her skin breathe, exhuming her face from its decade of burial under paint, once the topmost gray layer, which never saw the light of day, got some sun and warmth and vitamin D she'd probably discover a glowing, goyish complexion.

Not me. If Charles Haskell Revson—Revlon's Jew-boy cosmetics magnate, whose surname was Yiddish for *rabbi's son,* who had once famously yelled from a control room he didn't realize was miked, only two hours before shooting a live Revlon commercial to be seen by 50,000,000 viewers of *The $64,000 Question,* in reference to his model, "Get rid of that girl! She looks too Jewish!"—had designed a cosmetics line for pale-faced Jew-girls who looked as afflicted as I did now, he would have called it

Shtetl Girl. To bring the optical illusion of good health to my cheeks, he'd have concocted a blusher, a pale-ish, pinkish, abraded-looking shade, named *Chicken*. For wear underneath all other beauty products in the *Shtetl Girl* line, he'd have mixed a liquid foundation that perfectly matched my skin tone and called the shade *Pulled Tooth*. A blood-red lipstick, *Pogrom,* for when I was feeling impetuous, and a dramatic, neo-Gothic, dark-gray eye shadow, *Ashes,* for same. For romantic, sexy nights out, like my date with Chan, he would have formulated an extravagant perfume, christened it with a musical, tintinnabulary name, *Kristallnacht,* packaged it in an elaborately angular, desecrated-looking stained-glass bottle, and advertised it with the slogan, *For Those Unforgettable Nights Out.* The bottle's stopper might be a glittering, shattered Star of David. Before bedtime I'd soak a cotton ball in a clear, liquid astringent, *The Final Solution,* and rub it all over my face to remove any residual, undesirable elements. Then I'd apply an overnight moisturizer—*Creamatorium*—to help slow the formation of wrinkles caused by millennia of anxiety and persecution.

Perhaps God—not Charlotte's obsession, but *Adoshem in himel*—would strike me down for amusing myself this way, but I had to busy my brain somehow, so I wouldn't contemplate what I was about to do.

One time when I was a kid, I'd heard the word spoken, and I'd asked Dad what a *mitzvah* was. He answered with a joke. "The one about the Jew who's about to kill himself jumping off a bridge. The Jew says, 'I can't go on! I want to die! I can't take it anymore!' A Jewish cop shows up and says, 'If you jump, it's my job to jump in after you, to rescue you. But I don't know how to swim. Surely you wouldn't want a man with a wife and six beautiful kids—God bless them, *kayn eyn-hore*—to die? You want I should drown in the line of duty? Listen to me. Be a good Jew. Do me a mitzvah. Get down off this bridge. Go home. Relax. Get comfortable. Then go hang yourself.'"

In the stall I worried an unused roll of toilet paper from its cramped dispenser. In formulating my hypothesis about tears' selection advantage in not being disgusting, I'd erroneously omitted the mucous factor. Mucus nudged tears toward disgust's next realm. Maybe tears were disgusting after all, maternity itself being the selective adaptation, and if babies wept shit the species would use its higher reasoning to finesse the belief that shit wasn't itself vile. The institutional-supply toilet paper felt coarse in my hands. For the $25,000 a year we paid or borrowed to go to this *farshtinkener* College, they could've stocked something decent for wiping shit from the *tuchas* and mucus from the nose.

Chan was a cough—a nagging, contagious cough—and I'd caught it. He'd passed it on to me, and now it was mine to tend to or to disregard. As I opened the lecture hall's doors, permitting the glare of the killing fields to pierce my unaccustomed, forced-open pupils, the simple fact that he and I were *landsleit*—two people born in the same town in the Old Country—pierced me, too. In the presence of a weeping *landsman,* a *balbatisheh mensch* can do no more, and no less, than to sit her skinny, peasant ass down, hand over the toilet paper, and lean inward, inward into his storm.

Ellen Miller

Chanveasna Chan is based on a Cambodian student I knew. Once, after several coincidences, accidents, and social faux pas, we went to the movies. Together we were horrified to discover we were in the wrong theater, which was showing the movie mentioned in the excerpt. My response wasn't Beth's. Beth has a sense of humor about her predicament; in the factual moment nothing was funny at all, but like Beth, I was conscious then of feeling responsible for bearing witness to his historical agony. I'm using responsible *not in the causal sense, not to suggest blame or guilt or collective moral culpability, but to mean* able to respond. *I can't say whether my having felt able to respond arose from my being the particular per-*

son I am, being Jewish, or being Holocaust-haunted, because I've never not been the particular person I am, and I've never not been Jewish or Holocaust-haunted. The incident's most potent dimension was my witnessing the immediate inextricability of language and memory, the power of human voices, speaking in left-behind language, to transport someone so thoroughly back to a left-behind life, to a land—and with it, a language—fled.

How to Make It to the Promised Land

Ellen Umansky

Here is the game they want us to play. Bobby Z., the camp director, explains it to us the night before. First, he reads us the names: Treblinka, Birkenau, Terezin, Auschwitz. "This is what happened to so many of the Jews of Europe," he says, as if we didn't know. "But what about the ones who got away?" He asks this, and then he splits us up. We are no longer the three dozen fifteen-year-olds attending Camp Shalom in the summer of 1991. Tomorrow will be November 1, 1940, and we will be in Lodz, which was invaded by the Nazis last September. Two-thirds of us are Polish Jews, living in the ghetto. The remaining third are "officials"—Polish, German, or SS guards. The challenge, for the Jews, is to escape deportation.

We are handed yellow stars and strands of plastic beads that will double as currency. We are given purple, ink-smudged maps of camp on which everything has been renamed. All the Hebrew names are gone: my bunk, formerly called Machon, is the Polish Passport Agency. Bunk Alonim is the bank. The kitchen is the town's desecrated synagogue and is entirely off-limits. The old canyon fire road is the Polish border. We are also given ID cards. I am not Lizzie Lenthem, fifteen, of Topanga, California, but Anya Ossevsheva, twenty-one, of Lodz. I have four kids. I have a long aquiline nose and a hard unsmiling mouth. I look nothing like me.

We are told: "You will have to make it across the Polish border by sundown." We are advised to try the official routes first. A very few of us are lucky, our names already on visa lists. But most of us are not; we will try to trade our pathetic beads, acquire visas, meet up with relatives and friends who are better off, masquerade as goys, charm guards into letting us stow away on a train to Zurich or a boat to Buenos Aires. How will we do this? Who among us has money? Who doesn't? Bobby Z. won't tell us. "Go to the bank. Try the passport office," he says. "You will see."

We are told: "The wood between the girls' and boys' camps is Central Europe; the goal is to move beyond it, past the fire road, to the old tennis courts, to America. The guards will try to prevent this—the soccer field will be used for roundups—but if you have the proper papers, there is nothing they can do." Bobby Z. says: "Do not enter the synagogue; do not try to trade real goods or real money; and do not, I repeat, do not try any funny business, or you'll never leave this camp, let alone Poland." Any of these rules can change at any time, we are warned. We are told all this, and the next morning we are sent on our way.

Except I don't go on my way. What do I know? I am the newcomer. When I was a kid, I once asked an old woman on a Santa Monica beach if the numbers tattooed on her arm were her phone number. I spent last Yom Kippur with my Filipino boyfriend, making out in the parking lot of the Wendy's on Pico, eating double bacon cheeseburgers. The only reason I'm here is that my mother (Israeli, atheist) wants to piss off my father (Bostonian, Presbyterian), who is six months behind on child support. She sent me here so she could "rejuvenate," she said. Where's the rejuvenation in steaming off wallpaper and installing new bathroom tiles? That's all she seems to do these days. I haven't answered a single one of her letters since I've been here. But one thing I do know is this: Malibu in 1991 just isn't Lodz during the war. And I'm not going to pretend otherwise.

We are forced up and out of our bunks before the summer sun has warmed the air or dried the dew on the clumps of yellowing grass, and the basketball court we assemble in is buzzing in the bluish morning light.

A small group settles down on the blacktop, just inches away from Bobby Z., all anxious and excited. They're kids like Leslie Epstein and David Margolis, who are always offering to lead one of the million prayers that I still don't know, sending those stupid Shabbat-o-grams back and forth to one another, or saying, "You haven't been bat-mitzvahed?" as if I'm some kind of alien. They cup their IDs in their hands. They have already pinned on their stars.

Then there are the boys in loose flannels throwing mock lay-ups into the sagging basketball net, and a knot of languid lip-glossed girls in little white shorts and tanks, who don't seem to notice the cold, stretching out their legs, exchanging looks. A girl with a great smear of purple eyeshadow is braiding Jill Simon's long lush hair; Jill is drawing a bunch of daisies on her knee. In front of them, in a bright pile of shifting colors, are their IDs and stars. There's no way they're going to put them on until they have to.

This is the difference between cool and not cool here: who wears the stars and who doesn't. And this is just one of many reasons I can't stand this Jew-camp hell, which everyone else has been coming to since they were fetuses. I am sitting behind the basketball net, away from everyone else, just as I've been doing all summer. In order not to look for Rafi, whom I look for far too often, I am staring at the distant hay-colored hills. Rafi is a *madreich,* a counselor for the little kids, a guitar-playing junior from Santa Cruz, with sleepy silvery eyes and a mass of jet-black curls, who hitched around the Golan Heights last summer. You'd think everyone else would be after him too, that all those lip-glossed girls would try to sidle up to him during meals, and the fact that they don't just proves what I've known since I first set foot in this camp: They know nothing.

"You'll have an hour here in the 'town square,'" Bobby Z.

tells us, slicing his fingers through the air to form quotation marks. "You can trade items with one another, you can look for family members—it will be easier to get across as a unit than alone." His wide bearded face breaks into a grin; nothing in his look lets on that his camp is on its way down, that parents now prefer Ramah or Wilshire Boulevard camps to Shalom. "You must wear your star and ID at all times. Failure to do so will jeopardize your chances of obtaining a visa."

"Fascist," I hear a low voice say. It is Kron, with her crazy red hair and dozens of black rubber bracelets wallpapering her pale wrists, the closest thing I have to a friend in this place.

"You're lucky to be here in America. All of us are. For just one day we'd like you to pretend otherwise," Bobby Z. concludes.

Names are being called out: "Rosie Glass, Wolfe Gootman, Lev Levy." People are milling about, searching for family, grabbing their friends. I am doing none of this. I am not interested in finding Anya's husband. In my family (my real family, my only family, that is), marriage is a burden, not a boon, and one that the women of every generation have worked hard to shake off.

A boy with a moon face comes by. "Have you seen Helen Markowitz?" he asks. I study him for a moment. He should be at the other end of the basketball court, where people really care about this stupid game, where counselors are pointing out wives and distributing extra safety pins and tips on how to make it to the promised land.

"Helen is dead," I say.

His face shifts colors, from pink to purplish red—I see it happen.

"Dead?"

For a second, I feel bad—I don't even know him—but I continue. "Of course, she's dead. You're dead, she's dead, Anya Ossevsheva is dead too," I say, thrusting my ID in his face. "It's only a game."

He looks at me and scowls. "Thanks a lot."

I smile. "You're welcome."

"Bitch."

"Asshole."

He leaves. I look at the ID in my hand. I stare until the photograph of Anya no longer looks like a face. It becomes something else: a fingerprint, maybe, or a scattering of sand, or an oil stain. It looks like everything and nothing at the same time. I fold it up and stick it in my back pocket.

"The bank and Passport Control are opening up," Bobby Z. says, getting excited. "Get moving."

The weak sun is now casting a pale glare. The basketball court clears out. Clutching their plastic beads, kids file past the red-painted iron sculpture that looks like dueling tampons. I see them line up in front of Bunk Machon, then circle back to Alonim.

Bobby Z. and the couple of counselors who didn't take the younger kids to the water slides in San Marino are walking around, sweeping the place. "Time to get going," Orna Lewis says. "No dilly-dallying in Poland."

"If this is Poland, how come we're not speaking Polish?"

She just scowls at me. "Let's go," she says. "There's KP duty in Poland, too."

I head down the slope toward the dining hall, acting as if I know where I'm going. Kron appears by my side. Her red hair is wild, each curl going off in its own direction, disobeying the laws of gravity. She looks at me and says, serious, "How are we supposed to remember what we never knew in the first place?"

It's a good question. Kron occupies the only single bed in our bunk; no other girl wanted to be near the black netting she draped over her bed, the weird atonal music she plays. She and I started hanging out a couple of weeks ago, eating at those empty tables in the back of the dining hall; still, I don't know much about her. The counselors call her Karen, but she insists that her name is Kron, that she was born on the planet of Lamu. She moves her bracelets up and down her wrist, following my eyes.

I don't know what makes me say it: her bracelets, her sad serious face, or mine? "Let's get out of here," I say.

I lead the way through a raggedy stand of pines and up a back path that I like to take to the dining hall. If you climb far enough up this hill, you can sometimes spot a glint of metal— cars streaming up and down the black strip of the Pacific Coast Highway, heading north to Santa Barbara or south to L.A.

Somehow we manage to reach the kitchen without running into any guards. You'd think there'd be someone here to acknowledge the building's transformation into a desecrated synagogue, but in a way I'm not surprised. My mother has told me stories about her uncle Avi, a fat, black-hatted father of eight with disarmingly pale blue eyes and a sour-pickle smell; he refused to join the army, railing against the godless Israeli state and his heathen relatives, while he ripped off his business partner and cheated on his wife. The more pious they look, the more hypocritical they are, she'd say. She thinks this and yet she still sent me here?

I rattle the screen door and call Yarden's name. Yarden is from Honduras and has skin the color of milky tea. Sometimes when I'm supposed to be at swimming or archery I sneak in here and plant myself on the counter, helping him to peel potatoes until they form a pyramid. He tells me about the importance of breathing through the diaphragm, his long fingers resting on his ribs, or he tells me about the mangroves back home. I am beautiful and smart, he says, but I shouldn't be so down on makeup. "A girl should never be afraid to wear a little color," he says firmly as he chops onions, the tip of his knife gleaming.

"Yarden?" I hiss again. No answer. Kron stays several feet back, on patrol.

"It's better that he's not around," I say. "We'll just pop off the screen window, and you'll crawl in."

I give her a leg up, guide her to the loose part of the screen. She is as light as a bird. I am loving this. We are misfits, we are outlaws. We won't be around for deportation. If we were in Poland, we would be the ones to survive.

"This is a bad idea," Kron whispers.

I boost her up even higher. "It's the best idea I've had all summer," I say.

She twists around. "I don't think—"

"That's right," I say. "Don't think at all." That had been my policy all summer: not thinking, trying to forget, trying to imagine that the person stuck here with a freak as her only friend is someone else, that it's someone else standing under the weak shower spray, tears mixing with the lukewarm water, wondering, why me?

Finally, Kron gets the screen off and slips through the window. A minute later, she is at the back door, opening it for me.

"I bet you they're all inbred," I say, inside the dark narrow kitchen with its cracked linoleum. "They probably have those weird diseases, like the Amish or the English royal family."

We are discussing the girls in our bunk, or rather, I'm discussing them. Kron isn't nearly as interested as I am in Jill Simon's breeding. There's only the scratch scratch of her pencil as she sits on the floor, drawing.

I lean over. On the yellow cardboard face of her star, she's sketching a disk with radiating spokes. It's creepy, but kind of cool too. I'm wondering what it's supposed to represent, when Kron, in her small, flat voice, says, "It's not so bad in here."

"No, it's not," I say, thinking that we could stay here for days, weeks even. Yarden would come back and the two of us could help him in the kitchen, hanging out in this sanctuary of warmth, away from the onslaught of activity after activity performed in the name of "camp spirit" and "Jewish community." "If they wanted to make sure the Holocaust never happens again," I say, "they'd be teaching us stuff so we don't end up like them."

Kron snorts. "What kind of stuff?"

I'm thinking of my mother's two years in the army. "Stuff so we could kick ass, so no one could push us around."

Kron doesn't say anything but she doesn't laugh either. A minute or two pass with the sound of her scratchings. Then she says, "If we get caught—"

"We're not going to get caught."

"If we do," Kron says again, flatly, "we meet at the canteen at three. No one will bother us there."

"Okay." I sit back, grateful that she's taking charge. "Tell me about Lamu," I say. Kron gives me a look. I shrug. "What's the weather like? Who lives there?"

"Some things are better left unsaid," she says beneath the curtain of her hair. "You know, Anne Frank survived years in an attic, barely talking above a whisper."

"Good for Anne Frank," I say. I pluck a pan off a hook above the industrial chrome stove and stare into it. The surface is all scratched up, but I can just make out my face. An old-looking face I've been told ("classic," my mother says)—the hard jaw, the formerly blond hair that has settled into a harmless and unexciting shade of brown, the tiny nose and light-blue eyes that I'm told are dead ringers for my father's. Not that I see him often enough to know. It's an okay face, not great, not terrible. I say, "I'm surprised they didn't make me a guard or a Nazi or something."

Kron looks up.

"Are there Jews on Lamu?" I try. "Jews who look like me?"

"Lamu does not host organized religions," she says after a pause. "We don't believe in them."

"That's good," I say, softly.

I am looking out the window to see if I can spot Rafi but I see only Bunk Machon. A couple of girls are sitting back to back, their chins upturned to the sun. Some guys are playing tic-tac-toe with sticks in the dirt. Nobody looks anxious. Nobody looks Polish. Nobody cares about anyone but themselves.

I hear footsteps behind me. "Kron?" I say.

"Whatsa matter, Lizzie?" a voice says. "You afraid of being a Jew?"

I turn around. Orna Lewis taps her fingers against the clipboard she clutches to her chest and flicks a strand of stringy blond hair behind her ear. "Game over," she says impatiently. "Let's go."

"The game's over?" I say slowly. She could send us to the soccer field for deportation, if she wanted to. "We can go back to the bunk now?"

She bangs her clipboard against the counter. "You have to get your papers and get out of Poland. Now! Let's go! Both of you!"

I start to move, but Kron doesn't. She's sprawled out, lying prostrate on the dirty linoleum, her pale birdlike arms at her sides, her hair spreading around her. Orna nudges her foot against Kron's butt. "Karen! I'm serious!" she says, but Kron doesn't respond. Her eyes flutter open. She looks at Orna, she looks at me. She smiles, and out flies pale-colored vomit from her mouth—elegantly, in an arc, it flies up and shoots down on Orna's woven open-toed sandals.

"Oh," Kron says.

Orna shrieks and stomps around, light brown drops flinging around like wet paint. I freeze. I live in fear of throwing up. The last time I did I was in fifth grade. It was a rainy Wednesday, and I was having dinner with my father at a restaurant. I twirled great masses of spaghetti and clams around my fork, my eyes fixed on the Dodger game on the TV set above the bar. He talked about his new office, the great view he had of the Hudson.

"You mean, New Jersey," I said.

His eyes crinkled blue. "How did you know that?"

"Geography," I said, and my voice filled with exasperation. "We learned that in fourth grade."

On the way back to my mother's, not knowing when I would see him again, I threw up in his rental car. I am remembering his "Jesus! Jesus!" when I hear Orna yell, "She needs to go to the infirmary!"

"Orna," I moan, clutching my stomach, "the chicken, I think it was . . ." But I am two beats too late.

"Don't even try it!" she says. "You're going to Machon. Now."

Orna stomps across the linoleum. Kron turns around, raises her sharp eyebrows. "Canteen at three," she mouths to me.

The sun is on full blast. We pass the empty basketball court, its black asphalt glittering in the heat, and a ring of campers standing around with clipboards like Orna's. They watch as she marches me to the Machon line. I stare right back at them and wave, just to let them know that I'm still around, but I'm feeling a little nervous with Kron gone. Orna deposits me at the back of the line, where the rumors are flying. "You don't even need a visa." "No one is getting across." "Kids are disappearing; no one's seen Leslie Epstein for hours." "Bobby Z. is standing at the gates, making you pay real money; it's all a front so he can make a little extra cash." But they don't stray from the line.

I am not here, I tell myself. I am not here at all. If I concentrate hard enough, I can put myself behind the counter at Häagen-Dazs on Seventeenth Street, where I should be, scooping shivery happiness for anyone with $1.49.

Jill Simon, the premier girlie girl of my bunk, saunters up to the line with her boyfriend Jesse, a short guy with thick hair who acts inches taller than he is.

"We could be at Zuma right now," Jesse says. "Out there, in the water." He traces the line of skin between Jill's shorts and her top.

"You can't go surfing," Jill says. "We have visas to worry about." She guides his hand to her navel, laughs lightly, as if no one were around for miles.

I cough, loudly.

"What?" she says, as if interested in my response, but there is a hitch to her tone that tells me everything. "What are you looking at?"

"Nothing," I say. "Nothing at all."

"Let her watch all she wants," Jesse says. "If that's how she gets her kicks." He flings an arm over Jill's shoulders.

"Yes, you're splendid entertainment."

"You don't think I could entertain you?" Jesse says in a voice knitted with sweetness. I feel his eyes travel up my body. I know what he's looking at. Earlier this year, my body took off without me; this was the year that my mother and I spent too many hours at Bullock's shopping for bras. Last week, Jesse came up to me in the dining hall and leered at my chest as I held a glass under the soda machine's spigot. "Go bother your Barbie doll of a girl-friend," I said, but that did nothing to wipe his smirk off. Now his lips curve into a smile.

I cross my arms. "In your dreams."

But it is as if I've said nothing at all. And I do what I've been doing all summer, I concentrate so hard that a hum starts up in my ears and light wavers in front of my eyes. I pull my ID out of my back pocket, and I stare again at Anya's face. Thick eyebrows set far apart, a narrow bridge of a nose, dark hair that hangs down heavy over her cheeks. It's a strange look, but not unat-tractive. I wonder what her life was like. Did she really have four kids? What happened to them? What happened to her? Was she one of the people they were talking about last night? I think of those train tracks, skin stretched thin over bones, and those in my family who never made it out. I won't let that happen to me.

It takes close to an hour, but when I finally get inside the bunk is cool and dark. The fans click. As my eyes adjust and the shadowy shapes sharpen, my heart does a dance. I should've come here hours ago.

Someone has pushed all the bunk beds against the far wall, their metal legs peeking out beneath the mint-green sheets they're using as curtains. In front, sitting, resplendent, as if on some kind of stage, is Rafi, beautiful Rafi. He is in charge of pass-ports. He is in control.

A rectangle of butcher paper is covered with a grid of names,

X's and O's marching down in columns. In front of me, a fat girl in orange hightops is arguing with a short, sallow-skinned boy whose name I also don't know. "I'm not selling the painting just to get across," she hisses.

Rafi waves them over. They hand their papers to him. Rafi's fingers fly. They waltz across the keys of the adding machine, they flip through the IDs. They are long and limber with a life of their own. They could be anywhere, those hands—tapping on a glass-topped table in Paris, unbuttoning an Israeli Army jacket, caught in the tangle of my hair. I can't say if it is minutes or seconds later—time is a slippery, iridescent glaze—but soon Rafi stamps their cards and is calling to me.

"Hey," he says, folding his hands in front of him. "Look who we have here." He is smiling. Tiny holes ring the neck of his worn T-shirt, which reads "Once Is Never Enough."

I breathe. "Hey," I say and smile back.

He brushes hair out of his eyes, clears his throat. He asks for my papers.

"You're married," he says, "with four kids." He tells me this like he's telling me: You can stay out all night.

I bite my lip. "I've been busy," I say.

He laughs. "Clearly," he says. And I laugh, too.

He swivels around, checking names on the paper behind him. I stare at the curve of his tanned neck, the point at which his curls stop and the knob of his spine appears. There is a dime-sized patch of peeling skin, and I resist the urge to reach out and tear it off. Maybe he'll give me a train pass for later this afternoon; maybe I'll get to wait here for hours with him.

Rafi turns back around, places his hands flat on the table. Can he tell that I've been with older guys before? That I'm not just some silly fifteen-year-old who doesn't know anything?

"I can't let you through."

"What?" Stupidly, I smile some more.

He leans closer; his lips are a little chapped. His skin smells like clean laundry. "I can't give you a stamp."

"What do you mean?" I say, and I badly need to swallow. "You can let me through. I know you can."

He shrugs. "Sorry."

I hate myself for what happens next. It's just a game. But the tears well up anyway. "I don't understand," I say, and my voice is a pathetic whisper. "Please."

"You'll be fine." He tips his chair back on its hind legs, gives me what I'm sure he thinks is an encouraging nod. "See you on the other side."

The sky is too blue, hard with color and cleared of any clouds. The basketball court is a ghost town. The back door to the kitchen is padlocked shut; the window Kron and I crawled through is now covered with yellow caution tape. There is the soft hum of a generator, and an oceany rush that I know is the flow of cars on the PCH.

I peek through the back window of the infirmary, but all the beds are empty. Where is Kron? Why didn't she warn me she was going to throw up? I would have told her that I couldn't do it. Maybe she knew that; maybe she wanted to get rid of me and go over to the other side. Maybe everyone will make it but me. I lean against the stuccoed wall of the dining hall. I'll do what I should have done in the first place, what I should have done that first week of camp. I'll hike down to the cars careering up and down the highway, and I'll hitch a ride north to Santa Barbara or Los Ojos. I'll learn to waitress, to balance plates on my arm and know what people want before they ask. I unlace my sneakers, easing my sticky heels out of the canvas. The smell is so strong, so deep and purely rank that for a second I breathe in, impressed. I close my eyes and daydream about Topanga and my mother; her hard freckled shoulders and her cigarettes and the orangy-brown lipstick she's been wearing since I was four. She'd probably hate this game, even more than I do, and I'm thinking about how the summer will be over in three weeks and maybe I should write her back when I feel something brush against my foot. I slit my eyes open.

Standing above me is a boy I recognize from archery. He has a wide, sun-dusted face, and the stiffest hair I've ever seen, sand-colored hair that must add two inches to his height. Larry, Gary? He is cooing "who, who" at me.

"Hey." I blink.

"Hello, Jew." He toes his right sneaker in the dirt, pointing it into the ground and making a hole. "Jew, let's see your papers."

I can't even speak. His eyes are dark, water-slicked rocks. "Jew, where's your star?"

Jew? "Bullshit," I feel like spitting. I want to say: No, I'm not. Not in real life. But I am and I know it and I just stare. None of this can be happening. None of it at all.

"Get out of here." He taps the words out against my bare leg with his dirt-encrusted toe. "You should be long gone."

He could haul me in; he could march me down to the soccer field and collect whatever stupid reward they're handing out. This should make me hold my tongue, but I don't. "Why don't you go bother a midget your own size?"

He kicks my ankle. "Because I can bother you, Jew."

Tears spring to my eyes. "Fuck you," I say, and grab his leg with both my hands. I throw him off-balance, and he spins around, hopping. I give it a furious yank, and he falls. "You're a Jew, too."

"Not now I'm not." We're both in the dirt, and he's grabbing me, clutching my mouth, my throat. He pins my arms back so far; I swear something inside of me crests and breaks.

"Okay, okay!" I start laughing. "Please, stop, please."

He moves his mouth to my ear. "Why should I?"

"Because I'm asking you nicely. Please."

His fingers are still around my collarbone. He speaks in almost a pleasant tone. "Okay. Get the fuck out of here."

And I do.

He has my shoes. The bastard has my sneakers. I run hard anyway, wincing as I step on sharp rocks, twigs that scrape against the softness of my soles. I try to tell myself that I don't care, that it's good for me. My feet need to toughen up anyway. But I do care, I do.

I head up the incline, fast. There is the shallow rhythm of my breathing, the sound of leaves and twigs cracking beneath my feet. My forehead is covered in a fine light mist. This fucked-up game isn't funny anymore. I'm almost at the top of the hill when I hear a tangle of noises. I reach one of the stone arches that leads into the amphitheater. The noise is now a steady hum. An orange banner hangs limply at the entrance, a remnant of the color wars held last week. I was picked second to last for green and spent most of the time on the sidelines, cheering for blue.

My feet hurt. I am hot and tired and I can't imagine the noises being anything good. Why should I go inside? I wonder this and it's as if the wondering is my answer. Stepping gingerly on the balls of my sore feet, I pass under the orange flag.

The amphitheater is ours. Hot damp bodies crowd the stage. They throng the makeshift aisles, stepping over piles of clothing, pools of brightly colored plastic beads, bins of sneakers and flip-flops, pyramids of baseball caps. There are Walkmans and head-less Barbies and Gameboys galore. There are dozens of voices braiding together, high and low-pitched throbs that vibrate long past the words. All are clamoring for attention. Nothing is not for sale.

"A pass for a dozen beads. Get your passage here!"

"Exit for exchanges."

"Music for cash!"

It is a quick business. People don't linger. They file out like a steady stream. They want to get to the other side.

I hang back, stunned. Has this been going on all day? Has everyone known about it but me? I notice that Jill and Jesse have beat me here, and I watch as they hand over a fistful of beads and a Lakers cap for sweat-stained visas.

Everyone is going to the other side. Why can't I?

"What do you have?"

I turn. "Excuse me?"

He is pale and rail-thin. Sam, if I remember right. A really good tennis player who practices all day long. You can hear the thwack, catch the gleam of the moving ball, as you leave the dining hall in the falling darkness. Secretly I like him for that, for the way he avoids everyone and everything for the only thing he cares about.

"Hi," I say, smiling at him now.

"Hello." His amber-colored eyes slide over the surface of my face. His oxford shirt, the kind everyone else saves for Shabbat, is tucked neatly into his khakis, and his topsiders are polish-bright. He reaches out, brushes his hand against my cheek.

"Hey!" My hands fly up.

"What do you want for the earrings?"

"Nothing," I say, touching the small braided hoops that I'd forgotten I was wearing. They were my paternal grandmother's, and except for a dark-blue fraternity tie that my mother used to hang on our refrigerator door as a joke, the earrings are the only thing I have from my father's side of the family. I step back, almost trip over a wicker basket.

He grabs my elbow. "Watch yourself," he says.

"I'm just fine," I say.

Behind him, a tall girl with legs like a stork hands over a box of jujubes; a freckled boy readjusts his Dodgers cap and screams, "Two hours! We've got two hours to get out of here!"

"I could get you to America in no time with those," he says, his eyes on my ears.

"We are in America," I say.

"Right," he says, smiling. "Do we have a trade or not?"

"I can't sell the earrings," I explain.

"Fine," he says, annoyed, and begins scanning the crowd for the next prospect.

"Sam—" I blurt out his name and touch his sleeve; I'm that desperate. "There's got to be something else you'd want."

"From you?" He raises his eyebrows, looking me up and down.

I flush, embarrassed. Who is he to do this to me? Who are any of these people? I look down at his diver's watch; the digits glow 2:38 P.M. I want out so badly. I feel as if I'm peering over the edge of a cliff when I say, "What if I have information on a fugitive?"

"Look around you," he says, looking bored. "They're everywhere."

"It's Kron." I say it and wind whistles in my ears. "I know where you can find her."

"Kron from Lamu?" He says it quickly. "Now that's a different story."

I nod, tired.

"Where is she?"

"Visa first," I say.

This time, when I cut through no man's land, through the stand of eucalyptus trees where the ground is freckled by shadows, I walk more slowly. I feel a little sick, but I tell myself that Kron is fine, that she never showed up to the canteen, that she is worlds away.

"We've made it," I say to Anya, and I'm surprised to hear my voice out loud. I pass the creek, which is little more than a trickle. The rocks lie gleaming, dry, white, and smooth as calcified bones. A lizard skitters from one to another. Its head is enormous and ugly, weighted down by a spiky, prehistoric-looking crown. I stop as it leaps closer to me, its tail wiping the rock. It is more graceful than anything I've ever seen. I lean over, holding my finger out. The lizard's body goes rigid. Except for the slight quiver of skin hanging beneath its chin, you wouldn't know it's alive. I think: I could hurt it, if I wanted to. I could.

"Hello, Mr. Lizard," I say, softly. "I won't hurt you."

"Hello."

I jump, and the lizard darts off. Jesse is behind me. He is

perched on a rock, his tanned legs dangling down, the bare soles of his feet flashing.

For a moment, neither of us says a word. Finally, he speaks. "You crossing?"

I take a step back. "Where's Jill?"

He jerks his head around. "Around. Somewhere." He hops off the rock, takes a step toward me. The air shifts—it becomes heavier somehow—but I don't look away. "I haven't seen her in a while. Everyone seems to be disappearing. Where's your freaky double?"

"Around," I say carefully.

He nods, moves even closer. "What about your papers?" He asks this easily, smiling. But before I can stop him, he reaches around me and pulls my ID and visa out of my back pocket.

"Hey!"

He backs away, laughing and shaking his head. He lets out a low whistle. "This is funny, you know. You and I."

"Funny?"

"Just—well, you are my wife."

I stare. "Your wife?"

He pulls a green square out of his back pocket. "Moishe," he reads. "I'm Moishe Ossevsheva. You're Anya."

He can't do that. I don't care if it's just a game. I feel a force pressing down against my temples. He has no right to me. He has no right to Anya.

"I heard we got a divorce."

"Really?" He folds his arms and looks down at my chest with a little smile as if my body is telling him something else. "Why would we want that? If we're married, I can help you get across. I hear you'll do lots of things to get across." Still smiling, he puts my visa and ID in his back pocket. "Why are you shaking, Anya?" He moves his mouth close to mine. "It's only a game."

"Don't touch me," I hear myself say. "Don't you dare."

"Oh, please," he says. "As if this isn't what you've wanted all along."

And his lips are on mine and he's right but oh so wrong and I feel both small and large, beautiful and grotesque, so unlike myself that I'm not sure I'm even there. He pulls me down to the rocky ground and wraps his legs around mine. And I don't want to think about Kron and Anya, but they're all I see. I'm horrible and I'll do anything and his elbow is digging into my ribs and his hands are everywhere and mine are too. It's probably only seconds but it feels like centuries later when we both hear it—a sharp noise, a crackling somewhere in the distance.

"Shit," he says. He twists around fast and scrambles to his feet. "Where did that come from?" I get up too, pulling my shirt back down. "Jill?" He scans the wall of trees, brushing his fingers through his hair.

"It's not her," I say, and somehow I manage to reach over, grab the papers fanning out of his pocket.

"What are you doing?" Jesse twists around, blinking—his eyes are strangely lidded, thin and opaque—just like the lizard's.

"You don't even have a visa, Jew. This isn't going to get you far." My voice trembles. I feel an unbearable urge to pee. "You thought you were going to touch me? You and your dirty Jewish ways?"

I'm shivering as I rip up his ID, letting the pieces fall through my fingers like glitter. "Jew," I practically coo. "Now why would I ever have married a Jew like you?"

"Freak."

"Fuck you."

"You'd like that, wouldn't you?" Jesse gives me a withering look and turns and lumbers away.

Now I'm shivering even more. I feel my way over to a boulder still warm with sun and I flatten my hands against it. I look at my own ID one last time, at that face, those eyes, so familiar, staring back at me, and I am dizzy with recognition. Carefully, I tear the green slip of paper apart. Anya's face becomes speckles on the rocks in the drying creek. As much as I wish it were otherwise, the speckles remain; there isn't enough stream to carry them away.

Ellen Umansky

A couple of years ago, I was talking to a friend, and something she said prompted me to remember an episode at camp that I hadn't thought of in decades. One summer morning, when I couldn't have been more than ten or eleven, we were told that the camp had become the Soviet Union, and we were all Russian refuseniks, desperate to escape to the United States or Israel. The details were extremely hazy to me (the only one that I could recall with clarity was the shame I felt when I couldn't escape), and the more I tried to remember the game, the stranger and eerier it became in my mind. I couldn't shake it, and so I found myself writing about it.

I moved the game from the early 1980s in Russia to 1940 Poland because I was interested in imagining the worst-case scenario and the cruelty it could inspire, and partly too because it allowed me to explore some things I had been thinking about for a while—that is, how do you try to explain the unexplainable? I wondered how teenagers in the well-off, secure world of West Los Angeles in the 1990s (in particular, a girl who finds herself decidedly the outsider at Jewish camp) would make sense of the Holocaust, how such horrors would, or wouldn't, be assimilated into their lives.

THE ARGUMENT

Rachel Kadish

Kreutzer reads in the newspaper. Sipping coffee that is lukewarm, he reads about a thing called False Memory Syndrome. This is a new syndrome, just discovered. It happens when
something terrible a person thinks they remember turns out not
to have happened after all. Kreutzer sighs. Imagine. Such relief.

The quote from one of the girls interviewed in the paper
reminds him of someone, he can't think who. "But if it never happened," the girl says, "why do I feel so terrible?"

Jacobson's room in the nursing home is decorated in pastels. He
wears a stained powder-blue sweater; there is a yellow scarf
across his legs. The colors of springtime.

Today Jacobson's mind has turned to opposites. "What is the
opposite of a curtain?" he asks his guest.

Leaning heavily against the wall, Kreutzer breathes. The long
flight of stairs has tired him. He looks at the sun-filled curtains.

"A carpet," Jacobson answers. He bobs his bald head at
Kreutzer. There are crumbs in his beard.

Kreutzer clears his throat. He is not a cruel man, but he has a
job to do. There is a reason Kreutzer needs to quiz Jacobson: in
his former life Jacobson was also known as Rabbi Harold Jacobson. And a rabbi never stops being a rabbi, even when he thinks
the president of the Women's Division is her dead great-
grandmother. Even when he tells the sexton in front of the man's
entire family: I always liked you more than I liked your wife. You

have a sense of humor but she is wretched. Even ten years after his congregation and his own weary brain have fired him, a rabbi is still a rabbi. Especially when he knows the location of the deed to the land the synagogue stands on.

Which paperwork the synagogue needs if it is to avoid extra legal fees for the new building.

The congregation is ready to give up on the deed. It is digging into its pockets and hiring a lawyer. A search of the synagogue's files has revealed nothing. This is no surprise; the rabbi made it his habit to hide important documents in places known only to himself. Now Jacobson's mind has sailed to the highest branch of a tree and will not be coaxed back to earth. Even the rabbi's oldest friends have given up, not only on deeds but on words—it is impossible to have a conversation with the man.

Kreutzer, standing in his bathrobe in the kitchen while the president of the congregation made his plea over the telephone, toyed with this notion: the congregation was asking him to visit Jacobson in the hope it would spur Kreutzer, widower that he is, to become active in the synagogue once more. After brief reflection, however, Kreutzer found it unlikely the congregation hoped this. He finds it more likely the congregants think that because he and Jacobson are the same age, Kreutzer can enter the maze of the rabbi's mind. Kreutzer is not certain whether to be insulted.

But he agreed. And now he must do, although it will not be pleasant. The rabbi, as the president of the congregation informed him, is unaccustomed to visitors. Only the rebbetzin still comes, she knits beside her husband's bed; wife and husband do not always, Kreutzer knows, need words. As for the rabbi's son, he lives too far to visit—so says the rebbetzin, who loves her boy. The son, everyone knows, lives someplace far from Jersey City, someplace where there is snow that he skis on. Worse, the son moved to this someplace with a black girl. His wife. Together they ski. Kreutzer tries to imagine. Black people should not ski. They have no camouflage. Jews also, Kreutzer thinks, should not ski. If God meant them to ski He would have chosen Norway for a promised land. He would have written it in one of His books. The Book of Skis.

"What is the opposite of a Dorito?" Jacobson picks a chip from his lunch tray.

The man was a rabbi, thinks Kreutzer. He had conversations with God.

Rabbi Jacobson turns the chip in his palm, forlorn.

"Jacobson." Kreutzer leans forward, hands on his knees. Jacobson's gaze drifts in his direction like a rudderless ship. "Rabbi."

The rabbi's face registers alarm. Then, as Kreutzer waits, the rabbi grows solemn. "You may be seated," he says.

"Rabbi, I have a question for you."

But it is no good asking. The rabbi's head refuses to crack open like an oyster, revealing the tiniest pearl of information. The rabbi has never heard of a deed. He has never heard, it turns out, of a synagogue.

Kreutzer takes out the book he has brought: a holy book. Perhaps with some study of familiar words he will lull Jacobson into memory. All those years of training, of devout study, surely are lodged somewhere in the rabbi's mind. And if the rabbi can summon these memories, perhaps he will summon others. Unless—the thought gives Kreutzer pause—this contemplation of opposites is a code. Could it be that the rabbi has become a mystic? He has *chosen* forgetfulness—abandoned his Talmudic training and fooled them all, tiptoed beyond the everyday and vanished into the forests of kaballah.

Kreutzer eyes the rabbi. The rabbi, eyeing Kreutzer, passes wind noisily.

Kreutzer opens the book. In as patient a tone as he can muster, he addresses the rabbi. "We begin with the laws of kashruth."

Kreutzer knows now who he was reminded of. The girl in the newspaper reminded him of his daughter Marjorie. Marjorie who used also words like terrible. The pollution of the environment?

It was terrible. The attitudes of Kreutzer and Kreutzer's wife and everyone they knew: terrible. Also, always, the war in Vietnam. He thinks of Marjorie in high school with her terribles. He thinks of her the summer she was twenty-two years old. That was the summer she packed her things in borrowed suitcases and left. Jersey City wasn't close enough for her, she had to move right up in its face and breathe its polluted breath: Manhattan. She stopped seeing movies and started seeing films. She met people named Portia and Nikita, and within two years she married a violinist.

A violinist.

And now, this. Marjorie, with news.

This reunion with the rabbi is bitter, thinks Kreutzer as he watches Jacobson pick through his cup of fruit cocktail with a gritty teaspoon. Bitter not because of the man's health; the rabbi is not in pain. Today Jacobson is eight years old. Hitler has not come to power, the Brooklyn Dodgers sign baseballs even when handed them by Jewish boys. Jacobson is happy.

Bitter because unfair.

Rabbi Jacobson was a learned man. Few people know Kreutzer appreciated this; out loud, Kreutzer spoke only of the rabbi's faults. But for twenty years Kreutzer relished his Sunday morning ritual. His wife swept in the kitchen, his daughter Marjorie sat upstairs listening to her radio; Gabriel, Kreutzer's studious son, read the newspaper as Kreutzer passed it to him, section by section. And when Kreutzer had read the news, he sat at the coffee table and began his letter. *To Rabbi Jacobson with regards*, he wrote. Sometimes he read aloud to Gabriel as he composed. *I attended your sermon this Sabbath.*

And although I respect your intentions in choosing your subject, I believe you have erred in the following manner.

It was certain omissions of detail, certain liberal tendencies with the text, that irked Kreutzer. *You of all people will agree,*

Kreutzer scratched onto the paper, *our nature as Jews is to pre-serve*. It bothered him when Jacobson did not mention minor commentators who had dissented in an interpretation, even if all agreed that the majority was clearly in the right. The rabbi should have mentioned the dissenters in his sermon, for the sake of thoroughness. And then there were their disagreements over the state of Israel—not, Kreutzer admitted, true disagreements. But in the formation of a state every nuance counts, and so he took it as his responsibility to correct Rabbi Jacobson when the rabbi strayed.

When Kreutzer argued he felt his muscles tense and the blood breathe in his veins. It felt right. Life was not easy and neither was argument, but both necessary. When Kreutzer was a boy in heder, the rabbis talked to him about his soul. The rabbis did not use this word, but Kreutzer knew when they encouraged the boys to debate one line of the Bible for hours, this is what they were after. Souls are not easy to talk about, even for rabbis. In the public school hallway when lockers slammed and gym-class teammates cursed him, he was Kreutzer. But in the soften-ing evening hours of heder, he was David. The rabbis rounded his name, added the diminutive. *Duvidl.* Gently Duvidl was instructed in the proper posture for highest prayer: the three bows, the backward step at the prayer's finish, for one must never turn one's back to God. Paired with another boy—for a Jew must study with a partner, a co-counsel in the court of the One True Judge—Duvidl was instructed in the skills of debate. *When God's people debate His tradition, He knows they love Him.* True faith, the rabbis taught, was an unresolved argument. Jews argued; in His heavens God laughed and was satisfied. And how He loved their labor. For a week once the heder boys were made to write essays not in regular Hebrew script, but in the cockeyed alphabet of the great sage Rashi. Even the learned man's hand-writing, the rabbis intoned as the boys worked, even the slight-est twist he put on the letters of the Hebrew alphabet in his rush to commit his thoughts to parchment, must be preserved. God rewarded vigilance; God rewarded devotion; not a single nuance must be forgotten.

A block from the heder the Italian and black boys from Leonard Young Elementary School waited to pound a Jewish soul until it bled from the nose and cried hot shaming tears. Kreutzer could not ask for help at home; evenings he tiptoed through the entry so as not to distract his father, seated at the kitchen table worrying over the books of his faltering real estate office. Kreutzer's mother was easily frightened, and if she knew she would insist on walking him home from heder; the other boys would see. David Kreutzer turned to God. He looked in the Torah and saw that Moses defended his people against the slavedriver. He understood that God wanted him to hit back. Kreutzer was eleven years old. He whispered his prayer and stepped out the heder door. Better their faces should break my hand than God should be disappointed in one of His people. Kreutzer repeated this to himself as the boys approached. And God guided his fist to the face of Anthony Marcetti. After that the Italian and black boys left him alone. God was good in other ways also. Duvidl was not the smartest boy, the rabbis said, but he worked. Kreutzer's father came to pick him up early for a rare weekend outing and the rabbi turned to the man fidgeting in the entryway waiting for his son and said the compliment loud enough for all to hear: The boy *thinks*.

Kreutzer was not saying, he explained to his son Gabriel while folding his letter to Rabbi Jacobson, that writing an essay in the handwriting of a man dead nine centuries was the only way to learn. Just that it taught a principle.

On Wednesdays came the rabbi's replies. *In haste*, they began. In haste was Rabbi Jacobson, in haste enough to warn Kreutzer this would be a short letter, but not so much as to prevent his defending himself on each point. Rebuttal filled a page of the synagogue's stationery, sometimes both sides. There was a period of years when the rabbi responded mildly—*I have reread*

*the text as you suggest. And while I believe you are mistaken, I do
see whence your interpretation arises.* Other times, particularly the
year the rabbi's son brought home his fiancée as well as a handful
of Black Panther pamphlets, the rabbi's letters were longer than
Kreutzer's. *Will you contradict the wisdom of our great sages? Must
you mock the tradition?* The rabbi's thick script cried out on the
paper in Kreutzer's hands.

In person he and the rabbi were polite, although it was not
lost on Kreutzer that the rabbi managed to position himself across
the room from him at synagogue gatherings. This did not concern
Kreutzer; a rabbi needed someone to keep him on his toes. Jews
studied in pairs. This was the nature of the world. Kreutzer came
to understand it as a duty. He stayed home from backyard barbe-
cues and poker games to write his letters.

Now Rabbi Harold Jacobson, his old sparring partner, was
sprung from memory like a schoolboy on holiday. It was inde-
cent—a coward's way out of an argument. The disgrace was not
that the rabbi had skipped out on an argument with Kreutzer.
The disgrace was the other argument the rabbi was trying to
escape: with God.

Sitting opposite the rabbi, book open on the table between
them, Kreutzer pauses. For the past hour he has led the rabbi
through legal reasoning. Now he ventures a test. "When a
kosher pot is accidentally touched by non-kosher metal, what is
the ruling?"

"If the metal is cold, kosher," the rabbi responds without
hesitation. "If hot, the pot must be repurified."

Kreutzer is elated. With patience he has cajoled the rabbi
into precious memory. Now he will make him confess the where-
abouts of the deed.

They have closed the book; Kreutzer makes a solemn nod to
Jacobson.

"What is the opposite of a spider?" the rabbi asks Kreutzer
happily.

Kreutzer places a hand to his chest. This sudden beating

against his ribs, can it be a heart attack? He thinks he cannot bear this cresting tension another minute. He thinks he hates the rabbi.

He hadn't meant any disrespect to the shiksas. He was simply stating a fact. It was the shiksas that killed Moe Roth, who was the next-door neighbor when Marjorie was a girl. Marjorie had asked, What ever happened to the next-door family from all those years ago? So Kreutzer was telling. The shiksas in Moe's factory unionized, and it was the stress of it what killed Moe. Moe was a good boss. There wasn't any need for union.

But Marjorie, who they had named for Iris's mother Malka, got mad. "Your racism is staggering," Marjorie told him. Kreutzer had thought racism was shvartzes and white people. He was careful about shvartzes. About *Negroes*, he corrected himself. *Black people*. But no one told him shiksas counted. "Do you have any plans whatsoever to even visit the modern era?" Marjorie was not finished. "I certainly hope you'll let us know if you're coming. We'll leave a light on for you." Marjorie had a mouth. Always she wanted something different from what you put in front of her. Extracurricular activities. Guitar lessons. Food with seaweed in it, like a person ate in Japan. Food that looked like the Japanese person already ate it. When Iris was alive she would defend it. *It's a new world*, Iris said. *Let's give our daughter a chance to explore it.*

"It's a new world." Marjorie stood with her hands on her hips. "In case you haven't noticed. In case you haven't noticed, Dad, you're a dinosaur."

And Yuri, Yuri the violinist who converted to Judaism just in order that Kreutzer's daughter can now ignore everything she knew all her life about Jewish customs—can even have a Christmas tree in her living room and still Marjorie calls the house Jewish, because officially both the people who live there are. *Dad, I do have a Jewish home.* Like a home was a thing you circumcised and then no matter what it did, it was still part of the tribe; even if the house went out and ate pork sausages with milk all night long, still when it dropped its pants to take a leak, right there carved on its doorpost was the message: Still a Jew.

Yuri the violinist took Marjorie by the shoulder. "Easy, sweetheart," he said.

Marjorie closed her mouth.

Kreutzer does not know what women see in violinists.

And now suddenly he cannot sleep. Kreutzer who always could fall into dreams like a baby instead lies looking at shadows. His brain is a fountain; all what he knows pools in his head. He cannot stop the fountain's spigot from running. Details threaten to overflow his mind. The address of a man he once did business with. Names of a couple he met who said they would invite him for a dinner. Surely he copied their telephone number into his address book? By the light of the bed lamp his pajama legs look shabby. The stripes remind him of prison uniforms; he stops this thought but cannot keep his brain from pivoting elsewhere. There in his own handwriting in his address book is the number of the couple. Should he? Accept a social invitation, get out into circulation as everyone urged him after Iris's death? If Iris were still alive, she would tell him to stop worrying and call. *David*, she would say, *it's no shame for a man to reach out for company*. No, Kreutzer corrects himself: She would not say this. She would have called already.

The clock flips a papery card: three twenty-five in the A.M. Maybe in the daylight he will call.

When at last Kreutzer sleeps he cannot dream a regular dream. He can only dream what was real, what he will not allow himself to think in waking hours. Thoughts that punch through darkness to torment. He does not know why suddenly this should be happening, yet there is no denying it: these dreams have visited him nightly since he heard Marjorie's news.

In his dream his son Gabriel is once more seventeen years old and tells Kreutzer he is thinking of being a rabbi. Kreutzer can imagine his son at the pulpit; his son the rabbi's words sing out. The congregation sits rapt. But to Gabriel he says only, *So. So everybody thinks they can be rabbi*. He does not let Gabriel know it would please him. Same as he never shows his disappointment when Gabriel chooses doctor instead.

Kreutzer slips from sleep, he presses a heavy palm to his forehead, he is not dreaming but remembering. In his waking remembering mind a fountain has spilled over, now he is unable to keep the thoughts away. Of his son Gabriel, a doctor in the war in Asia. Kreutzer sees once more Marjorie. Marjorie protesting on a college campus while Gabriel finishes his medical school training and applies for air force commission. "It's that or get drafted," Gabriel says to his sister's turned back. "At least this way I have some choice about where I end up." Marjorie will not speak. "Run away to Canada," she writes on the piece of paper she throws at her brother before stalking out of the room. "Defect to Russia. Have some imagination."

"Thailand is beautiful," Gabriel's letter reads that spring. "Although smelly if you get close to the canals."

The legs of the chair Kreutzer sits in are spindly. He imagines them breaking, his weight crashing to the floor. A sack of flour, Kreutzer is. A sack of meal. He can't think what he is a sack of. Something soft, heavier than is reasonable. He imagines the nursing home aides running to help. In his imagination, the rabbi sits watching Kreutzer swimming on the floor. Belly and liver spots and gray tired face. The rabbi's expression is thoughtful.

"Your letters," says Kreutzer now to the rabbi, "ended always the same. *Thank you for your response to my ministry*. Tell me, Jacobson. Did they teach you to say this in rabbinical school?"

The rabbi looks at Kreutzer as at a form spied through a wall of glass brick.

Three weeks of visits and such is Kreutzer's reward: today Jacobson refuses even to recognize him. Kreutzer halves his donut and passes a portion across the table. The rabbi mutters a blessing—the correct one—and bites, scattering shards of glazed sugar over his sweater.

"Did you wonder," Kreutzer asks, "why I stopped writing to you?"

The rabbi picks the pieces of sugar off his sweater with care and deposits them on his tongue. "Did you wonder why I stopped coming to synagogue except on highest holidays?"

Pleasantly the rabbi nods.

On Jacobson's windowsill, an envelope from a state where there is skiing. A son, even a son who defies his father, sends a letter now and again. They are perplexing, such rebellious tenacious children. This son and Marjorie would have made a good pair. Just as Kreutzer thinks to tell the rabbi this, he notices that the son's letter is unopened, and at the same moment he is assaulted by a rapid slide show: Shutting his burning eyes he sees his own son Gabriel leaving for Thailand without even a good-bye from his sister. He sees Gabriel's airmail letters to Marjorie crumpled unopened in the wastebasket. Since there is no satisfaction in not speaking to someone who's far away, now Marjorie, a freshman in college, refuses to speak to Kreutzer.

Forcing his eyes open, Kreutzer thinks: Young people can afford to believe their parents know nothing. They can afford to cram their heads with liberal ideas. They marry people who play violin on ski slopes. They run through the woods eating marijuana. Kreutzer pictures young people stirring marijuana into their coffee at breakfast.

He and the rabbi know better. They know that life is no joke. They have argued commentary together. They have argued six presidents, three wars in the Mideast. Kreutzer has in his house two letters of condolence from the rabbi. Together they have seen life.

Yet now Kreutzer does not understand what is happening to him. He can feel the weight of the air in the room, pressing down. Air denser than any air he has ever felt.

"I am a dinosaur," he says to Jacobson.

The rabbi gives an amiable smile. "I also."

"Perhaps," Kreutzer concedes. "But tomorrow you will be a butterfly. Tuesday a horse or woodpecker. And I? Again a dinosaur."

The rabbi pulls on his beard.

Kreutzer thinks he knows the reason he cannot sleep. Why his daughter Marjorie has not had children before now is a mystery to Kreutzer. Iris would have asked, but Iris has been gone since before anyone noticed Marjorie forgot to have children.

Because he does not know why there have been no children all this time, the reason Marjorie has decided to have a child now, at the age of forty, is also a mystery to Kreutzer. But now she is pregnant. It has been over a week since she and the violinist drove to Jersey City to inform him. There is something about Marjorie's pregnancy that seems significant. Momentous. The pregnancy is like a verse of Torah; it cries out for interpretation. For days Kreutzer has been trying in vain to figure out what it means. It means—he has been able to proceed no further than this—she is going to have a baby.

For no reason he can fathom, he cleans his attic. In a box beneath a trunk he discovers a notebook Iris must have saved from the garbage, a memento from his boyhood. In the margins in painstaking hand is the script of the great sage Rashi. *"And Abraham went and took the ram and offered it up as a sacrifice in place of his son." Rashi teaches: The ram had been waiting for this duty ever since the six days of creation.*

Kreutzer takes the notebook downstairs. He takes it into his bed. A foolish postulate: It might help him sleep. Before shutting the light he peers once more into the notebook, furtive like a spy. Inside, handwriting inscribed centuries ago. Bit by bit, without his being aware, Kreutzer's own boyhood has receded, now it is as ancient to him as this argument nine centuries past. Yet there is no denying: once he was a boy. Before *Sputnik,* before Hitler, before the Dodgers left Brooklyn. Then a skinny teenager. He was a virgin when he married Iris and she too. That night she was so shy, he had to learn boldness or they would never have been man and wife. How he loved her, her gray eyes, her pale shy hands, that night and after. Later he became a father. He became a man in the world. Those years are lost to him. When he tries to think of them, he can remember little more than finishing his morning prayers: unwrapping his tefillin, buttoning his shirt. Walking out the front door. He does not understand how this can have happened. He does not understand why his wife and his growing children are not vivid in the pictures he summons from those years when they were all young. Only the hardships are real to him this last week: memories he has banished so forcefully they have come back to haunt him. With the greatest of will he tries to summon his wife's face; instead, he sees before him the one face in this world that most resembles hers. Helpless as if watching a film on a screen before him, Kreutzer is witness to the single time he nearly hit Marjorie, weeks after the solemn visit from the air force officer. 1971. Marjorie is twenty; letting herself into the house at midnight she stumbles into the door. Kreutzer and his wife, roused from sleeplessness, hurry silent into the living room to discover her kicking the door, cursing the pain. Their daughter is foul-mouthed in her rage, she is made up as though she would give herself to any man for a nickel. It freezes Kreutzer to his heartstrings. He wants to shake her, wake her out of this madness that has reigned in his home since the news from Thailand. He calls Marjorie's name; she looks at him with wild flat eyes he does not recognize, a distorted mirror of Iris's gray eyes, and he is certain now of the worst, he is certain it is marijuana. Kreutzer turns to his wife. And a thing happens that has never happened before: Iris gazes back at him as if she can look through him. Kreutzer does not recognize his own wife's eyes. There is nothing in this world he can control. Suddenly Iris cries out. She huddles Marjorie in her arms, she will not let him near. Kreutzer hears his daughter's muffled words as she sobs against her mother's blouse: *I hate him.*

That week he reads in Marjorie's diary. *Shooting up with James and Portia at Portia's apartment. Late afternoon.* Kreutzer cannot force himself to close the diary. *That feeling when it takes command of your pulse and your body fights at first but then after a while you submit to that new rhythm and just feel quieted. I said to James, Isn't it spooky the way it makes your heart jump in its cage, like playing jazz on the car radio with the bass cranked, windows sealed tight. James said, That's it, exactly. I think James likes me. For once this afternoon I didn't think about opening a vein.* Kreutzer closes the diary. He is not a father. He is not a man. He is nothing. There is a knock on his door; Rabbi Harold Jacobson wanting to plan a memorial service for the one month anniversary of Gabriel's death. Kreutzer shuts the door in the rabbi's face. He does not understand who James is or where his daughter is spending her time but he wants to cry out to Marjorie, *Your mother has lost already. I myself am beyond forgiveness but you are young. Don't do the one thing that cannot be forgiven. Don't break your mother's heart.*

Memory is cruel. The days Kreutzer would like to relive, the sweet days, are lost to him. How can the good years have disappeared? How can a man disappear from himself? Yet it is true: this ancient heder notebook and the letters from Rabbi Jacobson are the sole evidence Kreutzer has of a life vanished. Now, in the mornings, the night's visions swirl about him; the stubble on his face is white. He is an old man. How he longs for a single thread of argument to shepherd him past his sleeplessness—the clear pulse of debate in which he used to feel the murmuring of God. He would like to bring a case before the ancient court of rabbis; he imagines assembling the Sanhedrin to hear his argument. If Kreutzer cannot summon the good times, if he cannot recall the years of innocence, he would like to murder the bad. Would it be so wrong? If a man kills a year, Kreutzer would petition the assembled sages, what is his punishment? If he murders the day of a rasping doorbell chime, the day of an air force officer on his stoop, what penalty? Opinions vary. If a day kills a man, the sages say two thousand souls have been lost. A first rabbi poses the question, Who has been killed: the day or the man? If either, says another rabbi, a goat must be sacrificed. If both, a third rabbi insists, slaughter the man's ox and divide the value among the family. Price an uninjured day in the marketplace and compensate the wronged party for the loss of value.

Kreutzer cannot sleep.

At dawn he dials. "I wanted to know, is there anything you need for the baby?"

There is a long pause. "Dad?" says Marjorie.

Immediately Kreutzer regrets his foolishness. He has insulted her. His daughter is a grown woman. She will soon be, in fact, an enormous woman. Why would she need from him? "I'm sure there is nothing you need," he says.

In the background is the sound of the violinist yawning. "Who is it, honey?"

Marjorie's voice sounds strange. "No, Dad," she says. "I guess there isn't."

Kreutzer dozes. The sun is pressing a pink radiance through his swollen lids when Gabriel visits. *Dad*, he begins. Kreutzer plugs his ears. Gabriel is trying to forgive him. Kreutzer will not be forgiven. With his fingers in his ears he gazes upon his son trying in vain to address him. The boy is suntanned. His eyes, green-brown like Kreutzer's own, were always so gentle Kreutzer worried for the boy. Now these eyes, they refuse to convict. *You are my father*, Gabriel tells him.

You are my son.

He wakes in a sweat. The telephone is ringing. It is Marjorie calling back. Holding the receiver, Kreutzer glances at the clock and realizes it is time for prayers. His thoughts lurch. If his daughter learns he no longer prays, she will think he has admitted she was right to marry the violinist. So Kreutzer tells her, "I will call you back. I have to pray."

He watches the clock. After twenty minutes he calls.

"I'm wondering," Marjorie says, "what time will you be at the cemetery tomorrow?"

Something about Marjorie's question is not right. Kreutzer has a feeling in his gut. Marjorie should not be in the cemetery. He isn't yet certain why, but he is sure she must not go—not now that she is pregnant. Kreutzer remains rational. "You could fall," he says.

"I'm fine," Marjorie says. "I'm stronger than you are."

"We're not going this year," he insists. "It's dangerous."

Marjorie sighs heavily to be sure Kreutzer knows he is frustrating her. "I'll call you back when you've had time to come to your senses. Will you be home this afternoon?"

"I'm visiting with the rabbi."

"Jesus, Dad. You tormented the poor man all his professional life. Can't you let him retire in peace?"

"We enjoy each other's company is a fact." Kreutzer is surprised at the anger in his voice. "We study Torah together."

"Dad, if he recognized you he'd bolt for the door. Even Rabbi Jacobson didn't care about every dot and comma of the Bible. You were a thorn in his side."

"I won't be home this afternoon," he enunciates. "I have to visit the rabbi."

"Fine, so this evening." Marjorie hesitates. "Dad. Why do you hate him so much?"

"Hate?"

"You're obsessed with him, and you're obsessed with digging up that deed. Look, what's lost is lost, okay? It's *lost,* Dad. They've already had another deed made up, they've broken ground on the new building."

———

He tries to shave before going to see the rabbi. Iris would tell him to. He lathers but cannot bring himself to lift the razor. He gazes at it, heavy in his hand. The words float through his mind: *an old man's blood*. Afraid, he looks in the mirror. Clear as day he sees the scribes fluttering around him with wings of ink; each brush against the walls leaves a searing paragraph. Kreuzer blinks at the black spots floating in his mirror. Bit by bit his bathroom walls are being covered in tiny script like bird-prints. "I am ashamed," he tells the scribes scaling the reflected bathroom walls. They write down his words, and immediately surround them with interpretation: minuscule lettering that stretches from ceiling to floor. "I should not be alive," Kreutzer says.

The scribes, angry, stop writing and are gone.

After a while he towels the shaving cream from his face, leaves the towel folded neatly over the lip of the sink.

At the nursing home, under the rabbi's gaze, Kreutzer produces the clipping from the previous day's paper. His hands are shaking. He points to the phrase on the newsprint. "See here," he says.

It is an article about politics in today's Israel, but that is not the important thing. What is important is this reference to the time of Palestine under British Mandate. *Mandatory Palestine*, the newspaper says. When Kreutzer first read these two words, they meant only 1930s Palestine, Palestine when it flew British flags. But by the time he set down the paper to rummage for scissors he understood the words meant more. "Mandatory Palestine": now *that* was Jewish. Palestine because you had to. Palestine because Jews owed allegiance there and no place else. Jewish wasn't marijuana and oblivion and T-shirts telling you to drop out. Jewish wasn't a Christmas tree in a living room. Jewish was Jewish. Was holding on tight. What was so bad about guilt? Why was everyone so eager to bury hatchets, forget deeds? So what if the rest of the world thought guilt was a nasty word?

Jews proudly fought a War of Atonement. Jews had memory even if it hurt.

"Banana?" Jacobson offers the fruit.

On the rabbi's windowsill is the envelope from the son with the black wife. The son who still lives, breathes, wants communication with his father. The envelope is unopened. Kreutzer's head feels swollen as if someone banged on it through the night. All those precious letters from Gabriel, he thinks. Envelope after envelope, white with red and blue stripes, each holding one of his son's carefully penned pages. Kreutzer must tell the rabbi something. "A son's letters are important," he says. "My son wrote to me every week during the war."

"War?"

The banana waves slowly in the air. Kreutzer is nauseous. "The war in Vietnam."

"There is a war?"

Kreutzer stands. The room reels about him. Pastel fabrics swirl, a field of fluttering flowers; he staggers against the wall. He wants to murder the rabbi. He wants to punch the rabbi until he bleeds from his nose. "Gabriel was a good boy!" he shouts at Jacobson.

The rabbi cowers in his chair. His eyes widen, then begin to tear.

In the doorway appears a nurse. Holding one hand to his temple, Kreutzer nods to her. From the corner come soft whimpering noises: Jacobson crying, his arms wrapped around his waist, a quivering cocoon. The nurse watches Kreutzer put on his jacket.

Leaving, Kreutzer pauses beside Jacobson's doubled form. He sets a heavy hand on the back of the rabbi's chair. "What is the opposite of Alzheimer's?" Kreutzer demands.

The rabbi's gaze wavers in confusion.

"Jewish," Kreutzer curses him.

———

In the parking lot and on the access ramp to the highway, Kreutzer's anger is so great he cannot concentrate on his driving. That he, Kreutzer, should be trapped by memory, while the rabbi—a rabbi, who has chosen to shoulder the suffering of the Jewish people—is excused, is too much to bear.

But as he passes the airport, planes thundering into the sky, Kreutzer thinks. He is not a mystical man but it occurs to him that maybe the rabbi is showing him something. On the way home the thought grows in Kreutzer's mind. He is so excited he nearly drives past his exit. What if the rabbi has found the answer, not only for himself but for everyone? What if God has sent the rabbi to show Kreutzer the truth?

If you can't forget, at least you can forgive, Iris used to say. *David, I forgive you.* Kreutzer never knew how his wife could say this. He will never forgive himself for his son's death. But there is—he now sees—another option.

Reaching home, he composes his first letter to Jacobson in over twenty years. *Dear Rabbi, at last I understand: Word and deed are dispensable to you. You have defeated suffering. Others linger in yesterday; you soar past.* Kreutzer is so excited he feels feverish. He will not be selfish and save this discovery for his own sole benefit. He will bring the world's Jews to Rabbi Jacobson's feet, let them learn oblivion under the rabbi's instruction. *Never forget* was a mistaken rallying cry; together they would erase the painful memory of Inquisitions, of the Holocaust. Kreutzer tries to picture it: his whole people with Alzheimer's, millennia of troubles gone in a flash. What couldn't the Jews be without the last two thousand years? And beneath all, Kreutzer is a compassionate man; he will see to it that not only the Jews benefit. If the shiksas and shvartzes and Italians need, Kreutzer will bring them to the rabbi also. Kreutzer will lead the parade of forgetfulness, all who have suffered thronging at his heels. Together they will become innocents, babes, far from any reminder of sorrow.

And now Kreutzer knows he must call his daughter. His finger swerves over the dial; the telephone is too slow. Marjorie is right—he is a dinosaur. He with his rotary telephone. Kreutzer laughs at the folly of his life. "You can go to the cemetery," he explains when Marjorie picks up her telephone. "But not the baby."

During the few seconds' silence he thinks he has convinced her.

"Funny thing is, Dad, right now the baby and I are rather inseparable. If I go to the cemetery, she has to go too."

"She?"

Marjorie giggles. Kreutzer is almost certain it is a giggle. "I wasn't going to tell."

She meets him at the gate. Together they walk to the grave. She is bundled in a jacket and her belly sticks out.

"You're staring at me."

He cannot deny. He needs to tell her what he understands now about her pregnancy. But first he must explain to her why they need the rabbi's help. "Do you ever think about Gabriel?" he asks.

"Do I think about him?" Now Marjorie stares. "Dad, I think about him every single day."

Kreutzer is so surprised he does not utter a word. That Marjorie should also think of Gabriel at every turn? Marjorie who refused to hear his name after he went to Thailand, Marjorie who called her brother Traitor?

Marjorie who wears now a serious expression on her face. A hopeful expression. As if for the first time in her life maybe her father said something not entirely terrible. Standing beside her brother's gravestone, she speaks. "I think about everything. I think about the stupid fake advice he used to give me about boys. I think about the time he convinced me to put Alka-Seltzer up my nose. I think about the day we heard about the plane crash, when the captain came to our house."

There is more that Marjorie thinks. There is, it turns out, no end to her thoughts. Every detail of Gabriel she recalls, the blond hair that darkened as he grew older, the A's on his homework, his tears the time he received a C. Marjorie dredges up the names of both girls her brother asked to his senior promenade—the one who refused and the one who agreed. Things Kreutzer never knew about his son. Kreutzer is drowning. He cannot breathe. At this very moment, when he has determined to shed all, his contrary, bewildering daughter insists on parading her memories. She insists on remembering how she refused to speak to her brother. She refused to speak to him and then he died. Marjorie is crying.

It has never occurred to him that Marjorie might have guilt. Not in all the years since he pleaded with her silently at the dinner table, *Help your mother*; and his daughter looked out at the world through stringy bangs and would not speak. And Iris grew silent and Marjorie was silent and the great silence that engulfed Kreutzer's home drove him to silences of his own until he could no longer speak even the most intimate speech of all: he could no longer pray. And why now? Now that he has at last decided that there will be no more memories, nor guilt, nor struggle, now that he has decided to embrace oblivion with all his being? Why now should his daughter speak?

"I was high for years after Gabriel died. If not for Yuri I'd be dead in a gutter somewhere."

Suddenly Kreutzer sees. Tears threaten to overflow his own lids; blinking them back, he tells himself for the first time since Gabriel's death: *I am a father.* Joy floods his heart—there is something, after all these years, he can give to his daughter. For his mission will bring peace not only to himself, but to Marjorie as well. Quickly, before the baby is born, they both will learn to forget. All their guilt will be absolved. And Marjorie will share Kreutzer's joy at what he has foreseen: her baby will be a new generation, protected from sorrow, raised according to the wisdom of the rabbi.

Marjorie has finished. They stand together on the grass.

Kreutzer regards his daughter, wind blowing her jacket against her belly. There are fine lines around her eyes. Kreutzer is overwhelmed with a love so powerful he cannot move a muscle. He knows his daughter cannot feel the same way about him. How could she?

"Will you come for lunch tomorrow?" Marjorie says.

If he could speak, he would tell her that by tomorrow noon everything will be different. But a nod is all he can muster.

"Dad," she says. Then she does something. She stands heavily on her toes, and kisses him on the cheek. "I'm glad we had this talk."

Dear Iris, Kreutzer would say, if he could. *I bid farewell to you tonight, because soon I will no longer remember. And I want you to know I am sorry to lose these things. Your quiet and your loveliness.*

He lies awake, tears slide down both cheeks and pool in his ears. With all his strength he will endure this last night of memory.

Dear Iris, he would say. *You told me I did not cause Gabriel to die. But in this one matter you were wrong. There are things between a man and his son. There are things. Sometimes, when he is frightened, a son turns to his father.*

A son comes to his father in wartime. A son—a son who is close to his father—does not make an important decision like this without consulting.

"It's a choice," Gabriel tells him.

Gabriel in jeans and a T-shirt, pale from his medical studies. Gabriel with a buzzed haircut that makes his ears stick out.

"Either I accept this commission in Thailand, Dad, or I refuse it. If I accept it, I'll be working in a hospital far from the fighting."

If not, he will be drafted. The next assignment, the one he will be forced to accept, might be a base in Europe. It might be

Plattsburgh: a couple of dull years in upstate New York, not too far from home.

Or it might be Vietnam. Gabriel knows a surgeon who refused an air force assignment in Thailand; at this very moment he is on a plane to the heart of combat in Vietnam.

They sit in the living room. The sunset is stretched across the carpeted floor. Outside, the evening newspaper lands on the doorstep with a thump. Slowly, irregularly, thumps recede down the street.

"If Thailand is safe," says Kreutzer.

Rabbi Jacobson beside the window, under a blanket of pink and yellow. Braiding the tassels of the blanket like fringes on a prayer shawl.

Kreutzer is nervous, and excited. Who will he be once oblivion descends? What will it feel like to learn the rabbi's secret?

He is willing to lose his mind. He will forget the soft voices of long-dead teachers who called him *Duvidl*, forget his own father's shadowed tired face; he will sacrifice the years of earning his family's livelihood, the curl of the great sage's pen, everything that makes him David Kreutzer. And along with it will disappear all that makes his daughter Marjorie weep. Marjorie will forget guilt, she will forget fury, she will forget wanting to drown her own heartbeat in some other hot, jarring rhythm. She will change her mind about naming the baby Gabrielle; the rabbi, in his wisdom, will not permit such a tribute, for the child must not bear a single old sorrow. Such they will be: old man, mother, child, all washed of memory.

"Rabbi," Kreutzer breathes.

The rabbi smiles a cordial smile.

Kreutzer opens his mouth to tell Jacobson about the baby, how she will be born into forgetfulness. But he sees something on the floor. It is an envelope, fallen from the sunlit windowsill.

Unopened. "Jacobson," he stumbles. "Have you not reconciled with your son?"

"My son," says the rabbi, "married a wonderful girl."

"So you have forgiven his intermarriage."

"My son married a Jewish girl. The whole congregation danced at the wedding." The rabbi pats his stomach, pleased. "There was almond soup."

Kreutzer remembers that soup. Iris so wanted the recipe, she went on the sly into the kitchen to ask. The cook, preparing dessert in a rush of steam and barked orders, ejected her back onto the dance floor with a flurry of curses. Iris was embarrassed and they left early; Kreutzer remembers that almond soup well.

"That was your nephew's wedding," Kreutzer says. "Not your son's."

Jacobson beams. "My son's wedding."

What matters a detail from the past? Forgetfulness is best; how sweet its honey will taste on his eager tongue.

Yet he cannot let it rest. "Your nephew's," says Kreutzer.

"No," says the rabbi gently. He sighs.

It is the moment Kreutzer has awaited. But something in this conversation is not right. A son has written a letter; it must be answered. The son is loyal despite transgressions, he is waiting for the father to forgive. How can the rabbi excuse himself for condemning his boy? Whatever a man feels, mustn't he be mindful of his children? Kreutzer pictures Marjorie standing in the cemetery with her belly. He pictures Marjorie with her terribles.

The smile on Kreutzer's face tumbles, it feels to him it will never stop tumbling.

Forgiveness. There is no escaping it. Marjorie has forgiven him; this Kreutzer is forced to see. In the cemetery she peered at him through tears as if to say: A child needs a grandfather. Even one who rails about Christmas trees. And a daughter, a daughter needs a father. She looked at him with eyes that were, after all these years, Iris's eyes. Telling him: *Forgive.*

Yet if he absolves himself? For years he has known he mustn't. Because if Kreutzer admits his own powerlessness, if he admits there was nothing he could have done different, then there is only one other to blame for what should never have happened—for an airplane failing mid-landing; smashing into the single building along the base's airstrip that was occupied. The building in which David Kreutzer's son lay on his cot reading.

He looks at the rabbi. The sweetness of oblivion is so near Kreutzer is light-headed. But the muddy business of life will not be ignored. A wrong has been done and it must be righted. Not all may ever be well between a man and his family once there has been difficulty. But a father has a responsibility to try.

"We are old men," he tells Jacobson. "We have little to offer. But what we can, we must."

The rabbi considers Kreutzer.

"Forgive him," Kreutzer says. "Forgive your son."

The rabbi makes no answer. Shifting his attention to his blanket, he unbraids a single tassel, then rebraids.

Kreutzer lifts weary eyes to the clock. It is noon. His daughter has invited him to lunch.

He stands. He is an old man, the chains of gravity are heavy. For years he has made the greatest sacrifice, a sacrifice worthy of the sages: He has blamed himself and spared another his rage. Now he will forgive himself; David Kreutzer will rejoin the world as best as he—dinosaur, racist, fool—is able. But at what cost. For now he must call to account the one with whom he has held the longest silence. Dreadful words form in his mouth: words to which there can be no rebuttal.

As Kreutzer steps past Jacobson's chair, the rabbi stretches a hand to touch Kreutzer's sleeve. He does not reach it; his fingers plait empty air. He chants quietly. "The responsive reading is on page one hundred and five. The Torah remains in the ark."

Kreutzer's voice is empty. "And the deed to the synagogue's land?"

"In the storage room of Temple Beth Shalom, beneath a box

of hagaddahs. Twelve Grove Street, second floor." The rabbi purses his lips, meditative. "We turn to page one hundred and five for the responsive reading. We begin with blessings for a sweet new year."

With a wave Kreutzer deflects Jacobson's piety. The rabbi follows his gaze. In tandem they face the sharp haze of the window, blinding as the brightness of heaven. "No blessings without atonement," says Kreutzer.

"Atonement," echoes the rabbi. His head bobs slightly as in prayer. "At the new year, atonement must be made for both types of sin. Two categories: man against man, man against God."

"You are wrong," says Kreutzer. "There is a third category of sin."

"Two only," murmurs the rabbi. An anxious flicker of his eyes says to Kreutzer, *Stay.*

Kreutzer stares: at the luminous window, at the spare furnishings, at the rabbi wrapped in a tassled blanket, mottled neck tremoring. With a leaden step, he turns his back. "Rabbi," Kreutzer says. The corridor before him is silent. He drapes his jacket over his arms. "God has picked my pocket."

Rachel Kadish

The character of David Kreutzer came to life when I borrowed a few traits from each of my grandfathers—one raised in a hard-scrabble, racist environment during the Depression; the other a highly educated and argumentative European refugee—and began inventing from there. Kreutzer's intimate struggle with faith moved me deeply. Now that I'm no longer writing his story, I miss him—his bluntness, his irascible humor, his deep if confused integrity.

In subject and in voice, "The Argument" is identifiably Jewish (though as I type these words I practically hear Kreutzer's protest:

"As if a story was a thing you circumcised . . . ?"). And I under-stand that labels such as "Jewish writer" or "woman writer" can be in some way helpful to readers. I choose, however, to consider myself simply a writer. Much of my work is about Jews; some is not. Some focuses on women, some on men. I'm fortunate in that my life includes contact with a broad range of people and cultures. I trea-sure and insist on my freedom to write about the full range of sub-jects that fascinate me.

PART THREE

Mystics, Seekers,
and Fanatics

BEE SEASON

Myla Goldberg

The spelling bee registrar's face has a worn-out shoe leather softness to it specific to upper middle-aged women. She holds Eliza's library card in her hands. "Eliza Naumann." Her eyes scan her list. She crosses through Eliza's name with a red pen. The soft folds of her neck remind Eliza of turtle skin. "Do you happen to have a picture ID?"

"A picture ID?"

The registrar's glasses have slipped to the end of her nose, magnifying the age spots on her cheeks. One of them is shaped like Ohio. "You didn't hear about Bucks County?"

Eliza shakes her head.

"A boy takes fifth place and it turns out he wasn't even on the list. Turns out he lost his school bee but Mom wanted him to try again at the district. So I'm supposed to ask for a picture, but it's okay if you don't have one. What kind of little kid carries a picture ID? Besides, I can tell you belong."

She winks. The air current created by her arm as she points Eliza in the direction of the auditorium smells of cigars and talcum powder.

The auditorium has cushy seats, a balcony, and a large stage concealed by a heavy purple curtain. Aaron chooses a seat toward the back, figuring it will be easier to make a quick exit without attracting notice. He expects they will be leaving early.

The bee contestants are split according to gender between two backstage dressing rooms. The girls' has large mirrors along one cinder block wall, each mirror framed by light bulbs. A thick layer of dust has settled along each bulb, few of which are actually lit. One flickers like an amorous lightning bug.

A group of girls crowds around one mirror, mechanically brushing and rebrushing their bangs. One of the smaller girls seems to be praying. A few stand frozen as their mouths form strings of silent, hopeful letters. The only adult in the room is a badged bee chaperone. She sits ineffectually in the corner, splitting the silence at irregular intervals to remind the girls to pee.

Eliza is the only one not wearing a skirt or a dress. She sees word booklets and spelling lists from which girls are quizzing each other. She can't believe she wasted the week waiting for her father's nod when she could have been studying. She is suddenly grateful for Saul's absence, realizes that having him here would have meant watching his face fold into disappointment on a larger scale than ever before.

When it is time for the bee to begin, the children are led onstage and told to take their seats according to their numbers. It's a much bigger stage than the one in McKinley's cafeteria, the first real stage Eliza has ever been on. She grasps her number tightly in her hands and gazes at the *Times-Herald* Spelling Bee banner for reassurance.

Children shuffle to their seats like convalescents who have hopelessly strayed from the hospital grounds and are waiting to be retrieved. A small boy in the back row quietly hyperventilates. Two rows up, a girl tears her cuticles with her teeth. Another energetically sucks her hair.

The curtain opens with a whoosh of heavy fabric, the creak of rusty pulleys, and isolated gasps from startled children. The impression of the audience as a wave about to crash over them is heightened by the sound of applause. One startled fifth grader cries out, "Mo—" stopping himself before the incriminating final M, his gaffe mercifully concealed by the clapping. The same woman who moments ago had been exhorting Eliza and the others to urinate approaches the microphone. Her voice sounds like a soft-focus greeting card cover.

"Hello. I'm Katherine Rai and I'd like to welcome all of you here today to the *Times-Herald* District Spelling Bee." More applause. "The spelling bee is a truly American tradition, one that encourages learning and greater familiarity with our language. Each young person sitting on this stage is a winner. Each is here because he or she has exhibited superior abilities and knowledge. Each is an example of the best and brightest in our area. We are not competing *against* each other today. This is not a competition. It's a celebration. Of spelling and of achievement. Parents, remember that no matter what place your child comes in today, he or she is a winner. Spellers, be proud. Be proud of yourselves and be proud that you are here."

More applause. Eliza isn't sure if people are applauding because they feel they should or because they actually believe this woman's lies.

The woman continues, her voice the live embodiment of gently curved Hallmark lettering in a gender-appropriate pastel. "I'd like to introduce our word pronouncer for today's bee. Mr. Stanley Julien, Norristown Area High's own principal, has graciously volunteered his time and vocal talents to these youngsters. Stan?"

Mr. Julien walk-jogs onstage like a late-night talk show host with his own theme song. More applause. Mr. Julien smiles and waves his way to where a book, a microphone, and a gavel are waiting.

"Thank you, Kathy. Ms. Rai is our school's resource counselor and she does a great job, a great job. I also understand she was once a spelling bee contestant herself, isn't that right, Kathy?"

Every year, the same script. Katherine still remembers the mortification of having to pee midway through the sixth round. By round eight, when she could hold it no longer, she misspelled her word just for the chance to get offstage. She smiles too broadly at Stanley in response, her teeth luminous in the stage lights.

As Ms. Rai lowers herself into the seat beside Mr. Julien, her fuzzy demeanor and calligraphic voice are replaced by a primal predator hunting its next meal. Ms. Rai's manicured hand becomes a bloodied talon, her gavel rising like a guillotine blade waiting to descend upon the trembling, outstretched neck of the next spelling victim. When the gavel comes crashing down and Ms. Rai growls *"Incorrect,"* all sweetness and light are gone from her voice. Her victims sometimes limp offstage as if the gavel has smashed the smaller bones of their feet.

But not Eliza. From the first time she steps to the microphone the words are there, radiant as neon. She hears the word and suddenly it is inside her head, translated from sound into physical form. Sometimes the letters need a moment to arrange themselves behind her closed eyes. An E will replace an I, a consonant will double. Eliza is patient. She is not frightened by Ms. Rai's gavel hand. She knows when a word has reached its perfect form, SCALLION and BUTANE and ORANGUTAN blazing pure and incontrovertible in her mind.

By the time it comes down to Eliza and Number 24, a small boy in a blue shirt the color of deodorized toilet water, time itself is measured in syllables. The sounds of chairs scraping, footfalls echoing on the stage, and the screech of the improperly adjusted microphone are all transformed into letters, the world one vibrant text spelling itself before her. There is no hesitation in Eliza's voice as she tackles LEGUME and PORTENT. Her pre-bee trepidation is forgotten. She stands confident, no longer caring that she is the only girl in pants. Each turn at the microphone, she spells to a different person in the audience, as if that word is the person's most secret wish.

Eliza wins the district bee with VACUOUS. Her trophy is crowned with a gold-tinted bee figurine wearing glasses and a tasseled miter board. The bee clutches a dictionary to its chest and holds aloft a flaming torch. Eliza poses for a photographer from the *Norristown Times-Herald* alone, with her fellow runners-up, with Aaron, and with Mr. Julien and Ms. Rai. Eliza learns that if she dies or becomes too ill to attend the state competition, she is to inform the Spelling Board as soon as possible so that they can notify Number 24. She learns that Number 24 is named Matthew Harris and that he has a defective pituitary gland, but that he is going to be starting growth hormone therapy in a week. She is too happy to notice that Aaron doesn't talk much on the way home or that he spends his time at stoplights observing her as if she is a formerly passive dog who has killed its first small animal. Elly spends the car ride silently spelling the words she hears on the radio, her trophy clutched tightly in both hands.

On day of his bar mitzvah, Aaron attends to each button on his new blue suit with geriatric care. His new shoes, professionally polished, are the first he has ever owned requiring a shoehorn. He slips his feet into them with underwater slowness. He gets his tie perfect on his first attempt and without any help. The day is a Tootsie Pop he must try to lick without giving in to the urge to bite through its chocolate center. He is determined to make it last longer than any other day of his life.

Aaron's regular visits to his father's study segued so seamlessly into studying for his bar mitzvah that Aaron isn't exactly certain how long they have been preparing. It seems that bits and pieces may have been around as early as sixth grade, when Saul first opened his study doors. Aaron remembers playing games in which he learned the *trup*, the special symbols indicating how the ancient words of the Torah and Haftorah are to be chanted. If Aaron had any doubts about becoming a rabbi, the time spent studying with his father has erased them. His father's pride in him seeps into his skin, infuses his blood, and whispers his future.

The service is flawless. Aaron acts as cantor and rabbi, leading the congregation through both the prayers and responsive readings, chanting the *Hatzi Kaddish* like a pro. He is self-assured. He doesn't slouch. As he recites each prayer from memory, his gaze moves confidently between the faces assembled before him. When he chants his Torah portion, Rabbi Mayer doesn't have to correct him even once.

Aaron's earlier habit of looking for God in everyday objects has devolved into a less focused sense of anticipation. Though Aaron no longer whispers questions to God during the Silent Amidah, part of him has never stopped praying for revelation.

Aaron is on the *bimah*, speeding through the final *brachot* after completing his Haftorah portion when a warm flush starts at his toes and spreads, opening like a feather fan, to the top of his head. Suddenly, every particle of him is shimmering. He can sense each part of his body, down to each hair on his head, but at the same time feels he is one fluid whole. Though his mouth keeps moving, he is no longer focused on the prayers before him. They have become body knowledge, so deeply ingrained that they flow as naturally as air from his lungs. Aaron can sense the approach of something larger, a sea swell building up to a huge wave. Then, in a moment so intense Aaron has no idea he is still standing, it hits.

Every person in the room becomes part of him. He can suddenly see the temple from forty-six different perspectives, through forty-six pairs of eyes. He is linked. He feels the theme and variation of forty-six heartbeats, the stretch and release of forty-six pairs of lungs, the delicate interplay of warm and cool air currents on a congregation of arms, hands, and faces. For one breathtaking moment, Aaron is completely unself-conscious. He feels total acceptance and total love.

The moment passes. Aaron realizes he has finished the *brachot* and that his father is presenting him with a twelve-string guitar. Already the transformative moment feels distant, a dream he must struggle to recall upon waking. Rabbi Mayer proclaims this to be the most impressive bar mitzvah he has ever attended and presents Aaron with *The Jewish Book of Why* on behalf of the congregation. Everyone adjourns to the back room where the kosher caterers have set up lunch. Politely ignored is the fact that some of the broiled chicken breasts were not thoroughly defeathered.

A DJ is spinning Duran Duran, Eurythmics, and Flock of Seagulls, songs to which Aaron does not listen but knows are popular. When Aaron dances with Stacey Lieberman, he doesn't worry that she might only be dancing with him to be polite. When he asks for a second dance, he can tell that she's really sorry her heel hurts too much to say yes. He decides he will call her next week to ask her to a movie.

Aaron accepts congratulations and a fat slice of cake. He is contemplatively sucking on a sugar flower when he decides that what he experienced on the *bimah* was God. His early years of whispered prayer and the cloud and cookie watching have been rewarded. He knows it was really God because there was no booming voice, no beam of light. His experience was something as momentous and private and unexpected as seeing a red pulsing light inside a cloud. He keeps it to himself.

When Eliza arrives home, Saul's first thought is how nice it is that the district bee gives away such huge consolation trophies. It takes him a few moments of hearing his daughter's *"I won! I won!"* and feeling her arms wrapped around his waist to comprehend that the trophy is no consolation. He scoops his little girl into his arms and tries to hold her above his head but realizes, midway, that he hasn't tried to do this for at least five or six years. He puts her back down, silently resolving to start exercising.

"Elly, that's fantastic! I wish I could have been there. I bet it was something else, huh, Aaron?"

Aaron smiles and nods, tries to think of what a good older brother would say. "She beat out a lot of kids, Dad. You would have loved it."

"I know, I know. And I didn't even think to give you the camera." Saul shakes his head. "But now I get another chance. You're going on to the next level, right?"

Eliza nods. "The area finals are in a month. In Philadelphia."

Saul claps his hands. "Perfect! We'll all go. A family trip. A month should give your mother enough time to clear the day. I'm so proud of you, Elly. I knew it was just a matter of time until you showed your stuff. A month. I can barely wait."

At which point Eliza realizes that she has only four weeks in which to study.

Studying has always been a chore on the level of dish-washing and room-cleaning, approached with the same sense of distraction and reluctance. Eliza fears that studying will leech her of spelling enthusiasm. The days following her spelling win, she resolutely maintains her after-school schedule of television reruns, pretends not to notice her father's raised eyebrows at the sight of her in her regular chair, nary a spelling list or dictionary in sight. More than her father's unspoken expectations, it is Eliza's growing suspicion that she has stumbled upon a skill that convinces her to break out the word lists. She realizes she has never been naturally good enough at anything to want to get better before. She renames studying "practice." Spelling is her new instrument, the upcoming bee the concert for which she must prepare her part.

Within a few days Eliza has developed a routine. After two TV reruns, she retreats to her room. Though she knows there is little chance of anyone disturbing her, she closes and locks her door. She likes the idea, however unlikely, of Saul or Aaron stuck outside, reduced to slipping a note under her door or to waiting for her to emerge. After dinner, she allows herself one prime-time show and then, with Aaron and Saul playing guitar in the study and her mother either cleaning the kitchen or reading her maga-zines, she returns to her room. The click of the bedroom door becomes one of her favorite sounds, filling her with a sense of well-being.

When Eliza studies, it is like discovering her own anatomy. The words resonate within her as if rooted deep inside her body. She pictures words lining her stomach, expanding with each stretch of her lungs, nestling in the chambers of her heart. She is thankful to have been spared from fracture, tonsillitis, or appendectomy. Such incidents might have resulted in words being truncated or removed altogether, reducing her internal vocabulary. Elly contemplates growing her hair long; it could give her an extra edge. When she closes her eyes to picture a word she imagines a communion of brain and body, her various organs divulging their lingual secrets.

Eliza starts walking around with the kind of smile usually associated with Mona Lisas and sphinxes. *I am the best speller on this bus,* she thinks on the way home from school. After a few days of studying, when she's feeling more daring, she goes as far as *I am the best speller at the dinner table,* Saul, Miriam, and Aaron innocently eating around her. Eliza knows that something special is going on. On Wednesday, she remembers the words she studied on Monday and Tuesday. On Thursday, she remembers all the old words, plus the new ones from the day before. The letters are magnets, her brain a refrigerator door.

Eliza finally understands why people enjoy entering talent shows or performing in recitals. She stops hating Betsy Hurley for only doing double-Dutch jump rope at recess. If Eliza could, she would spell all the time. She starts secretly spelling the longer words from Ms. Bergermeyer's droning class lessons and from the nightly TV news broadcasts. When Eliza closes her eyes to spell, the inside of her head becomes an ocean of consonants and vowels, swirling and crashing in huge waves of letters until the word she wants begins to rise to the surface. The word spins and bounces. It pulls up new letters and throws back old ones, a fisherman sorting his catch, until it is perfectly complete.

Eliza can sense herself changing. She has often felt that her outsides were too dull for her insides, that deep within her there was something better than what everyone else could see. Per-

haps, like the donkey in her favorite bedtime story, she has been
turned into a stone. Perhaps, if she could only find a magic pebble, she could change. Walking home from school, Eliza has often
looked for a pebble, red and round, that might transform her
from her unremarkable self. When Eliza finds this pebble in her
dreams, her name becomes the first the teacher memorizes at the
beginning of the school year. She becomes someone who gets
called to come over during Red Rover, Red Rover, someone for
whom a place in the lunch line is saved to guarantee a piece of
chocolate cake. In the dream, Eliza goes to sleep with this magic
pebble under her head. The dream is so real that she wakes up
reaching beneath her pillow. Her sense of loss doesn't fade no
matter how many times she finds nothing there.

After a week of studying, Eliza begins sleeping with a word
list under her head. In the morning it is always there, waiting.

Eliza feels invigorated by her rejection of Saul's offer of help. Her
power to cause her father's emergence from his study in the name
of spelling is made all the sweeter by her decision not to employ
it. Rather than block out her father's and brother's guitar music
she now incorporates it into her own pursuits, her words gliding
on the muted chords rising up through the air vents. Even her
mother's solitary habits have lost the feeling of a party to which
Eliza is not invited. Miriam's typing lends Eliza's studies rhythm
and tempo.

Paging through the dictionary is like looking through a
microscope. Every word breaks down into parts with unique
properties—prefix, suffix, root. Eliza gleans not only the natural
laws that govern the letters but their individual behaviors. R, M,
and D are strong, unbending and faithful. The sometimes silent B
and G and the slippery K follow strident codes of conduct. Even
the redoubtable H, which can make P sound like F and turn
ROOM into RHEUM, obeys etymology. Consonants are the
camels of language, proudly carrying their lingual loads.

Vowels, however, are a different species, the fish that flash and glisten in the watery depths. Vowels are elastic and inconstant, fickle and unfaithful. E can sound like I or U. -IBLE and -ABLE are impossible to discern. There is no combination the vowels haven't tried, exhaustive and incestuous in their couplings. E will just as soon pair with A, I, or O, leading the dance or being led. Eliza prefers the vowels' unpredictability and, of all vowels, favors Y. Y defies categorization, the only letter that can be two things at once. Before the bee, Eliza had been a consonant, slow and unsurprising. With her bee success, she has entered vowelhood. Eliza begins to look at life in alphabetical terms. School is consonantal in its unchanging schedule. God, full of possibility, is a vowel. Death: the ultimate consonant.

Toward the end of the Silent Amidah, Aaron and Eliza play a game called Sheep that both claim to have invented. At the Amidah's beginning, Rabbi Mayer tells the entire congregation to rise. The congregants are supposed to remain standing for as long as they wish to pray, sitting down when they have finished. A lot of people actually do begin by praying, but most stop soon after they start. They become distracted by thoughts of the evening's prime-time television lineup or by how awful the perfume is of the old lady with dyed hair who always sits in the seat under the air duct so that the smell of her goes everywhere.

Because of this, knowing when to sit down is a problem. People want to appear prayerful, but they also want the service to end in time for *Remington Steele* or *Dallas* or *Falcon Crest*. After a period that is short enough to move things along but long enough to seem respectable, they look for a cue. That is what Sheep is all about.

The best nights to play Sheep are bar mitzvah Fridays. The synagogue is filled with people whose nephew or cousin or boss's son is becoming a man the next morning. These people occupy the back half of the synagogue even though there are seats available up front. When they stand for the Silent Amidah they never know whether to focus on the prayerbook or upon a distant point, looking thoughtful.

The key is to make scraping noises. When Eliza or Aaron chooses the moment they feel represents the perfect prayerful/let's-get-on-with-it ratio, they rattle their chairs and rub one or two of the chair legs against the floor to make it sound as if more than one person is actually descending. Their efforts carry to the back where it is determined that if the front rows are sitting, the other rows are allowed to sit down as well. Once Eliza timed it so around three-fourths of the congregation followed her into their chairs like an elaborate chain of dominoes. Even Aaron had been forced to admit she'd set a new record.

This Friday night not being a bar mitzvah, neither Aaron nor Eliza nets any followers, the regulars making it a point of pride to have a unique time to reseat themselves. Three prayers, a Mourner's Kaddish, and two responsive readings later come the weekly announcements, which precede the final prayer. It's the same as usual—Sisterhood meetings, Sunday school classes, and singles retreats—until Saul includes a special announcement.

"Eliza Naumann has won the honor of representing our district tomorrow in the bee finals for our area. We wish her mazel tov and best of luck."

Then he moves on to something about adult education, as though what he has just said is the most normal thing in the world. Eliza starts smiling so hard her cheek muscles hurt. Aaron makes a point of not looking at her.

After the last prayer, everyone proceeds to the back room for *oneg,* where a table is waiting with tea, coffee, juice, and cookies. Eliza loves *oneg* even though the juice is watered down and there are better cookies at home. On the cookie plate are always a few chocolate wafers, but the majority are chalky shortbreads that crumble into little pieces unless the whole thing is ingested at once. On someone's birthday, there is a store-bought cake sparsely decorated with candy flowers.

The trick is to get one of the wafer cookies or, if it is a birthday, a slice of cake with a flower. This takes practice. Eliza and Aaron can't just race to the back room after the last prayer and grab what they want. They have to wait until Rabbi Mayer has come to the table and said a prayer over the food. In a way, this is lucky because sitting in the front row would put them at a distinct disadvantage if it were first come, first serve, especially with the Kaplan kids, who always sit in the back.

The key to snagging a good cookie is placement. Eliza puts herself nearest to the side of the cookie plate with the good cookies on it, then casually rests her hand by the edge of the plate. As soon as the prayer is over, her hand is in prime position.

Getting a flower is trickier. An adult always cuts the cake and there is a line. Eliza never knows what slicing method the cake cutter will use, so it is hard to anticipate where in the cake line she should be to net a flower. It is generally smarter to notice which adults get flowers and to casually ask for one. This is especially effective with women, who usually make a show of handing over their flowers in the service of the diet of the moment. With men, it isn't as sure a bet. They may hand over their flower to prove what great guys they are, but they are just as likely to make a joke about not giving over their flower to spotlight their lingering youthfulness in the face of galloping middle age. Eliza has a standing cake agreement with Mrs. Schoenfeld, who doesn't have children of her own and likes to think that giving Eliza her occasional flower gives them a special bond.

The pre-bee service happens to fall on a birthday week, so there is cake. When it is Eliza's turn Mrs. Schwartz, who is the de facto slicer and prides herself on not playing favorites, actually cuts a piece out of sequence in order to give Eliza a flower, saying that it will bring luck.

Aaron tells himself he isn't jealous. Dad's announcement is no big deal. Eliza deserves the attention, she doesn't usually get any, and the state bee is important. Except that Aaron has been to the state science fair a few times and Saul has never told the congregation about it. When Mrs. Schoenfeld offers him her flower he declines. He's too old to care about such things.

Once Eliza loots the *oneg* table, she generally drifts outside to play tag until it's time to go home. Usually this is no problem, but tonight grownups want to talk to her. Mrs. Lieberman corners Eliza by the Siddur table and kisses her on both cheeks. Eliza wonders if her lipstick has left pucker marks.

". . . is a wonderful thing that can open doors to wonderful places."

Eliza misses the first half. She has been watching Aaron, an *oneg* pro, walk outside with neither cake flower nor good cookie, a sure sign that something is amiss. She feels a strange mixture of anxiety and pride at the thought that she may have something to do with it.

Mr. Schwartz announces he is going to quiz her, one spelling champion to another. Up close, he has a brown front tooth and more wrinkles than Eliza thought. He sips his tea so loudly that she has to repeat NEIGHBOR three times before Mrs. Schwartz comes to her rescue, admonishing Phil for tiring Eliza out before the real thing. The sound of Mr. Schwartz's until now unknown first name allows Eliza to picture Mr. Schwartz in some place other than the synagogue, wearing something other than a brown-striped tie with a stained tip.

Eliza is steps away from freedom when George finds her. George, who lives in the apartment complex nearby, isn't Jewish but comes to services every Friday and attends Saul's adult education classes. Eliza once overheard him talking to her father about religious conversion, and George's belief that if he is going to do it, he wants to "go all the way," but that he isn't sure he is "strong enough." Eliza has no idea what George was talking about even though Aaron has told her he was once in the bathroom when George was peeing and saw that George was uncircumcised.

George tells Eliza she will be representing not only her district tomorrow but Her People. George holds Eliza's shoulders as he speaks and spits in his earnestness, the wetter syllables arcing harmlessly over Eliza's head.

"For centuries, the Jewish nation has been persecuted and exiled. Tomorrow is your chance to manifest the same spirit that has kept the Chosen People alive and faithful through their wanderings in the desert. What you're doing is courageous."

Eliza's eyes are at the level of George's zipper. She squelches the urge to shout "Uncircumcised," though still unsure of its meaning. Instead she silently spells the word. She smiles and nods at George as the letters dance and swirl inside her head until they are perfect, the word that is George's secret spelled out in all its mysterious glory.

The Philadelphia Spectrum serves as concert venue, hockey rink, basketball court and, every so often, books the Ice Capades. Aaron has not attended a Flyers game since learning firsthand that blood bounces on ice.

The morning of the area finals is the closest the stadium comes to the best-of-breed tent at a county fair. Friends and relatives scan the spellers, trying to predict the blue ribbon winner. Eyes travel between contestants, gauging preparedness, intelligence, and spelling savvy. Some parents attempt last-minute changes to their entries. One speller stands frozen beneath a hand smoothing a cowlick. Another melts into the floor as his mother rains words like hailstones upon his slumped shoulders. A morbid camaraderie has arisen between spellers, numbered placards drooping from their necks like turkey wattles. Shared smiles and briefly held gazes acknowledge mutual doom.

This is lost on Eliza, who is too excited by her family's presence to notice. The singularity of their collective appearance outside the house lends a holiday air to their actions. They walk the stadium concourse as if beyond lies Disneyworld or Mesa Verde, this the closest they have come to the family vacation Saul has been promising since Eliza was born.

As far as Eliza can remember, this is the first time she has ever held both parents' hands at once. She swings her arms back and forth, penduluming them the way she's seen happy children do on Kodak commercials. Miriam wears the smile she usually reserves for discovering one of her letters to the editor in print. Saul whistles a klezmer tune between snapping pictures with film that has been in his camera since the Iranian hostage crisis. Even Aaron is talking a few levels louder than usual. When the time comes for Eliza to journey backstage, she is reluctant to go. She would be content to pass by the statue of Rocky Balboa, circling seating sections A–Z until the sky turned purple if it meant they could keep looking the way TV families look by the end of the show.

The area finals can be distinguished from the district bee in the details. The folding chairs for the contestants are cushioned. There is a bell instead of a gavel. The introductory speeches, while of identical content, are given by local politicians instead of school administrators. Three minutes after the applause for the stageful of winners dies down, the first speller—a thin girl with limp hair and large, sad eyes—is eliminated. Her sigh as she leaves the stage, more than the raising of the curtain, signifies that the bee has truly begun.

Tension runs between the spellers like an invisible steel cable. When one rises to approach the microphone, everyone in the row feels the pull. Many are unconscious of the fact they are spelling along with each contestant. As their mouths form the letters, the effect is that of a choir of mutes accompanying every word.

From the third row, it is impossible for Eliza to see anything but the backs of other spellers' heads. The tights Miriam picked out for her itch horribly. Eliza uses the relative privacy accorded by her seat to scratch.

Spellers can ask for word pronunciation, definition, etymology, and use in a sentence, but once they start spelling, there is no turning back. A misspoken letter is irreversible, the equivalent of a nervous tic during brain surgery.

The hardest to watch are those who know they have made a mistake. Sometimes they stop mid-word, the air knocked out of them. Even then they are expected to continue until the word is finished. They flinch their way to the word's end, mere shadows of the child they were before the mistake was made. Finally, the misspelled word is complete, its mistaken A or extra T dangling like a flap of dead skin.

There is a pause, like the split second between touching the thing that's too hot and feeling the burn. Then, the bell.

Ding.

It is the sound of an approaching bicycle, harmless as a sugar ant, but here it takes on atomic, fifties sci-fi proportions. Just as in the movies, its hapless victim stands immobile while the correct spelling, monstrous with huge, flesh-rending jaws, comes at them from the pronouncer's mouth.

It is worst when the speller stands there, nodding like a spring-loaded lawn ornament. A couple times, the fatal moment functions like some kind of psychological glue trap: even after the pronouncer completes the word, the speller remains frozen in place. One boy stands with his hand in front of him, thumb pressing an invisible button on what appears to be an invisible remote control, willing the world to rewind.

Eliza begins to wish she were closer to the front. The wait is like the slow *tic-tic-tic* of a roller coaster climbing to its summit before the stomach-plunging drop. She would gladly trade the ability to scratch at her tights unseen for a shorter ascent, a briefer fall. She is most afraid that some fatal blockage will occur between her brain and mouth, preventing the word from emerging whole. She can hear it happen with other children. She can tell they know the word by the way they intone it, but then some kind of home accident occurs. The word trips over the edge of the tongue and plunges headlong into a tooth. A letter is twisted, I into E, T into P, or there is a pause and the last letter is repeated. Eliza knows it could happen to anyone, that possessing the right spelling is only half the battle.

By the time it is her turn, Eliza is ready for the worst. Instead, she gets ELEMENT. She practically sings the word into the microphone.

Aaron didn't want to come but knew better than to say anything. There are certain times when it's easier to go along with what his father says. When the words "as a family" are used is one of those times. Saul gets a look in his eye, like that of a dominant lion, that means either act like one of the pride or prepare to be attacked by the alpha male. Aaron is grateful for these irregular demands on his filial devotion. They reinforce the idea that the four of them are bound by more than a shared roof.

With that in mind, Aaron puts on his most attentive, brotherly face as he tries to discern his sister among the rows of preadolescents squirming in their chairs like insect specimens that weren't asphyxiated before being pinned. He wants to be able to support his sister's newfound spelling abilities. It's silly, he tells himself. It's immature. But he can't help but notice the way Saul's gaze has been fixed upon the stage ever since enough spellers were eliminated for Eliza to become visible. Even when it's nowhere near her turn, Saul sits at attention, immune from the monotony of each round. The pronouncer's voice, the heavy pauses as the children buy time at the microphone, the recurring requests—"Please repeat the word, please repeat the definition"—have no effect. Saul's gaze is fixed on Eliza. He is looking at her the way a parent looks at an infant too new to be taken for granted.

Aaron remembers that look. He is six years old. Baby Eliza is fresh from the hospital. As Saul introduces Aaron to his new sister, he cannot believe anything that small could actually be alive. He grasps one of his sister's doll hands and examines the tiny fingers. Aaron is not even aware of putting the finger into his mouth, of testing it with his teeth. His sister's scream interrupts his reverie. Saul snatches the tiny hand away. Aaron is terrified, expects the bitten finger to fall off onto the table in a shower of blood, his fragile sister forever fractured. He can barely believe his eyes when the hand emerges whole, the skin unbroken, only a slight ring of indentations left by his teeth. "NO," his father commands, the menace in his voice a physical presence.

Aaron flinches, expecting reprisal. Instead, his father's voice suddenly softens.

"Be gentle. Your sister needs your love. Look how small she is. She will never be as big or old as you. Will you help me look out for her? She needs us both."

Aaron nods, his eyes large from the shock of his actions and his unexpected reprieve. Marvin Bussy and Billy Mamula are years away. He is still a boy who believes he has the power to protect.

A lot of time is spent raising and lowering the mike stand between contestants who have hit puberty and those still waiting to grow. Eliza wishes that those who didn't know their words would just guess instead of stalling until they're asked to start spelling by the judges. In the time it takes some spellers to get started, Eliza has spelled their word a few times, fought the temptation to just take off her tights, and repeatedly sung through the theme from *Star Wars* which, for some reason, she is unable to get out of her head.

Without realizing it, she has developed a routine. Three turns before her own, she blocks out the sounds of the bee and closes her eyes. Since she was very small, Eliza has thought of the inside of her head as a movie theater, providing herself with an explanation for the origin of bad dreams. Nightmares are rationalized away with the private assurance that she has accidentally stepped into an R-rated movie and needs only to return herself to the G-rated theater to remedy the situation. Using the mental movie theater construct, Eliza pictures the inside of her head as a huge blank screen upon which each word will be projected.

It doesn't occur to her to be self-conscious about closing her eyes at the microphone. How else is she to see her word? Not having observed the others' faces, she is unaware that most spell with their eyes open after a brief period of face-clenched concentration indigenous to constipation and jazz solos. Eliza opens her eyes only after uttering the last letter, the word inside her head as real as her nose and just as unmistakable. She has no fear of the *ding*. It's not meant for her.

By Round 7, the words have gotten serious. Eliza has a moment's hesitation with CREPUSCULE, but when she closes her eyes a second time, the word is there, waiting. After she spells it correctly, she spots her father in the audience when he is the only one standing during the applause. She considers waving but decides that it is too uncool. She tries a droll wink but is unable to manage the eyelid coordination and looks instead as if she has something stuck in her eye.

Though they haven't spoken, Eliza has developed an affection for the speller next to her, an intense and careful girl whose numbered placard lies at an upward tilt because of her boobs. When the girl is eliminated with SANSEVIERIA, Eliza feels a loss. After the girl is gone Eliza avoids touching her empty chair.

At the beginning of Round 12, the surviving spellers are consolidated into the front row. Eliza sits with Numbers 8 and 32, two serious-looking Pakistani boys, and Number 17, a red-haired girl with dark circles under her eyes. They are all older and Eliza keeps having to readjust the microphone. Between turns, the red-haired girl whispers a mantra which sounds to Eliza like, "My bear, my bear, my bear." Number 8 alternates between sitting on his hands and chewing his cuticles. Eliza stares into the audience, trying to find her family, but is blinded by the stage lights, which make identifying individual spectators impossible. In quick succession, 17 is dinged by DAGUERREOTYPE and 8 by CZARINA. It is down to Eliza and Number 32, the shorter of the Pakistanis.

He carries himself like a middle-aged businessman forced into early retirement. He wears blocky glasses with tinted lenses.

Before starting his words he runs his fingers through his hair as if he's collecting letters from his scalp. He and Eliza avoid eye contact. When Eliza accidentally brushes his thigh with her hand as he sits down and she stands up, he jerks his leg back as if he's been burned.

Time stops sometime after PHARMACOPOEIA. Eliza knows Number 32's body as well as her own: the inflamed hangnail on his left index finger, the two gray hairs near the back of his head, the way he walks heels first when approaching the mike. He has the annoying habit of grinding his teeth, a quirk that intensifies as the rounds continue. By Round 20, it has become so loud Eliza is sure it can be heard by the spectators in the back rows. The bee has become a war of attrition. If nothing else, Number 32 will turn fifteen before Eliza, at which point he will become too old to qualify.

Despite the incredible tension, despite the fact that Number 32 has obviously been doing this longer than she has, and despite the fact that her stomach is about to tear itself into tiny pieces and explode in a bright cloud of confetti from her mouth, Eliza feels overwhelmingly, intensely alive. She can feel her lungs expanding, the rush of blood traveling from her heart to her fingers. The words hit her at a level of cognition that outpaces conscious thought, resonating somewhere where spelling doesn't need to happen because it already has, each word exploding upon entering her ear. She loves it. She loves everything about it. And she is fully prepared to spend the next year of her life on this stage, trading words into the microphone with Number 32 until his fifteenth birthday finally arrives, the judges forcibly remove him from the stage and announce Eliza to be the *Times-Herald*'s Greater Philadelphia Metro Area Spelling Champion.

Saul doesn't know what he is expecting to happen in Philadelphia, but it certainly isn't the realization that his daughter is a mystical prodigy. And yet, with Eliza standing over the exact spot where Dave "The Hammer" Schulz pummeled Dale Rolfe's

face, that is exactly what happens. He watches, stunned, as Eliza
stands at the microphone, eyes closed, body perfectly relaxed, waiting faithfully and patiently for the next word to materialize. Round
after round—while the other children nod, shake, or bounce, their
hands scratching and picking—his Eliza stands perfectly centered,
in complete concentration, employing the techniques of the ancient
rabbis.

Saul wants to jump to his feet and dance where he stands. He
wants to sing, raising his hands in gratitude and humility. Even
Isaac Luria needed a teacher. Even Shabbatai Zvi and Rabbi Nah-
man of Bratzlav required instruction to reach mystical greatness.
Saul learned long ago that he was not meant to be another Abulafia. Instead, he has been hoping to encounter a student of
whom history is made.

But that it should be Eliza! His own quiet, unassuming Elly-
belly who does little more than go through the motions of the
Shabbat service every Friday and who, until the day before the
district bee, had never set foot inside his study. He would like to
think he has kept his distance in order to protect his daughter
from his unfulfilled hopes. He did not want Eliza to sense paternal expectations as unrealistic as they were immutable. Saul—
who chose books over cars, Naumann over Newman—knows too
well the feeling of becoming something a parent does not intend.
At least, Saul had told himself, *if I cannot prevent myself from my
father's faults, I can protect my daughter from their effect.*

As Saul watches his daughter go head to head with the
serious-looking boy two years her senior, he realizes something
with illogical and unexplainable certainty: his daughter is going
to surpass his greatest expectations. She is going to win.

When Number 32 stumbles over GLISSANDO, the audience
gasps as if the missing second S has left them short of breath. The
ding causes the boy's body to go rigid. For everyone but Saul,
who suddenly feels as if he is watching his destiny unfold, it is
like witnessing an execution.

Number 32 doesn't leave the stage. If Eliza misspells her

word, the bee will continue. As she approaches the microphone, every muscle in Number 32's body is tense, his teeth by now surely reduced to blighted stumps.

"Number 26," the pronouncer intones with the solemnity of the keeper of the Book of Life, "your word is EYRIR."

"Ay-reer?"

"Ay-reer."

Doubt hits Saul like a cold wave. His certainty, so strong seconds ago, seems more space than substance. He can already feel disappointment cooling his blood. He wants to run to his daughter standing so completely still onstage with her eyes closed and yell, before it is too late, *Quick. Open your eyes. This is what I look like when I believe in you.*

EYRIR is a supernova inside Eliza's head, unexpected but breathtakingly beautiful. The lights transform the audience into a sea of vague shapes, the alien syllables echoing in the auditorium's corners. It is strangely quiet. The word fills Eliza's mouth with a sweet, metallic taste.

Suddenly, it is as though she is living underwater. Light wavers on its course to her eyes. The stadium ripples as if painted in ink on a lake's surface. EYRIR is a dank thing exuding heat and threat, its dark fur tangled from years in the forest. EYRIR is the nameless, shapeless fear that haunts sleepless nights. Eliza wants EYRIR to disappear like a fever vision at the touch of her father's hand. Instead, she asks for a definition.

"It's a unit of currency," the pronouncer explains, eyes unreadable. "Used in Iceland."

"Ay-reer." Eliza pauses. *A? AI?* She closes her eyes. She doesn't think about Number 32 glowering behind her or about the fact that she will be required to start spelling soon or about her family somewhere in the audience. She waits patiently, faithfully, for the word to reveal itself. Then, as her eyelids glow red from the stage lights, it does. Eliza takes a deep breath to give the word strength.

Y, the slippery snake. Y that can change from vowel to conso-
nant like water to ice.

"E-Y-" She lets out her breath. "R-I-R. Eyrir." She waits.

Resounding, palpable silence. Nothing moves. Eliza wonders
if death is not a sleep you can't wake up from but life reduced to
one inescapable moment.

The pronouncer's voice cracks the silence, a thickened shell
protecting sweet meat.

"That is correct."

Applause pounds the stage like colored pebbles. An internal
mute button that Eliza didn't even know existed disengages. It is
like hearing the ocean after years of watching waves silently
crash upon the sand.

And then Eliza sees her father. Saul is not walking but running to the stage. He is oblivious to the rows of chairs, to the
clusters of people and journalists, his body reminding Eliza of a
bumper car as he bounces off them on his stageward trajectory,
eyes locked on her. His face is like a page from Eliza's illustrated
Old Testament: Jew beholding Promised Land. Eliza feels like
Moses. She feels like Superman. She holds her trophy aloft, the
stage her Mount Sinai, Saul her Jimmy Olsen. When Saul reaches
the stage and lifts her into a hug like manna in the desert, Eliza is
flying.

Myla Goldberg

When Bee Season *came out I was completely taken by surprise*
when some people started calling it a Jewish novel and myself a
Jewish writer. Of course, in retrospect it makes sense since the fam-
ily is Jewish and the whole book—like this excerpt—is peppered
with the arcane practices of Abraham Abulafia, but the thing I
want to know is this: will the people who considered Bee Season *to*
be a Jewish book and myself to be a Jewish writer still think that
way about me and my work when they read the next book, which

features an Irish-Catholic woman living in South Boston? Jewish
culture is always going to influence my perspective on the world and
my writing, but not always in as literal a way as it did in Bee Season. *If Jewish culture and thought are to remain relevant and*
vibrant through the next century, it is crucial we recognize that Jew-
ish imaginations and minds need to tackle a world much wider than
the specifically Jewish past and present that has traditionally com-
posed the Jewish literary and cultural canon.

A Poland, a Lithuania, a Galicia

Tova Mirvis

Two dish racks had appeared overnight, and they were sitting innocently in Evelyn Newman's kitchen sink as if they had always been there. This wasn't the only unusual occurrence in the house. On Monday, the mezuzahs were unscrewed from the doorposts and taken to the rabbi to be checked for any smudged or missing letter that would render them non-kosher. A day later, having apparently been declared kosher, they were put back. On Wednesday, large plastic cups intended for morning ritual washing had been placed in each of the bathrooms. And now, Thursday, it was dish racks. It was as if a team of religious elves had been let loose in the neighborhood. Instead of green hats and turned-up shoes, these elves wore black hats and white beards and scurried from house to house, waving wands and leaving kosher in their wake. But Evelyn, standing in her kitchen, knew who was behind this transformation. It wasn't her daughter Ilana or her husband, David. It was their son Bryan, who had just returned home from his second year of yeshiva in Israel, filled with religious fervor and a love for the letter of the law.

He had gone to Israel between high school and college, as all his friends had done. This was the path David and Evelyn laid out for their kids, this line of moderation, this Modern Orthodoxy. They believed in the integration of religious and secular. They sent their kids to a yeshiva high school that doubled as a feeder for the Ivy League. In coed classes, in jeans and sneakers, they studied English and math half the day, Jewish law and Bible

the other half. They kept Shabbos and kosher and played on basketball teams wearing blue and white uniforms with matching
yarmulkes. And before they ventured out of this world where
everything was consistent, or at least consistently inconsistent,
they spent a year in Israel.

Before he left for yeshiva, Bryan had worried whether he'd
have enough time to play basketball. But after a few months, having undergone some transformation his parents couldn't understand, he worried that he didn't have enough time to study
Talmud. He begged for a second year and they had reluctantly
agreed, in accordance with their principle that kids need room to
grow and explore. And in accordance with their principle that
two years in yeshiva were more than enough, they made him
promise that after his second year in Israel, he would attend
Columbia University as planned.

But instead, he had come home and informed them that he no
longer wanted to be called Bryan. He wanted to use his Hebrew
name, Baruch, which they hadn't intended for use in the secular
world. Because Baruch carried with it the dreaded *ch*, the
modern-day shibboleth. As in Chana and Chaviva and Yechiel.
Chaim, Nechama, Zacharyah, and Achiezer. Not a *ch*, like Charlie,
not a *sh*, like Shirley, but a guttural sound that came from the
back of those throats that had been trained from birth.

They thought his fervor was the result of age, the kind of
certitude only a nineteen-year-old could muster. They had seen
their friends' children pass through this stage of fervent religiosity. It was one of the milestones on the road to adulthood, as normal and yet as disconcerting as puberty. They had heard stories
about children who came home from Israel and cleared out all the
dishes in the house and carted them off in the middle of the night
to be dunked in the local *mikvah*. Children who, if they could,
would kidnap their parents and dunk them too. They rattled off
for their parents every commandment they trespassed upon,
eager to let them know why they and all their friends were hyp-
ocrites. And these were the more pliant children. Others refused

to set foot back on American soil. The only way they would leave Israel was kicking and screaming.

Roots to grow and wings to soar, Evelyn had written on birthday and graduation cards. Until Bryan had taken this far too seriously and searched for roots that went deeper than Middleton, New Jersey, where they lived. Their son wanted to pass through Ellis Island in reverse, to find a Poland, a Lithuania, a Galicia he was sure still existed somewhere. And when he found where these roots lead, he had taken the wings they had given him and flown right off the deep end. But still, they didn't expect their son to permanently join the growing ranks of the nouveau yeshiva-ish. They reassured themselves that all it took was a few weeks back in America to even out. He had been home for five days and, in the hopes that he would soon return to a more comfortable middle ground, they were tiptoeing around him and waiting.

Bryan, or Baruch, was in his bedroom reciting the morning prayers. He was wrapped in the black leather straps of his tefillin *(You shall wear them as frontlets between your eyes)* and in a guilt that encircled him. Jet lag and laziness had conspired against him and he had slept late, through minyan at shul, which he was commanded by God to attend. *(He who prays with his community is to be praised.)* Before he left yeshiva, his rabbi had warned him against being lulled into the complacency of his parents' so called Modern Orthodox world *(You shall not imitate the ways of the other nation)*, where one wasn't required to go to great pains to fulfill the word of God. Five days in America and this was what he had become.

He was trying to make up for this failure with an extra measure of concentration. In yeshiva, when he davened, he saw arms wrapped in tefillin, backs cloaked in the black and white stripes of the tallis, and he had felt certain he was standing in God's shadow. After davening, he sat in front of his Talmud and learned. He ate lunch, then learned more. At night, he returned to the beit midrash to review what they had learned during the day. *(And you shall be occupied with it day and night.)* He had studied Talmud in high school for the fifty-minute period squeezed between Algebra and AP American History. But when he spent the whole day immersed in its study, he had nowhere to go but deeper into the miles-long stretch of pages. In the seemingly dry rabbinic discussions of Jewish law, he saw the shadow of God peeking out from behind the words.

If two men find an object, the law read, they should split it. But what is meant by *find*, what is meant by *object*? He who sees it first or he who holds it first? What about a case in which both men claimed it was theirs? What about a contradictory text, a standing principle? A proof text was brought from here, an opposing opinion from there. Baruch followed along with the sages as they parsed each word for a hint of God's law. The folio pages of the Talmud became his world. The tiny black letters unhooked themselves from their intended shape and became small square huts with triangular roofs. They lined up one rectangle next to another and become rows of houses, stacked themselves and became modern skyscrapers. Then they changed shape again and became open doors and tunnels, pathways, caves, and alleyways leading him deeper into this world. Behind every door, he found another door. Behind every answer, another question.

But now that Baruch was home, this world that had existed so fully for him threatened to collapse, the words losing dimension and becoming nothing but flat black scribbling on a page. About to say Shema and proclaim God's oneness, he tried to bury himself in his prayers. But this sort of concentration was impossible, because coming not from his own heart but from the stereo in his sister's room was distraction itself. She was blasting her music, the same rock music he had once listened to. God worked in strange and wondrous ways, and here, The Holy One Blessed Be He was using the Top 40 to test him, just as He tested Avraham on Mount Moriah, Moses with the rock. Baruch put his siddur in front of his face, and he *shuckled* and swayed with more fervor. When it was no use—her music imbedded too deeply under his skin, mingled with the words of his prayer—he decided he would have to say something to Ilana. He knocked lightly on her door, then louder when she of course couldn't hear him with her music playing so loudly. Finally he opened the door.

"Ilana, I'm trying to daven and I would appreciate it if you lowered the music."

He had to restrain himself from adding that he wished she understood that he was trying to be someone new. He wished she could make it easier, not harder. He also wished that though he had become a different person, he could still have the same relationship with her. But shackled by the new awkwardness in their relationship, he knew that none of this would be said: all of it one more heartfelt, if futile, prayer.

In the first week of summer vacation, in the thirteenth year of her life, Ilana was lying on her bed, talking on the phone, having just said good-bye to the eighth grade at the Middleton Hebrew Academy.

"I've got to go," she said into the phone and hung up.

In the five days since he had come home from Israel, everyone was trying to pretend that things were fine. She knew that they weren't. She and Bryan had once been close, but these past few days, she had barely spoken to him. She had tried, but even when the words came rushing out of her mouth, they were met by silence or disinterest or worse. But willing to give him another chance, she took his presence in her room as a hopeful sign that this would pass.

"Come in," she invited him.

"I'm in the middle of davening," he said.

In the doorway, he shuffled from foot to foot. He looked away from her. It was as if his entire body had turned against her. She watched him brace his arm against the door frame and stand there, as if he dared not enter further. His expression, so serious and self-righteously perturbed, was sending out warning signs: Do Not Enter or No Passing Zone. It made her feel that she shouldn't be lying down. She felt the urge to tuck away anything that might be incriminating.

But there was nothing she could do about her room. Once-worn clothes were draped over her desk chair. Dirty clothes were inside out on the floor, in the vicinity of the hamper her mother had placed there as a suggestion. A tangle of shoes filled the remaining space on the floor—one sneaker, the socks balled up inside, two black platform shoes, a sandal paired with a clog. The mess in her room was well past the stage where she could be told to clean up. It had taken on the dimension of family project, something for which several days would need to be allocated. But in this family, where no one liked to tell anyone what to do, those days would just be vaguely alluded to: a suggestion, a recommendation, a wish, a dream. In her defense, she claimed her room as a vehicle for creative expression. An art form in its own right. "I know you think it's random," she liked to say, "but a lot of thought goes into it." She smiled and coaxed from her parents their agreement that *her personal sanctuary* wouldn't be interfered with.

"So what's up?" she asked, hesitantly.

"The music," he said. "Would you turn it down?"

She lowered the volume, hoping this gesture would eliminate the distance brewing between them. "Okay, Bryan," she said.

"You know my name is Baruch now," he said.

She leaned back into her pillows and stared at him. "That might be what you're making us call you, but technically your name is still Bryan. You can ask us to call you by a different name and we can agree if we want to, but you can't say we have an obligation to listen to you."

"If I want to use my Hebrew name, why would you object to that?"

"I'm just saying that for some of us, it's still a free country and you can't force us to do anything we don't want to do."

"No, I can't force you. But I am *asking* you, as your older brother, to respect my wishes and call me Baruch. And I'm also trying to daven, which I'm sure you didn't do today, and that is why I am *asking* you to lower the music."

"Whatever."

She scowled at him, and remembered the hurt feelings that she had been nursing since his arrival. At the airport, she had screamed his name and thrown her arms around him. He didn't stop her, but his shoulders tensed and his body drew back as he perfunctorily returned the hug. She was so happy to see him that she hadn't thought anything of it. Later that evening, she sat on the floor of his room and watched him unpack. Still so excited to have him home, she moved to hug him again and this time, he didn't just tense. He disentangled himself.

"Ilana," he had said. "It says in the *Shulchan Aruch* that after the age of bar mitzvah, a brother isn't allowed to hug his sister."

Still in hugging range, she stared at him.

"What are you talking about?" she asked.

"It's *assur*," he said. Forbidden.

"That's crazy."

"It's not saying that there would be anything going on. Just that it's improper."

It was all so impersonal. A theoretical brother. A theoretical sister. A theoretical hug. She stepped back and held her hands up in surrender. "Fine. No problem," she had said and wondered if the rabbis would object to her smacking her brother. In their estimation was that sort of contact inappropriate as well? But inside this anger, she had felt something that surprised her. She felt ashamed, as if these rabbis and her brother were accusing her of a sort of incestuous rabbinic sluttiness.

But that was five days ago. She was over it. Looking at this stranger in the doorway, she laughed that she had been naive enough to think that having her brother home meant having him back. But she wasn't going to listen to this new Baruch boy who had returned in her brother's body. The Invasion of the Body Snatchers, that was how she thought of the rabbis he was always quoting. She scowled at him, and he turned away and went back to his room. As he closed his door, she hurled after him, like it was a curse word, *Bryan*.

Bryan, Bryan, Bryan, Bryan. The music, which Ilana had turned louder, seemed to be screaming his name. But he wasn't going to allow the forces of good to be so easily drowned out by the forces of evil. Opening his bedroom door, he sang aloud: *"Shema Yisroel, HaSem Elohaynu, HaSem Echad."*

Hear O Israel, the Lord is our God, the Lord is One: these words ought to be able to hold out against I want to kiss you, I want to love you, please let me touch you. He imagined his words like soldiers armed only with their piety going off to fight the corrupt and militarily superior words of Britney Spears.

"Mee chamocha ba'elim Elohim," he sang. Who is like you, God, in your glory and majesty, in your manifestations of holiness, in your goodness and your truth.

She opened her door too: I want to rock all night, come on baby, dance with me.

When it was time to recite the silent Shemoneh Esray, he could think of no source that allowed him to say it out loud, even to combat the forces of rebelliousness and rock music. He let her music play while he stood, feet together, lips moving, and blessed the God of Abraham, Isaac and Jacob. But when he finished, he resumed his battle cry.

"Ashrei yoshvei veitecha." Happy is he who sits in God's House.

"Aleinu leshabeach la'adon hakol." It is incumbent upon us to praise the Master of all.

His first year in Israel, he had tried not to be one of the boys so influenced by the rabbis that they gave up everything. In Yeshiva, he spent the first six months trying to escape the rabbi's inquisitive eye. He went to *shiur* most of the time, and spent his evenings hanging out on Ben Yehudah Street with other Americans. Then he grew bored going out and there was nothing to do but learn. He immersed himself in the Talmud and spent late nights in the beit midrash. When his rabbi delivered *shiur,* Baruch saw that he wasn't simply lecturing, presenting, explicating. He was living, breathing the words. Once he saw this, it was like trying to walk against the wind.

"Face it," Baruch had said to his friends who were struggling with the same questions. "What our parents do is not really right." His parents were minimally Orthodox. They went to shul, they kept kosher. But they didn't, he was sure, see the law of God as binding. Picking and Choosing, this was their true religion. In this family where anything could presumably be discussed, all he wanted to ask his parents was if in their hearts, with all their souls, with all their might, they believed.

But Baruch believed. He had peeled back his outer layers of doubt and cynicism, ego and desire, and underneath he found a hard luminescent core of faith. He knew that if confronted, his parents would extol the virtues of moderation and secular education. They would talk about integrating and assimilating the best of both worlds. They would claim that math and science, art and literature were also from God. His mother would say that religion is a journey and we are all in the continuous process of finding ourselves and our belief. His father would quote Rav Solveitchik about dialectics, duality, faith, struggle, and doubt. He would extol the benefits of living in two worlds at once. He wouldn't understand that Baruch wanted one world, authentic and whole.

There was something else his parents didn't know and wouldn't understand. They, whom he was commanded to honor, assumed that in two months he would be starting his first year at Columbia. His parents, he was sure, imagined him wearing the blue and white Columbia sweatshirt he bought when he went for his interview. They imagined their son living in a coed dorm, enrolled in classes in literature and science and philosophy. And as soon as he worked up the courage, he would tell them. He wasn't going to college, not this year, not next year, not ever.

He had friends who submitted to the will of their parents and considered themselves passive resisters as they attended their first-year orientations. At the Ivy League school of their parent's choice, they read the books on the syllabi but didn't allow them to penetrate their minds. He had a friend at Yale who returned from Israel and refused to live in the dorms. He organized his classes around minyan and shiur. Another friend at Penn claimed he was majoring in "honoring my mother and father." And by the end of their sophomore years, after incremental steps toward the middle ground, both of them were going to football games and majoring in comparative religion. But he wasn't going to be one of these boys. He was going back to Israel, back to yeshiva where he would fulfill God's commandment to immerse himself in the study of Torah day and night. He wanted the real thing: the unadulterated God.

His rebbe said that change starts at home, so he took a look around his room: a different boy had once lived here. Yankees pennants on the walls. A Derek Jeter poster over his bed. Bookshelves lined with spy novels, a bulletin board covered with old sports schedules. From his desk, he pulled out a stack of *Playbills* from musicals he had seen, pictures from camp with his arms around various girls. He made a pile in the middle of his room, and he added to this his high school yearbook, guides to the SAT, copies of *Sports Illustrated,* regular and swimsuit issues. He tossed in the knit yarmulkes he had once worn. They were a modern Orthodox mating ritual, crocheted by the girls as flirtatious gestures and inscribed in contrasting colors, "To Bryan, Luv Hadassah." They came in hot pink and hunter green, trimmed according to the fashion of the day, argyle and Pacman giving way to Nike swooshes and Bart Simpson. If these knit yarmulkes were the religious equivalent of a sports car, Baruch had traded his in for a somber four-door: the black velvet yarmulke.

Toward the front of his closet were the new clothes he had bought in Israel, identical black wool dress pants next to identical white long-sleeve shirts. Pushed to the back were Tommy Hilfiger shirts and Gap blue jeans, Nike sneakers, ripped, sloganed T-shirts and cable-knit sweaters. He piled them up, filling bags, until all that was left behind were empty hangers and the starkness of so much black and white. If it weren't illegal, he would have made a bonfire and set the pile aflame. Instead of a ram and two he-goats, this would be his Karban Olah, his burnt offering. But in the time of the holy temple (as in the days of old, may they speedily be restored, he intoned automatically) one who wanted to repent was required to bring two sacrifices. So he added to the top of this pile a Karban Chatat, his most heartfelt sin offering: the navy blue sweatshirt with the white letters proclaiming Columbia.

Dish racks in hand, Evelyn listened to Baruch and Ilana fighting. She had stood in this position before, disagreements swirling about, and she in the center trying to hold everything together. She was used to knowing what to do with her kids. She had read the books, switched from Dr. Spock to Penelope Leach back to Dr. Spock. She followed their new stages with new books. *The Wonder Years, Siblings Without Rivalry, How to Talk So Kids Will Listen.* She believed in Harriet Lerner and *The Dance of Anger, The Dance of Intimacy, The Dance of Motherhood.* She had committed to memory the entire Adele Faber canon. She subscribed to late toilet training, emerging literacy, anger management. She didn't yell, didn't, God forbid, hit. Instead, she had said, "No, Bryan, little sisters are not for biting. Dustpans are not for eating." "I know you want a chocolate chip cookie, Ilana," she had learned to say. "Wouldn't it be great if the whole world were one giant cookie and we could take a bite whenever we wanted?"

"Don't Adele Faber me," Ilana had once responded.

But even with this setback (Ilana, at ten, had taken the book from Evelyn's nightstand and read it too), these books, with opposing opinions and contradictory experts, had coalesced into something of a philosophy. She wasn't going to force her kids to do anything. Suggest, encourage, recommend, persuade. But never stuffing food into their mouths, throwing them into the swimming pool, extricating from the car sort of parenting style. And they, as a result, were good kids. They studied, they had nice friends, they played on sports teams, they got good grades.

She tried to be accepting of whatever ideas and friends they brought home. This openness, she believed, was the way to turn out good kids: give them space and let them grow.

But this was where that philosophy had gotten her. She was like the biblical Rebecca, who carried the warring Esau and Jacob in her womb. When she passed a synagogue, she felt a kick from one side of her belly. When she passed a house of sin, she felt a kick from the other side. This schizophrenic baby, Rebecca must have thought; he doesn't know who he is or what he wants. Then she realized with a start, not one baby, but two. And not only two babies, but two ideologies, two nations.

But this was her family. These were her children. Even Rebecca must have loved both sons equally. The text may not have been explicit on this point, but Evelyn knew how to see past the actual words. She could fill the white spaces between the lines with her own commentary. After a few more moments of listening, she realized that the noises from upstairs could blend together, and she listened closely to hear it. Soon, it almost sounded as if Baruch was setting the morning prayers to a rock beat, as if Ilana's music was incorporating a cantorial undertone. With some deep breathing and a sense of humor, maybe the summer wouldn't be so difficult after all. She put the dish racks in the cabinet under the sink, and as she left the kitchen, this music created, at least in Evelyn's ears, a cacophony that was pleasurable, a harmonious blending of worlds.

An hour later, Evelyn went back into the kitchen and the dish racks were in the sink again. She narrowed her eyes at them as if they were the naughty child. Once again, she put them away. She wasn't going to give up so easily. She wasn't going to be put off by Baruch's righteousness which so easily veered into self-righteousness. Since he had come home, they had been peering at him from a distance, trying to locate any remnant of their funny, easygoing son inside the vestments of this other world. But this time she had him cornered. If he, for a reason she didn't yet understand, wanted dish racks, he was going to have to pass through her first. Positive attitude in hand, she sat down at the kitchen table, drank her coffee, and waited.

Two cups later, Baruch emerged from his room. It was ninety degrees and he was wearing black wool pants, a dark blazer, and a white, long-sleeve dress shirt. His tzitzit hung from inside his pants, eight white strings on each side, left out for all to see. On his head, his black velvet yarmulke stood proudly, ready to proclaim that there was a God above. He went straight for the sink. He pulled out the dish racks and was about to return them to their new location.

"Is there a reason you've taken a sudden interest in dish racks?" Evelyn asked.

He startled and feigned innocence or at least incomprehension. "What?" he asked.

"The dish racks?" she asked, reminding herself to keep her voice friendly and open, her face relaxed.

"Oh," he said. "Right. Maybe you didn't know, but with porcelain sinks, you're supposed to use dish racks."

"Why?" she asked.

"Because there's no way to *kasher* them."

This already was a kosher kitchen. All the dishes came two by two: two sets of plates, two sets of pots, one for meat, one for milk. But the laws of kosher were details upon details. A kitchen could always be more kosher; the rules could always be applied more strictly. But in the beginning, the Torah merely prohibited cooking a goat in its mother's milk. From this, the rabbis derived the separation of all things meat and milk. They extrapolated from not eating them together to waiting six hours between eating one and the other. They separated them even further: from don't eat them together to don't cook them together, to don't use the same dishes for one and then the other. And so, he explained to her in the singsong tune of the Gemarah, if their kitchen sinks had been metal, which was nonporous, even if they had been used by the previous homeowners for non-kosher, they could be made kosher again with boiling water. But porcelain was porous, so the *treif* has become, so to, speak, part of the actual sink. Which meant that there was no way to make them kosher again. Which also meant that her otherwise kosher dishes couldn't touch the porcelain without themselves becoming *treif*.

"Okay," she said, though he had lost her somewhere along the way. "That's fine. But I'd like you to show me where it says that."

"Trust me. My rebbe says—"

She shook her head. "If you want dish racks, you're going to have to show me."

"I'm not making this up," he said. "Do you think I'm pulling this out of thin air?"

"Come on, Baruch. Humor me."

He went to his room and returned a few minutes later holding a maroon volume with gilded Hebrew letters on the cover.

He had the page bookmarked. "It's right here," and he pointed his finger to the line.

Evelyn looked. At least according to Rav Moshe Feinstein, Baruch was right: porcelain sinks without dish racks weren't allowed. Here, in the twenty-first century, she and her son were fighting about dish racks, and her son could pull a book from his shelf and their argument could be traced back into rabbinic conversations from centuries before, in the sources and principles passed down from one generation to the next, stretching, all the way back, she imagined, to Sinai. And because he could point the passage out to her, in her own appliance-filled kitchen, she too was connected. She relaxed at this feeling of inclusion. Baruch was inviting her to step into the pages of his texts and she was eager to follow.

"The alternative would be for me not to eat in your house," he said.

The pleasurable feeling that she was bound up in rabbinic tradition dissipated. "Are you crazy? You're acting like we're not religious at all. We are. This is a kosher kitchen. Remember?"

He looked away from her, down into his book and she regretted what she had said. She had seen, a second too late, the look of hopefulness in his eyes as she studied the page of text. And she had also seen, for that moment, her son. It didn't matter what he had on, what he said his name was. But then the open look in his eyes was gone. His mask of surety was back in place.

"If it means that much to you," she decided, "the dish racks can stay."

"You can still be a good person," Baruch offered as he picked up the dish racks and returned them to the sink. "But if you really want to consider yourself a *frum* Jew, then this is non-negotiable."

She felt, at the same time, an urge to shake her son and grab him in a hug. "I thought maybe we could all do something fun today," she said instead.

"Thanks, Imma," he said, using the Hebrew for Mother. "But I can't today. I have some things I need to do, in Brooklyn." As if to make up for this, for all of this, he kissed her on the cheek, one thing which, according to Baruch and his rabbi and their laws, was apparently still permissible.

Lying in bed next to David that night, Evelyn asked, "Do you think Baruch is right about us?"

Her daytime attempts at openness had given way to an edgy, worrisome night. With the house quiet, everyone long ago disappeared to their own corners, a discomforting feeling buzzed inside her. It was true, their observance wasn't perfect. Evelyn didn't cover her hair. She wore pants. She and David went mixed swimming. They ate salad and fruit in non-kosher restaurants and didn't worry whether the knife used to cut these otherwise kosher foods had been used for something *treif*. On vacation, they ate tuna and bagels and sushi, which were probably fine but had no official certification. They had no problem with interdenominational dialogue or R-rated movies. They had no patience for the added strictures of Glatt kosher meat or separate seating at weddings. They didn't wrestle with whether it was wrong to be involved in the secular world. They managed to find space for the modern and possibly problematic concepts of pluralism and multiplicity of interpretations.

"Are you serious?" David asked. "Don't tell me you're going to let what his rebbe says affect you."

"It's just that I wonder where this is all coming from. Maybe there's something we should have done differently."

"It's coming from being nineteen years old and thinking that you know everything. It's coming from spending two years up in yeshiva where you're taught to obey whatever your rabbis say. And what the rabbis say is that the outside world is bad, that your parents are bad, that college is bad and working is bad, that everything except sitting and learning all day is bad."

"Did you tell him how you feel?" she asked.

"I'm sure he's more than aware."

"Today he told me that we need to use dish racks in the sink. Because there's no way to *kasher* porcelain."

"I hope you told him that when he has a kitchen of his own, he's welcome to use all the dish racks he wants."

"I told him that we'd use the dish racks. He said he wouldn't eat in our house otherwise."

"Look, Evelyn. For every rabbi who says one thing, I can find two who say the opposite."

"What do you want me to tell him? We want you to be religious, just not this religious, to take it as seriously as we do, but no more, thank you?"

"That might work," he said. "Maybe in the morning, you could sit him down and say that."

"You're kidding."

"I'm not."

"How could I say that? It goes against everything we've always taught them." She looked at him again. Though he was staring at her deadpan, she saw at the corners of his mouth the start of a smile. "You are kidding."

"Unless you have a better idea."

Though they had been veering into argument, they laughed.

They curled into each other, as if assuming crash position. They differed on how to deal with their newly pious, some would say fanatical, son. Lay down the law, David said. With a gentle hand and patient heart, Evelyn believed. But despite this disagreement, they were more or less on the same side. This newfound crack in the family didn't separate them into opposing camps.

"You know what? I think it's going to be okay," she said. "He just needs some time. It's hard to come home. He's having culture shock."

"*He's* having culture shock?" David said.

"I mean it," she said. "By the end of the summer, he'll be back to himself, and we'll look back at this and laugh. And there are worse things than being very religious, right?"

He didn't answer, but she wondered if, in the scheme of things, maybe they were getting off easy. She saw how some of the kids looked these days. In shul, they sat zombie-like. They went through the motions, hoping no one would do anything to shake them or wake them. They cloaked inside their school-sanctioned outfits the thrusts of rebellion. Boys wore ever-shrinking yarmulkes on top of stiff, gelled, angry hair. The girls had on skirts long but so tight that Evelyn wondered how they could walk. Through their guises of nonchalance, she felt their anger at something, at everything, at everyone, burning on the surface.

With Shabbos starting in an hour, there wasn't time to think about the dish racks or ideological divides of the previous day. Shabbos started eighteen minutes before sundown and she couldn't be late. Though some rules could be bent, when it came to Shabbos, there was no room for negotiation. Once it was Shabbos, the Newman house would feel calm. Everything that was going to get done would be done. The food would be ready, the table would be set, and the candles would burn. But until that moment, a busy chaos ran the house.

She cooked, without a recipe in sight, everything done from memory and estimation. She added dashes of this to pinches of that. She saw no reason not to stir in some more noodles, add extra sauce, try something new. When she ran out of one ingredient, she substituted another. Three pots of water boiled in front of her, the mixer going, food processor whirring. She juggled dishes, trying to remember which pot needed rice, which colander of noodles needed egg and oil, which just needed the final dash of seasoning. It was a perfectly run system tottering at the edge of chaos. She gave a quick thanks that the house hummed with quiet. Baruch was in his room, with all but a Do Not Disturb sign hanging there. Ilana had rushed out of the house a little while before, calling over her shoulder some quick, unintelligible sentence about meeting friends. One phone call, one interruption from her children, and everything would be mixed together.

Out of the oven came two roast chickens, the vegetables, and the kugels. She lined them on trivets on her countertops, their timely completion one more miracle for which she ought to be thankful. She crossed these from her list and checked her watch: one hour to go. Just once, she wanted to bring Shabbos in calmly. Everything done ahead of time, so she could sit back those final few minutes before lighting candles and reflect on the week that had passed, on the week that was coming.

Even David had promised to be home earlier. Usually he cut it close, especially in the winter, when Shabbos started as early as four-thirty. And then there was the traffic; going out to New Jersey on a Friday afternoon felt like the exodus from Egypt, the turnpike bumper to bumper with people trying to make it home in time for Shabbos. David didn't usually go to shul on Friday night—three hours on Shabbos morning was enough for him.

"You should go with Baruch to shul tonight," Evelyn had urged David that morning. "It would be nice for both of you."

David had eventually agreed. She called him twice to remind him, and her nudging paid off. He walked in as she was taking the last kugel out of the oven: thirty minutes to go. She kissed him and he went upstairs to get ready. Now, with twenty minutes to go, all she needed was the cake to finish baking, Ilana to come home, and everyone to get along.

In his room once again, Baruch stood in front of his mirror and tried on his black hat, a Borsalino fedora. The black hat wasn't just an item of clothing, but a term of identity; not a description of what he was wearing but who he was. As he and his friends made their pilgrimages to Meah Shearim to buy their hats, they described it to each other as a way of sealing their new identities. He bought a hat box and stuffed the hat with tissue paper and packed it into his suitcase so he wouldn't have to explain its presence to his parents until he was ready. The black hat made an unequivocal statement about where he belonged. The Charedim whom he admired wore the long coats and fur-trimmed streimels of a long-ago Polish nobility. They proved that it was possible to create a different world. Why, they seemed to ask, do we have to live in the year in which we happened to be born? Who is to say that time travel is quite so impossible?

It was nearly Shabbos. He took one final look in the mirror. The hat sealed his identity. It was not a costume, not a disguise. This was who he was now. He looked forward to the day when he didn't have to wrestle with these two halves of a whole. Until this happened, it was hard to leave his room. In less than a week, he had transformed it into an appropriate space for a yeshiva boy. His bedroom had become his holy temple, the rest of the house the interminable exile. But he remembered that after the temple was destroyed, the oral law was written down so that it wouldn't be lost and dispersed. Compiled and recorded, it became fixed into a solid unchanging entity. The Jews carried it with them wherever they went, law like walls, buildings fashioned from commandment instead of wood. He would have to do the same, carry his belief wherever he went and let it build a protective wall around him.

He went down the stairs wearing the hat. He paused and adjusted the brim, trying to shore up his confidence. He told himself that his parents shouldn't be surprised by the appearance of this hat, which fit in with everything else he had brought home. And even if they were surprised, he was old enough to make his own decisions. When he finally descended, he walked carefully, as if he were balancing a melon on his head.

His parents were standing by the front door, conferring in urgent, hushed tones. "Good Shabbos," he said.

They looked at him. No, they stared at him. His father's eyes didn't move from the hat. His mother glanced at it, then quickly looked away, her eyes darting to his suit, to the floor, forcing herself to look at anything but the hat. Pretending not to see it, they said nothing, the same nothing they said about everything. They were now in the final minutes before Shabbos started, the eighteen minutes of leeway intended for emergencies but used universally as a buffer zone. All over Middleton, preparations for Shabbos were coming to a hurried end. Squares of toilet paper were ripped, refrigerator lightbulbs unscrewed, bedroom lights turned off, bathroom lights left on. Automatic timers were set, ovens switched off, Crock-Pots turned to low, candles lit.

"I don't know where Ilana is," Evelyn said and checked her watch again. "This is so unlike her, to be so late. I don't want to light without her but—"

Baruch checked his watch. "What's wrong with her? Doesn't she know what time Shabbos starts?" he said.

"Of course she knows. She was going out with her friends. I was so surprised she was going out so close to Shabbos, but . . . maybe she lost track of time. She's probably on her way home right now. I'm sure she'll slip in at the last minute."

"It already is the last minute," Baruch said.

"Don't worry about Ilana," David said.

"Someone needs to worry about her," Baruch said.

Again, they looked at the hat, and Baruch searched for something to say. He didn't know whether to make it better or worse. He could emulate Aaron who pursued peace at all costs. Or he could be like Pinchas the zealot, who raised his sword and saw no shades of gray. He was stuck between these two. He didn't know how to reach out and push away at the same time. And because it had been rising in his throat all day, a question, a declaration, a request, he blurted it out.

"I'm not going to Columbia."

"What do you mean?" Evelyn asked. "Of course you are."

"No," Baruch said. "I'm going back to yeshiva."

With this statement, his voice grew stronger. He shed the questionlike intonation and it became more solidly a statement of fact. And his parents just stood there and stared. His father opened his mouth, then closed it without saying a word. His mother gave a barely visible shrug. They exchanged glances, a quick plotting of how to handle this: we could ignore him, we could yell at him, we could humor him, we could punish him, we could reason with him, we could bribe him. A silent, coded negotiation passed swiftly before his eyes.

"Remember, honey," his mother finally said, "we had an agreement. You were going to go back to yeshiva for one more year and then—"

"I know," he said, "but I've changed my mind. This is what I'm doing."

"No sir. No, you're not," David said. "A deal's a deal."

"I'm nineteen years old. I can do what I want," Baruch protested.

"You need to go to college. Everyone does," Evelyn said.

"You can't force me to go."

"Why don't we talk about this later," Evelyn said.

"There's nothing to talk about. My rebbe says that—"

"This isn't up to your rebbe," David said.

"You two need to get going if you're going to make it to shul on time," Evelyn said. "It's already ten past."

David and Baruch still weren't moving, not wanting to walk the five blocks to shul where they would either have to continue this conversation or come up with another one in order to avoid it. That they used to talk easily felt like an impossibility now.

They looked at each other and, in a brief, unintentional meeting of minds, they wondered: This is my father? This is my son?

With one minute to go until Shabbos, the front door opened and Ilana breezed in. She took in the anger on their faces and felt the tension crackling through the house.

"Where have you been? Do you realize that Shabbos is starting right now?" Evelyn asked, now angry herself.

"I made it, though, didn't I?" she said and looked at her watch. "I even have another forty-five seconds."

Ilana kissed her mother, then her father, on the cheek. She flashed her most innocent smile. She didn't know why they were standing there, not moving or speaking to each other. Something had clearly happened. Or was about to. But whatever it was, she wasn't going to be dragged into it. Poised on the staircase, about to go upstairs, she turned back to them.

"Oh, and by the way, Bryan," she called. "Nice hat."

Tova Mirvis

I once saw a family portrait where the parents in the picture looked suburban, thoroughly modern. The children, in their black hats and black jackets, looked as if they had just stepped off the boat from a nineteenth-century Polish shtetl. I was struck by this seeming reversal of time and history. Looking at this family, it was hard to tell what was past and what was future. This intermingling reminded me of the Talmud, which is spoken of in the present tense, as if these ancient voices can step off the pages and argue across the generations. This is one of the ways I want to use Jewish issues, texts, and images in my work. They provide me with inspiration and with additional layers to work with. I proudly call myself a Jewish writer. I think there is a fear of wearing this or other adjectives before "writer." But I don't see any of them as limiting me in terms of subject matter or audience. I feel the gift of a wealth of material, a vast source of ideas that I can shape and use as I wish.

Consent

Ben Schrank

"Have you spoken to your father recently?" my mother asks. "I went up and saw him a couple of months ago," I say. "He told me that profits in the small-cap sector were making him cry with joy."

Payard Patisserie is where my mother's brought me. It's a French restaurant. We've been led up a flight of stairs to a special seating area with sepia walls and a tin ceiling. I look across at her over the yellow tablecloth, which is set with china edged in gold. There's one white candle between us. Behind my mother's head there's a glowing oval setback in the wall that frames a dimly lit painting of two horses wandering down a country lane.

"That's how he speaks to you?" she asks.

"How else would he?" I stare at her. Just now, I can't think how else he has ever spoken to me. I'm not sure what else he'd have to say. I'm not sure what else he's ever said.

"I guess you're right," she says. "How else would he speak? I don't know either." And she shrugs. She was always sarcastic when she was with him, and now the only time she acts that way is when he comes up in conversation. The rest of the time, she fairly glows with the prospect of her new frontiers. She's staying at the St. Moritz with her new husband, Lawrence Gold. They're here for the spring antiques show because they're interior decorators. They're a team.

My mom, gone from Elizabeth Zabusky of Manhattan to Liz Gold of La Jolla, California. I've always suspected that she wanted to take steps in a Christian direction. And now I wonder if she hasn't begun to grow some anti-Jewish sentiment. I've tried to discuss this with her and the result was not good. "Did I ever deny that I'm a Jew?" This is what she kept asking me. "Did I ever in my entire life deny to anyone that I'm a Jew? And who took you to see *Joseph and the Amazing Technicolor Dreamcoat*? Me, that's who. Remember, your father wouldn't have any part of it." She got pretty angry. And no, I don't recall her ever denying that we were Jews. But she doesn't talk about religion, at least not with me. We can still get through a dinner, though. We don't dislike each other.

My mother divorced my father when I was still an undergraduate, before I got married. She was quick to marry Lawrence Gold, who used to license sunglass designs to Ralph Lauren's company. Lawrence made a mint and retired into my mother's business. Now they both put tremendous thought into the way things in a house look when they're positioned in relation to one another. I visited them once out in La Jolla and watched as they pondered and enjoyed the effect they got when they set out a cherry side table and put a thick gardening book next to a pewter plate next to a vase with hyacinths in it. Then they adjusted these elements and cooed at each other while they worked. In a way, I'm proud of my mom. She's certainly living somebody's dream.

"It's fine for me not to have a relationship with him," she says. "That's okay. But I expect different from you."

"I'm sure I'll see him again," I say. "We agreed to do a better job of being in touch."

"You met his girlfriend? Sarah Jane something—a Protestant surname."

"Caldwell, yes," I say. "She was there."

My mother sighs. She touches her gold necklace and tries to smile at me, but it isn't easy. She's a more attractive woman now than she was when I was young, with her hair dyed up to a rich brown and her skin looking creamy, with hardly any hints of age.

I remember a thinness in her upper lip when I was younger. Late on a Saturday afternoon I'd watch her outline her lips with a dark brown pencil while I stood in the doorway of the bathroom, waiting for my father to come home from doing whatever extra work Max Asherberg assigned to him. We would all stroll across town to eat at Keens Chophouse. I'd try to count the thousands of antique pipes on the ceiling while I munched on celery, black olives, and pickles, and all the time I wondered at the new shape of my mother's lips.

Looking at her now, in the ivory yellow light of this restaurant, it seems possible that she's had something injected into her lips to make them full. Either that or perhaps now that she's disconnected from my father, even her face has relaxed.

"What were the specials again?" she asks. I close my eyes and reel them off: celery root soup, yellowfin tuna carpaccio, stuffed French sardines, Chilean sea bass, codfish, lamb. As I've said, my memory is good. It isn't photographic; I'm nothing for images, but language stays with me forever.

"The other night Lawrence and I stayed up and watched *Young Frankenstein* on AMC, and I thought of you and your monster. Tell me its name again . . ."

"The Golem?"

"Of course, that's it. It's amazing the things I've forgotten from my own childhood. The monsters are similar. That's what I told Lawrence. He was asleep but I woke him up and told him about the connection."

"They're not the same at all," I say.

"I don't see much difference," she says. "I'll bet you've never had a risotto with Parmesan foam on top. It's wonderful. We'll ask them to make it."

"Look, Mom, if you want to know what I'm doing, you need to forget Frankenstein. Close your eyes and forget this restaurant. Pretend you're in a movie. Imagine a group of Hasidic mystics in Germany, back in the thirteenth century. Put yourself in peasant garb. It's late at night and you see into a courtyard where they're doing rituals that involve combinations of the Hebrew alphabet and the material form of the universe. They do all this, they say some names, they create a monster."

"Mute and thoughtless, just like Frankenstein," she says. She flips over the butter knife and examines its markings.

"Fine—like Frankenstein, if you must. But let's imbue him with the will of the Jewish people. Let's let God get involved, too. The Golem we create is larger than a big man, but only by a head or so. He's got *emeth*, or 'truth,' on his forehead, and the way to turn him off is to erase the first letter, so he's *meth*, which is 'death.' They use him for holy missions, to save the people of the ghetto when they get into trouble or find themselves unfairly persecuted."

"I remember last year with Lawrence on Christmas Eve, when you told us all the story of the dead babies and the bloody Passover matzos."

"I'm sorry about that."

"Unforgettable," she says. She shakes her head. I love that story, of when Rabbi Loeb of the Prague ghetto uses the Golem to keep peace in the ghetto. But when I told my mother and her husband and their friends, they found it stereotypical and distasteful. It is a bit graphic, what with the grave digging and the idea that Jews would need the blood of Christian babies to make their matzos, but it is also deeply inspirational. The Golem helped the Jews to control the unjust forces that conspired against them. The Golem is as simple and good as that.

"All the work you did with Jung, and you're reduced to this?" She sips from her glass of wine and then holds on to the glass by the stem, as if she may need it again soon, if I keep going. So I rush.

"I know. But I believe there's beauty in the reduction. Imagine this: Once the Golem becomes a hero, he grows more intelligent and dreams of being able to speak and to love, like a man with a soul. One night the rabbi forgets to remove the letter of power from the Golem's forehead and the Golem's unquenchable desire drives him wild. Even the Jews are afraid of him. Then when the monster is sleeping, the rabbi has to get up on a stool and erase the letter of life from his forehead. The Golem turns to mud and falls on him and kills him. He destroys his master."

"An archetypal story," she says. "The metaphor of the monster run amok." She looks glum, and I find her easy familiarity with my subject matter confusing. She's just the same as Weingarden in this respect. They both act as if what I'm studying were only a part of everyday life, instead of folklore. Maybe they're the ones who are looking for more complexity and I'm not. I watch my mother scan the room around me. A waiter passes by and she taps her glass.

"I'm sorry," she says, "but I can't see what you'll do with all of this, I just can't."

I know that part of what makes her good at her job is that she can listen to anybody rattle on about anything, but listening and making the effort to extract a clear understanding are quite different things.

"Couldn't you use your memory to take apart something besides folklore? What about picking stocks with your father. I hated all that, as you know, but it wouldn't hurt, would it? A little sideline?"

"I've got to like something to remember it," I say.

"If only life were so sweet that you could go along and remember only things you like. Really, Mike, I want to understand your work, because you're my son and I love you, but lately it feels as if your thoughts are running in circles. Your father and I are practical people. I don't see where all of this comes from, not a bit of it."

I smile at my mother, even as I choose not to suggest that this is exactly why I am so in love with myth. Of course my inclination to bend reality exists in opposition to my parents' practicality. And my memory has been a wonderful ally in the struggle to adjust facts to serve my needs. My memory explains how I excelled in college and how I managed to become a professional graduate student. I memorized all of Jung, most of Freud, and lots of different religious and gnostic tracts. I remember things slightly wrong, with varying degrees of awareness. My inclination to change events and theories caused or created by others has, so far, made me guilty not of lying but of innovation. I am also aware that such a malleable memory can be used another way—as protection.

In turn, my fascination with Jewish mysticism arises directly from an interest in trying to weave together disparate, even wholly disconnected ideas using strings of stories that are bound together only by our collective notion of time. Jewish mysticism has a wildly fragmented history. It is a far more extreme version of the traditional notion of our Diaspora. Doubly hidden and reviled, and yet, like so many other broken, illogical, but entirely human sets of ideas, even after many centuries of worldly disdain, mysticism lives.

If I were religious, the fragile connections that make up Jewish mysticism would be inspiring. But I'm not a religious person. I appreciate mysticism's tenacity and I continue to want to be involved with it, but only in a spirited, cheerleading kind of way.

"When you saw your father, were you able to talk to him about your work?" she asks.

"Sure," I say. "He wanted to hear all about what I'm doing—he was really interested—I guess because he's finally happy up in Roosevelt."

"I don't know if I believe that," she says. "I bet that's your hope talking, rather than your honesty. But it's good to at least have open lines of communication—for both your sakes."

My mother looks down then at her menu and begins to read carefully.

I owe my father one large debt, which stems from a kind act he did for me, which occurred when my own marriage was falling apart. He came and sat with me for a few crucial days in Chicago. Two years after I graduated, I married a woman called Alexis, who was a few years older than me. She convinced me that we should stay in Chicago and build our lives there. Back then, apartments were inexpensive, and there was a burgeoning music scene.

Alexis was the lead singer of a band called Art Collection. They sounded a lot like Sleater-Kinney, though Alexis had a voice that was more reminiscent of Siouxsie Sioux or Cait O'Riordan. Meanwhile, I had my job at Exodus Travel. We nursed each other's affection for drugs, and when we weren't looking, the marriage dissolved into what I realize now was a combination of betrayal and addiction so horrifying that it turned into satire.

Alexis left me for the bass player in her band, who was a friend of mine and lived in the apartment above ours. I fell under the influence of a drug dealer who worked at the window desk in my travel agency. I'm grateful to my father for flying into town and forcing me to laugh about the childishness of the mess I'd made with Alexis, while I sweated out all the indignity. He's a bit crude, my father—old Jefferson Gerard Zabusky. He knew just how to handle that unpleasantness.

"I'll call him again soon," I say.

"Thank you," my mother says, and she breathes hard through her mouth. "Remember what he says? *Got zol mich bentshen ich zol nit broichen mentshen.*"

"What? 'God should—'"

"'God should bless me so that I don't need people.'"

"But I thought he didn't believe in God," I say.

"That's the joke," she says. "No love for God or people, either. You've got to help him fight against his impulses. Only in Yiddish would anyone say such a thing. You know what I say? *Nor a shteyn zol zayn aleyn.*"

"'Only a stone should be alone'?" I ask.

"That's right—my goodness, Michael, I didn't know you'd learned Yiddish. But that language, it's too brutal. I make sure not to speak it anymore. And you shouldn't either," she says, and she doesn't smile. I watch as she looks around the room. None of the other women are smiling either. But they can't all be worried about their ex-husbands. More probably, it's this economy. It's making all of us tense, but those who wear multiple pieces of gold jewelry without irony—real estate brokers and boutique owners, dress designers and interior decorators—they're really crackling with fear.

"What reason could you have to be worried about him?"

"You don't see it? He's lonely, no matter what he says to you. It's that house, and the life he chose up there. He should never have bought it."

"What's the matter with the house? I was up there, it's beautiful. He's the luckiest man in the world."

"Wrong—wrong on both counts," my mother says. "He's lonely, and it's lousy. A shithouse." She wipes at her eyes.

The room I have here at the Gouverneur is pretty nice. I pay a convention rate, minus maid and phone service, since I use my cell phone for everything. This gets me down to under forty dollars a night. When I'm really broke, I take evening shifts for Blake, who works the front desk. Sometimes I'll fill out a tax form for Lisa, the maid who works the fifth floor, or I'll tutor her kid, and then she'll vacuum and change my sheets.

There was a time when this neighborhood was filled with young people, and in those years it looked like the Lower East Side would never be poor again, but recently, gentrification has slowed. Now the boarded-up storefronts hide failed clothing boutiques and bars, rather than pizza places and bodegas. Unfortunately, my father's parents' store, Louis Zabusky's Housewares and Locksmith, which was just a few blocks away, on Essex Street, won't be coming back. They closed it more than twenty years ago. Now it's a Chinese salon called New Century Hair Center.

My father worked there all through high school, weighing out pounds of nails and cutting keys for the local landlords. He was forced to work every afternoon, right after he was finished at Brooklyn Tech. Now, aside from the occasional complaint about how his parents ruined his high school career, he hates to talk about it. He grew up on Howard Avenue in Crown Heights, Brooklyn, which is where his parents went the moment they could afford to get out of the Lower East Side. He hated it there, too. He and my mother moved away from both their parents to the relative anonymity of Stuyvesant Square as quickly as they could.

Now most of the Jews left around here are Hasidic. They maintain a presence that seems almost sentimental. Sometimes middle-class Jews come in from the suburbs on Sundays to visit the Henry Street Settlement or the Tenement Museum, but that's all. I've been to the museum and seen the room that illustrates how my grandparents lived when they came here. It isn't pretty, with its bad wallpaper and uncomfortable bed, but if I hadn't lucked into my hotel room, I'd be living that way now.

If the economy continues to falter, the only people left will be the poor and the truly hip, all of us walking around in black suits with tarnished white shirts. They look a little like the Hasidic Jews, and sometimes, still, so do I. Some nights I'll fall asleep and dream that I'm still what I was at twenty-four. I've returned to being thin-faced, long-nosed, string-haired, wearing shoddy black shoes, white socks, a white shirt, a yellow undershirt, that pervasive greasy sheen on my suit knees and ass. I wake up pulling on a thin beard that isn't there and I'll be trying to tear their black hat off my head. But I was not Hasidic back then. I was only a punk working in a travel agency, with no real religion of my own.

Save the year I was thirteen, I've never been a member of a temple, but I can read Hebrew. I've learned German, Polish—whatever a book demands. I work hard to get close to texts, since my spiritual connection does not come naturally.

The only training I had came in the form of the bar mitzvah I went through for the benefit of my father's family, now mostly passed away. My father's parents gave me a tool kit they assembled themselves and a check for a thousand dollars, to be saved for a trip to Israel. I spent it on a Pioneer stereo with fat dials and pulsing red lights and Fleetwood Mac and Heart records. My father didn't care that I spent the money. He encouraged me to laugh at their traditions. My mother was okay with all that, too.

I stand at the window and look over Straus Square, toward

uptown, and Kazan Street, which is hazy with yellow streetlight. A few teenagers play a game of dice against a newly boarded-up Japanese T-shirt store. I'm not going to do any work. I pick up my phone and quickly dial Katherine's number, with no rehearsal. The number hasn't left me since I learned it, and all this time I've been working hard not to think about her, so that when I do speak to her I'll have some chance at sounding natural. She answers immediately.

"Hello," I say, "this is—"

"Oh it's you, from the other night?" she says. "Hold for just a moment, will you?"

She gets off the other line. I've got that at least. I beat the other line. I button my shirt to the top, so I'm tightened and sober. My stomach clenches around nothing—my body telling me that though I'm excited, I'm empty.

"That was something, wasn't it?" she says. I hear her rustling, adjusting furniture—a desk perhaps, or better, a bed.

"You're in Brooklyn?"

"Yes—listen, were you serious with me the other night?"

"I was," I say. I blow hot air onto my windowpane and draw the balls and talons of that bathtub.

"Because I don't want to talk to you unless you were really serious about kissing me," she says. "I don't kiss people unless there's a future involved."

"It's so nice to hear you say that," I say. "This is no joke."

"No?"

"No," I say. "When can I see you?"

"Mike—I don't know. I'm overwhelmed with work and I'm scheduled to see friends on the few nights I'm not working. So, maybe—what about next Wednesday?"

I'm quiet. I want to see her sooner than that. I don't want to give her time to resist her own inclination toward being serious.

"What about later tonight?" I ask, and I make my voice slow.

"Tonight? Mmm. Why don't you come and meet me at—no, at Chez Omar. It's just around the corner from where I live."

Eight or so minutes later I'm in a cab headed up Bedford Avenue, to the spot where Fort Greene meets Bedford-Stuyvesant. I arrive in front of Chez Omar and stand there for half an hour. This is an odd place to have chosen for a midnight meeting, as it's not a bar at all but a restaurant. But I don't worry too much about being stood up. The one thing I know about her is that she's curious.

When she does come up the street, because I've never seen her from this distance before, it's the movement of her hips inside her skirt that beats away my reserve. I'm feeling good, suddenly, and highly aware.

"I see the place I've chosen is closed," she says. She reaches forward and gives me a kiss that melts between my cheek and lip.

We step into Bier and Wasser, a bar across the street, where a few people watch as the Knicks slowly beat the Heat. She sets her purse down. It is a massive thing, stuffed full of indistinct objects, no real color left to the leather, held up by a frayed strap at the point of tearing. The purse, duffel bag—it pulses at me. I go and get us tap beer from the bartender. She says it's just the kind she would have chosen. But she doesn't taste it.

I sit down and bend forward, my lower ribs pressed up against the table. Not because she's whispering. Rather, I'm catching sight of lines on her face, a small vertical scar at the top right of her lip, smile lines between her mouth and cheek. I'm smelling her as hard as I can, taking deep breaths that are full of the underlying scent of her.

"You told me you were doing something on religious texts?" she asks. "Some sort of exegesis?"

I nod but I say nothing. I had begun to hope that she'd forgotten the moment where I revealed my Golem obsession.

"I used to think about religion," she says. "There was a point when I was filled up with Faulkner. I was working in Mississippi and reading his novels exclusively, and I started to grow really horrified at what people do to each other. Then I lost my sister. I decided that I only loved God. I was sure I'd become a nun, but that passed."

"What do you mean—you lost your sister?"

The space behind her is dark, so her face is framed by shadows. She looks down at her hands and then twines her fingers together. She's quiet, and it looks as if she's angry with herself for revealing too much.

"Oh, I don't want to explain that. I shouldn't have said anything. When I saw that I couldn't be a nun, I figured out that I could do the next best thing, and never get married."

"Never? Why not?" I ask.

"Too much awfulness seems to surround the waiting for that sort of love," she says. Then she smiles. So I smile back. I don't mention my own failed marriage. Instead, I worry if she's telling the truth. But I'm calm, and I remember that saying never to love that way is just a thing to say—it's just an early-date thing to say.

"But I could see being very serious with you," she says. "I can imagine being comfortably in love with you."

So I see that my array of indicators, which were never terribly accurate, are useless here.

"I want you to be comfortable with me," I say. She takes up her glass and sips long from it, while she watches me. It's more than half done when she puts it down.

She says, "Yes, let's be comfortable and serious and safe. I need all that, as I've just been involved in something unpleasant. A married man. I can't have that again for a while." She shakes her head and looks away from me. She exaggerates her mouth into a sneer, but she doesn't look mean or angry.

She says, "At the beginning, he didn't tell me that he was married. And now I'm paying for his lie. That was him the other night—the man you wanted to throw out of a window. I know he was less than charming then. But at the beginning—I got bowled over, I really did."

"When you grew up, did you have a car?" I ask.

What I would like to say is, I could kill that man for you. Or I hate that man for you. But that won't sound right. I'd end up sounding vulnerable and weak, when I'd like to sound strong.

Cars are safe, though. Everybody has a car story, some old car they loved.

"I had a black Rabbit convertible, Cabriolet, a freakishly fast car. I bought it at an auction in—where I'm from. Tin can, though, real rattler. Hey, it wasn't *easy,* you know? He's thirteen years older, and it's just been such a mess. I mean, I ended up having to talk to his wife about it—we had to have dinner together, to save his marriage. A real pleasure, what I had to go through. I've done things in my past that I only blame myself for, but this was not one of them."

"Where's that car now?"

"I gave it to an old boyfriend, and he sold it without telling me. I see, you're one of those. You'd just as soon not listen to the tougher parts of a woman's history." But she smiles when she says this.

"No," I say, and I concentrate, and measure my words. "It's just that I want to hear more about you, and less about this man whom you no longer care for."

I cannot recall that man's face, but I remember the foolish thing he said. I would like to believe that this married man must have only been fodder for her, to keep her busy before she met me, and yet we're discussing him now. If he's fodder, I'd like her to spit him out. She sighs.

"Leah would love that, how pointed you were just now," she says.

"Leah?"

"My housemate. You called right when we got back from yoga and we were feeling so good—she encouraged me to come out with you."

"Please thank Leah for me," I say. I pick up my pint to finish it, but the glass is empty.

"But she won't believe that I'm talking like this to you, after what I just went through with him. I hardly ever sleep anymore, not that I need any sleep. I'm going to make you listen anyway. He'd been offered a job in Berlin and he was going to take it. We were going to run away together. I had a bag packed before something stopped me. I remember sitting down on my bed, a little while ago, and just stopping, seeing how absurd my situation was. And then there he was at that party, acting so incredibly hostile. Maybe what sat me down was that I was hoping to meet you."

"Where are you from?"

"It doesn't matter. Here. New York. It was just—if I ran away with Adam, I'd only be quitting one more life, running into his fantasy this time. That's not moving forward. I hated to admit all that to myself and to end it with him. The reality of my horrible job saved me, I think. It's a kind of last stand. You see, these last months haven't been easy."

"Where in New York?" I ask. "Where is here?"

"It doesn't matter. Think of a place you like but don't know well—that's where I'm from."

Her eyes well up. I quiet down and I see that she's like me in this way. She's comfortable with incomplete disclosure. There's a quiver around her mouth. Though I've been staring at her all along, it's as if I've gotten better at staring at her now, and her eyes are wet. I take up her hands.

We lighten our talk. We shift to faraway places, trips she's made to Guatemala, Eritrea, Morocco. In between the no more than two years that she's ever spent in any one place, there were months-long trips, alone or with lovers, when no one could find her.

It is past three when we stand, and the time has knifed past so quickly that I believe we've got something, Katherine and I. I just can't name it. I don't even want to try, not yet. I'd love to believe that I don't like to name things, because of all that I've learned about Jewish mystics and the danger of speaking the name of God aloud. But it bothers me that this is the only way I've found to connect with being a Jew—by being hesitant to name my passion, as if it were nearly as sublime as the search for the name of God. This is why I like the Golem. Unlike studying the lives and writings of real mystics, like Moses Maimonides or Jacob ben Jacob ha-Kohen, the Golem is just a story, and thoughts of him are easy to carry through a night like this.

"Hey," she says, "do you want to walk me home?"

We walk back slowly and stop in front of her stoop. Her street is thick with trees and because of this it is darker here than the night. Some televisions are still on, so a few rooms bounce white light against other windows and onto our faces. I watch as she takes a few long breaths and closes her eyes. I draw on the concrete with my shoe and look up at her house.

"The whole brownstone is yours?" I ask.

"Leah owns it," she says. "Bud bought a jingle. It's a funny story, but I won't tell you now."

I stare up at the house and I don't have to remember the address or the name of the street. It is ingrained in me, and other information gives way to it. For instance, where I live or what I do, none of that matters. But the Golem stays with me. Down at the bottom of the street, behind the Plymouth Fury and the oak tree, that's where he is. He stands there, mute, watching over us.

"Don't invite me in," I say. "Unless you want to."

"I won't. We're far too intense with each other already to ruin it with that." And then she closes her impossible eyes.

It's not just a kiss good night, it's a brain-scrambling embrace, and I find myself pulling her tighter because her body is rolling with me and because I've gone so thoughtless—without her I'm sure I'd stagger and fall. I slide my fingers down her back and around and touch where we were so hard against each other the other night. Now, even though we are on the street and there are so many clothes between us, I feel as near to her as I did then.

We come apart and she goes up her stairs. She says good night. I stare up at her and she looks back at me for an instant. I listen to the oiled clicks of her lock, and then she is gone.

Ben Schrank

When I was a senior in college I took a course on Jewish mysticism with Joseph Dan, who was visiting from Israel, where he is Ger-

shom Scholem Professor of Kabbalah in the Department of Jewish Thought at the Hebrew University of Jerusalem. *The class met at four in the afternoon. Professor Dan usually began by reading from prepared notes in a low voice with a dense accent. After thirty or so minutes of droning, he'd get excited. He'd start to yell and spit his lecture at us while he stared at a point above our heads. His lecture on the Golem was deafening, as was his analysis of a little-known text called the* Shiur Qomah. *The latter is a particularly heretical document because it attempts to measure the size of God. I wrote a paper that compared Marx's* Theses on Feuerbach *to the* Shiur Qomah. *Professor Dan found it amusing. He'd attempted something similar when he was in school.*

Seven years later, I'd broken my heart enough times to think that I could make a fictional entertainment out of the experience. It was then that I knew I'd found the right outlet for what I'd learned from Professor Dan. In Consent *(both this story and the novel), my narrator, Mike Zabusky, would incorrectly internalize some aspects of Jewish mysticism and use them to grapple with love. Since he's alienated from the communal aspect of religious practice, he tries to shove his burgeoning religiosity onto a love affair which is delicate and new and can't bear any sort of weight—much less the theory he throws at it. The affair ends and he's left with an introduction to the* Shiur Qomah, *and a hint about what it might mean to pray. Like most novelists, I repeatedly reconstructed aspects of my history while I wrote* Consent. *Now I see that during that time I became a journeyman writer, able only to grapple with what I'd learned from Professor Dan as a possible method of answering fictional questions, rather than religious ones.*

Ten Plagues

Simone Zelitch

The Pharaoh Merneptah had aged well. Morning walks along the wadi banks kept his flesh firm and clear, and his round head was smooth, save for a crease between his eyebrows. Most days he sat with his maps, a scribe on either hand. Most nights before he went to bed, he shot quail in the dark, and even at an age when the eyes of men grow weak, Merneptah never missed his mark. His cooks were hard-put to roast all the game, and so grew tales of pots which never emptied and feather coverlets piled to the sky.

For Merneptah was also a wizard, a sage and a holy man. Never had a more pious Pharaoh sat in Goshen. His tomb made his father's look like a footstool. He laid such bounty at the temple doors that they seemed made more of gold than stone. Around his throne were ten wise men from Thebes, Memphis and Persia, and there had not been such men since the beginning of the world. Each stood seven feet tall, and it was said that a single blink of their eyes could shut the sky like a window. Yet none of those men could cure the queen's madness, or open her closed womb.

Bityah had been mad since time remembered. Her white hair spilled across her shoulders as quickly as her slaves could bind it up again, and her hands rattled and twitched. She had tried to take her own life ten times. Yet for all of that, she was still impossibly beautiful. These days, she kept a silence which made her seem less a woman than a shaft of light. When Bityah sat on her throne, it quivered as with pleasure. When she lay beside the pool in the south garden, the orange fish would surface and draw their round eyes over the rim of the water. Merneptah's advisers often said: Take a younger wife, one who will bear a child. Yet Merneptah would not forsake Bityah, and on that matter he would not be crossed.

One day, the handmaid who held Bityah still to bind her gown found that it was tight across the bosom. When three months had passed, all the court wondered at her belly; it was round as a ball, and she held it with trembling hands as though she was afraid it would roll off her frame and out the door.

In secret, some spoke of artifice; she was too big for three months' time. In deeper secrecy yet, in the tiny painted room where he kept his maps, Merneptah conferred with the only man in the world he trusted, the Greek physician, and he said, "It isn't possible."

"You," the physician said, his wry face turned off toward the window, "the most pious of men, don't believe in the power of your sacred seed?"

"Shut up!" Merneptah snapped. He cracked his hands against his knees in a gesture of anger and bewilderment. "It's a tumor."

"Very likely," the physician said at last. He set his hand upon Merneptah's and said, "It would be a mercy, you must know."

"It's a tumor," Merneptah repeated, as though he had not heard, and then he bowed his head and studied a map of the sea which flowed off the world's edge, until the physician let him be.

He read until nightfall made the map too dark to see, and then he paced out into a court swimming in moonlight, followed by his long, strong shadow. Most nights, he slept soundly enough, but that night, as many years before, restlessness kept him strutting back and forth with his arrow and quiver strung across his back, and his shoulder aching like any old man's.

As a youth, he had climbed the wall of that forbidden garden where Bityah had kept a pet who asked a lot of questions. That pet had haunted the wall's summit, not on guard but waiting. Waiting for him, he'd thought. Now no one waited. Now the garden was just another garden, well tended and empty of meaning.

That night, something stirred on that wall, dark and round. At once, he set an arrow, let it speed, and waited. Something hit the stone.

Another quail, fat, plain and female. By rights, he should call in one of his wise men and read an auspice. He picked the quail up by its feet so that a few loose feathers floated and hovered. The spring air was very clear and smelled of almonds.

Was it a tumor or a son? He knew: It was a tumor. Yet memory mixed with feathers and with moonlight, and he knew that stranger things than sons had happened in his world, even if he'd sooner they had not.

And Merneptah made peace with his fortune and the next day, as instructed, he sent grain and oil to the temple of Seth and asked the god if Bityah was with child.

The answer took this form: Merneptah was conferring with his wise men in the map room, and the Canaanite turned pale and spoke abruptly. "Am I dismissed?"

Merneptah had no quarrel with the man, who had crossed rivers and deserts beyond number and could read many maps. He said, "Why do you think that I would dismiss you?"

"You have called another nomad," the wise man said, and in the doorway stood Moses.

The Pharaoh was so dumbstruck that he was not his own master. The man wore moldy rags; his face was pocked with burn marks; his beard hung in greasy strands. But it was Moses; it could be no other. It was Moses who looked straight through him with the familiar, stunned, unreadable expression. There was a minor priest as well, and he was saying something, but the Pharaoh did not hear a word. Rather, his eyes ate Moses.

Finally, the Pharaoh asked, "Why are you here?"

It was the priest who answered, in smooth Egyptian. "I speak for him. He comes from a true god who works wonders."

"I am a true god," the Pharaoh said. "I work wonders."

The priest said, "There is only one true god!" Then he dropped his little rod on the stone floor where it bounced twice and slithered.

Illusion, then. Fair enough. It could all be an illusion. He could fling back the curtains and let light pass through Moses and turn him to dust and memory. Still, can an illusion stink? And can it stare?

"Throw down your wands!" the Pharaoh called to his wise men, and at once ten green snakes slipped out of their hands. All might have gone well then, but from behind came Bityah.

She leaned between two handmaids, weighed down by her round belly and by gold, walking with tiny, shaking steps. Then she raised her eyes.

"Aie!" She spun through wizards and snakes and she threw herself at the feet of Moses and clamped her hands around his ankles. "You're back! You're back! Aie—love!" Her white hair spread around his filthy feet, and as Moses looked down, his face broke in two, and his mouth opened wider, wider.

"Monster!" Merneptah cried out, leaping forward and taking his wife up under the arms. "Traitor! Murderer!" Dragging Bityah backwards he kicked away snake after snake, and they passed into the mouth of the silver viper of the priest, which turned into a rod as he took it up again, so that when Merneptah threw his wife into the arms of her handmaids, he stood with bare stone between himself and Moses.

The priest asked, "Will you let us serve our god in Sinai, or will you harden your heart?"

"You bring me this man and speak of hardened hearts?" The Pharaoh's voice shook as he struggled toward composure. "I protect Goshen from men without hearts, from the wild tribes of Amaleke, from hunger and thirst and death without burial."

"The true god does not love death," the priest said.

"If he does not love death," Merneptah said, "he cannot know this man."

The two departed from the presence of the Pharaoh on the first day. The wise men called for sacred wood to carve new wands, and the Pharaoh ordered the place where Moses had stood cleaned with lye, meaning to blot it out, yet there remained a circle of uncanny whiteness where the lye had eaten into the stone.

As for Bityah, all that afternoon cries rose from her throat and her hands pulled at nothing. She did not try to tear herself away from Merneptah. She did not try to tear herself away from bed. She wanted silence, but the cries kept coming, and she knew that so long as she cried he would never come back again.

Merneptah whispered, "No more," as he had many times before. And again, "We are nearing the end of long lives and no more will we have luck or trouble."

Yet all the while, the hard, round belly with his son curled inside of it turned those words false. Bityah pressed both hands against the belly now, and it was as though it lifted her from her husband's hands and into others.

In her chamber, two maidservants were weeping. Bityah watched without understanding. How could anyone weep when her beloved had returned from a long journey? She wanted to tell them he had returned, and she thought she had risen from her bed and walked to the smaller, prettier girl and kissed her on the mouth, but then she knew she had not so much as raised her coverlet.

"My lady, my beauty," the little one called across the room. Her mouth was pink; her slant eyes were like jewels. "When your time comes, let me stand by you."

Bityah thought she had said yes and had given the girl a gold ring from her finger. The girl's hands were empty and her smooth, pale palms spread themselves along her skirt as she turned to her tall friend.

"She's sleeping now."

By and by they would leave; now they have left. Bityah rested her cheek in her long, white hair and waited. By and by she would hear footsteps, heavy as the Pharaoh's. There they were. A rush of something like wind, only sweeter. Bityah looked up at a face that hung above her own face like the moon.

"I knew you would come tonight," Bityah said. And when she spoke to Miriam, Miriam answered.

"Well met, Princess." Her big hands made a cup around Bityah's belly. "Ha! And he rocks in your womb with his big flat feet tucked under, la la la."

Bityah sat up and laid hold of Miriam's ears which poked below her head-rag. "Let loose your hair."

"Ow! I told you, Princess. No."

"I want to see it rain."

"You'll see rain enough, of all sorts—ow! Leave go!" Miriam laughed, no maiden's laughter but a wild dark booming that made Bityah roll backwards and start to laugh herself. Miriam's freed ears vibrated like tambourines. She shook her head and once again Bityah hoped that her head rag would fall free so she could see her hair again.

She had only seen it twice. The first time, she was a young girl, and above a baby in a basket, through the rain, she had seen something sitting in the reeds, a sleek darkness with two hard, glittering eyes. She had moved closer with the basket in her arms and out of the darkness, out of her hair, stepped Miriam. The second time, scant months ago, Bityah, who had spent countless years beneath a curtain, woke one morning to find that curtain's stuff had turned from blood to fine black hair. She raised an arm and rent that curtain, rising toward friendly light.

Behind that hair was a face she knew, the gold earrings, the mouth sticky with dates. In her hand was a flask shaped like a key.

"This opens," she said, and she spilled a drop between the legs of Bityah so that it seeped into her womb.

Then she moved toward the window, singing: "La la," and the key smashed underfoot, and dancing, she was pulled, hair first, out the window, into a rainy sky.

Yet, she returned each day. She made Bityah bind the fragments of that flask into a handkerchief, and now Bityah kept the handkerchief between her breasts. She touched it often; the edges of that broken flask were sharp enough to draw blood. When her time would come, she would know how to use them.

Merneptah did not speak even to the physician about his encounter with Moses. In truth, he was ashamed. He had acted without forethought, like a child who felt betrayed. Taking a broad view, what did Moses matter? If the flight of Moses left a trail of evil consequences, those consequences could just as easily be traced back to his stubborn father or to Bityah, even to himself. Why bear old grudges? This Moses was clearly harmless now. Once he had mistaken the voice of Moses for the voice of his own heart. Now Moses didn't speak at all.

The priest was a different story. His voice Merneptah knew, and he knew the man's position. That day, he made a point of finding out the name of Aaron's four sons, and at once he had them relieved of their stations. He confiscated the land of Aaron's wife. He considered having wife and sons brought before him, but let matters close.

It was with a cheerful spirit that he took his morning walk beside the wadi. He walked alone, bareheaded, as he had since childhood, carrying only a spear for hunting. His slaves whispered that he gathered water there for magic, and spoke to holy fish. In fact, he gathered nothing and spoke to no one. He only took his sandals in his hand and let his feet drag through the silt and watched the sky.

The sky above the rushes was slate blue. Merneptah drew up

first one foot and then the other to replace his sandals, and he turned back to the palace. There stood Aaron, alone.

"Hello," Merneptah said. "Your sons and wife are destitute."

"Hear the word of the true god." Aaron's well-modulated voice trembled. He looked the worse for wear, mud spattered on his gown, most of his neck bands gone. "If you do not let us go to serve him," Aaron said, "he will turn water to blood."

"Will he?" Merneptah smiled and poked his spear into the mud. "What did you say you were to this god?"

"His voice," Aaron said.

Merneptah laughed and Aaron turned so red that for a moment Merneptah felt pity and would have given the poor man anything he asked for had he not, at that moment, caught sight of Moses. He was obscured by rushes and he looked the way he had looked years ago, doggedly expectant. In a fury, Merneptah let his answer fly.

"Turn it to blood," he said, "and I'll taste water. Turn it to blood, but I'll smell water, feel, touch water, hear water rushing. I know what is false from what is true."

"You have closed your heart?" Aaron asked.

Merneptah looked not at Aaron, but at Moses who did not ask his own questions. He said, "I live by truth alone. I do not swear false vows."

So did Merneptah turn his back to the palace with his wet feet slippery in their sandals. Behind him came, thick, unmistakable, the smell of blood.

For three days there was no water in Egypt. The basins were brown with blood. There was blood in the kneading bowls, blood in the bread and blood in the beer. Yet in the palace of Merneptah, all of Egypt knew, the Pharaoh had fresh water. They knew because they saw him bathe and drink.

Never had Merneptah drunk so much as he did in those three days. He called for a jar of water in the morning which he downed with a hunk of brown bread. He called for water always at his feet and at his elbow. Water must moisten his lips as he read his maps and water must wash the stones of the palace. "Water," said Merneptah to all who would listen, "is sacred, the stuff of life. I dedicate these days to the holiness and purity of water."

The servants of the palace kept handkerchiefs over their noses as they baked and stirred and scrubbed with blood. At the end of the third day, every wall and floor of the palace was an even brown, except for a single patch of white in the map room where once a servant scrubbed a circle of lye.

Finally the physician found the nerve to approach Merneptah. He found him sitting, sipping a cup of blood, with his keen yellow eyes moving along the ledger of a book of accounts.

"Look," said the physician. "This is nonsense. There's poison in the water and you're killing yourself. Who would have the throne when you are gone?"

"My son," said the Pharaoh.

The physician ignored his answer and said, "It's clear enough the Hebrews have poisoned the spring where the wadi begins. Purify it. If you want to cover yourself, have your wise men say a prayer or two and wave their wands."

"They have no wands," said the Pharaoh.

The physician rolled his eyes. "Oh, surely they can find a few that haven't crawled away."

Looking at his friend's ironical and sensible face, Merneptah felt so foolish that he spat out the blood in his mouth and said, "You're right." He smiled. His teeth were caked with blood, and he rubbed them clean with his thick fingers and shook his head. "I don't know what possessed me. I'll call that priest here."

"And his brother," said the physician. "That is the one I'd watch for."

Merneptah's throat tightened. "Why?"

After a pause, the physician very tentatively said, "Nomads know things."

"I cannot stand," Merneptah said, "the way all of this blood has made my head ache." Throwing open the shutters of his map room, he took a breath of sour air and vomited into the court below.

The people of Egypt rejoiced when the Pharaoh turned the blood back into water. They drank and drank until they wept, and when some noticed that the Goshen slaves did not drink with them, the rumors were confirmed that every tribe's well had run clear. On this matter, they questioned the god Seth who, in a voice transformed, spoke of ruin for all who crossed the will of Pharaoh.

Merneptah himself seemed like a new man. He sent for Moses and Aaron, calling them not into the map room, but into his great court, for an official audience. This time he did not let himself look at Moses, but motioned Aaron forward with such simplicity that Aaron himself seemed disarmed. He asked Aaron, "What do you want then? You will have it."

Aaron shivered, as though he had a fever. He raised his absurd silver rod. "Three days in Sinai to serve our god."

"Sinai?" Merneptah asked pleasantly. "The wilderness? Where snakes live?"

"Sinai," said Aaron. The days had not been easy for him. His linen was grey with sweat and dust, and all of his gold was gone. He seemed to have stopped shaving, as there was stubble on his skull.

"A powerful god," Merneptah said. "Powerful gods need temples. Why not build a temple here in Goshen?"

Aaron did not answer. He moved his weight from one foot to the other. The wise men who stood at Pharaoh's throne pressed close to hear, for in that new god's temple they might find a place. All around them rose the rank smell of Moses, yet Merneptah, who had made himself drink blood, thought it no heavy matter to bear the stench without seeing the man.

Merneptah went on. "We have the means to complete a small sanctuary before winter. Of course, a true temple will take years, but a sanctuary, yourself as High Priest, with a tithe of young bulls for sacrifice, with temple slaves—"

"Slaves?"

It was not Aaron. Merneptah's chest resounded and at last he knew he had no choice. As surely as his stomach knew blood, his ears knew that voice. Moses had spoken to Aaron.

"Slaves?" he asked again, and he croaked out the word as if it couldn't fit through his throat, and once released, it hovered, and Aaron caught his arm and pulled him back, whispering:

"Brother, if we—"

Merneptah shouted: "Speak for yourself! Ask for something I can give!" He realized he was on his feet, and his eyes were smarting and his heart turned as if it was fastened to a wheel. He shouted: "Do not speak at all! There is nothing I can give you! Nothing!"

But now the two brothers had fled into the dusty sunlight out of which leapt a sudden stream of frogs.

A guard appeared at the Pharaoh's elbow. "What would you have me do?"

"Close the door," Merneptah heard himself say. Then he rose from his seat and kicked great heaps of frogs aside and locked the door with his own hand.

During those days, he walked the palace hallway, room to room, and by the striped light from the shuttered window, he studied lists of gods. Soon, the drone of frogs made reading impossible. Later, a pounding broke the tablets in his hands, so he read papyrus. His scribes repeated tales of every god they knew, but each tale was split in half by a wild kick at the door. Small gnats forced themselves between gaps of wood and clung to Merneptah's face. To flee those gnats, he closed off the north wing and lay in the dark, gathering many thoughts together only to feel them slip away and leave him empty of anything but anger. His bed, clammy with dead gnats, soon fell to pieces, and then he sat

on his stone chair with his hands pressed on his knees and felt
such wild, white hatred that the walls of his room glowed.

A voice broke through. "Open up, you fool!"

It was the physician, the only man in Egypt with nerve
enough to at last demand to see the Pharaoh. The Pharaoh
unlatched the door and stood before someone almost unrecogniz-
able. The physician's face was spattered with venom and his eyes
poked out from greenish sockets. As he stepped into the room,
with him traveled a cloud of flies. He grasped Merneptah by the
shoulders and he shouted:

"Are you mad! Are you mad!"

Merneptah shook him off and frowned. "Are you? What
would you have me do?"

"Give them what they ask for."

"Them?" The voice of Merneptah rang like ice. "Hebrew
slaves? I offered them a temple. What else would you have me
give them?"

"If it means this ends, give them everything," the physician
pleaded. "Look, they have come three times to see if you will give
them what they want."

"Which is?" Merneptah asked.

"Leave for themselves and their flocks—"

"Flocks?" Merneptah pushed the physician out of the way
and started down the hall, so he had to trail after him, calling:

"Yes, flocks. Our own cattle are dead, but theirs are thriving. They want their flocks with them when they serve their
god. They will take sheep, cattle, and all the gold they can
carry."

"Gold?" Merneptah shouted. He stomped toward the open
where the walls were black with blood and flies and gnats, and
the corners were blue and green with rotting piles of frogs.

The Persian wizard, the most powerful of all, whose long
curled beard once was a wonder of the east, staggered toward the
Pharaoh on crooked legs and presented a chin eaten half bare

with boils and lice. "I fear," he said, "that if you make them stay, their god will eat our gods."

Merneptah pushed him to the ground and stomped up toward the throne. "I know the god," he said at last.

The wise men clustered near, trembling and moaning, eager for wisdom.

"I know the god," Merneptah said. "I know how to meet him, and it is not with gold and oil and grain."

"But his name——" they all brayed out. "His name. We must know his name."

Before the feet of Merneptah bowed all of his scribes, his servants, his musicians, cooks and stewards who spoke in one voice: "For the sake of those who suffer, let them go."

Merneptah laughed. "What do I care if you suffer?"

Then through the prone Egyptians came a cloaked figure holding a staff, and all around him the air was clear of flies. Merneptah felt at his side for a spear, for he knew, at this time as at no other, that the name of the god was Anger and he might, at last, kill Moses.

The hood of the cloak dropped away, and there was a rosy old man who dropped to his knees and cried out: "Lord! Master! God!"

The Pharaoh looked him up and down and frowned. The man's long beard was curled at the tip, and his kohled, yearning eyebrows arched above weak eyes.

"Lord! Master! God!" he said again. "I am Hur, the elder of the tribe of Levi, and I have come many miles to beg, for the sake of slaves who serve you and love you."

The Pharaoh rose from his seat and gazed down in black amazement. "Slaves who love me?"

"More than we love water, sunlight, and life. For who else gives us a home? Who else would protect us from the demons who would make us homeless wanderers?"

With a cough like a laugh, Merneptah took up his spear. "If I ran you through, would you still love me?"

"Oh yes, Lord, Master, God." Hur sputtered out the words.

"And this Moses who has kept you sound while all of Egypt suffers, him you hate?"

"More than thirst, darkness, or death," Hur replied, "for because of these plagues we are so hated in Goshen that we will all find death at the hands of our neighbors."

"And your god?" Merneptah asked him.

"You are our god," Hur said, and he threw himself at Merneptah's feet. Merneptah did not kill Hur, but said rather, "Tell Moses to come here without the priest."

Hur sprang up and shuffled backwards with even, soft steps, and the flies parted around him like fog. Merneptah looked after him, and anger was so mixed with disgust now that his whole body felt like a boil. Turning to the Persian who still lingered by his shoulder, Merneptah said, "Bring me a looking glass."

"Lord," the Persian pleaded. "God and Master."

"Bring it to me," the Pharaoh said again.

The Persian turned and called for a looking glass to be brought to Merneptah, and Merneptah held it to his face and nodded, for the face was one loose boil. It could not be otherwise; there was no beauty in the world, or truth, and no answer, no answer at all.

No beauty, he thought again, and he let the looking glass drop to the floor and then, out loud, said: "Bityah."

What had become of Bityah? Merneptah sucked in a breath, and ran as quickly as he could to her chamber. He slipped on frogs and flies and gnats, and the boils on the soles of his feet sent a wild ache up his loins, yet still he ran, hitting doorway after doorway, forgetting where she lay, calling at last with all his strength, "Bityah! Bityah!" He shouted over cracks that hit the walls and roof top, and his voice broke everything to pieces as he called again: "Bityah!"

He found her in bed, covered by a brown blanket. The physician stood over her, his hands hovering above her belly. Her Hebrew maidservants had left long ago.

"Friend," Merneptah cried out, "how is Bityah?"

The physician looked up at the Pharaoh, and his face was a stranger's. He raised his hands, and as he did the blanket parted, and there was a fluttering of hard, brown wings. "Locusts," he said.

Merneptah feared to take another step. He stared. The locusts cracked and sank from Bityah's head to her feet, and they made a curve around her belly. Finally, Merneptah said, "I have gone mad."

"You are not mad," said the physician. His voice, too, was a stranger's. Then softly, he added, "She is in labor."

Those terrible words made Merneptah suck in a throat full of locusts, and he tried to cry out, but his hacking drove him blindly down the hall, and at last into the small room where he kept his maps. He locked the door.

And the Pharaoh knew he was no longer angry. He was lonely. It was as though that loneliness filled his emptiness to bursting.

Why could he not kill Moses? Because he wanted, more than anything, to be with him again, talking all night about the truth. When Moses shouted about slaves, the word hung in the air and turned like a bird shifting direction, and Merneptah wanted to shout some wild grand statement in reply, only to find, in Moses' cracked voice, a question. And his love for Bityah, what did it matter when he could not speak of it to anyone? Merneptah took his knees in his arms and wept.

There was a small knock. Merneptah did not look up to answer. In spite of locked doors, somehow, there was Moses.

"You called for me?" Moses said.

Merneptah could not rise at once. His knees were useless and his arms lacked the strength even to find the floor. So it was Moses who stepped forward and lifted Merneptah up to place him on a bench of stone.

Again Moses said to Merneptah, "You called for me?"

Through scarred lips, Merneptah said to Moses, "Open the door. I would have air and light."

Moses answered, "There is no light."

"Light," Merneptah said again. He raised his hand toward Moses, though he could not see him, and he said, "These days I have lived in a small dark place which cannot be unlocked."

Moses laid his hand behind Merneptah's head so that it would not rest upon cold stone. "You do not need to talk."

"Once," Merneptah said to Moses, "we pledged friendship in the name of truth. I know now we made a false pledge."

"That is wrong," said Moses.

Merneptah said, "Speak the truth then. How can I open my heart?"

"Walk," said Moses, and his voice was the quiet voice Merneptah knew, that voice that stopped midway up the throat and softened there. "Along the hallway you will feel between your toes fragments of glass and gold. Gather them and follow."

Merneptah reached again for Moses, but his fingers were too broken and they only hovered. Finally, he said, "You help me up."

Moses bore the Pharaoh from the stone seat, and he opened the door and left him in the hallway in a darkness five shades darker than night, so deep that nothing could be seen or felt, heard, touched or tasted. In such a darkness, pain could not live, so Merneptah found himself able to stand with assistance. He could not see Moses go.

Yet into the hands of Merneptah fell, singly, the fragments. They met each other, and in his mind's eye as he moved from piece to piece those pieces fell together. Who led him from fragment to fragment? Who brings pieces together? Who opens?

He asked, was it always so? Yet he expected no answer and so answered himself: Always, it was so.

The last piece clung to the edge of the gold key. Darkness smoothed into twilight, and against that twilight lay his wife, Bityah, in her third day of labor.

The Pharaoh watched from behind, as her white hair streamed backwards down her frail, golden arms, and she clenched the end of a table. Her mouth opened, and dark thinned just enough to make way for her voice as she cried: "Miriam! Miriam!"

Miriam! Merneptah knew that name. Now between the thighs of Bityah he saw Miriam attending, draped in a cloak, draped in her hair, draped in the scent of dates, but when he rushed to pull her from his wife, the hood fell back. There was his own physician.

"Thank God!" Merneptah shouted, and he cried with pure relief.

"Which god?" the physician asked in his dry voice. "Or do you know?" It was then the Pharaoh realized that the man who was drawing forth the head of his son was not his physician, but the Angel of Death.

At once, the Pharaoh knew what must be done. He turned from the Angel of Death and spoke not to Moses, but to God.

"So now they cannot turn back," he said. "So they must go to Sinai, for they will never be allowed to stay in Goshen now that you are killing in their name. And now I will tell them to take their flocks and gold and never to return."

From behind, the Angel of Death rose with the Pharaoh's dead son in his arms. His face was just as dry and just as intelligent as the face of the physician, and it was with the physician's voice that he said, "You know they will not go until they're forced."

The Pharaoh smiled, and he clapped the Angel of Death on both shoulders and said, "You speak, and it's with the voice of my own heart! I'll mount a chariot and call my swiftest men, and we won't give them time enough to bake a journey's bread before they're gone."

Through the last rag ends of dark, the Pharaoh mounted a bright chariot, and all of Egypt wondered at his holy anger as he drove the twelve tribes from the wadi for the sake of his dead son. Through the rushes, arrows flew, until at last those tribes were trapped against a deep Red Sea.

Yet closed things open. When Merneptah felt for the gold key, he found that it was gone. He himself was the key, and he drove himself into the open gap of water through which swarmed his enemies, until, over his head, the waves closed up.

Simone Zelitch

When I was a senior at Akimbo Hebrew Academy, my favorite novel was Kazantzakis's Last Temptation of Christ. *Jesus interested me far less than Judas, and Judas less than Martha. Then, as now, I favored minor characters. My edition had a big cross on the cover, and I think it got some of my teachers worried, but really, I found the book to be familiar territory. It was a midrash. I'd been fascinated by midrash ever since I first got a peek at Ginzberg's marvelous* Legends of the Jews *and read embroidered versions of Bible stories as juicy and electrifying as anything out of the* Arabian Nights. *What struck me most about those legends was the way that every miracle had an emotional foundation. When Moses hears God speak from the burning bush, it is with the voice of his own father. The Red Sea only parts when an obscure Hebrew has courage enough to jump in headlong, and risk drowning. Years later, I saw this same pattern in* One Hundred Years of Solitude, *a blurry line between passion and magic that lends both intensity. I wrote* Moses in Sinai *with Kazantzakis, Ginzberg, and Marquez all in mind. Consider "Ten Plagues" an example of Jewish magic realism.*

SEEKERS IN THE HOLY LAND

Joan Leegant

He has chosen Safed because the kabbalists came here. The streets are hilly, some of the roads rocky—this is what he wants, what he came for, the ancient feeling, the hard-to-get-there feeling—and from time to time he has to pull up on his backpack, shrug each shoulder through his bulky jacket to keep it from slipping and pulling him down into the old stones that pave these streets and could take him under. Though he'd gladly go, that's how much he wants to know this place. He is tired of Jerusalem, tired of his fellow Americans posing at the modern yeshiva, not even a yeshiva, an Institute it calls itself, to attract the university-conscious who need the pretext of a graduate school. As if they were there for a credential, a degree; as if that was what being there was about. He hadn't understood this when he sent in his forms, what did he know, reading the brochure in his apartment in Boston. An immersion in study. He thought the other students would be like him, but they're not. They come to the classes and act like it matters, but really all they want is to have a good time. To get away from their parents or colleges, hang out on Ben Yehuda and meet American girls on exchange programs, and get high and go to Egypt and Petra and then return home after the year and tell their friends they had a mystical experience.

He has found his way from the bus station to the old section of the city, the streets narrow and winding like in the pictures, like in the guidebooks, like in parts of Jerusalem. The weather is like Jerusalem, too. Cold, the altitude, December, and it can be raw, not like home, of course, but still raw, wet, you never get warm. His roommates are complaining about the heat in their building, on for only certain hours of the day and never enough. So far he is succeeding pretty well in ignoring the tourist buses clogging the narrow streets. And most of those will be pulling out of Safed now because it's Friday afternoon and there's nowhere for the tourists to stay. They'll go to Tiberias or Haifa to the big hotels. Old synagogues and artists in Safed, that's it, a daytime show, you don't want to be here Friday night, the tour guide would say. Nothing to do. Not even restaurants open.

As if on cue, a charter bus rumbles past him down the hill on its way out of town. Blank faces at the windows, some in those perky cotton hats, faux kibbutz, given free with the tour agency's shoulder bags. Too quiet to be Americans. Probably some guilty Europeans—Danish, Swiss, the ever-present Germans. He catches a woman's eye, knows what she sees: the oversized kippa, the tzitzit fringes dangling, exposed, near his belt, though the hair is too long to be really religious, really Orthodox. But she probably doesn't know that. *Young Jews reclaiming their heritage*, she's thinking. *Isn't that nice*. The bus rounds a curve and disappears, he hears the bounce of the shocks. He sees them all over the country, his parents' age, born after the war, sincere, prosperous-looking people—the old ones, he thinks, wouldn't dare come, or want to. But even these he finds offensive, as if they're atoning; as if boating on the Kinneret or buying ceramic candlesticks for their friends back home were atonement. He's been watching tourists in this country for five months now and likes the Japanese best because he can't understand their language, not a single syllable, and because they seem so game. Jews? What are Jews? Interesting. Let's go see. They seem to know little, unlike the Europeans who know too much. The Japanese women are always wearing the wrong kinds of shoes, high heels or flimsy ladies' sandals, and the men wear formal, pressed pants. They don't know how to dress for the climate or the terrain. Watching them at a war memorial full of rubble or at a dig with its treacherous potholes and insufficiently roped-off areas, he wonders if somehow they got to this country by mistake; if they hadn't meant instead to go to Rome or Madrid or some more civilized place, better paved, but got on the wrong plane.

A dumpster juts onto the sidewalk—overflowing plastic bags, a moldy rug—and he steps around it, catches a streak of gray, the wide whine of a cat. The hostel, he's been told, is at the bottom of one of these hilly streets, a ten-minute walk to the synagogue he wants to find. He heard about the synagogue from Aryeh, one of his teachers. A plum piece of intelligence. Not listed in the guidebooks, the tourists don't know about it. *The real thing, sometimes they still do secret ceremonies, anointing initiates, those who've learned the Way. They study for years, practice, they're not young.* In truth, he knows almost nothing about the mystics, the Seven Sefirot, the Infinite Ein-Sof, the migration of souls, they're only phrases he's read; knows almost nothing about the religion altogether, a juvenile Hebrew School education, a couple of courses in college. But he knows this is where he belongs, in Safed, at this synagogue. He wants to drink from this well, and Aryeh saw it, recognized it, told only him.

At the corner he checks his directions, then shifts the pack and turns right, leaving Arlozorov Street. Behind a cracking stone archway, off a tiny building practically buried in weeds, a man all in white is standing on a porch, eyes closed, silently rocking. A meditation. A flock of birds squawks overhead, and the man opens his eyes. He hurries on. There are probably dozens, maybe hundreds of people concentrating like that at this very moment, right here, the highest elevation in the country, the closest point to heaven. He turns down a side street, passes a florist, its metal shutters pulled closed. He should be on that porch, too, he's wasting his time in Jerusalem.

The street narrows, and it is mazelike where he's walking, winding streets within winding streets. And quiet. Too quiet.

Where is the hustle and bustle, the children coming home from school early, the women rushing back from the markets to cook? He passes silent doorways, a few toys left out against the cement buildings—a tricycle, a child's battered wagon—then checks his watch, a fleeting worry he's lost track. Two o'clock. He lifts his wrist to his ear, hears it ticking, squints anyway at a clock through a window in a partially shuttered candy store and confirms the time again: only two. Maybe this is the influence of the kabbalists, Shabbat brought in with silence and contemplation, even the streets paying attention to their breath.

And now he is there, where the hostel is supposed to be. Malachim Street. Street of the Angels. He looks to the top. Arlozorov is at the other end, he has been walking in a circle. There is no number 35. He looks again at the slip of paper, at Aryeh's scrawly handwriting, a crude map of the hostel and the synagogue, a dark circle colored in at each. The synagogue location was from Aryeh but the hostel was in the guidebook: 35 Malachim.

He finds 14, 27, 48, 63, walking the length of it, a short street with mismatched numbers. A car appears at the top, a dusty white Peugeot; he edges up against a building just in time to let it speed past. He combs the street again, looking for a sign—hostel, hotel, pension—spots a battered metal Coca-Cola placard hanging off a single nail, another one for Strauss Ice Cream. But the buildings are shuttered, whatever they are—restaurants, groceries, kiosks—closed. The whole block looks vacated, an aura of having been fled. But Safed is not a city to be fled, not like the towns on the northern border, Kiryat Shmona or Metulla, whose residents routinely go underground.

He has exhausted the little street and also himself. He sits heavily on a stoop, puts his backpack by his feet. His boots are covered in dust, he could write his name across the leather. *Neal Fox.* He wants to change it, Naftali or Natan. Maybe Nachum, after the great seer of Bratslav, if he can work up the nerve. He flexes his shoulders, rotates his arms. The pack is too heavy, he could lose the second bottle of water, the camera—what was he thinking? it's Shabbat—his three books. Across from him the Coca-Cola sign flutters on its nail. This is not the first time something like this has gone wrong, it happens all the time in this country: buses regularly off schedule, businesses out of business, addresses listed wrong. No one is ever surprised. *Y'hiyeh b'seder*. It'll be all right. He has two hours before sundown. He's twenty-one and strong. There's a hostel somewhere in this city, he just has to find it. The next car, the next passerby—he'll ask.

Meanwhile he pulls one of the water bottles from his pack and drinks. Waits. No cars come. The sky is deepening pink. He knows it's close to three. Shabbat begins at four-thirty.

She appears at the top of the street, at Arlozorov, blond, a day-glo orange ski jacket, a pack almost identical to his, only smaller. She's wearing a skirt and knee socks like his sister Carly when Carly was in eighth grade. Only this person is not fourteen.

"Excuse me, can you help me?" she says in Hebrew, an accent he can't place. "Do you know where is the hostel?"

Her Hebrew, he is certain even from this little bit, is better than his—the speed, the pronunciation, his gut sense that whatever her native tongue, she doesn't want to use it—and to show her he knows she's only a tourist, why is she trying Hebrew, he answers in English, "Do you speak English?"

"Oh. Sorry," she says. "I am looking for the youth hostel." She says *looking* like *loooking*, that extra *ooh*, and he finds it appealing. The fine blond hair, the pretty blue eyes, the earnest face, the accent, the knee socks: she is like Heidi, like the cast from *The Sound of Music*, like Gretel in an opera he once saw on TV. Like a German.

"Yeah, well, me too," he says, picking up his bottle.

She glances around, confused. "It's not here?"

"Doesn't seem to be." He takes another swig, puts the bottle away. He's seen these tourists, too. Young Europeans traveling alone, crisscrossing the world in six months or a year with a single small backpack. A girl from Finland once showed him the contents of hers. A quarter of a washcloth, neatly cut, a hand towel, one skirt, one pair of pants, one sweater, one shirt, one undershirt, two pairs of thin socks, two pairs of underpants, a half-size toothbrush, and two tampons—enough until you get somewhere to buy, she said, oddly the only thing she commented on. Often he meets them on the way back from Turkey or Egypt or Iran, Israel a modern relief.

"Perhaps the guidebook had it wrong," she says, looking up to Arlozorov. "Perhaps it's not Malachim but HaPalmach or Rimonim, the next ones over," she says, turning, scanning, her street pronunciations polished, studied, expert.

"Perhaps." He folds his hands, looks past the hem of her skirt, which is eye level from where he's sitting, and wonders about the socks. Is it for comfort? Or did someone on the bus tell her to put on a skirt, slip it on over her pants, then take the pants off, the rules of modesty; in religious sections Jewish women don't wear pants. She would respect local customs. A seasoned traveler, no doubt, like the Finn.

"Aren't you going to look?" she says.

He hadn't gotten that far. But now that she's here, so efficient, he feels compelled to justify his inertia. "I was considering the situation," he says. "Thinking it through."

She makes a little *Oh* with her lips, then goes to the bottom of Malachim. Something makes him leave his pack and follow her, and they comb five streets. He knows where she got her Hebrew, has seen people like her in the ulpan studying with the new immigrants and Jewish students like him. They're good with languages, already know English and French in addition to German, and are pleasant to everyone; the Russian women want to bring them home and feed them. Some of them are Christians, there to proselytize, to get the Jews to join them so they can have their Second Coming; the Jews are holding it up. But you don't find that out for weeks, even months.

They walk through open gates, knock at unmarked doors. A lone pedestrian crosses the street and ignores them when they try to ask.

Back at Malachim they compare slips of paper. Hers is also in English; she copied it from the same guidebook.

"So the guidebook is mistaken," she declares, studying her paper. Her pack seems featherlight; she has not yet put it down, while his remains on the stoop.

"Evidently." He makes a show of looking at his watch, pulling back his jacket cuff, wiping off the face. "If you hurry you can catch a bus to Tiberias, stay there instead."

She looks up. "What good will that do me?"

"It's a place to stay. There are two or three hostels there." He makes a sweeping gesture. "Unlike here."

"I will find."

He shrugs and goes toward his pack.

"And you?" she says, behind him.

He hoists the straps. "I guess I will find, too."

"Where do you need to be? Where are you going in Safed?"

He will not tell her. He wants his synagogue to be his own discovery; wants to be, for once, in a place unsullied by outsiders, by spectators there to gawk and paste the experience into some mental scrapbook. *Look how pious, how devoted.* He knows of course that he's an outsider, too, but he will do his best to fit in, be inconspicuous. "I want to be near one of the synagogues," he says, shifting the pack. It feels like there are bricks inside, extra weight accumulated since he first set it down, as if the cement of the building has seeped in through the canvas.

"Me, too."

"Yeah, well, good luck," he says, and starts to walk away.

"Which one?" she calls. "Which synagogue?"

He stops, thinks quickly and turns around. Her hair has fanned out with the wind, a yellow curtain against the deepening rose of the sky. "You want to know which one to visit? Go to the Joseph Caro or the Ari, they're famous, everyone goes there.

They're in all the guidebooks." He points to the top of the street, to Arlozorov. "Go to any of the shops, they'll tell you where."

She stares a moment longer. He has finessed her, that's not what she meant. She wanted to know where he was going.

But she knows she's been dismissed. She's well brought up, or perhaps more timid than he thought. She straightens up, her backpack almost floating, as if filled with air, gives a small comradely wave, starts up Malachim. He moves off in the other direction, then turns. In her orange jacket, her back to him, she looks like a frail bird.

At the only grocery still open the proprietor tells him of a woman who takes in guests, Mrs. Baghdadi at 36 Montefiore. He loves these surnames, Baghdadi, heavy with place and history, while what does he have to show for himself? Fox, whatever gave it life—Folkshtein, Foxman, Feuerstein—long since chopped off at the root.

He buys a small jar of peanut butter, the three rolls left in the bin, the last two borekas, a liter of apple juice, a container of cottage cheese. Somewhere in his pack he hopes there's a spoon and a plastic knife. He was told the hostel served breakfast and would provide a cold supper Friday night if given enough notice, but now he's on his own. He thanks the proprietor excessively, grateful the store is still open this close to candlelighting, and the man gives a lengthy reply. Neal's Hebrew isn't good enough to fully understand, though he suspects it is the story of the man's life—he picks up something about Yemen, a wife, nine children—and he waits for a pause while the man collects his thoughts, then nods vigorously and says a too-loud *Shabbat shalom* and heads out.

It's turned cold, a chilly damp that feels like rain. Two men hurry past, their heads down, hair wet, and he sees then the tiny sign on a low stone building. *Mikveh.* For men. He's just recently found out about such a thing, men immersing themselves before holy days. For the truly devout, every week. He should do this, why hadn't he heard of it before? An old man is closing up, lock-ing the gate, and Neal turns left, berates himself. Next time. Next time he'll come earlier, be smarter, better prepared. At 36 Monte-fiore there's a gate opening onto a thorny courtyard. He picks his way over broken stones and dead geranium petals, the bright red decayed to black along the edges, as if burned, and finds the door, knocks.

The woman who answers is like from a lithograph: shrunken, kerchiefed, wizened. He asks for Mrs. Baghdadi and the old lady shakes her head. Not here? Wrong name? Did he misunderstand? Immediately she begins talking in rapid-fire Hebrew. He can't understand a word and pain is pulling across his shoulders from the weight of his pack.

"One hundred shekels," the woman says, interrupting her-self and holding out her hand.

"One hundred?" The hostel cost thirty-five, about nine dollars.

"One hundred," she repeats. When he hesitates she says, her Hebrew louder as if he were deaf instead of American, "All of Shabbat. Tonight, tomorrow, you can stay until after dark, or the next morning. Room is clean."

What choice does he have? He gives her the money, follows her to a room at the end of a long hall, the dense smell of cumin and cinnamon hovering above them. Inside are four bare beds cramped together, two of them perpendicular so that someone's feet would be up against someone else's head. He takes the one closest to the wall in case she's still doing business later, guaran-teeing privacy at least on one side.

The woman appears with a sheet and a pillow. The word for blanket has suddenly evaporated from his already rudimentary vocabulary.

"More?" he manages, smoothing the top of the bed. She shakes her head, obviously annoyed. What could he want, more what?

He puts his arms around himself and pretends to shiver. "Something for cold," he says.

She leaves, returns with a rubber thing shaped like a kidney. A hot water bottle, he presumes. He sinks onto the bed. The springs creak like an old song. There is always his jacket.

The synagogue is dark. He was not expecting floodlights, but he knows before even trying the door that no one is there.

Yet it is a synagogue, the synagogue. It's got the two lion heads on the gate that Aryeh told him about, the broken arch at the street, the two Stars of David carved over the door, one above the other. Even the address is right: 18 Eliyahu HaNavi. *Do you know who is Eliyahu?* Aryeh said, eyes flaming, drawing the little map. *Carried to heaven on a fiery chariot, his horse went through the sun, better than Icarus!* When Aryeh told him this, Neal felt himself shaking: this was what he wanted, to fly into the center and merge with that heat, with that sun. Isn't that why he came, not just to Safed but to the country altogether, to find something true, a way? His Jewish friends at home were doing yoga, Buddhism; one was considering becoming a priest. Because what was there in America if you were Jewish? Temples with health clubs? Fund-raisers? Rabbis like at his parents' synagogue, Rabbi Shore, preoccupied with building campaigns, numbers, membership rolls? Or, on the other side, rules, fetishistic rules, a black and white orthodoxy. But for the soul, what was there?

He tries the door one more time, then walks around the low building, looks in through two small windows. Prayer books stacked up, a table in the middle, next to it a wooden ark, chairs in a disorganized semicircle. And books, papers, lamps, stray articles of clothing cluttering the corners.

Perhaps he is early. He thinks not; he has passed several synagogues on his way and they've all started. But perhaps here they begin later, do it differently. At the Ari and Joseph Caro they have to toe the line, be routine, otherwise they lose their guidebook listings and, with them, American dollars. Ones and fives dropped into the shammes's wooden bowl on the way out after the tours on weekdays, loose change if the tourists are feeling cheap or unsatisfied. He's heard about these shammeses, toothless old men who don't wash, shuffle in and out. Ancients who wanted to be disciples, initiates, who are still hoping. They sweep and clean the toilets, and when the tourists come they give the men little cardboard hats like pyramids, the women bits of lace, and suffer with the wooden bowl for donations, murmuring, head down, from Psalms.

He glances around the courtyard, then to the neighboring buildings, shadows and candles in the windows, music, a female singer, Ofra Haza on someone's CD. There is no place to sit. He leans with his back to the building, then slides down, hunches up against the concrete. The ground is rocky and damp. He takes off his jacket, sits on it, hugs himself for warmth.

But this too is cold. He puts the jacket back on, searches his pockets for something to put between himself and the ground—a hat, gloves, a map, anything, where is his backpack when he needs it?—and, empty-handed, leans back, shuts his eyes, and tells himself to concentrate on his breath, on the drifting music, on the descending blanket of dusk. To allow contentment to spread within, that he is where he wants to be, not in Jerusalem for a noisy Shabbat with his roommates and the girls they met from the School for Overseas Students, the pickup scene they will all flock to later, downtown. And not in Boston where he wouldn't be having Shabbat at all.

He is hungry. His breath is not holding his attention. He tastes the bland cottage cheese and the doughy roll he managed to down before walking over, wishes he had a candy bar. And then there is the German girl with her blue eyes and expert Hebrew wanting to know where he was going, probably doing penance for her SS grandparents, or a proselytizer wanting to convert him. Interlopers, they can't leave the Jews alone, even in their own country. As if the Crusades and the Inquisition weren't enough. And the old lady at Mrs. Baghdadi's. He was ripped off, should have bargained, when will he learn that in this country everything is open to negotiation?

He opens his eyes. His pants are damp. The courtyard is a bluish black. At the edge of the property is a bench sitting amid tangled vines. How could he have missed it?

He dries the seat of his pants as best he can and walks to the bench. It's stone, and cold, the vines reaching as if trying to touch it, but it's better than the ground. The sky is turning to night. From where he sits the synagogue is disappearing into darkness.

In his dream the men are singing *L'cha Dodi*. There are fifteen or twenty of them, all old, sitting in the semicircle of chairs. When, at the last stanza, they stand and turn to the door to bow and welcome the Sabbath Bride, she comes in, still in her knee socks and skirt and the orange jacket. Her yellow hair gives off a shimmering light, and she smiles, radiant—Meira, they call her, *radiance*—and while they sing, she moves to the center, next to the ark, and takes off her clothes. First the jacket, then the skirt, then a pair of pants hidden beneath, then the sweater, the shirt, the undershirt, the two pairs of underpants, the knee socks, a second set inside them, and last, slipping out of her, the two tampons, pristine and smooth and white. At that, the men finish the song and move en masse, graceful and slow, as if in a ballet, and surround her, their eyes closed, their faces turned upward, and inhale slowly and deeply. She is a vapor, a white wind, a genie uncorked, floating inside the circle, and the men stand, enraptured, breathing in again and again until they have taken in all there is, and all that's left of her are the clothes lying in an orange heap on the floor.

He opens his eyes. The courtyard is black. He is horrified. The European—what European? the German!—as the Sabbath Bride! What is she doing in his dream, in his Shabbat, in the most unsullied synagogue in Safed! She has no right. The Nazi, the Jew-killer, masquerading as the messenger of Shabbat! She has polluted his mind; worse, she is standing naked before the most pious of men, men who'd sooner die than have to look at an unclothed woman.

His hands are numb, and he rubs them together, then runs them over his face. And there, again, he sees, under his palms, the heap of clothes, the naked girl—soft, white, blond. The dream is continuing but now is no longer a dream but a living thing, and he cannot stop watching. The men are smiling now at the girl, who is not vapor but flesh. She begins to dance, a slow undulating movement in the center of the circle, revealing herself, parting her legs, and the men stare, breathless, then begin to touch themselves through their clothes, their hands moving up and down, up and down, preparing to enter her.

He is appalled; he has to stop the dream, stop the reel! He gets up from the bench and shakes his head violently from side to side, then his hands, as if he might shake the girl loose, send her flying, then makes for the gate, groping along spindly vines, a thin tree, trips once, twice, hits something hard with his foot. A stone wall. He feels his way, finds the entrance, pushes himself out onto the path leading to the street.

Light. He stops, catches his breath. Shadows move in the windows of the buildings. He has no idea what time it is. Under a streetlamp he checks his watch, four-forty, not possible, the time he arrived at the synagogue, listens for ticking. Silence. He hurries back to Mrs. Baghdadi's. The front door is unlocked. In the hall he smells not cinnamon and cumin but roasted meat, sweet peppers, apples. He is famished. But whoever ate and whenever the meal was, it is now long since over because the apartment is dark. If he is alone in his room he will eat another roll or one of the borekas, it will help him sleep.

But he is not alone. Two of the other beds are taken. They have been pushed together, the blankets spread across both— two men, two women, one of each, he has no idea, because it is too dark to tell. He goes out, finds his way to the toilet. There is no light. He does his business, washes his hands and face, returns, and in his clothes, lies down on his bed. Something cushiony meets his face. A blanket. He takes off his shoes, his jacket, his pants, shoves them under the bed with his backpack, and covers himself. After a few minutes he feels himself growing calmer, beginning to drift off, his terrible dream receding. Though all night he is stirred out of sleep again and again by the murmuring of coupling, unidentifiable sounds neither high nor low, three, four, five times, rising from the other side of the room.

They are gone. And so is his backpack.

In the bright light of morning he finds his pants under his bed, checks the pockets. His wallet is there, the contents intact. His apartment key is safe, mixed in with his change.

He is hungry. In his jacket pocket he finds a package of peanuts and eats them quickly, washes away the dryness with water cupped in his hand at the bathroom sink. He smoothes back his hair, searches for toothpaste, finds none and rinses his mouth again.

Outside, the sky is winter white, and it's late; everywhere, the morning services have already begun. He checks his watch, then remembers, hurries off in the direction of the Joseph Caro and the Ari. The trip needn't be a total loss, surely they are fine places, who is he to judge. But as he nears the street he should turn down, he finds himself walking in another direction, toward Eliyahu. He'll just check; maybe they don't meet Friday night, have only a morning minyan. *Hidden, obscure,* Aryeh whispered.

He takes the last part of the street in a run, can see into the courtyard and through the windows, and yes! there is movement inside. He is so lucky! Everything is going as it should, even his backpack. He is released from its burden, and isn't that a sign, the material world no longer weighing him down? Confirmation that he's doing what he must, that in Safed he is on the right path.

Outside the synagogue he catches his breath, straightens his jacket, then softly opens the door so as not to disturb. The men are standing in a tight semicircle in front of the chairs, twelve, fifteen of them, their white tallises over their heads. Perhaps it is the silent Amidah. The prayer books are up front. He waits to see the men moving, rocking with their prayers, murmuring. But the men are still, so close together their tallises form a giant curtain.

A rustling, a soft shuffling. There is movement on the other side, someone inside the circle. It is the ceremony, there is an initiate. He can't believe his good fortune, can't wait to tell Aryeh. He was so right to come back.

He tiptoes to the ring of huddled men. One moves a hand, and he glimpses between the curtain of cloth into the opening.

It is she, the girl. She is standing in the middle, a huge tallis over her shoulders reaching all the way to the floor, her eyes closed.

"She is a German!" he shouts. "A child of Nazis!"

The men turn, and he sees her fully now, the skirt, those socks, the orange jacket visible through the white cloth, absurd, preposterous. Even more preposterous than the socks. "How can she be one of them? One of you! You have to be old, you have to be Jewish! She's a proselytizer, a usurper! She took our lives, our histories, now she wants our Path, our Way! She cannot have it!"

"Anyone can have it!" the men shout. "It is open to all! All with a pure heart, all who cleave unto heaven with humility and awe!"

"But she wants to destroy us!"

"Yes!" There are thirty, fifty, a hundred men, with ancient faces and modern faces, bearded and clean-shaven, forty years old and sixty years old and two hundred years old, all merging and blending. "She is your enemy, your hatred! She is everything you despise and judge and fear!"

The floor is shaking, the room loosening from its foundations. It is dark, and the center is spinning. It is the girl, she is transforming, melting, whirling before him. Now she is Mrs. Baghdadi, now the Yemenite proprietor, now an SS man, a Crusader on a white horse swinging a giant cross. She is his parents,

Rabbi Shore, Aryeh, the other Americans at the Institute. "You must merge with *all* worlds!" the voices thunder. "*This* is the unity of One-ness! Not with God but with your enemy. Not with some old man in heaven but with your judgment. With all that you despise and demean and diminish and pity! You must merge with the All That Divides You!"

The girl melts, re-forms, melts again. She is a lion, an eagle, a cyclone whirling red, orange, yellow. The center is a blinding, scorching light. Neal buries his face in his arms. He will be burned and his eyes will be seared.

"Neal! Neal!"

A thin reed amid the thunder. It is she, that accent, that voice. She knows his name and is calling him. She wants to save him.

"Neal! Neal!"

He lifts his head, looks. She is a pillar of flame hurling toward him, a giant furnace. She will take him to the sun—she *is* the sun—and will leave him there.

"Neal!" he hears again, and understands. *Kneel!* She is commanding him to get down.

It is the fury of heaven, and he scrambles to the floor and presses his face into the stone, squeezes his eyes shut and cries into the foundations for mercy, prays he will not be consumed.

There are noises. Buses, car radios. He is on the floor, his skin sticky with dried sweat. A wave of Led Zeppelin floats by. He pulls himself up, looks at the window. Night. Saturday night, the restaurants open, the shops, people selling CDs and silver jewelry from folding tables.

He runs a hand over his hair, then over his face. Stubble, as if days, not hours, have passed. His jacket is torn and his shoes are missing. A bus exhaust belches loudly, there is the powerful squeal of brakes. A charter has parked in front of the courtyard. A large man in a baseball cap motions a parade of middle-aged people down the bus steps and into a line, then leads them up the path and through the gate to the synagogue door.

"'Allo? 'Allo?"

Neal stands in shadow in a corner. The tour guide adjusts his cap, flicks on a light, and motions in his charges. They file in, wait in a cluster in the middle.

"Everyone inside?" the guide booms, his English thick with an Israeli accent. "Come, Mrs. Feld, join us in the center." The door closes, heels clicking on the floor. "Now, this is the oldest synagogue in Safed, built in the 1490s, recently renovated and open to tourists. Most of it was destroyed in the great earthquake of 1837 but parts survived." Someone's flash goes off. A man takes out a handkerchief, blows his nose. The guide glances at the domed ceiling, at the intricate woodwork, and Neal pushes himself farther into the shadow. "The kabbalists founded this one, too," the guide says, his voice echoing in the cavernous room, "just like the others we passed. You see how the ark faces south rather than east? And this one also has the special Chair of Elijah—you see? Back there?" Murmurs, more flashes. "Watch out—if you sit there you'll have a baby within a year."

They laugh, make jokes. *What do they put in there, Viagra? Who wants to go first?* They disperse, pick up prayer books, examine the carved doors of the ark and look at the decorations on the walls, elaborate framed writings, calligraphed letters snaking up the sides and along the bottoms. Neal tries to shrink into the corner. "It was near here, in a cave in Meron, that Shimon Bar Yochai wrote *The Zohar*," the guide says. He's standing by the ark, the doors now open, two ancient Torahs watching. "Thirteen years it took him. The most famous book of mystical teachings, they study it still. Sit, contemplate, study. Union with God, that's what they wanted."

"Sounds like my son who went to India," one woman says, wandering over to the ark. "Last summer." She runs a hand over the velvet covering of one of the scrolls. Neal flinches as if she were touching him. "Now he meditates all day while on our money he's flunking out of NYU."

"Nu? Shammes!" calls the guide, looking around. "Where's the shammes?" He pivots, then lights on Neal, strides over and snaps something in Hebrew, waves at his baseball cap.

Neal sees on a low shelf near the prayer books the box with the cardboard pyramids and lace snippets, goes over and picks it up, hands it to the guide.

"Not me, you fool—to them!" the guide whispers in Hebrew. "Don't you want them to tip?"

Neal shuffles to the Americans and offers the box, his head down. A few take. One woman brushes past him. "Dov," she says, loud, to the guide, "can you ask the janitor where's the bathroom?"

Neal looks at her. The guide barks something to him, and Neal points to the back, a guess, though he is certain he is right. The woman bumps him with her pocketbook on the way; he smells a trail of cigarette smoke.

"How much longer, Dov?" the man with the handkerchief calls. "We're starving." Neal goes back to his corner. He is cold, especially his feet. He looks down. His socks are thinner than he thought, and there are holes.

"A few more minutes," the guide says. "As soon as Mrs. Goodman comes out of the bathroom."

"Oh, that Lynn," someone says from the back. "Everywhere we go, a pit stop."

"You think maybe she's pregnant?" someone else calls out, and everyone laughs, maybe she's been here before, has already used the chair. They have all lost interest in the synagogue except one couple who has been studying the walls, looking at the framed texts. They are standing five or six feet from Neal.

"What do you think it is?" the woman says to her husband, pointing at the frame. "Hebrew? Aramaic?"

"I don't know." He shrugs and tips his head toward Neal. "Ask him."

"He doesn't speak English. And, besides, he's just the janitor."

"Not a janitor," the man says. "The sexton takes care of the place. Like at the shul your father used to go to. They always know."

The woman smiles quickly at Neal, embarrassed, then calls to the guide. "Dov, do you know what this is?" she says, pointing to the frame.

Dov walks over, looks, then beckons to Neal.

Neal doesn't move.

"Come look," the guide tells him in Hebrew. "Tell them what it is."

Neal opens his palms, shakes his head. He doesn't know and can't speak, not in his terrible Hebrew nor in his perfect English.

"Fool!" the guide whispers, coming closer. "Make busy, make it up! They'll tip! This is what they want. To feel they've been near something old, from the very religious! Something real, something true! You understand?"

Neal inches over to the couple. Behind them Mrs. Goodman closes the bathroom door, complains loudly that the light doesn't work.

The couple stand politely at the frame. Neal looks at it. He has no idea what it is. It's long, four, five paragraphs, and it could be anything. He is ignorant, a stupid Jew who knows nothing, understands nothing. He needs twenty, thirty, fifty years before he will understand a single letter.

"Tefila," he mutters. It's a prayer.

"Tefilat ha-derech!" the guide booms, making it up, covering for him. "Prayer for a safe journey. Very good choice, Mrs. Weiss, because now we will continue our journey. Everyone ready?"

They line up like schoolchildren, make jokes about the crazy Israeli drivers, they should all pray good and hard for such a journey. A few talk about dinner, what are they having, Dov— fish? Italian? Someone heard in Safed there's now even Chinese.

Dov goes to the door, to the head of the line. "Shammes!" he calls, and Neal understands that it's for him. He walks over, spots the wooden bowl, picks it up. The guide nods. Neal stands by the door with his head bowed, eyes lowered, as the visitors file out, the bills floating down and landing softly on the bottom, the silence punctuated now and then by the clinking of falling coins.

Joan Leegant

I've been interested for a long time in Jewish religious seekers, especially in young Jewish Americans who go to Israel looking for a more authentic and spiritual Judaism than what seems available in our often sterile American Jewish life. Indeed, having been on the outskirts of such a community myself for two years in Jerusalem, and drawn to religious life at that time for precisely the same reasons, I was, and still am, sympathetic to such seekers. But almost twenty years would have to pass before I could write about it. And then my initial attempts would fail. My characters would be overly earnest, and the stories could never come together. It was only after I tapped into a darker side of that spiritual searching—an arrogance that assumes the right to a sort of instant enlightenment without the long cultivation of knowledge and awe—that a story could come together.

THE VERY RIGID SEARCH

Jonathan Safran Foer

My legal name is Alexander Perchov. But all of my many friends dub me Alex, because that is a more flaccid-to-utter version of my legal name. My mother dubs me Alexi-stop-spleening-me!, because I am always spleening her. My father used to dub me Shapka, for the fur hat I would don even in the summer month. He stopped dubbing me that because I ordered him to stop dubbing me that. It sounded boyish to me, and I have always thought of myself as very potent and generative. As for me, I was sired in 1977, the same year as Jonathan Safran Foer, who is the hero of this story. In truth, my life has been very ordinary. I dig American movies. I dig Negroes, particularly Michael Jackson. I dig to disseminate very much currency at famous discothèques in Odessa. Lamborghini Countaches are excellent, and so are cappuccinos. Many girls want to be carnal with me in many good arrangements, notwithstanding the Inebriated Kangaroo, the Gorgky Tickle, and the Unyielding Zoo Keeper. But, nonetheless, it is evident that my life is ordinary. That is why I was so effervescent to go to Lutsk and translate for Jonathan Safran Foer. It would be unordinary.

My mother is a humble woman. She toils at a small café one hour distant from our home. She says to me, "All day I am doing things I do not like. You want to know why? It is for you, Alexi-stop-spleening-me! One day, you will do things for me that you do not like. That is what it means to be a family." What she does not clutch is that I already do things for her that I do not like. I

listen to her when she talks, and I resist bewailing about my
pygmy allowance. But I do not do these things because we are a
family. I do them because they are common decencies. That is an
idiom that the hero taught me. I do them because I am not a big
fucking asshole. That is another idiom that the hero taught me.

My father toils for a travel agency here in Odessa. It is denom-
inated Heritage Touring. It is for Jewish people, like the hero,
who have cravings to leave that ennobled country America, and
visit humble towns in Poland and Ukraine. My father's business
scores a translator, guide, and driver for the Jews, who try to find
places where their families once existed. Jewish people are at
intervals having shit between their brains. But Jonathan Safran
Foer is not having shit between his brains. He is an ingenious Jew.

Now I will begin the story. My father obtained a telephone call
from the American office of Heritage Touring. They required a
driver, guide, and translator for a young man who would be in
Lutsk at the dawn of the month of July. "Shapka," my father said
to me, "what was the language you studied this year at school?"
"Do not call me Shapka," I said. "Alex," he said, "what was the
language you studied this year at school?" "The language of English," I told him. "Are you good and fine at it?" he asked me. "I
am fluid," I told him. "Excellent, Shapka," he said. "Do not call
me that," I said. "Excellent, Alex. You must nullify any plans you
possess for the first week of the month of July." "I do not possess
any plans," I said. "Yes, you do," he said. "Your grandfather and
you are going to Lutsk."

Now is a befitting time to mention my grandfather. I will
mention him. He has gold teeth, and dubs me Sasha. He toiled for
fifty years at many employments, primarily farming, and later
machine manipulating. His final employment was at Heritage
Touring, where he persevered until several years of yore. But
now he is retarded. My grandmother died two years ago of a cancer in her brain, and my grandfather became very melancholy,

and also, he says, blind. My father does not believe him, but purchased a seeing-eye bitch for him, nonetheless, because a seeing-eye bitch is not only for blind people but also for people who pine for the antonym of loneliness—a word I am unable to discover because that page of my very useful thesaurus has vanished. (And I should not have used "purchased" because in truth my father did not purchase her, but only accepted currency to take her from the home for forgotten dogs. Because of this, she is not a real seeing-eye bitch, and is also mentally deranged.) If you're conjecturing what the bitch's name is, it is Sammy Davis, Jr., Jr. She has this name because Sammy Davis, Jr., was my grandfather's beloved singer.

After telephoning me, my father informed my grandfather that he would be the driver of our journey at the dawn of July. If you want to know who would be the guide, the answer is there would be no guide. My father said that a guide was not an indispensable thing, because my grandfather knew a beefy amount from his years at Heritage Touring. But when my grandfather and I roosted in my father's house that night to converse the journey, my grandfather said, "I do not want to do it. I did not become a retarded person in order to have to perform shit such as this." "I do not care what you want," my father told him. That was the end of the conversation. In my family, my father has become a world expert at ending conversations. So we made schemes to procure the hero at the Lvov train station, on 2 July, 1999, at 15:00 of the afternoon. From there, we would drive to Lutsk and the neighboring villages. "He is looking for the town his grandfather came from, and someone who salvaged his grandfather from the war," my father said. "He may have low-grade brains. The American office informs me that he telephones them every day and manufactures numerous half-witted queries about eating and the hazard of rapid bowel proceedings." Here I will repeat that the hero is a very ingenious Jew.

My grandfather and I viewed television for several hours after my father reposed. We viewed an American program that had the words in Russian at the bottom of the screen. It was about a Chinaman who was resourceful with a bazooka. Amid my grandfather and I was a silence you could cut with a scimitar. The only time that either of us spoke was when he rotated to me during an advertisement for McDonald's beefburgers and said, "I do not want to drive ten hours to an ugly city to attend to a spoiled American."

It made my girls very mirthless that I should be away for many days. I told them all, "If possible, I would be here with only you forever. But we need currency for famous discothèques, yes? I am doing something I hate for you! This is what it means to be in love." But, in truth, that was not the truth. I was electrified to go.

A few days before the hero was to arrive, I inquired my father if I could go forth to America when I made to graduate from university. "No," he said. "But I want to," I informed him. "I do not care what you want," he said, and that is usually the end of the conversation, but it was not this time. "Why?" I asked. "If you want to know why," he said, unclosing the refrigerator, "it is because your great-grandfather was from Odessa, and your grandfather was from Odessa, and your father, me, was from Odessa, and your boys will be from Odessa." "But what if I want my boys to grow up someplace superior, with superior things, and more things?" I asked. My father excavated three pieces of ice from the refrigerator, closed the refrigerator, and punched me. "Put these on your face," he said, "so you do not look terrible and manufacture disasters in Lvov." This was the end of the conversation.

It was agreed that my grandfather and I would go forth to Lvov at midnight of 1 July. This would present us with fifteen hours. It was agreed that my grandfather would wait with patience in the car at the Lvov train station, while I waited on the tracks for the hero, holding a sign that my father had given me: "Jon-fen!" The drive with my grandfather was not made easier by Sammy Davis, Jr., Jr., whom my grandfather required to bring along. "You are being a fool," my father informed him. "I need her to help me see the road," my grandfather said, pointing his finger at his eyes. "I am blind." "You are not blind, and you are not bringing the bitch. It is not professional for the bitch to go along." "It is either I go with the bitch, or I do not go." My father was in a position. Not like the Latvian Home Stretch, but like amid a rock and a rigid place, which is, in truth, somewhat similar to the Latvian Home Stretch.

Notwithstanding that we had a deranged bitch in the car, the drive was also rigid because the car is so much shit that it would not travel any faster than as fast as I could run, which is sixty kilometres per the hour. Many cars passed us, which made me feel second-rate, especially when the cars were heavy with families, and when they were bicycles. My grandfather and I did not say words pending the drive, which is not abnormal, because we have never said multitudinous words. I made efforts not to spleen him, but did sometimes. For one example, I forgot to examine the map, and we missed our entrance to the superway. "Do not become very spleened," I said, "but I made a miniature error with the map." My grandfather punched the stop pedal, and my face became sociable with the front window. He did not say anything for the major of a minute. "Did I ask you to drive the car?" he asked. "No," I said. "Did I ask you to prepare me breakfast while you roost there?" he asked. "No," I said. "Did I ask you to invent a new kind of wheel?" he asked. "No," I said. "How many things did I ask you to do?" he asked. "Merely one," I said, and I knew that he would yell at me for some durable time, and perhaps even punch me. But he did not. If you want to know what he did, he rotated the car around, and we drove back to where I fashioned the error. Twenty minutes it captured. "If you blunder again," my grandfather said, when we arrived at the location, "I will stop the car and you will get out with a foot in the backside. It will be my foot. It will be your backside. Is this a thing you understand?"

We arrived in Lvov in only eleven hours, but the train station was rigid to find, and we became lost many times. "I hate

Lvov," my grandfather said. Lvov is a big, impressive city, but not like Odessa. Odessa is very beautiful, with many famous beaches where girls are lying on their backs and announcing their first-rate bosoms. Lvov is a city like New York City in America. It has very tall buildings, and comprehensive streets and many cellular phones. I have never witnessed a place fashioned of so much concrete. But Lvov is not very impressive from inside the train station. This is where I loitered for the hero for more than four hours. I was spleened to have to loiter there with nothing to do, without even a hi-fi, and when the hero's train finally arrived, both of my legs were needles and nails from being an upright person for such a duration. I would have roosted, but the floor was very dirty, and I wore my peerless blue jeans to impress the hero. I did not know what the hero's appearance would be, and he did not know how tall and aristocratic I would appear. This was something we made much repartee about after. He was very nervous, he said. He made shit of a brick. I said to him that I also made shit of a brick, but it was not that I would not recognize him. An American in Ukraine is flaccid to recognize. I made shit of a brick because I desired to show him that I, too, could be an American.

I held the sign with his name and looked into the eyes of every person that walked past. I was trying to select him. The one with the satchel? No. The one with the red hairs? No. When I found the hero, I was very flabbergasted by his appearance. This is an American? I thought. He was severely short. He wore spectacles and had diminutive hairs which rested on his head like a shapka. He did not appear like the Americans I had witnessed in magazines, with yellow hairs and muscles. In truth, he did not look like anything special at all.

He must have witnessed the sign I was holding, because he punched me on the shoulder and said, "Alex?" I told him yes. "You're my translator, right?" I asked him to manufacture brakes, because I could not fathom him. He spoke very rapidly, and in truth I was making a brick wall of shits. "Lesson one. Hello. How are you doing this day?" "What?" "Lesson two. Is not the weather full of delight?" "You're my translator," he said, "yes?" "Yes," I said, presenting him my hand. "I am Alexander Perchov. I am your humble translator." "It would not be nice to beat you," he said. "What?" I said. "I said," he said, "it would not be nice to beat you." "Oh yes," I laughed, "it would not be nice to beat you also. I implore you to forgive my speaking of English. I am not so premium with it." "Jonathan Safran Foer," he said, and presented me his hand. "I am Alex," I said. "I know," he said. "Did someone hit you?" He examined at my right eye. "It was nice for my father to beat me," I said. I took his bags from him, and we went forth to the car.

"Your train ride appeased you?" I asked. "Oh, God," he said, "twenty-six hours, fucking unbelievable." This girl Unbelievable must be very majestic, I thought. "You were able to Z Z Z Z Z?" I asked. "What?" "Did you manufacture any Zs?" "I don't understand." "Repose." "What?" "Did you repose?" "Oh. No," he said, "didn't repose at all." "And the guards at the border?" "It was nothing," he said. "I've heard so much about them, that they would, you know, give me a hard time. But they came in, checked my passport, and didn't bother me at all." "What?" I asked. "I had heard it might be a problem, but it wasn't a problem." "You had heard about them?" "Oh yeah, I was making shit of a brick." In truth, I was flabbergasted that the hero did not have any tribulations with the border guards. They have an unsavory habit for taking things without asking. I have also been informed stories of travellers who must present currency to the guards in order to receive their documents in return. For Americans, it is best if the guard is in love with America, and wants to overawe the American by being a premium guard. This kind of guard thinks that he will encounter the American again one day in America, and that the American will offer to take him to a Chicago Bulls game, and buy him blue jeans and delicate toilet paper. The other kind of guard is also in love with America, but he will hate the American for being an American. This is worst. This guard knows he will never go to America or meet the American again. He will burgle the American, and spleen the American, only to demonstrate that he can. My father told me this, and I am certain that it is faithful.

When we arrived at the car, my grandfather was waiting with patience as my father had ordered him to. He was very patient. He was snoring. He was snoring with such volume that the hero and I could hear him even though the windows were elevated. "This is our driver," I said. I observed distress in the smile of our hero. "Is he O.K.?" he asked. "With certainty," I said. "But I must tell you, I am very familiar with this driver. He is my grandfather." At this moment, Sammy Davis, Jr., Jr., made herself evident, because she jumped up from the back seat and barked in volumes. "Jesus Christ!" the hero said with terror, and he moved distant from the car. "Do not be distressed," I informed him as Sammy Davis, Jr., Jr., punched her head against the window. "That is only the driver's seeing-eye bitch. She is deranged," I explained, "but so so playful."

"Grandfather," I said. "Grandfather, he is here." I was able to move my grandfather from his repose. If you want to know how, I fastened his nose with my fingers so that he could not breathe. He did not know where he was. "Anna?" he asked. That was the name of my grandmother. "No, Grandfather," I said, "it is me. Alex." He was very shamed. I could perceive this because he rotated his face away from me. "We should go forth to Lutsk," I suggested, "as Father ordered." "What?" the hero inquired. "I told him that we should go forth to Lutsk." "Yes, Lutsk. That's where I was told we would go. And from there to Trachimbrod, my grandfather's village." "Correct," I said. "Where's the dog going to be?" the hero inquired. "What?" "Where's . . . the . . . dog . . . going . . . to . . . be?" "I do not understand." "I'm afraid of dogs," he said. "I've had some bad experiences with them." I told this to my grandfather, who was still half of himself in repose. "No one is afraid of dogs," he said. "My grandfather informs me that no one is afraid of dogs." The hero moved his shirt up to exhibit me the remains of a wound. "That's from a dog bite," he said. "What is?" "That." "What?" "This thing." "What

thing?" "Here. It looks like two intersecting lines." "I don't see
it." "Right here," he said, and I said, "Oh yes," although in truth
I still could not witness a thing. "So?" "So I'm afraid of dogs." I
clutched the situation now. "Sammy Davis, Jr., Jr., must roost in
the front with us," I told my grandfather. "Get in the fucking
car," he said, having misplaced all of the patience that he had
while reposing. "The bitch and the American will share the back
seat. It is vast enough for both of them." I did not mention how
the back seat was not vast enough for even one of them.

Sammy Davis, Jr., Jr., had made her mouth with blood from mas-
ticating her own tail. Next she converted her attention to trying
to lick clean the hero's spectacles. "Can you please get this dog
away from me," the hero said, making his body into a ball.
"Please. I really don't like dogs." "She is only making games with
you," I told him when she put her body on top of his and kicked
him with her back legs. "It signifies that she likes you." I will
now mention that Sammy Davis, Jr., Jr., is very often sociable
with her new friends, but I had never witnessed a thing like this.
I conjectured that she was in love with the hero. "Are you donning
cologne?" I asked. "What?" "Are you donning any cologne?" He
rotated his body so that his face was in the seat, away from the
bitch. "Maybe a little," he said, defending the back of his head
with his hands. "Because she loves cologne. It makes her sexually
stimulated." "Great." "She is trying to sex you. This is a good sign.
It signifies that she will not bite." "Help!" he said, as Sammy
Davis, Jr., Jr., rotated to do a sixty-nine. "He does not like her," I
told my grandfather. "Yes, he does," he said.

I do not think there was a person in the car that was surprised when we became lost amid the Lvov train station and the
superway to Lutsk. "I hate Lvov," my grandfather rotated to tell
the hero. "What's he saying?" the hero asked me. "He said it will
not be long," I told him, which was a befitting lie. "Long until
what?" the hero asked. "I hate Lvov, I hate Lutsk, I hate the Jew
in the back seat of this car that I hate," my grandfather said. "You

are not making this any cinchier," I said. "What?" the hero asked. "He says it will not be long until we get to Lutsk," I said.

It captured five very long hours. If you want to know why, it is because my grandfather is my grandfather first and a driver second. He made us lost often and became on his nerves. I had to translate his anger into useful information for the hero. "Fuck," my grandfather said. "He says if you look at the statues, you can see that some no longer endure. Those are where Communist statues used to be." "Fucking fuck, fuck!" my grandfather shouted. "Oh," I said, "he wants you to know that that building, that building, and that building, are all important." "Why?" the hero inquired. "Fuck!" my grandfather said. "He cannot remember," I said.

"Could you turn on some air-conditioning?" the hero commanded. I was humiliated to the highest degree possible. "This car does not have air-conditioning," I said. "What?" "I am apologetic," I said. "Well, can we roll down the windows? It's really hot in here, and it smells like something died." "Sammy Davis, Jr., Jr., will jump out." "Who?" "The bitch. Her name is Sammy Davis, Jr., Jr." "Is that a joke?" "No, she will truly go forth from the car." "No, his name." "Her name," I rectified him, because I am first-rate with pronouns. "Tell him to Velcro his lips together," my grandfather said. "He says that the bitch was named for his favorite singer, who was Sammy Davis, Jr." "A Jew," the hero said. "What?" "Sammy Davis, Jr., was a Jew." "This is not possible," I said. "A convert. He found the Jewish God or something." I told this to my grandfather. "Sammy Davis, Jr., was not a Jew!" he said, more on his nerves than I would have conjectured. "He was the Negro of the Rat Pack!" "But the American is certain of it." "The Music Man? A Jew?" "He is certain." "Dean Martin, Jr.!" my grandfather hollered to the back seat. "Get up here! Get away from the American!"

It was pending this five-hour car drive from the Lvov train station to Lutsk that the hero explained to me why he came to Ukraine. He excavated several items from his bag. First he exhibited me a photograph. It was yellow and folded and had many pieces of affixative affixing it together. "See this?" he said. "This here is my grandfather." He pointed to a young man, who I am implored to say appeared very much like the hero. "This was taken during the war." "From whom?" "No, not taken like that. The photograph was made." "I understand." "Well, these people he is with are the family that saved him from the Nazis. He escaped the Nazi raid on Trachimbrod. Everyone else was killed. He lost a wife and a baby." "And how will we find this family?" "We're not really looking for the family, so much as this girl in the picture. She would be the only one still alive. If she is still alive." He moved his finger along the face of a girl in the photograph. "I want to see Trachimbrod," the hero said, "to see what it's like, how my grandfather grew up, where I would be now if it weren't for the war." "You would be Ukrainian," I said. "Like me." "I guess." "Only not like me because you would be a farmer in an unimpressive village, and I live in Odessa, which is very much like Miami." "I want to see what it's like now," he said. "I don't think there are any Jews left there, but maybe there are. The shtetls weren't only Jews." "The what?" "Shtetl. It's like a village." "Why don't you merely dub it a village?" "It's a Jewish word, like 'schmuck.'" "What does it mean 'schmuck'?" "A schmuck is someone who does something that you don't agree with." "Teach me another." "'Putz.'" "What does that mean?" "It's like 'schmuck.'" "Teach me another." "'Schmendrik.'" "What does that mean?" "It's also like 'schmuck.'" "Do you know any words that are not like 'schmuck'?" He pondered for a moment. "'Shalom,'" he said, "but that's Hebrew, not Yiddish. The Eskimos have four hundred words for snow, and the Jews have four hundred words for schmuck."

"So we will sightsee the shtetl?" "I figured it would be a good place to begin our search." "Search?" "For Augustine." "Who is Augustine?" "The girl in the photograph." It was very silent for a moment. "And then," I said, "if we find her?" The hero was a pensive person. "I don't know what then. I suppose I'd thank her." "For saving your grandfather." "Yes." "And I am querying, how do you know that her name is Augustine?" "I don't really. On the back, see, here, is written a few words, in my grandfather's writing, I think. It says, 'This is me with Augustine, 1942.'" "Do you think he loved her?" "What?" "Because he remarks only her." "So?" "So perhaps he loved her." "It's funny that you should think that. I've wondered. He was eighteen, and she was, what, about fifteen? He had just lost a wife and daughter when the Nazis raided his town. It seems so improbable that he could have loved her. But isn't there something strange about the picture, the closeness between them, even though they're not looking at each other? The *way* that they aren't looking at each other. It's very powerful, don't you think?" "Yes." "And that we should both think about the possibility of his loving her is also strange." "How did you obtain this photograph?" I asked, holding it to the window. "My grandmother gave it to my mother two years ago, and she said that this was the family that had saved my grandfather from the Nazis." "Why merely two years ago?" "She has her reasons." "What are these reasons?" "I don't know. We couldn't ask her about it." "Why not?" "She held on to the photograph for fifty-five years. If she wanted to tell us anything about it, she would have. I couldn't even tell her I was coming to the Ukraine." "Why is this?" "Her memories of the Ukraine aren't good. Her shtetl is only a few kilometres from Trachimbrod. But all of her family was killed, everyone—mother, father, sisters, grandparents." "Did a Ukrainian save her?" "No, she fled before the war." "It surprises me that no one saved her family." "It shouldn't. The Ukrainians were terrible to the Jews. At the beginning of the war, a lot of Jews wanted to go to the Nazis to be protected from the Ukrainians." "This is not true," I said. "It is." "I cannot believe what you are saying." "Look it up in the history books. Ukrainians were known for being terrible to the Jews. So were the Poles. Listen, I don't mean to offend you. It's

got nothing to do with you. We're talking about fifty years ago."
"It does not say this in history books," I told the hero. "I don't
know what to say, then." "Say that you are mistaken." "I can't."
"You must."

"Here are my maps," he said, excavating a few pieces of
paper from his bag. He pointed to one that was wet from Sammy
Davis, Jr., Jr. Her tongue, I hoped. "This is Trachimbrod. This is
Lutsk. This is Kolky. It's an old map. Some of the places we're
looking for aren't on new maps. Here," he said, and presented it
to me. "You can see where we have to go. This is all I have, these
maps and the photograph. It's not much." "I promise you that we
will find this Augustine," I said. I could perceive that this made
the hero appeased. It also made me appeased. "Grandfather," I
said, and I explained everything that the hero had just uttered to
me about Augustine, and the maps, and the hero's grandmother.
"Augustine," my grandfather said, and pushed Sammy Davis, Jr.,
Jr., onto me. He scrutinized at the photograph while I fastened
the wheel. He put it close to his face, like he wanted to smell it, or
touch it with his eyes. "Augustine." "She is the one we are looking for," I said. He moved his head to and fro. "We will find her,"
he said. "I know," I said. But I did not know, and nor did my
grandfather.

When we reached Lutsk, it was already commencing darkness.
"Let us eat," my grandfather said. "You are hungry?" I asked the
hero, who was again the sexual object of Sammy Davis, Jr., Jr.
"Get it off of me," he said. "Are you hungry?" I echoed. "Get the
dog away from me, please." I called to her, and, when she did not
respond, I punched her in the face. She moved to her side of the
back seat, because now she understood what it means to be
stupid with the wrong person. "I'm famished," the hero said, lifting his head from amid his knees. "What?" "Yes, I'm hungry."
"You are hungry." "Yes." "Then we will eat," I said. "Good," the
hero said. "One thing, though." "What?" "You should know . . ."
"Yes?" "I am a vegetarian." "I do not understand." "I don't eat

meat." "Why not?" "I just don't." "How can you not eat meat?" "I just don't." "He does not eat meat," I told my grandfather. "Yes, he does," he informed me. "Yes, you do," I likewise informed the hero. "No, I don't." "Why not?" I inquired him again. "I just don't. No meat." "Pork?" "No." "Steak?" "No." "Chickens?" "No." "Do you eat veal?" "Oh, God. Absolutely no veal." "What about sausage?" "No sausage, either." I told my grandfather this, and he presented me a very distressed look. "What is wrong with him?" he asked. "What is wrong with you?" I asked him. "It's just the way I am," he said. "Hamburger?" "No hamburger." "Tongue?" "It's very popular in America to be vegetarian. It's very cool." "What did he say is wrong with him?" my grandfather asked. "It is just the way he is," I said.

"What do you mean he does not eat meat?" the waitress asked, and my grandfather put his head in his hands. "What is wrong with him?" she asked. "It is only the way that he is." "He does not eat any meat at all?" she inquired me. "It is very cool to be like that in America," I told her. "Everyone is that way." "Sausage?" she asked. "No sausage," my grandfather said. "Maybe you could eat some meat," I suggested to the hero, "because they do not have anything that is not meat." "Don't they have potatoes or something?" he asked. "Do you have potatoes?" I asked the waitress. "You only receive a potato with the meat," she said. I told the hero. "Couldn't I just get a plate of potatoes?" "What?" "Couldn't I get two or three potatoes, without meat?" I asked the waitress, and she said she would go to the chef and inquire him. "Ask him if he eats liver," my grandfather said.

The waitress returned and said, "Here is what I have to say. We can make concessions to give him two potatoes, but they are served with a piece of meat on the plate. The chef says that this cannot be negotiated. He will have to eat the meat." When the food arrived, the hero asked for me to remove the meat off his plate. "I'd prefer not to touch it," he said. This spleened me to the maximum. I took the meat off his plate, because I knew that is what my father would have desired me to do, and I did not utter a thing. "We will commence very early in the morning tomor-

row," my grandfather said. "Let me inspect at his maps." I asked
the hero for the maps. As he was reaching into his side bag, he
kicked the table, which made his plate move. One of the potatoes
descended to the floor. When it hit the floor it made a sound.
Plomp. It rolled over, and then was inert. My grandfather and I
examined each other. I did not know what to do. "A terrible
thing has occurred," my grandfather said. The hero viewed the
potato on the floor. It was a dirty floor. It was one of his two potatoes. "This is awful," my grandfather said quietly, and moved his
plate to the side. "Awful." He was correct. The waitress returned
to our table with the colas we ordered. "Here are . . ." she began,
but then she witnessed the potato on the floor. She put the colas
on our table, and walked away with warp speed. The hero was
still witnessing the potato on the floor. He did not do anything.
We remained silent, and witnessing the potato. Then my grandfather inserted his fork in the potato, picked it up from the floor,
and put it on his plate. He cut it into four pieces, and gave one to
Sammy Davis, Jr., Jr., under the table, one to me, and one to the
hero. He cut off a piece from his piece, and ate it. Then he looked
at me. I did not want to, but I knew that I had to. To say that it
was not delicious would be an overstatement. Then we looked at
the hero. He looked at the floor, and then at his plate. He cut off
a piece from his piece, and looked at it. He ate it and smiled at us.
"Welcome to Ukraine," my grandfather said to him, and punched
me on the back, which was a thing I relished very much. Then
my grandfather started laughing. Then I started laughing. Then
the hero started laughing. We laughed for a long time. Each of us
was manufacturing tears at his eyes. It was not until much in the
posterior that I understood that each of us was laughing for a
different reason, for our own reason, and that not one of those
reasons had a thing to do with the potato. As for Sammy Davis,
Jr., Jr., she did not eat her piece of the potato.

The hero and I spoke very much at dinner, mostly about America. "Tell me about having things that you have in America," I

said. "What do you want to know about?" "You have many good schools for accounting in America, yes?" "I guess, I don't really know. I could find out for you when I get back." "Thank you," I said, because now I had a connection in America, and was not alone. "What do you study?" I asked. "This and that." "What does it mean this and that?" "I don't know, just what it sounds like, some of this, and some of that." "Why do you not inform me?" "Writing, things like that." "It is a good career?" "What?" "Writing." "If you're good at it, I suppose." "Why do you want to write?" "I don't know. I used to think it was what I was born to do." "That is how I feel about accounting." "You're lucky. I don't feel that way anymore." "Now what do you feel like you were born to do?" "I don't know. Maybe writing. But it sounds terrible to say it. Cheap." "It sounds nor terrible nor cheap." "I want to express myself." "The same is faithful for me." "I'm looking for my voice." "It is in your mouth." "The other voice. The voice that can't be spoken." "I understand this." "I want to do something I'm not ashamed of," he said. "Something you are proud of, yes?" "Not even. I just don't want to be ashamed." "If I may partake in a different theme: How much currency would an accountant receive in America?" "I'm not sure. A lot, I imagine, if he or she is good." "She!" "Or he." "Are there Negro accountants?" "There are African-American accountants. You don't want to use that word, though, Alex." "And homosexual accountants?" "There are homosexual everythings. There are homosexual garbage men." "How much currency would a Negro homosexual accountant receive?" "You shouldn't use that word." "Which word?" "The one before homosexual." "What?" "The N-word. Well, it's not *the* N-word, but—" "Negro?" "Shhh!" "I dig Negroes." "You really shouldn't say that." "But I dig them all the way. They are premium people." "It's that word, though. You shouldn't say the N-word." "Negro?" "Please." "What's wrong with Negroes?" "Shhh!" "How much does a cup of coffee cost in America?" "Oh, it depends. Maybe one dollar." "One dollar! This is like giving it for free! In Ukraine one cup of coffee is five dollars!" "Oh, well, I didn't men-

tion cappuccinos. They can be as much as five or six dollars." "Cappuccinos," I said, elevating my hands above my head, "there is no
maximum! What about the girls in America?" "What about them?"
"They are very informal with their vaginas, yes?" "You hear
about girls like that, but nobody I know has ever met one of
them." "Are you carnal very often?" "Are you?" "I inquired you.
Are you?" "Are you?" "I inquired headmost. Are you?" "Not
really." "What do you intend by 'not really'?" "I'm not a priest,
but I'm not John Holmes, either." "I know of this John Holmes." I
lifted my hands to my sides. "With the premium penis." "That's
the one," he said, and laughed. I made him laugh with my funny.
"In Ukraine, everyone has a penis like that." He laughed again.
"Even the women?" he asked. "You made a funny?" I asked.
"Yes," he said. So I laughed. "Do you think the women in Ukraine
are first-rate?" "I haven't seen many since I've been here." "Do
you have women like this in America?" "There's at least one of
everything in America." "Do you have many motorcycles in
America?" "Of course." "And fax machines?" "Yes, but they're
very passé." "What does it mean 'passé'?" "They're out of date.
Paper is so tedious." "Tedious?" "It makes you fatigued." "I
understand what you are telling me, and I harmonize. I would not
ever use paper. It makes me a sleeping person. Do most young
people have impressive cars in America? Lotus Esprit V8 twin tur-
bos? DeLorean DMC-12s?" "I certainly don't. I have a piece-of-
shit Honda." "It is brown?" "No, it's an expression." "How can
your car be an expression?" "I have a car that is like a piece of
shit. You know, it stinks like shit, and looks shitty." "And if you
are a good accountant, you could buy an impressive car?"
"Absolutely." "What kind of wife would a good accountant
have?" "Who knows?" "Would she have rigid tits?" "I couldn't
say for sure." "Probably, although?" "I guess." "I dig this. I dig
rigid tits." "But there are also accountants who have ugly wives.
That's just the way it works." "If John Holmes was a first-rate
accountant, he could have any woman he would like for his wife,
yes?" "Probably." "My penis is very big." "O.K."

After dinner, we drove back to the hotel. It was an unimpressive hotel. When we unclosed the door to the hero's room, I could perceive that he was distressed. "It's fine," he said, because he could perceive that I could perceive that he was distressed. "Really, it's just for sleeping." "You do not have hotels like this in America!" I made a funny. "No," he said, and he was laughing. We were like friends. "Make sure you secure the door," I told him. "I do not want to make you a petrified person, but there are many dangerous people who want to take things without asking from Americans, and also kidnap them. Good night." The hero laughed again, but he laughed because he did not know that I was very serious.

"Come on Sammy Davis, Jr., Jr.," my grandfather called to the bitch, but she would not leave the hero's door. "Come on!" he bellowed, but she would not dislodge. I tried to sing to her, which she relishes, especially when I sing "Billie Jean Is Not My Lover," by Michael Jackson. But Sammy Davis, Jr., Jr., only pushed her head against the door to the hero's room. I knocked on the door, and the hero had a toothbrush in his mouth. "Sammy Davis, Jr., Jr., will manufacture Zs with you this evening," I told him, although I knew that it would not be successful. "No," he said, and that was all. "She will not depart from your door," I told him. "Then let her sleep in the hall." "But she is compassionate," I said. "Listen," the hero said. "If she needs to sleep in the room, I'll be happy to sleep in the hall. But if I'm in the room, I'm alone in the room." "Perhaps you could both sleep in the hall," I suggested.

After we left the hero and the bitch to repose—hero in room, bitch in hall—my grandfather and I went downstairs to the hotel bar for drinks of vodka. It was my grandfather's notion. In truth, I was a petite amount terrified of being alone with him. "He is a good boy," my grandfather said. I could not perceive if he was inquiring me, or tutoring me. "He seems good," I said. "We should try inflexibly to help him." "We should," I said. "I would like very much to find Augustine," he said. "So would I." That was all the talking for the night. We had three vodkas each and watched the weather report on the television at the bar, and then we went up to our room. "I will repose on the bed, and you will repose on the floor," my grandfather said. "Of course," I said. We had spent the day thinking what the hero's grandfather did during the war. That night—my grandfather on the bed, me on the floor—there was a new question: what did *my* grandfather do during the war?

The alarm made a noise at six of the morning. "Go get the Jew," my grandfather said. "I will loiter downstairs." "Breakfast?" I asked. "Oh," he said, "let us descend to the restaurant and eat breakfast. Then you will get the Jew." "What about his breakfast?" "They will not have anything without meat, so we should not make him an uncomfortable person." "You are smart," I told him. When we roosted at the restaurant my grandfather said, "Eat very much. It will be a long day, and who could be certain when we will eat next?" For this reason we ordered three breakfasts for the two of us, and ate very much sausage, which is a delicious food. "Get the Jew," my grandfather said, when we had finished. "I will loiter with patience in the car."

I am certain that the hero was not reposing, because before I could punch for the second time he unclosed the door. He was already in clothing. "Listen," he said, "what do you say we have a little breakfast?" "What?" "Breakfast," he said, putting his hands on his stomach. "No," I said, "I think it is superior if we commence the search. We want to search as much as possible while light still exists." "But it's only six-thirty." "Yes, but it will not be six-thirty forever. Look," I said, and pointed to my watch, which is a Rolex from Bulgaria, "it is already six-thirty-one. We are misplacing time." "Maybe a little something?" he said. "What?" "I'm really hungry." "This cannot be negotiated. I think it is best—" "We have a minute, or two. What's that on your breath?" "You will have one cappuccino in the restaurant downstairs, and that will be the end of the conversation." "What do you mean that's the end—" I put my fingers on my lips. This signified "SHUT UP!"

"Back for more breakfast?" the waitress asked. "She says good morning, would you like a cappuccino?" "Oh," he said. "Tell her yes. And maybe some bread, or something." "He is an American," I said. "I know," she said. "I can see." "But he does not eat meat, so just give him a cappuccino." "What are you telling her?" "I told her not to make it too watery." "Good. I hate it when it's watery." "So just one cappuccino will be adequate," I told the waitress, who was a very beautiful girl with the most breasts I had ever seen. "Would you like to go to a famous discothèque with me tonight?" I added. "Will you bring the American?" she asked. This spleened me. "He is a Jew," I said, and I know that I should not have uttered that, but I was beginning to feel very awful about myself. The problem is that I felt more awful after uttering it. "Oh," she said. "I have never seen a Jew before. Can I see his horns?" I told her to attend to her own affairs and merely bring a cappuccino for the Jew and two more orders of sausage for the bitch, because who could be certain when she would eat again.

"How do we get there?" my grandfather inquired me when the hero and I entered the car. "I do not know," I said. "Inquire Jon-fen," he ordered, so I did. "I don't know," he said. "He does not know." "What do you mean he does not know? We are in the car. We are primed to go forth on our journey. How can he not know?" His voice was now with volume, and it frightened Sammy Davis, Jr., Jr., making her bark. "What do you mean you do not know?" "I told you everything I know. I thought one of you was supposed to be a certified Heritage guide." My grandfather punched the car's horn, and it made a sound: *Honk*. "My grandfather is certified!" I informed him, which was faithful, although he was certified to operate an automobile, not find lost history. *Honk*. "Please!" I said at my grandfather. "Please! You are making this impossible!" *Honk*. *Bark*. "Shut up," he said, "and shut the Jew up!" *Bark*. "You're sure he's certified?" "Of course," I said. *Honk*. "I would not deceive." *Bark*. "Do something," I told my grandfather. *Honk*. "Not that!" I said with volume.

My grandfather drove us to a petrol store that we had passed on the way to the hotel the night yore. A man came to the window. "Yes?" the man asked. "We are looking for Trachimbrod," my grandfather said. "We do not have any," the man said. "It is a place. We are trying to find it." The man turned to a group of men standing in front of the store. "Do we have anything called 'trachimbrod'?" They all elevated their shoulders, and continued to talk to themselves. "Apologies," he said, "we do not have any." "Present me the map," I said to the hero. He investigated his bag. "It's gone. I think Sammy Davis, Jr., Jr., ate it." "Impossible!" I said, although I knew that it was possible. I told the hero to mention the petrol man some of the other names of towns, and perhaps one would sound informal. "Kovel," the hero said, "Kivertsy, Sokeretchy . . ." "Yes, yes," the man said, "I have heard of these towns." "And you could direct us to them?" I asked. "Of course. They are very proximal. Maybe thirty kilometres distant. No more. Merely travel north on the superway, and then east through the farm lands." "Here," the hero said. He was holding a package of Marlboro cigarettes at the petrol man. "What the hell is he doing?" my grandfather inquired. "What the hell is he doing?" the petrol man inquired. "What the hell are you doing?" I inquired. "For his help," he said. "I read in a guidebook that it's hard to get Marlboro cigarettes here, and that you should bring several packs with you wherever you go, and give them as tips." "What is a tip?" "It's something you give someone in exchange for help." "You are informed that you will be paying for this trip with currency, yes?" "No, not like that," he said, "tips are for small things, like directions." "He does not eat meat," my grandfather told the petrol man.

It was already seven-ten when we were driving again. I must confess that it was a beautiful day, with much light of the sun. "It is beautiful, yes?" I said to the hero. "What?" "The day. It is a beautiful day." "Yes," he said. "It's absolutely beautiful." This made me proud, and I told my grandfather, and he smiled. "Inform him about Odessa," my grandfather said. "Inform him how beautiful it is there." "In Odessa," I said to the hero, "it is more beautiful than even this. You have never witnessed a thing similar to it."

"Inform him," my grandfather said, "that Odessa is the most wonderful place to become in love, and also to make a family." "Do you think this is true?" I inquired. "Of course," he said. "I know that it is true." So I informed the hero. "Odessa," I said, "is the most wonderful place to become in love, and also to make a family." "Have you ever fallen in love?" he inquired me, which seemed like such a queer inquiry, so I returned it to him. "Have you?" "I don't know," he said. "Nor I," I said. "I don't think so," he said. "I do not think so, either." "I've been close to love." "Yes." "Really close, like almost there." "Almost." "But never, I don't think." "No." "Maybe I should go to Odessa," he said. "I could fall in love." We both laughed. "Have you ever had a girlfriend?" I asked the hero. "Have you?" "I am inquiring you." "I sort of have," he said. "What do you signify with 'sort of'?" "Nothing formal, really. Not a girlfriend girlfriend, really. I've dated, I guess. I don't want to be formal." "It is the same state of affairs with me," I said. "I also do not want to be formal. I do not want to be handcuffed to only one girl." "Exactly," he said. "I mean, I've fooled around with girls." "Of course," I said. "Blow jobs." "Yes, of course." "But once you get a girlfriend, well, you know." "I know very well."

"Can I view Augustine again?" I asked the hero. He presented me the photograph. I observed it while he observed the beautiful day. Augustine had short hairs. They did not arrive at her shoulders. They were thin hairs. I did not need to touch them to be certain. "Look at those fields," the hero said, with his finger outside of the car. "They're so green." "Tell him that the land is premium for farming." "My grandfather desires me to tell you that the land is very premium for farming." "Look at those people working in the fields," the hero said. "Some of those women must be sixty, or even seventy." I inquired my grandfather about this. "It is not so unusual," he said. "In the fields, you toil until you are not able to toil. My father died in the fields." "Did your mother work in the fields?" "She was working with him when he died." "What is he saying?" the hero inquired, which prohibited my grandfather from continuing. It was the first occasion that I

had ever heard my grandfather speak of his parents, and I wanted
to know very much more of them. What did they do during the
war? Who did they save? But I felt that it was a common decency
for me to be silent on the matter. He would speak when he
needed to speak. So I did what the hero and bitch did, which was
look out the window. I do not know how much time tumbled, but
a lot of time tumbled. "It would be reasonable to inquire someone
how to get to Trachimbrod," my grandfather said. "I do not think
that we are more than ten kilometres distant." "This seems reasonable," I said, because I did not know what to say. "Of course it
seems reasonable," he said. "It is reasonable."

We moved the car to the side of the road. "Go inquire someone," my grandfather said. "And bring the Jew with you."
"Come," I informed the hero. "Where?" I pointed at a herd of
men in the field who were smoking. "You want me to go with
you?" "Of course," I said, because I desired the hero to feel that
he was included in every aspect of the voyage. But, in truth, I
was also afraid of the men in the field. I had never talked to people like that, poor farming people, and, similar to most people
from Odessa, I speak a fusion of Russian and Ukrainian, and they
spoke only Ukrainian, and people who speak only Ukrainian
sometimes hate people who speak a fusion of Russian and
Ukrainian, because very often people who speak a fusion of
Russian and Ukranian think they are superior to people who
speak only Ukranian. We think this because we *are* superior, but
that is for another story. I commanded the hero not to speak,
because at times people who speak Ukranian who hate people
who speak a fusion of Russian and Ukranian also hate people
who speak English. It is for the selfsame reason that I brought
Sammy Davis, Jr., Jr., with us. "Why?" the hero inquired. "Why
what?" "Why can't I talk?" "It distresses some people greatly to
hear English. We will have a more flaccid time procuring assistance if you keep your lips together." "What?" "Shut up."

"I have never heard of it," said one of the men, with his cigarette at the side of his mouth. "Nor have I," said another, and

they exhibited their backs. "Thank you," I said. I rotated my head to inform the hero that they did not know. "Maybe you've seen this woman," the hero said, taking out the photograph of Augustine. "Put that back," I said. "What are you intending here?" one of the men inquired, and cast his cigarette to the ground. "What did he say?" the hero asked. "We are searching for the town Trachimbrod," I informed them, and I could perceive that I was not selling like hotcakes. "I told you, there is no place Trachimbrod." "So stop bothering us," one of the other men said. "Do you want a Marlboro cigarette?" I proposed, because I could not design anything else. "Get out of here," one of the men said. "Go back to Kiev." "I am from Odessa," I said, and this made them laugh with very much violence. "Then go back to Odessa." "Can they help us?" the hero inquired. "Do they know anything?" "Come," I said, and we walked back to the car. I was humbled to the maximum. "Come on, Sammy Davis, Jr., Jr.!" But she would not come, even though the smoking men harassed her. There was merely one option remaining. "Billy Jean is not my lover." The maximum of humbling was made maximumer.

"What in hell were you doing uttering English!" I said. "I commanded you not to speak English! You understood me, yes?" "Yes." "Then why did you speak English?" "I don't know." "You don't know! Did I ask you to prepare breakfast?" "What?" "Did I ask you to invent a new kind of wheel?" "I don't—" "I asked you to do merely one thing, and you made a disaster of it!" "I just thought it would be helpful." "But it was not helpful. You contaminated everything!" "Sorry, I just thought, the picture—" "I will do the thinking. You will do the silence." "I'm sorry." "I am the one who is sorry! I am sorry that I brought you with me on this journey!"

I was very shamed by the manner of how the men spoke to me, and I did not want to inform my grandfather of what occurred, because I knew that it would shame him also. But when we returned to the car, I realized that I did not have to inform him a thing. If you want to know why, it is because I first had to move him from his repose. "Grandfather," I said, touching his arm. "Grandfather." "Anna?" "No, Grandfather. It is me, Sasha." "I was dreaming," he said. "They did not know where Trachimbrod is." "Well, enter the car," he said. "We will persevere to drive, and search for another person to inquire."

We ferreted many other people to inquire, but in truth, every person regarded us in the same manner. "Go away," an old man uttered. "Why now?" a woman in a yellow dress inquired. Not one of them knew where Trachimbrod was, and not one of them had ever heard of it, but all of them became spleened or silent when I inquired. We persevered to drive, now unto subordinate roads, lacking any markings. The houses were less proximal to one another, and it was an abnormal thing to see anyone at all. "I have lived here my whole life," one old man said, without amputating himself from his seat under a tree, "and I can inform you that there is no place called Trachimbrod." Another old man, who was escorting a cow across the dirt road, said, "You should stop searching now. I can promise you that you will not find anything." I did not tell this to the hero. Perhaps this is because I am a good person. Perhaps it is because I am a bad one. I told him that each person told us to drive more, and that if we drove more we would discover some person who knew where Trachimbrod was. We would drive until we found Trachimbrod, and drive until we found Augustine. So we drove more, because we were severely lost, and because we did not know what else to do.

It was already the center of the day. "What are we going to do?" my grandfather inquired me. "We have been driving for six hours, and we are no more proximal than six hours yore." "This is a very rigid situation," I said. We persevered to drive. We drove more, farther and farther in the same circles. The car became fixed in the ground many times, and the hero and I had to get out to impel it. "It's not easy," the hero said. "No, it is not," I yielded. "But I guess we should keep driving. Don't you think? If that's what people have been telling us to do?" We drove beyond many of the towns that the hero named to the petrol man. Kolky. Sokeretchy.

Kivertsi. But there were approximately no people anywhere, and, when there was a person, the person could not help us. "Go away." "There is no Trachimbrod here." "You are lost." It was seeming as if we were in the wrong country, or the wrong century, or as if Trachimbrod had disappeared, and so had the memory of it.

We drove more, and then drove more. We followed roads that we had already followed, we witnessed parts of the land that we had already witnessed. We drove in circles, and both my grandfather and I were desiring that the hero was not aware of this. I remembered when I was a boy and my father would punch me, and after he would say, "It does not hurt. It does not hurt." And the more he would utter it, the more it was faithful. I believed him, in some measure because he was my father, and in some measure because I, too, did not want it to hurt. This is how I felt with the hero as we persevered to drive. It was as if I were uttering to him, "We will find her. We will find her." I was deceiving him, and I am certain that he desired to be deceived.

"There," my grandfather said, as darkness was verging, and pointed his finger at a person roosting on the steps of a very diminutive house. It was the first person that we had viewed in many minutes. He arrested the car. "Go." Because I did not know what else to say, I said, "O.K." I said to the hero, "Come!" There was no rejoinder. "Come," I said, and rotated. The hero was manufacturing Zs, and so was Sammy Davis, Jr., Jr. There is no necessity for me to move them from repose, I said to my brain. I took with me the photograph of Augustine, and was very circumspect not to disturb them as I closed the car's door.

The house was white wood that was falling off of itself. As I walked more proximal, I could perceive that it was a woman roosting on the steps. She was very aged, and peeling the skin off of corn. "Leniency," I said, while I was still a petite amount distant. I said this so that I would not make her a terrified person. "I have a query for you." She was donning a white shirt and a white dress, but they were covered with dirt and places where liquids had dried. I could perceive that she was a very poor woman. All of the people in the small towns are very poor, but she was more poor. This was clear-cut because of how svelte she was, and how broken all of her belongings were.

She smiled as I became proximal to her, and I could see that she did not have any teeth. Her hairs were white, her skin had brown marks, and her eyes were blue. She was not so much of a woman, and what I signify here is that she was very petite, and appeared as if she could be obliterated with one finger. "Leniency," I said, "I do not want to pester you—" "How could anything pester me on such a beautiful evening?" "Yes, it is beautiful." "Where are you from?" she asked. This shamed me. I rotated over in my head what to manufacture. "Odessa." She put down one piece of corn and picked up another. "I have never been to Odessa," she said, and moved hairs that were in front of her face to behind her ear. It was not until this moment that I perceived how her hairs were as long as her. "You must go there," I said. "I know. I know I must. I am sure there are many things that I must do." "And many things that you must not do also." I was trying to make her a sedate person, and I accomplished. She laughed. "You are a sweet boy." "Have you ever heard of a town dubbed Trachimbrod?" I inquired. "I was informed that someone proximal to here would know of it." She put her corn on her lap. "What?" "I do not want to pester you, but have you ever heard of a town dubbed Trachimbrod?" "No," she said, picking up her corn and removing its skin. "I have never heard of that." "I am sorry to have confiscated your time," I said. "Have a good day." She presented me with a sad smile.

I commenced to perambulate away, but I felt so awful. What would I inform the hero when he was no longer manufacturing Zs? What would I inform my grandfather? For how long could we fail until we surrendered? Darkness was near, and I felt as if all the weight was residing on me. There are only so many times that you can utter "It does not hurt" before that begins to hurt even more than the hurt. Not-truths hung in front of me like fruit. Which could I pick for the hero? Which could I pick for my grandfather? Which for myself? Then I remembered that I had the photograph of Augustine, and, although I do not know what it was that coerced me to do it, I rotated back around and exhibited the photograph to the woman. "Have you ever witnessed anyone in this photograph?"

She examined it for several moments. "No."

I do not know why, but I inquired again. "Have you ever witnessed anyone in this photograph?"

"No," she said again, although this second *no* did not seem like a parrot, but like a different variety of "no."

"Have you ever witnessed anyone in this photograph?" I inquired, and this time I held it very proximal to her face.

"No," she said again, and this seemed like a third variety of "no."

I put the photograph in her hands. "Have you ever witnessed anyone in the photograph?"

"No," she said, but in her "no" I was certain that I could hear, Please persevere. Inquire me again.

So I did. "Have you ever witnessed anyone in the photograph?"

She moved her thumbs over the faces, as if she were attempting to erase them. "No."

"Have you ever witnessed anyone in the photograph?"

"No," she said, and she put the photograph on her lap.

"Have you ever witnessed anyone in the photograph?" I inquired.

"No," she said, still examining it, but only from the angles of her eyes.

"Have you ever witnessed anyone in the photograph?"

"No."

"Have you ever witnessed anyone in the photograph?"

"No," she said. "No."

I saw a tear descend to her white dress.

"Have you ever witnessed anyone in the photograph?" I

inquired, and I felt cruel, I felt like an awful person, but I was certain that I was performing the right thing.

"No," she said, "I have not. They all look like strangers."

Darkness was amid us. I perilled everything. "Has anyone in this photograph ever witnessed you?"

"I have been waiting for you for so long."

I pointed to the car. "We are searching for Trachimbrod."

"Oh," she said, and she released a river of tears. "You are here. I am it."

Jonathan Safran Foer

People sometimes ask me where the idea for the voice of Alex came from. If I knew where such things came from, I would always be there, instead of here. The truth is, I don't know. I never met anyone like Alex, and I don't remember being inspired by anything I'd seen or read. I don't even remember trying to create him. Which is not to say that his voice came in some beautiful, inspirational flash. No. It was much more mundane than that. Like most important things in my life, it came unexpectedly. I sat down and started to write like him. Soon enough, I was speaking like him. I've spent the time since trying to shake him.

"The Very Rigid Search" is a cobbling together of passages from my novel Everything Is Illuminated. *Before I wrote the book, I never considered myself someone to whom Judaism was important. And I suppose I still don't consider myself particularly Jewish. (Actually, the whole notion of "considering myself" at all is fairly new to me, and still feels somewhat false and ridiculous.) So if I learned any great lesson with the writing of the novel, it was that you can be wrong about who you think you are. Because when I look over the book, I see writing of a very Jewish person.*

GOODBYE, EVIL EYE

Gloria DeVidas Kirchheimer

It is not common knowledge that a woman sailed with Christopher Columbus. There are references to her in the peculiar melange of languages Columbus sometimes used in his diaries. This from a marginal note in his second Viaje: "*Et mulia tiene moltos sognos* [cares or dreams?] *sed mare* [or *madre*—ms. unclear] *non fecit.*" Perhaps she was of noble family, in hiding because of her religion (Jewish) or her pregnancy or both.

In the manner of Anastasia, women have come forward over the centuries, claiming to be descended from Columbus and his mysterious companion. With the exception of one Eli Matarasso, formerly of Izmir, Turkey, and later of Astoria, Queens, no other male has made this claim.

Flora Maimon had been born a Bar-David in Alexandria, Egypt. The official on Ellis Island, hearing the name Bar-David, wrote it as Bar *Doved* (having heard a little Yiddish in his time). The French word for dove is *colombe*, and one can only conjecture that Flora, a woman of great beauty and culinary prowess, did not fail to note the singular coincidence between the bird and the explorer. She had been primed by Arab fortune-tellers to believe that she was a princess and would cross the sea, as she had in another life, accompanied by an admiral. She had indeed crossed the sea, accompanied by a porcelain salesman, her husband Salvo Maimon. Perhaps while correcting the spelling of her maiden name, Flora showed the harried official the tiny cruciform scar in the crook of her left elbow, a small disfiguration with calligraphic indentations at each of the four extremities (north, south, east, etc.).

Her daughter Louise also bore this mark and assumed that, like buck teeth, it was a hereditary flaw. Flora had not revealed the scar's probable significance, this being one of the many mysteries Sephardic young women were expected to unravel through their own efforts.

Louise Maimon grew up surrounded by innuendo, learning to translate almost before she could speak. Her mother's invitation to a guest to loosen his necktie could be translated as: "Louise, open the window, I am dying of the heat." If Salvo said to Louise, "Correct me if I'm wrong," it meant that any disagreement between father and daughter would seriously undermine the very foundation of Jewish life and might well be the leading cause of heart attacks in Nassau County.

All of Louise's childhood illnesses were attended by the evil eye ritual administered by her mother. Who can say that it was not effective? Chicken pox and measles had left no trace on that olive-skinned, slightly surly countenance. Sitting at her daughter's bedside and clutching an ounce of salt in her right hand, Flora would recite her incantation, a mixture of begats and blessings, partly in Hebrew and partly in Ladino, the ancestral language still spoken in the Maimon home. If the spell was working, Flora found herself yawning uncontrollably. While Louise mimicked and giggled, Flora would continue to wave her hand over her daughter's head, never missing a word and smiling occasionally through her yawns. The incantation over, Louise was forced to endure the application of a little salt to her palate while the rest was thrown away over her left shoulder.

Once, during her freshman year, Louise made the mistake of enacting the ritual for the amusement of her friends in the NYU cafeteria. She poured a handful of salt from the greasy salt cellar and proceeded to wave her hand about, reciting whatever she could recall. To her astonishment she found herself yawning violently. Spilling the salt all over her advanced calculus book, she vowed never again to attempt the demonstration.

At thirty, Louise knew her family considered her a failure: no husband nor any prospects of one, and no hobbies. Recently she had dropped out of graduate school, the only woman in a doctoral program in mathematics, and was working intermittently for a public opinion firm.

One evening, while amusing herself with square roots and round numbers, she received an excited call from her father. He was phoning from Long Beach, Long Island, where her parents had a modest summer home. Her cousin Eliot would be arriving from California for a short visit the following Friday, and her father wanted Louise to come out to the house so she could drive them all to the airport to pick him up. Eliot had said he was coming "on urgent family business."

"Is it Eliot or his brother who's in genetic engineering?" she asked. "You know, cloning hardboiled eggs with our tax money?"

"This is America," her father said angrily. "People have opportunities here. You never had to walk barefoot to school like I did."

"Calm down, Dad. I'll be there."

Having met Eliot and his older brother Steve when they were all children, Louise was moderately curious about her relatives in California, of whom there were many. She visualized the two branches of the Maimon family on opposite coasts, keeping an entire continent in check between them. Her aunt Helen, Eliot and Steve's mother, was purportedly unstable because of her Lithuanian ancestry. According to family lore, she had led a "fast life" before her marriage. She and Salvo's brother Marco had eloped and, soon after, she gave birth "prematurely" to Steve. Aside from enjoying vacations without her husband, sign enough of mental illness, Helen's personality lacked what the Sephardim called *pimienta*, or pepper. She wore harlequin-shaped eyeglasses and continued to hope, after more than thirty years, that working with Chicano ladies would endear her to the Maimon family.

To Louise's father, California signified madness and blood. People who barbecued all day and drove 100 miles per hour on their freeways and who buried their pets with benefit of clergy were bound to be mad. Blood, on the other hand, meant family, and family was holiness. To Salvo, the shortest distance between New York and California was the number of relatives one could count on for accommodations. Blood was not always a guarantee of amity, however. During his brother Marco's last visit, the two men had nearly assaulted each other over the privilege of picking up the check at the International House of Pancakes. Each had flung upon the table an awesome wad of bills; Salvo's face turned purple, his veins stood out, a veritable Noh mask of rage. Each brother had cursed the other in his zeal to convey the depth of his familial passion, but the proprietor intervened and the check was split.

How long was her cousin staying, Louise asked as she drove to the airport on Friday.

"These people don't tell you anything," Flora said.

"It's not nice to ask," Salvo said. "We can't chase him out of the house."

"Perhaps he would prefer a hotel," Louise suggested, thinking of the cramped house by the sea.

"Out of the question," her father said crisply. "It's not proper." Or, what would they say in California if we let him stay in a hotel? "Too bad my brother couldn't come too."

"Thank God," Flora said, sotto voce. "Marco would drive your father crazy. Californians have a different mentality."

At the airport, Salvo ran from one computer screen to another looking for information on the arrival of the flight. "Nobody gives you the right time of day," he fumed after failing to locate what he was looking for. "I always knew Pan Am was a lousy airline."

"But you said it was TWA," Louise said, checking the screen again. She dragged her parents off to the gate where passengers were just being discharged.

"Steve! Steve!" Salvo waved a frantic all-clear signal to a young man who had just emerged.

"*Steve?*" Louise said. "Eliot's brother? You told me Eliot was coming. Didn't Dad say Eliot was coming?"

"How can Eliot come?" her father called over his shoulder while pushing his way forward. "He's doing work for the government."

Steve—what was it Louise had been told about him, years ago? That he was a "drifter," because with a master's in sociology he had become a vegetarian, a day-care teacher, then a salesman for massage equipment. She had no idea what he was doing now. She knew that he had once been picked up for vagrancy because he was taking a walk on the road at night near his home. In California, it was understood that unless you had a dog, you did not walk.

Louise's first impression of her cousin was one of restrained ferocity. Perhaps it was his complexion, so unevenly dark that she could imagine him stubbornly sitting outdoors in the Sierras and letting the winds lash at him. No resemblance to anyone in the family, she decided. Good-looking for a cousin.

"You won't believe this," Louise said, maneuvering the car out of the lot, "but I was told your brother was coming."

"Eliot? He's busy making germs for the Pentagon."

Salvo slapped his nephew on the back. "What a sense of humor, just like your old man. No left turn here."

Seeing the sign pointing away from the city, Steve said he had made a hotel reservation.

"We'll cancel it," Salvo said.

"Besides, I bet you haven't had good Sephardic food in years," Flora said.

The party line, Louise thought. "How long are you staying?" She figured she would be doing her parents a favor by asking. "There's a lot to see."

"I'm just here for the weekend. I came for a particular reason. I want to see our grandfather's grave."

"There's a good show at the Music Hall," Salvo said.

"Poor kid," Flora murmured to her husband. "Lithuanians are morbid people."

"I hear you are in the appliance business," Salvo said.

"I used to sell massage equipment for motels. But that was a long time ago. Before I went into medicine." He explained that he was interning at a local hospital near L.A. It was rare for him to have an entire weekend off, but this was important. "I really want to visit your father's grave, Uncle Salvo."

"It's nice to be respectful," Salvo said uneasily as they turned into Oceanside Road.

The house in Long Beach was a far cry from the ancestral home by the Mediterranean, this bungalow facing a bike shop on the boardwalk and a frozen custard stand. No terraced hills or Moorish villas here, just green and pink stucco, split Georgian or nouveau saltbox houses, lawns decorated with reindeer or whitewashed jockeys holding lanterns, and a stretch of formerly genteel hotels now given over to the elderly and the deranged. It was not unusual to see a crone wandering up and down Beech Street in the middle of the night calling for her insurance agent. The great attraction was the sea air which, as everyone knew, cured all maladies. "I hope everyone is breathing," Flora said as she supervised installation on the porch.

"We'd be dead if we weren't," Louise said.

"But we have an eminent doctor with us," Salvo said, jovially, pointing to his nephew.

"Just an intern at North Hollywood General," Steve said. "Now about Grandpa . . ."

Seeing everyone inhaling satisfactorily, Flora retired to the kitchen. Aside from the ocean and the air, Long Beach was a wilderness for her. No friends, no music, no theater. Only dullards dropping in. Of course, she was always prepared. Four pounds of *borekas* happened to be ready at this very moment as well as two trays of *kadaif*, just in case. Certain people she could count on. Leon Habib was sure to make his appearance just at dinnertime. Naturally, she would ask him to stay.

Flora sighed. What happened to those promises made by the Arab fortune tellers of her youth? What good had it done her to be descended from Christopher Columbus? She was lucky if Salvo condescended to take her out in a fishing boat.

On the porch, Steve was attempting to elicit some information about his grandfather. His father Marco had told him so little, he explained. Mostly along the lines of "Grandpa told us never to be fresh to our parents." Marco always added, "Wisdom worth a million bucks," before switching to the latest gossip about who was seen with whom at El Morocco.

"My father may he rest in peace was very wise, no question about it." Salvo tapped his fingers on the table. This boy's curiosity was unhealthy. What did he want to go poking around a grave for, especially one shrouded in bitterness. They had enough bodies in medical school. "How about the Boston Pops in Jones Beach? They are doing a tribute to Régine Crespin."

Louise rolled her eyes. Her father's musical taste stopped with John Philip Sousa, an Ur-American whose music made his chest swell with pride. But in a house where a taste for classical music was usually deemed a sign of a daughter's snobbery, Régine Crespin took the honors. The famous singer was Sephardic—*de los muestros,* one of our people—and was no doubt related to Salvo's childhood friend from Turkey, Alberto Crespin, otherwise known as *peppino,* or cucumber.

"Dad," Louise said firmly, "Steve wants to see Grandpa's grave."

"A few *borekas*?" Flora appeared with a tray.

"It's far," Salvo said. "Hard to get to. It's in Brooklyn."

"I thought it was in Queens," his daughter said.

"Queens, Brooklyn, it's a big place."

"The sun is so hot." Flora fanned herself. "I don't care, but Louise thought we should have an awning."

"Oh yes," Louise said almost automatically. "I'm just dying to have a blue scalloped awning here."

"Her father can't refuse her anything," Flora said fondly.

"Next year, God willing, we'll fix up this place."

"God has nothing to do with it," Louise said. "Macy's has them on sale."

"Is there some secret about where he's buried?" Steve asked. "Can't you just tell me?"

But Louise's parents had risen just then to greet a neighbor on the adjoining balcony.

"They can't tell you much because they don't know," Louise said, taking a perverse delight in Steve's persistence. "Or rather, there are different versions of everything. For instance, my dad will say that he was born in 1927, then another time it will be 1928. Some days the name of the cemetery is Cedars of Lebanon, other times it's Cypress Hills."

Steve looked uncomfortably at his aunt and uncle who had resumed their seats. Salvo was smiling and nodding, Flora was surreptitiously loosening her brassiere to facilitate respiration.

"I paid my respects last month," Salvo said, "but Leon was driving so I didn't pay attention."

"So we should call this Leon," Steve prompted.

"No need," his cousin said. "He is number one moocher and should be turning the corner in exactly five seconds."

"He's an old friend," Salvo said.

"Louise is right," his wife said. "Now we'll be stuck with him all evening." She leaned over the railing. "Yoo-oo, Leon . . ."

Leon Habib: old schoolfellow of Salvo's from Turkey, former U.S. Army major, and present-day miser. He likes to drop in for lunch at the Nahums, for dinner at the Maimons, for coffee at the Bensignors. Everyone vies for his company: Flora because of her reputation as cook; the Soninos because, known as "the Vatican," they feel an obligation to those less fortunate; the Hamaouis because they cheated Leon's family two centuries earlier in Iraq. Everyone complains of his stinginess, the lack of reciprocity (not that they would want to go to his apartment, moldy with bachelor life). Occasionally he brings a minuscule box of chocolate kisses, such as the one he now presents to Flora while welcoming Steve to the bosom ("if I may be so bold") of the family.

"Leon is taking us out to dinner," Salvo announces.

"With pleasure," answers Leon, roaring with laughter.

Salvo says, "You can't take it with you."

"But he can try," says Louise.

"Now, now, young lady . . ." Leon wags his finger. "I knew you when you had a bare bottom. What happened to that boyfriend of yours, the Russian fellow?"

"He got me pregnant and I had an abortion. Then he decided he was gay."

"Mon dieu." Leon blushes. *"Quelle histoire."*

"She's teasing," Flora says. "Have some salad."

Steve's eyes meet Louise's. She blushes. Didn't one of the Ptolemys marry his sister? Cousins were a much healthier combination.

"Your uncle tells me you are in the appliance business."

"Es medico," Salvo says in Ladino as though he were revealing shameful information.

"How come I'm the first doctor in the family? After all, Maimonides was the great healer and our name is Maimon."

"We can't stand the sight of blood," Louise said.

"The name is just a coincidence," Salvo said. "Besides, Maimonides was a radical."

"We are registered Democrats," Flora said, offering round yet another tray of food.

"About that grave . . ."

"Ah yes," Leon said, "if I recall correctly, it is near a fence." Leon was the treasurer of the burial society and spoke with some authority. The society had been formed for the sole purpose of burying its members who, in the meantime, held frequent picnics and boat rides.

"Just follow the highway," Salvo said. "Cypresses of Lebanon. It's closed on Saturdays."

"I'll go on Sunday then. I'll change my flight to a later one."

"Can't you go another time, dear?" Flora asked. "The beach will be so lovely this weekend, according to the weather reports." How would it look, writing to the relatives: *We showed him the sights and then took him to the cemetery?*

"I can't give you the precise location since I am only the treasurer of the society and our records keeper is recovering from his prostate. However, when you get there—it's Cedars of Lebanon—they will tell you." Leon looked at his watch and abandoned his seat with regret. He was due at the next house for dessert.

"What's your hurry?" asked Salvo. "The night is young. You don't mind taking down the garbage, do you?"

It was too early for bed, so the two young people went for a stroll on the boardwalk. Louise wondered if he was seeing anyone. What a pity they were related. "You seem pretty well-balanced for someone from California," she said.

"But you're wondering why I want to spend time at a grave instead of going to hear some jazz with a beautiful cousin, right? I'll tell you why."

When he was pre-med, an angel had appeared to him in a dream and confirmed what he had always suspected: The Maimons were indeed descended from Moses Maimonides, the great physician. In the dream the angel held the caduceus in one hand—that winged staff with the two snakes coiled around it, the symbol of the medical profession—and in the other hand, a jar of yogurt. (Yes, Louise remembered, the pioneer who had brought yogurt to America had been *de los muestros*.) The angel had commanded Steve to found a clinic based on Maimonides' teachings.

"But how did the angel know you were pre-med?" she asked—then caught herself. "Of course, there was no pre-med in Maimonides' time," she added. But they did have mathematics. She thought with sudden nostalgia of infinite and irrational numbers, the glimpses she'd had into charmed quarks and astrophysics.

Louise looked up at the stars. "The Ptolemaic system," she murmured. "Earth as the center of the universe. Ptolemy was also from Alexandria, like my mom." Dreamily she rubbed the scar on her elbow. Steve looked at her. He seemed to understand.

With rain threatening on Saturday morning, Flora suggested that the young people drive to Coney Island to visit their grandmother at the Sephardic senior citizens home, thereby permitting her and Salvo to skip their biweekly visit. The idea was greeted with enthusiasm by Steve who thought that perhaps Nona might know where her husband's grave was.

"She doesn't even know her own son," Flora said, draining her cup of Turkish coffee and peering into the grounds. "My goodness, what do I see?"

"I don't know," Louise said rhetorically, "what do you see?"

"I don't see the sugar," Salvo said, waving his spoon.

"Louise is going to be very lucky." Flora studied the dregs.

"That's what you told me last time, Mom."

"What nonsense," Salvo said. "You call yourselves liberated women? Isn't there any sugar in this house?"

"Louise is going on a trip," Flora said.

"I stopped tripping in high school."

"Make fun," her mother said, "I don't mind."

"Remind me to show you my blue stone," Louise said. "It's supposed to keep the evil eye away from me."

"It seems to be working so far," Steve said.

"Bravo," his aunt said. "I'm glad you understand."

"I just remembered," Louise said. "There's a fortune teller in town. A friend of mine went to her recently. She might be able to locate a grave."

Salvo laughed. "I don't think they work on Saturdays. They probably have a union. Goddam unions." He frowned.

Flora was putting together a parcel for Salvo's mother, the candies Leon had brought and a woolen sweater. Nona would probably complain about the color. "Last time she wanted blue," Flora said, "I brought her blue. Then she said she preferred brown. Tell her this is brown." It was purple.

"You know she can't eat those candies, *chérie*."

"They can't go empty-handed. I don't want to hear that her children neglect her. Let her give the candy to the nurses." The old woman would probably cram everything underneath her mattress.

The veranda of the Coney Island Sephardic Senior Home was lined with aluminum chairs where the elderly sat on warm days, looking out at the ocean. For the visitor, entering was like running the gauntlet. Arms reached out to touch, canes waved imperiously, intimate questions were asked. "Do you have a husband?" "Is your belly fruitful?" And now to Louise, "Are you Shemaria's granddaughter?" Pointing to Steve, "Is he one of us?" (Not, is he gentile? but, is he Sephardic or one of the others, an Ashkenazi?) Followed by Steve, Louise went down the receiving line, smiling (how her parents would have been surprised). "Be healthy," she said in Ladino. "May you live a long time." Hands tugged at her. "I knew your grandfather," a fierce looking man said and Steve gasped with joy. His Ladino was rudimentary but serviceable.

Nona's room faced the sea and the "Cyclone" roller coaster. She was eighty-eight and illiterate. Great tufts of white hair protruded from her ears like antennae. Without turning at their entrance she said in Ladino, "Are you Salvo's wife?"

Louise went around and faced her grandmother.

"Look, Nona, I'm your granddaughter and this is your grandson Steve."

"My grandsons never come to see me. Where is Salvo?"

"He couldn't come, he had work to do," Louise lied.

"You shouldn't work on the Sabbath," Nona said and began

to rock in her chair. Steve had taken her hand but she seemed not to notice. She stopped rocking and said, "They told me he wouldn't come. Bring me a thimble next time."

Louise slowly explained who Steve was.

"His mother is that Lithuanian woman." Nona lapsed into vehement Armenian, perhaps cursing.

A staff worker came in with a tray. "Come on honey, here's your lunch."

"This one stole my package," Nona said.

"She saying I stole her package again? Is this it, sweetie?" She produced a paper bag from a drawer.

"I don't want it. Tell her to throw it away."

"She'll want it later. I'll just set it down here on the shelf." The woman went out.

Nona poured her coffee into her soup. "They left me here to die," she said with satisfaction. "Where is the sweater?" But before Louise could open the parcel she said, "Hide it or they'll steal it. Under the mattress, quick!"

Steve jumped up and did as she asked.

"Why didn't they let me dance at your wedding?" she asked. "I can't walk but I can dance."

Downstairs someone was playing a Greek song on the piano and people were stamping in rhythm.

"Nona," Steve said, "tell me about your husband." He spoke slowly, unsure of his Ladino.

"The wife must obey the husband," Nona said. "It's the law." Suddenly she began to cry. "He was the light of my life. The boys quarreled." Tears were streaming down her face. "I couldn't do anything."

Louise put her arm around her. "We're here now. See, this is Steve. He came from far away."

Nona smiled through her tears. "I knew he would come. It says so in the holy book." She turned toward the window. The roller coaster was descending. She began to rock again. It was clear that there was no point in asking her where her husband was buried.

"Let's go to your fortune teller," Steve said when they got back to the car.

"You? A man of science?"

"Whatever works." There was a slightly mad glint in his eye. The ocean was shimmering like plastic, and shots could be heard from the penny arcade.

Reverend B. Jonas practiced her ministry at the Church of All Souls on the second floor above the Eclair Konditorei where fortunate members of Central Europe went for *Kaffee und Kuchen*.

A large middle-aged woman ushered them into a small chapel whose walls were covered with wallpaper resembling stained glass. She led them to the back and sat down at a desk facing them. Several drawing pens were hooked neatly into her jacket pocket as though messages from different regions of the underworld were conveyed in specific colors. There was nothing on the desk except a clock and a container of coffee.

"Twenty-five dollars in advance," she said. "Cash or any major credit card. Try and deduct it from your major medical. You come here because your soul is ailing."

After handing over the money, Steve said he wanted to locate a grave since no one seemed to know where it was.

Dr. Jonas closed her eyes. A cat moved across the floor and sat at Louise's feet. She shifted nervously.

"I see an elderly lady in a polyester suit carrying an umbrella. Not a relative, a teacher maybe . . . someone who has passed on."

"I don't know any old teachers," Steve said dubiously.

"I tell it as it is given," the Reverend said sharply, eyes still closed. "There is an old man with a goatee. . . . He greets you."

"Grandpa," Louise breathed.

"He is happy. He has a flower in his buttonhole, a pink—" Suddenly she sneezed. "Excuse me, I'm allergic to roses." She opened her eyes, which were watering, and blew her nose. Resuming, "He is—uhmm—singing." She began a low hum that sounded like "Swing Low, Sweet Chariot." The cat put one paw up on Louise's chair. She shrank back.

"Wait," Dr. Jonas said. "This man, he did not go to his rest in peace. Oh no no. These people at the grave, they are arguing. The priest—"

"Rabbi," Louise said.

"In the spirit world all are ministers of the Lord and if you want a cheap job you all can go next door to the gypsy lady. I tell it as it is given to me. By the way, don't leave your camera in the car."

"Too late," Steve said.

"I see—a hospital. Old man writing. He's got a little black box, shining. A shining . . . it's not clear. Wait—it's in the eyes— it is the eyes. Someone else has his eyes. Is it you, darling?"

"Giving his eyes to science!" Steve whispered. "It all ties in."

"Oh my, oh my. The old man's sons, they are having some fracas. He wants to tell me something. I see a wall. A stone, a stone near a tower."

Steve gripped Louise's hand.

"In the sea there's a tower, in the tower there's a window. . . . At the window she calls to sailors. Oh, why are you seasick, dear?"

Louise swallowed. The ground seemed to be tilting. Salt was on her tongue. "That's from a song," she told Steve. "Nona used to sing it." To Reverend Jonas, "How come you're giving the words in English?"

"In the world of the soul, all languages are one."

Louise took a deep breath.

"Take it easy," Steve said, holding her hand.

"It passes," Reverend Jonas said. "All journeys end. There's that desert again."

"What desert?" Louise asked faintly.

"California," Steve said.

"It's the land of the fair . . . the old man has gone to the land of the fair—Pharaoh."

"Maimonides," Steve said quietly.

Of course. The great teacher had gone into exile in Egypt. Even Louise knew that. Knew the story about the emperor Saladin who had called on Maimonides to attend his captive, Richard the Lion-Hearted. This was one of the few highlights of eight stultifying years of Hebrew school.

Dr. Jonas opened her eyes. "If you want more, it's another twenty-five dollars. I charge by the hour. Maybe you all would like to know which stocks are going up?" Her fingers played temptingly with her pens, but the two cousins were already at the door.

Saturday morning services at the Sephardic synagogue in Long Beach were extremely refined, as befitted the descendants of grandees. To go to the Ashkenazi temple would have been unthinkable. Flora shuddered at their pronunciation and the unseemly emotion of the rabbi, who sobbed while praying.

She settled back in her balcony seat and looked around critically. There was Mrs. Camhi with her green eyeshadow and plain daughter. What a pity Louise refused to join the young adult group here.

The new rabbi walked slowly to the pulpit and folded his hands. Perhaps they were shaking. He was trying hard, one had to say that for him. Always apologizing for being born an Ashkenazi (the congregation had had to take him for lack of qualified Sephardic candidates). But to give him credit, he had recently written an article about Associate Justice Benjamin Cardozo who was *de los muestros*.

"Today," he began, "I should like to speak about the personal habits of the Jew at war. . . ." Flora's mind ran back to her oven: one spinach, one tomato, one leek pie. Enough for a dozen unexpected guests.

". . . The soldier must maintain the highest moral and hygienic standards. The law prescribes that the soldier shall have a place outside the camp wherein he shall attend to his bodily functions. With his gear he shall have a shovel . . ."

What a soothing voice he had. If only he were ten years younger and unmarried.

". . . The personal habits of the soldier of Israel are part of his artillery." Flora unbuttoned the top button of her blouse. She was feeling warm. Politics did not belong in the synagogue.

The rabbi raised his arms impressively. "Contagion can mean disaster." My God, was he talking about venereal disease? Why had Louise broken off with her last boyfriend? "He contaminated me," was all she would volunteer; then she went off to Philadelphia and returned almost emaciated, a fearful reminder of how she had been at sixteen. Anorexia, Louise had called it, a lovely name like that of a Greek goddess, but the ultimate cruelty to a mother.

Down below in the men's section, Salvo was thinking that this rabbi had no style. Speaking about war like a milquetoast. Louise couldn't abide the poor rabbi. But she had strange ideas, expecting a clergyman to be out protesting and sleeping with the homeless. An odd child, his daughter. He remembered her studying "probability" and arguing with him. Salvo laughing and wondering what there was to study. Probability meant that something might happen or it might not. Marriage would shape her up. And never mind love. His brother Marco had been in love and see where that had gotten him.

Love, to Salvo, denoted illicit relationships such as those between business executives and their mistresses. Husbands and wives, in Salvo's vocabulary, should like each other and get along. Marco was so besotted with his wife that for each of her birthdays he had built an addition to their house in Santa Monica. Salvo had seen with his own eyes the wishing well, the sauna, the orchids in the greenhouse, and God knows what.

How misguided this boy was to look for the old man's grave.

Only Salvo's vigilance had prevented disaster when his revered father died. No one had taken the elder Maimon seriously when he announced on his deathbed that he wished to give his body to science, stating it in his will, with a separate clause for the eyes. Never, said Salvo, it was against holy law.

The old man, so orthodox, had become unhinged. Marco had been willing to bargain. "Maybe not the whole body, but just the eyes? It's his last wish." But Salvo had been adamant; if not for him, their father would not now be lying peacefully between two shopping centers in Long Island—or Queens—but would have been chopped in pieces for "science." Science was good, it was important, even the rabbi was talking about it now: technology in war, shovels, trenches . . . but there had to be a limit.

The service over, Salvo folded up his prayer shawl and went to find his wife with whom he got along so well.

The cousins found a restaurant overlooking the water where they could gorge themselves on shellfish, forbidden food to be con-'
sumed, always, with a slight frisson of guilt.

"Another reason for coming east is that I wanted to get a feel for the family," Steve said.

"The great myth of family," Louise grimaced. "What was it like growing up in California?" she asked.

Steve's mother hated California, she learned. His parents quarreled constantly, shouting at each other from opposite ends of the family room where the furniture was arranged for maximum lack of communication. One time when he was very young, his father said something so dreadful to his mother that she clapped her hands over the boy's ears. "I heard it anyway, but I can't remember it. All I remember is that she said he didn't mean it, that he really loved me. As though what he said was some kind of attack on me. That part of it stuck in my mind."

He seemed to be turning morose. To divert him, Louise asked what he was planning to specialize in.

"Family medicine," he said, which struck them both as absurd.

The Cedars of Lebanon straddled the no-man's-land between Queens and Brooklyn, with the Expressway dividing the waves of headstones. It was early Sunday morning. Steve looked pale. "There's something wrong," he said. "I can feel it."

"You're right. It's not open yet. I could have slept another hour." Louise was beginning to tire of his obsession.

"Here's this angel," Steve said slowly. Was he talking to her or to himself? "There's a staff in the angel's hand. He tells me to found a clinic. He's holding a jar of yogurt. That's the part I don't understand."

"Maybe you should start a health food restaurant instead."

At that moment the gates swung open, probably activated by remote control.

The place was immense. Every trade, every lodge had its resting place. Knights of Pythias, Elks, Moose, Friends of Wildlife (how did they get in here?), Oddfellows . . . They continued walking, past the United Jewish Printers, Amalgamated Tailors, Furriers, Leatherworkers, the Association of Jews from Sofia, Monastir, Salonika, Rhodes, Izmir. And then they stopped in front of a black gate with a sign. Home ground for the Sephardic Burial Society.

A tremor went through the young man. "Hey," Louise said and touched his shoulder. Steve's teeth were chattering. She drew him to a nearby bench and made him sit down.

Directly facing the bench was a headstone with a miniature oval photograph propped against it, a young woman in a high-necked dress. The inscription on the stone said, in Ladino, "You are gone but we remember you, Sarina." Sarina had been born on the isle of Corfu. Perhaps she had crossed the Atlantic in a rickety boat, eating nothing but olives and biscuits.

"You know, I realized very early in my life that my dad preferred my brother Eliot," Steve said. "He still hasn't forgiven me for turning down his graduation present, a paid night with a whore. He laughed when I said it was undignified for a descendant of Maimonides. Then he said, 'It's okay, I love you just the same,' and I was reminded of that time I told you about, when he said something my mother didn't want me to hear, years back." Steve shook his head and stood up. "I've tried to remember what it was so many times, but it just escapes me."

They picked their way through paths overgrown with perpetual care and found the grave at last, topped by a nondescript slab, etched with the name in Hebrew and English, date of birth and death. Nothing more. Steve closed his eyes. Louise moved away, leaving him free for whatever revelation might be forthcoming.

After a moment he opened his eyes wide, his mouth twisted. "I remember," he shouted and staggered toward her. "I remember what he said to her. He said, 'You and your brat.' Not his brat. *Somebody else's.*" His voice was hoarse. *"My father was— somebody else—a stranger."*

Soon after Steve's return to Los Angeles, Salvo received an irate letter from his brother Marco, saying that he'd been compelled to tell Steve the truth about his parentage. Besides Helen, of course, Salvo was the only other person who knew the secret. Not even Flora knew.

Marco was not Steve's father. Before he married Helen she had had an affair and gotten pregnant; the father had disappeared. Marco had married her anyway, despite his brother's disapproval.

Marco also had to tell Steve about (may he rest in peace) the old man's thwarted desire to donate his organs to science and accused Salvo of aiding and abetting the boy in his ridiculous search for the grave.

Salvo was furious. So much for the Maimon family motto ("Peace at any price"). Had Marco taken Salvo's advice years ago, he would not have fallen in love and would not have had to bring up another man's son.

The information was given to Louise at the tail end of a phone conversation with her mother about Xavier Cugat, the Latin bandleader known as the king of the conga, rhumba, cha-cha, etc., and his ascension to the ranks of *los muestros,* courtesy of the Sephardic community of Long Beach.

The news about Steve was like the discovery of a new solar system.

Give him time, Louise said to herself. He'll call when he's ready. In the meantime, after several recurring dreams about parabolas and vectors, she decided to return to graduate school. Some dreams were reliable.

"This is your former cousin," Steve said when he finally phoned after a month. "I've learned that angels make mistakes too. Even your fortune teller was taken in." He had started a search for his real father. Also, he was switching from family medicine to psychiatry, a profession unrecognized in the Sephardic enclaves of New York, Los Angeles, and possibly Seattle.

"And what about you?" he inquired. Might she come out for a visit—to relatives?

Something lurched inside her. "Stay tuned for lift-off," she said. It became suddenly clear to Louise that if Steve could investigate the inner workings of the mind, she could explore the outer reaches of the universe, either as an astronaut or, more likely, as a cartographer of outer space. In the meantime there were earthly delights to contemplate, since Steve had promised to stay in touch.

When after a year it became clear that Louise was flying out to the West Coast more often than was healthy, and no other man was spoken about save her thesis advisor, Flora began to allow herself to plan. Surely the union between a California doctor and the putative descendant of Christopher Columbus would merit being recorded in History rather than in the *Long Island Daily Press*.

And it came to pass in one of those wedding palaces off the Sunrise Highway that the rabbi proclaimed in suburban Hebrew the authenticity of the marriage contract drawn up several thousand years ago in the original Aramaic (holding it up for viewing) and now validated in Roslyn Heights. But once the bandleader had ordered all those couples who married for sex, for love, for money, out on the floor, and when he had done with asking for applause for the happy couple (a quick glance at his notes for the names), then blood took over, the blood of the Sephardim. It fired up the instrumentalists, and cowed the rabbi and the small Ashkenazi contingent on the groom's mother's side, and music erupted. The women threw back their heads, and shimmied, while the men, aged but smoldering, stamped their feet provocatively. The Greek guests did their decorous ceremonial dance. There was even a belly dancer, Marco's present, quivering her body as men stuffed dollar bills into her sequined bosom.

Louise's mother insisted that her daughter wear around her neck the hand-shaped talisman, the *hamsa*, she had received from her own mother before coming to America. Within the amulet was a piece of parchment with faded Hebrew lettering. The words, however, would not be Hebrew but Ladino: "*El Almirante estaba enamorado de* . . . [blurred] *mujer, hija de David.*" The admiral loved . . . [?] woman, daughter of David.

Like the compass-shaped scar on Louise's elbow, this was another link to the illustrious explorer, which she would have to discover on her own.

Gloria DeVidas Kirchheimer

I was "doodling" verbally when I set down what I thought was a preposterous premise: that Christopher Columbus had a woman companion onboard during one of his voyages. The statement seemed so intriguing to me after I looked at it that I wanted to explore it. I realized that it reflected one of the primary tenets of Sephardic lore, namely, that Columbus was Jewish. It then seemed appropriate to play out the idea in terms of a specific family. The story enabled me to incorporate many of the various elements of growing up in a Sephardic household that I had always found bizarre, delightful, and maddening.

THE KING OF THE KING
OF FALAFEL

Jon Papernick

Mordechai HaLevi was still very young—only seventeen years old—when his father, Boaz, the King of Falafel, tried to run over his chief competitor with his rusty Toyota truck and was sentenced to three years in prison in the outskirts of Jerusalem.

The King of the King of Falafel had opened business across the busy thoroughfare of King George Street only six months earlier, undercutting the King of Falafel, selling two falafels for the price of one. Boaz told his son that Benny Ovadiah, the newly crowned king, must have been scraping vegetables off the floor of the Mahane Yehuda market and selling them in his sandwiches for such a price.

"He's using rat meat to make his shwarmas. I know it," Mordechai's father said. "How else can a man sell falafels so cheap and still keep the rain off his head?"

"Maybe the angels," Mordechai said.

"The only angel I know is the Angel of Death," his father answered, turning his wedding ring on his thick finger.

The week before his father went berserk, Mordechai was sent across the street to plead with Benny Ovadiah, who was a war hero, saved by golden-winged angels at the Allenby Bridge. He was a religious man and would listen to reason.

Manufactured air blew into Mordechai's face as he entered the gleaming oasis of polished marble and glass where twisting rams horns, bronze water pipes, and wide-eyed *hamsas* hung decorously from the walls. Hungry patrons sat in plush chairs covered with richly embroidered swirling Yemenite stitchwork beneath a sky-blue domed ceiling. They ate from round marble tables that were smoother than ice and whiter than snow. Mordechai wiped his brow, leaving the heat of King George Street behind. Pictures of the great mystics—the Baba Sali, Ovadiah Yosef, and others—were taped on the glass beside the mandate-era cash register that ka-chinged with annoying regularity.

Benny Ovadiah stood behind the counter wearing a large black *kippah* pulled low onto his forehead.

"My father wants you to move away," Mordechai said. "He is the King of Falafel."

"But, I am the King of the King of Falafel," Benny Ovadiah said, throwing a falafel ball in the air and catching it in an open pita.

He was right. His prep men juggled their falafel balls in the air, tapped their tongs on the counter, and sang *Heenay Ma' Tov* as they made their sandwiches. The King of the King of Falafel offered thirty-two different toppings, including thick hummus, zesty tahini, tomatoes, cucumbers, pickled turnips, radishes, olives, eggplant, red peppers, onions, and chips.

"Give this to your father," Benny Ovadiah said, handing Mordechai the fully dressed falafel.

"But when will you leave?" Mordechai asked.

"When the Messiah comes."

When Mordechai returned to the falafel stand to tell his father, he had to shout above the noise of the ancient ceiling fan that clattered like battling swords. His father slammed Benny Ovadiah's falafel against the wall and said, "The fucking Messiah! I'll kill him!"

Mordechai did not love falafels, but he did love his father, so he agreed to run the business while his father was away. With the help of his friend Shuki he secretly planned to drive the King of the King of Falafel out of business to honor his departed father.

Shuki was a juvenile delinquent who did not want to serve

in the army and did his best to convince society that he was unfit to die in Lebanon. He wore a T-shirt that said "Rage," smoked filterless cigarettes, and spat on the street as he walked. He whispered ideas in Mordechai's ear and laughed like a sick braying beast.

They paid a Russian farmer from the north to deliver pork to Benny Ovadiah's back door, but the King of the King of Falafel could smell *treif* a mile away and threw it in the street in front of Mordechai's falafel stand. The flies buzzed above the meat all afternoon until Benny Ovadiah approached Mordechai at the end of the day as he was sweeping the floor. Only an autographed team photograph of the *Betar Yerushalayim* football club hung on the wall next to a yellowing dogeared kashruth certificate.

"Not many customers today," Benny Ovadiah said. "The smell is difficult, the flies are worse."

"It is not so bad," Mordechai said, wondering if Benny Ovadiah smelled of body odor or cumin powder.

"You are losing money. Come and work for me. You can buy cigarettes to send your father in prison."

"I want you to leave," Mordechai said. "Go to Katamonim. We don't want you here."

"You are a punk, but there is hope for you. You honor your father even though he is a maniac. It's a commandment of God."

"But I don't love my neighbor," Mordechai said, sure now that no cumin powder in the world could smell so rank as Benny Ovadiah.

"Leave!" Mordechai shouted.

"When the Messiah comes," Benny Ovadiah said, laughing.

"There cannot be two kings of falafel."

"Why don't you call yourself the King of Shwarma, or the King of *Fuul*, or," Benny Ovadiah said in English, "the King of Fools." He grabbed his rounded belly and laughed again. "Or, maybe, the son of the King of Fools," he said, opening the door to King George Street.

To gain leverage over his enemy, Mordechai stayed open on

Shabbat to take advantage of hungry tourists wandering the empty streets of Jerusalem. For a while, he did a brisk business until the black-hatted Ultraorthodox from Mea Shearim caught wind of it and pelted stones and bags of dung at his falafel stand.

"Go back to Germany and destroy the sabbath," they shouted.

Cars packed with families arrived from as far away as Nahariya, Afula, and Yeroham to savor the delights of Benny Ovadiah's King of the King of Falafel.

"What spell has he put on them?" Mordechai wondered. "What angel watches over him?"

Even his most loyal customer, Reuven the Watcher, walked away from the King of Falafel saying, "Your falafel tastes like sand. I wouldn't feed it to the dead."

Mordechai gave away free samples, concocted the fruit falafel, painted a new bright red sign, shouted down his adversary through a megaphone, and continued to lose business to Benny Ovadiah. He even considered calling himself the King of the King of the King of Falafel, but did not have enough space on his tiny storefront.

Shuki suggested they steal the pita bread that was delivered to Benny Ovadiah's front door hours before the King of the King of Falafel opened for business.

"Falafel without pita is like the Dead Sea without salt," Shuki said.

They were amazed to discover that without his pitas, the King of the King of Falafel did not fold up and blow away. He thrived, in fact. People lined up all along the street, jockeyed for position, and shouted across to Mordechai and his empty stand. Finally a policeman on horseback arrived to calm the crowd, but he too dismounted and joined the hungry line.

"What's going on?" Mordechai shouted to one of the patrons.

"It's amazing," a young girl called back. "He is serving falafel on manna from heaven."

When his father wrote him asking how business was,

Mordechai lied; when he asked after the nudnik who called him-self 'king,' Mordechai said the filthy dog was on the run: "He's in the *mikvah* now, preparing for the Messiah."

"He should drown," his father said.

One day Shuki drank a jar of olive oil and bit into a shwarma at Benny Ovadiah's restaurant. He threw up on the floor right in front of the King of the King of Falafel and screamed, "Bad lamb! Bad lamb!"

But Benny Ovadiah had seen Shuki hanging out with Mordechai and beat him with a broom.

"Don't break your teeth. I'm not leaving," Benny Ovadiah shouted as he brought the broom down onto Shuki's head.

"What about the Messiah?" Shuki said.

"Show me the Messiah."

Frustrated and tired of falafel, they ate hamburgers at the new McDonald's, where Shuki tried to lighten the mood, moving the buns of his burger like the mouth of a hand puppet. "I am the red heifer. I taste better with cheese." And he bit into the burger, laughing.

"I am the pink heifer," Mordechai said, holding his burger. "Cook me some more, please."

"Stupid!" Shuki said, hitting Mordechai on the forehead with the palm of his hand. "Don't you remember from religion class in school where God told the children of Israel to purify themselves?"

"Take a shower," Mordechai said, laughing. "With soap!"

"He told them to sacrifice a red heifer, a pure red heifer with-out blemish or spot, because only the ashes of a red heifer can purify Jews so they can rebuild the Temple." Shuki paused and beat a drum roll on the table. "And-bring-the-Messiah-the-King-of-Israel."

"But there hasn't been a red heifer in Israel in over two thousand years," Mordechai said, remembering the mysterious passage.

"Yes," Shuki said, "that is true. But now . . ." And he began to hum, and then Mordechai joined in and they were singing, "Moshiach, Moshiach, Moshiach!"

They drove out of the city under a starless sky toward the west and the coastal plain. The air became warmer as they descended. Shuki rolled down his window and lit a cigarette. Mordechai fiddled with the radio dial as they drove, finding Jordan Radio in English, then *Arutz Sheva*, the Jewish settlers' pirate station, and finally *Galei Tzahal*, Army wave radio, where they sang out together "Wonderwall," by Oasis.

"Remember when we were young?" Mordechai asked Shuki as they turned off the highway.

Shuki knew the kibbutz guard by name, because he used to hitch down every week to make out in the banana fields with a girl he'd met on a school trip to the Holocaust museum. They waved and drove by him, but they didn't stop at the girl's room, they kept going along the dirt road past the bulls kicking up dust, and on to the dairy. The air smelled of fresh cow manure and trees.

"Cows are so dumb," Mordechai said. "All they do is shit. They live in shit, they sleep in shit. . . ."

"Quiet," Shuki said. "Operation Secret Messiah."

The frightened cows moved away from them as one, their hooves rumbling against the earth. Mordechai and Shuki followed them twice around the pen under the moonless sky. The cows were brown and black and some were just brown.

"Okay," Shuki said, "Let's get this one, she's stopped moving."

"She's too big," Mordechai said, laughing. "Even bigger than Tamar."

"My sister's having twins, idiot. Just grab one," Shuki answered. "Grab it by the tail."

But they couldn't catch the other cows who kept circling around and around the pen in the darkness.

"Let's get this one before she wakes up," Mordechai said, slapping the fat sleepy cow on the rump. *"Yala!"*

It wasn't easy to get the giant brown cow into the truck. She wouldn't move after being prodded out of the pen. When she finally did move she stepped on Mordechai's foot and then didn't move again.

"Ouch," Mordechai called. "She's on my foot."

"Punch her," Shuki said.

"What?"

"In the nose."

"No. You punch her."

"Tickle her, then," Shuki said, spitting onto the ground. "Like she's your girlfriend."

When they finally got her into the truck they covered her with a tarp and gunned the engine past the guard when his back was turned.

When they pulled back onto the highway, Mordechai and Shuki sang the song that they thought was so hilarious calling for the Messiah. "Moshiach, Moshiach, Moshiach! Ai, ai, ai, ai . . ."

"We should call her 'one million burgers,'" Mordechai said as they drove back up toward the holy city.

"She's the red heifer," Shuki said. "And I'm a blond."

In the alleyway behind the King of Falafel they slathered red paint onto the cow and worked it into her coat.

"The hairdresser at work," Mordechai said.

"If that will keep me from the army," Shuki said, kissing the cow dramatically on the forehead.

The cow stood still, big-eyed, oblivious.

It was nearly four o'clock in the morning when they led the red painted cow across King George Street. Mordechai and Shuki were as red as the cow, their hands and faces smeared with paint. They were high from the paint fumes.

"Ai, ai ai, ai, wo-o, wo-o, wo-o . . ." Mordechai sang.

"Quiet," Shuki said.

"Jews are depending on you, big girl," Mordechai whispered. "In the morning they will wake to trumpets and flutes and harps . . ."

"Shut up," Shuki said, leading the cow into the alleyway behind the King of the King of Falafel.

"At last the Messiah can come," Mordechai added, patting her on the head. "Isn't that right, Red?"

Not even a moo.

Shuki jimmied open the back door of Benny Ovadiah's King of the King of Falafel with a pocket knife he carried in his jeans. They had difficulty leading the beefy cow through the back door, her wet paint rubbing off against the door, but they forced her through, laughing as they went.

"Through the red door, destiny awaits," Mordechai said.

They left her standing alone in the dark, in the middle of the restaurant.

From across the street they could hear the red-painted cow rattling around in the darkness, a breaking of glass, battering against the steel shutter that said: King of the King of Falafel, and then the graffito, "Is the king of nothing." They heard hooves stamping and long, loud, moos.

Mordechai imagined Benny Ovadiah's unblemished marble tables shattering on the floor, his tapestries trod upon, his bronze *tchotchkes* battered and stomped on. He imagined the Lubavitcher rebbe climbing out of the photo from beside the mandate-era register to sweep the cluttered floor muttering lamentations, and the frightened cow nuzzling close, dripping snot on the black-clad rabbi.

From the time they locked the cow inside, there was not a moment of silence. Afraid that the paint fumes had made her crazy as a bull, they agonized all night under the moonless sky, without a star to wish on.

"You go see her," Mordechai said.

"No! You!"

"She's destroying the place."

"She's destroying the place," Shuki repeated, and they both broke out laughing.

Mordechai's insides heaved as he laughed and he felt a warm

glow inside him. He laughed so hard he could not tell if sweat or tears poured down his face.

For a moment before the sun rose, the sky filled with stars and then morning burst out of the east to greet them.

Things were not so hilarious by the time Benny Ovadiah arrived to open the King of the King of Falafel. Both Mordechai and Shuki were exhausted and a little afraid.

"Caught with red hands," Shuki said, but he did not laugh.

The sun was out now, and there was nowhere for the two boys to hide. They stood by the side of the road and could hear Benny Ovadiah screaming and cursing, calling them sons of whores, sons of bitches, sons of shit. Mordechai turned to Shuki and offered a prayer for his soul. He was only half joking.

When Benny Ovadiah emerged from his battered restaurant, he was completely red, covered in paint or blood or both.

He carried a bloody butcher knife in his shaking hand. "You had better hope the Messiah comes now," Benny Ovadiah shouted, stepping into the street. "Then, the dead can rise again. And you will be the first."

"You can't kill us," Mordechai said.

"Why not? I can share a cell with your father."

He reached the sidewalk and grabbed Mordechai by the hair.

"It was just a joke," Mordechai said, almost in tears.

"I've slaughtered your joke," Benny Ovadiah boomed.

"But, we're neighbors," Mordechai said, the words almost swallowed. "Look," he said, pointing to the pathetic sight of Benny Ovadiah's ruined falafel restaurant across the street.

"No! Look!" Shuki cried, wide-eyed.

And, from behind an overturned table, Mordechai saw a little red calf stumble unsteadily out of the wreckage, its legs buckling like a drunk, as it mooed and stepped out to join the morning traffic.

Jon Papernick

"The King of the King of Falafel" is a story that was born from its title. When I lived in Israel, it seemed that there was a falafel stand on every corner, and whenever a new restaurant opened on the block it also seemed to be another falafel stand. Many of these restaurants were called the King of Falafel, or some variation on that theme. My roommate mentioned that he had once seen a restaurant called the King of the King of Falafel and wouldn't that be a funny title for a story. So I began to write, inspired only from the title. I knew the story was going to take a humorous tone, as the silliness and the one-upmanship of the title automatically made me smile. But when I got down to writing, I was surprised where the story went, particularly by the ending. The title came to take on a double meaning that I hadn't initially intended. I see the "King of the King of Falafel" as a religious story, a story of coming to faith, but a teacher of mine read it differently, more ominously, as the first step to the violent religious extremism found in many of my other stories.

The Contributors

Steve Almond's fiction has appeared in magazines and journals such as *Playboy, Ploughshares*, and *Tin House*. His story collection, *My Life in Heavy Metal: Stories* (Grove), was published last year. A prolific writer and a nominee for several Pushcart Prizes (including one for "A Dream of Sleep"), Almond is the recipient of a 2002 Pushcart Prize and was also a 2001 National Magazine Award finalist for fiction. He lives in Somerville, Massachusetts, and teaches creative writing at Boston College.

Aimee Bender's stories have appeared in *Granta, GQ, Story, Harper's, The Antioch Review*, and other publications. She is the author of *The Girl in the Flammable Skirt* (Doubleday) and a novel, *An Invisible Sign of My Own* (Doubleday). She lives in Los Angeles and is at work on her second novel.

Gabriel Brownstein's stories have appeared in *Zoetrope: All-Story, The Northwest Review, The Literary Review*, and *The Hawaii Review*. His story collection, *The Curious Case of Benjamin Button Apt. 3W* (W. W. Norton), won the 2000 PEN/Hemingway Award for best first book of fiction. He lives in Brooklyn, New York.

Judy Budnitz's stories have appeared in *Harper's, Story, The Paris Review, Glimmer Train*, and in collections including *Prize Stories 2000: The O. Henry Awards* and *25 and Under*. She is the author of *Flying Leap* (Picador USA), a collection of stories. Her novel, *If I Told You Once* (Picador USA), was short-listed for England's prestigious Orange Prize in 2000. Budnitz teaches creative writing at Brown and Columbia Universities.

Nathan Englander grew up in an Orthodox Jewish community on Long Island, a background that has helped shape his stories about Hasidic and ultra-Orthodox Jews. His short fiction has appeared in *The Atlantic Monthly*, *The New Yorker*, and several prize anthologies including *The Best American Stories*, *The O. Henry Awards*, and the *Pushcart Prize* collection. Englander's story collection, *For the Relief of Unbearable Urges* (Knopf), was an international bestseller, and earned him a PEN/Faulkner Malamud Award and the American Academy of Arts and Letters Sue Kauffman Prize. More recently he was awarded a 2003 Guggenheim Fellowship and the Bard Fiction Prize. He lives in New York City and is at work on a novel.

Jonathan Safran Foer's short fiction has appeared in *The New Yorker*, *The Paris Review,* and *Conjunctions*, among other publications. He also the editor of *A Convergence of Birds: Original Fiction and Poetry Inspired by the Work of Joseph Cornell*. An excerpt of Foer's first novel, *Everything Is Illuminated* (Houghton Mifflin), appeared in *The New Yorker* in 2001 as "The Very Rigid Search." The story, reprinted here, helped to create a critical buzz for the then twenty-five-year-old writer. The novel was an international bestseller, and has been translated into nineteen languages. Foer is at work on a second novel, scheduled to appear in 2004.

Myla Goldberg's first novel, *Bee Season* (Doubleday), was published to wide acclaim in 2000. A recipient of the 2001 Harold U. Ribalow Prize (administered by *Hadassah Magazine*), *Bee Season* was also a *New York Times* Notable Book. Goldberg's short fiction has appeared in *Harper's*, as well as the *Virgin Fiction* anthology. Goldberg lives in Brooklyn, New York, and is completing a new novel, *Wickett's Remedy*, set in Boston during the 1918 influenza epidemic.

Ehud Havazelet is the author of two critically acclaimed story collections, *Like Never Before* (Doubleday) and *What Is It Then Between Us?* (Collier). His stories have appeared in such journals as *DoubleTake, New England Review, The Southern Review, ZYZZYVA, Iowa Review, Ontario Review*, and *Crazyhorse*, and have been selected for four Pushcart Prizes. Havazelet was also the recipient of fellowships from the Guggenheim Foundation and the Whiting Foundation, and was a Wallace Stegner Fellow at Stanford University. He directs the fiction program at the University of Oregon.

Dara Horn's first novel, *In the Image* (W. W. Norton), was published in 2002. Her award-winning nonfiction writing has appeared in *Hadassah, American Heritage, Science*, and the *Christian Science Monitor*. Horn is also a doctoral candidate in comparative literature at Harvard University, studying Hebrew and Yiddish. She lives with her husband in New York City.

Rachel Kadish is the author of a novel, *From a Sealed Room* (Penguin Putnam), and her writing has appeared in leading magazines such as *Zoetrope: All-Story, Story*, and *Tin House*, as well as in the anthologies *Daughters of Kings* and *Traveling Souls: Contemporary Pilgrimage Stories*. Kadish is the recipient of several awards, including a recent NEA fiction fellowship. Her story "The Argument" is part of a forthcoming story collection, *Collect Call from Mars*. Kadish is also at work on a novel, *Soon Also for You*, and a memoir about Holocaust reparation claims.

Gloria DeVidas Kirchheimer grew up in a multilingual Sephardic household in New York City; her parents spoke more than seven languages between them. Her writing has been published in several literary quarterlies and anthologies, including *With Signs and Wonder* (Invisible Cities Press). She is coauthor (with Manfred Kirchheimer) of *We Were So Beloved: Autobiography of a German Jewish Community*. Her story collection, *Goodbye,*

Evil Eye (Holmes & Meier) was a finalist for the 2000 National Jewish Book Award.

Binnie Kirshenbaum is the author of two story collections, *History on a Personal Note* (Fromm International) and *Married Life and Other True Adventures* (Crossing Press), and four novels, most recently *Pure Poetry* (Simon & Schuster) and *Hester Among the Ruins* (W. W. Norton). Kirshenbaum is the recipient of a 1996 Critic's Choice Award for *History on a Personal Note*. The same year she was also named one of the fifty-two Best Young American Novelists by *Granta* magazine. Kirshenbaum currently teaches writing at Columbia University's School of the Arts in New York City.

Joan Leegant's fiction has appeared in *Prairie Schooner, Columbia, Nimrod, Crazyhorse, Pakn Treger, American Literary Review*, and the anthology *With Signs and Wonder* (Invisible Cities Press). Her story collection, *An Hour in Paradise* (W. W. Norton), will be published in 2003. "Seekers in the Holy Land" (reprinted in *Lost Tribe*) was a finalist in the 2002 *Moment Magazine* Contest. Leegant has received an Artist Grant from the Massachusetts Cultural Council and two fellowships at the MacDowell Colony. She lives in Boston and teaches writing at Harvard University.

Michael Lowenthal is the author of two novels, *The Same Embrace* (Dutton) and *Avoidance* (Graywolf Press). His short stories and personal essays have appeared in publications such as *The New York Times Magazine, The Kenyon Review, The Southern Review, Tin House, Witness*, and *Nerve*, and have been anthologized in more than a dozen books, including *Neurotica, Best American Gay Fiction*, and *Wrestling with the Angel*. Lowenthal lives in Boston and teaches creative writing at Boston College.

Ellen Miller is the author of a novel, *Like Being Killed* (Dutton). Her fiction has appeared in the anthologies *Full Frontal Fiction:*

The Best of Nerve.com and *110 Stories: New York Writes After September 11*. She has taught fiction writing at New York University, the New School, and the Metropolitan Correction Center. She lives in New York City, where she is currently at work on her second novel, an excerpt of which appears in *Lost Tribe*.

Tova Mirvis grew up in the tight-knit Orthodox Jewish world of Memphis, Tennessee. She began to write her first novel *The Ladies' Auxiliary Club* (W.W. Norton) while she was an M.F.A. student at Columbia University. The novel, which is a perennial favorite among book clubs, was selected by Barnes & Noble for the 1999 Discover Great New Writers Program. Mirvis lives in New York City and is at work on a second novel, an excerpt of which appears in *Lost Tribe*.

Peter Orner's debut collection, *Esther Stories* (Houghton Mifflin), has achieved extraordinary critical acclaim, with stories appearing in *The Best American Stories 2001* and the Pushcart Prize 2001 collections. The collection was also a finalist for the Pen/Hemingway Prize and was a *New York Times* Notable Book. Orner is the recipient of the 2002 Rome Prize from the American Academy of Arts and Letters, and the 2002 Samuel Goldberg Prize from the National Foundation for Jewish Culture. He lives in San Francisco.

Jon Papernick, who was born and raised in Toronto, Canada, spent much of the 1990s in Israel. He spent time working on an army base, lived on a kibbutz in the Jezreel Valley, studied at a yeshiva in Jerusalem, and worked as a journalist for United Press International and the Associated Press. These experiences helped to serve as a background for his stories, published as *The Ascent of Eli Israel and Other Stories* (Arcade) in 2002. He lives in Brooklyn, New York, and is currently at work on a novel.

Nelly Reifler's stories have been published in magazines and journals including *The Florida Review, Exquisite Corpse, Bomb,*

Post Road, and *Black Book*, and the anthology *110 Stories: New York Writes After September 11*. Reifler's fiction was awarded a Henfield Prize in 1995 and a U.A.S. Explorations Prize in 1998. Her story collection, *See Through* (Simon & Schuster), will be published in 2003. She lives in Brooklyn, New York, with her husband, painter Josh Dorman.

Ben Schrank is the author of two novels, *Miracle Man* (Quill) and most recently *Consent* (Random House). He lives in Brooklyn, New York, and teaches in the creative writing program at Brooklyn College. His story "Consent" is excerpted from his novel.

Suzan Sherman's writing has appeared in the *New York Times*, the *New York Observer, Bookforum, Bomb*, the *Mississippi Review, Mr. Beller's Neighborhood, The Forward*, and the fiction anthology *110 Stories: New York Writes After September 11*. "Knitting One" is part of a story collection-in-progress, *My Hidden Children*, exploring issues of adoption and identity.

Gary Shteyngart was born in Leningrad in 1972. He is the author of a novel, *The Russian Debutante's Handbook* (Riverhead), and his fiction has appeared in *The New Yorker, Granta*, and other publications. He lives in New York City.

Aryeh Lev Stollman is the author of two novels, *The Illuminated Soul* (Riverhead) and *The Far Euphrates* (Riverhead), which won a Wilbur Award, a Lambda Award, and was selected as an American Library Association Notable Book of 1997. Stollman's fiction and essays have appeared in *Story, American Short Fiction, The Yale Review*, and elsewhere. The story "Die Grosse Liebe" will be included in his collection, *The Dialogues of Time and Entropy* (Riverhead), published in 2003. Dr. Stollman is a neuroradiologist at the Mount Sinai Medical Center in New York City.

Ellen Umansky's fiction and nonfiction have appeared in the *New York Times, The Forward, Salon*, and *Playboy*, among other publications. A graduate of Columbia's M.F.A. program, she was most recently the features editor of the *New York Sun*. She lives in Brooklyn, New York, with her husband and is at work on her first novel.

Simone Zelitch is the author of three novels, including *The Confession of Jack Straw* (Black Heron Press) and *Louisa* (Penguin Putnam), which received the 2000 Samuel Goldberg Prize from the National Foundation for Jewish Culture. Her story "Ten Plagues" is excerpted from her most recent novel, *Moses in Sinai* (Black Heron Press). Zelitch teaches writing at the Community College of Philadelphia.